S TEPHEN JONES is the winner of two World Fantasy Awards, the Horror Writers of America Bram Stoker Award, and nine-time recipient of The British Fantasy Award. A full-time columnist, film-reviewer, television producer/director and genre movie publicist (all three *Hellraiser* films, *Nightbreed*, *Split Second* etc.), he is the co-editor of *Horror: 100 Best Books*, *The Best Horror from Fantasy Tales*, *Gaslight & Ghosts*, *Now We Are Sick* and the *Fantasy Tales*, *Best New Horror* and *Dark Voices* series. He has also compiled *Clive Barker's The Nightbreed Chronicles*, *The Mammoth Book of Terror*, *Clive Barker's Shadows in Eden*, *The Hellraiser Chronicles* and *James Herbert: By Horror Haunted*.

The Mammoth Book of
VAMPIRES

The Mammoth Book of
VAMPIRES

Edited by
STEPHEN JONES

Carroll & Graf Publishers, Inc.
New York

Carroll & Graf Publishers, Inc.
260 Fifth Avenue
New York
NY 10001

First published in Great Britain 1992

First Carroll & Graf edition 1992

ISBN 0–88184–796–8

Typeset by Hewer Text Composition Services, Edinburgh
Printed in Great Britain.

10 9 8 7 6 5 4

CONTENTS

ACKNOWLEDGEMENTS

"Human Remains" copyright © 1984 by Clive Barker. Originally published in *Books of Blood Volume 3*. Reprinted by permission of Sphere Books.

"Necros" copyright © 1986 by Brian Lumley. Originally published in *The Second Book of After Midnight Stories*. Reprinted by permission of the author and the author's agent.

"The Man Who Loved the Vampire Lady" copyright © 1988 by Brian Stableford. Originally published in *The Magazine of Fantasy and Science Fiction*, Vol.75, No.2, August 1988. Reprinted by permission of the author.

"For the Blood is the Life" by F. Marion Crawford. Originally published in *Wandering Ghosts* (1911).

"The Brood" copyright © 1980 by Ramsey Campbell. Originally published in *Dark Forces*. Reprinted by permission of the author.

"Hungarian Rhapsody" copyright © 1958 by Ziff-Davis Publishing Co. Originally published in *Fantastic*, June 1958. Reprinted by permission of the author and the author's agent.

"Ligeia" by Edgar Allan Poe. Originally published in *Baltimore American Museum* (1838).

"Vampire" copyright © 1986 by Richard Christian Matheson. Originally published in *Cutting Edge*. Reprinted by permission of the author.

"Stragella" copyright © 1932 by The Clayton Magazines, Incorporated. Originally published in *Strange Tales*, June 1932. Reprinted by permission of the author.

"A Week in the Unlife" copyright © 1991 by David J. Schow. Originally published in *A Whisper of Blood*. Reprinted by permission of the author.

"The House at Evening" copyright © 1982 by Stuart David Schiff. Originally published in *Whispers* No.15–16, March 1982. Reprinted by permission of the author.

"The Labyrinth" copyright © 1974 by Ronald Chetwynd-Hayes. Originally published in *The Elemental*. Reprinted by permission of the author.

"Beyond Any Measure" copyright © 1982 by Stuart David Schiff. Originally published in *Whispers* No.15–16, March 1982. Reprinted by permission of the author.

"Doctor Porthos" copyright © 1968 by Basil Copper. Originally published in *The Midnight People*. Reprinted by permission of the author.

"Dracula's Guest" by Bram Stoker. Originally published in *Dracula's Guest and Other Weird Stories* (1914).

For Ronald Chetwynd-Hayes,
a true gentleman and a
vampire's best friend.

Introduction

The Children of the Night

THE UNDEAD ... *Nosferatu* ... *Children of the Night* ... Call them what you will, what they all have in common is a need to suck the life-force from the living to prolong their own unnatural existence and propagate. For the classic vampire, The Blood *is* the Life.

But in recent years, many novels and anthologies have elected to show the vampire in a somewhat different light—as a sympathetic, misunderstood character, a victim of its own affliction; or as a creature that feeds upon the human mind or bodily fluids other than blood (in the latter case, enhancing the vampire's identification with a dark sexuality). All these approaches are perfectly valid, and some have even produced modern classics of the genre.

However, I usually prefer a more traditional approach to vampire fiction.

The Mammoth Book of Vampires collects together twenty-nine classic and contemporary stories and one poem. As to be expected in any representative collection, there are a few of the modern type of vampire stories I referred to above, but for the most part the bloodsuckers you'll find within these pages are the real thing.

From Hugh B. Cave's pulp thriller 'Stragella' through to Howard Waldrop's bizarre blend of vampires and Nazis, 'Der Untergang Des Abendlandesmenschen', you'll discover a modern mix of vampire fiction by such masters of the macabre as Clive Barker, Brian Lumley, Ramsey Campbell, Robert Bloch and Karl Edward Wagner, amongst others. F. Paul Wilson and Les Daniels are represented by two powerful short novels, and there is original fiction from Graham Masterton, Steve Rasnic Tem and Kim Newman.

However, no volume of traditional vampire stories would be complete without a sampling of the classics of the genre. Therefore you'll also find included five examples of the best vampire fiction ever written, from such renowned authors as Bram Stoker, Edgar Allan Poe, M.R. James, E.F. Benson and F. Marion Crawford.

As usual, all of the stories in this volume were chosen because they are particular favourites of mine. I have also attempted to put together a collection that offers a relatively unfamiliar line-up of tales to even the most jaded vampire aficionado.

So, before turning the page, make sure that the garlic is in place at window and door, and that a wooden stake is close to hand. Just in case . . .

I bid you, welcome.

Stephen Jones
London

Clive Barker

Human Remains

Clive Barker recently enjoyed a stay in the bestseller lists on both sides of the Atlantic with two new books: his epic novel of erotic chills, Imajica, *and* The Hellbound Heart, *which formed the basis for the* Hellraiser *series of movies.*

As usual, various editions of his classic short story collections, Books of Blood, *continue to appear, and all his novels—*The Damnation Game, Weaveworld, Cabal *and* The Great and Secret Show—*are in print. On the comics front a bewildering variety of titles are being published, based on his stories and concepts, and 1991 saw the publication of two non-fiction volumes about the writer:* Pandemonium *and* Clive Barker's Shadows in Eden.

Barker is currently preparing a multi-million dollar science fiction epic for Universal Pictures, which he will direct, and his story 'The Forbidden' was recently filmed as Candyman.

The story that follows in one of the author's earliest, it is also one of his most poignant. Prepare to meet a very different type of vampire . . .

SOME TRADES ARE best practised by daylight, some by night. Gavin was a professional in the latter category. In midwinter, in midsummer, leaning against a wall, or poised in a doorway, a fire-fly cigarette hovering at his lips, he sold what sweated in his jeans to all comers.

Sometimes to visiting widows with more money than love, who'd hire him for a weekend of illicit meetings, sour, insistent kisses and perhaps, if they could forget their dead partners, a dry hump on a lavender-scented bed. Sometimes to lost husbands, hungry for their own sex and desperate for an hour of coupling with a boy who wouldn't ask their name.

Gavin didn't much care which it was. Indifference was a trademark of his, even a part of his attraction. And it made leaving him, when the deed was done and the money exchanged, so much simpler. To say, "Ciao", or "Be seeing you", or nothing at all to a face that scarcely cared if you lived or died: that was an easy thing.

And for Gavin, the profession was not unpalatable, as professions went. One night out of four it even offered him a grain of physical pleasure. At worst it was a sexual abattoir, all steaming skins and lifeless eyes. But he'd got used to that over the years.

It was all profit. It kept him in good shoes.

By day he slept mostly, hollowing out a warm furrow in the bed, and mummifying himself in his sheets, head wrapped up in a tangle of arms to keep out the light. About three or so, he'd get up, shave and shower, then spend half an hour in front of the mirror, inspecting himself. He was meticulously self-critical, never allowing his weight to fluctuate more than a pound or two to either side of his self-elected ideal, careful to feed his skin if it was dry, or swab it if it was oily, hunting for any pimple that might flaw his cheek. Strict watch was kept for the smallest sign of venereal disease—the only type of lovesickness he ever suffered. The occasional dose of crabs was easily dispatched, but gonorrhoea, which he'd caught twice, would keep him out of service for three weeks, and that was bad for business; so he policed his body obsessively, hurrying to the clinic at the merest sign of a rash.

It seldom happened. Uninvited crabs aside there was little to do in that half-hour of self-appraisal but admire the collision of genes that had made him. He was wonderful. People told him that all the time. Wonderful. The face, oh the face, they would say, holding him tight as if they could steal a piece of his glamour.

Of course there were other beauties available, through the agencies, even on the streets if you knew where to search. But most of the hustlers Gavin knew had faces that seemed, beside his, unmade. Faces that looked like the first workings of a sculptor rather than the finished article: unrefined, experimental. Whereas he was made, entire. All that could be done had been; it was just a question of preserving the perfection.

Inspection over, Gavin would dress, maybe regard himself for another five minutes, then take the packaged wares out to sell.

He worked the street less and less these days. It was chancey; there was always the law to avoid, and the occasional psycho with an urge to clean up Sodom. If he was feeling really lazy he could pick up a client through the Escort Agency, but they always creamed off a fat portion of the fee.

He had regulars of course, clients who booked his favours month after month. A widow from Fort Lauderdale always hired him for a few days on her annual trip to Europe; another woman whose face he'd seen once in a glossy magazine called him now and then, wanting only to dine with him and confide her marital problems. There was a man Gavin called Rover, after his car, who would buy him once every few weeks for a night of kisses and confessions.

But on nights without a booked client he was out on his own finding a spec and hustling. It was a craft he had off perfectly. Nobody else working the street had caught the vocabulary of invitation better; the subtle blend of encouragement and detachment, of putto and wanton. The particular shift of weight from left foot to right that presented the groin at the best angle: so. Never too blatant: never whorish. Just casually promising.

He prided himself that there was seldom more than a few minutes between tricks, and never as much as an hour. If he made his play with his usual accuracy, eyeing the right disgruntled wife, the right regretful husband, he'd have them feed him (clothe him sometimes), bed him and bid him a satisfied goodnight all before the last tube had run on the Metropolitan Line to Hammersmith. The years of half-hour assignations, three blow-jobs and a fuck in one evening, were over. For one thing he simply didn't have the hunger for it any longer, for another he was preparing for his career to change course in the coming years: from street hustler to gigolo, from gigolo to kept boy, from kept boy to husband. One of these days, he knew it, he'd marry one of the widows; maybe the matron from Florida. She'd told him how she could picture him spread out beside her pool in Fort Lauderdale, and it was a fantasy he kept warm for her. Perhaps he hadn't got there yet, but he'd turn the trick of it sooner or later. The problem was that these rich blooms needed a lot of tending, and the pity of it was that so many of them perished before they came to fruit.

Still, this year. Oh yes, this year for certain, it had to be this year. Something good was coming with the autumn, he knew it for sure.

Meanwhile he watched the lines deepen around his wonderful mouth (it was, without doubt, wonderful) and calculated the odds against him in the race between time and opportunity.

It was nine-fifteen at night. September 29th, and it was chilly, even in the foyer of the Imperial Hotel. No Indian summer to bless the streets this year: autumn had London in its jaws and was shaking the city bare.

The chill had got to his tooth, his wretched, crumbling tooth. If he'd gone to the dentist's, instead of turning over in his bed and sleeping another hour, he wouldn't be feeling this discomfort. Well, too late now, he'd go tomorrow. Plenty of time tomorrow. No need for an appointment. He'd just smile at the receptionist, she'd melt and tell him she could find a slot for him somewhere, he'd smile again, she'd blush and he'd see the dentist then and there instead of waiting two weeks like the poor nerds who didn't have wonderful faces.

For tonight he'd just have to put up with it. All he needed was one lousy punter—a husband who'd pay through the nose for taking it in the mouth—then he could retire to an all-night club in Soho and content himself with reflections. As long as he didn't find himself with a confession-freak on his hands, he could spit his stuff and be done by half ten.

But tonight wasn't his night. There was a new face on the reception desk of the Imperial, a thin, shot-at face with a mismatched rug perched (glued) on his pate, and he'd been squinting at Gavin for almost half an hour.

The usual receptionist, Madox, was a closet-case Gavin had seen prowling the bars once or twice, an easy touch if you could handle that kind. Madox was putty in Gavin's hand; he'd even bought his company for an hour a couple of months back. He'd got a cheap rate too—that was good politics. But this new man was straight, and vicious, and he was on to Gavin's game.

Idly, Gavin sauntered across to the cigarette machine, his walk catching the beat of the muzack as he trod the maroon carpet. Lousy fucking night.

The receptionist was waiting for him as he turned from the machine, packet of Winston in hand.

"Excuse me . . . Sir." It was a practised pronounciation that was clearly not natural. Gavin looked sweetly back at him.

"Yes?"

"Are you actually a resident at this hotel . . . Sir?"

"Actually— "

"If not, the management would be obliged if you'd vacate the premises immediately."

"I'm waiting for somebody."

"Oh?"

The receptionist didn't believe a word of it.

"Well just give me the name— "

"No need."

"Give me the name— ", the man insisted, "and I'll gladly check to see if your . . . contact . . . is in the hotel."

The bastard was going to try and push it, which narrowed the options. Either Gavin could choose to play it cool, and leave the foyer, or play the outraged customer and stare the other man down. He chose, more to be bloodyminded than because it was good tactics, to do the latter.

"You don't have any right— " he began to bluster, but the receptionist wasn't moved.

"Look, sonny— " he said, "I know what you're up to, so don't try and get snotty with me or I'll fetch the police." He'd lost control of his elocution: it was getting further south of the river with every syllable. "We've got a nice clientele here, and they don't want no truck with the likes of you, see?"

"Fucker," said Gavin very quietly.

"Well that's one up from a cocksucker, isn't it?"

Touché.

"Now, sonny—you want to mince out of here under your own steam or be carried out in cuffs by the boys in blue?"

Gavin played his last card.

"Where's Mr Madox? I want to see Mr Madox: he knows me."

"I'm sure he does," the receptionist snorted, "I'm bloody sure he does. He was dismissed for improper conduct— " The artificial accent was re-establishing itself "—so I wouldn't try dropping his name here if I were you. OK? On your way."

Upper hand well and truly secured, the receptionist stood back like a matador and gestured for the bull to go by.

"The management thanks you for your patronage. Please don't call again."

Game, set and match to the man with the rug. What the hell; there were other hotels, other foyers, other receptionists. He didn't have to take all this shit.

As Gavin pushed the door open he threw a smiling "Be seeing you" over his shoulder. Perhaps that would make the tick sweat a little one of these nights when he was walking home and he heard a young man's step on the street behind him. It was a petty satisfaction, but it was something.

The door swung closed, sealing the warmth in and Gavin out. It was colder, substantially colder, than it had been when he'd stepped into the foyer. A thin drizzle had begun, which threatened to worsen as he hurried down Park Lane towards South Kensington. There were a couple of hotels on the High Street he could hole up in for a while; if nothing came of that he'd admit defeat.

The traffic surged around Hyde Park Corner, speeding to Knightsbridge or Victoria, purposeful, shining. He pictured himself standing on the concrete island between the two contrary streams of cars, his fingertips thrust into his jeans (they were too tight for him to get more than the first joint into the pockets), solitary, forlorn.

A wave of unhappiness came up from some buried place in him. He was twenty-four and five months. He had hustled, on and off and on again, since he was seventeen, promising himself that he'd find a marriageable widow (the gigolo's pension) or a legitimate occupation before he was twenty-five.

But time passed and nothing came of his ambitions. He just lost momentum and gained another line beneath the eye.

And the traffic still came in shining streams, lights signalling this imperative or that, cars full of people with ladders to climb and snakes to wrestle, their passage isolating him from the bank, from safety, with its hunger for destination.

He was not what he'd dreamed he'd be, or promised his secret self.

And youth was yesterday.

Where was he to go now? The flat would feel like a prison tonight, even if he smoked a little dope to take the edge off the room. He wanted, no, he *needed* to be with somebody tonight. Just to see his beauty through somebody else's eyes. Be told how perfect his proportions were, be wined and dined and flattered stupid, even if it was by Quasimodo's richer, uglier brother. Tonight he needed a fix of affection.

The pick-up was so damned easy it almost made him forget the episode in the foyer of the Imperial. A guy of fifty-five or so, well-heeled: Gucci shoes, a very classy overcoat. In a word: quality.

Gavin was standing in the doorway of a tiny art-house cinema, looking over the times of the Truffaut movie they were showing, when he became aware of the punter staring at him. He glanced at the guy to be certain there was a pick-up in the offing. The direct look seemed to unnerve the punter; he moved on; then he seemed to change his mind, muttered something to himself, and retraced his steps, showing patently false interest in the movie schedule. Obviously not too familiar with this game, Gavin thought; a novice.

Casually Gavin took out a Winston and lit it, the flare of the match in his cupped hands glossing his cheekbones golden. He'd done it a thousand times, as often as not in the mirror for his own pleasure. He had the glance up from the tiny fire off pat: it always did the trick. This time when he met the nervous eyes of the punter, the other didn't back away.

He drew on the cigarette, flicking out the match and letting it drop. He hadn't made a pick-up like this in several months, but he was well satisfied that he still had the knack. The faultless recognition of a potential client, the implicit offer in eyes and lips, that could be construed as innocent friendliness if he'd made an error.

This was no error, however, this was the genuine article. The man's eyes were glued to Gavin, so enamoured of him he seemed to be hurting with it. His mouth was open, as though the words of introduction had failed him. Not much of a face, but far from ugly. Tanned too often, and too quickly: maybe he'd lived abroad. He was assuming the man was English: his prevarication suggested it.

Against habit, Gavin made the opening move.

"You like French movies?"

The punter seemed to deflate with relief that the silence between them had been broken.

"Yes," he said.

"You going in?"

The man pulled a face.

"I . . . I . . . don't think I will."

"Bit cold . . ."

"Yes. It is."

"Bit cold for standing around, I mean."

"Oh—yes."

The punter took the bait.

"Maybe . . . you'd like a drink?"

Gavin smiled.

"Sure, why not?"

"My flat's not far."

"Sure."

"I was getting a bit cheesed off, you know, at home."

"I know the feeling."

Now the other man smiled. "You are . . .?"

"Gavin."

The man offered his leather-gloved hand. Very formal, business-like. The grip as they shook was strong, no trace of his earlier hesitation remaining.

"I'm Kenneth," he said, "Ken Reynolds."

"Ken."

"Shall we get out of the cold?"

"Suits me."

"I'm only a short walk from here."

A wave of musty, centrally-heated air hit them as Reynolds opened the door of his apartment. Climbing the three flights of stairs had snatched Gavin's breath, but Reynolds wasn't slowed at all. Health freak maybe. Occupation? Something in the city. The handshake, the leather gloves. Maybe Civil Service.

"Come in, come in."

There was money here. Underfoot the pile of the carpet was lush, hushing their steps as they entered. The hallway was almost bare: a calendar hung on the wall, a small table with telephone, a heap of directories, a coat-stand.

"It's warmer in here."

Reynolds was shrugging off his coat and hanging it up. His gloves remained on as he led Gavin a few yards down the hallway and into a large room.

"Let's have your jacket," he said.

"Oh . . . sure."

Gavin took off his jacket, and Reynolds slipped out into the hall with it. When he came in again he was working off his gloves; a slick of sweat made it a difficult job. The guy was still nervous: even on his home ground. Usually they started to calm down once they were safe behind locked doors. Not this one: he was a catalogue of fidgets.

"Can I get you a drink?"

"Yeah; that would be good."

"What's your poison?"

"Vodka."

"Surely. Anything with it?"

"Just a drop of water."

"Purist, eh?"

Gavin didn't quite understand the remark.

"Yeah," he said.

"Man after my own heart. Will you give me a moment—I'll just fetch some ice."

"No problem."

Reynolds dropped the gloves on a chair by the door, and left

Gavin to the room. It, like the hallway, was almost stiflingly warm, but there was nothing homely or welcoming about it. Whatever his profession, Reynolds was a collector. The room was dominated by displays of antiquities, mounted on the walls, and lined up on shelves. There was very little furniture, and what there was seemed odd: battered tubular frame chairs had no place in an apartment this expensive. Maybe the man was a university don, or a museum governor, something academic. This was no stockbroker's living room.

Gavin knew nothing about art, and even less about history, so the displays meant very little to him, but he went to have a closer look, just to show willing. The guy was bound to ask him what he thought of the stuff. The shelves were deadly dull. Bits and pieces of pottery and sculpture: nothing in its entirety, just fragments. On some of the shards there remained a glimpse of design, though age had almost washed the colours out. Some of the sculpture was recognisably human: part of a torso, or foot (all five toes in place), a face that was all but eaten away, no longer male or female. Gavin stifled a yawn. The heat, the exhibits and the thought of sex made him lethargic.

He turned his dulled attention to the wall-hung pieces. They were more impressive than the stuff on the shelves but they were still far from complete. He couldn't see why anyone would want to look at such broken things; what was the fascination? The stone reliefs mounted on the wall were pitted and eroded, so that the skins of the figures looked leprous, and the Latin inscriptions were almost wiped out. There was nothing beautiful about them: too spoiled for beauty. They made him feel dirty somehow, as though their condition was contagious.

Only one of the exhibits struck him as interesting: a tombstone, or what looked to him to be a tombstone, which was larger than the other reliefs and in slightly better condition. A man on a horse, carrying a sword, loomed over his headless enemy. Under the picture, a few words in Latin. The front legs of the horse had been broken off, and the pillars that bounded the design were badly defaced by age, otherwise the image made sense. There was even a trace of personality in the crudely made face: a long nose, a wide mouth; an individual.

Gavin reached to touch the inscription, but withdrew his fingers as he heard Reynolds enter.

"No, please touch it," said his host. "It's there to take pleasure in. Touch away."

Now that he'd been invited to touch the thing, the desire had melted away. He felt embarrassed; caught in the act.

"Go on," Reynolds insisted.

Gavin touched the carving. Cold stone, gritty under his finger-tips.

"It's Roman," said Reynolds.

"Tombstone?"

"Yes. Found near Newcastle."

"Who was he?"

"His name was Flavinus. He was a regimental standard-bearer."

What Gavin had assumed to be a sword was, on closer inspection, a standard. It ended in an almost erased motif: maybe a bee, a flower, a wheel.

"You an archaeologist, then?"

"That's part of my business. I research sites, occasionally oversee digs; but most of the time I restore artifacts."

"Like these?"

"Roman Britain's my personal obsession."

He put down the glasses he was carrying and crossed to the pottery-laden shelves.

"This is stuff I've collected over the years. I've never quite got over the thrill of handling objects that haven't seen the light of day for centuries. It's like plugging into history. You know what I mean?"

"Yeah."

Reynolds picked a fragment of pottery off the shelf.

"Of course all the best finds are claimed by the major collections. But if one's canny, one manages to keep a few pieces back. They were an incredible influence, the Romans. Civil engineers, road-layers, bridge builders."

Reynolds gave a sudden laugh at his burst of enthusiasm.

"Oh hell," he said, "Reynolds is lecturing again. Sorry. I get carried away."

Replacing the pottery-shard in its niche on the shelf, he returned to the glasses, and started pouring drinks. With his back to Gavin, he managed to say: "Are you expensive?"

Gavin hesitated. The man's nervousness was catching and the sudden tilt of the conversation from the Romans to the price of a blow-job took some adjustment.

"It depends," he flannelled.

"Ah . . ." said the other, still busying himself with the glasses, "you mean what is the precise nature of my—er—requirement?"

"Yeah."

"Of course."

He turned and handed Gavin a healthy-sized glass of vodka. No ice.

"I won't be demanding of you," he said.

"I don't come cheap."

"I'm sure you don't," Reynolds tried a smile, but it wouldn't stick to his face, "and I'm prepared to pay you well. Will you be able to stay the night?"

"Do you want me to?"

Reynolds frowned into his glass.

"I suppose I do."

"Then yes."

The host's mood seemed to change, suddenly: indecision was replaced by a spurt of conviction.

"Cheers," he said, clinking his whisky-filled glass against Gavin's. "To love and life and anything else that's worth paying for."

The double-edged remark didn't escape Gavin: the guy was obviously tied up in knots about what he was doing.

"I'll drink to that," said Gavin and took a gulp of the vodka.

The drinks came fast after that, and just about his third vodka Gavin began to feel mellower than he'd felt in a hell of a long time, content to listen to Reynolds' talk of excavations and the glories of Rome with only one ear. His mind was drifting, an easy feeling. Obviously he was going to be here for the night, or at least until the early hours of the morning, so why not drink the punter's vodka and enjoy the experience for what it offered? Later, probably much later to judge by the way the guy was rambling, there'd be some drink-slurred sex in a darkened room, and that would be that. He'd had customers like this before. They were lonely, perhaps between lovers, and usually simple to please. It wasn't sex this guy was buying, it was company, another body to share his space awhile; easy money.

And then, the noise.

At first Gavin thought the beating sound was in his head, until Reynolds stood up, a twitch at his mouth. The air of well-being had disappeared.

"What's that?" asked Gavin, also getting up, dizzy with drink.

"It's all right— " Reynolds, palms were pressing him down into his chair. "Stay here— "

The sound intensified. A drummer in an oven, beating as he burned.

"Please, please stay here a moment. It's just somebody upstairs."

Reynolds was lying, the racket wasn't coming from upstairs. It was from somewhere else in the flat, a rhythmical thumping, that speeded up and slowed and speeded again.

"Help yourself to a drink," said Reynolds at the door, face flushed. "Damn neighbours. . ."

The summons, for that was surely what it was, was already subsiding.

"A moment only," Reynolds promised, and closed the door behind him.

Gavin had experienced bad scenes before: tricks whose lovers appeared at inappropriate moments; guys who wanted to beat him up for a price—one who got bitten by guilt in a hotel room and smashed the place to smithereens. These things happened. But Reynolds was different: nothing about him said weird. At the back of his mind, at the very back, Gavin was quietly reminding himself that the other guys hadn't seemed bad at the beginning. Ah hell; he put the doubts away. If he started to get the jitters every time he went with a new face he'd soon stop working altogether. Somewhere along the line he had to trust to luck and his instinct, and his instinct told him that this punter was not given to throwing fits.

Taking a quick swipe from his glass, he refilled it, and waited.

The noise had stopped altogether, and it became increasingly easier to rearrange the facts: maybe it had been an upstairs neighbour after all. Certainly there was no sound of Reynolds moving around in the flat.

His attention wandered around the room looking for something to occupy it awhile, and came back to the tombstone on the wall. Flavinus the Standard-Bearer.

There was something satisfying about the idea of having your likeness, however crude, carved in stone and put up on the spot where your bones lay, even if some historian was going to separate bones and stone in the fullness of time. Gavin's father had insisted on burial rather than cremation: How else, he'd always said, was he going to be remembered? Who'd ever go to an urn, in a wall, and cry? The irony was that nobody ever went to his grave either: Gavin had been perhaps twice in the years since his father's death. A plain stone bearing a name, a date, and a platitude. He couldn't even remember the year his father died.

People remembered Flavinus though; people who'd never known him, or a life like his, knew him now. Gavin stood up and touched the standard-bearer's name, the crudely chased "FLAVINVS" that was the second word of the inscription.

Suddenly, the noise again, more frenzied than ever. Gavin turned away from the tombstone and looked at the door, half-expecting Reynolds to be standing there with a word of explanation. Nobody appeared.

"Damn it."

The noise continued, a tattoo. Somebody, somewhere, was very angry. And this time there could be no self-deception: the drummer was here, on this floor, a few yards away. Curiosity nibbled Gavin, a coaxing lover. He drained his glass and went out into the hall. The noise stopped as he closed the door behind him.

"Ken?" he ventured. The word seemed to die at his lips.

The hallway was in darkness, except for a wash of light from the far end. Perhaps an open door. Gavin found a switch to his right, but it didn't work.

"Ken?" he said again.

This time the enquiry met with a response. A moan, and the sound of a body rolling, or being rolled, over. Had Reynolds had an accident? Jesus, he could be lying incapacitated within spitting distance from where Gavin stood: he must help. Why were his feet so reluctant to move? He had the tingling in his balls that always came with nervous anticipation; it reminded him of childhood hide-and-seek: the thrill of the chase. It was almost pleasurable.

And pleasure apart, could he really leave now, without knowing what had become of the punter? He had to go down the corridor.

The first door was ajar; he pushed it open and the room beyond was a book-lined bedroom/study. Street lights through the curtainless window fell on a jumbled desk. No Reynolds, no thrasher. More confident now he'd made the first move Gavin explored further down the hallway. The next door—the kitchen—was also open. There was no light from inside. Gavin's hands had begun to sweat: he thought of Reynolds trying to pull his gloves off, though they stuck to his palm. What had he been afraid of? It was more than the pick-up: there was somebody else in the apartment: somebody with a violent temper.

Gavin's stomach turned as his eyes found the smeared hand-print on the door; it was blood.

He pushed the door, but it wouldn't open any further. There was something behind it. He slid through the available space, and into the kitchen. An unemptied waste bin, or a neglected vegetable rack, fouled the air. Gavin smoothed the wall with his palm to find the light switch, and the fluorescent tube spasmed into life.

Reynolds' Gucci shoes poked out from behind the door. Gavin pushed it to, and Reynolds rolled out of his hiding place. He'd obviously crawled behind the door to take refuge; there was something of the beaten animal in his tucked up body. When Gavin touched him he shuddered.

"It's all right . . . it's me." Gavin prised a bloody hand from Reynolds' face. There was a deep gouge running from his temple to his chin, and another, parallel with it but not as deep, across the middle of his forehead and his nose, as though he'd been raked by a two pronged fork.

Reynolds opened his eyes. It took him a second only to focus on Gavin, before he said:

"Go away."

"You're hurt."

"Jesus' sake, go away. Quickly. I've changed my mind . . . You understand?"

"I'll fetch the police."

The man practically spat: "Get the fucking hell out of here, will you? Fucking bum-boy!"

Gavin stood up, trying to make sense out of all this. The guy was in pain, it made him aggressive. Ignore the insults and fetch something to cover the wound. That was it. Cover the wound, and then leave him to his own devices. If he didn't want the police that was his business. Probably he didn't want to explain the presence of a pretty-boy in his hot-house.

"Just let me get you a bandage— "

Gavin went back into the hallway.

Behind the kitchen door Reynolds said: "Don't," but the bum-boy didn't hear him. It wouldn't have made much difference if he had. Gavin liked disobedience. Don't was an invitation.

Reynolds put his back to the kitchen door, and tried to edge his way upright, using the door-handle as purchase. But his head was spinning: a carousel of horrors, round and round, each horse uglier than the last. His legs doubled up under him, and he fell down like the senile fool he was. Damn. Damn. Damn.

Gavin heard Reynolds fall, but he was too busy arming himself to hurry back into the kitchen. If the intruder who'd attacked Reynolds was still in the flat, he wanted to be ready to defend himself. He rummaged through the reports on the desk in the study and alighted on a paper knife which was lying beside a pile of unopened correspondence. Thanking God for it, he snatched it up. It was light, and the blade was thin and brittle, but properly placed it could surely kill.

Happier now, he went back into the hall and took a moment to work out his tactics. The first thing was to locate the bathroom, hopefully there he'd find a bandage for Reynolds. Even a clean towel would help. Maybe then he could get some sense out of the guy, even coax him into an explanation.

Beyond the kitchen the hallway made a sharp left. Gavin turned the corner, and dead ahead the door was ajar. A light burned inside: water shone on tiles. The bathroom.

Clamping his left hand over the right hand that held the knife, Gavin approached the door. The muscles of his arms had become rigid with fear: would that improve his strike if it was required? he wondered. He felt inept, graceless, slightly stupid.

There was blood on the door-jamb, a palm-print that was clearly Reynolds'. This was where it had happened—Reynolds had thrown out a hand to support himself as he reeled back from his assailant. If the attacker was still in the flat, he must be here. There was nowhere else for him to hide.

Later, if there was a later, he'd probably analyse this situation and call himself a fool for kicking the door open, for encouraging this confrontation. But even as he contemplated the idiocy of the action he was performing it, and the door was swinging open across tiles strewn with water-blood puddles, and any moment there'd be a figure there, hook-handed, screaming defiance.

No. Not at all. The assailant wasn't here; and if he wasn't here, he wasn't in the flat.

Gavin exhaled, long and slow. The knife sagged in his hand, denied its pricking. Now, despite the sweat, the terror, he was disappointed. Life had let him down, again—snuck his destiny out of the back door and left him with a mop in his hand not a medal. All he could do was play nurse to the old man and go on his way.

The bathroom was decorated in shades of lime; the blood and tiles clashed. The translucent shower curtain, sporting stylised fish and seaweed, was partially drawn. It looked like the scene of a movie murder: not quite real. Blood too bright: light too flat.

Gavin dropped the knife in the sink, and opened the mirrored cabinet. It was well-stocked with mouth-washes, vitamin supplements, and abandoned toothpaste tubes, but the only medication was a tin of Elastoplast. As he closed the cabinet door he met his own features in the mirror, a drained face. He turned on the cold tap full, and lowered his head to the sink; a splash of water would clear away the vodka and put some colour in his cheeks.

As he cupped the water to his face, something made a noise behind him. He stood up, his heart knocking against his ribs, and turned off the tap. Water dripped off his chin and his eyelashes, and gurgled down the waste pipe.

The knife was still in the sink, a hand's-length away. The sound was coming from the bath, from *in* the bath, the inoffensive slosh of water.

Alarm had triggered flows of adrenalin, and his senses distilled the air with new precision. The sharp scent of lemon soap, the brilliance of the turquoise angel-fish flitting through lavender kelp

on the shower curtain, the cold droplets on his face, the warmth
behind his eyes: all sudden experiences, details his mind had passed
over 'til now, too lazy to see and smell and feel to the limits of
its reach.

You're living in the real world, his head said (it was a revelation),
and if you're not very careful you're going to die there.

Why hadn't he looked in the bath? Asshole. Why not the bath?

"Who's there?" he asked, hoping against hope that Reynolds had
an otter that was taking a quiet swim. Ridiculous hope. There was
blood here, for Christ's sake.

He turned from the mirror as the lapping subsided—do it! do
it!—and slid back the shower curtain on its plastic hooks. In his
haste to unveil the mystery he'd left the knife in the sink. Too late
now: the turquoise angels concertinaed, and he was looking down
into the water.

It was deep, coming up to within an inch or two of the top of the
bath, and murky. A brown scum spiralled on the surface, and the
smell off it was faintly animal, like the wet fur of a dog. Nothing
broke the surface of the water.

Gavin peered in, trying to work out the form at the bottom,
his reflection floating amid the scum. He bent closer, unable to
puzzle out the relation of shapes in the silt, until he recognised the
crudely-formed fingers of a hand and he realised he was looking at
a human form curled up into itself like a foetus, lying absolutely still
in the filthy water.

He passed his hand over the surface to clear away the muck, his
reflection shattered, and the occupant of the bath came clear. It was a
statue, carved in the shape of a sleeping figure, only its head, instead
of being tucked up tight, was cranked round to stare up out of the
blur of sediment towards the surface. Its eyes were painted open, two
crude blobs on a roughly carved face; its mouth was a slash, its ears
ridiculous handles on its bald head. It was naked: its anatomy no
better realised than its features: the work of an apprentice sculptor.
In places the paint had been corrupted, perhaps by the soaking, and
was lifting off the torso in grey, globular strands. Underneath, a core
of dark wood was uncovered.

There was nothing to be frightened of here. An *objet d'art* in a
bath, immersed in water to remove a crass paint-job. The lapping
he'd heard behind him had been some bubbles rising from the thing,
caused by a chemical reaction. There: the fright was explained.
Nothing to panic over. Keep beating my heart, as the barman
at the Ambassador used to say when a new beauty appeared on
the scene.

Gavin smiled at the irony; this was no Adonis.

"Forget you ever saw it."

Reynolds was at the door. The bleeding had stopped, staunched by an unsavoury rag of a handkerchief pressed to the side of his face. The light of the tiles made his skin bilious: his pallor would have shamed a corpse.

"Are you all right? You don't look it."

"I'll be fine . . . just go, please."

"What happened?"

"I slipped. Water on the floor. I slipped, that's all."

"But the noise . . ."

Gavin was looking back into the bath. Something about the statue fascinated him. Maybe its nakedness, and that second strip it was slowly performing underwater: the ultimate strip: off with the skin.

"Neighbours, that's all."

"What is this?" Gavin asked, still looking at the unfetching doll-face in the water.

"It's nothing to do with you."

"Why's it all curled up like that? Is he dying?"

Gavin looked back to Reynolds to see the response to that question, the sourest of smiles, fading.

"You'll want money."

"No."

"Damn you! You're in business aren't you? There's notes beside the bed; take whatever you feel you deserve for your wasted time— "
He was appraising Gavin. "—and your silence."

Again the statue: Gavin couldn't keep his eyes off it, in all its crudity. His own face, puzzled, floated on the skin of the water, shaming the hand of the artist with its proportions.

"Don't wonder," said Reynolds.

"Can't help it."

"This is nothing to do with you."

"You stole it . . . is that right? This is worth a mint and you stole it."

Reynolds pondered the question and seemed, at last, too tired to start lying.

"Yes. I stole it."

"And tonight somebody came back for it— "

Reynolds shrugged.

"—Is that it? Somebody came back for it?"

"That's right. I stole it . . ." Reynolds was saying the lines by rote, ". . . and somebody came back for it."

"That's all I wanted to know."

"Don't come back here, Gavin whoever-you-are. And don't try anything clever, because I won't be here."

"You mean extortion?" said Gavin, "I'm no thief."

Reynolds' look of appraisal rotted into contempt.

"Thief or not, be thankful. If it's in you." Reynolds stepped away from the door to let Gavin pass. Gavin didn't move.

"Thankful for what?" he demanded. There was an itch of anger in him; he felt, absurdly, rejected, as though he was being foisted off with a half-truth because he wasn't worthy enough to share this secret.

Reynolds had no more strength left for explanation. He was slumped against the door-frame, exhausted.

"Go," he said.

Gavin nodded and left the guy at the door. As he passed from bathroom into hallway a glob of paint must have been loosened from the statue. He heard it break surface, heard the lapping at the edge of the bath, could see, in his head, the way the ripples made the body shimmer.

"Goodnight," said Reynolds, calling after him.

Gavin didn't reply, nor did he pick up any money on his way out. Let him have his tombstones and his secrets.

On his way to the front door he stepped into the main room to pick up his jacket. The face of Flavinus the Standard-Bearer looked down at him from the wall. The man must have been a hero, Gavin thought. Only a hero would have been commemorated in such a fashion. He'd get no remembrance like that; no stone face to mark his passage.

He closed the front door behind him, aware once more that his tooth was aching, and as he did so the noise began again, the beating of a fist against a wall.

Or worse, the sudden fury of a woken heart.

The toothache was really biting the following day, and he went to the dentist mid-morning, expecting to coax the girl on the desk into giving him an instant appointment. But his charm was at a low ebb, his eyes weren't sparkling quite as luxuriantly as usual. She told him he'd have to wait until the following Friday, unless it was an emergency. He told her it was: she told him it wasn't. It was going to be a bad day: an aching tooth, a lesbian dentist receptionist, ice on the puddles, nattering women on every street corner, ugly children, ugly sky.

That was the day the pursuit began.

Gavin had been chased by admirers before, but never quite like this. Never so subtle, so surreptitious. He'd had people follow him round for days, from bar to bar, from street to street, so dog-like it almost drove him mad. Seeing the same longing face night after night, screwing up the courage to buy him a drink, perhaps offering him a watch, cocaine, a week in Tunisia, whatever. He'd rapidly come to loathe that sticky adoration that went bad as quickly as milk, and stank to high Heaven once it had. One of his most ardent admirers, a knighted actor he'd been told, never actually came near him, just followed him around, looking and looking. At first the attention had been flattering, but the pleasure soon became irritation, and eventually he'd cornered the guy in a bar and threatened him with a broken head. He'd been so wound up that night, so sick of being devoured by looks, he'd have done some serious harm if the pitiful bastard hadn't taken the hint. He never saw the guy again; half thought he'd probably gone home and hanged himself.

But this pursuit was nowhere near as obvious, it was scarcely more than a feeling. There was no hard evidence that he had somebody on his tail. Just a prickly sense, every time he glanced round, that someone was slotting themselves into the shadows, or that on a night street a walker was keeping pace with him, matching every click of his heel, every hesitation in his step. It was like paranoia, except that he wasn't paranoid. If he was paranoid, he reasoned, somebody would tell him.

Besides, there were incidents. One morning the cat woman who lived on the landing below him idly enquired who his visitor was: the funny one who came in late at night and waited on the stairs hour after hour, watching his room. He'd had no such visitor: and knew no-one who fitted the description.

Another day, on a busy street, he'd ducked out of the throng into the doorway of an empty shop and was in the act of lighting a cigarette when somebody's reflection, distorted through the grime on the window, caught his eye. The match burned his finger, he looked down as he dropped it, and when he looked up again the crowd had closed round the watcher like an eager sea.

It was a bad, bad feeling: and there was more where that came from.

Gavin had never spoken with Preetorius, though they'd exchanged an occasional nod on the street, and each asked after the other in the company of mutual acquaintances as though they were dear friends. Preetorius was a black, somewhere between forty-five and assassination, a glorified pimp who claimed to be descended from

Napoleon. He'd been running a circle of women, and three or four
boys, for the best part of a decade, and doing well from the business.
When he first began work, Gavin had been strongly advised to ask for
Preetorius' patronage, but he'd always been too much of a maverick
to want that kind of help. As a result he'd never been looked upon
kindly by Preetorius or his clan. Nevertheless, once he became a
fixture on the scene, no-one challenged his right to be his own man.
The word was that Preetorius even admitted a grudging admiration
for Gavin's greed.

Admiration or no, it was a chilly day in Hell when Preetorius
actually broke the silence and spoke to him.

"White boy."

It was towards eleven, and Gavin was on his way from a bar off
St Martin's Lane to a club in Covent Garden. The street still buzzed:
there were potential punters amongst the theatre and movie-goers,
but he hadn't got the appetite for it tonight. He had a hundred in
his pocket, which he'd made the day before and hadn't bothered to
bank. Plenty to keep him going.

His first thought when he saw Preetorius and his pie-bald goons
blocking his path was: they want my money.

"White boy."

Then he recognised the flat, shining face. Preetorius was no street
thief; never had been, never would be.

"White boy, I'd like a word with you."

Preetorius took a nut from his pocket, shelled it in his palm, and
popped the kernel into his ample mouth.

"You don't mind do you?"

"What do you want?"

"Like I said, just a word. Not too much to ask, is it?"

"OK. What?"

"Not here."

Gavin looked at Preetorius' cohorts. They weren't gorillas, that
wasn't the black's style at all, but nor were they ninety-eight pound
weaklings. This scene didn't look, on the whole, too healthy.

"Thanks, but no thanks." Gavin said, and began to walk, with as
even a pace as he could muster, away from the trio. They followed.
He prayed they wouldn't, but they followed. Preetorius talked at
his back.

"Listen. I hear bad things about you," he said.

"Oh yes?"

"I'm afraid so. I'm told you attacked one of my boys."

Gavin took six paces before he answered. "Not me. You've got
the wrong man."

"He recognised you, trash. You did him some serious mischief."

"I told you: not me."

"You're a lunatic, you know that? You should be put behind fucking bars."

Preetorius was raising his voice. People were crossing the street to avoid the escalating argument.

Without thinking, Gavin turned off St Martin's Lane into Long Acre, and rapidly realised he'd made a tactical error. The crowds thinned substantially here, and it was a long trek through the streets of Covent Garden before he reached another centre of activity. He should have turned right instead of left, and he'd have stepped onto Charing Cross Road. There would have been some safety there. Damn it, he couldn't turn round, not and walk straight into them. All he could do was walk (not run; never run with a mad dog on your heels) and hope he could keep the conversation on an even keel.

Preetorius: "You've cost me a lot of money."

"I don't see— "

"You put some of my prime boy-meat out of commission. It's going to be a long time 'til I get that kid back on the market. He's shit scared, see?"

"Look . . . I didn't do anything to anybody."

"Why do you fucking lie to me, trash? What have I ever done to you, you treat me like this?".

Preetorius picked up his pace a little and came up level with Gavin, leaving his associates a few steps behind.

"Look . . ." he whispered to Gavin, "kids like that can be tempting, right? That's cool. I can get into that. You put a little boy-pussy on my plate I'm not going to turn my nose up at it. But you hurt him: and when you hurt one of my kids, I bleed too."

"If I'd done this like you say, you think I'd be walking the street?"

"Maybe you're not a well man, you know? We're not talking about a couple of bruises here, man. I'm talking about you taking a shower in a kid's blood, that's what I'm saying. Hanging him up and cutting him everywhere, then leaving him on my fuckin' stairs wearing a pair of fuckin' socks. You getting my message now, white boy? You read my message?"

Genuine rage had flared as Preetorius described the alleged crimes, and Gavin wasn't sure how to handle it. He kept his silence, and walked on.

"That kid idolised you, you know? Thought you were essential reading for an aspirant bum-boy. How'd you like that?"

"Not much."

"You should be fuckin' flattered, man, 'cause that's about as much as you'll ever amount to."

"Thanks."

"You've had a good career. Pity it's over."

Gavin felt iced lead in his belly: he'd hoped Preetorius was going to be content with a warning. Apparently not. They were here to damage him: Jesus, they were going to hurt him, and for something he hadn't done, didn't even know anything about.

"We're going to take you off the street, white boy. Permanently."

"I did nothing."

"The kid knew you, even with a stocking over your head he knew you. The voice was the same, the clothes were the same. Face it, you were recognised. Now take the consequences."

"Fuck you."

Gavin broke into a run. As an eighteen year old he'd sprinted for his county: he needed that speed again now. Behind him Preetorius laughed (such sport!) and two sets of feet pounded the pavement in pursuit. They were close, closer—and Gavin was badly out of condition. His thighs were aching after a few dozen yards, and his jeans were too tight to run in easily. The chase was lost before it began.

"The man didn't tell you to leave," the white goon scolded, his bitten fingers digging into Gavin's biceps.

"Nice try." Preetorius smiled, sauntering towards the dogs and the panting hare. He nodded, almost imperceptibly, to the other goon.

"Christian?" he asked.

At the invitation Christian delivered a fist to Gavin's kidneys. The blow doubled him up, spitting curses.

Christian said: "Over there." Preetorius said: "Make it snappy," and suddenly they were dragging him out of the light into an alley. His shirt and his jacket tore, his expensive shoes were dragged through dirt, before he was pulled upright, groaning. The alley was dark and Preetorius' eyes hung in the air in front of him, dislocated.

"Here we are again," he said. "Happy as can be."

"I . . . didn't touch him," Gavin gasped.

The unnamed cohort, Not-Christian, put a ham hand in the middle of Gavin's chest, and pushed him back against the end wall of the alley. His heel slid in muck, and though he tried to stay upright his legs had turned to water. His ego too: this was no time to be courageous. He'd beg, he fall down on his knees and lick their soles if need be, anything to stop them doing a job on him. Anything to stop them spoiling his face.

That was Preetorius' favourite pastime, or so the street talk went: the spoiling of beauty. He had a rare way with him, could maim beyond hope of redemption in three strokes of his razor, and have the victim pocket his lips as a keepsake.

Gavin stumbled forward, palms slapping the wet ground. Something rotten-soft slid out of its skin beneath his hand.

Not-Christian exchanged a grin with Preetorius.

"Doesn't he look delightful?" he said.

Preetorius was crunching a nut. "Seems to me— " he said, "—the man's finally found his place in life."

"I didn't touch him," Gavin begged. There was nothing to do but deny and deny: and even then it was a lost cause.

"You're guilty as hell," said Not-Christian.

"*Please.*"

"I'd really like to get this over with as soon as possible," said Preetorius, glancing at his watch, "I've got appointments to keep, people to pleasure."

Gavin looked up at his tormentors. The sodium-lit street was a twenty-five-yard dash away, if he could break through the cordon of their bodies.

"Allow me to rearrange your face for you. A little crime of fashion."

Preetorius had a knife in his hand. Not-Christian had taken a rope from his pocket, with a ball on it. The ball goes in the mouth, the rope goes round the head—you couldn't scream if your life depended on it. This was it.

Go!

Gavin broke from his grovelling position like a sprinter from his block, but the slops greased his heels, and threw him off balance. Instead of making a clean dash for safety he stumbled sideways and fell against Christian, who in turn fell back.

There was a breathless scrambling before Preetorius stepped in, dirtying his hands on the white trash, and hauling him to his feet.

"No way out, fucker," he said, pressing the point of the blade against Gavin's chin. The jut of the bone was clearest there, and he began the cut without further debate—tracing the jawline, too hot for the act to care if the trash was gagged or not. Gavin howled as blood washed down his neck, but his cries were cut short as somebody's fat fingers grappled with his tongue, and held it fast.

His pulse began to thud in his temples, and windows, one behind the other, opened and opened in front of him, and he was falling through them into unconsciousness.

Better to die. Better to die. They'd destroy his face: better to die.

Then he was screaming again, except that he wasn't aware of making the sound in his throat. Through the slush in his ears he tried to focus on the voice, and realised it was Preetorius' scream he was hearing, not his own.

His tongue was released; and he was spontaneously sick. He staggered back, puking, from a mess of struggling figures in front of him. A person, or persons, unknown had stepped in, and prevented the completion of his spoiling. There was a body sprawled on the floor, face up. Not-Christian, eyes open, life shut. God: someone had killed for him. *For him.*

Gingerly, he put his hand up to his face to feel the damage. The flesh was deeply lacerated along his jawbone, from the middle of his chin to within an inch of his ear. It was bad, but Preetorius, ever organised, had left the best delights to the last, and had been interrupted before he'd slit Gavin's nostrils or taken off his lips. A scar along his jawbone wouldn't be pretty, but it wasn't disastrous.

Somebody was staggering out of the mêlée towards him— Preetorius, tears on his face, eyes like golf-balls.

Beyond him Christian, his arms useless, was staggering towards the street.

Preetorius wasn't following: why?

His mouth opened; an elastic filament of saliva, strung with pearls, depended from his lower lip.

"Help me," he appealed, as though his life was in Gavin's power. One large hand was raised to squeeze a drop of mercy out of the air, but instead came the swoop of another arm, reaching over his shoulder and thrusting a weapon, a crude blade, into the black's mouth. He gargled it a moment, his throat trying to accommodate its edge, its width, before his attacker dragged the blade up and back, holding Preetorius' neck to steady him against the force of the stroke. The startled face divided, and heat bloomed from Preetorius' interior, warming Gavin in a cloud.

The weapon hit the alley floor, a dull clank. Gavin glanced at it. A short, wide-bladed sword. He looked back at the dead man.

Preetorius stood upright in front of him, supported now only by his executioner's arm. His gushing head fell forward, and the executioner took the bow as a sign, neatly dropping Preetorius' body at Gavin's feet. No longer eclipsed by the corpse, Gavin met his saviour face to face.

It took him only a moment to place those crude features: the startled, lifeless eyes, the gash of a mouth, the jug-handle ears. It was Reynolds' statue. It grinned, its teeth too small for its

head. Milk-teeth, still to be shed before the adult form. There
was, however, some improvement in its appearance, he could see
that even in the gloom. The brow seemed to have swelled; the face
was altogether better proportioned. It remained a painted doll, but
it was a doll with aspirations.

The statue gave a stiff bow, its joints unmistakably creaking, and
the absurdity, the sheer absurdity of this situation welled up in
Gavin. It bowed, damn it, it smiled, it murdered: and yet it couldn't
possibly be alive, could it? Later, he would disbelieve, he promised
himself. Later he'd find a thousand reasons not to accept the reality
in front of him: blame his blood-starved brain, his confusion, his
panic. One way or another he'd argue himself out of this fantastic
vision, and it would be as though it had never happened.

If he could just live with it a few minutes longer.

The vision reached across and touched Gavin's jaw, lightly,
running its crudely carved fingers along the lips of the wound
Preetorius had made. A ring on its smallest finger caught the light:
a ring identical to his own.

"We're going to have a scar," it said.

Gavin knew its voice.

"Dear me: pity," it said. It was speaking with *his* voice. "Still, it
could be worse."

His voice. God, his, his, his.

Gavin shook his head.

"Yes," it said, understanding that he'd understood.

"Not me."

"Yes."

"Why?"

It transferred its touch from Gavin's jawbone to its own, marking
out the place where the wound should be, and even as it made the
gesture its surface opened, and it grew a scar on the spot. No blood
welled up: it had no blood.

Yet wasn't that his own, even brow it was emulating, and the piercing eyes, weren't they becoming his, and the wonderful mouth?

"The boy?" said Gavin, fitting the pieces together.

"Oh the boy . . ." It threw its unfinished glance to Heaven. "What
a treasure he was. And how he snarled."

"You washed in his blood?"

"I need it." It knelt to the body of Preetorius and put its fingers in
the split head. "This blood's old, but it'll do. The boy was better."

It daubed Preetorius' blood on its cheek, like war-paint. Gavin
couldn't hide his disgust.

"Is he such a loss?" the effigy demanded.

The answer was no, of course. It was no loss at all that Preetorius was dead, no loss that some drugged, cocksucking kid had given up some blood and sleep because this painted miracle needed to feed its growth. There were worse things than this every day, somewhere; huge horrors. And yet—

"You can't condone me," it prompted, "it's not in your nature is it? Soon it won't be in mine either. I'll reject my life as a tormentor of children, because I'll see through *your* eyes, share *your* humanity . . ."

It stood up, its movements still lacking flexibility.

"Meanwhile, I must behave as I think fit."

On its cheek, where Preetorius' blood had been smeared, the skin was already waxier, less like painted wood.

"I am a thing without a proper name," it pronounced. "I am a wound in the flank of the world. But I am also that perfect stranger you always prayed for as a child, to come and take you, call you beauty, lift you naked out of the street and through Heaven's window. Aren't I? Aren't I?"

How did it know the dreams of his childhood? How could it have guessed that particular emblem, of being hoisted out of a street full of plague into a house that was Heaven?

"Because I am yourself," it said, in reply to the unspoken question, "made perfectable."

Gavin gestured towards the corpses.

"You can't be me. I'd never have done this."

It seemed ungracious to condemn it for its intervention, but the point stood.

"Wouldn't you?" said the other. "I think you would."

Gavin heard Preetorius' voice in his ear. "A crime of fashion." Felt again the knife at his chin, the nausea, the helplessness. Of course he'd have done it, a dozen times over he'd have done it, and called it justice.

It didn't need to hear his accession, it was plain.

"I'll come and see you again," said the painted face. "Meanwhile—if I were you— " it laughed, "—I'd be going."

Gavin locked eyes with it a beat, probing it for doubt, then started towards the road.

"Not that way. This!"

It was pointing towards a door in the wall, almost hidden behind festering bags of refuse. That was how it had come so quickly, so quietly.

"Avoid the main streets, and keep yourself out of sight. I'll find you again, when I'm ready."

Gavin needed no further encouragement to leave. Whatever the explanations of the night's events, the deeds were done. Now wasn't the time for questions.

He slipped through the doorway without looking behind him: but he could hear enough to turn his stomach. The thud of fluid on the ground, the pleasurable moan of the miscreant: the sounds were enough for him to be able to picture its toilet.

Nothing of the night before made any more sense the morning after. There was no sudden insight into the nature of the waking dream he'd dreamt. There was just a series of stark facts.

In the mirror, the fact of the cut on his jaw, gummed up and aching more badly than his rotted tooth.

In the newspapers, the reports of two bodies found in the Covent Garden area, known criminals viciously murdered in what the police described as a "gangland slaughter".

In his head, the inescapable knowledge that he would be found out sooner or later. Somebody would surely have seen him with Preetorius, and spill the beans to the police. Maybe even Christian, if he was so inclined, and they'd be there, on his step, with cuffs and warrants. Then what could he tell them, in reply to their accusations? That the man who did it was not a man at all, but an effigy of some kind, that was by degrees becoming a replica of himself? The question was not whether he'd be incarcerated, but which hole they'd lock him in, prison or asylum?

Juggling despair with disbelief, he went to the casualty department to have his face seen to, where he waited patiently for three and a half hours with dozens of similar walking wounded.

The doctor was unsympathetic. There was no use in stitches now, he said, the damage was done: the wound could and would be cleaned and covered, but a bad scar was now unavoidable. Why didn't you come last night, when it happened? the nurse asked. He shrugged: what the hell did they care? Artificial compassion didn't help him an iota.

As he turned the corner with his street, he saw the cars outside the house, the blue light, the cluster of neighbours grinning their gossip. Too late to claim anything of his previous life. By now they had possession of his clothes, his combs, his perfumes, his letters—and they'd be searching through them like apes after lice. He'd seen how thorough-going these bastards could be when it suited them, how completely they could seize and parcel up a man's identity. Eat it up, suck it up: they could erase you as surely as a shot, but leave you a living blank.

There was nothing to be done. His life was theirs now to sneer at and salivate over: even have a nervous moment, one or two of them, when they saw his photographs and wondered if perhaps they'd paid for this boy themselves, some horny night.

Let them have it all. They were welcome. From now on he would be lawless, because laws protect possessions and he had none. They'd wiped him clean, or as good as: he had no place to live, nor anything to call his own. He didn't even have fear: that was the strangest thing.

He turned his back on the street and the house he'd lived in for four years, and he felt something akin to relief, happy that his life had been stolen from him in its squalid entirety. He was the lighter for it.

Two hours later, and miles away, he took time to check his pockets. He was carrying a banker's card, almost a hundred pounds in cash, a small collection of photographs, some of his parents and sister, mostly of himself; a watch, a ring, and a gold chain round his neck. Using the card might be dangerous—they'd surely have warned his bank by now. The best thing might be to pawn the ring and the chain, then hitch North. He had friends in Aberdeen who'd hide him awhile.

But first—Reynolds.

It took Gavin an hour to find the house where Ken Reynolds lived. It was the best part of twenty-four hours since he'd eaten and his belly complained as he stood outside Livingstone Mansions. He told it to keep its peace, and slipped into the building. The interior looked less impressive by daylight. The tread of the stair carpet was worn, and the paint on the balustrade filthied with use.

Taking his time he climbed the three flights to Reynolds' apartment, and knocked.

Nobody answered, nor was there any sound of movement from inside. Reynolds had told him of course: don't come back—I won't be here. Had he somehow guessed the consequences of sicking that thing into the world?

Gavin rapped on the door again, and this time he was certain he heard somebody breathing on the other side of the door.

"Reynolds . . ." he said, pressing to the door, "I can hear you."

Nobody replied, but there was somebody in there, he was sure of it. Gavin slapped his palm on the door.

"Come on, open up. Open up, you bastard."

A short silence, then a muffled voice. "Go away."

"I want to speak to you."

"Go away, I told you, go away. I've nothing to say to you."

"You owe me an explanation, for God's sake. If you don't open this fucking door I'll fetch someone who will."

An empty threat, but Reynolds responded: "No! Wait. Wait."

There was the sound of a key in the lock, and the door was opened a few paltry inches. The flat was in darkness beyond the scabby face that peered out at Gavin. It was Reynolds sure enough, but unshaven and wretched. He smelt unwashed, even through the crack in the door, and he was wearing only a stained shirt and a pair of pants, hitched up with a knotted belt.

"I can't help you. Go away."

"If you'll let me explain— " Gavin pressed the door, and Reynolds was either too weak or too befuddled to stop him opening it. He stumbled back into the darkened hallway.

"What the fuck's going on in here?"

The place stank of rotten food. The air was evil with it. Reynolds let Gavin slam the door behind him before producing a knife from the pocket of his stained trousers.

"You don't fool me," Reynolds gleamed, "I know what you've done. Very fine. Very clever."

"You mean the murders? It wasn't me."

Reynolds poked the knife towards Gavin.

"How many blood-baths did it take?" he asked, tears in his eyes. "Six? Ten?"

"I didn't kill anybody."

". . . monster."

The knife in Reynolds' hand was the paper knife Gavin himself had wielded. He approached Gavin with it. There was no doubt: he had every intention of using it. Gavin flinched, and Reynolds seemed to take hope from his fear.

"Had you forgotten what it was like, being flesh and blood?"

The man had lost his marbles.

"Look . . . I just came here to talk."

"You came here to kill me. I could reveal you . . . so you came to kill me."

"Do you know who I am?" Gavin said.

Reynolds sneered: "You're not the queer boy. You look like him, but you're not."

"For pity's sake . . . I'm Gavin . . . Gavin— "

The words to explain, to prevent the knife pressing any closer, wouldn't come.

"Gavin, you remember?" was all he could say.

Reynolds faltered a moment, staring at Gavin's face.

"You're sweating," he said. The dangerous stare fading in his eyes.

Gavin's mouth had gone so dry he could only nod.

"I can see," said Reynolds, "you're sweating."

He dropped the point of the knife.

"It could never sweat," he said, "Never had, never would have, the knack of it. You're the boy . . . not it. The boy."

His face slackened, its flesh a sack which was almost emptied.

"I need help," said Gavin, his voice hoarse. "You've got to tell me what's going on."

"You want an explanation?" Reynolds replied, "you can have whatever you can find."

He led the way into the main room. The curtains were drawn, but even in the gloom Gavin could see that every antiquity it had contained had been smashed beyond repair. The pottery shards had been reduced to smaller shards, and those shards to dust. The stone reliefs were destroyed, the tombstone of Flavinus the Standard-Bearer was rubble.

"Who did this?"

"I did," said Reynolds.

"Why?"

Reynolds sluggishly picked his way through the destruction to the window, and peered through a slit in the velvet curtains.

"It'll come back, you see," he said, ignoring the question.

Gavin insisted: "Why destroy it all?"

"It's a sickness," Reynolds replied. "Needing to live in the past."

He turned from the window.

"I stole most of these pieces," he said, "over a period of many years. I was put in a position of trust, and I misused it."

He kicked over a sizeable chunk of rubble: dust rose.

"Flavinus lived and died. That's all there is to tell. Knowing his name means nothing, or next to nothing. It doesn't make Flavinus real again: he's dead and happy."

"The statue in the bath?"

Reynolds stopped breathing for a moment, his inner eye meeting the painted face.

"You I thought I was it, didn't you? When I came to the door."

"Yes. I thought it had finished its business."

"It imitates."

Reynolds nodded. "As far as I understand its nature," he said, "yes, it imitates."

"Where did you find it?"

"Near Carlisle. I was in charge of the excavation there. We found it lying in the bathhouse, a statue curled up into a ball beside the remains of an adult male. It was a riddle. A dead man and a statue, lying together in a bathhouse. Don't ask me what drew me to the thing, I don't know. Perhaps it works its will through the mind as well as the physique. I stole it, brought it back here."

"And you fed it?"

Reynolds stiffened.

"Don't ask."

"I *am* asking. You fed it?"

"Yes."

"You intended to bleed me, didn't you? That's why you brought me here: to kill me, and let it wash itself— "

Gavin remembered the noise of the creature's fists on the sides of the bath, that angry demand for food, like a child beating on its cot. He'd been so close to being taken by it, lamb-like.

"Why didn't it attack me the way it did you? Why didn't it just jump out of the bath and feed on me?"

Reynolds wiped his mouth with the palm of his hand.

"It saw your face, of course."

Of course: it saw my face, and wanted it for itself, and it couldn't steal the face of a dead man, so it let me be. The rationale for its behaviour was fascinating, now it was revealed: Gavin felt a taste of Reynolds' passion, unveiling mysteries.

"The man in the bathhouse. The one you uncovered— "

"Yes . . .?"

"He stopped it doing the same thing to him, is that right?"

"That's probably why his body was never moved, just sealed up. No-one understood that he'd died fighting a creature that was stealing his life."

The picture was near as damn it complete; just anger remaining to be answered.

This man had come close to murdering him to feed the effigy. Gavin's fury broke surface. He took hold of Reynolds by shirt and skin, and shook him. Was it his bones or teeth that rattled?

"It's almost got my face." He stared into Reynolds' bloodshot eyes. "What happens when it finally has the trick off pat?"

"I don't know."

"You tell me the worst—Tell me!"

"It's all guesswork," Reynolds replied.

"Guess then!"

"When it's perfected its physical imitation, I think it'll steal the one thing it can't imitate: your soul."

Reynolds was past fearing Gavin. His voice had sweetened, as though he was talking to a condemned man. He even smiled.

"Fucker!"

Gavin hauled Reynolds' face yet closer to his. White spittle dotted the old man's cheek.

"You don't care! You don't give a shit, do you?"

He hit Reynolds across the face, once, twice, then again and again, until he was breathless.

The old man took the beating in absolute silence, turning his face up from one blow to receive another, brushing the blood out of his swelling eyes only to have them fill again.

Finally, the punches faltered.

Reynolds, on his knees, picked pieces of tooth off his tongue.

"I deserved that," he murmured.

"How do I stop it?" said Gavin.

Reynolds shook his head.

"Impossible," he whispered, plucking at Gavin's hand. "Please," he said, and taking the fist, opened it and kissed the lines.

Gavin left Reynolds in the ruins of Rome, and went into the street. The interview with Reynolds had told him little he hadn't guessed. The only thing he could do now was find this beast that had his beauty, and best it. If he failed, he failed attempting to secure his only certain attribute: a face that was wonderful. Talk of souls and humanity was for him so much wasted air. He wanted his face.

There was rare purpose in his step as he crossed Kensington. After years of being the victim of circumstance he saw circumstance embodied at last. He would shake sense from it, or die trying.

In his flat Reynolds drew aside the curtain to watch a picture of evening fall on a picture of a city.

No night he would live through, no city he'd walk in again. Out of sighs, he let the curtain drop, and picked up the short stabbing sword. The point he put to his chest.

"Come on," he told himself and the sword, and pressed the hilt. But the pain as the blade entered his body a mere half inch was enough to make his head reel: he knew he'd faint before the job was half-done. So he crossed to the wall, steadied the hilt against it, and let his own body-weight impale him. That did the trick. He wasn't sure if the sword had skewered him through entirely, but by the amount of blood he'd surely killed himself. Though he tried to arrange to turn, and so drive the blade all the way home as he fell on it, he fluffed the gesture, and instead fell on his side. The impact made him aware of the sword in his body, a stiff, uncharitable presence transfixing him utterly.

It took him well over ten minutes to die, but in that time, pain apart, he was content. Whatever the flaws of his fifty-seven years, and they were many, he felt he was perishing in a way his beloved Flavinus would not have been ashamed of.

Towards the end it began to rain, and the noise on the roof made him believe God was burying the house, sealing him up forever. And as the moment came, so did a splendid delusion: a hand, carrying a light, and escorted by voices, seemed to break through the wall, ghosts of the future come to excavate his history. He smiled to greet them, and was about to ask what year this was when he realised he was dead.

The creature was far better at avoiding Gavin than he'd been at avoiding it. Three days passed without its pursuer snatching sight of hide or hair of it.

But the fact of its presence, close, but never too close, was indisputable. In a bar someone would say: "Saw you last night on the Edgware Road" when he'd not been near the place, or "How'd you make out with that Arab then?" or "Don't you speak to your friends any longer?"

And God, he soon got to like the feeling. The distress gave way to a pleasure he'd not known since the age of two: ease.

So what if someone else was working his patch, dodging the law and the street-wise alike; so what if his friends (what friends? Leeches) were being cut by this supercilious copy; so what if his life had been taken from him and was being worn to its length and its breadth in lieu of him? He could sleep, and know that he, or something so like him it made no difference, was awake in the night and being adored. He began to see the creature not as a monster terrorising him, but as his tool, his public persona almost. It was substance: he shadow.

He woke, dreaming.

It was four-fifteen in the afternoon, and the whine of traffic was loud from the street below. A twilight room; the air breathed and rebreathed and breathed again so it smelt of his lungs. It was over a week since he'd left Reynolds to the ruins, and in that time he'd only ventured out from his new digs (one tiny bedroom, kitchen, bathroom) three times. Sleep was more important now than food or exercise. He had enough dope to keep him happy when sleep wouldn't come, which was seldom, and he'd grown to like the staleness of the air, the flux of light through the curtainless window, the sense of a world elsewhere which he had no part of or place in.

Today he'd told himself he ought to go out and get some fresh air, but he hadn't been able to raise the enthusiasm. Maybe later, much later, when the bars were emptying and he wouldn't be noticed, then he'd slip out of his cocoon and see what could be seen. For now, there were dreams—

Water.

He'd dreamt water; sitting beside a pool in Fort Lauderdale, a pool full of fish. And the splash of their leaps and dives was continuing, an overflow from sleep. Or was it the other way round? Yes; he had been hearing running water in his sleep and his dreaming mind had made an illustration to accompany the sound. Now awake, the sound continued.

It was coming from the adjacent bathroom, no longer running, but lapping. Somebody had obviously broken in while he was asleep, and was now taking a bath. He ran down the short list of possible intruders: the few who knew he was here. There was Paul: a nascent hustler who'd bedded down on the floor two nights before; there was Chink, the dope dealer; and a girl from downstairs he thought was called Michelle. Who was he kidding? None of these people would have broken the lock on the door to get in. He knew very well who it must be. He was just playing a game with himself, enjoying the process of elimination, before he narrowed the options to one.

Keen for reunion, he slid out from his skin of sheet and duvet. His body turned to a column of gooseflesh as the cold air encased him, his sleep-erection hid its head. As he crossed the room to where his dressing gown hung on the back of the door he caught sight of himself in the mirror, a freeze frame from an atrocity film, a wisp of a man, shrunk by cold, and lit by a rainwater light. His reflection almost flickered, he was so insubstantial.

Wrapping the dressing gown, his only freshly purchased garment, around him, he went to the bathroom door. There was no noise of water now. He pushed the door open.

The warped linoleum was icy beneath his feet; and all he wanted to do was to see his friend, then crawl back into bed. But he owed the tatters of his curiosity more than that: he had questions.

The light through the frosted glass had deteriorated rapidly in the three minutes since he'd woken: the onset of night and a rain-storm congealing the gloom. In front of him the bath was almost filled to overflowing, the water was oil-slick calm, and dark. As before, nothing broke surface. It was lying deep, hidden.

How long was it since he'd approached a lime-green bath in a lime-green bathroom, and peered into the water? It could have been yesterday: his life between then and now had become one long night. He looked down. It was there, tucked up, as before, and asleep, still wearing all its clothes as though it had had no time to undress before it hid itself. Where it had been bald it now sprouted a luxuriant head of hair, and its features were quite complete. No trace of a painted face remained: it had a plastic beauty that was his own absolutely, down to the last mole. Its perfectly finished hands were crossed on its chest.

The night deepened. There was nothing to do but watch it sleep, and he became bored with that. It had traced him here, it wasn't likely to run away again, he could go back to bed. Outside the rain had slowed the commuters' homeward journey to a crawl, there were accidents, some fatal; engines overheated, hearts too. He listened to the chase; sleep came and went. It was the middle of the evening when thirst woke him again: he was dreaming water, and there was the sound as it had been before. The creature was hauling itself out of the bath, was putting its hand to the door, opening it.

There it stood. The only light in the bedroom was coming from the street below; it barely began to illuminate the visitor.

"Gavin? Are you awake?"

"Yes," he said.

"Will you help me?" it asked. There was no trace of threat in its voice, it asked as a man might ask his brother, for kinship's sake.

"What do you want?"

"Time to heal."

"Heal?"

"Put on the light."

Gavin switched on the lamp beside the bed and looked at the figure at the door. It no longer had its arms crossed on its chest, and Gavin saw that the position had been covering an appalling shotgun wound. The flesh of its chest had been blown open, exposing its colourless innards. There was, of course, no blood: that it would never have. Nor, from this distance, could Gavin see anything in its interior that faintly resembled human anatomy.

"God Almighty," he said.

"Preetorius had friends," said the other, and its fingers touched the edge of the wound. The gesture recalled a picture of the wall of his mother's house. Christ in Glory—the Sacred Heart floating inside the Saviour—while his fingers, pointing to the agony he'd suffered, said: "This was for you."

"Why aren't you dead?"

"Because I'm not yet alive," it said.

Not yet: remember that, Gavin thought. It has intimations of
mortality.

"Are you in pain?"

"No," it said sadly, as though it craved the experience, "I feel
nothing. All the signs of life are cosmetic. But I'm learning." It
smiled. "I've got the knack of the yawn, and the fart." The idea
was both absurd and touching; that it would aspire to farting, that
a farcical failure in the digestive system was for it a precious sign of
humanity.

"And the wound?"

"—is healing. Will heal completely in time."

Gavin said nothing.

"Do I disgust you?" it asked, without inflection.

"No."

It was staring at Gavin with perfect eyes, his perfect eyes.

"What did Reynolds tell you?" it asked.

Gavin shrugged.

"Very little."

"That I'm a monster? That I suck out the human spirit?"

"Not exactly."

"More or less."

"More or less," Gavin conceded.

It nodded. "He's right," it said. "In his way, he's right. I need
blood: that makes me monstrous. In my youth, a month ago, I bathed
in it. Its touch gave wood the appearance of flesh. But I don't need it
now: the process is almost finished. All I need now— "

It faltered; not, Gavin thought, because it intended to lie, but
because the words to describe its condition wouldn't come.

"What do you need?" Gavin pressed it.

It shook its head, looking down at the carpet. "I've lived several
times, you know. Sometimes I've stolen lives and got away with it.
Lived a natural span, then shrugged off that face and found another.
Sometimes, like the last time, I've been challenged, and lost— "

"Are you some kind of machine?"

"No."

"What then?"

"I am what I am. I know of no others like me; though why should
I be the only one? Perhaps there *are* others, many others: I simply
don't know of them yet. So I live and die and live again, and
learn nothing— " the word was bitterly pronounced, "—of myself.
Understand? You know what you are because you see others like you.
If you were alone on earth, what would you know? What the mirror
told you, that's all. The rest would be myth and conjecture."

The summary was made without sentiment.

"May I lie down?" it asked.

It began to walk towards him, and Gavin could see more clearly the fluttering in its chest-cavity, the restless, incoherent forms that were mushrooming there in place of the heart. Sighing, it sank face-down on the bed, its clothes sodden, and closed its eyes.

"We'll heal," it said. "Just give us time."

Gavin went to the door of the flat and bolted it. Then he dragged a table over and wedged it under the handle. Nobody could get in and attack it in sleep: they would stay here together in safety, he and it, he and himself. The fortress secured, he brewed some coffee and sat in the chair across the room from the bed and watched the creature sleep.

The rain rushed against the window heavily one hour, lightly the next. Wind threw sodden leaves against the glass and they clung there like inquisitive moths; he watched them sometimes, when he tired of watching himself, but before long he'd want to look again, and he'd be back staring at the casual beauty of his outstretched arm, the light flicking the wrist-bone, the lashes. He fell asleep in the chair about midnight, with an ambulance complaining in the street outside, and the rain coming again.

It wasn't comfortable in the chair, and he'd surface from sleep every few minutes, his eyes opening a fraction. The creature was up: it was standing by the window, now in front of the mirror, now in the kitchen. Water ran: he dreamt water. The creature undressed: he dreamt sex. It stood over him, its chest whole, and he was reassured by its presence: he dreamt, it was for a moment only, himself lifted out of a street through a window into Heaven. It dressed in his clothes: he murmured his assent to the theft in his sleep. It was whistling: and there was a threat of day through the window, but he was too dozy to stir just yet, and quite content to have the whistling young man in his clothes live for him.

At last it leaned over the chair and kissed him on the lips, a brother's kiss, and left. He heard the door close behind it.

After that there were days, he wasn't sure how many, when he stayed in the room, and did nothing but drink water. This thirst had become unquenchable. Drinking and sleeping, drinking and sleeping, twin moons.

The bed he slept on was damp at the beginning from where the creature had laid, and he had no wish to change the sheets. On the contrary he enjoyed the wet linen, which his body dried out too soon. When it did he took a bath himself in the water the thing had

lain in and returned to the bed dripping wet, his skin crawling with
cold, and the scent of mildew all around. Later, too indifferent to
move, he allowed his bladder free rein while he lay on the bed, and
that water in time became cold, until he dried it with his dwindling
body-heat.

But for some reason, despite the icy room, his nakedness, his
hunger, he couldn't die.

He got up in the middle of the night of the sixth or seventh day,
and sat on the edge of the bed to find the flaw in his resolve. When
the solution didn't come he began to shamble around the room much
as the creature had a week earlier, standing in front of the mirror to
survey his pitifully changed body, watching the snow shimmer down
and melt on the sill.

Eventually, by chance, he found a picture of his parents he
remembered the creature staring at. Or had he dreamt that? He
thought not: he had a distinct idea that it had picked up this picture
and looked at it.

That was, of course, the bar to his suicide: that picture. There
were respects to be paid. Until then how could he hope to die?

He walked to the Cemetery through the slush wearing only a pair
of slacks and a tee-shirt. The remarks of middle-aged women and
school-children went unheard. Whose business but his own was it
if going barefoot was the death of him? The rain came and went,
sometimes thickening towards snow, but never quite achieving its
ambition.

There was a service going on at the church itself, a line of brittle
coloured cars parked at the front. He slipped down the side into
the churchyard. It boasted a good view, much spoiled today by the
smoky veil of sleet, but he could see the trains and the high-rise flats;
the endless rows of roofs. He ambled amongst the headstones, by no
means certain of where to find his father's grave. It had been sixteen
years: and the day hadn't been that memorable. Nobody had said
anything illuminating about death in general, or his father's death
specifically, there wasn't even a social gaff or two to mark the day:
no aunt broke wind at the buffet table, no cousin took him aside to
expose herself.

He wondered if the rest of the family ever came here: whether
indeed they were still in the country. His sister had always threatened
to move out: go to New Zealand, begin again. His mother was
probably getting through her fourth husband by now, poor sod,
though perhaps she was the pitiable one, with her endless chatter
barely concealing the panic.

Here was the stone. And yes, there were fresh flowers in the marble urn that rested amongst the green marble chips. The old bugger had not lain here enjoying the view unnoticed. Obviously somebody, he guessed his sister, had come here seeking a little comfort from Father. Gavin ran his fingers over the name, the date, the platitude. Nothing exceptional: which was only right and proper, because there'd been nothing exceptional about him.

Staring at the stone, words came spilling out, as though Father was sitting on the edge of the grave, dangling his feet, raking his hair across his gleaming scalp, pretending, as he always pretended, to care.

"What do you think, eh?"

Father wasn't impressed.

"Not much, am I?" Gavin confessed.

You said it, son.

"Well I was always careful, like you told me. There aren't any bastards out there, going to come looking for me."

Damn pleased.

"I wouldn't be much to find, would I?"

Father blew his nose, wiped it three times. Once from left to right, again left to right, finishing right to left. Never failed. Then he slipped away.

"Old shithouse."

A toy train let out a long blast on its horn as it passed and Gavin looked up. There he was—himself—standing absolutely still a few yards away. He was wearing the same clothes he'd put on a week ago when he'd left the flat. They looked creased and shabby from constant wear. But the flesh! Oh, the flesh was more radiant than his own had ever been. It almost shone in the drizzling light; and the tears on the doppelganger's cheeks only made the features more exquisite.

"What's wrong?" said Gavin.

"It always makes me cry, coming here." It stepped over the graves towards him, its feet crunching on gravel, soft on grass. So real.

"You've been here before?"

"Oh yes. Many times, over the years— "

Over the years? What did it mean, over the years? Had it mourned here for people it had killed?

As if in answer:

"—I come to visit Father. Twice, maybe three times a year."

"This isn't your father," said Gavin, almost amused by the delusion. "It's mine."

"I don't see any tears on your face," said the other.

"I feel . . ."

"Nothing," his face told him. "You feel nothing at all, if you're honest."

That was the truth.

"Whereas I . . ." the tears began to flow again, its nose ran, "I will miss him until I die."

It was surely playacting, but if so why was there such grief in its eyes: and why were its features crumpled into ugliness as it wept. Gavin had seldom given in to tears: they'd always made him feel weak and ridiculous. But this thing was proud of tears, it gloried in them. They were its triumph.

And even then, knowing it had overtaken him, Gavin could find nothing in him that approximated grief.

"Have it," he said. "Have the snots. You're welcome."

The creature was hardly listening.

"Why is it all so painful?" it asked, after a pause. "Why is it loss that makes me human?"

Gavin shrugged. What did he know or care about the fine art of being human? The creature wiped its nose with its sleeve, sniffed, and tried to smile through its unhappiness.

"I'm sorry," it said, "I'm making a damn fool of myself. Please forgive me."

It inhaled deeply, trying to compose itself.

"That's all right," said Gavin. The display embarrassed him, and he was glad to be leaving.

"Your flowers?" he asked as he turned from the grave.

It nodded.

"He hated flowers."

The thing flinched.

"Ah."

"Still, what does he know?"

He didn't even look at the effigy again; just turned and started up the path that ran beside the church. A few yards on, the thing called after him:

"Can you recommend a dentist?"

Gavin grinned, and kept walking.

It was almost the commuter hour. The arterial road that ran by the church was already thick with speeding traffic: perhaps it was Friday, early escapees hurrying home. Lights blazed brilliantly, horns blared.

Gavin stepped into the middle of the flow without looking to right or left, ignoring the squeals of brakes, and the curses, and began to walk amongst the traffic as if he were idling in an open field.

The wing of a speeding car grazed his leg as it passed, another almost collided with him. Their eagerness to get somewhere, to arrive at a place they would presently be itching to depart from again, was comical. Let them rage at him, loathe him, let them glimpse his featureless face and go home haunted. If the circumstances were right, maybe one of them would panic, swerve, and run him down. Whatever. From now on he belonged to chance, whose Standard-Bearer he would surely be.

Brian Lumley

Necros

If anyone knows about vampires, it should be Brian Lumley. He has had a huge success on both sides of the Atlantic (and in translation) with the five-volume 'Necroscope' series: Necroscope, Wamphyri!, The Source, Deadspeak *and* Deadspawn, *and he is currently at work on a follow-up trilogy, 'Brian Lumley's Vampire World'.*

Other recent books include The Transition of Titus Crow, The Burrowers Beneath, House of Cthulhu, Tarra Khash: Hrossak!, The House of Doors, Sorcery in Shad *and* Demogorgon, *while a handsome hardcover collection,* The Compleat Khash: Volume One, Never a Backward Glance, *was published in 1991. Short stories have appeared in* Best New Horror, Dark Voices 2 *and* 3, Final Shadows *and* The Mammoth Book of Terror, *amongst others.*

'Necros' is one of Lumley's best—a clever twist on the vampire theme, with an ending that is guaranteed to come as a surprise.

I

AN OLD WOMAN in a faded blue frock and black head-square paused in the shade of Mario's awning and nodded good-day. She smiled a gap-toothed smile. A bulky, slouch-shouldered youth in jeans and a stained yellow T-shirt—a slope-headed idiot, probably her grand-son—held her hand, drooling vacantly and fidgeting beside her.

Mario nodded good-naturedly, smiled, wrapped a piece of stale *fucaccia* in greaseproof paper and came from behind the bar to give it to her. She clasped his hand, thanked him, turned to go.

Her attention was suddenly arrested by something she saw across the road. She started, cursed vividly, harshly, and despite my meager knowledge of Italian I picked up something of the hatred in her tone. "Devil's spawn!" She said it again. "Dog! Swine!" She pointed a shaking hand and finger, said yet again: "Devil's spawn!" before making the two-fingered, double-handed stabbing sign with which the Italians ward off evil. To do this it was first necessary that she drop her salted bread, which the idiot youth at once snatched up.

Then, still mouthing low, guttural imprecations, dragging the shuffling, *fucaccia*-munching cretin behind her, she hurried off along the street and disappeared into an alley. One word that she had repeated over and over again stayed in my mind: "*Necros! Necros!*" Though the word was new to me, I took it for a curse-word. The accent she put on it had been poisonous.

I sipped at my Negroni, remained seated at the small circular table beneath Mario's awning and stared at the object of the crone's distaste. It was a motorcar, a white convertible Rover and this year's model, inching slowly forward in a stream of holiday traffic. And it was worth looking at it only for the girl behind the wheel. The little man in the floppy white hat beside her—well, he was something else, too. But *she* was—just something else.

I caught just a glimpse, sufficient to feel stunned. That was good. I had thought it was something I could never know again: that feeling a man gets looking at a beautiful girl. Not after Linda. And yet—

She was young, say twenty-four or -five, some three or four years my junior. She sat tall at the wheel, slim, raven-haired under a white, wide-brimmed summer hat which just missed matching that of her companion, with a complexion cool and creamy enough to pour over peaches. I stood up—yes, to get a better look—and right then the traffic came to a momentary standstill. At that moment, too, she turned her head and looked at me. And if the profile had stunned me . . . well, the full frontal knocked me dead. The girl was simply, classically, beautiful.

Her eyes were of a dark green but very bright, slightly tilted and perfectly oval under straight, thin brows. Her cheeks were high, her lips a red Cupid's bow, her neck long and white against the glowing yellow of her blouse. And her smile—

—Oh, yes, she smiled.

Her glance, at first cool, became curious in a moment, then a little angry, until finally, seeing my confusion—that smile. And as she turned her attention back to the road and followed the stream of traffic out of sight, I saw a blush of color spreading on the creamy surface of her cheek. Then she was gone.

Then, too, I remembered the little man who sat beside her. Actually, I hadn't seen a great deal of him, but what I had seen had given me the creeps. He too had turned his head to stare at me, leaving in my mind's eye an impression of beady bird eyes, sharp and intelligent in the shade of his hat. He had stared at me for only a moment, and then his head had slowly turned away; but even when he no longer looked at me, when he stared straight ahead, it seemed to me I could feel those raven's eyes upon me, and that a query had been written in them.

I believed I could understand it, that look. He must have seen a good many young men staring at him like that—or rather, at the girl. His look had been a threat in answer to my threat—and because he was practiced in it I had certainly felt the more threatened!

I turned to Mario, whose English was excellent. "She has something against expensive cars and rich people?"

"Who?" he busied himself behind his bar.

"The old lady, the woman with the idiot boy."

"Ah!" he nodded. "Mainly against the little man, I suspect."

"Oh?"

"You want another Negroni?"

"OK—and one for yourself—but tell me about this other thing, won't you?"

"If you like—but you're only interested in the girl, yes?" He grinned.

I shrugged. "She's a good-looker . . ."

"Yes, I saw her." Now he shrugged. "That other thing—just old myths and legends, that's all. Like your English Dracula, eh?"

"Transylvanian Dracula," I corrected him.

"Whatever you like. And Necros: that's the name of the spook, see?"

"Necros is the name of a vampire?"

"A spook, yes."

"And this is a real legend? I mean, historical?"

He made a fifty-fifty face, his hands palms-up. "Local, I guess. Ligurian. I remember it from when I was a kid. If I was bad, old Necros sure to come and get me. Today," again the shrug, "it's forgotten."

"Like the bogeyman," I nodded.

"Eh?"

"Nothing. But why did the old girl go on like that?"

Again he shrugged. "Maybe she think that old man Necros, eh? She crazy, you know? Very backward. The whole family."

I was still interested. "How does the legend go?"

"The spook takes the life out of you. You grow old, spook grows young. It's a bargain you make: he gives you something you want, gets what he wants. What he wants is your youth. Except he uses it up quick and needs more. All the time, more youth."

"What kind of bargain is that?" I asked. "What does the victim get out of it?"

"Gets what he wants," said Mario, his brown face cracking into another grin. "In your case the girl, eh? *If* the little man was Necros . . ."

He got on with his work and I sat there sipping my Negroni. End of conversation. I thought no more about it—until later.

II

Of course, I should have been in Italy with Linda, but . . . I had kept her "Dear John" for a fortnight before shredding it, getting mindlessly drunk and starting in on the process of forgetting. That had been a month ago. The holiday had already been booked and I wasn't about to miss out on my trip to the sun. And so I had come out on my own. It was hot, the swimming was good, life was easy and the food superb. With just two days left to enjoy it, I told myself it hadn't been bad. But it would have been better with Linda.

Linda . . . She was still on my mind—at the back of it, anyway—later that night as I sat in the bar of my hotel beside an open bougainvillaea-decked balcony that looked down on the bay and the seafront lights of the town. And maybe she wasn't all that far back in my mind—maybe she was right there in front—or else I was just plain daydreaming. Whichever, I missed the entry of the lovely lady and her shriveled companion, failing to spot and recognize them until they were taking their seats at a little table just the other side of the balcony's sweep.

This was the closest I'd been to her, and—

Well, first impressions hadn't lied. This girl *was* beautiful. She didn't look quite as young as she'd first seemed—my own age, maybe—but beautiful she certainly was. And the old boy? He must be, could only be, her father. Maybe it sounds like I was little naive, but with her looks this lady really didn't need an old man. And if she did need one it didn't have to be *this* one.

By now she'd seen me and my fascination with her must have been obvious. Seeing it she smiled and blushed at one and the same time, and for a moment turned her eyes away—but only for a moment. Fortunately her companion had his back to me or he must have known my feelings at once; for as she looked at me again—fully upon me this time—I could have sworn I read an invitation in her eyes, and in that same moment any bitter vows I may have made melted away completely and were forgotten. God, *please* let him be her father!

For an hour I sat there, drinking a few too many cocktails, eating olives and potato crisps from little bowls on the bar, keeping my eyes off the girl as best I could, if only for common decency's sake. But . . . all the time I worried frantically at the problem of how to introduce myself, and as the minutes ticked by it seemed to me that the most obvious way must also be the best.

But how obvious would it be to the old boy?

And the damnable thing was that the girl hadn't given me another glance since her original—invitation? Had I mistaken that look of hers?—or was she simply waiting for me to make the first move? *God, let him be her father*!

She was sipping Martinis, slowly; he drank a rich red wine, in some quantity. I asked a waiter to replenish their glasses and charge it to me. I had already spoken to the bar steward, a swarthy, friendly little chap from the South called Francesco, but he hadn't been able to enlighten me. The pair were not resident, he assured me; but being resident myself I was already pretty sure of that.

Anyway, my drinks were delivered to their table; they looked surprised; the girl put on a perfectly innocent expression, questioned the waiter, nodded in my direction and gave me a cautious smile, and the old boy turned his head to stare at me. I found myself smiling in return but avoiding his eyes, which were like coals now, sunken deep in his brown-wrinkled face. Time seemed suspended—if only for a second—then the girl spoke again to the waiter and he came across to me.

"Mr Collins, sir, the gentleman and the young lady thank you and request that you join them." Which was everything I had dared hope for—for the moment.

Standing up I suddenly realized how much I'd had to drink. I willed sobriety on myself and walked across to their table. They didn't stand up but the little chap said, "Please sit." His voice was a rustle of dried grass. The waiter was behind me with a chair. I sat.

"Peter Collins," I said. "How do you do, Mr—er?— "

"Karpethes," he answered. "Nichos Karpethes. And this is my wife, Adrienne." Neither one of them had made the effort to extend their hands, but that didn't dismay me. Only the fact that they were married dismayed me. He must be very, very rich, this Nichos Karpethes.

"I'm delighted you invited me over," I said, forcing a smile, "but I see that I was mistaken. You see, I thought I heard you speaking English, and I— "

"Thought we were English?" she finished it for me. "A natural error. Originally I am Armenian, Nichos is Greek, of course. We do not speak each other's tongue, but we do both speak English. Are you staying here, Mr Collins?"

"Er, yes—for one more day and night. Then— " I shrugged and put on a sad look, "—back to England, I'm afraid."

"Afraid?" the old boy whispered. "There is something to fear in a return to your homeland?"

"Just an expression," I answered. "I meant I'm afraid that my holiday is coming to an end."

He smiled. It was a strange, wistful sort of smile, wrinkling his face up like a little walnut. "But your friends will be glad to see you again. Your loved ones—?"

I shook my head. "Only a handful of friends—none of them really close—and no loved ones. I'm a loner, Mr Karpethes."

"A loner?" His eyes glowed deep in their sockets and his hands began to tremble where they gripped the table's rim. "Mr Collins, you don't— "

"We understand," she cut him off. "For although we are together, we too, in our way, are loners. Money has made Nichos lonely, you see? Also, he is not a well man and time is short. He will not waste what time he has on frivolous friendships. As for myself—people do not understand our being together, Nichos and I. They pry, and I withdraw. And so I too am a loner."

There was no accusation in her voice, but still I felt obliged to say: "I certainly didn't intend to pry, Mrs— "

"Adrienne," she smiled. "Please. No, of course you didn't. I would not want you to think we thought that of you. Anyway I will *tell* you why we are together, and then it will be put aside."

Her husband coughed, seemed to choke, struggled to his feet. I stood up and took his arm. He at once shook me off—with some distaste, I thought—but Adrienne had already signaled to a waiter. "Assist Mr Karpethes to the gentleman's room," she quickly instructed in very good Italian. "And please help him back to the table when he has recovered."

As he went Karpethes gesticulated, probably tried to say something to me by way of an apology, choked again and reeled as he allowed the waiter to help him from the room.

"I'm . . . sorry," I said, not knowing what else to say.

"He has attacks." She was cool. "Do not concern yourself. I am used to it."

We sat in silence for a moment. Finally I began. "You were going to tell me— "

"Ah, yes! I had forgotten. It is a symbiosis."

"Oh?"

"Yes. I need the good life he can give me, and he needs . . . my youth? We supply each other's needs." And so, in a way, the old woman with the idiot boy hadn't been wrong after all. A sort of bargain had indeed been struck. Between Karpethes and his wife. As that thought crossed my mind I felt the short hairs at the back of my neck stiffen for a moment. Gooseflesh grawled on my arms. After all, "Nichos" was pretty close to "Necros," and now this youth thing again. Coincidence, of course. And after all, aren't all relationships bargains of sorts? Bargains struck for better or for worse.

"But for how long?" I asked. "I mean, how long will it work for you?"

She shrugged. "I have been provided for. And he will have me all the days of his life."

I coughed, cleared my throat, gave a strained, self-conscious laugh. "And here's me, the non-pryer!"

"No, not at all, I wanted you to know."

"Well," I shrugged, "—but it's been a pretty deep first conversation."

"First? Did you believe that buying me a drink would entitle you to more than onε conversation?"

I almost winced. "Actually, I— "

But then she smiled and my world lit up. "You did not need to buy the drinks," she said. "There would have been some other way."

I looked at her inquiringly. "Some other way to—?"

"To find out if we were English or not."

"Oh!"

"Here comes Nichos now," she smiled across the room. "And we must be leaving. He's not well. Tell me, will you be on the beach tomorrow?"

"Oh—yes!" I answered after a moment's hesitation. "I like to swim."

"So do I. Perhaps we can swim out to the raft . . .?"

"I'd like that very much."

Her husband arrived back at the table under his own steam. He looked a little stronger now, not quite so shriveled somehow. He did not sit but gripped the back of his chair with parchment fingers, knuckles white where the skin stretched over old bones. "Mr Collins," he rustled, "—Adrienne, I'm sorry . . ."

"There's really no need," I said, rising.

"We really must be going." She also stood. "No, you stay here, er, Peter? It's kind of you, but we can manage. Perhaps we'll see you on the beach." And she helped him to the door of the bar and through it without once looking back.

III

They weren't staying at my hotel, had simply dropped in for a drink. That was understandable (though I would have preferred to think that she had been looking for me) for *my* hotel was middling tourist-class while theirs was something else. They were up on the hill, high on the crest of a Ligurian spur where a smaller, much more exclusive place nested in Mediterranean pines. A place whose lights spelled money when they shone up there at night, whose music came floating down from a tiny open-air disco like the laughter of high-living elementals of the air. If I was poetic it was because of her. I mean, that beautiful girl and that weary, wrinkled dried up walnut of an old man. If anything I was sorry for him. And yet in another way I wasn't.

And let's make no pretense about it—if I haven't said it already, let me say it right now—I wanted her. Moreover, there had been that about our conversation, her beach invitation, which told me that she was available.

The thought of it kept me awake half the night . . .

I was on the beach at 9:00 a.m.—they didn't show until 11:00. When they did, and when she came out of her tiny changing cubicle—

There wasn't a male head on the beach that didn't turn at least twice. Who could blame them? That girl, in *that* costume, would have turned the head of a sphynx. But—there was something, some little nagging thing different about her. A maturity beyond

her years? She held herself like a model, a princess. But who was
it for? Karpethes or me?

As for the old man: he was in a crumpled lightweight summer
suit and sunshade hat as usual, but he seemed a bit more perky
this morning. Unlike myself he'd doubtless had a good night's sleep.
While his wife had been changing he had made his way unsteadily
across the pebbly beach to my table and sun umbrella, taking the
seat directly opposite me; and before his wife could appear he had
opened with:

"Good morning, Mr Collins."

"Good morning," I answered. "Please call me Peter."

"Peter, then," he nodded. He seemed out of breath, either from his
stumbling walk over the beach or a certain urgency which I could
detect in his movements, his hurried, almost rude "let's get down
to it" manner.

"Peter, you said you would be here for one more day?"

"That's right," I answered, for the first time studying him closely
where he sat like some strange garden gnome half in the shade of
the beach umbrella. "This is my last day."

He was a bundle of dry wood, a pallid prune, a small, umber
scarecrow. And his voice, too, was of straw, or autumn leaves blown
across a shady path. Only his eyes were alive. "And you said you
have no family, few friends, no one to miss you back in England?"

Warning bells rang in my head. Maybe it wasn't so much urgency
in him—which usually implies a goal or ambition still to be realized—but eagerness in that the goal was in sight. "That's correct. I
am, was, a student doctor. When I get home I shall seek a position.
Other than that there's nothing, no one, no ties."

He leaned forward, bird eyes very bright, claw hand reaching
across the table, trembling, and—

Her shadow suddenly fell across us as she stood there in that
costume. Karpethes jerked back in his chair. His face was working,
strange emotions twisting the folds and wrinkles of his flesh into
stranger contours. I could feel my heart thumping against my ribs
... why I couldn't say. I calmed myself, looked up at her and
smiled.

She stood with her back to the sun, which made a dark silhouette
of her head and face. But in that blot of darkness her oval eyes were
green jewels. "Shall we swim, Peter?"

She turned and ran down the beach, and of course I ran after her.
She had a head start and beat me to the water, beat me to the raft,
too. It wasn't until I hauled myself up beside her that I thought
of Karpethes: how I hadn't even excused myself before plunging

after her. But at least the water had cleared my head, bringing me completely awake and aware.

Aware of her incredible body where it stretched almost touching mine, on the fiber deck of the gently bobbing raft.

I mentioned her husband's line of inquiry, gasping a little for breath as I recovered from the frantic exercise of our race. She, on the other hand, already seemed completely recovered. She carefully arranged her hair about her shoulders like a fan, to dry in the sunlight, before answering.

"Nichos is not really my husband," she finally said, not looking at me. "I am his companion, that's all. I could have told you last night, but . . . there was the chance that you really were curious only about our nationality. As for any veiled threats he might have issued: that is not unusual. He might not have the vitality of younger men, but jealousy is ageless."

"No," I answered, "he didn't threaten—not that I noticed. But jealousy? Knowing I have only one more day to spend here, what has he to fear from me?"

Her shoulders twitched a little, a shrug. She turned her face to me, her lips inches away. Her eyelashes were like silken shutters over green pools, hiding whatever swam in the deeps. "I am young, Peter, and so are you. And you are very attractive, very . . . eager? Holiday romances are not uncommon."

My blood was on fire. "I have very little money," I said. "We are staying at different hotels. He already suspects me. It is impossible."

"What is?" she innocently asked, leaving me at a complete loss.

But then she laughed, tossed back her hair, already dry, dangled her hands and arms in the water. "Where there's a will . . ." she said.

"You know that I want you— " The words spilled out before I could control or change them.

"Oh, yes. And I want you." She said it so simply, and yet suddenly I felt seared. A moth brushing the magnet candle's flame.

I lifted my head, looked toward the beach. Across seventy-five yards of sparkling water the beach umbrellas looked very large and close. Karpethes sat in the shade just as I had last seen him, his face hidden in shadow. But I knew that he watched.

"You can do nothing here," she said, her voice languid—but I noticed now that she, too, seemed short of breath.

"This," I told her with a groan, "is going to kill me!"

She laughed, laughter that sparkled more than the sun on the sea. "I'm sorry," she sobered. "It's unfair of me to laugh. But—your case is not hopeless."

"Oh?"

"Tomorrow morning, early, Nichos has an appointment with a specialist in Genova. I am to drive him into the city tonight. We'll stay at a hotel overnight."

I groaned my misery. "Then my case *is* quite hopeless. I fly tomorrow."

"But if I sprained my wrist," she said, "and so could not drive . . . and if he went into Genova by taxi while I stayed behind with a headache—because of the pain from my wrist— " Like a flash she was on her feet, the raft tilting, her body diving, striking the water into a spray of diamonds.

Seconds for it all to sink in—and then I was following her, laboring through the water in her churning wake. And as she splashed from the sea, seeing her stumble, go to her hands and knees in Ligurian shingle—and the pained look on her face, the way she held her wrist as she came to her feet. As easy as that!

Karpethes, struggling to rise from his seat, stared at her with his mouth agape. Her face screwed up now as I followed her up the beach. And Adrienne holding her "sprained" wrist and shaking it, her mouth forming an elongated "O." The sinuous motion of her body and limbs, mobile marble with dew of ocean clinging saltily. . . .

If the tiny man had said to me: "I am Necros. I want ten years of your life for one night with her," at that moment I might have sealed the bargain. Gladly. But legends are legends and he wasn't Necros, and he didn't, and I didn't. After all, there was no need. . . .

IV

I suppose my greatest fear was that she might be "having me on," amusing herself at my expense. She was, of course, "safe" with me—insofar as I would be gone tomorrow and the "romance" forgotten, for her, anyway—and I could also see how she was starved for young companionship, a fact she had brought right out in the open from the word go.

But why me? Why should I be so lucky?

Attractive? Was I? I had never thought so. Perhaps it was because I *was* so safe: here today and gone tomorrow, with little or no chance of complications. Yes, that must be it. *If* she wasn't simply making a fool of me. She might be just a tease—

—But she wasn't.

At 8:30 that evening I was in the bar of my hotel—had been there

for an hour, careful not to drink too much, unable to eat—when
the waiter came to me and said there was a call for me on the
reception telephone. I hurried out to reception where the clerk
discreetly excused himself and left me alone.

"Peter?" Her voice was a deep well of promise. "He's gone. I've
booked us a table, to dine at 9:00. Is that all right for you?"

"A table? Where?" my own voice breathless.

"Why, up here, of course! Oh, don't worry, it's perfectly safe. And
anyway, Nichos knows."

"Knows?" I was taken aback, a little panicked. "What does he
know?"

"That we're dining together. In fact he suggested it. He didn't
want me to eat alone—and since this is your last night . . ."

"I'll get a taxi right away," I told her.

"Good. I look forward to . . . seeing you. I shall be in the bar."

I replaced the telephone in its cradle, wondering if she always
took an *apéritif* before the main course. . . .

I had smartened myself up. That is to say, I was immaculate.
Black bow tie, white evening jacket (courtesy of C & A), black
trousers and a lightly-frilled white shirt, the only one I had ever
owned. But I might have known that my appearance would never
match up to hers. It seemed that everything she did was just
perfectly right. I could only hope that that meant literally everything.

But in her black lace evening gown with its plunging neckline,
short wide sleeves and delicate silver embroidery, she was stunning.
Sitting with her in the bar, sipping our drinks—for me a large
whiskey and for her a tall Cinzano—I couldn't take my eyes off
her. Twice I reached out for her hand and twice she drew back
from me.

"Discreet they may well be," she said, letting her oval green
eyes flicker toward the bar, where guests stood and chatted, and
back to me, "but there's really no need to give them occasion to
gossip."

"I'm sorry, Adrienne," I told her, my voice husky and close to
trembling, "but— "

"How is it," she demurely cut me off, "that a good-looking man
like you is—how do you say it?—going short?"

I sat back, chuckled. "That's a rather unladylike expression," I
told her.

"Oh? And what I've planned for tonight is ladylike?"

My voice went huskier still. "Just what is your plan?"

"While we eat," she answered, her voice low, "I shall tell you." At which point a waiter loomed, towel over his arm, inviting us to accompany him to the dining room.

Adrienne's portions were tiny, mine huge. She sipped a slender, light white wine, I gulped blocky rich red from a glass the waiter couldn't seem to leave alone. Mercifully I was hungry—I hadn't eaten all day—else that meal must surely have bloated me out. And all of it ordered in advance, the very best in quality cuisine.

"This," she eventually said, handling me her key, "fits the door of our suite." We were sitting back, enjoying liqueurs and cigarettes. "The rooms are on the ground floor. Tonight you enter through the door, tomorrow morning you leave via the window. A slow walk down to the seafront will refresh you. How is that for a plan?"

"Unbelievable!"

"You don't believe it?"

"Not my good fortune, no."

"Shall we say that we both have our needs?"

"I think," I said, "that I may be falling in love with you. What if I don't wish to leave in the morning?"

She shrugged, smiled, said: "Who knows what tomorrow may bring?"

How could I ever have thought of her simply as another girl? Or even an ordinary young woman? Girl she certainly was, woman, too, but so . . . *knowing*! Beautiful as a princess and knowing as a whore.

If Mario's old myths and legends were reality, and if Nichos Karpethes were really Necros, then he'd surely picked the right companion. No man born could ever have resisted Adrienne, of that I was quite certain. These thoughts were in my mind—but dimly, at the back of my mind—as I left her smoking in the dining room and followed her directions to the suite of rooms at the rear of the hotel. In the front of my mind were other thoughts, much more vivid and completely erotic.

I found the suite, entered, left the door slightly ajar behind me.

The thing about an Italian room is its size. An entire suite of rooms is vast. As it happened I was only interested in one room, and Adrienne had obligingly left the door to that one open.

I was sweating. And yet . . . I shivered.

Adrienne had said fifteen minutes, time enough for her to smoke another cigarette and finish her drink. Then she would come to me. By now the entire staff of the hotel probably knew I was in here, but this was Italy.

V

I shivered again. Excitement? Probably.

I threw off my clothes, found my way to the bathroom, took the quickest shower of my life. Drying myself off, I padded back to the bedroom.

Between the main bedroom and the bathroom a smaller door stood ajar. I froze as I reached it, my senses suddenly alert, my ears seeming to stretch themselves into vast receivers to pick up any slightest sound. For there had been a sound, I was sure of it, from that room. . . .

A scratching? A rustle? A whisper? I couldn't say. But a sound, anyway.

Adrienne would be coming soon. Standing outside that door I slowly recommenced toweling myself dry. My naked feet were still firmly rooted, but my hands automatically worked with the towel. It was nerves, only nerves. There had been no sound, or at worst only the night breeze off the sea, whispering in through an open window.

I stopped toweling, took another step toward the main bedroom, heard the sound again. A small, choking rasp. A tiny gasping for air.

Karpethes? What the hell was going on?

I shivered violently, my suddenly chill flesh shuddering in an uncontrollable spasm. But . . . I forced myself to action, returned to the main bedroom, quickly dressed (with the exceptions of my tie and jacket) and crept back to the small room.

Adrienne must be on her way to me even now. She mustn't find me poking my nose into things, like a suspicious kid. I must kill off this silly feeling that had my skin crawling. Not that an attack of nerves was unnatural in the circumstances, on the contrary, but I wasn't about to let it spoil the night. I pushed open the door of the room, entered into darkness, found the lightswitch. Then—

—I held my breath, flipped the switch.

The room was only half as big as the others. It contained a small single bed, a bedside table, a wardrobe. Nothing more, or at least nothing immediately apparent to my wildly darting eyes. My heart, which was racing, slowed and began to settle toward a steadier beat. The window was open, external shutters closed—but small night sounds were finding their way in through the louvers. The distant sounds of traffic, the toot of horns—holiday sounds from below.

I breathed deeply and gratefully, and saw something projecting from beneath the pillow on the bed. A corner of card or of dark leather, like a wallet or—

—Or a passport!

A Greek passport, Karpethes', when I opened it. But how could it be? The man in the photograph was young, no older than me. His birthdate proved it. And there was his name: Nichos Karpethes. Printed in Greek, of course, but still plain enough. His son?

Puzzling over the passport had served to distract me. My nerves had steadied up. I tossed the passport down, frowned at it where it lay upon the bed, breathed deeply once more . . . and froze solid!

A scratching, a hissing, a dry grunting—from the wardrobe.

Mice? Or did I in fact smell a rat?

Even as the short hairs bristled on the back of my neck I knew anger. There were too many unexplained things here. Too much I didn't understand. And what was it I feared? Old Mario's myths and legends? No, for in my experience the Italians are notorious for getting things wrong. Oh, yes, notorious . . .

I reached out, turned the wardrobe's doorknob, yanked the doors open.

At first I saw nothing of any importance or significance. My eyes didn't know what they sought. Shoes, patent leather, two pairs, stood side by side below. Tiny suits, no bigger than boys' sizes, hung above on steel hangers. And—my God, my God—a waistcoat!

I backed out of that little room on rubber legs, with the silence of the suite shrieking all about me, my eyes bugging, my jaw hanging slack—

"Peter?"

She came in through the suite's main door, came floating toward me, eager, smiling, her green eyes blazing. Then blazing their suspicion, their anger as they saw my condition. "Peter!"

I lurched away as her hands reached for me, those hands I had never yet touched, which had never touched me. Then I was into the main bedroom, snatching my tie and jacket from the bed, (don't ask me why!) and out of the window, yelling some inarticulate, choking thing at her and lashing out frenziedly with my foot as she reached after me. Her eyes were bubbling green hells. "*Peter!*"

Her fingers closed on my forearm, bands of steel containing a fierce, hungry heat. And strong as two men she began to lift me back into her lair!

I put my feet against the wall, kicked, came free and crashed backward into shrubbery. Then up on my feet, gasping for air, running, tumbling, crashing into the night, down madly tilting slopes, through black chasms of mountain pine with the Mediterranean stars winking overhead, and the beckoning, friendly lights of the village seen occasionally below . . .

In the morning, looking up at the way I had descended and remembering the nightmare of my panic-flight, I counted myself lucky to have survived it. The place was precipitous. In the end I *had* fallen, but only for a short distance. All in utter darkness, and my head striking something hard. But . . .

I did survive. Survived both Adrienne and my flight from her.

And waking with the dawn, and gently fingering my bruises and the massive bump on my forehead, I made my staggering way back to my still slumbering hotel, let myself in and *locked* myself in my room—then sat there trembling and moaning until it was time for the coach.

Weak? Maybe I was, maybe I am.

But on my way into Genova, with people round me and the sun hot through the coach's windows, I could think again. I could roll up my sleeve and examine that claw mark of four slim fingers and a thumb, branded white into my suntanned flesh, where hair would never more grow on skin sere and wrinkled.

And seeing those marks I could also remember the wardrobe and the waistcoat—and what the waistcoat contained.

That tiny puppet of a man, alive still but barely, his stick-arms dangling through the waistcoat's armholes, his baby's head projecting, its chin supported by the tightly buttoned waistcoat's breast. And the large bull-dog clip over the hanger's bar, its teeth fastened in the loose, wrinkled skin of his walnut head, holding it up. And his skinny little legs dangling, twig-things twitching there; and his pleading, pleading eyes!

But eyes are something I mustn't dwell upon.

And green is a color I can no longer bear . . .

Brian Stableford

The Man Who Loved the Vampire Lady

Brian Stableford's The Empire of Fear *was one of the most acclaimed fantasy novels of the past few years, and the story which follows eventually became the first chapter of that epic alternate history of a world ruled by vampires.*

More recently he's done the same thing for lycanthropes in the novel Werewolves of London, *and some of his best short stories have been collected in* Sexual Chemistry. *As a writer, critic and academic, Stableford has also written a great deal of non-fiction and edited several anthologies, including* Tales of the Wandering Jew *and* The Dedalus Book of English Fantasy: The 19th Century.

'The Man Who Loved the Vampire Lady' is a touchingly romantic evocation of the vampire that also sets the scene for Stableford's longer work.

> *A man who loves a vampire lady may not die young,*
> *but cannot live forever.* WALACHIAN PROVERB

IT WAS THE thirteenth of June in the Year of Our Lord 1623. Grand Normandy was in the grip of an early spell of warm weather, and the streets of London bathed in sunlight. There were crowds everywhere, and the port was busy with ships, three having docked that very day. One of the ships, the *Freemartin*, was from the Moorish enclave and had produce from the heart of Africa, including ivory and the skins of exotic animals. There were rumors, too, of secret and more precious goods: jewels and magical charms; but such rumors always attended the docking of any vessel from remote parts of the world. Beggars and street urchins had flocked to the dockland, responsive as ever to such whisperings, and were plaguing every sailor in the streets, as anxious for gossip as for copper coins. It seemed that the only faces not animated by excitement were those worn by the severed heads that dressed the spikes atop the Southwark Gate. The Tower of London, though, stood quite aloof from the hubbub, its tall and forbidding turrets so remote from the streets that they belonged to a different world.

Edmund Cordery, mechanician to the court of the Archduke Girard, tilted the small concave mirror on the brass device that rested on his workbench, catching the rays of the afternoon sun and deflecting the light through the system of lenses.

He turned away and directed his son, Noell, to take his place. "Tell me if all is well," he said tiredly. "I can hardly focus my eyes, let alone the instrument."

Noell closed his left eye and put his other to the microscope. He turned the wheel that adjusted the height of the stage. "It's perfect," he said. "What is it?"

"The wing of a moth." Edmund scanned the polished tabletop, checking that the other slides were in readiness for the demonstration. The prospect of Lady Carmilla's visit filled him with a complex anxiety that he resented in himself. Even in the old days, she had not come to his laboratory often, but to see her here—on his own territory, as it were—would be bound to awaken memories that were untouched by the glimpses that he caught of her in the public parts of the Tower and on ceremonial occasions.

"The water slide isn't ready," Noell pointed out.

Edmund shook his head. "I'll make a fresh one when the time comes," he said. "Living things are fragile, and the world that is in a water drop is all too easily destroyed."

He looked farther along the bench-top, and moved a crucible, placing it out of sight behind a row of jars. It was impossible—and unnecessary—to make the place tidy, but he felt it important to conserve some sense of order and control. To discourage himself from fidgeting, he went to the window and looked out at the sparkling Thames and the strange gray sheen on the slate roofs of the houses beyond. From this high vantage point, the people were tiny; he was higher even than the cross on the steeple of the church beside the Leathermarket. Edmund was not a devout man, but such was the agitation within him, yearning for expression in action, that the sight of the cross on the church made him cross himself, murmuring the ritual devotion. As soon as he had done it, he cursed himself for childishness.

I am forty-four years old, he thought, *and a mechanician. I am no longer the boy who was favored with the love of the lady, and there is no need for this stupid trepidation.*

He was being deliberately unfair to himself in this private scolding. It was not simply the fact that he had once been Carmilla's lover that made him anxious. There was the microscope, and the ship from the Moorish country. He hoped that he would be able to judge by the lady's reaction how much cause there really was for fear.

The door opened then, and the lady entered. She half turned to indicate by a flutter of her hand that her attendant need not come in with her, and he withdrew, closing the door behind him. She was alone, with no friend or favorite in tow. She came across the room carefully, lifting the hem of her skirt a little, though the floor was not dusty. Her gaze flicked from side to side, to take note of the shelves, the beakers, the furnace, and the numerous tools of the mechanician's craft. To a commoner, it would have seemed a threatening environment, redolent with unholiness, but her attitude was cool and controlled. She arrived to stand before the brass instrument that Edmund had recently completed, but did not look long at it before raising her eyes to look fully into Edmund's face.

"You look well, Master Cordery," she said calmly. "But you are pale. You should not shut yourself in your rooms now that summer is come to Normandy."

Edmund bowed slightly, but met her gaze. She had not changed in the slightest degree, of course, since the days when he had been intimate with her. She was six hundred years old—hardly younger than the archduke—and the years were impotent as far as her appearance was concerned. Her complexion was much darker than his, her eyes a deep liquid brown, and her hair jet black. He had not stood so close to her for several years, and he could not help the tide of memories rising in his mind. For her, it would be different: his hair was gray now, his skin creased; he must seem an altogether different person. As he met her gaze, though, it seemed to him that she, too, was remembering, and not without fondness.

"My lady," he said, his voice quite steady, "may I present my son and apprentice, Noell."

Noell bowed more deeply than his father, blushing with embarrassment.

The Lady Carmilla favored the youth with a smile. "He has the look of you, Master Cordery," she said—a casual compliment. She returned her attention then to the instrument.

"The designer was correct?" she asked.

"Yes, indeed," he replied. "The device is most ingenious. I would dearly like to meet the man who thought of it. A fine discovery—though it taxed the talents of my lens grinder severely. I think we might make a better one, with much care and skill; this is but a poor example, as one must expect from a first attempt."

The Lady Carmilla seated herself at the bench, and Edmund showed her how to apply her eye to the instrument, and how to adjust the focusing wheel and the mirror. She expressed surprise at the appearance of the magnified moth's wing, and Edmund took her through the series of prepared slides, which included other parts of insects' bodies, and sections through the stems and seeds of plants.

"I need a sharper knife and a steadier hand, my lady," he told her. "The device exposes the clumsiness of my cutting."

"Oh no, Master Cordery," she assured him politely. "These are quite pretty enough. But we were told that more interesting things might be seen. Living things too small for ordinary sight."

Edmund bowed in apology and explained about the preparation of water slides. He made a new one, using a pipette to take a drop from a jar full of dirty river water. Patiently, he helped the lady search the slide for the tiny creatures that human eyes were not equipped to perceive. He showed her one that flowed as if it were semiliquid itself, and tinier ones that moved by means of cilia. She was quite captivated, and watched for some time, moving the slide very gently with her painted fingernails.

Eventually she asked: "Have you looked at other fluids?"

"What kind of fluids?" he asked, though the question was quite clear to him and disturbed him.

She was not prepared to mince words with him. "Blood, Master Cordery," she said very softly. Her past acquaintance with him had taught her respect for his intelligence, and he half regretted it.

"Blood clots very quickly," he told her. "I could not produce a satisfactory slide. It would take unusual skill."

"I'm sure that it would," she replied.

"Noell has made drawings of many of the things we *have* looked at," said Edmund. "Would you like to see them?"

She accepted the change of subject, and indicated that she would. She moved to Noell's station and began sorting through the drawings, occasionally looking up at the boy to compliment him on his work. Edmund stood by, remembering how sensitive he once had been to her moods and desires, trying hard to work out now exactly what she was thinking. Something in one of her contemplative glances at Noell sent an icy pang of dread into Edmund's gut, and he found his more important fears momentarily displaced by what might have been anxiety for his son, or simply jealousy. He cursed himself again for his weakness.

"May I take these to show the archduke?" asked the Lady Carmilla, addressing the question to Noell rather than to his father. The boy nodded, still too embarrassed to construct a proper reply. She took a selection of the drawings and rolled them into a scroll. She stood and faced Edmund again.

"We are most interested in this apparatus," she informed him. "We must consider carefully whether to provide you with new assistants, to encourage development of the appropriate skills. In the meantime, you may return to your ordinary work. I will send someone for the instrument, so that the archduke can inspect it at his leisure. Your son draws very well, and must be encouraged. You and he may visit me in my chambers on Monday next; we will dine at seven o'clock, and you may tell me about all your recent work."

Edmund bowed to signal his acquiescence—it was, of course, a command rather than an invitation. He moved before her to the door in order to hold it open for her. The two exchanged another brief glance as she went past him.

When she had gone, it was as though something taut unwound inside him, leaving him relaxed and emptied. He felt strangely cool and distant as he considered the possibility—stronger now—that his life was in peril.

When the twilight had faded, Edmund lit a single candle on the bench and sat staring into the flame while he drank dark wine from a flask. He did not look up when Noell came into the room, but when the boy brought another stool close to his and sat down upon it, he offered the flask. Noell took it, but sipped rather gingerly.

"I'm old enough to drink now?" he commented dryly.

"You're old enough," Edmund assured him. "But beware of excess, and never drink alone. Conventional fatherly advice, I believe."

Noell reached across the bench so that he could stroke the barrel of the microscope with slender fingers.

"What are you afraid of" he asked.

Edmund sighed. "You're old enough for that, too, I suppose?"

"I think you ought to tell me."

Edmund looked at the brass instrument and said: "It were better to keep things like this dark secret. Some human mechanician, I daresay, eager to please the vampire lords and ladies, showed off his cleverness as proud as a peacock. Thoughtless. Inevitable, though, now that all this play with lenses has become fashionable."

"You'll be glad of eyeglasses when your sight begins to fail," Noell told him. "In any case, I can't see the danger in this new toy."

Edmund smiled. "New toys," he mused. "Clocks to tell the time, mills to grind the corn, lenses to aid human sight. Produced by human craftsmen for the delight of their masters. I think we've finally succeeded in proving to the vampires just how very clever we are—and how much more there is to know than we know already."

"You think the vampires are beginning to fear us?"

Edmund gulped wine from the flask and passed it again to his son. "Their rule is founded in fear and superstition," he said quietly. "They're long-lived, suffer only mild attacks of diseases that are fatal to us, and have marvelous powers of regeneration. But they're not immortal, and they're vastly outnumbered by humans. Terror keeps them safe, but terror is based in ignorance, and behind their haughtiness and arrogance, there's a gnawing fear of what might happen if humans ever lost their supernatural reverence for vampirekind. It's very difficult for them to die, but they don't fear death any the less for that."

"There've been rebellions against vampire rule. They've always failed."

Edmund nodded to concede the point. "There are three million people in Grand Normandy," he said, "and less than five thousand vampires. There are only forty thousand vampires in the entire imperium of Gaul, and about the same number in the imperium of Byzantium—no telling how many there may be in the khanate of Walachia and Cathay, but not so very many more. In Africa the vampires must be outnumbered three or four thousand to one. If people no longer saw them as demons and demi-gods, as unconquerable forces of evil, their empire would be fragile. The centuries through which they live give them wisdom, but longevity seems to be inimical to creative thought—they learn, but they don't *invent*. Humans remain the true masters of art and science, which are forces of change. They've tried to control that—to turn it to their advantage—but it remains a thorn in their side."

"But they do have power," insisted Noell. "They *are* vampires."

Edmund shrugged. "Their longevity is real—their powers of regeneration, too. But is it really their magic that makes them so? I don't know for sure what merit there is in their incantations and rituals, and I don't think even *they* know—they cling to their rites because they dare not abandon them, but where the power that makes humans into vampires really comes from, no one knows. From the devil? I think not. I don't believe in the devil—I think it's something in the blood. I think vampirism may be a kind of disease—but a disease that makes men stronger instead of weaker, insulates them against death instead of killing them. If that *is* the case—do you see now why the Lady Carmilla asked whether I had looked at blood beneath the microscope?"

Noell stared at the instrument for twenty seconds or so, mulling over the idea. Then he laughed.

"If we could *all* become vampires," he said lightly, "we'd have to suck one another's blood."

Edmund couldn't bring himself to look for such ironies. For him, the possibilities inherent in discovering the secrets of vampire nature were much more immediate, and utterly bleak.

"It's not true that they *need* to suck the blood of humans," he told the boy. "It's not nourishment. It gives them . . . a kind of pleasure that we can't understand. And it's part of the mystique that makes them so terrible . . . and hence so powerful." He stopped, feeling embarrassed. He did not know how much Noell knew about his sources of information. He and his wife never talked about the days of his affair with the Lady Carmilla, but there was no way to keep gossip and rumor from reaching the boy's ears.

Noell took the flask again, and this time took a deeper draft from it. "I've heard," he said distantly, "that humans find pleasure, too . . . in their blood being drunk."

"No," replied Edmund calmly. "That's untrue. Unless one counts the small pleasure of sacrifice. The pleasure that a human man takes from a vampire lady is the same pleasure that he takes from a human lover. It might be different for the girls who entertain vampire men, but I suspect it's just the excitement of hoping that they may become vampires themselves."

Noell hesitated, and would probably have dropped the subject, but Edmund realized suddenly that he did not want the subject dropped. The boy had a right to know, and perhaps might one day *need* to know.

"That's not entirely true," Edmund corrected himself. "When the Lady Carmilla used to taste my blood, it did give me pleasure, in a way. It pleased me because it pleased *her.* There *is* an excitement in loving a vampire lady, which makes it different from loving an ordinary woman . . . even though the chance that a vampire lady's lover may himself become a vampire is so remote as to be inconsiderable."

Noell blushed, not knowing how to react to this acceptance into his father's confidence. Finally he decided that it was best to pretend a purely academic interest.

"Why are there so many more vampire women than men?" he asked.

"No one knows for sure," Edmund said. "No humans, at any rate. I can tell you what I believe, from hearsay and from reasoning, but you must understand that it is a dangerous thing to think about, let alone to speak about."

Noell nodded.

"The vampires keep their history secret," said Edmund, "and they try to control the writing of human history, but the following facts are probably true. Vampirism came to western Europe in the fifth century, with the vampire-led horde of Attila. Attila must have known well enough how to make more vampires—he converted both Aëtius, who became ruler of the imperium of Gaul, and Theodosius II, the emperor of the east who was later murdered. Of all the vampires that now exist, the vast majority must be converts. I have heard reports of vampire children born to vampire ladies, but it must be an extremely rare occurrence. Vampire men seem to be much less virile than human men—it is said that they couple very rarely. Nevertheless, they frequently take human consorts, and these consorts often become vampires. Vampires usually claim that this is a gift, bestowed deliberately by magic, but I am not so sure they can control the process. I think the semen of vampire men carries some kind of seed that communicates vampirism much as the semen of humans makes women pregnant—and just as haphazardly. That's why the male lovers of vampire ladies don't become vampires."

Noell considered this, and then asked: "Then where do vampire lords come from?"

"They're converted by other male vampires," Edmund said. "Just as Attila converted Aëtius and Theodosius." He did not elaborate, but waited to see whether Noell understood the implication. An expression of disgust crossed the boy's face and Edmund did not know whether to be glad or sorry that his son could follow the argument through.

"Because it doesn't always happen," Edmund went on, "it's easy for the vampires to pretend that they have some special magic. But some women never become pregnant, though they lie with their husbands for years. It is said, though, that a human may also become a vampire by drinking vampire's blood—if he knows the appropriate magic spell. That's a rumor the vampires don't like, and they exact terrible penalties if anyone is caught trying the experiment. The ladies of our own court, of course, are for the most part onetime lovers of the archduke or his cousins. It would be indelicate to speculate about the conversion of the archduke, though he is certainly acquainted with Aëtius."

Noell reached out a hand, palm downward, and made a few passes above the candle flame, making it flicker from side to side. He stared at the microscope.

"*Have* you looked at blood?" he asked.

"I have," replied Edmund. "And semen. Human blood, of course—and human semen."

"And?"

Edmund shook his head. "They're certainly not homogeneous fluids," he said, "but the instrument isn't good enough for really detailed inspection. There are small corpuscles—the ones in semen have long, writhing tails—but there's more . . . much more . . . to be seen, if I had the chance. By tomorrow this instrument will be gone—I don't think I'll be given the chance to build another."

"You're surely not in danger! You're an important man—and your loyalty has never been in question. People think of you as being almost a vampire yourself. A black magician. The kitchen girls are afraid of me because I'm your son—they cross themselves when they see me."

Edmund laughed, a little bitterly. "I've no doubt they suspect me of intercourse with demons, and avoid my gaze for fear of the spell of the evil eye. But none of that matters to the vampires. To them, I'm only a human, and for all that they value my skills, they'd kill me without a thought if they suspected that I might have dangerous knowledge."

Noell was clearly alarmed by this. "Wouldn't. . . ." He stopped, but saw Edmund waiting for him to ask, and carried on after only a brief pause. "The Lady Carmilla . . . wouldn't she . . .?"

"Protect me?" Edmund shook his head. "Not even if I were her favorite still. Vampire loyalty is to vampires."

"She was human once."

"It counts for nothing. She's been a vampire for nearly six hundred years, but it wouldn't be any different if she were no older than I."

"But . . . she did love you?"

"In her way," said Edmund sadly. "In her way." He stood up then, no longer feeling the urgent desire to help his son to understand. There were things the boy could find out only for himself and might never have to. He took up the candle tray and shielded the flame with his hand as he walked to the door. Noell followed him, leaving the empty flask behind.

*   *   *

Edmund left the citadel by the so-called Traitor's Gate, and crossed the Thames by the Tower Bridge. The houses on the bridge were in darkness now, but there was still a trickle of traffic; even at two in the morning, the business of the great city did not come to a standstill. The night had clouded over, and a light drizzle had begun to fall. Some of the oil lamps that were supposed to keep the thoroughfare lit at all times had gone out, and there was not a lamplighter in sight. Edmund did not mind the shadows, though.

He was aware before he reached the south bank that two men were dogging his footsteps, and he dawdled in order to give them the impression that he would be easy to track. Once he entered the network of streets surrounding the Leathermarket, though, he gave them the slip. He knew the maze of filthy streets well enough—he had lived here as a child. It was while he was apprenticed to a local clockmaker that he had learned the cleverness with tools that had eventually brought him to the notice of his predecessor, and had sent him on the road to fortune and celebrity. He had a brother and a sister still living and working in the district, though he saw them very rarely. Neither one of them was proud to have a reputed magician for a brother, and they had not forgiven him his association with the Lady Carmilla.

He picked his way carefully through the garbage in the dark alleys, unperturbed by the sound of scavenging rats. He kept his hands on the pommel of the dagger that was clasped to his belt, but he had no need to draw it. Because the stars were hidden, the night was pitch-dark, and few of the windows were lit from within by candlelight, but he was able to keep track of his progress by reaching out to touch familiar walls every now and again.

He came eventually to a tiny door set three steps down from a side street, and rapped upon it quickly, three times and then twice. There was a long pause before he felt the door yield beneath his fingers, and he stepped inside hurriedly. Until he relaxed when the door clicked shut again, he did not realize how tense he had been.

He waited for a candle to be lit.

The light, when it came, illuminated a thin face, crabbed and wrinkled, the eyes very pale and the wispy white hair gathered imperfectly behind a linen bonnet.

"The lord be with you," he whispered.

"And with you, Edmund Cordery," she croaked.

He frowned at the use of his name—it was a deliberate breach of etiquette, a feeble and meaningless gesture of independence. She did not like him, though he had never been less than kind to her. She did not fear him as so many others did, but she considered him tainted.

They had been bound together in the business of the Fraternity for nearly twenty years, but she would never completely trust him.

She led him into an inner room, and left him there to take care of his business.

A stranger stepped from the shadows. He was short, stout, and bald, perhaps sixty years old. He made the special sign of the cross, and Edmund responded.

"I'm Cordery," he said.

"Were you followed?" The older man's tone was deferential and fearful.

"Not here. They followed me from the Tower, but it was easy to shake them loose."

"That's bad."

"Perhaps—but it has to do with another matter, not with our business. There's no danger to you. Do you have what I asked for?"

The stout man nodded uncertainly. "My masters are unhappy," he said. "I have been asked to tell you that they do not want you to take risks. You are too valuable to place yourself in peril."

"I am in peril already. Events are overtaking us. In any case, it is neither your concern nor that of your . . . masters. It is for me to decide."

The stout man shook his head, but it was a gesture of resignation rather than a denial. He pulled something from beneath the chair where he had waited in the shadows. It was a large box, clad in leather. A row of small holes was set in the longer side, and there was a sound of scratching from within that testified to the presence of living creatures.

"You did exactly as I instructed?" asked Edmund.

The small man nodded, then put his hand on the mechanician's arm, fearfully. "Don't open it, sir, I beg you. Not here."

"There's nothing to fear," Edmund assured him.

"You haven't been in Africa, sir, as I have. Believe me, *everyone* is afraid—and not merely humans. They say that vampires are dying, too."

"Yes, I know," said Edmund distractedly. He shook off the older man's restraining hand and undid the straps that sealed the box. He lifted the lid, but not far—just enough to let the light in, and to let him see what was inside.

The box contained two big gray rats. They cowered from the light.

Edmund shut the lid again and fastened the straps.

"It's not my place, sir," said the little man hesitantly, "but I'm not sure that you really understand what you have there. I've seen the cities of West Africa—I've been in Corunna, too, and Marseilles. They remember other plagues in those cities, and all the horror stories are emerging again to haunt them. Sir, if any such thing ever came to London. . . ."

Edmund tested the weight of the box to see whether he could carry it comfortably. "It's not your concern," he said. "Forget everything that has happened. I will communicate with your masters. It is in my hands now."

"Forgive me," said the other, "but I must say this: there is naught to be gained from destroying vampires, if we destroy ourselves, too. It would be a pity to wipe out half of Europe in the cause of attacking our oppressors."

Edmund stared at the stout man coldly. "You talk too much," he said. "Indeed, you talk a *deal* too much."

"I beg your pardon, sire."

Edmund hesitated for a moment, wondering whether to reassure the messenger that his anxiety was understandable, but he had learned long ago that where the business of the Fraternity was concerned, it was best to say as little as possible. There was no way of knowing when this man would speak again of this affair, or to whom, or with what consequence.

The mechanician took up the box, making sure that he could carry it comfortably. The rats stirred inside, scrabbling with their small clawed feet. With his free hand, Edmund made the sign of the cross again.

"God go with you," said the messenger, with urgent sincerity.

"And with thy spirit," replied Edmund colorlessly.

Then he left, without pausing to exchange a ritual farewell with the crone. He had no difficulty in smuggling his burden back into the Tower, by means of a gate where the guard was long practiced in the art of turning a blind eye.

When Monday came, Edmund and Noell made their way to the Lady Carmilla's chambers. Noell had never been in such an apartment before, and it was a source of wonder to him. Edmund watched the boy's reactions to the carpets, the wall hangings, the mirrors and ornaments, and could not help but recall the first time *he* had entered these chambers. Nothing had changed here, and the rooms were full of provocations to stir and sharpen his faded memories.

Younger vampires tended to change their surroundings often, addicted to novelty, as if they feared the prospect of being changeless themselves. The Lady Carmilla had long since passed beyond this phase of her career. She had grown used to changelessness, had transcended the kind of attitude to the world that permitted boredom and ennui. She had adapted herself to a new aesthetic of existence, whereby her personal space became an extension of her own eternal sameness, and innovation was confined to tightly controlled areas of her life—including the irregular shifting of her erotic affections from one lover to another.

The sumptuousness of the lady's table was a further source of astonishment to Noell. Silver plates and forks he had imagined, and crystal goblets, and carved decanters of wine. But the lavishness of provision for just three diners—the casual waste—was something that obviously set him aback. He had always known that he was himself a member of a privileged elite, and that by the standards of the greater world, Master Cordery and his family ate well; the revelation that there was a further order of magnitude to distinguish the private world of the real aristocracy clearly made its impact upon him.

Edmund had been very careful in preparing his dress, fetching from his closet finery that he had not put on for many years. On official occasions he was always concerned to play the part of mechanician, and dressed in order to sustain that appearance. He never appeared as a courtier, always as a functionary. Now, though, he was reverting to a kind of performance that Noell had never seen him play, and though the boy had no idea of the subtleties of his father's performance, he clearly understood something of what was going on; he had complained acidly about the dull and plain way in which his father had made *him* dress.

Edmund ate and drank sparingly, and was pleased to note that Noell did likewise, obeying his father's instructions despite the obvious temptations of the lavish provision. For a while the lady was content to exchange routine courtesies, but she came quickly enough—by her standards—to the real business of the evening.

"My cousin Girard," she told Edmund, "Is quite enraptured by your clever device. He finds it most interesting."

"Then I am pleased to make him a gift of it," Edmund replied. "And I would be pleased to make another, as a gift for Your Ladyship."

"That is not our desire," she said coolly. "In fact, we have other matters in mind. The archduke and his seneschal have discussed certain tasks that you might profitably carry out. Instructions will be communicated to you in due time, I have no doubt."

"Thank you, my lady," said Edmund.

"The ladies of the court were pleased with the drawings that I showed to them," said the Lady Carmilla, turning to look at Noell. "They marveled at the thought that a cupful of Thames water might contain thousands of tiny living creatures. Do you think that our bodies, too, might be the habitation of countless invisible insects?"

Noell opened his mouth to reply, because the question was addressed to him, but Edmund interrupted smoothly.

"There are creatures that may live upon our bodies," he said, "and worms that may live within. We are told that the macrocosm reproduces in essence the microcosm of human beings; perhaps there is a small microcosm within us, where our natures are reproduced again, incalculably small. I have read. . . ."

"I have read, Master Cordery," she cut in, "that the illnesses that afflict humankind might be carried from person to person by means of these tiny creatures."

"The idea that diseases were communicated from one person to another by tiny seeds was produced in antiquity," Edmund replied, "but I do not know how such seeds might be recognized, and I think it very unlikely that the creatures we have seen in river water could possibly be of that character."

"It is a disquieting thought," she insisted, "that our bodies might be inhabited by creatures of which we can know nothing, and that every breath we take might be carrying into us seeds of all kinds of change, too small to be seen or tasted. It makes me feel uneasy."

"But there is no need," Edmund protested. "Seeds of corruptibility take root in human flesh, but yours is inviolate."

"You know that is not so, Master Cordery," she said levelly. "You have seen me ill yourself."

"That was a pox that killed many humans, my lady—yet it gave to you no more than a mild fever."

"We have reports from the imperium of Byzantium, and from the Moorish enclave, too, that there is plague in Africa, and that it has now reached the southern regions of the imperium of Gaul. It is said that this plague makes little distinction between human and vampire."

"Rumors, my lady," said Edmund soothingly. "You know how news becomes blacker as it travels."

The Lady Carmilla turned again to Noell, and this time addressed him by name so that there could be no opportunity for Edmund to usurp the privilege of answering her. "Are you afraid of me, Noell?" she asked.

The boy was startled, and stumbled slightly over his reply, which was in the negative.

"You must not lie to me," she told him. "You *are* afraid of me, because I am a vampire. Master Cordery is a skeptic, and must have told you that vampires have less magic than is commonly credited to us, but he must also have told you that I can do you harm if I will. Would you like to be a vampire yourself, Noell?"

Noell was still confused by the correction, and hesitated over his reply, but he eventually said: "Yes, I would."

"Of course you would," she purred. "All humans would be vampires if they could, no matter how they might pretend when they bend the knee in church. And men *can* become vampires; immortality is within our gift. Because of this, we have always enjoyed the loyalty and devotion of the greater number of our human subjects. We have always rewarded that devotion in some measure. Few have joined our ranks, but the many have enjoyed centuries of order and stability. The vampires rescued Europe from a Dark Age, and as long as vampires rule, barbarism will always be held in check. Our rule has not always been kind, because we cannot tolerate defiance, but the alternative would have been far worse. Even so, there are men who would destroy us—did you know that?"

Noell did not know how to reply to this, so he simply stared, waiting for her to continue. She seemed a little impatient with his gracelessness, and Edmund deliberately let the awkward pause go on. He saw a certain advantage in allowing Noell to make a poor impression.

"There is an organization of rebels," the Lady Carmilla went on. "A secret society, ambitious to discover the secret way by which vampires are made. They put about the idea that they would make all men immortal, but this is a lie, and foolish. The members of this brotherhood seek power for themselves."

The vampire lady paused to direct the clearing of one set of dishes and the bringing of another. She asked for a new wine, too. Her gaze wandered back and forth between the gauche youth and his self-assured father.

"The loyalty of your family is, of course, beyond question," she eventually continued. "No one understands the workings of society like a mechanician, who knows well enough how forces must be balanced and how the different parts of a machine must interlock and support one another. Master Cordery knows well how the cleverness of rulers resembles the cleverness of clockmakers, do you not?"

"Indeed, I do, my lady," replied Edmund.

"There might be a way," she said, in a strangely distant tone, "that a good mechanician might earn a conversion to vampirism."

Edmund was wise enough not to interpret this as an offer or a promise. He accepted a measure of the new wine and said: "My lady, there are matters that it would be as well for us to discuss in private. May I send my son to his room?"

The Lady Carmilla's eyes narrowed just a little, but there was hardly any expression in her finely etched features. Edmund held his breath, knowing that he had forced a decision upon her that she had not intended to make so soon.

"The poor boy has not quite finished his meal," she said.

"I think he has had enough, my lady," Edmund countered. Noell did not disagree, and, after a brief hesitation, the lady bowed to signal her permission. Edmund asked Noell to leave, and, when he was gone, the Lady Carmilla rose from her seat and went from the dining room into an inner chamber. Edmund followed her.

"You were presumptuous, Master Cordery," she told him.

"I was carried away, my lady. There are too many memories here."

"The boy is mine," she said, "if I so choose. You do know that, do you not?"

Edmund bowed.

"I did not ask you here tonight to make you witness the seduction of your son. Nor do you think that I did. This matter that you would discuss with me—does it concern science or treason?"

"Science, my lady. As you have said yourself, my loyalty is not in question."

Carmilla laid herself upon a sofa and indicated that Edmund should take a chair nearby. This was the antechamber to her bedroom, and the air was sweet with the odor of cosmetics.

"Speak," she bade him.

"I believe that the archduke is afraid of what my little device might reveal," he said. "He fears that it will expose to the eye such seeds as carry vampirism from one person to another, just as it might expose the seeds that carry disease. I think that the man who devised the instrument may have been put to death already, but I think you know well enough that a discovery once made is likely to be made again and again. You are uncertain as to what course of action would best serve your ends, because you cannot tell whence the greater threat to your rule might come. There is the Fraternity, which is dedicated to your destruction; there is plague in Africa, from which even vampires may die; and there is the new sight, which renders visible what previously lurked unseen. Do you want my advice, Lady Carmilla?"

"Do you *have* any advice, Edmund?"

"Yes. Do not try to control by terror and persecution the things that are happening. Let your rule be unkind *now*, as it has been before, and it will open the way to destruction. Should you concede power gently, you might live for centuries yet, but if you strike out . . . your enemies will strike back."

The vampire lady leaned back her head, looking at the ceiling. She contrived a small laugh.

"I cannot take advice such as that to the archduke," she told him flatly.

"I thought not, my lady," Edmund replied very calmly.

"You humans have your own immortality," she complained. "Your faith promises it, and you all affirm it. Your faith tells you that you must not covet the immortality that is ours, and we do no more than agree with you when we guard it so jealously. You should look to your Christ for fortune, not to us. I think you know well enough that we could not convert the world if we wanted to. Our magic is such that it can be used only sparingly. Are you distressed because it has never been offered to you? Are you bitter? Are you becoming our enemy because you cannot become our kin?"

"You have nothing to fear from me, my lady," he lied. Then he added, not quite sure whether it was a lie or not: "I loved you faithfully. I still do."

She sat up straight then, and reached out a hand as though to stroke his cheek, though he was too far away for her to reach.

"That is what I told the archduke," she said, "when he suggested to me that you might be a traitor. I promised him that I could test your loyalty more keenly in my chambers than his officers in theirs. I do not think you could delude me. Edmund. Do you?"

"No my lady," he replied.

"By morning," she told him gently, "I will know whether or not you are a traitor."

"That you will," he assured her. "That you will, my lady."

He woke before her, his mouth dry and his forehead burning. He was not sweating—indeed, he was possessed by a feeling of desiccation, as though the moisture were being squeezed out of his organs. His head was aching, and the light of the morning sun that streamed through the unshuttered window hurt his eyes.

He pulled himself up to a half-sitting position, pushing the coverlet back from his bare chest.

So soon! he thought. He had not expected to be consumed so quickly, but he was surprised to find that his reaction was one of relief rather than fear or regret. He had difficulty collecting his thoughts, and was perversely glad to accept that he did not need to.

He looked down at the cuts that she had made on his breast with her little silver knife; they were raw and red, and made a strange contrast with the faded scars whose crisscross pattern still engraved the story of unforgotten passions. He touched the new wounds gently with his fingers, and winced at the fiery pain.

She woke up then, and saw him inspecting the marks.

"Have you missed the knife?" she asked sleepily. "Were you hungry for its touch?"

There was no need to lie now, and there was a delicious sense of freedom in that knowledge. There was a joy in being able to face her, at last, quite naked in his thoughts as well as his flesh.

"Yes, my lady," he said with a slight croak in his voice. "I had missed the knife. Its touch . . . rekindled flames in my soul."

She had closed her eyes again, to allow herself to wake slowly. She laughed. "It is pleasant, sometimes, to return to forsaken pastures. You can have no notion how a particular *taste* may stir memories. I am glad to have seen you again, in this way. I had grown quite used to you as the gray mechanician. But now. . . ."

He laughed, as lightly as she, but the laugh turned to a cough, and something in the sound alerted her to the fact that all was not as it should be. She opened her eyes and raised her head, turning toward him.

"Why, Edmund," she said, "you're as pale as death!"

She reached out to touch his cheek, and snatched her hand away again as she found it unexpectedly hot and dry. A blush of confusion spread across her own features. He took her hand and held it, looking steadily into her eyes.

"Edmund," she said softly. "What have you done?"

"I can't be sure," he said, "and I will not live to find out, but I have tried to kill you, my lady."

He was pleased by the way her mouth gaped in astonishment. He watched disbelief and anxiety mingle in her expression, as though fighting for control. She did not call out for help.

"This is nonsense," she whispered.

"Perhaps," he admitted. "Perhaps it was also nonsense that we talked last evening. Nonsense about treason. Why did you ask me to make the microscope, my lady, when you knew that making me a party to such a secret was as good as signing my death warrant?"

"Oh Edmund," she said with a sigh. "You could not think that it was my own idea? I tried to protect you, Edmund, from Girard's fears and suspicions. It was because I was your protector that I was made to bear the message. What have you done, Edmund?"

He began to reply, but the words turned into a fit of coughing.

She sat upright, wrenching her hand away from his enfeebled grip, and looked down at him as he sank back upon the pillow.

"For the love of God!" she exclaimed, as fearfully as any true believer. "It is the plague—the plague out of Africa!"

He tried to confirm her suspicion, but could do so only with a nod of his head as he fought for breath.

"But they held the *Freemartin* by the Essex coast for a full fortnight's quarantine," she protested. "There was no trace of plague aboard."

"The disease kills men," said Edmund in a shallow whisper. "But animals can carry it, in their blood, without dying."

"You cannot know this!"

Edmund managed a small laugh. "My lady," he said, "I am a member of that Fraternity that interests itself in everything that might kill a vampire. The information came to me in good time for me to arrange delivery of the rats—though when I asked for them, I had not in mind the means of using them that I eventually employed. More recent events. . . ." Again he was forced to stop, unable to draw sufficient breath even to sustain the thin whisper.

The Lady Carmilla put her hand to her throat, swallowing as if she expected to feel evidence already of her infection.

"You would destroy me, Edmund?" she asked, as though she genuinely found it difficult to believe.

"I would destroy you all," he told her. "I would bring disaster, turn the world upside down, to end your rule. . . . We cannot allow you to stamp out learning itself to preserve your empire forever. Order must be fought with chaos, and chaos is come, my lady."

When she tried to rise from the bed, he reached out to restrain her, and though there was no power left in him, she allowed herself to be checked. The coverlet fell away from her, to expose her breasts as she sat upright.

"The boy will die for this, Master Cordery," she said. "His mother, too."

"They're gone," he told her. "Noell went from your table to the custody of the society that I serve. By now they're beyond your reach. The archduke will never catch them."

She stared at him, and now he could see the beginnings of hate and fear in her stare.

"You came here last night to bring me poisoned blood," she said. "In the hope that this new disease might kill even me, you condemned yourself to death. What did you do, Edmund?"

He reached out again to touch her arm, and was pleased to see her flinch and draw away: that he had become dreadful.

"Only vampires live forever," he told her hoarsely. "But anyone may drink blood, if they have the stomach for it. I took full measure from my two sick rats . . . and I pray to God that the seed of this fever is raging in my blood . . . and in my semen, too. You, too, have received full measure, my lady . . . and you are in God's hands. now like any common mortal. I cannot know for sure whether you will catch the plague, or whether it will kill you, but I—an unbeliever—am not ashamed to pray. Perhaps you could pray, too, my lady, so that we may know how the Lord favors one unbeliever over another."

She looked down at him, her face gradually losing the expressions that had tugged at her features, becoming masklike in its steadiness.

"You could have taken our side, Edmund. I trusted you, and I could have made the archduke trust you, too. You could have become a vampire. We could have shared the centuries, you and I."

This was dissimulation, and they both knew it. He had been her lover, and had ceased to be, and had grown older for so many years that now she remembered him as much in his son as in himself. The promises were all too obviously hollow now, and she realized that she could not even taunt him with them.

From beside the bed she took up the small silver knife that she had used to let his blood. She held it now as if it were a dagger, not a delicate instrument to be used with care and love.

"I thought you still loved me," she told him. "I really did."

That, at least, he thought, might be true.

He actually put his head farther back, to expose his throat to the expected thrust. He wanted her to strike him—angrily, brutally, passionately. He had nothing more to say, and would not confirm or deny that he did still love her.

He admitted to himself now that his motives had been mixed, and that he really did not know whether it was loyalty to the Fraternity that had made him submit to this extraordinary experiment. It did not matter.

She cut his throat, and he watched her for a few long seconds while she stared at the blood gouting from the wound. When he saw her put stained fingers to her lips, knowing what she knew, he realized that after her own fashion, she still loved him.

F. Marion Crawford

For the Blood is the Life

Francis Marion Crawford (1854–1909) was an American, born in Italy but educated in the United States. A Sanskrit scholar, he mastered eighteen languages and lived for many years in India, where he worked as a newspaper editor. He finally returned to Italy and died in Sorrento.

One of the most popular and commercially successful authors of his day, he wrote more than forty books, several in the fantasy and horror genres. However, his reputation as a short story writer rests on a single collection of seven stories, Wandering Ghosts *(UK:* Uncanny Tales*), published posthumously in 1911.*

'For the Blood is the Life' contains all the archetypal trappings we have come to associate with the vampire story, yet after more than eighty years it still evokes a delightful shudder of dread . . .

WE HAD DINED at sunset on the broad roof of the old tower, because it was cooler there during the great heat of summer. Besides, the little kitchen was built at one corner of the great square platform, which made it more convenient than if the dishes had to be carried down the steep stone steps broken in places and everywhere worn with age. The tower was one of those built all down the west coast of Calabria by the Emperor Charles V early in the sixteenth century, to keep off the Barbary pirates, when the unbelievers were allied with Francis I against the Emperor and the Church. They have gone to ruin, a few still stand intact, and mine is one of the largest. How it came into my possession ten years ago, and why I spend a part of each year in it, are matters which do not concern this tale. The tower stands in one of the loneliest spots in Southern Italy, at the extremity of a curving, rocky promontory, which forms a small but safe natural harbour at the southern extremity of the Gulf of Policastro, and just north of Cape Scalea, the birthplace of Judas Iscariot, according to the old local legend. The tower stands alone on this hooked spur of the rock, and there is not a house to be seen within three miles of it. When I go there I take a couple of sailors, one of whom is a fair cook, and when I am away it is in charge of a gnome-like little being who was once a miner and who attached himself to me long ago.

My friend, who sometimes visits me in my summer solitude, is an artist by profession, a Scandinavian by birth, and a cosmopolitan by force of circumstances.

We had dined at sunset; the sunset glow had reddened and faded again, and the evening purple steeped the vast chain of the mountains that embrace the deep gulf to eastward and rear themselves higher and higher towards the south. It was hot, and we sat at the landward corner of the platform, waiting for the night breeze to come down from the lower hills. The colour sank out of the air, there was a little interval of deep-grey twilight, and a lamp sent a yellow streak from the open door of the kitchen, where the men were getting their supper.

Then the moon rose suddenly above the crest of the promontory, flooding the platform and lighting up every little spur of rock and knoll of grass below us, down to the edge of the motionless water. My friend lighted his pipe and sat looking at a spot on the hillside. I knew that he was looking at it, and for a long time past I had wondered whether he would ever see anything there that would fix his attention. I knew that spot well. It was clear that he was interested at last, though it was a long time before he spoke. Like most painters, he trusts to his own eyesight, as a lion trusts his strength and a stag his speed, and he is always disturbed when he cannot reconcile what he sees with what he believes that he ought to see.

"It's strange," he said. "Do you see that little mound just on this side of the boulder?"

"Yes," I said, and I guessed what was coming.

"It looks like a grave," observed Holger.

"Very true. It does look like a grave."

"Yes," continued my friend, his eyes still fixed on the spot. "But the strange thing is that I see the body lying on the top of it. Of course," continued Holger, turning his head on one side as artists do, "it must must be an effect of light. In the first place, it is not a grave at all. Secondly, if it were, the body would be inside and not outside. Therefore, it's an effect of the moonlight. Don't you see it?"

"Perfectly; I always see it on moonlight nights."

"It doesn't seem to interest you much," said Holger.

"On the contrary, it does interest me, though I am used to it. You're not so far wrong, either. The mound is really a grave."

"Nonsense!" cried Holger incredulously. "I suppose you'll tell me that what I see lying on it is really a corpse!"

"No," I answered, "it's not. I know, because I have taken the trouble to go down and see."

"Then what is it?" asked Holger.

"It's nothing."

"You mean that it's an effect of light, I suppose?"

"Perhaps it is. But the inexplicable part of the matter is that it makes no difference whether the moon is rising or setting, or waxing or waning. If there's any moonlight at all, from east or west or overhead, so long as it shines on the grave you can see the outline of the body on top."

Holger stirred up his pipe with the point of his knife, and then used his finger for a stopper. When the tobacco burned well he rose from his chair.

"If you don't mind," he said, "I'll go down and take a look at it."

He left me, crossed the roof, and disappeared down the dark steps. I did not move, but sat looking down until he came out of the tower below. I heard him humming an old Danish song as he crossed the open space in the bright moonlight, going straight to the mysterious mound. When he was ten paces from it, Holger stopped short, made two steps forward, and then three or four backward, and then stopped again. I know what that meant. He had reached the spot where the Thing ceased to be visible—where, as he would have said, the effect of light changed.

Then he went on till he reached the mound and stood upon it. I could see the Thing still, but it was no longer lying down; it was on its knees now, winding its white arms round Holger's body and looking up into his face. A cool breeze stirred my hair at that moment, as the night wind began to come down from the hills, but it felt like a breath from another world.

The Thing seemed to be trying to climb to its feet helping itself up by Holger's body while he stood upright, quite unconscious of it and apparently looking toward the tower, which is very picturesque when the moonlight falls upon it on that side.

"Come along!" I shouted. "Don't stay there all night!"

It seemed to me that he moved reluctantly as he stepped from the mound, or else with difficulty. That was it. The Thing's arms were still round his waist, but its feet could not leave the grave. As he came slowly forward it was drawn and lengthened like a wreath of mist, thin and white, till I saw distinctly that Holger shook himself, as a man does who feels a chill. At the same instant a little wail of pain came to me on the breeze—it might have been the cry of the small owl that lives among the rocks—and the misty presence floated swiftly back from Holger's advancing figure and lay once more at its length upon the mound.

Again I felt the cool breeze in my hair, and this time an icy thrill of dread ran down my spine. I remembered very well that I had once gone down there alone in the moonlight; that presently, being near, I had seen nothing; that, like Holger, I had gone and had stood upon the mound; and I remembered how when I came back, sure that there was nothing there, I had felt the sudden conviction that there was something after all if I would only look behind me. I remembered the strong temptation to look back, a temptation I had resisted as unworthy of a man of sense, until, to get rid of it, I had shaken myself just as Holger did.

And now I knew that those white, misty arms had been round me, too; I knew it in a flash, and I shuddered as I remembered that I had heard the night owl then, too. But it had not been the night owl. It was the cry of the Thing.

I refilled my pipe and poured out a cup of strong southern wine; in less than a minute Holger was seated beside me again.

"Of course there's nothing there," he said, "but it's creepy, all the same. Do you know, when I was coming back I was so sure that there was something behind me that I wanted to turn round and look? It was an effort not to."

He laughed a little, knocked the ashes out of his pipe, and poured himself out some wine. For a while neither of us spoke, and the moon rose higher and we both looked at the Thing that lay on the mound.

"You might make a story about that," said Holger after a long time.

"There is one," I answered. "If you're not sleepy, I'll tell it to you."

"Go ahead," said Holger, who likes stories.

*   *   *

Old Alario was dying up there in the village behind the hill. You remember him, I have no doubt. They say that he made his money by selling sham jewellery in South America, and escaped with his gains when he was found out. Like all those fellows, if they bring anything back with them, he at once set to work to enlarge his house, and as there are no masons here, he sent all the way to Paola for two workmen. They were a rough-looking pair of scoundrels—a Neapolitan who had lost one eye and a Sicilian with an old scar half an inch deep across his left cheek. I often saw them, for on Sundays they used to come down here and fish off the rocks. When Alario caught the fever that killed him the masons were still at work. As he had agreed that part of their pay should be their board and lodging, he made them sleep in the house. His wife was dead, and he had an only son called Angelo, who was a much better sort than himself. Angelo was to marry the daughter of the richest man in the village, and, strange to say, though the marriage was arranged by their parents, the young people were said to be in love with each other.

For that matter, the whole village was in love with Angelo, and among the rest a wild, good-looking creature called Cristina, who was more like a gipsy than any girl I ever saw about here. She had very red lips and very black eyes, she was built like a greyhound, and had the tongue of the devil. But Angelo did not care a straw for her. He was rather a simpleminded fellow, quite different from his old scoundrel of a father, and under what I should call normal circumstances I really believe that he would never have looked at any girl except the nice plump little creature, with a fat dowry, whom his father meant him to marry. But things turned up which were neither normal nor natural.

On the other hand, a very handsome young shepherd from the hills above Maratea was in love with Cristina, who seems to have been quite indifferent to him. Cristina had no regular means of subsistence, but she was a good girl and willing to do any work or go on errands to any distance for the sake of a loaf of bread or a mess of beans, and permission to sleep under cover. She was especially glad when she could get something to do about the house of Angelo's father. There is no doctor in the village, and when the neighbours saw that old Alario was dying they sent Cristina to Scalea to fetch one. That was late in the afternoon, and if they had waited so long it was because the dying miser refused to allow any such extravagance while he was able to speak. But while Cristina was gone matters grew rapidly worse, the priest was brought to the bedside, and when he had done what he could he gave it as his opinion to the bystanders that the old man was dead, and left the house.

You know these people. They have a physical horror of death. Until the priest spoke, the room had been full of people. The words were hardly out of his mouth before it was empty. It was night now. They hurried down the dark steps and out into the street.

Angelo, as I have said, was away, Cristina had not come back—the simple woman-servant who had nursed the sick man fled with the rest, and the body was left alone in the flickering light of the earthen oil lamp.

Five minutes later two men looked in cautiously and crept forward toward the bed. They were the one-eyed Neapolitan mason and his Sicilian companion. They knew what they wanted. In a moment they had dragged from under the bed a small but heavy iron-bound box, and long before anyone thought of coming back to the dead man they had left the house and the village under cover of the darkness. It was easy enough, for Alario's house is the last toward the gorge which leads down here, and the thieves merely went out by the back door, got over the stone wall, and had nothing to risk after that except that possibility of meeting some belated countryman, which was very small indeed, since few of the people use that path. They had a mattock and shovel, and they made their way without accident.

I am telling you this story as it must have happened, for, of course, there were no witnesses to this part of it. The men brought the box down by the gorge, intending to bury it until they should be able to come back and take it away in a boat. They must have been clever enough to guess that some of the money would be in paper notes, for they would otherwise have buried it on the beach in the wet sand, where it would have been much safer. But the paper would have rotted if they had been obliged to leave it there long, so they dug their hole down there, close to that boulder. Yes, just where the mound is now.

Cristina did not find the doctor in Scalea, for he had been sent for from a place up the valley, half-way to San Domenico. If she had found him he would have come on his mule by the upper road, which is smoother but much longer. But Cristina took the short cut by the rocks, which passes about fifty feet above the mound, and goes round that corner. The men were digging when she passed, and she heard them at work. It would not have been like her to go by without finding out what the noise was, for she was never afraid of anything in her life, and, besides, the fishermen sometimes come ashore here at night to get a stone for an anchor or to gather sticks to make a little fire. The night was dark and Cristina probably came close to the two men before she could see what they were doing. She knew them, of course, and they knew her, and understood instantly that they were in her power. There was only one thing to be done for their safety, and they did it. They knocked her on the head, they dug the hole deep, and they buried her quickly with the iron-bound chest. They must have understood that their only chance of escaping suspicion lay in getting back to the village before their absence was noticed, for they returned immediately, and were found half an hour later gossiping quietly with the man who was making Alario's coffin. He was a crony of theirs, and had been working at the repairs in the old man's house. So far as I have been able to make out, the only persons who were supposed to know where Alario kept his treasure were Angelo and the one woman-servant I have mentioned. Angelo was away; it was the woman who discovered the theft.

It is easy enough to understand why no one else knew where the money was. The old man kept his door locked and the key in his pocket when he was out, and did not let the woman enter to clean the place unless he was there himself. The whole village knew that he had money somewhere, however, and the masons had probably discovered the whereabouts of the chest by climbing in at the window in his absence. If the old man had not been delirious until he lost consciousness he would have been in frightful agony of mind for his riches. The faithful woman-servant forgot their existence only for a few moments when she fled with the rest, overcome by the horror of death. Twenty minutes had not passed before she returned with the two hideous old hags who are always called in to prepare the dead for burial. Even then she had not at first the courage to go near the bed with them, but she made a pretence of dropping something, went down on her knees as if to find it, and looked under the bedstead. The walls of the room were newly whitewashed down to the floor, and she saw at a glance that the chest was gone. It had been there in the afternoon, it had therefore been stolen in the short interval since she had left the room.

There are no carabineers stationed in the village; there is not so much as a municipal watchman, for there is no municipality. There never was such a place, I believe. Scalea is supposed to look after it in some mysterious way, and it takes a couple of hours to get anybody from there. As the old woman had lived in the village all her life, it did not even occur to her to apply to any civil authority for help. She simply set up a howl and ran through the village in the dark, screaming out that her dead master's house had been robbed. Many of the people looked out, but at first no one seemed inclined to help her. Most of them, judging her by themselves, whispered to each other that she had probably stolen the money herself. The first man to move was the father of the girl whom Angelo was to marry;

having collected his household, all of whom felt a personal interest in the wealth which was to have come into the family, he declared it to be his opinion that the chest had been stolen by the two journeymen masons who lodged in the house. He headed a search for them, which naturally began in Alario's house and ended in the carpenter's workshop, where the thieves were found discussing a measure of wine with the carpenter over the half-finished coffin, by the light of one earthen lamp filled with oil and tallow. The search-party at once accused the delinquents of the crime, and threatened to lock them up in the cellar till the carabineers could be fetched from Scalea. The two men looked at each other for one moment, and then without the slightest hesitation they put out the single light, seized the unfinished coffin between them, and using it as a sort of battering ram, dashed upon their assailants in the dark. In a few moments they were beyond pursuit.

That is the end of the first part of the story. The treasure had disappeared, and as no trace of it could be found the people naturally supposed that the thieves had succeeded in carrying it off. The old man was buried, and when Angelo came back at last he had to borrow money to pay for the miserable funeral, and had some difficulty in doing so. He hardly needed to be told that in losing his inheritance he had lost his bride. In this part of the world marriages are made on strictly business principles, and if the promised cash is not forthcoming on the appointed day, the bride or the bridegroom whose parents have failed to produce it may as well take themselves off, for there will be no wedding. Poor Angelo knew that well enough. His father had been possessed of hardly any land, and now that the hard cash which he had brought from South America was gone, there was nothing left but debts for the building materials that were to have been used for enlarging and improving the old house. Angelo was beggared, and the nice plump little creature who was to have been his, turned up her nose at him in the most approved fashion. As for Cristina, it was several days before she was missed, for no one remembered that she had been sent to Scalea for the doctor, who had never come. She often disappeared in the same way for days together, when she could find a little work here and there at the distant farms among the hills. But when she did not come back at all, people began to wonder, and at last made up their minds that she had connived with the masons and had escaped with them.

I paused and emptied my glass.

"That sort of thing could not happen anywhere else," observed Holger, filling his everlasting pipe again. "It is wonderful what a natural charm there is about

murder and sudden death in a romantic country like this. Deeds that would be simply brutal and disgusting anywhere else become dramatic and mysterious because this is Italy, and we are living in a genuine tower of Charles V built against genuine Barbary pirates."

"There's something in that," I admitted. Holger is the most romantic man in the world inside of himself, but he always thinks it necessary to explain why he feels anything.

"I suppose they found the poor girl's body with the box," he said presently.

"As it seems to interest you," I answered, "I'll tell you the rest of the story."

The moon had risen had by this time; the outline of the Thing on the mound was clearer to our eyes than before.

The village very soon settled down to its small dull life. No one missed old Alario, who had been away so much on his voyages to South America that he had never been a familiar figure in his native place. Angelo lived in the half-finished house, and because he had no money to pay the old woman-servant, she would not stay with him, but once in a long time she would come and wash a shirt for him for old acquaintance' sake. Besides the house, he had inherited a small patch of ground at some distance from the village; he tried to cultivate it, but he had no heart in the work, for he knew he could never pay the taxes on it and on the house, which would certainly be confiscated by the Government, or seized for the debt of the building material, which the man who had supplied it refused to take back.

Angelo was very unhappy. So long as his father had been alive and rich, every girl in the village had been in love with him; but that was all changed now. It had been pleasant to be admired and courted, and invited to drink wine by fathers who had girls to marry. It was hard to be stared at coldly, and sometimes laughed at because he had been robbed of his inheritance. He cooked his miserable meals for himself, and from being sad became melancholy and morose.

At twilight, when the day's work was done, instead of hanging about in the open space before the church with young fellows of his own age, he took to wandering in lonely places on the outskirts of the village till it was quite dark. Then he slunk home and went to bed to save the expense of a light. But in those lonely twilight hours he began to have strange waking dreams. He was not always alone, for often when he sat on the stump of a tree, where the narrow path turns down the gorge, he was sure that a woman came up noiselessly over the rough stones, as if her feet were bare; and she stood under a clump of chestnut trees only half a dozen yards down the path, and beckoned to him without speaking. Though she was in the shadow he knew that her lips were red, and that when they parted a little and smiled at him she showed two small sharp teeth. He knew this at first rather than saw it, and he knew that it was Cristina, and that she was dead. Yet he was not afraid; he only wondered whether it was a dream, for he thought that if he had been awake he should have been frightened.

Besides, the dead woman had red lips, and that could only happen in a dream. Whenever he went near the gorge after sunset she was already there waiting for him, or else she very soon appeared, and he began to be sure that she came a little nearer to him every day. At first he had only been sure of her blood-red mouth, but now each feature grew distinct, and the pale face looked at him with deep and hungry eyes.

It was the eyes that grew dim. Little by little he came to know that someday the dream would not end when he turned away to go home, but would lead him down the gorge out of which the vision rose. She was nearer now when she beckoned to him. Her cheeks were not livid like those of the dead, but pale with starvation, with the furious and unappeased physical hunger of her eyes that devoured him. They feasted on his soul and cast a spell over him, and at last they were close to his own and held him. He could not tell whether her breath was as hot as fire, or as cold as ice; he could not tell whether her red lips burned his or froze them, or whether her five fingers on his wrists seared scorching scars or bit his flesh like frost; he could not tell whether he was awake or asleep, whether she was alive or dead, but he knew that she loved him, she alone of all creatures, earthly or unearthly, and her spell had power over him.

When the moon rose high that night the shadow of that Thing was not alone down there upon the mound.

Angelo awoke in the cool dawn, drenched with dew and chilled through flesh, and blood, and bone. He opened his eyes to the faint grey light, and saw the stars still shining overhead. He was very weak, and his heart was beating so slowly that he was almost like a man fainting. Slowly he turned his head on the mound, as on a pillow, but the other face was not there. Fear seized him suddenly, a fear unspeakable and unknown; he sprang to his feet and fled up the gorge, and he never looked behind him until he reached the door of the house on the outskirts of the village. Drearily he went to his work that day, and wearily the hours dragged themselves after the sun, till at last it touched the sea and sank, and the great sharp hills above Maratea turned purple against the dove-coloured eastern sky.

Angelo shouldered his heavy hoe and left the field. He felt less tired now than in the morning when he had begun to work, but he promised himself that he would go home without lingering by the gorge, and eat the best supper he could get himself, and sleep all night in his bed like a Christian man. Not again would he be tempted down the narrow way by a shadow with red lips and icy breath; not again would he dream that dream of terror and delight. He was near the village now; it was half an hour since the sun had set, and the cracked church bell sent little discordant echoes across the rocks and ravines to tell all good people that the day was done. Angelo stood still a moment where the path forked, where it led toward the village on the left, and down to the gorge on the right, where a clump of chestnut trees overhung the narrow way. He stood still a minute, lifting his battered hat from his head and gazing at the fast-fading sea westward, and his lips moved as he silently repeated the familiar evening prayer. His lips moved, but the words that followed them in his brain lost their meaning and turned into others, and ended in a name that he spoke aloud—Cristina! With the name, the tension of his will relaxed suddenly, reality went out and the dream took him again, and bore him on swiftly and surely like a man walking in his sleep, down, down, by the steep path in the gathering darkness. And as she glided beside him, Cristina whispered strange, sweet things in his ear, which somehow, if he had been awake, he knew that he could not quite have understood; but now they were the most wonderful words he had ever heard in his life. And she kissed him also, but not upon his mouth. He felt her sharp kisses upon his white throat, and he knew that her lips were red. So the wild dream sped on through twilight and darkness and moonrise, and all the glory of the summer's night. But in the chilly dawn he lay as one half dead upon the mound down there, recalling and not recalling, drained of his blood, yet strangely longing to give those red lips more. Then came the fear, the awful nameless panic, the mortal horror that guards the confines of the world we see not, neither know of as we know of other things, but which we feel when its icy chill freezes our bones and stirs our hair with the touch of a ghostly hand. Once more Angelo sprang from the mound and fled up the gorge in the breaking day, but his step was less sure this time, and he panted for breath as he ran; and when he came to the bright spring of water that rises half way up the hillside, he dropped upon his knees and hands and plunged his whole face in and drank as he had never drunk before—for it was the thirst of the wounded man who has lain bleeding all night long upon the battle-field.

She had him fast now, and he could not escape her, but would come to her every evening at dusk until she had drained him of his last drop of blood. It was in vain that when the day was done he tried to take another turning and to go home by a path that did not lead near the gorge. It was in vain that he made promises to himself each morning at dawn when he climbed the lonely way up from the shore to the village. It was all in vain, for when the sun sank burning into the sea, and the coolness of the evening stole out as from a hiding-place to delight the weary world, his feet turned toward the old way, and she was waiting for him in the shadow under the chestnut trees; and then all happened as before, and she fell to kissing his white throat even as she flitted lightly down the way, winding one arm about him. And as his blood failed, she grew more hungry and more thirsty every day, and every day when he awoke in the early dawn it was harder to rouse himself to the effort of climbing the steep path to the village; and when he went to his work his feet dragged painfully, and there was hardly strength in his arms to wield the heavy hoe. He scarcely spoke to anyone now, but the people said he was "consuming himself" for love of the girl he was to have married when he lost his inheritance; and they laughed heartily at the thought, for this is not a very romantic country. At this time Antonio, the man who stays here to look after the tower, returned from a visit to his people, who live near Salerno. He had been away all the time since before Alario's death and knew nothing of what had happened. He has told me that he came back late in the afternoon and shut himself up in the tower to eat and sleep, for he was very tired. It was past midnight when he awoke, and when he looked out the waning moon was rising over the shoulder of the hill. He looked out toward the mound, and he saw something, and he did not sleep again that night. When he went out again in the morning it was broad daylight, and there was nothing to be seen on the mound but loose stones and driven sand. Yet he did not go very near it; he went straight up the path to the village and directly to the house of the old priest.

"I have seen an evil thing this night," he said; "I have seen how the dead drink the blood of the living. And the blood is the life."

"Tell me what you have seen," said the priest in reply.

Antonio told him everything he had seen.

"You must bring your book and your holy water to-night," he added. "I will be here before sunset to go down with you, and if it pleases your reverence to sup with me while we wait, I will make ready."

"I will come," the priest answered, "for I have read in old books of these strange beings which are neither quick nor dead, and which lie ever fresh in their graves, stealing out in the dusk to taste life and blood."

Antonio cannot read, but he was glad to see that the priest understood the business; for, of course, the books must have instructed him as to the best means of quieting the half-living Thing for ever.

So Antonio went away to his work, which consists largely in sitting on the shady side of the tower, when he is not perched upon a rock with a fishing-line catching nothing. But on that day he went twice to look at the mound in the bright sunlight, and he searched round and round it for some hole through which the being might get in and out; but he found none. When the sun began to sink and the air was cooler in the shadows, he went up to fetch the old priest, carrying a little wicker basket with him; and in this they placed a bottle of holy water, and the basin, and sprinkler, and the stole which the priest would need; and they came down and waited in the door of the tower till it should be dark. But while the light still lingered very grey and faint, they saw something moving, just there, two figures, a man's that walked, and a woman's that flitted beside him, and while her head lay on his shoulder she kissed his throat. The priest has told me that, too, and that his teeth chattered and he grasped Antonio's arm. The vision passed and disappeared into the shadow. Then Antonio got the leathern flask of strong liquor, which he kept for great occasions, and poured such a draught as made the old man feel almost young again; and gave the priest his stole to put on and the holy water to carry, and they went out together toward the spot where the work was to be done. Antonio says that in spite of the rum his own knees shook together, and the priest stumbled over his Latin. For when they were yet a few yards from the mound the flickering light of the lantern fell upon Angelo's white face, unconscious as if in sleep, and on his upturned throat, over which a very thin red line of blood trickled down into his collar; and the flickering light of the lantern played upon another face that looked up from the feast, upon two deep, dead eyes that saw in spite of death—upon parted lips, redder than life itself—upon two gleaming teeth on which glistened a rosy drop. Then the priest, good old man, shut his eyes tight and showered holy water before him, and his cracked voice rose almost to a scream; and then Antonio, who is no coward after all, raised his pick in one hand and the lantern in the other, as he sprang forward, not knowing what the end should be; and then he swears that he heard a woman's cry, and the Thing was gone, and Angelo lay alone on the mound unconscious, with the red line on his throat and the beads of deathly sweat on his cold forehead. They lifted him, half-dead as he was, and laid him on the ground close by; then Antonio went to work, and the priest helped him, though he was old and could not do much; and they dug deep, and at last Antonio, standing in the grave, stooped down with his lantern to see what he might see.

His hair used to be dark brown, with grizzled streaks about the temples; in less than a month from that day he was as grey as a badger. He was a miner when he was young, and most of these fellows have seen ugly sights now and then, when accidents have happened, but he had never seen what he saw that night—that Thing which is neither alive nor dead, that Thing that will abide neither above ground nor in the grave. Antonio had brought something with him which the priest had not noticed. He had made it that afternoon—a sharp stake shaped from a piece of tough old driftwood. He had it with him now, and he had his heavy pick, and he had taken the lantern down into the grave. I don't think any power on earth could make him speak of what happened then, and the old priest was too frightened to look in. He says he heard Antonio breathing like a wild beast, and moving as if he were fighting with something almost as strong as himself; and he heard an evil sound also, with blows, as of something violently driven through flesh and bone; and then, the most awful sound of all—a woman's shriek, the unearthly scream of a woman neither dead nor alive, but buried deep for many days. And he, the poor old priest, could only rock himself as he knelt there in the sand, crying aloud his prayers and exorcisms to drown these dreadful sounds. Then suddenly a small iron-bound chest was thrown up and rolled over against the old man's knee, and in a moment more Antonio was beside him, his face as white as tallow in the flickering light of the lantern, shovelling the sand and pebbles into the grave with furious haste, and looking over the edge till the pit was half full; and the priest said that there was much fresh blood on Antonio's hands and on his clothes.

I had come to the end of my story. Holger finished his wine and leaned back in his chair.

"So Angelo got his own again," he said. "Did he marry the prim and plump young person to whom he had been betrothed?"

"No; he had been badly frightened. He went to South America, and has not been heard of since."

"And that poor thing's body is there still, I suppose," said Holger. "Is it quite dead yet, I wonder?"

I wonder, too. But whether it be dead or alive, I should hardly care to see it, even in broad daylight. Antonio is as grey as a badger, and he has never been quite the same man since that night.

Ramsey Campbell

The Brood

Ramsey Campbell is arguably Britain's most respected living horror writer. He was recently named "The horror writer's horror writer" by The Observer *magazine, and 1991 saw a clutch of awards headed his way, including his third World Fantasy Award and sixth British Fantasy Award for co-editing the* Best New Horror *series, and a seventh British Fantasy Award for his novel* Midnight Sun.

On the book front, his latest novel, The Count of Eleven, *and a new collection,* Waking Nightmares, *both appeared towards the end of 1991. The pseudonymous* Night of the Claw *will be reissued on both sides of the Atlantic under his own byline, and Arkham House will be publishing a thirty-year retrospective collection of short stories, illustrated by J.K. Potter, probably titled* Alone With the Horrors. *He is currently at work on a new supernatural novel,* The Long Lost.

Although "The Brood" uses all the traditional trappings of vampire fiction, it remains firmly rooted in Campbell's unique world-view of mental and urban disintegration.

HE'D HAD AN almost unbearable day. As he walked home his self-control still oppressed him, like rusty armour. Climbing the stairs, he tore open his mail: a glossy pamphlet from a binoculars firm, a humbler folder from the Wild Life Preservation Society. Irritably he threw them on the bed and sat by the window, to relax.

It was autumn. Night had begun to cramp the days. Beneath golden trees, a procession of cars advanced along Princes Avenue, as though to a funeral; crowds hurried home. The incessant anonymous parade, dwarfed by three stories depressed him. Faces like these vague twilit miniatures—selfishly ingrown, convinced that nothing was their fault—brought their pets to his office.

But where were all the local characters? He enjoyed watching them, they fascinated him. Where was the man who ran about the avenue, chasing butterflies of litter and stuffing them into his satchel? Or the man who strode violently, head down in no gale, shouting at the air? Or the Rainbow Man, who appeared on the hottest days obese with sweaters, each of a different garish colour? Blackband hadn't seen any of these people for weeks.

The crowds thinned; cars straggled. Groups of streetlamps lit, tinting leaves sodium, unnaturally gold. Often that lighting had meant—Why, there she was, emerging from the side street almost on cue: the Lady of the Lamp.

Her gait was elderly. Her face was withered as an old blanched apple; the rest of her head was wrapped in a tattered grey scarf. Her voluminous ankle-length coat, patched with remnants of colour, swayed as she walked. She reached the central reservation of the avenue, and stood beneath a lamp.

Though there was a pedestrian crossing beside her, people deliberately crossed elsewhere. They would, Blackband thought sourly: just as they ignored the packs of stray dogs that were always someone else's responsibility—ignored them, or hoped someone would put them to sleep. Perhaps they felt the human strays should be put to sleep, perhaps that was where the Rainbow Man and the rest had gone!

The woman was pacing restlessly. She circled the lamp, as though the blurred disc of light at its foot were a stage. Her shadow resembled the elaborate hand of a clock.

Surely she was too old to be a prostitute. Might she have been one, who was now compelled to enact her memories? His binoculars drew her face closer: intent as a sleepwalker's, introverted as a foetus. Her head bobbed against gravel, foreshortened by the false perspective of the lenses. She moved offscreen.

Three months ago, when he'd moved to this flat, there had been two old women. One night he had seen them, circling adjacent lamps. The other woman had been slower, more sleepy. At last the Lady of the Lamp had led her home; they'd moved slowly as exhausted sleepers. For days he'd thought of the two women in their long faded coats, trudging around the lamps in the deserted avenue, as though afraid to go home in the growing dark.

The sight of the lone woman still unnerved him, a little. Darkness was crowding his flat. He drew the curtains, which the lamps stained orange. Watching had relaxed him somewhat. Time to make a salad.

The kitchen overlooked the old women's house. See The World from the Attics of Princes Avenue. All Human Life Is Here. Backyards penned in rubble and crumbling toilet sheds; on the far side of the back street, houses were lidless boxes of smoke. The house directly beneath his window was dark, as always. How could the two women—if both were still alive—survive in there? But at least they could look after themselves, or call for aid; they were human, after all. It was their pets that bothered him.

He had never seen the torpid woman again. Since she had vanished, her companion had begun to take animals home; he'd seen her coaxing them toward the house. No doubt they were company for her friend; but what life could animals enjoy in the lightless, probably condemnable house? And why so many? Did they escape to their homes, or stray again? He shook his head: the women's loneliness was no excuse. They cared as little for their pets as did those owners who came, whining like their dogs, to his office.

Perhaps the woman was waiting beneath the lamps for cats to drop from the trees, like fruit. He meant the thought as a joke. But when he'd finished preparing dinner, the idea troubled him sufficiently that he switched off the light in the main room and peered through the curtains.

The bright gravel was bare. Parting the curtains, he saw the woman hurrying unsteadily toward her street. She was carrying a kitten: her head bowed over the fur cradled in her arms; her whole body seemed to enfold it. As he emerged from the kitchen again, carrying plates, he heard her door creak open and shut. Another one, he thought uneasily.

By the end of the week she'd taken in a stray dog, and Blackband was wondering what should be done.

The women would have to move eventually. The houses adjoining theirs were empty, the windows shattered targets. But how could they take their menagerie with them? They'd set them loose to roam or, weeping, take them to be put to sleep.

Something ought to be done, but not by him. He came home to rest. He was used to removing chicken bones from throats; it was suffering the excuses that exhausted him—Fido always had his bit of chicken, it had never happened before, they couldn't understand. He would nod curtly, with a slight pained smile. "Oh yes?" he would repeat tonelessly "Oh yes?"

Not that that would work with the Lady of the Lamp. But then, he didn't intend to confront her: what on earth could he have said? That he'd take all the animals off her hands? Hardly. Besides, the thought of confronting her made him uncomfortable.

She was growing more eccentric. Each day she appeared a little earlier. Often she would move away into the dark, then hurry back into the flat bright pool. It was as though light were her drug.

People stared at her, and fled. They disliked her because she was odd. All she had to do to please them, Blackband thought, was be normal: overfeed her pets until their stomachs scraped the ground, lock them in cars to suffocate in the heat, leave them alone in the house all day then beat them for chewing. Compared to most of the owners he met, she was Saint Francis.

He watched television. Insects were courting and mating. Their ritual dances engrossed and moved him: the play of colours, the elaborate racial patterns of the life-force which they instinctively decoded and enacted. Microphotography presented them to him. If only people were as beautiful and fascinating!

Even his fascination with the Lady of the Lamp was no longer unalloyed; he resented that. Was she falling ill? She walked painfully slowly, stooped over, and looked shrunken. Nevertheless, each night she kept her vigil, wandering sluggishly in the pools of light like a sleepwalker.

How could she cope with her animals now? How might she be treating them? Surely there were social workers in some of the cars nosing home, someone must notice how much she needed help. Once he made for the door to the stairs, but already his throat was parched of words. The thought of speaking to her wound him tight inside. It wasn't his job, he had enough to confront. The spring in his guts coiled tighter, until he moved away from the door.

One night an early policeman appeared. Usually the police emerged near midnight, disarming people of knives and broken glass, forcing them into the vans. Blackband watched eagerly. Surely the man must escort her home, see what the house hid. Blackband glanced back to the splash of light beneath the lamp. It was deserted.

How could she had moved so fast? He stared, baffled. A dim shape lurked at the corner of his eyes. Glancing nervously, he saw the woman standing on the bright disc several lamps away, considerably farther from the policeman than he'd thought. Why should he have been so mistaken?

Before he could ponder, sound distracted him: a loud fluttering, as though a bird were trapped and frantic in the kitchen. But the room was empty. Any bird must have escaped through the open window. Was that a flicker of movement below, in the dark house? Perhaps the bird had flown in there.

The policeman had moved on. The woman was trudging her island of light; her coat's hem dragged over the gravel. For a while Blackband watched, musing uneasily, trying to think what the fluttering had resembled more than the sound of a bird's wings.

Perhaps that was why, in the early hours, he saw a man stumbling through the derelict back streets. Jagged hurdles of rubble blocked the way; the man clambered, panting dryly, gulping dust as well as breath. He seemed only exhausted and uneasy, but Blackband could see what was pursuing him: a great wide shadow-colored stain, creeping vaguely over the rooftops. The stain was alive, for its face mouthed—though at first, from its color and texture, he thought the head was the moon. Its eyes gleamed hungrily. As the fluttering made the man turn and scream, the face sailed down on its stain toward him.

Next day was unusually trying: a dog with a broken leg and a suffering owner, you'll hurt his leg, can't you be more gentle, oh come here, baby, what did the nasty man do to you; a senile cat and its protector, isn't the usual vet here today, he never used to do that, are you sure you know what you're doing. But later, as he watched the woman's obsessive trudging, the dream of the stain returned to him. Suddenly he realized he had never seen her during daylight.

So that was it! he thought, sniggering. She'd been a vampire all the time! A difficult job to keep when you hadn't a tooth in your head. He reeled in her face with the focusing-screw. Yes, she was toothless. Perhaps she used false fangs, or sucked through her gums. But he couldn't sustain his joke for long. Her face peered out of the frame of her grey scarf, as though from a web. As she circled she was muttering incessantly. Her tongue worked as though her mouth were too small for it. Her eyes were fixed as the heads of grey nails impaling her skull.

He laid the binoculars aside, and was glad that she'd become more distant. But even the sight of her trudging in miniature troubled him. In her eyes he had seen that she didn't want to do what she was doing.

She was crossing the roadway, advancing toward his gate. For a moment, unreasonably and with a sour uprush of dread, he was sure she intended to come in. But she was staring at the hedge. Her hands fluttered, warding off a fear; her eyes and her mouth were stretched wide. She stood quivering, then she stumbled toward her street, almost running.

He made himself go down. Each leaf of the hedge held an orange-sodium glow, like wet paint. But there was nothing among the leaves, and nothing could have struggled out, for the twigs were intricately bound by spiderwebs, gleaming like gold wire.

The next day was Sunday. He rode a train beneath the Mersey and went tramping the Wirral Way nature trail. Red-faced men, and women who had paralyzed their hair with spray, stared as though he'd invaded their garden. A few butterflies perched on flowers, their wings settled together delicately, then they flickered away above the banks of the abandoned railway cutting. They were too quick for him to enjoy, even with his binoculars; he kept remembering how near death their species were. His moping had slowed him, he felt barred from his surroundings by his inability to confront the old woman. He couldn't speak to her, there were no words he could use, but meanwhile her animals might be suffering. He dreaded going home to another night of helpless watching.

Could he look into the house while she was wandering? She might leave the door unlocked. At some time he had become intuitively sure that her companion was dead. Twilight gained on him, urging him back to Liverpool.

He gazed nervously down at the lamps. Anything was preferable to his impotence. But his feelings had trapped him into committing himself before he was ready. Could he really go down when she emerged? Suppose the other woman was still alive, and screamed? Good God, he needn't go in if he didn't want to. On the gravel, light lay bare as a row of plates on a shelf. He found himself thinking, with a secret eagerness, that she might already have had her wander.

As he made dinner, he kept hurrying irritably to the front window. Television failed to engross him; he watched the avenue instead. Discs of light dwindled away, impaled by their lamps. Below the kitchen window stood a block of night and silence. Eventually he went to bed, but heard fluttering—flights of litter in the derelict streets, no doubt. His dreams gave the litter a human face.

Throughout Monday he was on edge, anxious to hurry home and be done; he was distracted. Oh poor Chubbles, is the man hurting you! He managed to leave early. Day was trailing down the sky as he reached the avenue. Swiftly he brewed coffee and sat sipping, watching.

The caravan of cars faltered, interrupted by gaps. The last

homecomers hurried away, clearing the stage. But the woman failed to take her cue. His cooking of dinner was fragmented; he hurried repeatedly back to the window. Where was the bloody woman, was she on strike? Not until the following night, when she had still not appeared, did he begin to suspect he'd seen the last of her.

His intense relief was short-lived. If she had died of whatever had been shrinking her, what would happen to her animals? Should he find out what was wrong? But there was no reason to think she'd died. Probably she, and her friend before her, had gone to stay with relatives. No doubt the animals had escaped long before—he'd never seen or heard any of them since she had taken them in. Darkness stood hushed and bulky beneath his kitchen window.

For several days the back streets were quiet, except for the flapping of litter or birds. It became easier to glance at the dark house. Soon they'd demolish it; already children had shattered all the windows. Now, when he lay awaiting sleep, the thought of the vague house soothed him, weighed his mind down gently.

That night he awoke twice. He'd left the kitchen window ajar, hoping to lose some of the unseasonable heat. Drifting through the window came a man's low moaning. Was he trying to form words? His voice was muffled, blurred as a dying radio. He must be drunk; perhaps he had fallen, for there was a faint scrape of rubble. Blackband hid within his eyelids, courting sleep. At last the shapeless moaning faded. There was silence, except for the feeble, stony scraping. Blackband lay and grumbled, until sleep led him to a face that crept over heaps of rubble.

Some hours later he woke again. The lifelessness of four o'clock surrounded him, the dim air seemed sluggish and ponderous. Had he dreamed the new sound? It returned, and made him flinch: a chorus of thin, piteous wailing, reaching weakly upward toward the kitchen. For a moment, on the edge of dream, it sounded like babies. How could babies be crying in an abandoned house? The voices were too thin. They were kittens.

He lay in the heavy dark, hemmed in by shapes that the night deformed. He willed the sounds to cease, and eventually they did. When he awoke again, belatedly, he had time only to hurry to work.

In the evening the house was silent as a draped cage. Someone must have rescued the kittens. But in the early hours the crying woke him: fretful, bewildered, famished. He couldn't go down now, he had no light. The crying was muffled, as though beneath stone. Again it kept him awake, again he was late for work.

His loss of sleep nagged him. His smile sagged impatiently, his nods were contemptuous twitches. "Yes," he agreed with a woman who said she'd been careless to slam her dog's paw in a door, and when she raised her eyebrows haughtily: "Yes, I can see that." He could see her deciding to find another vet. Let her, let someone else suffer her. He had problems of his own.

He borrowed the office flashlight, to placate his anxiety. Surely he wouldn't need to enter the house, surely someone else—He walked home, toward the darker sky. Night thickened like soot on the buildings.

He prepared dinner quickly. No need to dawdle in the kitchen, no point in staring down. He was hurrying; he dropped a spoon, which reverberated shrilly in his mind, nerve-racking. Slow down, slow down. A breeze piped incessantly outside, in the rubble. No, not a breeze. When he made himself raise the sash he heard the crying, thin as wind in crevices.

It seemed weaker now, dismal and desperate: intolerable. Could nobody else hear it, did nobody care? He gripped the windowsill; a breeze tried feebly to tug at his fingers. Suddenly, compelled by vague anger, he grabbed the flashlight and trudged reluctantly downstairs.

A pigeon hobbled on the avenue, dangling the stump of one leg, twitching clogged wings; cars brisked by. The back street was scattered with debris, as though a herd had moved on, leaving its refuse to manure the paving stones. His flashlight groped over the heaped pavement, trying to determine which house had been troubling him.

Only by standing back to align his own window with the house could he decide, and even then he was unsure. How could the old woman have clambered over the jagged pile that blocked the doorway? The front door sprawled splintered in the hall, on a heap of the fallen ceiling, amid peelings of wallpaper. He must be mistaken. But as his flashlight dodged about the hall, picking up debris then letting it drop back into the dark, he heard the crying, faint and muffled. It was somewhere within.

He ventured forward, treading carefully. He had to drag the door into the street before he could proceed. Beyond the door the floorboards were cobbled with rubble. Plaster swayed about him, glistening. His light wobbled ahead of him, then led him toward a gaping doorway on the right. The light spread into the room, dimming.

A door lay on its back. Boards poked like exposed ribs through the plaster of the ceiling; torn paper dangled. There was no carton full of starving kittens; in fact, the room was bare. Moist stains engulfed the walls.

He groped along the hall, to the kitchen. The stove was fat with grime. The wallpaper had collapsed entirely, draping indistinguishable shapes that stirred as the flashlight glanced at them. Through the furred window, he made out the light in his own kitchen, orange-shaded, blurred. How could two women have survived here?

At once he regretted that thought. The old woman's face loomed behind him: eyes still as metal, skin the colour of pale bone. He turned nervously; the light capered. Of course there was only the quivering mouth of the hall. But the face was present now, peering from behind the draped shapes around him.

He was about to give up—he was already full of the gasp of relief he would give when he reached the avenue—when he heard the crying. It was almost breathless, as though close to death: a shrill feeble wheezing. He couldn't bear it. He hurried into the hall.

Might the creatures be upstairs? His light showed splintered holes in most of the stairs; through them he glimpsed a huge symmetrical stain on the wall. Surely the woman could never have climbed up there—but that left only the cellar.

The door was beside him. The flashlight, followed by his hand, groped for the knob. The face was near him in the shadows; its fixed eyes gleamed. He dreaded finding her fallen on the cellar steps. But the crying pleaded. He dragged the door open; it scraped over rubble. He thrust the flashlight into the dank opening. He stood gaping, bewildered.

Beneath him lay a low stone room. Its walls glistened darkly. The place was full of debris: bricks, planks, broken lengths of wood. Draping the debris, or tangled beneath it, were numerous old clothes. Threads of a white substance were tethered to everything, and drifted feebly now the door was opened.

In one corner loomed a large pale bulk. His light twitched toward it. It was a white bag of some material, not cloth. It had been torn open; except for a sifting of rubble, and a tangle of what might have been fragments of dully painted cardboard, it was empty.

The crying wailed, somewhere beneath the planks. Several sweeps of the light showed that the cellar was otherwise deserted. Though the face mouthed behind him, he ventured down. For God's sake, get it over with; he knew he would never dare return. A swath had been cleared through the dust on the steps, as though something had dragged itself out of the cellar, or had been dragged in.

His movements disturbed the tethered threads; they rose like feelers, fluttering delicately. The white bag stirred, its torn mouth worked. Without knowing why, he stayed as far from that corner as he could.

The crying had come from the far end of the cellar. As he picked his way hurriedly over the rubble he caught sight of a group of clothes. They were violently coloured sweaters, which the Rainbow Man had worn. They slumped over planks; they nestled inside one another, as though the man had withered or had been sucked out.

Staring uneasily about, Blackband saw that all the clothes were stained. There was blood on all of them, though not a great deal on any. The ceiling hung close to him, oppressive and vague. Darkness had blotted out the steps and the door. He caught at them with the light, and stumbled toward them.

The crying made him falter. Surely there were fewer voices, and they seemed to sob. He was nearer the voices than the steps. If he could find the creatures at once, snatch them up and flee—He clambered over the treacherous debris, toward a gap in the rubble. The bag mouthed emptily; threads plucked at him, almost impalpably. As he thrust the flashlight's beam into the gap, darkness rushed to surround him.

Beneath the debris a pit had been dug. Parts of its earth walls had collapsed, but protruding from the fallen soil he could see bones. They looked too large for an animal's. In the centre of the pit, sprinkled with earth, lay a cat. Little of it remained, except for its skin and bones; its skin was covered with deep pock-marks. But its eyes seemed to move feebly.

Appalled, he stooped. He had no idea what to do. He never knew, for the walls of the pit were shifting. Soil trickled scattering as a face the size of his fist emerged. There were several; their limbless mouths, their sharp tongues flickered out toward the cat. As he fled they began wailing dreadfully.

He chased the light toward the steps. He fell, cutting his knees. He thought the face with its gleaming eyes would meet him in the hall. He ran from the cellar, flailing his flashlight at the air. As he stumbled down the street he could still see the faces that had crawled from the soil: rudimentary beneath translucent skin, but beginning to be human.

He leaned against his gatepost in the lamplight, retching. Images and memories tumbled disordered through his mind. The face crawling over the roofs. Only seen at night. Vampire. The fluttering at the window. Her terror at the hedge full of spiders. *Calyptra*, what was it, *Calyptra eustrigata*. Vampire moth.

Vague though they were, the implications terrified him. He fled into his building, but halted fearfully on the stairs. The things must be destroyed: to delay would be insane. Suppose their hunger brought them crawling out of the cellar tonight, toward his flat—Absurd though it must be, he couldn't forget that they might have seen his face.

He stood giggling, dismayed. Whom did you call in these circumstances? The police, an exterminator? Nothing would relieve his horror until he saw the brood destroyed, and the only way to see that was to do the job himself. Burn. Petrol. He dawdled on the stairs, delaying, thinking he knew none of the other tenants from whom to borrow the fuel.

He ran to the nearby garage. "Have you got any petrol?"

The man glared at him, suspecting a joke. "You'd be surprised. How much do you want?"

How much indeed! He restrained his giggling. Perhaps he should ask the man's advice! Excuse me, how much petrol do you need for—"A gallon," he stammered.

As soon as he reached the back street he switched on his flashlight. Crowds of rubble lined the pavements. Far above the dark house he saw his orange light. He stepped over the debris into the hall. The swaying light brought the face forward to meet him. Of course the hall was empty.

He forced himself forward. Plucked by the flashlight, the cellar door flapped soundlessly. Couldn't he just set fire to the house? But that might leave the brood untouched. Don't think, go down quickly. Above the stairs the stain loomed.

In the cellar nothing had changed. The bag gaped, the clothes lay emptied. Struggling to unscrew the cap of the petrol can, he almost dropped the flashlight. He kicked wood into the pit and began to pour the petrol. At once he heard the wailing beneath him. "Shut up!" he screamed, to drown out the sound. "Shut up! Shut up!"

The can took its time in gulping itself empty; the petrol seemed thick as oil. He hurled the can clattering away, and ran to the steps. He fumbled with matches, gripping the flashlight between his knees. As he threw them, the lit matches went out. Not until he ventured back to the pit, clutching a ball of paper from his pocket, did he succeed in making a flame that reached his goal. There was a whoof of fire, and a chorus of interminable feeble shrieking.

As he clambered sickened toward the hall, he heard a fluttering above him. Wallpaper, stirring in a wind: it sounded moist. But there was no wind, for the air clung clammily to him. He slithered over the rubble into the hall, darting his light about. Something white bulked at the top of the stairs.

It was another torn bag. He hadn't been able to see it before. It slumped emptily. Beside it the stain spread over the wall. That stain was too symmetrical; it resembled an inverted coat. Momentarily he thought the paper was drooping, tugged perhaps by his unsteady light, for the stain had begun to creep down toward him. Eyes glared at him from its dangling face. Though the face was upside down he knew it at once. From its gargoyle mouth a tongue reached for him.

He whirled to flee. But the darkness that filled the front door was more than night, for it was advancing audibly. He stumbled, panicking, and rubble slipped from beneath his feet. He fell from the cellar steps, onto piled stone. Though he felt almost no pain, he heard his spine break.

His mind writhed helplessly. His body refused to heed it in any way, and lay on the rubble, trapping him. He could hear cars on the avenue, radio sets and the sounds of cutlery in flats, distant and indifferent. The cries were petering out now. He tried to scream, but only his eyes could move. As they struggled, he glimpsed through a slit in the cellar wall the orange light in his kitchen.

His flashlight lay on the steps, dimmed by its fall. Before long a rustling darkness came slowly down the steps, blotting out the light. He heard sounds in the dark, and something that was not flesh nestled against him. His throat managed a choke shriek that was almost inaudible, even to him. Eventually the face crawled away toward the hall, and the light returned. From the corner of his eye he could see what surrounded him. They were round, still, practically featureless: as yet, hardly even alive.

Robert Bloch

Hungarian Rhapsody

Over the years, Robert Bloch has written numerous stories about vampires, and choosing one for this collection proved to be more difficult than I expected. In the end I picked 'Hungarian Rhapsody' because it hadn't been anthologised quite so often as some of his other tales, and it is a fine example of '50s paranoia and the Psycho *author's renowned sense of black humour.*

1991 saw the publication of a special issue of Weird Tales *honouring the writer's work, as well as a number of new books, including a collaborative novel with Andre Norton,* The Jekyll Legacy; *his third book about the Bates Motel,* Psycho House; *a collection of some of his best recent fiction,* Midnight Pleasures, *and a new anthology,* Psycho-Paths. *He also has a short poem in* Now We Are Sick, *and is set to have a story in the anthology movie* Tales of the Darkside II *and others adapted for a new theatrical version of the celebrated* Grand Guignol.

Since making his professional debut in 1935, Bloch has continued to turn out fiction that is a unique blend of psychological terror and grim graveyard humour, for which he was recently hounoured with the first World Horror Award in Nashville. He adds: "I currently have an autobiography in the hands of my agent in New York. It is my intention to go on living it until the last chapter. And maybe I can come up with a surprise ending . . .!"

RIGHT AFTER LABOR Day the weather turned cold and all the summer cottage people went home. By the time ice began to form on Lost Lake there was nobody around but Solly Vincent.

Vincent was a big fat man who had purchased a year-round home on the lake early that spring. He wore loud sports-shirts all summer long, and although nobody ever saw him hunting or fishing, he entertained a lot of weekend guests from the city at his place. The first thing he did when he bought the house was to put up a big sign in front which read SONOVA BEACH. Folks passing by got quite a bang out of it.

But it wasn't until fall that he took to coming into town and getting acquainted. Then he started dropping into Doe's Bar one or two evenings a week, playing cards with the regulars in the back room.

Even then, Vincent didn't exactly open up. He played a good game of poker and he smoked good cigars, but he never said anything about himself. Once, when Specs Hennessey asked him a direct question, he told the gang he came from Chicago, and that he was a retired business man. But he never mentioned what business he had retired from.

The only time he opened his mouth was to ask questions, and he didn't really do that until the evening Specs Hennessey brought out the gold coin and laid it on the table.

"Ever see anything like that before?" he asked the gang. Nobody said anything, but Vincent reached over and picked it up.

"German, isn't it?" he mumbled. "Who's the guy with the beard—the Kaiser?"

Specs Hennessey chuckled. "You're close," he said. "That's old Franz Joseph. He used to be boss of the Austro-Hungarian Empire, forty–fifty years ago. That's what they told me down at the bank."

"Where'd you get it, in a slot-machine?" Vincent wanted to know.

Specs shook his head. "It came in a bag, along with about a thousand others."

That's when Vincent really began to look interested. He picked up the coin again and turned it in his stubby fingers. "You gonna tell what happened?" he asked.

Specs didn't need any more encouragement. "Funniest damn thing," he said. "I was sitting in the office last Wednesday when this dame showed up and asked if I was the real-estate man and did I have any lake property for sale. So I said sure, the Schultz cottage over at Lost Lake. A mighty fine bargain, furnished and everything, for peanuts to settle the estate.

"I was all set to give her a real pitch but she said never mind that, could I show it to her? And I said, of course, how about tomorrow, and she said why not right now, tonight?

"So I drove her out and we went through the place and she said she'd take it, just like that. I should see the lawyer and get the papers ready and she'd come back Monday night and close the deal. Sure enough, she showed up, lugging this big bag of coins. I had to call Hank Felch over from the bank to find out what they were and if they were any good. Turns out they are, all right. Good as gold." Specs grinned. "That's how come I know about Franz Joseph." He took the coin from Vincent and put it back in his pocket. "Anyway, it looks like you're going to have a new neighbor out there. The Schultz place is only about a half-mile down the line from yours. And if I was you, I'd run over and borrow a cup of sugar."

Vincent blinked. "You figure she's loaded, huh?"

Specs shook his head. "Maybe she is, maybe she isn't. But the main thing is, she's stacked." He grinned again. "Name's Helene Esterhazy. Helene, with an *e* on the end. I saw it when she signed. Talks like one of them Hungarian refugees—figure that's what she is, too. A countess, maybe, some kind of nobility. Probably busted out from behind the Iron Curtain and decided to hole up some place where the Commies couldn't find her. Of course I'm only guessing, because she didn't have much to say for herself."

Vincent nodded. "How was she dressed?" he asked.

"Like a million bucks." Specs grinned at him. "What's the idea, you figuring on marrying for money, or something? I tell you, one look at this dame and you'll forget all about dough. She talks something like this ZaZa Gabor. Looks something like her, too, only she has red hair. Boy, if I wasn't a married man, I'd— "

"When she say she was moving in?" Vincent interrupted.

"She didn't say. But I figure right away, in a day or so."

Vincent yawned and stood up.

"Hey, you're not quitting yet, are you? The game's young— "

"Tired," Vincent said. "Got to hit the sack."

And he went home, and he hit the sack, but not to sleep. He kept thinking about his new neighbor.

Actually, Vincent wasn't too pleased with the idea of having anyone for a neighbor, even if she turned out to be a beautiful redheaded refugee. For Vincent was something of a refugee himself, and he'd come up north to get away from people; everybody except the few special friends he invited up during summer weekends. Those people he could trust, because they were former business associates. But there was always the possibility of running into former business rivals—and he didn't want to see any of them. Not ever. Some of them might nurse grudges, and in Vincent's former business a grudge could lead to trouble.

That's why Vincent didn't sleep very well at night, and why he always kept a little souvenir of his old business right under the pillow. You never could tell.

Of course, this sounded legitimate enough; the dame probably was a Hungarian refugee, the way Specs Hennessey said. Still, the whole thing might be a very clever plant, a way of moving in on Vincent which wouldn't be suspected.

In any case, Vincent decided he'd keep his eye on the old Schultz cottage down the line and see what happened. So the next morning he went into town again and bought himself a very good pair of binoculars, and the day after that he used them when the moving van drove into the drive of the Schultz place half a mile away.

Most of the leaves had fallen from the trees and Vincent got a pretty clear view from his kitchen window. The moving van was a small one, and there was just the driver and a single helper, carrying in a bunch of boxes and crates. Vincent didn't see any furniture and that puzzled him until he remembered the Schultz cottage had been sold furnished. Still, he wondered about the boxes, which seemed to be quite heavy. Could the whole story be on the up-and-up and the boxes maybe filled with more gold coins? Vincent couldn't make up his mind. He kept waiting for the woman to drive in, but she didn't show, and after a while the men climbed into their van and left.

Vincent watched most of the afternoon and nothing happened. Then he fried himself a steak and ate it, looking out at the sunset over the lake. It was then that he noticed the light shining from the cottage window. She must have sneaked in while he was busy at the stove.

He got out his binoculars and adjusted them. Vincent was a big man, and he had a powerful grip, but what he saw nearly caused the binoculars to drop from his fingers.

The curtain was up in her bedroom, and the woman was lying on the bed. She was naked, except for a covering of gold coins.

Vincent steadied himself and propped both hands up on the sill as he squinted through the binoculars.

There was no mistake about it—he saw a naked woman, wallowing in a bed strewn with gold. The light reflected from the coins, it danced and dazzled across her bare body, it radiated redly from her long auburn hair. She was pale, wide-eyed, and voluptuously lovely, and her oval face with its high cheekbones and full lips seemed transformed into a mask of wanton ecstasy as she caressed her nakedness with handfuls of shimmering gold.

Then Vincent knew that it wasn't a plant, she wasn't a phoney. She was a genuine refugee, all right, but that wasn't important. What was important was the way the blood pounded in his temples, the way his throat tightened up until he almost choked as he stared at her, stared at all that long, lean loveliness and the white and the red and the gold.

He made himself put down the binoculars, then. He made himself pull the shade, and he made himself wait until the next morning even though he got no rest that night.

But bright and early he was up, shaving close with his electric razor, dressing in the double-breasted gab that hid his paunch, using the lotion left over from summer when he used to bring the tramps up from the city. And he put on his new tie and his big smile, and he walked very quickly over to the cottage and knocked on the door.

No answer.

He knocked a dozen times, but nothing happened. The shades were all down, and there wasn't a sound.

Of course he could have forced the lock. If he'd thought she was a plant, he'd have done so in a moment, because he carried the souvenir in his coat-pocket, ready for action. And if he'd had any idea of just getting at the coins he would have forced the lock, too. That would be the ideal time, when she was away.

Only he wasn't worried about plants, and he didn't give a damn about the money. What he wanted was the woman. Helene Esterhazy. Classy name. Real class. A countess, maybe. A writhing redhead on a bed of golden coins—

Vincent went away after a while, but all day long he sat in the window and watched. Watched and waited. She'd probably gone into town to stock up on supplies. Maybe she visited the beauty parlor, too. But she ought to be back. She had to come back. And when she did—

This time he missed her because he finally had to go to the bathroom, along about twilight. But when he returned to his post and saw the light in the front room, he didn't hesitate. He made the half-mile walk in about five minutes, flat, and he was puffing a little. Then he forced himself to wait on the doorstep for a moment before knocking. Finally his ham-fist rapped, and she opened the door.

She stood there, staring startled into the darkness, and the lamplight from behind shone through the filmy transparency of her long hostess-gown, then flamed through the long red hair that flowed loosely across her shoulders.

"Yes?" she murmured.

Vincent swallowed painfully. He couldn't help it. She looked like a hundred-a-night girl; hell, make it a thousand-a-night, make it a million. A million in gold coins, and her red hair like a veil. That was all he could think of, and he couldn't remember the words he'd rehearsed, the line he'd so carefully built up in advance.

"My name's Solly Vincent," he heard himself saying. "I'm your neighbor, just down the lake a ways. Heard about you moving in and I thought I ought to, well, introduce myself."

"So."

She stared at him, not smiling, not moving, and he got a sick hunch that she knew just what he'd been thinking.

"Your name's Esterhazy, isn't it? Tell me you're Hungarian, something like that. Well, I figured maybe you're a stranger here, haven't got settled yet, and— "

"I'm quite satisfied here." Still she didn't smile or move. Just stared like a statue; a cold, hard, goddam beautiful statue.

"Glad to hear it. But I just meant, maybe you'd like to stop in at my place, sort of get acquainted. I got some of that Tokay wine and a big record-player, you know, classic stuff. I think I even have that piece, that *Hungarian Rhapsody* thing, and— "

Now what had he said?

Because all at once she was laughing. Laughing with her lips, with her throat, with her whole body, laughing with everything except those ice-green eyes.

Then she stopped and spoke, and her voice was ice-green too. "No thank you," she said. "As I say, I am quite satisfied here. All I require is that I am not disturbed."

"Well, maybe some other time— "

"Let me repeat myself. I do not wish to be disturbed. Now or at any time. Good evening, Mr— " The door closed.

She didn't even remember his name. The stuckup bitch didn't even remember his name. Unless she'd pretended to forget on purpose. Just like she slammed the door in his face, to put him down.

Well, nobody put Solly Vincent down. Not in the old days, and not now, either.

He walked back to his place and by the time he got there he was himself again. Not the damfool square who'd come up to her doorstep like a brush salesman with his hat in his hand. And not the jerk who had looked at her through the binoculars like some kid with hot pants.

He was Solly Vincent, and she didn't have to remember his name if she didn't want to. He'd show her who he was. And damned soon.

In bed that night he figured everything out. Maybe he'd saved himself a lot of grief by not getting involved. Even if she was a real disheroo, she was nuttier'n a fruitcake. Crazy foreigner, rolling around in a pile of coins. All these Hunky types, these refugees, were nuts. God knows what might have happened if he'd gotten mixed up with her. He didn't need a woman, anyway. A guy could always have himself a woman, particularly if he had money.

Money. That was the important thing. She had money. He'd seen it. Probably those crates were full of dough. No wonder she was hiding out here; if the Commies knew about her haul, they'd be right on the spot. That's the way he figured it, that's the way Specs Hennessey, the real-estate man, had figured it.

So why not?

The whole plan came to him at once. Call a few contacts in the city—maybe Carney and Fromkin, they could fence anything, including gold coins. Why the setup was perfect! She was all alone, there was nobody else around for three miles, and when it was over there wouldn't be any questions. It would look like the Commies had showed up and knocked the joint over. Besides, he wanted to see the look on her face when he came busting in—

He could imagine it now.

He imagined it all the next day, when he called Carney and Fromkin and told them to come up about nine. "Got a little deal for you," he said. "Tell you when I see you."

And he was still imagining it when they arrived. So much so that both Fromkin and Carney noticed something was wrong.

"What's it all about?" Carney wanted to know.

He just laughed. "Hope you got good springs in your Caddy," he said. "You may be hauling quite a load back to town."

"Give," Fromkin urged.

"Don't ask any questions. I've got some loot to peddle."

"Where is it?"

"I'm calling for it now."

And that's all he would say. He told them to sit tight, wait there at the house until he came back. They could help themselves to drinks if they liked. He'd only be a half-hour or so.

Then he went out. He didn't tell them where he was going, and he deliberately circled around the house in case they peeked out. But he doubled back and headed for the cottage down the way. The light was shining in the bedroom window, and it was time for the wandering boy to come home.

Now he could really let himself go, imagining everything. The way she'd look when she answered the door, the way she'd look when he grabbed her gown and ripped it away, the way she'd look when—

But he was forgetting about the money. All right, might as well admit it. The hell with the money. He'd get that too, yes, but the most important thing was the other. He'd show her who he was. She'd know, before she died.

Vincent grinned. His grin broadened as he noticed the light in the bedroom flicker and expire. She was going to sleep now. She was going to sleep in her bed of gold. So much the better. Now he wouldn't even bother to knock. He'd merely force the door, force it very quietly, and surprise her.

As it turned out, he didn't even have to do that. Because the door was unlocked. He tiptoed in very softly, and there was moonlight shining in through the window to help him find his way, and now there was the thickness in the throat again but it didn't come from confusion. He knew just what he was doing, just what he was going to do. His throat was thick because he was excited, because he could imagine her lying in there, naked on the heap of coins.

Because he could *see* her.

He opened the bedroom door, and the shade was up now so that the moonlight fell upon the whiteness and the redness and the golden glinting, and it was even better than he'd imagined because it was real.

Then the ice-green eyes opened and for a moment they stared in the old way. Suddenly there was a change. The eyes were flame-green now, and she was smiling and holding out her arms. Nuts? Maybe so. Maybe making love to all that money warmed her up. It didn't matter. What mattered was her arms, and her hair like a red veil, and the warm mouth open and panting. What mattered was to know that the gold was here and she was here and he was going to have them both, first her and then the money. He tore at his clothes, and then he was panting and sinking down to tear at her. She writhed and wriggled and his hands slipped on the coins and then his nails sank into the dirt beneath.

The dirt beneath—

There was dirt in her bed. And he could feel it and he could smell it, for suddenly she was above and behind him, pressing him down so that his face was rubbing in the dirt, and she'd twisted his hands around behind his back. He heaved, but she was very strong, and her cold fingers were busy at his wrists, knotting something tightly. Too late he tried to sit up, and then she hit him with something. Something cold and hard, something she'd taken from his own pocket; *my own gun*, he thought.

Then he must have passed out for a minute, because when he came to he could feel the blood trickling down the side of his face, and her tongue, licking it.

She had him propped up in the corner now, and she had tied

his hands and legs to the bedpost, very tightly. He couldn't move. He knew because he tried, God how he tried. The earth-smell was everywhere in the room. It came from the bed, and it came from her, too. She was naked, and she was licking his face. And she was laughing.

"You came anyway, eh?" she whispered. "You had to come, is that it? Well, here you are. And here you shall stay. I will keep you for a pet. You are big and fat. You will last a long, long time."

Vincent tried to move his head away. She laughed again.

"It isn't what you planned, is it? I know why you came back. For the gold. The gold and the earth I brought with me to sleep upon, as I did in the old country. All day I sleep upon it, but at night I awake. And when I do, you shall be here. No one will ever find or disturb us. It is good that you are strong. It will take many nights before I finish."

Vincent found his voice. "No," he croaked. "I never believed—you must be kidding, you're a refugee— "

She laughed again. "Yes. I am a refugee. But not a *political* refugee." Then she retracted her tongue and Vincent saw her teeth. Her long white teeth, moving against the side of his neck in the moonlight . . .

Back at the house Carney and Fromkin got ready to climb into the Cadillac.

"He's not showing up, that's for sure," Carney said. "We'll blow before there's any trouble. Whatever he had cooked up, the deal went sour. I knew it the minute I saw his face. He had a funny look, you know, like he'd flipped."

"Yeah," Fromkin agreed. "Something wrong with old Vincent, all right. I wonder what's biting him lately."

Edgar Allan Poe

Ligeia

Edgar Allan Poe (1809–49) has been described as "the father of modern horror".
He was born in Boston to parents who were itinerant actors, but the death of his
mother and desertion of his father resulted in the three-year-old Poe being made
the ward of a Virginia merchant who later disowned him.

Expelled from the University of Virginia for not paying his gambling debts
and dismissed from the West Point military academy for deliberate neglect of
duty, Poe finally embarked on a literary career.

He published a volume of poetry, Tamerlane and Other Poems, *in 1827*
but it wasn't until Poe wrote 'The Raven' (1845) that he became known as
'Mr Poe the poet'. He suffered from bouts of depression and madness, and his
state of mind is reflected in much of his fiction. Among his best stories are 'The
Fall of the House of Usher', 'The Murders in the Rue Morgue', 'The Black
Cat', 'The Tell-Tale Heart', 'The Pit and the Pendulum', 'The Premature
Burial' and 'The Facts in the Case of M. Valdemar'. Poe's only novel, The
Narrative of A. Gordon Pym *(1837), was left incomplete.*

'Ligeia' is rich in vampire imagery, as the spirit of a dead woman tries to
take possession of a living soul. It was filmed to great effect by Roger Corman
in 1964 as The Tomb of Ligeia, *starring Vincent Price.*

And the will therein lieth, which dieth not. Who knoweth the

*mysteries of the will, with its vigor? For God is but a great will
pervading all things by nature of its intentness. Man doth not yield
himself to the angels, nor unto death utterly, save only through the
weakness of his feeble will.*

JOSEPH GLANVILL

I CANNOT, FOR my soul, remember how, when, or even precisely
where, I first became acquainted with the lady Ligeia. Long years
have since elapsed, and my memory is feeble through much suffering.
Or, perhaps, I cannot *now* bring these points to mind, because, in
truth, the character of my beloved, her rare learning, her singular yet
placid cast of beauty, and the thrilling and enthralling eloquence of
her low musical language, made their way into my heart by paces
so steadily and stealthily progressive, that they have been unnoticed
and unknown. Yet I believe that I met her first and most frequently in
some large, old, decaying city near the Rhine. Of her family—I have
surely heard her speak. That it is of a remotely ancient date cannot
be doubted. Ligeia! Ligeia! Buried in studies of a nature more than
all else adapted to deaden impressions of the outward world, it is by
that sweet word alone—by Ligeia—that I bring before mine eyes in
fancy the image of her who is no more.

And now, while I write, a recollection flashes upon me that I have
never known the paternal name of her who was my friend and my
betrothed, and who became the partner of my studies, and finally
the wife of my bosom. Was it a playful charge on the part of my
Ligeia? or was it a test of my strength of affection, that I should
institute no inquiries upon this point? or was it rather a caprice of my
own—a wildly romantic offering on the shrine of the most passionate
devotion? I but indistinctly recall the fact itself—what wonder
that I have utterly forgotten the circumstances which originated
or attended it? And, indeed, if ever that spirit which is entitled
Romance—if ever she, the wan and the misty-winged *Ashtophet* of
idolatrous Egypt, presided, as they tell, over marriages ill-omened,
then most surely she presided over mine.

There is one dear topic, however, on which my memory fails me
not. It is the *person* of Ligeia. In stature she was tall, somewhat
slender, and, in her latter days, even emaciated. I would in vain
attempt to portray the majesty, the quiet ease of her demeanor,
or the incomprehensible lightness and elasticity of her footfall. She
came and departed as a shadow. I was never made aware of her
entrance into my closed study, save by the dear music of her low
sweet voice, as she placed her marble hand upon my shoulder. In
beauty of face no maiden ever equalled her. It was the radiance

of an opium-dream—an airy and spirit-lifting vision more wildly divine than the phantasies which hovered about the slumbering souls of the daughters of Delos. Yet her features were not of that regular mould which we have been falsely taught to worship in the classical labors of the heathen. "There is no exquisite beauty," says Bacon, Lord Verulam, speaking truly of all the forms and *genera* of beauty, "without some *strangeness* in the proportion." Yet, although I saw that the features of Ligeia were not of a classic regularity—although I perceived that her loveliness was indeed "exquisite" and felt that there was much of "strangeness" pervading it, yet I have tried in vain to detect the irregularity and to trace home my own perception of "the strange." I examined the contour of the lofty and pale forehead—it was faultless—how cold indeed that word when applied to a majesty so divine!—the skin rivalling the purest ivory, the commanding extent and repose, the gentle prominence of the regions above the temples; and then the raven-black, the glossy, the luxuriant, and naturally-curling tresses, setting forth the full force of the Homeric epithet, "hyacinthine!" I looked at the delicate outlines of the nose—and nowhere but in the graceful medallions of the Hebrews had I beheld a similar perfection. There were the same luxurious smoothness of surface, the same scarcely perceptible tendency to the aquiline, the same harmoniously curved nostrils speaking the free spirit. I regarded the sweet mouth. Here was indeed the triumph of all things heavenly—the magnificent turn of the short upper lip—the soft, voluptuous slumber of the under—the dimples which sported, and the color which spoke—the teeth glancing back, with a brilliancy almost startling, every ray of the holy light which fell upon them in her serene and placid yet most exultingly radiant of all smiles. I scrutinized the formation of the chin—and, here too, I found the gentleness of breadth, the softness and the majesty, the fulness and the spirituality of the Greek—the contour which the god Apollo revealed but in a dream, to Cleomenes, the son of the Athenian. And then I peered into the large eyes of Ligeia.

For eyes we have no models in the remotely antique. It might have been, too, that in these eyes of my beloved lay the secret to which Lord Verulam alludes. They were, I must believe, far larger than the ordinary eyes of our own race. They were even fuller than the fullest of the gazelle eyes of the tribe of the valley of Nourjahad. Yet it was only at intervals—in moments of intense excitement—that this peculiarity became more than slightly noticeable in Ligeia. And at such moments was her beauty—in my heated fancy thus it appeared perhaps—the beauty of beings either above or apart from the earth—the beauty of the fabulous Houri of the Turk. The hue of the orbs was the most brilliant of black, and, far over them, hung jetty lashes of great length. The brows, slightly irregular in outline, had the same tint. The "strangeness," however, which I found in the eyes was of a nature distinct from the formation, or the color, or the brilliancy of the features, and must, after all, be referred to the *expression*. Ah, word of no meaning! behind whose vast latitude of mere sound we intrench our ignorance of so much of the spiritual. The expression of the eyes of Ligeia! How for long hours have I pondered upon it! How have I, through the whole of a midsummer night, struggled to fathom it! What was it—that something more profound than the well of Democritus—which lay far within the pupils of my beloved? What *was* it? I was possessed with a passion to discover. Those eyes! those large, those shining, those divine orbs! they became to me twin stars of Leda, and I to them devoutest of astrologers.

There is no point, among the many incomprehensible anomalies of the science of mind, more thrillingly exciting than the fact—never, I believe, noticed in the schools—that in our endeavors to recall to memory something long forgotten, we often find ourselves *upon the very verge* of remembrance, without being able, in the end, to remember. And thus how frequently, in my intense scrutiny of Ligeia's eyes, have I felt approaching the full knowledge of their expression—felt it approaching—yet not quite be mine—and so at length entirely depart! And (strange, oh, strangest mystery of all!) I found, in the commonest objects of the universe, a circle of analogies to that expression. I mean to say that, subsequently to the period when Ligeia's beauty passed into my spirit, there dwelling as in a shrine, I derived, from many existences in the material world, a sentiment such as I felt always around, within me, by her large and luminous orbs. Yet not the more could I define that sentiment, or analyze, or even steadily view it. I recognized it, let me repeat, sometimes in the survey of a rapidly growing vine—in the contemplation of a moth, a butterfly, a chrysalis, a stream of running water. I have felt it in the ocean—in the falling of a meteor. I have felt it in the glances of unusually aged people. And there are one or two stars in heaven (one especially, a star of the sixth magnitude, double and changeable, to be found near the large star in Lyra) in a telescopic scrutiny of which I have been made aware of the feeling. I have been filled with it by certain sounds from stringed instruments, and not unfrequently by passages from books. Among innumerable other instances, I well remember something in a volume of Joseph Glanvill, which (perhaps merely from its quaintness—who shall say?) never failed to inspire me with the sentiment; "And the will therein lieth, which dieth not. Who knoweth the mysteries of the will, with its vigor? For God is but a great will pervading all things by nature of its intentness. Man doth not yield him to the angels, nor unto death utterly, save only through the weakness of his feeble will."

Length of years and subsequent reflection have enabled me to trace, indeed, some remote connection between this passage in the English moralist and a portion of the character of Ligeia. An *intensity* in thought, action, or speech was possibly, in her, a result or at least an index, of that gigantic volition which, during our long intercourse, failed to give other and more immediate evidence of its existence. Of all the women whom I have ever known, she, the outwardly calm, the ever-placid Ligeia, was the most violently a prey to the tumultuous vultures of stern passion. And of such passion I could form no estimate save by the miraculous expansion of those eyes which at once so delighted, and appalled me,—by the almost magical melody, modulation, distinctness, and placidity of her very low voice,—and by the fierce energy (rendered doubly effective by contrast with her manner of utterance) of the wild words which she habitually uttered.

I have spoken of the learning of Ligeia: it was immense—such as I have never known in woman. In the classical tongues was she deeply proficient, and as far as my own acquaintance extended in regard to the modern dialects of Europe, I have never known her at fault. Indeed upon any theme of the most admired because simply the most abstruse of the boasted erudition of the Academy, have I *ever* found Ligeia at fault? How singularly—how thrillingly, this one point in the nature of my wife has forced itself, at this late period only, upon my attention! I said her knowledge was such as I have never known in woman—but where breathes the man who has traversed, and successfully, *all* the wide areas of moral, physical, and mathematical science? I saw not then what I now clearly perceive, that the acquisitions of Ligeia were gigantic, were astounding; yet I was sufficiently aware of her infinite supremacy to resign myself, with a child-like confidence, to her guidance through the chaotic world of metaphysical investigation at which I was most busily occupied during the earlier years of our marriage. With how vast a triumph—with how vivid a delight—with how much of all that is ethereal in hope did I *feel*, as she bent over me in studies but little sought—but less known—that delicious vista by slow degrees expanding before me, down whose long, gorgeous, and all untrodden path, I might at length pass onward to the goal of a wisdom too divinely precious not to be forbidden!

How poignant, then, must have been the grief with which, after some years, I beheld my well-grounded expectations take wings to themselves and fly away! Without Ligeia I was but as a child groping benighted. Her presence, her readings alone, rendered vividly luminous the many mysteries of the transcendentalism in which we were immersed. Wanting the radiant lustre of her eyes, letters, lambent and golden, grew duller than Saturnian lead. And now those eyes shone less and less frequently upon the pages over which I pored. Ligeia grew ill. The wild eyes blazed with a too—too glorious effulgence; the pale fingers became of the transparent waxen hue of the grave; and the blue veins upon the lofty forehead swelled and sank impetuously with the tides of the most gentle emotion. I saw that she must die—and I struggled desperately in spirit with the grim Azrael. And the struggles of the passionate wife were, to my astonishment, even more energetic than my own. There had been much in her stern nature to impress me with the belief that, to her, death would have come without its terrors; but not so. Words are impotent to convey any just idea of the fierceness of resistance with which she wrestled with the Shadow. I groaned in anguish at the pitiable spectacle. I would have soothed—I would have reasoned; but in the intensity of her wild desire for life—for life—*but* for life—solace and reason were alike the uttermost of folly. Yet not until the last instance, amid the most convulsive writhings of her fierce spirit, was shaken the external placidity of her demeanor. Her voice grew more gentle—grew more low—yet I would not wish to dwell upon the wild meaning of the quietly uttered words. My brain reeled as I hearkened, entranced to a melody more than mortal—to assumptions and aspirations which mortality had never before known.

That she loved me I should not have doubted; and I might have been easily aware that, in a bosom such as hers, love would have reigned no ordinary passion. But in death only was I fully impressed with the strength of her affection. For long hours, detaining my hand, would she pour out before me the overflowing of a heart whose more than passionate devotion amounted to idolatry. How had I deserved to be so blessed by such confessions?—how had I deserved to be so cursed with the removal of my beloved in the hour of her making them? But upon this subject I cannot bear to dilate. Let me say only, that in Ligeia's more than womanly abandonment to a love, alas! all unmerited, all unworthily bestowed, I at length recognized the principle of her longing, with so wildly earnest a desire, for the life which was now fleeing so rapidly away. It is this wild longing—it is this eager vehemence of desire for life—*but* for life—that I have no power to portray—no utterance capable of expressing.

At high noon of the night in which she departed, beckoning me, peremptorily, to her side, she bade me repeat certain verses

composed by herself not many days before. I obeyed her. They were
these:—

> Lo! 'tis a gala night
>   Within the lonesome latter years!
> An angel throng, bewinged, bedight
>   In veils, and drowned in tears,
> Sit in a theatre, to see
>   A play of hopes and fears,
> While the orchestra breathes fitfully
>   The music of the spheres.
>
> Mimes, in the form of God on high,
>   Mutter and mumble low,
> And hither and thither fly;
>   Mere puppets they, who come and go
> At bidding of vast formless things
>   That shift the scenery to and fro,
> Flapping from out their condor wings
>   Invisible Woe!
>
> That motley drama!—oh, be sure
>   It shall not be forgot!
> With its Phantom chased for evermore,
>   By a crowd that seize it not,
> Through a circle that ever returneth in
>   To the self-same spot,
> And much of Madness, and more of Sin,
>   And Horror, the soul of the plot!
>
> But see, amid the mimic rout
>   A crawling shape intrude!
> A blood-red thing that writhes from out
>   The scenic solitude!
> It writhes!—it writhes!—with mortal pangs
>   The mimes become its food,
> And the seraphs sob at vermin fangs
>   In human gore imbued.
>
> Out—out are the lights—out all!
>   And over each quivering form,
> The curtain, a funeral pall,
>   Comes down with the rush of a storm—
> And the angels, all pallid and wan,
>   Uprising, unveiling, affirm
> That the play is the tragedy, "Man,"
>   And its hero, the conqueror Worm.

"O God!" half shrieked Ligeia, leaping to her feet and extending her arms aloft with a spasmodic movement, as I made an end of these lines—"O God! O Divine Father!—shall these things be undeviatingly so?—shall this conqueror be not once conquered? Are we not part and parcel in Thee? Who—who knoweth the mysteries of the will with its vigor? Man doth not yield him to the angels, *nor unto death utterly*, save only through the weakness of his feeble will."

And now, as if exhausted with emotion, she suffered her white arms to fall, and returned solemnly to her bed of death. And as she breathed her last sighs, there came mingled with them a low murmur from her lips. I bent to them my ear, and distinguished, again, the concluding words of the passage in Glanvill: "*Man doth not yield him to the angels, nor unto death utterly, save only through the weakness of his feeble will.*"

She died: and I, crushed into the very dust with sorrow, could no longer endure the lonely desolation of my dwelling in the dim and decaying city by the Rhine. I had no lack of what the world calls wealth. Ligeia had brought me far more, very far more, than ordinarily falls to the lot of mortals. After a few months, therefore, of weary and aimless wandering, I purchased and put in some repair, an abbey, which I shall not name, in one of the wildest and least frequented portions of fair England. The gloomy and dreary grandeur of the building, the almost savage aspect of the domain, the many melancholy and time-honored memories connected with both, had much in unison with the feelings of utter abandonment which had driven me into that remote and unsocial region of the country. Yet although the external abbey, with its verdant decay hanging about it, suffered but little alteration, I gave way, with a child-like perversity, and perchance with a faint hope of alleviating my sorrows, to a display of more than regal magnificence within. For such follies, even in childhood, I had imbibed a taste, and now they came back to me as if in the dotage of grief. Alas, I feel how much even of incipient madness might have been discovered in the gorgeous and fantastic draperies, in the solemn carvings of Egypt, in the wild cornices and furniture, in the Bedlam patterns of the carpets of tufted gold! I had become a bounden slave in the trammels of opium, and my labors and my orders had taken a coloring from my dreams. But these absurdities I must not pause to detail. Let me speak only of that one chamber, ever accursed, whither, in a moment of mental alienation, I led from the altar as my bride—as the successor of the unforgotten Ligeia— the fair-haired and blue-eyed Lady Rowena Trevanion, of Tremaine.

There is no individual portion of the architecture and decoration of that bridal chamber which is not now visibly before me. Where were the souls of the haughty family of the bride, when, through thirst of gold, they permitted to pass the threshold of an apartment *so* bedecked, a maiden and a daughter so beloved? I have said, that I minutely remember the details of the chamber—yet I am sadly forgetful on topics of deep moment; and here there was no system, no keeping, in the fantastic display, to take hold upon the memory. The room lay in a high turret of the castellated abbey, was pentagonal in shape, and of capacious size. Occupying the whole southern face of the pentagon was the sole window—an immense sheet of unbroken glass from Venice—a single pane, and tinted of a leaden hue, so that the rays of either the sun or moon passing through it, fell with a ghastly lustre on the objects within. Over the upper portion of this huge window, extended the trellis-work of an aged vine, which clambered up the massy walls of the turret. The ceiling, of gloomy-looking oak, was excessively lofty, vaulted, and elaborately fretted with the wildest and most grotesque specimens of a semi-Gothic, semi-Druidical device. From out the most central recess of this melancholy vaulting, depended, by a single chain of gold with long links, a huge censer of the same metal, Saracenic in pattern, and with many perforations so contrived that there writhed in and out of them, as if endued with a serpent vitality, a continual succession of parti-colored fires.

Some few ottomans and golden candelabra, of Eastern figure, were in various stations about; and there was the couch, too—the bridal couch—of an Indian model, and low, and sculptured of solid ebony, with a pall-like canopy above. In each of the angles of the chamber stood on end a gigantic sarcophagus of black granite, from the tombs of the kings over against Luxor, with their aged lids full of immemorial sculpture. But in the draping of the apartment lay, alas! the chief phantasy of all: The lofty walls, gigantic in height—even unproportionably so—were hung from summit to foot, in vast folds, with a heavy and massive-looking tapestry—tapestry of a material which was found alike as a carpet on the floor, as a covering for the ottomans and the ebony bed, as a canopy for the bed and as the gorgeous volutes of the curtains which partially shaded the window. The material was the richest cloth of gold. It was spotted all over, at irregular intervals, with arabesque figures, about a foot in diameter, and wrought upon the cloth in patterns of the most jetty black. But these figures partook of the true character of the arabesque only when regarded from a single point of view. By a contrivance now common, and indeed traceable to a very remote period of antiquity, they were made changeable in aspect. To one entering the room, they bore the appearance of simple monstrosities;

but upon a further advance, this appearance gradually departed; and, step by step, as the visitor moved his station in the chamber, he saw himself surrounded by an endless succession of the ghastly forms which belong to the superstition of the Norman, or arise in the guilty slumbers of the monk. The phantasmagoric effect was vastly heightened by the artificial introduction of a strong continual current of wind behind the draperies—giving a hideous and uneasy animation to the whole.

In halls such as these—in a bridal chamber such as this—I passed, with the Lady of Tremaine, the unhallowed hours of the first month of our marriage—passed them with but little disquietude. That my wife dreaded the fierce moodiness of my temper—that she shunned me, and loved me but little—I could not help perceiving; but it gave me rather pleasure than otherwise. I loathed her with a hatred belonging more to demon than to man. My memory flew back (oh, with what intensity of regret!) to Ligeia, the beloved, the august, the beautiful, the entombed. I revelled in recollections of her purity, of her wisdom, of her lofty—her ethereal nature, of her passionate, her idolatrous love. Now, then, did my spirit fully and freely burn with more than all the fires of her own. In the excitement of my opium dreams (for I was habitually fettered in the shackles of the drug), I would call aloud upon her name, during the silence of the night, or among the sheltered recesses of the glens by day, as if, through the wild eagerness, the solemn passion, the consuming ardor of my longing for the departed, I could restore her to the pathways she had abandoned—ah, *could* it be for ever?—upon the earth.

About the commencement of the second month of the marriage, the Lady Rowena was attacked with sudden illness, from which her recovery was slow. The fever which consumed her rendered her nights uneasy; and in her perturbed state of half-slumber, she spoke of sounds, and of motions, in and about the chamber of the turret, which I concluded had no origin save in the distemper of her fancy, or perhaps in the phantasmagoric influences of the chamber itself. She became at length convalescent—finally, well. Yet but a brief period elapsed, ere a second more violent disorder again threw her upon a bed of suffering; and from this attack her frame, at all times feeble, never altogether recovered. Her illnesses were, after this epoch, of alarming character, and of more alarming recurrence, defying alike the knowledge and the great exertions of her physicians. With the increase of the chronic disease, which had thus, apparently, taken too sure hold upon her constitution to be eradicated by human means, I could not fail to observe a similar increase in the nervous irritation of her temperament, and in her excitability by trivial causes of fear.

She spoke again, and now more frequently and pertinaciously, of the sounds—of the slight sounds—and of the unusual motions among the tapestries, to which she had formerly alluded.

One night, near the closing in of September, she pressed this distressing subject with more than usual emphasis upon my attention. She had just awakened from an unquiet slumber, and I had been watching, with feelings half of anxiety, half of vague terror, the workings of her emaciated countenance. I sat by the side of her ebony bed, upon one of the ottomans of India. She partly arose, and spoke, in an earnest low whisper, of sounds which she *then* heard, but which I could not hear—of motions which she *then* saw, but which I could not perceive. The wind was rushing hurriedly behind the tapestries, and I wished to show her (what, let me confess it, I could not *all* believe) that those almost inarticulate breathings, and those very gentle variations of the figures upon the wall, were but the natural effects of that customary rushing of the wind. But a deadly pallor, overspreading her face, had proved to me that my exertions to reassure her would be fruitless. She appeared to be fainting, and no attendants were within call. I remembered where was deposited a decanter of light wine which had been ordered by her physicians, and hastened across the chamber to procure it. But, as I stepped beneath the light of the censer, two circumstances of a startling nature attracted my attention. I had felt that some palpable although invisible object had passed lightly by my person; and I saw that there lay upon the golden carpet, in the very middle of the rich lustre thrown from the censer, a shadow—a faint, indefinite shadow of angelic aspect—such as might be fancied for the shadow of a shade. But I was wild with the excitement of an immoderate dose of opium, and heeded these things but little, nor spoke of them to Rowena. Having found the wine, I recrossed the chamber, and poured out a gobletful, which I held to the lips of the fainting lady. she had now partially recovered, however, and took the vessel herself, while I sank upon an ottoman near me, with my eyes fastened upon her person. It was then that I became distinctly aware of a gentle footfall upon the carpet, and near the couch; and in a second thereafter, as Rowena was in the act of raising the wine to her lips, I saw, or may have dreamed that I saw, fall within the goblet, as if from some invisible spring in the atmosphere of the room, three or four large drops of a brilliant and ruby-coloured fluid. If this I saw—not so Rowena. She swallowed the wine unhesitatingly, and I forbore to speak to her of a circumstance which must, after all, I considered, have been but the suggestion of a vivid imagination, rendered morbidly active by the terror of the lady, by the opium, and by the hour.

Yet I cannot conceal it from my own perception that, immediately subsequent to the fall of the ruby-drops, a rapid change for the worse took place in the disorder of my wife; so that, on the third subsequent night, the hands of her menials prepared her for the tomb, and on the fourth, I sat alone, with her shrouded body, in that fantastic chamber which had received her as my bride. Wild visions, opium-engendered, flitted, shadow-like, before me. I gazed with unquiet eye upon the sarcophagi in the angles of the room, upon the varying figures of the drapery, and upon the writhing of the parti-colored fires in the censer overhead. My eyes then fell, as I called to mind the circumstances of a former night, to the spot beneath the glare of the censer where I had seen the faint traces of the shadow. It was there, however, no longer; and breathing with greater freedom, I turned my glances to the pallid and rigid figure upon the bed. Then rushed upon me a thousand memories of Ligeia—and then came back upon my heart, with the turbulent violence of a flood, the whole of that unutterable woe with which I had regarded *her* thus enshrouded. The night waned; and still, with a bosom full of bitter thoughts of the one only and supremely beloved, I remained gazing upon the body of Rowena.

It might have been midnight, or perhaps earlier, or later, for I had taken no note of time, when a sob, low, gentle, but very distinct, startled me from my reverie. I *felt* that it came from the bed of ebony—the bed of death. I listened in an agony of superstitious terror—but there was no repetition of the sound. I strained my vision to detect any motion in the corpse—but there was not the slightest perceptible. Yet I could not have been deceived. I *had* heard the noise, however faint, and my soul was awakened within me. I resolutely and perseveringly kept my attention riveted upon the body. Many minutes elapsed before any circumstance occurred tending to throw light upon the mystery. At length it became evident that a slight, a very feeble, and barely noticeable tinge of color had flushed up within the cheeks, and along the sunken small veins of the eyelids. Through a species of unutterable horror and awe, for which the language of mortality has no sufficiently energetic expression, I felt my heart cease to beat, my limbs grow rigid where I sat. Yet a sense of duty finally operated to restore my self-possession. I could no longer doubt that we had been precipitate in our preparations—that Rowena still lived. It was necessary that some immediate exertion be made; yet the turret was altogether apart from the portion of the abbey tenanted by the servants—there were none within call—I had no means of summoning them to my aid without leaving the room for many minutes—and this I could not venture to do. I therefore struggled alone in my endeavors to call back the spirit still hovering. In a short period it was certain, however, that a relapse had taken place; the color disappeared from both eyelid and cheek, leaving a wanness even more than that of marble; the lips became doubly shrivelled and pinched up in the ghastly expression of death; a repulsive clamminess and coldness overspread rapidly the surface of the body; and all the usual rigorous stiffness immediately supervened. I fell back with a shudder upon the couch from which I had been so startlingly aroused, and again gave myself up to passionate waking visions of Ligeia. An hour thus elapsed, when (could it be possible?) I was a second time aware of some vague sound issuing from the region of the bed.

I listened—in extremity of horror. The sound came again—it was a sigh. Rushing to the corpse, I saw—distinctly saw—a tremor upon the lips. In a minute afterward they relaxed, disclosing a bright line of the pearly teeth. Amazement now struggled in my bosom with the profound awe which had hitherto reigned there alone. I felt that my vision grew dim, that my reason wandered; and it was only by a violent effort that I at length succeeded in nerving myself to the task which duty thus once more had pointed out. There was now a partial glow upon the forehead and upon the cheek and throat; a perceptible warmth pervaded the whole frame; there was even a slight pulsation at the heart. The lady *lived*; and with redoubled ardor I betook myself to the task of restoration. I chafed and bathed the temples and the hands, and used every exertion which experience, and no little medical reading, could suggest. But in vain. Suddenly, the color fled, the pulsation ceased, the lips resumed the expression of the dead, and, in an instant afterward, the whole body took upon itself the icy chilliness, the livid hue, the intense rigidity, the sunken outline, and all the loathsome peculiarities of that which has been, for many days, a tenant of the tomb.

And again I sank into visions of Ligeia—and again (what marvel that I shudder while I write?), *again* there reached my ears a low sob from the region of the ebony bed. But why shall I minutely detail the unspeakable horrors of that night? Why shall I pause to relate how, time after time, until near the period of the gray dawn, this hideous drama of revivification was repeated; how each terrific relapse was only into a sterner and apparently more irredeemable death; how each agony wore the aspect of a struggle with some invisible foe; and how each struggle was succeeded by I know not what of wild change in the personal appearance of the corpse? Let me hurry to a conclusion.

The greater part of the fearful night had worn away, and she who had been dead once again stirred—and now more vigorously than hitherto, although arousing from a dissolution more appalling in its utter hopelessness than any. I had long ceased to struggle or to move, and remained sitting rigidly upon the ottoman, a helpless prey to a whirl of violent emotions, of which extreme awe was perhaps the least terrible, the least consuming. The corpse, I repeat, stirred, and now more vigorously than before. The hues of life flushed up with unwonted energy into the countenance—the limbs relaxed—and, save that the eyelids were yet pressed heavily together, and that the bandages and draperies of the grave still imparted their charnel character to the figure, I might have dreamed that Rowena had indeed shaken off, utterly, the fetters of Death. But if this idea was not, even then, altogether adopted, I could at least doubt no longer, when, arising from the bed, tottering, with feeble steps, with closed eyes, and with the manner of one bewildered in a dream, the thing that was enshrouded advanced boldly and palpably into the middle of the apartment.

I trembled not—I stirred not—for a crowd of unutterable fancies connected with the air, the stature, the demeanor, of the figure, rushing hurriedly through my brain, had paralyzed—had chilled me into stone. I stirred not—but gazed upon the apparition. There was a mad disorder in my thoughts—a tumult unappeasable. Could it, indeed, be the *living* Rowena who confronted me? Could it, indeed, be Rowena *at all*—the fair-haired, the blue-eyed Lady Rowena Trevanion of Tremaine? Why, *why* should I doubt it? The bandage lay heavily about the mouth—but then might it not be the mouth of the breathing Lady of Tremaine? And the cheeks—there were the roses as in her noon of life—yes, these might indeed be the fair cheeks of the living Lady of Tremaine. And the chin, with its dimples, as in health, might it not be hers?—but *had she then grown taller since her malady?* What inexpressible madness seized me with that thought? One bound, and I had reached her feet! Shrinking from my touch, she let fall from her head, unloosened, the ghastly cerements which had confined it, and there streamed forth into the rushing atmosphere of the chamber huge masses of long and dishevelled hair; *it was blacker than the raven wings of midnight!* And now slowly opened *the eyes* of the figure which stood before me. "Here then, at least," I shrieked aloud, "can I never—can I never be mistaken—these are the full, and the black, and the wild eyes—of my lost love—of the lady—of the LADY LIGEIA."

Richard Christian Matheson

Vampire

The son of acclaimed science fiction writer Richard Matheson, over the past few years Richard Christian Matheson has proved himself to be the master of the short short horror story.

He's been an advertising copywriter, parapsychologist, rock 'n' roll drummer, songwriter, television scriptwriter and is now one of the hottest young producers in Hollywood. He's co-executive producing a major vampire movie, Red Sleep, *which he scripted with Mick Garris, marking his sixth sale of a screenplay written on speculation and sold for more than half-a-million dollars. He is also looking to direct one of his own original scripts within the next year or two.*

As if all that wasn't enough, Matheson's early short stories were collected in Scars and Other Distinguishing Marks, *and a second collection is due, along with his first novel* Created By, *a psychological thriller set in Hollywood, which Clive Barker describes as a "masterly fable".*

'Vampire' is the shortest story in this book. It is also one of the most powerful.

Man.
Late. Rain.
Road.
Man.
Searching. Starved. Sick.
Driving.
Radio. News. Scanners. Police. Broadcast.
Accident. Town.
Near.
Speeding. Puddles.
Aching.
Minutes.
Arrive. Park. Watch.
Bodies. Blood. Crowd. Sirens.
Wait.
Hour. Sit. Pain. Cigarette. Thermos. Coffee.
Sweat. Nausea.
Streetlights. Eyes. Stretchers. Sheets.
Flesh.
Death.
Shaking. Chills.
Clock. Wait.
More. Wait.
Car. Stink. Cigarette.
Ambulance. Crying. Tow truck. Bodies. Taken.
Crowd. Police. Photographers. Drunks. Leave.
Gone.
Street. Quiet.
Rain. Dark. Humid.
Alone.
Door. Out. Stand. Walk. Pain. Stare. Closer.
Buildings. Silent. Street. Dead.
Blood. Chalk. Outlines. Closer.
Step. Inside. Outlines. Middle.
Inhale. Eyes. Closed.
Think. Inhale. Concentrate. Feel. Breathe.
Flow.
Death. Collision. Woman. Screaming. Windshield. Expression.
Moment. Death.
Energy. Concentrate. Images. Exploding.
Moment.
Woman. Car. Truck. Explosion.
Impact. Moment.

Rush.
Feeling. Feeding.
Metal. Burning. Screams. Blood. Death.
Moment. Collision. Images. Faster.
Strength. Medicine.
Stronger.
Concentrate. Better.
Images. Collision. Stronger. Seeing. Death.
Moment. Healing. Moment.
Addiction.
Drug. Rush. Body. Warmer.
Death. Concentrating. Healing. Addiction. Drug.
Warm. Calm.
Death. Medicine.
Death.
Life.
Medicine.
Addiction. Strong.
Leave.
Car. Engine. Drive. Rain. Streets. Freeway. Map.
Drive. Relax. Safe. Warm. Rush. Good.
Radio. Cigarette. Breeze.
Night.
Searching. Accidents. Death.
Life.
Dash. Clock. Waiting.
Soon.

Hugh B. Cave

Stragella

Hugh B. Cave was born in 1910 in Chester, England, but emigrated to America with his family when he was five. While editing trade journals, he sold his first pulp magazine story, "Island Ordeal", to Brief Stories *in 1929.*

Cave quickly established himself as an inventive and prolific writer and became a regular contributor to Strange Tales, Weird Tales, Ghost Stories, Black Book Detective, Thrilling Mysteries, Spicy Mystery Stories, *and the so-called "shudder pulps",* Horror Stories *and* Terror Tales.

He then left the field for almost three decades, moving to Haiti and later Jamaica, where he established a coffee plantation and wrote two highly-praised travel books along with a number of mainstream novels. During this period he also contributed fiction regularly to The Saturday Evening Post *and other "slick-paper" magazines.*

In 1977 Karl Edward Wagner's Carcosa imprint published a hefty volume of Cave's best horror tales, Murgunstrumm and Others, *and he returned to the genre with stories in* Whispers *and* Fantasy Tales, *followed by a string of modern horror novels:* Legion of the Dead, The Nebulon Horror, The Evil, Shades of Evil, Disciples of Dread, The Lower Deep *and* Lucifer's Eye.

A new collection of shorter works, The Corpse Maker, *edited by Sheldon Jaffery, was recently issued by Starmont House, who also published a biography by Audrey Parent,* Pulp Man's Odyssey: The Hugh B. Cave Story. *In*

1991 the Horror Writers of America presented Cave with their highest honour, the Lifetime Achievement Award.
'Stragella' dates from Cave's most prolific period and is a classic vampire chiller written in the extravagant style of the pulp magazines of the '30s.

NIGHT, BLACK AS pitch and filled with the wailing of a dead wind, sank like a shapeless specter into the oily waters of the Indian Ocean, leaving a great gray expanse of sullen sea, empty except for a solitary speck that rose and dropped in the long swell.

The forlorn thing was a ship's boat. For seven days and seven nights it had drifted through the waste, bearing its ghastly burden. Now, groping to his knees, one of the two survivors peered away into the East, where the first glare of a red sun filtered over the rim of the world.

Within arm's reach, in the bottom of the boat, lay a second figure, face down. All night long he had lain there. Even the torrential shower, descending in the dark hours and flooding the dory with life-giving water, had failed to move him.

The first man crawled forward. Scooping water out of the tarpaulin with a battered tin cup, he turned his companion over and forced the stuff through receded lips.

"Miggs!" The voice was a cracked whisper. "Miggs! Good God, you ain't dead, Miggs? I ain't left all alone out here— "

John Miggs opened his eyes feebly.

"What—what's wrong?" he muttered.

"We got water, Miggs! Water!"

"You're dreamin' again, Yancy. It—it ain't water. It's nothin' but sea— "

"It rained!" Yancy screeched. "Last night it rained. I stretched the tarpaulin. All night long I been lyin' face up, lettin' it rain in my mouth!"

Miggs touched the tin cup to his tongue and lapped its contents suspiciously. With a mumbled cry he gulped the water down. Then, gibbering like a monkey, he was crawling toward the tarpaulin.

Yancy flung him back, snarling.

"No you won't!" Yancy rasped. "We got to save it, see? We got to get out of here."

Miggs glowered at him from the opposite end of the dory. Yancy sprawled down beside the tarpaulin and stared once again over the abandoned sea, struggling to reason things out.

They were somewhere in the Bay of Bengal. A week ago they had been on board the *Cardigan*, a tiny tramp freighter carrying its handful of passengers from Maulmain to Georgetown. The *Cardigan* had foundered in the typhoon off the Mergui Archipelago. For twelve hours she had heaved and groaned through an inferno of swirling seas. Then she had gone under.

Yancy's memory of the succeeding events was a twisted, unreal parade of horrors. At first there had been five men in the little boat. Four days of terrific heat, no water, no food, had driven the little Persian priest mad; and he had jumped overboard. The other two had drunk salt water and died in agony. Now he and Miggs were alone.

The sun was incandescent in a white hot sky. The sea was calm, greasy, unbroken except for the slow, patient black fins that had been following the boat for days. But something else, during the night, had joined the sharks in their hellish pursuit. Sea snakes, hydrophiinae, wriggling out of nowhere, had come to haunt the dory, gliding in circles round and round, venomous, vivid, vindictive. And overhead were gulls wheeling, swooping in erratic arcs, cackling fiendishly and watching the two men with relentless eyes.

Yancy glanced up at them. Gulls and snakes could mean only one thing—land! He supposed they had come from the Andamans, the prison isles of India. It didn't much matter. They were here. Hideous, menacing harbingers of hope!

His shirt, filthy and ragged, hung open to the belt, revealing a lean chest tattooed with grotesque figures. A long time ago—too long to remember—he had gone on a drunken binge in Goa. Jap rum had done it. In company with two others of the *Cardigan*'s crew he had shambled into a tattooing establishment and ordered the Jap, in a bloated voice, to "paint anything you damned well like, professor. Anything at all!" And the Jap, being of a religious mind and sentimental, had decorated Yancy's chest with a most beautiful Crucifix, large, ornate, and colorful.

It brought a grim smile to Yancy's lips as he peered down at it. But presently his attention was centered on something else—something unnatural, bewildering, on the horizon. The thing was a narrow bank of fog lying low on the water, as if a distorted cloud had sunk out of the sky and was floating heavily, half submerged in the sea. And the small boat was drifting toward it.

In a little while the fog bank hung dense on all sides. Yancy groped to his feet, gazing about him. John Miggs muttered something beneath his breath and crossed himself.

The thing was shapeless, grayish-white, clammy. It reeked—not with the dank smell of sea fog, but with the sickly, pungent stench of a buried jungle or a subterranean mushroom cellar. The sun seemed unable to penetrate it. Yancy could see the red ball above him, a feeble, smothered eye of crimson fire, blotted by swirling vapor.

"The gulls," mumbled Miggs. "They're gone."

"I know it. The sharks, too—and the snakes. We're all alone, Miggs."

An eternity passed, while the dory drifted deeper and deeper into the cone. And then there was something else—something that came like a moaning voice out of the fog. The muted, irregular, sing-song clangor of a ship's bell!

"Listen!" Miggs cackled. "You hear— "

But Yancy's trembling arm had come up abruptly, pointing ahead.

"By God, Miggs! Look!"

Miggs scrambled up, rocking the boat beneath him. His bony fingers gripped Yancy's arm. They stood there, the two of them, staring at the massive black shape that loomed up, like an ethereal phantom of another world, a hundred feet before them.

"We're saved," Miggs said incoherently. "Thank God, Nels— "

Yancy called out shrilly. His voice rang through the fog with a hoarse jangle, like the scream of a caged tiger. It choked into silence. And there was no answer, no responsive outcry—nothing so much as a whisper.

The dory drifted closer. No sound came from the lips of the two men as they drew alongside. There was nothing—nothing but the intermittent tolling of that mysterious, muted bell.

Then they realized the truth—a truth that brought a moan from Miggs' lips. The thing was a derelict, frowning out of the water, inanimate, sullen, buried in its winding-sheet of unearthly fog. Its stern was high, exposing a propeller red with rust and matted with clinging weeds. Across the bow, nearly obliterated by age, appeared the words: *Golconda—Cardiff*.

"Yancy, it ain't no real ship! It ain't of this world— "

Yancy stooped with a snarl, and picked up the oar in the bottom of the dory. A rope dangled within reach, hanging like a black serpent over the scarred hull. With clumsy strokes he drove the small boat beneath it; then, reaching up, he seized the line and made the boat fast.

"You're—goin' aboard?" Miggs said fearfully.

Yancy hesitated, staring up with bleary eyes. He was afraid, without knowing why. The *Golconda* frightened him. The mist clung to her tenaciously. She rolled heavily, ponderously in the long swell; and the bell was still tolling softly somewhere within the lost vessel.

"Well, why not?" Yancy growled. "There may be food aboard. What's there to be afraid of?"

Miggs was silent. Grasping the ropes, Yancy clambered up them. His body swung like a gibbet-corpse against the side. Clutching the rail, he heaved himself over; then stood there, peering into the layers of thick fog, as Miggs climbed up and dropped down beside him.

"I—don't like it," Miggs whispered. "It ain't— "

Yancy groped forward. The deck planks creaked dismally under him. With Miggs clinging close, he led the way into the waist, then into the bow. The cold fog seemed to have accumulated here in a sluggish mass, as if some magnetic force had drawn it. Through it, with arms outheld in front of him, Yancy moved with shuffling steps, a blind man in a strange world.

Suddenly he stopped—stopped so abruptly that Miggs lurched headlong into him. Yancy's body stiffened. His eyes were wide, glaring at the deck before him. A hollow, unintelligible sound parted his lips.

Miggs cringed back with a livid screech, clawing at his shoulder. "What—what is it?" he said thickly.

At their feet were bones. Skeletons—lying there in the swirl of vapor. Yancy shuddered as he examined them. Dead things they were, dead and harmless, yet they were given new life by the motion of the mist. They seemed to crawl, to wriggle, to slither toward him and away from him.

He recognized some of them as portions of human frames. Others were weird, unshapely things. A tiger skull grinned up at him with jaws that seemed to widen hungrily. The vertebrae of a huge python lay in disjointed coils on the planks, twisted as if in agony. He discerned the skeletonic remains of tigers, tapirs, and jungle beasts of unknown identity. And human heads, many of them, scattered about like an assembly of mocking, dead-alive faces, leering at him, watching him with hellish anticipation. The place was a morgue—a charnel house!

Yancy fell back, stumbling. His terror had returned with triple intensity. He felt cold perspiration forming on his forehead, on his chest, trickling down the tattooed Crucifix.

Frantically he swung about in his tracks and made for the welcome solitude of the stern deck, only to have Miggs clutch feverishly at his arm.

"I'm goin' to get out of here, Nels! That damned bell—these here things— "

Yancy flung the groping hands away. He tried to control his terror. This ship—this *Golconda*—was nothing but a tramp trader. She'd been carrying a cargo of jungle animals for some expedition. The beasts had got loose, gone amuck, in a storm. There was nothing fantastic about it!

In answer, came the intermittent clang of the hidden bell below decks and the soft lapping sound of the water swishing through the thick weeds which clung to the ship's bottom.

"Come on," Yancy said grimly. "I'm goin' to have a look around. We need food."

He strode back through the waist of the ship, with Miggs shuffling behind. Feeling his way to the towering stern, he found the fog thinner, less pungent.

The hatch leading down into the stern hold was open. It hung before his face like an uplifted hand, scarred, bloated, as if in mute warning. And out of the aperture at its base straggled a spidery thing that was strangely out of place here on this abandoned derelict—a curious, menacing, crawling vine with mottled triangular leaves and immense orange-hued blossoms. Like a living snake, intertwined about itself, it coiled out of the hold and wormed over the deck.

Yancy stepped closer, hesitantly. Bending down, he reached to grasp one of the blooms, only to turn his face away and fall back with an involuntary mutter. The flowers were sickly sweet, nauseating. They repelled him with their savage odor.

"Somethin'— " Miggs whispered sibilantly, "is watchin' us, Nels! I can feel it."

Yancy peered all about him. He, too, felt a third presence close at hand. Something malignant, evil, unearthly. He could not name it.

"It's your imagination," he snapped. "Shut up, will you?"

"We ain't alone, Nels. This ain't no ship at all!"

"Shut up!"

"But the flowers there—they ain't right. Flowers don't grow aboard a Christian ship, Nels!"

"This hulk's been here long enough for trees to grow on it," Yancy said curtly. "The seeds probably took root in the filth below."

"Well, I don't like it."

"Go forward and see what you can find. I'm goin' below to look around."

Miggs shrugged helplessly and moved away. Alone, Yancy descended to the lower levels. It was dark down here, full of shadows and huge gaunt forms that lost their substance in the coils of thick, sinuous fog. He felt his way along the passage, pawing the wall with both hands. Deeper and deeper into the labyrinth he went, until he found the galley.

The galley was a dungeon, reeking of dead, decayed food, as if the

stench had hung there for an eternity without being molested; as if
the entire ship lay in an atmosphere of its own—an atmosphere of
the grave—through which the clean outer air never broke.

But there was food here; canned food that stared down at him from
the rotted shelves. The labels were blurred, illegible. Some of the
cans crumbled in Yancy's fingers as he seized them—disintegrated
into brown, dry dust and trickled to the floor. Others were in fair
condition, air-tight. He stuffed four of them into his pockets and
turned away.

Eagerly now, he stumbled back along the passage. The prospects
of food took some of those other thoughts out of his mind, and he was
in better humor when he finally found the captain's cabin.

Here, too, the evident age of the place gripped him. The walls
were gray with mold, falling into a broken, warped floor. A single
table stood on the far side near the bunk, a blackened, grimy table
bearing an upright oil lamp and a single black book.

He picked the lamp up timidly and shook it. The circular base
was yet half full of oil, and he set it down carefully. It would come
in handy later. Frowning, he peered at the book beside it.

It was a seaman's Bible, a small one, lying there, coated with
cracked dust, dismal with age. Around it, as if some crawling slug
had examined it on all sides, leaving a trail of excretion, lay a peculiar
line of black pitch, irregular but unbroken.

Yancy picked the book up and flipped it open. The pages slid under
his fingers, allowing a scrap of loose paper to flutter to the floor. He
stooped to retrieve it; then, seeing that it bore a line of penciled script,
he peered closely at it.

The writing was an apparently irrelevant scrawl—a meaningless
memorandum which said crudely:

It's the bats and the crates. I know it now, but it is too late. God help me!

With a shrug, he replaced it and thrust the Bible into his belt,
where it pressed comfortingly against his body. Then he continued
his exploration.

In the wall cupboard he found two full bottles of liquor, which
proved to be brandy. Leaving them there, he groped out of the cabin
and returned to the upper deck in search of Miggs.

Miggs was leaning on the rail, watching something below. Yancy
trudged toward him, calling out shrilly:

"Say, I got food, Miggs! Food and brand— "

He did not finish. Mechanically his eyes followed the direction
of Miggs' stare, and he recoiled involuntarily as his words clipped
into stifled silence. On the surface of the oily water below, huge
sea snakes paddled against the ship's side—enormous slithering

shapes, banded with streaks of black and red and yellow, vicious and repulsive.

"They're back," Miggs said quickly. "They know this ain't no proper ship. They come here out of their hell-hole, to wait for us."

Yancy glanced at him curiously. The inflection of Miggs' voice was peculiar—not at all the phlegmatic, guttural tone that usually grumbled through the little man's lips. It was almost eager!

"What did you find?" Yancy faltered.

"Nothin'. All the ship's boats are hangin' in their davits. Never been touched."

"I found food," Yancy said abruptly, gripping his arm. "We'll eat; then we'll feel better. What the hell are we, anyhow—a couple of fools? Soon as we eat, we'll stock the dory and get off this blasted death ship and clear out of this stinkin' fog. We got water in the tarpaulin."

"We'll clear out? Will we, Nels?"

"Yah. Let's eat."

Once again, Yancy led the way below decks to the galley. There, after a twenty-minute effort in building a fire in the rusty stove, he and Miggs prepared a meal, carrying the food into the captain's cabin, where Yancy lighted the lamp.

They ate slowly, sucking the taste hungrily out of every mouthful, reluctant to finish. The lamplight, flickering in their faces, made gaunt masks of features that were already haggard and full of anticipation.

The brandy, which Yancy fetched out of the cupboard, brought back strength and reason—and confidence. It brought back, too, that unnatural sheen to Miggs' twitching eyes.

"We'd be damned fools to clear out of here right off," Miggs said suddenly. "The fog's got to lift sooner or later. I ain't trustin' myself to no small boat again, Nels—not when we don't know where we're at."

Yancy looked at him sharply. The little man turned away with a guilty shrug. Then hesitantly:

"I—I kinda like it here, Nels."

Yancy caught the odd gleam in those small eyes. He bent forward quickly.

"Where'd you go when I left you alone?" he demanded.

"Me? I didn't go nowhere. I—I just looked around a bit, and I picked a couple of them flowers. See."

Miggs groped in his shirt pocket and held up one of the livid, orange-colored blooms. His face took on an unholy brilliance as he held the thing close to his lips and inhaled its deadly aroma.

His eyes, glittering across the table, were on fire with sudden fanatic lust.

For an instant Yancy did not move. Then, with a savage oath, he lurched up and snatched the flower out of Miggs' fingers. Whirling, he flung it to the floor and ground it under his boot.

"You damned thick-headed fool!" he screeched. "You—God help you!"

Then he went limp, muttering incoherently. With faltering steps he stumbled out of the cabin and along the black passageway, and up on the abandoned deck. He staggered to the rail and stood there, holding himself erect with nerveless hands.

"God!" he whispered hoarsely. "God—what did I do that for? Am I goin' crazy?"

No answer came out of the silence. But he knew the answer. The thing he had done down there in the skipper's cabin—those mad words that had spewed from his mouth—had been involuntary. Something inside him, some sense of danger that was all about him, had hurled the words out of his mouth before he could control them. And his nerves were on edge, too; they felt as though they were ready to crack.

But he knew instinctively that Miggs had made a terrible mistake. There was something unearthly and wicked about those sickly sweet flowers. Flowers didn't grow aboard ship. Not real flowers. Real flowers had to take root somewhere, and, besides, they didn't have that drunken, etherish odour. Miggs should have left the vine alone. Clinging at the rail there, Yancy *knew* it, without knowing why.

He stayed there for a long time, trying to think and get his nerves back again. In a little while he began to feel frightened, being alone, and he returned below-decks to the cabin.

He stopped in the doorway, and stared.

Miggs was still there, slumped grotesquely over the table. The bottle was empty. Miggs was drunk, unconscious, mercifully oblivious of his surroundings.

For a moment Yancy glared at him morosely. For a moment, too, a new fear tugged at Yancy's heart—fear of being left alone through the coming night. He yanked Miggs' arm and shook him savagely; but there was no response. It would be hours, long, dreary, sinister hours, before Miggs regained his senses.

Bitterly Yancy took the lamp and set about exploring the rest of the ship. If he could find the ship's papers, he considered, they might dispel his terror. He might learn the truth.

With this in mind, he sought the mate's quarters. The papers had

not been in the captain's cabin where they belonged; therefore they
might be here.

But they were not. There was nothing—nothing but a chron-
ometer, sextant, and other nautical instruments lying in curious
positions on the mate's table, rusted beyond repair. And there were
flags, signal flags, thrown down as if they had been used at the last
moment. And, lying in a distorted heap on the floor, was a human
skeleton.

Avoiding this last horror, Yancy searched the room thoroughly.
Evidently, he reasoned, the captain had died early in the *Golconda*'s
unknown plague. The mate had brought these instruments, these
flags, to his own cabin, only to succumb before he could use them.

Only one thing Yancy took with him when he went out: a lantern,
rusty and brittle, but still serviceable. It was empty, but he poured
oil into it from the lamp. Then, returning the lamp to the captain's
quarters where Miggs lay unconscious, he went on deck.

He climbed the bridge and set the lantern beside him. Night was
coming. Already the fog was lifting, allowing darkness to creep in
beneath it. And so Yancy stood there, alone and helpless, while
blackness settled with uncanny quickness over the entire ship.

He was being watched. He felt it. Invisible eyes, hungry and
menacing, were keeping check on his movements. On the deck
beneath him were those inexplicable flowers, trailing out of the
unexplored hold, glowing like phosphorescent faces in the gloom.

"By God," Yancy mumbled, "I'm goin' to get out of here!"

His own voice startled him and caused him to stiffen and peer
about him, as if someone else had uttered the words. And then, very
suddenly, his eyes became fixed on the far horizon to starboard. His
lips twitched open, spitting out a shrill cry.

"Miggs! Miggs! A light! Look, Miggs— "

Frantically he stumbled down from the bridge and clawed his
way below decks to the mate's cabin. Feverishly he seized the signal
flags. Then, clutching them in his hand, he moaned helplessly and
let them fall. He realized that they were no good, no good in the dark.
Gibbering to himself, he searched for rockets. There were none.

Suddenly he remembered the lantern. Back again he raced through
the passage, on deck, up on the bridge. In another moment, with
the lantern dangling from his arm, he was clambering higher and
higher into the black spars of the mainmast. Again and again he
slipped and caught himself with outflung hands. And at length he
stood high above the deck, feet braced, swinging the lantern back
and forth. . . .

Below him, the deck was no longer silent, no longer abandoned.

From bow to stern it was trembling, creaking, whispering up at him.
He peered down fearfully. Blurred shadows seemed to be prowling
through the darkness, coming out of nowhere, pacing dolefully back
and forth through the gloom. They were watching him with a furtive
interest.

He called out feebly. The muted echo of his own voice came back
up to him. He was aware that the bell was tolling again, and the
swish of the sea was louder, more persistent.

With an effort he caught a grip on himself.

"Damned fool," he rasped. "Drivin' yourself crazy— "

The moon was rising. It blurred the blinking light on the horizon
and penetrated the darkness like a livid yellow finger. Yancy lowered
the lantern with a sob. It was no good now. In the glare of the
moonlight, this puny flame would be invisible to the men aboard
that other ship. Slowly, cautiously, he climbed down to the deck.

He tried to think of something to do, to take his mind off the fear.
Striding to the rail, he hauled up the water butts from the dory. Then
he stretched the tarpaulin to catch the precipitation of the night dew.
No telling how long he and Miggs would be forced to remain aboard
the hulk.

He turned, then, to explore the forecastle. On his way across the
deck, he stopped and held the light over the creeping vine. The
curious flowers had become fragrant, heady, with the fumes of an
intoxicating drug. He followed the coils to where they vanished into
the hold, and he looked down. He saw only a tumbled pile of boxes
and crates. Barred boxes which must have been cages at one time.

Again he turned away. The ship was trying to tell him something.
He felt it—felt the movements of the deck planks beneath his feet.
The moonlight, too, had made hideous white things of the scattered
bones in the bow. Yancy stared at them with a shiver. He stared
again, and grotesque thoughts obtruded into his consciousness. The
bones were moving. Slithering, sliding over the deck, assembling
themselves, gathering into definite shapes. He could have sworn it!

Cursing, he wrenched his eyes away. Damned fool, thinking such
thoughts! With clenched fists he advanced to the forecastle; but before
he reached it, he stopped again.

It was the sound of flapping wings that brought him about.
Turning quickly, with a jerk, he was aware that the sound emanated
from the open hold. Hesitantly he stepped forward—and stood rigid
with an involuntary scream.

Out of the aperture came two horrible shapes—two inhuman
things with immense, clapping wings and glittering eyes. Hideous;
enormous. *Bats!*

Instinctively he flung his arm up to protect himself. But the creatures did not attack. They hung for an instant, poised over the hatch, eyeing him with something that was fiendishly like intelligence. Then they flapped over the deck, over the rail, and away into the night. As they sped away towards the west, where he had seen the light of that other ship twinkling, they clung together like witches hell-bent on some evil mission. And below them, in the bloated sea, huge snakes weaved smoky, golden patterns—waiting!. . .

He stood fast, squinting after the bats. Like two hellish black eyes they grew smaller and smaller, became pinpoints in the moon-glow, and finally vanished. Still he did not stir. His lips were dry, his body stiff and unnatural. He licked his mouth. Then he was conscious of something more. From somewhere behind him came a thin, throbbing thread of harmony—a lovely, utterly sweet musical note that fascinated him.

He turned slowly. His heart was hammering, surging. His eyes went suddenly wide.

There, not five feet from him, stood a human form. Not his imagination. Real!

But he had never seen a girl like her before. She was too beautiful. She was wild, almost savage, with her great dark eyes boring into him. Her skin was white, smooth as alabaster. Her hair was jet black; and a waving coil of it, like a broken cobweb of pitch strings, framed her face. Grotesque hoops of gold dangled from her ears. In her hair, above them, gleamed two of those sinister flowers from the straggling vine.

He did not speak; he simply gaped. The girl was bare-footed, bare-legged. A short, dark skirt covered her slender thighs. A ragged white waist, open at the throat, revealed the full curve of her breast. In one hand she held a long wooden reed, a flute-like instrument fashioned out of crude wood. And about her middle, dangling almost to the deck, twined a scarlet, silken sash, brilliant as the sun, but not so scarlet as her lips, which were parted in a faint, suggestive smile, showing teeth of marble whiteness!

"Who—who are you?" Yancy mumbled.

She shook her head. Yet she smiled with her eyes, and he felt, somehow, that she understood him. He tried again, in such tongues as he knew. Still she shook her head, and still he felt that she was mocking him. Not until he chanced upon a scattered, faltering greeting in Serbian, did she nod her head.

"Dobra!" she replied, in a husky rich voice which sounded, somehow, as if it were rarely used.

He stepped closer then. She was a gipsy evidently. A Tzany of the

Serbian hills. She moved very close to him with a floating, almost ethereal movement of her slender body. Peering into his face, flashing her haunting smile at him, she lifted the flute-like instrument and, as if it were nothing at all unnatural or out of place, began to play again the song which had first attracted his attention.

He listened in silence until she had finished. Then, with a cunning smile, she touched her fingers to her lips and whispered softly:

"You—mine. Yes?"

He did not understand. She clutched his arm and glanced fearfully toward the west, out over the sea.

"You—mine!" she said again, fiercely. "Papa Bocito—Seraphino —they no have you. You—not go—to them!"

He thought he understood then. She turned away from him and went silently across the deck. He watched her disappear into the forecastle, and would have followed her, but once again the ship—the whole ship—seemed to be struggling to whisper a warning.

Presently she returned, holding in her white hand a battered silver goblet, very old and very tarnished, brimming with scarlet fluid. He took it silently. It was impossible to refuse her. Her eyes had grown into lakes of night, lit by the burning moon. Her lips were soft, searching, undeniable.

"Who are you?" he whispered.

"Stragella," she smiled.

"Stragella. . . . Stragella. . . ."

The name itself was compelling. He drank the liquid slowly, without taking his eyes from her lovely face. The stuff had the taste of wine—strong, sweet wine. It was intoxicating, with the same weird effect that was contained in the orange blooms which she wore in her hair and which groveled over the deck behind her.

Yancy's hands groped up weakly. He rubbed his eyes, feeling suddenly weak, powerless, as if the very blood had been drained from his veins. Struggling futilely, he staggered back, moaning half inaudibly.

Stragella's arms went about him, caressing him with sensuous touch. He felt them, and they were powerful, irresistible. The girl's smile maddened him. Her crimson lips hung before his face, drawing nearer, mocking him. Then, all at once, she was seeking his throat. Those warm, passionate, deliriously pleasant lips were searching to touch him.

He sensed his danger. Frantically he strove to lift his arms and push her away. Deep in his mind some struggling intuition, some half-alive idea, warned him that he was in terrible peril. This girl, Stregella, was not of his kind; she was a creature of the darkness, a denizen of a different, frightful world of her own! Those lips, wanting his flesh, were inhuman, too fervid—

Suddenly she shrank away from him, releasing him with a jerk. A snarling animal-like sound surged through her flaming mouth. Her hand lashed out, rigid, pointing to the thing that hung in his belt. Talonic fingers pointed to the Bible that defied her!

But the scarlet fluid had taken its full effect. Yancy slumped down, unable to cry out. In a heap he lay there, paralyzed, powerless to stir.

He knew that she was commanding him to rise. Her lips, moving in pantomime, formed soundless words. Her glittering eyes were fixed upon him, hypnotic. The Bible—she wanted him to cast it over the rail! She wanted him to stand up and go into her arms. Then her lips would find a hold. . . .

But he could not obey. He could not raise his arms to support himself. She, in turn, stood at bay and refused to advance. Then, whirling about, her lips drawn into a diabolical curve, beautiful but bestial, she retreated. He saw her dart back, saw her tapering body whip about, with the crimson sash outflung behind her as she raced across the deck.

Yancy closed his eyes to blot out the sight. When he opened them again, they opened to a new, more intense horror. On the *Golconda*'s deck, Stragella was darting erratically among those piles of gleaming bones. But they were bones no longer. They had gathered into shapes, taken on flesh, blood. Before his very eyes they assumed substance, men and beasts alike. And then began an orgy such as Nels Yancy had never before looked upon—an orgy of the undead.

Monkeys, giant apes, lunged about the deck. A huge python reared its sinuous head to glare. On the hatch cover a snow-leopard, snarling furiously, crouched to spring. Tigers, tapirs, crocodiles—fought together in the bow. A great brown bear, of the type found in the lofty plateaus of the Pamirs, clawed at the rail.

And the men! Most of them were dark-skinned—dark enough to have come from the same region, from Madras. With them crouched Chinamen, and some Anglo–Saxons. Starved, all of them. Lean, gaunt, mad!

Pandemonium raged then. Animals and men alike were insane with hunger. In a little struggling knot, the men were gathered about the number-two hatch, defending themselves. They were wielding firearms—firing pointblank with desperation into the writhing mass that confronted them. And always, between them and around them and among, darted the girl who called herself Stragella.

They cast no shadows, those ghost shapes. Not even the girl, whose arms he had felt about him only a moment ago. There was nothing real in the scene, nothing human. Even the sounds of the shots and the screams of the cornered men, even the roaring growls of the big cats, were smothered as if they came to him through heavy glass windows, from a sealed chamber.

He was powerless to move. He lay in a cataleptic condition, conscious of the entire pantomime, yet unable to flee from it. And his senses were horribly acute—so acute that he turned his eyes upward with an abrupt twitch, instinctively; and then shrank into himself with a new fear as he discerned the two huge bats which had winged their way across the sea. . . .

They were returning now. Circling above him, they flapped down one after the other and settled with heavy, sullen thuds upon the hatch, close to that weird vine of flowers. They seemed to have lost their shape, these nocturnal monstrosities, to have become fantastic blurs, enveloped in an unearthly bluish radiance. Even as he stared at them, they vanished altogether for a moment; and then the strange vapor cleared to reveal the two creatures who stood there!

Not bats! Humans! Inhumans! They were gipsies, attired in moldy, decayed garments which stamped them as Balkans. Man and woman. Lean, emaciated, ancient man with fierce white mustache; plump old woman with black, rat-like eyes that seemed unused to the light of day. And they spoke to Stragella—spoke to her eagerly. She, in turn, swung about with enraged face and pointed to the Bible in Yancy's belt.

But the pantomime was not finished. On the deck the men and animals lay moaning, sobbing. Stragella turned noiselessly, calling the old man and woman after her. Calling them by name.

"Come—Papa Bocito, Seraphino!"

The tragedy of the ghost-ship was being reenacted. Yancy knew it, and shuddered at the thought. Starvation, cholera had driven the *Golconda*'s crew mad. The jungle beasts, unfed, hideously savage, had escaped out of their confinement. And now—now that the final conflict was over—Stragella and Papa Bocito and Seraphino were proceeding about their ghastly work.

Stragella was leading them. Her charm, her beauty, gave her a hold on the men. They were in love with her. She had *made* them love her, madly and without reason. Now she was moving from one to another, loving them and holding them close to her. And as she stepped away from each man, he went limp, faint, while she laughed terribly and passed on to the next. Her lips were parted. She licked them hungrily—licked the blood from them with a sharp, crimson tongue.

How long it lasted, Yancy did not know. Hours, hours on end. He was aware, suddenly, that a high wind was screeching and wailing in the upper reaches of the ship; and, peering up, he saw that the spars were no longer bare and rotten with age. Great gray sails stood out against the black sky—fantastic things without any definite form or outline. And the moon above them had vanished utterly. The howling wind was bringing a storm with it, filling the sails to bulging proportions. Beneath the decks the ship was groaning like a creature in agony. The seas were lashing her, slashing her, carrying her forward with amazing speed.

Of a sudden came a mighty grinding sound. The *Golconda* hurtled back, as if a huge, jagged reef of submerged rock had bored into her bottom. She listed. Her stern rose high in the air. And Stragella with her two fellow fiends, was standing in the bow, screaming in mad laughter in the teeth of the wind. The other two laughed with her.

Yancy saw them turn toward him, but they did not stop. Somehow, he did not expect them to stop. This scene, this mad pantomime, was not the present; it was the past. He was not here at all. All this had happened years ago! Forgotton, buried in the past!

But he heard them talking, in a mongrel dialect full of Serbian words.

"It is done. Papa Bocito! We shall stay here forever now. There is land within an hour's flight, where fresh blood abounds and will always abound. And here, on this wretched hulk, they will never find our graves to destroy us!"

The horrible trio passed close. Stragella turned, to stare out across the water, and raised her hand in silent warning. Yancy, turning wearily to stare in the same direction, saw that the first streaks of daylight were beginning to filter over the sea.

With a curious floating, drifting movement the three undead creatures moved toward the open hatch. They descended out of sight. Yancy, jerking himself erect and surprised to find that the effects of the drug had worn off with the coming of dawn, crept to the hatch and peered down—in time to see those fiendish forms enter their coffins. He knew then what the crates were. In the dim light, now that he was staring directly into the aperture, he saw what he had not noticed before. Three of those oblong boxes were filled with dank grave-earth!

He knew then the secret of the unnatural flowers. They *had* roots! They were rooted in the soil which harbored those undead bodies!

Then, like a groping finger, the dawn came out of the sea. Yancy walked to the rail, dazed. It was over now—all over. The orgy was ended. The *Golconda* was once more an abandoned, rotted hulk.

For an hour he stood at the rail, sucking in the warmth and glory of the sunlight. Once again that wall of unsightly mist was rising out of the water on all sides. Presently it would bury the ship, and Yancy shuddered.

He thought of Miggs. With quick steps he paced to the companionway and descended to the lower passage. Hesitantly he prowled through the thickening layers of dank fog. A queer sense of foreboding crept over him.

He called out even before he reached the door. There was no answer. Thrusting the barrier open, he stepped across the sill—and then he stood still while a sudden harsh cry broke from his lips.

Miggs was lying there, half across the table, his arms flung out, his head turned grotesquely on its side, staring up at the ceiling.

"Miggs! Miggs!" The sound came choking through Yancy's lips. "Oh, God, Miggs—what's happened?"

He reeled forward. Miggs was cold and stiff, and quite dead. All the blood was gone out of his face and arms. His eyes were glassy, wide open. He was as white as marble, shrunken horribly. In his throat were two parallel marks, as if a sharp-pointed staple had been hammered into the flesh and then withdrawn. The marks of the vampire.

For a long time Yancy did not retreat. The room swayed and lurched before him. He was alone. Alone! The whole ghastly thing was too sudden, too unexpected.

Then he stumbled forward and went down on his knees, clawing at Miggs' dangling arm.

"Oh God, Miggs," he mumbled incoherently. "You got to help me. I can't stand it!"

He clung there, white-faced, staring, sobbing thickly—and presently slumped in a pitiful heap, dragging Miggs over on top of him.

It was later afternoon when he regained consciousness. He stood up, fighting away the fear that overwhelmed him. He had to get away, get away! The thought hammered into his head with monotonous force. Get away!

He found his way to the upper deck. There was nothing he could do for Miggs. He would have to leave him here. Stumbling, he moved along the rail and reached down to draw the small boat closer, where he could provision it and make it ready for his departure.

His fingers clutched emptiness. The ropes were gone. The dory was gone. He hung limp, staring down at a flat expanse of oily sea.

For an hour he did not move. He fought to throw off his fear long enough to think of a way out. Then he stiffened with a sudden jerk and pushed himself away from the rail.

The ship's boats offered the only chance. He groped to the nearest one and labored feverishly over it.

But the task was hopeless. The life boats were of metal, rusted through and through, wedged in their davits. The wire cables were knotted and immovable. He tore his hands on them, wringing blood from his scarred fingers. Even while he worked, he knew that the boats would not float. They were rotten, through and through.

He had to stop, at last, from exhaustion.

After that, knowing that there was no escape, he had to do something, anything, to keep sane. First he would clear those horrible bones from the deck, then explore the rest of the ship. . . .

It was a repulsive task, but he drove himself to it. If he could get rid of the bones, perhaps Stragella and the other two creatures would not return. He did not know. It was merely a faint hope, something to cling to.

With grim, tight-pressed lips he dragged the bleached skeletons over the deck and kicked them over the side, and stood watching them as they sank from sight. Then he went to the hold, smothering his terror, and descended into the gloomy belly of the vessel. He avoided the crates with a shudder of revulsion. Ripping up that evil vine-thing by the roots, he carried it to the rail and flung it away, with the mold of grave-earth still clinging to it.

After that he went over the entire ship, end to end, but found nothing.

He slipped the anchor chains then, in the hopes that the ship would drift away from that vindictive bank of fog. Then he paced back and forth, muttering to himself and trying to force courage for the most hideous task of all.

The sea was growing dark, and with dusk came increasing terror. He knew the *Golconda* was drifting. Knew, too, that the undead inhabitants of the vessel were furious with him for allowing the boat to drift away from their source of food. Or they *would* be furious when they came alive again after their interim of forced sleep.

And there was only one method of defeating them. It was a horrible method, and he was already frightened. Nevertheless he searched the deck for a marlin spike and found one; and, turning sluggishly, he went back to the hold.

A stake, driven through the heart of each of the horrible trio. . . .

The rickety stairs were deep in shadow. Already the dying sun, buried behind its wreath of evil fog, was a ring of bloody mist. He glanced at it and realized that he must hurry. He cursed himself for having waited so long.

It was hard, lowering himself into the pitch-black hold when he could only feel his footing and trust to fate. His boots scraped ominously on the steps. He held his hands above him, gripping the deck timbers.

And suddenly he slipped.

His foot caught on the edge of a lower step, twisted abruptly, and pitched him forward. He cried out. The marlin spike dropped from his hand and clattered on one of the crates below. He tumbled in a heap, clawing for support. The impact knocked something out of his belt. And he realized, even as his head came in sharp contact with the foremost oblong box, that the Bible, which had heretofore protected him, was no longer a part of him.

He did not lose complete control of his senses. Frantically he sought to regain his knees and grope for the black book in the gloom of the hold. A sobbing, choking sound came pitifully from his lips.

A soft, triumphant laugh came out of the darkness close to him. He swung about heavily—so heavily that the movement sent him sprawling again in an inert heap.

He was too late. She was already there on her knees, glaring at him hungrily. A peculiar bluish glow welled about her face. She was ghastly beautiful as she reached behind her into the oblong crate and began to trace a circle about the Bible with a chunk of soft, tarry, pitch-like substance clutched in her white fingers.

Yancy stumbled toward her, finding strength in desperation. She straightened to meet him. Her lips, curled back, exposed white teeth. Her arms coiled out, enveloping him, stifling his struggles. God, they were strong. He could not resist them. The same languid, resigned feeling came over him. He would have fallen, but she held him erect.

She did not touch him with her lips. Behind her he saw two other shapes take form in the darkness. The savage features of Papa Bocito glowered at him; and Seraphino's ratty, smoldering eyes, full of hunger, bored into him. Stragella was obviously afraid of them.

Yancy was lifted from his feet. He was carried out on deck and borne swiftly, easily, down the companionway, along the lower passage, through a swirling blanket of hellish fog and darkness, to the cabin where Miggs lay dead. And he lost consciousness while they carried him.

He could not tell, when he opened his eyes, how long he had been asleep. It seemed a long, long interlude. Stragella was sitting beside him. He lay on the bunk in the cabin, and the lamp was burning on the table, revealing Miggs' limp body in full detail.

Yancy reached up fearfully to touch his throat. There were no marks there; not yet.

He was aware of voices, then. Papa Bocito and the ferret-faced woman were arguing with the girl beside him. The savage old man in particular was being angered by her cool, possessive smile.

"We are drifting away from the prison isles," Papa Bocito snarled, glancing at Yancy with unmasked hate. "It is his work, lifting the anchor. Unless you share him with us until we drift ashore, we shall perish!"

"He is mine," Stragella shrugged, modulating her voice to a persuasive whisper. "You had the other. This one is mine. I shall have him!"

"He belongs to us all!"

"Why?" Stragella smiled. "Because he has looked upon the resurrection night? Ah, he is the first to learn our secret."

Seraphino's eyes narrowed at that, almost to pinpoints. She jerked forward, clutching the girl's shoulder.

"We have quarreled enough," she hissed. "Soon it will be daylight. He belongs to us all because he has taken us away from the isles and learned our secrets."

The words drilled their way into Yancy's brain. "The resurrection night!" There was an ominous significance in it, and he thought he knew its meaning. His eyes, or his face, must have revealed his thoughts, for Papa Bocito drew near to him and pointed into his face with a long, bony forefinger, muttering triumphantly.

"You have seen what no other eyes have seen," the ancient man growled bitterly. "Now, for that, you shall become one of us. Stragella wants you. She shall have you for eternity—for a life without death. Do you know what that means?"

Yancy shook his head dumbly, fearfully.

"We are the undead," Bocito leered. "Our victims become creatures of the blood, like us. At night we are free. During the day we must return to our graves. That is why"—he cast his arm toward the upper deck in a hideous gesture—"those other victims of ours have not yet become like us. They were never buried; they have no graves to return to. Each night we give them life for our own amusement, but they are not of the brotherhood—yet."

Yancy licked his lips and said nothing. He understood then. Every night it happened. A nightly pantomime, when the dead become alive again, reenacting the events of the night when the *Golconda* had become a ship of hell.

"We are gipsies," the old man gloated. "Once we were human, living in our pleasant little camp in the shadow of Pobyczdin Potok's

crusty peaks, in the Morava Valley of Serbia. That was in the time
of Milutin, six hundreds of years ago. Then the vampires of the hills
came for us and took us to them. We lived the undead life, until there
was no more blood in the valley. So we went to the coast, we three,
transporting our grave-earth with us. And we lived there, alive by
night and dead by day, in the coastal villages of the Black Sea, until
the time came when we wished to go to the far places."

Seraphino's guttural voice interrupted him, saying harshly:
"Hurry. It is nearly dawn!"

"And we obtained passage on this *Golconda*, arranging to have our
crates of grave-earth carried secretly to the hold. And the ship fell into
cholera and starvation and storm. She went aground. And—here we
are. Ah, but there is blood upon the islands, my pretty one, and so
we anchored the *Golconda* on the reef, where life was close at hand!"

Yancy closed his eyes with a shudder. He did not understand all of
the words; they were in a jargon of gipsy tongue. But he knew enough
to horrify him.

Then the old man ceased gloating. He fell back, glowering at
Stragella. And the girl laughed, a mad, cackling, triumphant laugh
of possession. She leaned forward, and the movement brought her
out of the line of the lamplight, so that the feeble glow fell full over
Yancy's prostrate body.

At that, with an angry snarl, she recoiled. Her eyes went wide
with abhorrence. Upon his chest gleamed the Crucifix—the tattooed
Cross and Savior which had been indelibly printed there. Stragella
held her face away, shielding her eyes. She cursed him horribly.
Backing away, she seized the arms of her companions and pointed
with trembling finger to the thing which had repulsed her.

The fog seemed to seep deeper and deeper into the cabin during
the ensuing silence. Yancy struggled to a sitting posture and cringed
back against the wall, waiting for them to attack him. It would be
finished in a moment, he knew. Then he would join Miggs, with
those awful marks on his throat and Stragella's lips crimson with his
sucked blood.

But they held their distance. The fog enveloped them, made them
almost indistinct. He could see only three pairs of glaring, staring,
phosphorescent eyes that grew larger and wider and more intensely
terrible.

He buried his face in his hands, waiting. They did not come.
He heard them mumbling, whispering. Vaguely he was conscious
of another sound, far off and barely audible. The howl of wolves.

Beneath him the bunk was swaying from side to side with the
movement of the ship. The *Golconda* was drifting swiftly. A storm had

risen out of nowhere, and the wind was singing its dead dirge in the rotten spars high above decks. He could hear it moaning, wheezing, like a human being in torment.

Then the three pairs of glittering orbs moved nearer. The whispered voices ceased, and a cunning smile passed over Stragella's features. Yancy screamed, and flattened against the wall. He watched her in fascination as she crept upon him. One arm was flung across her eyes to protect them from the sight of the Crucifix. In the other hand, outstretched, groping ever nearer, she clutched that hellish chunk of pitch-like substance with which she had encircled the Bible!

He knew what she would do. The thought struck him like an icy blast, full of fear and madness. She would slink closer, closer, until her hand touched his flesh. Then she would place the black substance around the tattooed cross and kill its powers. His defense would be gone. Then—those cruel lips on his throat. . . .

There was no avenue of escape. Papa Bocito and the plump old woman, grinning malignantly, had slid to one side, between him and the doorway. And Stragella writhed forward with one alabaster arm feeling . . . feeling. . . .

He was conscious of the roar of surf, very close, very loud, outside the walls of the fog-filled enclosure. The ship was lurching, reeling heavily, pitching in the swell. Hours must have passed. Hours and hours of darkness and horror.

Then she touched him. The sticky stuff was hot on his chest, moving in a slow circle. He hurled himself back, stumbled, went down, and she fell upon him.

Under his tormented body the floor of the cabin split asunder. The ship buckled from top to bottom with a grinding, roaring impact. A terrific shock burst through the ancient hulk, shattering its rotted timbers.

The lamp caromed off the table, plunging the cabin in semi-darkness. Through the port-holes filtered a gray glare. Stragella's face, thrust into Yancy's, became a mask of beautiful fury. She whirled back. She stood rigid, screaming lividly to Papa Bocito and the old hag.

"Go back! Go back!" she railed. "We have waited too long! It is dawn!"

She ran across the floor, grappling with them. Her lips were distorted. Her body trembled. She hurled her companions to the door. Then, as she followed them into the gloom of the passage, she turned upon Yancy with a last unholy snarl of defeated rage. And she was gone.

*   *   *

Yancy lay limp. When he struggled to his feet at last and went on deck, the sun was high in the sky, bloated and crimson, struggling to penetrate the cone of fog which swirled about the ship.

The ship lay far over, careened on her side. A hundred yards distant over the port rail lay the heaven-sent sight of land—a bleak, vacant expanse of jungle-rimmed shore line.

He went deliberately to work—a task that had to be finished quickly, lest he be discovered by the inhabitants of the shore and be considered stark mad. Returning to the cabin, he took the oil lamp and carried it to the open hold. There, sprinkling the liquid over the ancient wood, he set fire to it.

Turning, he stepped to the rail. A scream of agony, unearthly and prolonged, rose up behind him. Then he was over the rail, battling in the surf.

When he staggered up on the beach, twenty minutes later, the *Golconda* was a roaring furnace. On all sides of her the flames snarled skyward, spewing through that hellish cone of vapor. Grimly Yancy turned away and trudged along the beach.

He looked back after an hour of steady plodding. The lagoon was empty. The fog had vanished. The sun gleamed down with warm brilliance on a broad, empty expanse of sea.

Hours later he reached a settlement. Men came and talked to him, and asked curious questions. They pointed to his hair which was stark white. They told him he had reached Port Blair, on the southern island of the Andamans. After that, noticing the peculiar gleam of his blood-shot eyes, they took him to the home of the governor.

There he told his story—told hesitantly, because he expected to be disbelieved, mocked.

The governor looked at him cryptically.

"You don't expect me to understand?" the governor said. "I am not so sure, sir. This is a penal colony, a prison isle. During the past few years, more than two hundred of our convicts have died in the most curious way. Two tiny punctures in the throat. Loss of blood."

"You—you must destroy the graves," Yancy muttered.

The governor nodded silently, significantly.

After that, Yancy returned to the world, alone. Always alone. Men peered into his face and shrank away from the haunted stare of his eyes. They saw the Crucifix upon his chest and wondered why, day and night, he wore his shirt flapping open, so that the brilliant design glared forth.

But their curiosity was never appeased. Only Yancy knew; and Yancy was silent.

David J. Schow

A Week in the Unlife

David J. Schow is one of the most original stylists to emerge from the new wave of horror writers. His impressive short fiction began appearing a decade ago in the small press, and in 1985 he won The Twilight Zone Magazine*'s Dimension Award for 'Coming Soon to a Theatre Near You'. Two years later he picked up the World Fantasy Award for his story 'Red Light'.*

Following a string of pseudonymous novels and a TV reference book, he made his full-length debut in 1988 with The Kill Riff, *described as a "rock 'n' roll horror novel", while his second,* The Shaft, *remains published only in Britain. He edited* Silver Scream, *and the best of his stories have been collected in* Seeing Red *and* Lost Angels. *Other recent appearances are in* Fantasy Tales, Iniquities, Weird Tales, Dark Voices 3: The Pan Book of Horror, A Whisper of Blood *and* The Mammoth Book of Terror.

Schow's work for Hollywood includes scripts for Leatherface The Texas Chainsaw Massacre III, Critters 3 *and* 4, *and television's* Freddy's Nightmares. *He has also completed work on two segments of the Off-Broadway show* Grand Guignol, *based on Robert Bloch's stories.*

Schow believes that "It is the oversaturation of vampire lore, and the trivialist's lust to accumulate ever more of it, that is itself a new form of vampirism". As a reaction against this, he wrote the following story which he sums up as, "a vampire story with no vampires in it."

I

WHEN YOU STAKE a bloodsucker, the heartblood pumps out thick and black, the consistency of honey. I saw it make bubbles as it glurped out. The creature thrashed and squirmed and tried to pull out the stake—they always do, if you leave on their arms for the kill—but by the third whack it was, as Stoker might say, dispatched well and duly.

I lost count a long time ago. Doesn't matter. I no longer think of them as being even *former* human beings, and feel no anthropomorphic sympathy. In their eyes I see no tragedy, no romance, no seductive pulp appeal. Merely lust, rage at being outfoxed, and debased appetite, focused and sanguine.

People usually commit journals as legacy. So be it. Call me sentry, vigilante if you like. When they sleep their comatose sleep, I stalk and terminate them. When they walk, I hide. Better than they do.

They're really not as smart as popular fiction and films would lead you to believe. They do have cunning, an animalistic savvy. But I'm an experienced tracker; I know their spoor, the traces they leave, the way their presence charges the air. Things invisible or ephemeral to ordinary citizens, blackly obvious to me.

The journal is so you'll know, just in case my luck runs out.

Sundown. Nap time.

II

Naturally the police think of me as some sort of homicidal crackpot. That's a given; always has been for my predecessors. More watchers to evade. Caution comes reflexively to me these days. Police are slow and rational; they deal in the minutiae of a day-to-day world, deadly enough without the inclusion of bloodsuckers.

The police love to stop and search people. Fortunately for me, mallets and stakes and crosses and such are not yet illegal in this country. Lots of raised eyebrows and jokes and nudging but no actual arrests. When the time comes for them to recognize the plague that has descended upon their city, they will remember me, perhaps with grace.

My lot is friendless, solo. I know and expect such. It's okay.

City by city. I'm good at ferreting out the nests. To me, their kill-patterns are like a flashing red light. The police only see presumed loonies, draw no linkages; they bust and imprison mortals and never see the light.

I am not foolhardy enough to leave bloodsuckers lying. Even though the mean corpus usually dissolves, the stakes might be discovered. Sometimes there is other residue. City dumpsters and sewers provide adequate and fitting disposal for the leftovers of my mission.

The enemy casualties.

I wish I could advise the authorities, work hand-in-hand with them. Too complicated. Too many variables. Not a good control situation. Bloodsuckers have a maddening knack for vanishing into crevices, even hairline splits in logic.

Rule: Trust no one.

III

A female one, today. Funny. There aren't as many of them as you might suppose.

She had courted a human lover, so she claimed, like Romeo and Juliet—she could only visit him at night, and only after feeding, because bloodsuckers too can get carried away by passion.

I think she was intimating that she was a physical lover of otherworldly skill; I think she was fighting hard to tempt me not to eliminate her by saying so.

She did not use her mouth to seduce mortal men. I drove the stake into her brain, through the mouth. She was of recent vintage and did not melt or vaporize. When I fucked her remains, I was surprised to find her warm inside, not cold, like a cadaver. Warm.

With some of them, the human warmth is longer in leaving. But it always goes.

IV

I never met one before that gave up its existence without a struggle, but today I did, one that acted like he had been expecting me to wander along and relieve him of the burden of unlife. He did not deny what he was, nor attempt to trick me. He asked if he could talk a bit, before.

In a third-floor loft, the windows of which had been spray-painted flat black, he talked. Said he had always hated the taste of blood; said he preferred pineapple juice, or even coffee. He actually brewed a pot of coffee while we talked.

I allowed him to finish his cup before I put the ashwood length to his chest and drove deep and let his blackness gush. It dribbled, thinned by the coffee he had consumed.

V

Was thinking this afternoon perhaps I should start packing a Polaroid or somesuch, to keep a visual body count, just in case this journal becomes public record someday. It'd be good to have illustrations, proof. I was thinking of that line you hear overused in the movies. I'm sure you know it: *"But there's no such THING as a vampire!"* What a howler; ranks right up there alongside *"It's crazy—but it just might work!"* and *"We can't stop now for a lot of silly native superstitions!"*

Right; shoot cozy little memory snaps, in case they whizz to mist or drop apart to smoking goo. That bull about how you're not supposed to be able to record their images is from the movies, too. There's so much misleading information running loose that the bloodsuckers—the real ones—have no trouble at all moving through any urban center, *with impunity*, as they say on cop shows.

Maybe it would be a good idea to tape record the sounds they make when they die. Videotape them begging not to be exterminated. That would bug the eyes of all those monster movie fans, you bet.

VI

So many of them beleaguering this city, it's easy to feel outnumbered. Like I said, I've lost count.

Tonight might be a good window for moving on. Like them, I become vulnerable if I remain too long, and it's prudent operating procedure not to leave patterns or become predictable.

It's easy. I don't own much. Most of what I carry, I carry inside.

VII

They pulled me over on Highway Ten, outbound, for a broken left tail-light. A datafax photo of me was clipped to the visor in the Highway Patrol car. The journal book itself has been taken as evidence, so for now it's a felt-tip and high school notebook paper, which notes I hope to append to the journal proper later.

I have a cell with four bunks all to myself. The door is solid gray, with a food slot, unlike the barred cage of the bullpen. On the way back I noticed they had caught themselves a bloodsucker. Probably an accident; they probably don't even know what they have. There is no sunrise or sunset in the block, so if he gets out at night, they'll never know what happened. But I already know. Right now I will not say anything. I am exposed and at a disadvantage. The one I let slip today I can eliminate tenfold, next week.

VIII

New week. And I am vindicated at last.

I relaxed as soon as they showed me the photographs. How they managed documentation on the last few bloodsuckers I trapped, I have no idea. But I was relieved. Now I don't have to explain the journal—which, as you can see, they returned to me immediately. They had thousands of questions. They needed to know about the mallets, the stakes, the preferred method of killstrike. I cautioned them not to attempt a sweep and clear at night, when the enemy is stronger.

They paid serious attention this time, which made me feel much better. Now the fight can be mounted en masse.

They also let me know I wouldn't have to stay in the cell. Just some paperwork to clear, and I'm out among them again. One of the officials—not a cop, but a doctor—congratulated me on a stout job well done. He shook my hand, on behalf of all of them, he said, and mentioned writing a book on my work. This is exciting!

As per my request, the bloodsucker in the adjacent solitary cell was moved. I told them that to be really sure, they should use one of my stakes. It was simple vanity, really, on my part. I turn my stakes out of ashwood on a lathe. I made sure they knew I'd permit my stakes to be used as working models for the proper manufacture of all they would soon need.

When the guards come back I really must ask how they managed such crisp 8×10s of so many bloodsuckers. All those names and dates. First class documentation.

I'm afraid I may be a bit envious.

Frances Garfield

The House at Evening

Francis Garfield was born in Texas and has lived in Chapel Hill, North Carolina, since 1951 when she moved there with her husband, Manly Wade Wellman.

During the late 1930s and early '40s she had three stories published in Weird Tales *and another in* Amazing Stories. *After retiring from her job as a secretary in a school of public health, she kept thinking up ideas for horror stories and telling them to Wellman. He said they were "women's stories" and she would have to write them herself.*

So Garfield returned to her typewriter, and over the years the results have been published in The Year's Best Horror Stories, The Best Horror from Fantasy Tales, Whispers, Fantasy Book, Kadath, The Tome *and others.*

'The House at Evening' is a wonderfully atmospheric vampire story that should make us all glad she returned to the fold.

THE SUN HAD set and another twilight had begun. The western sky took on a rosy tinge, but none of the soft color penetrated into the lofty bedroom.

Claudia leaned toward the bureau. Her stormy black locks curtained her face as she brushed and brushed them. It was a luxurious, sensuous brushing. Her hair glistened in the light of the oil lamp.

Across the room sat Garland. She quickly combed her short blonde hair into an elfish mop of curls. "Thank goodness I don't have to worry about a great banner like yours," she said.

"Never you mind," Claudia laughed back. "We both know it's impressive."

They both applied makeup generously. Claudia fringed her silvery eyes with deep blue mascara and Garland brushed her pale eyebrows with brown. Each painted her lips a rosy red and smiled tightly to smooth the lipstick.

They finished dressing and went down the squeaking staircase to the big parlor. Darkness crept in, stealthily but surely. They picked up jugs of oil and went about, filling and lighting all the ancient glass-domed lamps. Light flickered yellow from table and shelf and glistened on the wide hardwood floor boards. Claudia took pride in those old expanses, spending hours on her knees to rub them to a glow. Garland arranged a bowl filled with colorful gourds on the mahogany table that framed the back of a brocaded couch. She put two scented candles into holders and lighted them.

Then they stood together to admire the effect of the soft light, Claudia in her red satin, Garland in her dark, bright blue. They checked each other for flaws and found none.

"I'd like to go walking outside, the way we used to do," said Garland. She glanced down at her high-heeled slippers. They weren't too high. "I'll only be gone a little while."

"There's not much to see out there," said Claudia. "Nobody much walks here anymore. It's been a long time since we've had company."

"Maybe I'm just being sentimental," smiled Garland. Her eyes twinkled for a moment, as if with some secret delight. "But maybe I'll bring somebody back."

"I'll stay here in case anybody calls," Claudia assured her.

The big wooden front door creaked shut behind Garland. She crossed the gray-floored piazza and ran down the steps to the path of old flagstones. Periwinkle overflowed them and knotted its roots everywhere. Ivy and honeysuckle choked the trees, autumn leaves poured down from the oaks. An old dead dogwood leaned wearily at the lawn's edge. Garland picked her way carefully.

An owl shrieked a message in the distance. Garland smiled to herself. She had worn no wrap out in the warm evening, but she nestled into the soft collar of her silky dress to feel its closeness. She breathed deeply of the night air.

Falling leaves whispered like raindrops. But there were only vagrant clouds in the sky. A young moon shone upon the old sidewalk, upon old houses along they way. They were large, pretentious houses, the sort called Victorian. They were ramshackle. No light shone from any window. Garland might have been the only moving creature in the neighborhood. Once this had been an elegant area on the edge of the old town that existed mainly for Ellerby College, but people had moved out. Deterioration had set in. Urban renewal threatened the neighborhood.

All at once Garland heard something—voices, hushed, furtive. She saw two tall young men coming toward her. She looked at them in the moonlight. They were handsome, sprucely dressed, looked like muscular young athletes. She hadn't seen their like for a while, and she felt a surge of warmth through her body.

They were near now, she could hear what they said.

"My Uncle Whit used to come here when he was in college," one young voice declared. "He said this was called Pink Hill. Said you'd be mighty well entertained."

Now she passed them, and turned at once to go back toward her house. She quickened her steps. For a moment she didn't know whether to be sad or happy. If only she hadn't lost her touch—but she knew her body, firm, sweet-looking. As she passed them again, she spoke.

"Hey," she greeted them.

One, tall with a neat, dark beard, spoke shyly, "Nice evening, isn't it?"

Garland smiled. If she had had dimples, she would have flashed them. "Yes, but there's a chill in the air. I think I'll just go back home. Maybe make some hot chocolate—or tea."

Away she walked ahead, her hips swinging a trifle, not so fast as to lose touch with them.

They seemed to be following her, all right. The bearded one was speaking, and Garland strained her ears to hear.

"After all," he was saying, "we did sort of think we were looking for experience."

The other, the fair-haired athletic one, said something too soft for Garland to hear. But it sounded like agreement.

She walked on, watching her feet on the treacherous pavement. There were so many cracks in that old cement. Sure enough, the two boys were coming along with her. Again she felt a flood of internal warmth. She felt almost young again, almost as young as she must look. Carefully she timed the sway of her hips. There was the house. Along the flagstones she minced happily, and up the steps and in at the door.

"We're going to have company, Claudia," she said.

Claudia swept the room with an appraising glance, and smiled a cool smile. "Tell me," she said quickly.

"Two really lovely young men, coming along to follow me. One with bright hair and a football body. The other tall, bearded, neat, sophisticated looking. We'll have to do them credit."

"Well, there's a bottle of port out, and some of those cheese biscuits I made." Claudia studied the table in the lamplight. "We'll be all right."

From outside they heard footsteps on the porch, and hesitant whispering.

"They're beautiful," said Garland.

Silence for an instant. Then a guarded tattoo of knocks on the panel of the door. A knock, Garland guessed, taught them by good old Uncle Whit.

"Okay, here we go," said Claudia, and gave Garland a triumphant look. "Remember your company manners."

She glided to the door, her red gown hugging her opulent hips and her slim waist. Her dress was long. It swept the floor and it accentuated every curve and hollow of the well-used body. She could be proud of how she looked, how she moved. She graduated magna cum laude in every way.

She opened the door, and the lamplight touched the two young men.

Garland had appraised them accurately. They wore well-fitting suits and open shirts. The taller one had a close-clipped beard, dark and sleek. Promising and intelligent. The other, of medium height but with broad shoulders, looked powerfully muscled. Undoubtedly undergraduates at Ellerby College. Fine prospects, both of them.

"Good evening, gentlemen," Claudia gave them her personal, hospitable smile.

"Good evening, ma'am," said the dark one, like a spokesman. He would be for Garland, thought Claudia. For her the other, the sturdy one.

"Well," said the tall one. "Well, we thought— " He paused embarrassedly.

"We thought we'd come walking this way," spoke up the other. "My name's Guy and this is Larry. We—we're students."

"Freshmen," added Larry. "We go to Ellerby."

"I see," Claudia soothed them. "Well, won't you come in?"

"Yes, ma'am," said Guy gratefully. They entered together and stood side by side. Their smiles were diffident. Claudia closed the door behind them.

Larry studied the parlor with politely curious eyes. "This is a great place," he offered. "Wonderful. It's—well, it's nostalgic."

"Thank you," Garland smiled to him. "Come sit here and see if this couch wasn't more or less made for you."

He hesitated, but only for a moment. Then he paced toward the couch. He wore handsome shiny boots. He and Garland sat down together and Claudia held out her hand to Guy.

"You look like somebody I used to know," she said, slitting her silvery eyes at him. "He played football at State. Came visiting here."

"Maybe all football players look alike," Guy smiled back. "I came to Ellerby to play tight end, if I can make it."

Beside Larry on the couch, Garland turned on her personality. It was as if she pressed a button to set it free.

"Would you like a glass of this port?" she asked. "It's very good."

"Let me do it." He took the bottle and poured. His hand trembled just a trifle. "Here." And he held out the glass.

"No, it's for you," she said. "I'll wait until later."

Larry sipped. "Delicious."

"Yes, only the best for our friends."

"We surely appreciate this, ma'am," he said, sipping again.

"You may call me Garland."

Claudia had seated Guy in a heavily soft armchair and had perched herself on its arm. They were whispering and chuckling together.

"Larry," said Garland, "you look to me as if you've been around a lot."

"Maybe my looks are deceptive," he said, brown eyes upon her. "I—I've never been at a place like this before."

Garland edged closer to him. "Tell me a little about yourself."

"Oh, I'm just a freshman at Ellerby. Nothing very exciting about that."

"But it must be." She edged even closer. "Just being on campus must be exciting. Come on, tell me more."

She put her hand on his. He took it in his warm clasp.

"Well, freshman year is rough." He seemed to have difficulty talking. "There's no hazing at Ellerby any more, not exactly, but you have to take a lot of stuff to get ready to be a sophomore."

She pulled his young arm around her shoulder and began to count the fingers on his hand with delicate little taps. Across the room, Claudia was sitting on Guy's lap, pulling his ear. They seemed to have come to good terms.

"This is really a great house," Larry said slowly. "It's— " He gulped. "It's nice," he said.

And right here it would come, Garland thought, something about how she was too lovely a girl to be in such a sordid business. To her relief, he didn't say it. Again she must take the initiative. She pulled his hand to where it could envelop her soft breast and held it there.

"Like it?" she whispered.

He must know what was coming, but plainly he was drowned in all sorts of conflicting emotions. Uncle Whit hadn't coached him, not nearly enough. He looked around the lamplit room with his eyes that were somehow plaintive. His beard seemed to droop.

"All right, Larry," said Garland, "come with me."

She got up and tugged his hand to make him get to his feet. He smiled. Of course, get him somewhere away from Claudia and Guy, there so cozy in the armchair. She picked up a lamp and led him into the hall.

"Wow," he said. "That staircase. Spiral. Looks like something in a historical movie."

"Does it?"

The staircase wound up into dark reaches. Gently Garland guided him and he seemed glad to be guided. She shepherded him past the torn spots in the carpeting, away from the shaky stretch of the balustrade, up to the hall above. She held up the lamp. It showed the faded roses on the carpet.

"Here," she said, "this is my room."

She opened the heavy door and pushed it inward. They stepped across the threshold together. She set the lamp on a table near the oriel window.

"I swear, Garland," he muttered, "this is great. That old four-poster bed, the bench—they must be worth a lot. They're old."

"Older than I am," she smiled at him.

"You're not old, Garland. You're beautiful."

"So are you," she told him truthfully.

They sat down on the bed. It had a cover of deep blue velvet with dim gold tassels. Larry seemed overwhelmed.

"I can't tell you how lovely all this is," he stammered.

"Then don't try. Put your feet up. That's right. Now relax."

He sank back. She pulled the loose shirt collar wider. "What a beautiful neck you have."

"Oh," he said, "it's Guy who's got the neck. All those exercises, those weights he lifts."

"Let Claudia attend to Guy. You're here with me."

Outside the door, a soft rustling. Garland paid no attention. Larry was quiet now, his eyes closed. Garland bent to him, her tender fingers massaging his temples, his neck. He breathed rhythmically, as though he slept. Closer Garland bent to him, her hands on his neck. Her fingers crooked, their tips pressed.

The lamplight shone on her red lips. They parted. Her teeth showed long and sharp. She crooned to him. She stopped. Her mouth opened above his neck.

Outside, voices spoke, faint, inhuman.

Garland rose quickly and went to the door. She opened it a crack.

Shapes hung there, gaunt and in ragged clothes. "Well," she whispered fiercely, "can't you wait?"

"Let me in," said one of them. Eyes gleamed palely. "Let me in," said another. "Hungry, hungry —"

"Can't you wait?" asked Garland again. "After I'm finished, you can have him. Have what's left."

She closed the door on their pleas, and hurried back to where Larry lay ready, motionless, dreaming, on the bed.

R. Chetwynd-Hayes

The Labyrinth

In 1988 Ronald Chetwynd-Hayes was awarded both The Horror Writers of America and The British Fantasy special awards for his services to the field.

Since 1973 he has edited some thirty-three anthologies (including twelve volumes of The Fontana Book of Great Ghost Stories*), published nineteen short story collections, two movie novelizations and nine novels, the latest of which are* The Curse of the Snake God *and* Kepple. *Two films have also been based on his work,* From Beyond the Grave *and* The Monster Club. *Recent short stories have appeared in* After Hours, Skeleton Crew, Fantasy Tales, The Mammoth Book of Terror *and* Dark Voices 4: The Pan Book of Horror.

"Me and vampires have always got on well together," explains the author, and to prove it here's a somewhat unusual twist on the theme . . .

THEY WERE LOST. Rosemary knew it and said so in forcible language. Brian also was well aware of their predicament but was unwilling to admit it.

"One cannot be lost in England," he stated. "We're bound to strike a main road if we walk in a straight line."

"But suppose we wander in a circle?" Rosemary asked, looking fearfully round at the Dartmoor landscape, "and finish up in a bog?"

"If we use our eyes there's no reason why bogs should bother us. Come on and stop moaning."

"We should never have left that track," Rosemary insisted. "Suppose we get caught out here when night falls?"

"Don't be daft," he snapped, "it's only mid-day. We'll be in Princetown long before nightfall."

"You hope." She refused to be convinced. "I'm hungry."

"So am I." They were walking up a steep incline. "But I don't keep on about it."

"I'm not keeping on. I'm hungry and I said so. Do you think we'll find a main road soon?"

"Over the next rise," he promised. "There's always a main road over the next rise."

But he was wrong. When they crested the next rise and looked down, there was only a narrow track which terminated at a tumbledown gate set in a low stone wall. Beyond, like an island girdled by a yellow lake, was a lawn-besieged house. It was built of grey stone and seemed to have been thrown up by the moors; a great, crouching monster that glared out across the countryside with multiple glass eyes. It had a strange look. The chimney stacks might have been jagged splinters of rock that had acquired a rough cylindrical shape after centuries of wind and rain. But the really odd aspect was that the sun appeared to ignore the house. It had baked the lawn to a pale yellow, cracked the paint on an adjacent summerhouse, but in some inexplicable way, it seemed to disavow the existence of the great, towering mass.

"Tea!" exclaimed Rosemary.

"What?"

"Tea." She pointed. "The old lady, she's drinking tea."

Sure enough, seated by a small table that nestled in the shade of a vast multi-coloured umbrella was a little white-haired old lady taking tea. Brian frowned, for he could not understand why he had not seen her, or at least the umbrella, before, but there she was, a tiny figure in a white dress and a floppy hat, sipping tea and munching sandwiches. He moistened dry lips.

"Do you suppose," he asked, "we dare intrude?"

"Watch me," Rosemary started running down the slope towards the gate. "I'd intrude on Dracula himself if he had a decent cup of tea handy."

Their feet moved on to a gravel path and it seemed whatever breeze stirred the sun-warm heather out on the moors did not dare intrude here. There was a strange stillness, a complete absence of sound, save for the crunch of feet on gravel, and this too ceased when they walked on to the parched lawn.

The old lady looked up and a slow smile gradually lit up a benign, wizened little face, while her tiny hands fluttered over the table, setting out two cups and saucers, then felt the teapot as though to make sure the contents were still hot.

"You poor children." Her voice had that harsh, slightly cracked quality peculiar to some cultured ladies of an advanced age, but the utterance was clear, every word pronounced with precision. "You look so hot and tired."

"We're lost," Rosemary announced cheerfully. "We've wandered for miles."

"I must apologise for intruding," Brian began, but the old lady waved a teaspoon at him as though to stress the impossibility of intrusion.

"My dear young man—please. You are most welcome. I cannot recall when I last entertained a visitor, although I have always hoped someone might pass this way again. The right kind of someone, of course."

She appeared to shiver momentarily, or perhaps tremble, for her hands and shoulders shook slightly, then an expression of polite distress puckered her forehead.

"But how thoughtless I am. You are tired having wandered so many miles and there are no chairs."

She turned her head and called out in a high-pitched, quivering voice. "Carlo! Carlo!"

A tall, lean man came out of the house and moved slowly towards them. He was dressed in a black satin tunic and matching trousers and, due possibly to some deformity, appeared to bound over the lawn, rather than walk. Brian thought of a wolf, or a large dog that has spotted intruders. He stopped a few feet from the old lady and stood waiting, his slate-coloured eyes watching Rosemary with a strange intensity.

"Carlo, you will fetch chairs," the old lady ordered, "then some more hot water."

Carlo made a guttural sound and departed in the direction of the summerhouse, leaping forward in a kind of loping run. He returned almost immediately carrying two little slatted chairs and presently Brian and Rosemary were seated under the vast umbrella, drinking tea from delicate china cups and listening to the harsh, cultivated voice.

"I must have lived alone here for such a long time. Gracious me, if I were to tell you how long, you would smile. Time is such an

inexhaustible commodity, so long as one can tap the fountainhead.
The secret is to break it down into small change. An hour does
not seem to be long until you remember it has three thousand,
six hundred seconds. And a week! My word, did you ever realise
you have six hundred and four thousand, eight hundred seconds to
spend every seven days? It's an enormous treasure. Do have another
strawberry jam sandwich, child."

Rosemary accepted another triangular, pink-edged sandwich,
then stared open-eyed at the house. At close quarters it looked
even more grim than from a distance. There was the impression
the walls had drawn their shadows above themselves like a ghostly
cloak, and although the house stood stark and forbidding in broad
daylight, it still seemed to be divorced from sunshine. Rosemary of
course made the obvious statement.

"It must be very old."

"It has lived," the old lady said, "for millions upon millions of
seconds. It has drunk deep from the barrel of time."

Rosemary giggled, then hastily assumed an extravagantly serious
expression as Brian glared at her. He sipped his tea and said: "This
is really most kind of you. We were fagged out—and rather scared
too. The moors seemed to go on and on and I thought we would
have to spend the night out there."

The old lady nodded, her gaze flickering from one young face to
the other.

"It is not pleasant to be lost in a great, empty space. Doubtless, if
you had not returned before nightfall, someone would have instigated
a search for you."

"Not on your nelly," Rosemary stated with charming simplicity.
"No one knows where we are. We're sort of taking a roaming
holiday."

"How adventurous," the old lady murmured, then called back
over one shoulder. "Carlo, the hot water, man. Do hurry."

Carlo came bounding out of the house carrying a silver jug in one
hand and a plate of sandwiches in the other. When he reached the
table his mouth was open and he was breathing heavily. The old
lady shot him an anxious glance.

"Poor old boy," she consoled. "Does the heat get you down, then?
Eh? Does the heat make you puff and pant? Never mind, you can
go and lie down somewhere in the shade." She turned to her guests
and smiled a most kindly, benign smile. "Carlo has mixed blood
and he finds the heat most trying. I keep telling him to practise
more self-control, but he will insist on running about." She sighed.
"I suppose it is his nature."

Rosemary was staring intently at her lap and Brian saw an ominous shake of her shoulders, so he hurriedly exclaimed:

"You really live all alone in that vast house? It looks enormous."

"Only a small portion, child." She laughed softly, a little silvery sound. "You see the windows on the ground floor which have curtains? That is my little domain. All the rest is closed up. Miles upon miles of empty corridors."

Brian re-examined the house with renewed interest. Six lower windows looked more wholesome than the others; the frames had, in the not-too-distant past, been painted white and crisp white curtains gave them a lived-in look, but the panes still seemed reluctant to reflect the sunlight and he frowned before raising his eyes to the upper storeys.

Three rows of dirt-grimed glass: so many eyes from behind which life had long since departed, save possibly for rats and mice. Then he started and gripped his knees with hands that were not quite steady. On the topmost storey, at the window third from the left, a face suddenly emerged and pressed its nose flat against the glass. There was no way of telling if the face were young or old, or if it belonged to a man, woman or child. It was just a white blur equipped with a pair of blank eyes and a flattened nose.

"Madam . . ." Brian began.

"My name," the old lady said gently, "is Mrs Brown."

"Mrs Brown. There's a . . ."

"A nice homely name," Mrs Brown went on. "Do you not think so? I feel it goes with a blazing fire, a singing kettle and muffins for tea."

"Madam—Mrs Brown. The window up there . . ."

. "What window, child?" Mrs Brown was examining the interior of the teapot with some concern. "There are so many windows."

"The third from the left." Brian was pointing at the face, which appeared to be opening and shutting its mouth. "There is someone up there and they seem to be in trouble."

"You are mistaken, my dear," Mrs Brown shook her head. "No one lives up there. And without life, there can be no face. That is logic."

The face disappeared. It was not so much withdrawn as blotted out, as though the window had suddenly clouded over and now it was just another dead man's eye staring out over the sun-drenched moors.

"I could swear there was a face," Brian insisted, and Mrs Brown smiled.

"A cloud reflection. It is so easy to see faces where none exist.

A crack in the ceiling, a damp patch on a wall, a puddle in moonlight—all become faces when the brain is tired. Can I press you to another cup?"

"No, thank you." Brian rose and nudged Rosemary to do the same. She obeyed with ill grace. "If you would be so kind as to direct us to the nearest main road, we will be on our way."

"I could not possibly do that." Mrs Brown looked most distressed. "We are really miles from anywhere and you poor children would get hopelessly lost. Really, I must insist you stay here for the night."

"You are most kind and do not think us ungrateful," Brian said, "but there must be a village not too far away."

"Oh Brian," Rosemary clutched his arm. "I couldn't bear to wander about out there for hours. And suppose the sun sets . . .?"

"I've told you before, we'll be home and dry long before then," he snapped, and Mrs Brown rose, revealing herself as a figure of medium height, whose bowed shoulders made her shorter than she actually was. She shook a playful finger at the young man.

"How could you be so ungallant? Can you not see the poor girl is simply dropping from fatigue?" She took Rosemary's arm and began to propel her towards the house, still talking in her harsh, precise voice. "These big strong men have no thought for us poor, frail women. Have they, my dear?"

"He's a brute." Rosemary made a face at Brian over one shoulder. "We wouldn't have got lost if he hadn't made us leave the main track."

"It is the restless spirit that haunts the best of them," Mrs Brown confided. "They must wander into strange and forbidden places, then come crying home to us when they get hurt."

They moved in through the open french windows, leaving the hot summer afternoon behind them, for a soft, clinging coolness leapt to embrace their bodies like a slightly damp sheet. Brian shivered, but Rosemary exclaimed: "How sweet."

She was referring to the room. It was full of furniture: chairs, table, sideboard, from which the sheen of newness had long since departed; the patterned carpet had faded, so had the wallpaper; a vase of dried flowers stood on the mantelpiece and from all around—an essential part of the coolness—came a sweet, just perceptible aroma. It was the scent of extreme old age which is timidly approaching death on faltering feet. For a moment, Brian had a mental picture of an open coffin bedecked with dying flowers. Then Mrs Brown spoke.

"There are two sweet little rooms situated at the rear. You will rest well in them."

Carlo emerged from somewhere; he was standing by the open

doorway, his slate-grey eyes watching Mrs Brown as she nodded gravely.

"Go with him, my dears. He will attend to your wants and presently, when you have rested, we will dine."

They followed their strange guide along a gloom-painted passage and he silently opened two doors, motioned Rosemary into one, then, after staring blankly at Brian, pointed to the other.

"You've been with Mrs Brown a long time?" Brian asked in a loud voice, assuming the man was deaf. "Must be rather lonely for you here."

Carlo did not answer, only turned on his heel and went back along the passage with that strange, loping walk. Rosemary giggled.

"Honestly, did you ever see anything like it?"

"Only in a horror film," Brian admitted. "Say, do you suppose he's deaf and dumb?"

"Fairly obviously," Rosemary shrugged. "Let's have a look at our rooms."

They were identical. Each held a four-poster bed, a Tudor-style chest of drawers and a bedside cupboard. The same faint odour prevailed here, but Rosemary did not seem to notice it.

"Do you suppose this place runs to a bath?" she asked, seating herself on Brian's bed.

Before he could answer, Carlo's lean form filled the doorway and he made a guttural sound while beckoning them to follow him. He led the way down the passage and at the very end opened a door and motioned them to enter the room beyond. It was empty save for a very ancient hip-bath and six leather buckets lined up against one wall.

They began to laugh, clinging to each other for support. Their silent guide watched them with an expressionless stare. Brian was the first to regain his powers of speech.

"Ask a silly question," he gasped, "and you'll get a ridiculous answer."

"I rarely eat."

Mrs Brown was sipping daintily from a glass of mineral water and watching the young people with lively interest as they each consumed a large steak and a generous helping of fresh salad.

"When you are my age," she went on, "one's fires need little fuel. A sip of water, an occasional nibble, the odd crumb."

"But you must eat," Rosemary looked at the old lady with some concern. "I mean—you have to."

"Child— " Mrs Brown beckoned to Carlo who started to collect the empty plates, "—food is not necessarily meat and vegetables. Passion will feed the soul and nourish the body. I recommend love as an *hors d'oeuvre*, hate as the *entrée* and fear as a chilly dessert."

Rosemary looked nervously at Brian, then took a long drink of water to hide her confusion. The young man decided to bring the conversation back to a more mundane plane.

"I am most interested in your house, Mrs Brown. It seems a shame that so little of it is used."

"I did not say it was not used, dear," Mrs Brown corrected gently. "I said no one lived in the region that lies outside this apartment. There is, as I am sure you will agree, a difference."

Carlo returned, carrying a dish of large, pink blancmange; this he deposited on the table after giving the girl and young man a long, expressionless stare.

"You must forgive Carlo," Mrs Brown said while she carved the blancmange into thin slices. "It is some time since we entertained guests and he is apt to stare at that which he is not allowed to touch."

Brian nudged Rosemary, who was watching the blancmange carving with undisguised astonishment. "Mrs Brown, you say the rest of the house is used, but not lived in. I'm sorry, but . . ."

"Does anyone live in your stomach?" Mrs Brown asked quietly.

He laughed, but seeing no smile on the wrinkled face opposite quickly assumed a serious expression.

"No, of course not."

"But it is used?" Mrs Brown persisted.

He nodded. "Yes indeed. Quite a lot."

"So with the house." She handed Rosemary a plate that contained three thin slices of pink blancmange and the girl said "Thank you" in a strangled voice. "You see, the house does not require people to live in it, for the simple reason that it is, in itself, a living organism."

Brian frowned as he accepted his plate of sliced blancmange.

"Why not?" The old lady appeared surprised that her word should be doubted. "Do you begrudge a house life?"

They both shook their heads violently and Mrs Brown appeared satisfied with their apparent acquiescence.

"After all, in ordinary houses, what are passages? I will tell you. Intestines. Bowels, if you wish. And the boiler which pumps hot water throughout the body of the house? A heart—what else could it be? In the same way, that mass of pipes and cisterns that reside up in the loft, what are they if not a brain?"

"You have a point," Brian agreed.

"Of course I have," Mrs Brown deposited another slice of blancmange on Rosemary's plate. "But of course I was referring to ordinary houses. This is not an ordinary house by any means. It really lives."

"I would certainly like to meet the builder," Brian said caustically. "He must have been a remarkable chap."

"Builder!" Mrs Brown chuckled. "When did I mention a builder? My dear young man, the house was not built. It grew."

"Nutty as a fruit cake." Rosemary spoke with strong conviction while she sat on Brian's bed.

"True," Brian nodded, "but the idea is rather fascinating."

"Oh, come off it. How can a house grow? And from what? A brick?"

"Wait a minute. In a way a house does grow. It is fathered by an architect and mothered by a builder."

"That's all very well," Rosemary complained, "but that old sausage meant the damned thing grew like a tree. Frankly, she gives me the willies. You know something? I think she's laughing at us. I mean to say, all that business of carving blancmange into thin slices."

"A house is an extension of a man's personality." Brian was thinking out loud. "In its early life it would be innocent, like a new-born baby, but after it had been lived in for a bit . . ." He paused, "then the house would take on an atmosphere . . . could even be haunted."

"Oh, shut up." Rosemary shivered. "I'm expected to sleep here tonight. In any case, as I keep saying, the old thing maintains the house grew."

"Even that makes a kind of mad logic." He grinned, mocking what he assumed to be her pretended fear. "We must reverse the process. The atmosphere came first, the house second."

"I'm going to bed." She got up and sauntered to the door. "If you hear me scream during the night, come a-running."

"Why bother to go?" Brian asked slyly. "If you stay here, I won't have to run anywhere."

"Ha, ha. Funny man. Not in this morgue." She smiled impishly from the doorway. "I'd be imagining all manner of things looking down at me from the ceiling."

Brian lay in his four-poster bed and listened to the house preparing for sleep. Woodwork contracted as the temperature dropped; floorboards creaked, window frames made little rattling noises, somewhere a door closed. Sleep began to dull his senses and he became only half-aware of his surroundings; he was poised on the brink of oblivion. Then, as though a bomb had exploded, he was blasted back into full consciousness. A long drawn-out moan had shattered the silence and was coming at him from all directions. He sat up and looked round the room. So far as he could see by the light of the rising moon that filtered through his lace curtains, the room was empty. Suddenly, the groan was repeated. He sprang out of bed, lit his candle, and looked wildly around him. The sound was everywhere—in the walls with their faded pink-rose wallpaper, in the cracked ceiling, the threadbare carpet. He covered his ears with shaking hands, but still the mournful groan continued, invading his brain, seeping down into his very being, until it seemed the entire universe was crying out in anguish. Then, as abruptly as it began, it ceased. A heavy, unnatural silence descended on the house like a great, enveloping blanket. Brian hastily scrambled into his clothes.

"Enough is enough." He spoke aloud. "We're getting out—fast."

Another sound came into being. It began a long way off. A slow, hesitant footstep, married to squeaking floorboards, a laborious picking up and putting down of naked feet, interspersed with a slow slithering which suggested the unseen walker was burdened with the tiredness of centuries. This time there was no doubt as to where the sound was coming from. It was up above. The soft, padding steps passed over the ceiling and once again the house groaned, but now it was a moan of ecstasy, a low cry of fulfilment. Brian opened the bedroom door and crept out into the corridor. The moaning cry and the slithering footsteps merged and became a nightmarish symphony, a two-toned serenade of horror. Then, again, all sound ceased and the silence was like a landmine that might explode at any moment. He found himself waiting for the moan, the slithering overhead footsteps to begin all over again—or perhaps something else, something that defied imagination.

He tapped on Rosemary's door, then turned the handle and entered, holding his candle high and calling her name.

"Rosemary, wake up. Rosemary, come on, we're getting out of here."

The flickering candle-flame made great shadows leap across the walls and dance over the ceiling; it cut ragged channels through the darkness until, at last, his questing eye saw the bed. It was empty. The sheets and blankets were twisted up into loose ropes and a pillow lay upon the floor.

"Rosemary!"

He whispered her name and the house chuckled. A low, harsh,

gurgling laugh, which made him run from the room, race down the long corridor, until he lurched into the dining-room. An old-fashioned oil lamp stood on the table, illuminating the room with a pale orange light and revealing Mrs Brown, seated in an armchair, calmly darning a sock. She looked up as Brian entered and smiled like a mother whose small son has strayed from his warm bed on a winter's night.

"I would put the candle down, dear," she said, "otherwise you will spill grease all over the carpet."

"Rosemary!" he shouted. "Where is she?"

"There's really no need for you to shout. Despite my advanced years, I am not deaf." She broke the wool, then turned the sock and examined her work with a certain pride. "That's better. Carlo is so hard on his socks." She looked up with a sly smile. "It is only to be expected, of course. He has hard feet."

"Where is she?" Brian set down the candle and moved closer to the old woman, who was now closing her work-basket. "She's not in her room and there are signs of a struggle. What have you done with her?"

Mrs Brown shook her head sadly.

"Questions, questions. How hungry youth is for knowledge. You demand to know the truth and, should I gratify your desire, how distressed you would become. Ignorance is a gift freely offered by the gods and so often it is spurned by misguided mortals. Even I sometimes wish I knew less, but . . ." Her sigh was one of sad resignation. "Time reveals all to those who live long enough. I should go back to bed, dear. The young need their sleep."

Brian advanced a few steps, then spoke in a carefully controlled voice.

"I am going to ask you for the last time, Mrs Brown, or whatever your name is—what have you done with Rosemary?"

She looked up and shook her head in sad reproof.

"Threats! How unwise. A sparrow should never threaten an eagle. It is so futile and such a waste of time."

Mrs Brown carefully placed her work-basket on the floor, then snapped in a surprisingly firm voice: "Carlo!"

There came, from somewhere to Brian's rear, a low, deep growl. Such a menacing sound might have issued from the throat of a large dog whose mistress has been threatened, or a she-wolf protecting her young, but when the young man spun round, he saw Carlo standing a few feet away. The man had his head tilted to one side and his large, yellow teeth were bared as he growled again. His stance was grotesque. He was leaning forward slightly as though preparing to spring and his fingers were curved, so that with their long, pointed nails, they looked uncannily like talons; his cheeks seemed to have shrunk and his black hair lay back over his narrow skull like a sleek, ebony mane.

"Will you believe me?" Mrs Brown said, and her voice was less harsh—much younger. "I have only to say one word and your windpipe will be hanging down your shirt-front."

"You are mad." Brian backed slowly away and Carlo moved forward, matching him step for step. "You are both mad."

"You mean," Mrs Brown came round and joined Carlo, "we are not normal by your standards. That much I grant you. Sanity is only a form of madness favoured by the majority. But I think the time has come for you to meet truth, since you are so eager to make her acquaintance."

"I only want to find Rosemary, then get out of here," Brian said.

"Find your little friend? Perhaps. Leave here? Ah . . ." Mrs Brown looked thoughtful. "That is another matter. But come, there is much for you to see, and please, no heroics. Carlo is on the turn. He is apt to be a little touchy when the moon is full."

They filed out into the hall, Mrs Brown leading the way with Brian following and the grim Carlo bringing up the rear. To the right of a great staircase was a black door and this Mrs Brown unlocked, then entered the room beyond, where she proceeded to light a lamp from Brian's candle.

The light crept outwards in ever-increasing circles as she turned up the wick, revealing oak-panelled walls and a cobweb-festooned ceiling. The room was bare, except for the portrait hanging over a dirt-grimed marble fireplace. To this the young man's eyes were drawn like a pin to a magnet.

The background was jet-black and the face corpse-white; the large black eyes glared an intense hatred for all living things and the thin-lipped mouth was shut tight, but so cunningly had the portrait been painted that Brian had the feeling it might open at any moment.

"My late husband," Mrs Brown stated, "was a partaker of blood."

The statement did not invite comment and Brian made none.

"It must be the best part of five hundred years since they came down from the village," Mrs Brown continued. "Chanting priests looking like black ravens, mewing peasants huddled together like frightened sheep. I recall it was night and the mists shrouded the moors and swirled about their thrice-accursed cross as though it wished to protect us from the menace it represented."

She paused and Brian realised that she looked much younger. The face was filling out, the shoulders were no longer bowed.

"They did not consider I was of great importance," Mrs Brown went on, "so I was merely tied to a tree and flogged, thereby providing entertainment for the herd of human cattle who liked nothing better than to see a woman writhe under the lash. But him. . . . They dug a hole, and laid him flat, having bound his body in cords that were sealed with the dreaded sign. Then they drove a stake through his heart. . . . Fools."

She glared at Brian and clenched her small fists.

"They left him for dead. Dead! His brain still lived. The blood was only symbolic, it was the vital essence we needed—still need: the force that makes the soul reach out for the stars, the hammer that can create beauty out of black depravity."

She went over to the portrait and stroked the white, cruel face with hands that had become long and slender.

"When they buried his beautiful body they planted a seed, and from that seed grew the house. A projection of himself."

"I don't believe you." Brian shook his head. "I won't—can't believe you."

"No!" She laughed and Carlo howled. "Then feel the walls. They are warm, flesh of his flesh. Moist. The body fluids seep out when he is aroused. Look." She pointed to a great double door set in one wall. "Look, the mouth. When I open the lips, food pops in. Succulent, living food and we all benefit. I, Carlo, who sprang from the old people—I still let him roam the moors when the moon is full—and, of course, He. The House. He needs all the sweet essence he can get. He sleeps after meat and no longer moans. I do not like to hear him moan."

"Where is Rosemary?" Brian asked again and knew what must follow.

"She passed through the lips an hour since." Mrs Brown laughed very softly and Carlo made a whining sound. "Now, if you would find her, there is not really much alternative. You must follow her through the great intestines, down into the mighty bowels. Wander and cry out, trudge on and on, until at last your will is broken and He can take from you what he needs."

"You want me to go through those doors?" Brian asked, and there was a glimmer of hope. "Then go wandering through the corridors of an empty house? When I find Rosemary, we will break out."

The woman smiled as she motioned to Carlo.

"Part the lips, Carlo."

The man, if indeed that which crept forward was a man, silently obeyed; the great doors groaned as they swung inwards and Brian saw a murky passage, lined with green tinted walls. A warm, sweet, cloying odour made his stomach heave and he drew back.

"She's waiting for you," Mrs Brown said softly, "and she must be very frightened wandering through the labyrinth, not exactly alone, but I doubt if she will appreciate the company. Most of them will be well digested by now."

Carlo was waiting, his hand on the handle of one door; his eyes were those of a hungry wolf who sees his prey about to be devoured by a lion. Brian, without a sideways glance, passed through the entrance and the doors slammed to behind him.

There were no stairs. The corridors sometimes sloped upwards, at others they spiralled down; there were stretches when the floor was comparatively level, but the corridors were never straight for long. They twisted, crossed other passages, suddenly split, leaving the wanderer with a choice of three or more openings; occasionally they came to a blank end, forcing him to retrace his footsteps. Light was provided by an eerie greenish glow radiating from the walls and ceiling and sometimes this light pulsated, suggesting it originated from some form of decay.

Brian stumbled onwards, shouting Rosemary's name, and his echo mocked him, went racing on ahead until it became a faraway voice calling back along the avenues of time. Once he stumbled and fell against the wall. Instantly, the moist, green surface contracted under his weight and there was an obscene sucking sound when he pulled himself free. A portion of his shirt sleeve remained stuck to the wall and there was a red mark on his arm.

When he had been walking for some thirty minutes he came upon the window passage. There was no other word to describe it, for one wall was lined with windows, each one set about six feet apart, and he gave a little cry of joy, certain this was the place from which he and Rosemary could make their escape. Then he saw—them. Before each window stood one, occasionally two, forms—hideously thin, scarecrow figures that pawed at the window panes with claw-like fingers and emitted little animal whimpers.

Brian approached the first window and gave a quick glance through the grimy panes. He was two floors, if that was the right expression, up, and he saw the lawn then, further out, the moors, all bathed in brilliant moonlight. Even as he watched, a great hound went bounding across the lawn. It cleared the low wall in a single leap, then streaked out across the moor. Something touched Brian's arm and he spun round to face one of the creatures that had silently crept along from the next window. He saw at close quarters the skeleton face covered with brown, wrinkled skin, and the vacant blue eyes that stared up at him with mute, suffering appeal. He judged the man to have been a tramp, or possibly a gypsy, for he wore the remnants of a red shirt and brown corduroy trousers. The claw-hands plucked feebly at his arm, the mouth opened, revealing toothless gums, and a hoarse whisper seeped out.

"The old cow said come in."

"How long have you been here?" Brian asked, uncomfortably aware that a number of other grotesque bundles of rag and bones were leaving their posts by the windows and slithering on naked feet towards him. The whisper came again.

"The old cow said come in."

"Have you seen a young girl?" Brian shouted. "Have any of you seen a girl?"

The man tried to grip his arm, but there was no strength left in the wasted frame and he could only repeat the single phrase:

"The old cow said come in."

They were all clustered round him. Three bore some resemblance to women, although their hair had fallen out, and one, a tall, beanstalk of a creature, kept mumbling: "Pretty boy," while she tried unsuccessfully to fasten her gums into his neck.

"Break the windows!" Brian shouted, pushing them away as gently as he could. "Listen, break the windows, then I'll be able to climb down and fetch help."

"The old cow said come in." The man could only repeat over and over the six ominous words, and a wizened, awful thing, no higher than a child, kept muttering: "Meat," as it tried to fasten its mouth on Brian's right hand.

Unreasoning terror made him strike the creature full in the face and it went crashing back against the wall. Instantly, the green surface bent inwards and a deep sigh ran through the house, making the ghastly pack go slithering along the corridor, their remaining spark of intelligence having presumably warned them this sound was something to be feared. The small, child-size figure was left, stuck to the wall like a fly on gummed paper, and, as the green light pulsated, the creature jerked in unison.

Brian pulled off one of his shoes and smashed the heel against the nearest window-pane. He might just as well have struck a slab of solid rock for all the impression he made, and at last he gave up and continued his search for Rosemary. After an hour of trudging wearily along green-tinted passages, he had no idea how far he had travelled, or if indeed he was just going round in a perpetual circle. He found himself dragging his feet, making the same hesitant, slithering footsteps that had so alarmed him in his bedroom, centuries ago.

The corridors were never silent, for there were always cries, usually some way off, and a strange thudding sound which came into being when the green light pulsated, but these offstage noises became as a murmur when the scream rang out. It was a cry of despair, a call for help, a fear-born prayer, and at once Brian knew who had screamed. He shouted Rosemary's name as he broke into a run, terrified lest he be unable to reach her, at the same time in dread of what he might find. Had she not screamed again he would doubtlessly have taken the wrong passage, but when the second shriek rang out he ran towards the sound and presently came to a kind of circular hall. They were clinging to her like leeches to a drowning horse. Their skeleton hands were tearing her dress, their toothless mouths fouled her flesh, and all the while they squealed like a herd of hungry pigs. He pulled them away and the soulless bodies went hurtling back against vibrating walls; bones snapped like frost-crisp twigs and despairing whimpers rose to an unholy chorus.

He took Rosemary in his arms and she clung to him as though he were life itself, clutching his shoulders in a terrified grip while she cried like a lost child. He murmured soft, unintelligible words, trying to reassure himself as much as her, then screamed at the pack who were again slowly moving in.

"Don't you understand, this is not real. It's the projection of a mad brain. A crazy nightmare. Try to find a way out."

It is doubtful if they heard, let alone understood what he was saying, and those that could still move were edging their way forward like rats whose hunger is greater than their fear.

"Can you walk?" he asked Rosemary and the girl nodded. "Good, then we must make our way downwards. The woman's apartment is on the ground floor and our only hope is to batter those doors in and escape across the lawn."

"It's impossible." Rosemary was clinging to his arm and they were leaving the creatures behind. "This place is a labyrinth. We will wander round and round these corridors until we drop."

"Nonsense." He spoke sharply. "The house can't be all that big and we are young and fit. So long as we go down, we're bound to find the doors."

This was easier said than done. Many corridors sloped down, only to slant up again, but presently they came out into a window passage and found they were somewhere at the rear of the house, but only one floor up.

"Now," Brian kissed Rosemary. "Only one more slope to go and we're there."

"But we're the wrong side of the house," Rosemary complained, "and even if we find the doors, how are you going to break through them?"

"One step at a time. Let's find them first, then, maybe, I'll use you as a battering ram."

It took an hour to find the next downward slope and then only after they had retraced their steps several times, but at last they were moving downwards, Rosemary shivered.

"It's getting colder."

"Yes, and that damned stink is becoming more pronounced. But never mind, we'll soon be there."

They went steadily downwards for another five minutes and then Rosemary began to cry.

"Brian, I can't go on much longer. Surely we've passed the ground floor ages ago? And there's something awful down here. I can feel it."

"It can't be more awful than what's up above," he retorted grimly. "We must go on. There's no turning back unless you want to finish up a zombie."

"Zombie!" She repeated dully.

"What did you imagine those things were, back there? They died long ago and only keep going because the house gives them a sort of half life. Mrs Brown and Carlo appear to be better provided for, but they died centuries ago."

"I can't believe all this." Rosemary shuddered. "How can a place like this exist in the twentieth century?"

"It doesn't. I should imagine we stumbled across the house at the right, or in our case, the wrong time. I suppose you might call it a time-trap."

"I don't know what you are talking about," Rosemary said, then added, "I very rarely do."

The passage was becoming steeper, spiralling round and sloping down until they had difficulty in remaining upright. Then the floor levelled out and after a space of about six feet came to an end.

"Earth." Brian felt the termination wall. "Good, honest earth."

"Earth," Rosemary repeated. "So what?"

Brian raised his eyes ceilingwards and then spoke in a carefully controlled voice. "So far we have been walking on a floor and between walls that are constructed of something very nasty. Right? Now we are facing a wall built or shovelled into place—I don't care—of plain, down to earth—earth. Got it?"

Rosemary nodded. "Yes, so we have got down to the house foundations. But I thought we were looking for the doors."

Brian gripped her shoulders.

"Say that again."

"Say what again? Look, you're hurting me."

He shook her gently. "The first bit."

She thought for a moment. "So we have got down to the house foundations. What's so important about that?"

He released her and went up close to the wall, where he stood for a few minutes examining its surface, then he came back and tilted her chin up so she was looking directly into his eyes.

"Will you try to be very, very brave?"

Fear came rushing back and she shivered.

"Why?"

"Because I am going to break down that wall." He spoke very slowly. "And on the other side we may find something very nasty indeed."

She did not move her head, only continued to gaze up into his eyes.

"Isn't there any other way?" she whispered.

He shook his head.

"None. None whatsoever."

There was a minute of complete silence, then:

"What are you going to use as a shovel?"

He laughed and went back to the wall which he pounded with his fist.

"I could say you have a point there, but I won't. Let's take an inventory. What have we that is pick- and shovel-worthy? Our hands, of course. Shoes? Maybe." He felt in his pocket and produced a bunch of keys and a penknife. "This might start things going, then I can pull the loose stuff out with my hands."

He sank the penknife blade into the soft, moist earth and traced the rough outline of a door, then he began to deepen the edges, digging out little lumps of earth that fell to the ground like gobbets of chewed meat. Brian then removed his shoes and used the heels to claw out a jagged hole.

"If I can work my way through," he explained, "it should be an easy matter to pull the entire thing down."

He dug steadily for another five minutes, then a glimmer of light appeared and, after a final effort, he was able to look through an opening roughly six inches in diameter.

"What can you see?" Rosemary asked, her tone suggesting she would rather not know.

"It seems to be some kind of large cave and it's lit up with that green light, just like the passages. I can see hunks of rock lying about, but not much else. Well, here goes."

He thrust his right hand through the aperture, curled his fingers round the inner wall and pulled. A large chunk came away, then he began to work with both hands, pulling, clawing, and the entire wall came tumbling down. He wiped his hands on already stained trousers, then put on his shoes.

"Now," he said, "for the moment of truth."

They were in a rough, circular cavern; it was perhaps twenty feet in diameter and an equal distance in height. Loose lumps of rock littered the floor, but there was no sign of anyone—alive or dead—and Brian gave a prolonged sigh of relief.

"I don't know what I expected to see, but thank heavens, I don't see it. Now, we must start looking for a way out. I'll go round the walls, you examine the floor. Never know, there might be a hole going down still further."

He turned his attention to the irregular walls, leaving Rosemary to wander miserably among the large rocks and boulders that formed a kind of fence round the centre of the cavern. He looked upwards and saw, some twenty feet from the ground, a fairly large hole. Deciding it would be worth investigating, he began to ascend the wall and found the task easier than he had supposed, for projecting rocks made excellent footholds. In a few minutes he had reached his objective. The hole was in fact a small cave that was about seven feet high and five across, but alas there was no exit.

He was about to descend and continue his search elsewhere when Rosemary screamed. Never before had he realised a human throat was capable of expressing such abject terror. Shriek after shriek rang out and re-echoed against the walls, until it seemed an army of banshees were forecasting a million deaths. He looked down and saw the girl standing just inside the fence of stones looking down at something he could not see; her eyes were dilated and seemed frozen into an expression of indescribable horror.

Brian scrambled down the wall and ran over to her; when he laid hands on her shoulders she flinched as though his touch were a branding iron, then her final shriek was cut off and she slid silently to the floor.

A few feet away there was a slight indentation, a shallow hole, and he experienced a terrifying urge not to look into it, but he knew he must, if for no other reason than a strange, compelling curiosity.

He dragged Rosemary well back and left her lying against one

wall, then he returned, creeping forward very slowly, walking on
tip-toe. At last he was on the brink of hell. He looked down.

Horror ran up his body in cold waves; it left an icy lump in his
stomach and he wanted to be sick only he had not the strength. He
had to stare down, concentrate all his senses and try to believe.

The head bore a resemblance to the portrait in Mrs Brown's
ante-room; it was dead-white, bloated, suggesting an excess of
nourishment consumed over a very long period. The hair was
at least six feet in length and was spread out over the loose rock
like a monstrous shroud. But the torso and arms grew out of the
ground. The shoulders and part of the forearms were flesh, but
further down the white skin assumed a greyish colour and, lower
still, gradually merged into solid rock. Most horrifying of all was
the profusion of fat, greenish, tubelike growths that sprouted out
from under forearms and neck and, so far as Brian could see, the
whole of the back. Obscene roots spreading out in every direction
until they disappeared into the black earth, writhing and pulsating,
carrying the vital fluid that circulated round the house.

The eyes were closed, but the face moved. The thin lips grimaced,
creating temporary furrows in the flabby fat. Brian withdrew from
the hole—the grave—and at last his stomach had its way and
allowed him to be violently sick. By the time he returned to Rosemary, he felt old and drained of strength. She was just returning to
consciousness and he smoothed back her hair.

"Are you fit enough to talk?" he asked.

She gave a little strangled gasp.

"That . . . that thing . . ."

"Yes, I know. Now listen. I am going to take you up there," He
pointed to the cave set high up on the opposite wall. "You'll be all
right there while I do what must be done."

"I don't understand." She shook her head. "What must you
do?"

"Mrs Brown told me her husband was a partaker of blood. In other
words, a vampire, and centuries ago the local lads did the traditional
things and drove a stake through his heart. She said something else.
It wasn't his body they should have destroyed, but his brain. Don't
you see? This house, the entire set-up, is a nightmare produced by
a monstrous intelligence?"

"I'll believe anything." Rosemary got to her feet. "Just get me out
of here. I'd rather walk the passages than spend another minute with
that . . . thing."

"No." He shook his head. "I must destroy the brain. The only
point is, when I do . . ." He looked round the cavern, then over

to the entrance of the green-walled passage. ". . . anything may happen."

"What about you?" she asked.

"So soon as the job is finished, I'll join you."

He might have added, "If I can," but instead guided Rosemary to the wall and assisted her up to the cave.

"Now," he instructed, "stay well back and don't, in any circumstances, so much as put your nose outside. Understand?"

"God, I'm petrified," she said.

"Don't let it get around," he nodded grimly, "but so am I."

He came back to the hole like a released spirit returning to hell. As he drew nearer, the terror grew until it required a desperate effort to raise one foot and put it down before the other. Only the memory of Rosemary up there in the cave kept his spark of courage alive. At last he again gazed down at that horrible growth; it groaned and the sound raced round the cavern and up through the house. The face grimaced and twitched, while the green tubes writhed like a nest of gorged worms. Brian selected a rock which was a little larger than the bloated head and, gripping it in both hands, prepared to hurl it down. He had tensed his muscles, and was turning slightly to one side, when the eyelids flicked back and he was staring into two pools of black hate.

The shock was so intense he automatically slackened his grip and the rock slid from his fingers and went crashing down somewhere behind him. The mouth opened and a vibrant whisper went racing up through the house.

"Elizabeth . . . Carlo . . ."

The words came out slowly, rather like a series of intelligible sighs, but from all around, from the walls, the floor, the high roof—never from the moving lips.

"Would . . . you . . . destroy . . . that . . . which . . . you . . . do . . . not . . . understand?"

Brian was fumbling for the rock, but he paused and the whispering voice went on.

"I . . . must . . . continue . . . to . . . be . . . I . . . must . . . grow . . . fill . . . the . . . universe . . . consume . . . take . . . strength . . ."

A padding of fast-running paws came from the passage entrance and a woman's voice was calling out.

"Petros, drink of his essence . . . will him into walking death."

There was a hint of fear in the terrible eyes. The whispering voice again ran through the house.

"He . . . is . . . an . . . unbeliever . . . he . . . is . . . the . . . young

... of ... a ... new ... age ... why ... did ... you ... let ...
him ... through ...?"

The great dog leapt over the loose earth and emerged from the
passageway; it was black as midnight, like a solid shadow newly
escaped from a wall, and it padded round the cavern before jumping
up on to a boulder and preparing to leap. Brian hurled a rock at it
and struck the broad, black snout. The beast howled and fell back
as Mrs Brown spoke from the entrance.

"You will not keep that up for long. Carlo cannot be killed by the
likes of you."

She had been transformed. The once white hair was now a rich
auburn, the face was as young as today, but the glorious eyes
reflected the evil of a million yesterdays. She wore a black evening
dress that left her arms and back bare and Brian could only stare
at her, forgetting that which lay behind him and Rosemary, up in
the cave. All he could see was white flesh and inviting eyes.

"Come away," the low, husky voice said. "Leave Petros to his
dream. He cannot harm you and it would be such a waste if Carlo
were to rip your nice body to shreds. Think of what I can offer. An
eternity of bliss. A million lifetimes of pleasure. Come."

He took one step forward, then another, and it seemed he was
walking into a forbidden dream; all the secret desires that up to
that moment he had not realised existed flared up and became
exciting possibilities. Then, just as he was about to surrender, go
running to her like a child to a beautiful toy, her voice lashed across
his consciousness.

"Carlo ... now."

The dog came snarling over the rocks and Brian fell back, suddenly
fully aware of the pending danger. He snatched up a piece of jagged
rock and threw it at the oncoming beast. He hit it just above the right
ear, then began to hurl stones as fast as he could pick them up. The
dog leapt from side to side, snarling with pain and rage, but Brian
realised it was coming forward more than it retreated and knew a
few minutes, at the most, must elapse before he felt those fangs
at his throat. By chance his hands closed round the original small
boulder—and it was then he understood what must be done.

He raised the rock high above his head, made as though to hurl it
at the dog, which momentarily recoiled, then threw it back—straight
at the head of Petros.

The house shrieked. One long-drawn-out scream and the dog was
no longer there; instead, Carlo ran towards his mistress, making
plaintive, guttural cries, before sinking down before her, plucking
frantically at the hem of her black dress.

Brian looked back and down into the hole and saw that the head was shattered and what remained of the flesh was turning black. The green tubes were now only streaks of deflated tissue and the life-giving fluid no longer flowed up into the body of the house. From up above came a deep rumbling sound and a great splintering, as though a mountain of rocks were grinding together. Brian ran towards the far wall and, quickly scrambling up into the cave, found Rosemary waiting to welcome him with outstretched arms.

"Keep down," he warned. "All hell is going to break loose at any moment."

They lay face down upon the floor, and Brian had to raise his head to see the final act. The green light was fading, but before it went he had a last glimpse of the woman staring blankly at the place where Petros had lain. She was patting Carlo's head. Then the ceiling came down and for a while there was only darkness filled with a mighty rumbling and crashing of falling rock. Fantasy tumbling down into the pit of reality. Time passed and the air cleared as the dust settled and presently, like a glimmer of hope in the valley of despair, a beam of light struck the entrance to the cave. Brian looked out, then up. Twenty feet above was a patch of blue sky.

They came up from the pit, bruised, clothes torn, but happy to be alive. They trudged hand-in-hand out across the moors and after a while looked back to see a pile of rocks that, at this distance, could have been mistaken for a ruined house.

"We will never talk about this to anyone," Brian said. "One does not talk about one's nightmares. They are so ridiculous in the light of day."

Rosemary nodded. "We slept. We dreamed. Now we are awake."

They walked on. Two figures that distance diminished until they became minute specks on a distant horizon. Then they were gone.

The early morning breeze caressed the summer grass, harebells smiled up at a benign sky and a pair of rabbits played hide and seek among the fallen rocks. To all outward appearances the moors were at peace.

Then a rabbit screamed and a stoat raised blood-dripping jaws.

Karl Edward Wagner

Beyond Any Measure

Not only is Karl Edward Wagner one of the finest horror writers working in the field today, he has also edited twelve volumes of The Year's Best Horror Stories, *currently being reprinted in omnibus hardcovers as* Horrorstory.

The adventures of his heroic fantasy character Kane are chronicled in Darkness Weaves, Death Angel's Shadow, Bloodstone, Dark Crusade, Night Winds *and* The Book of Kane, *while Wagner's short fiction has been showcased in the collections* In a Lonely Place, Why Not You and I? *and* Unthreatened by the Morning Light.

The multiple British and World Fantasy Award winner is currently working on a major graphic novel, Tell Me, Dark, *with artist Kent Williams for DC Comics, and a new novel,* The Fourth Seal.

As Wagner explains: "Beyond Any Measure *explores the relationships of eroticism and horror—and the title is from Richard O'Brien's* The Rocky Horror Picture Show: *'Erotic nightmares beyond any measure and sensual daydreams to treasure forever.' It was written as an intended screenplay, and the story contains cinematic references and homages beyond counting. Fans of* The Avengers *television series will be quick to recognise the play on the infamous 'A Touch of Brimstone' episode, shown only in later reruns on American TV . . ."* The story justifiably won a World Fantasy Award for Best Novella.

I

"IN THE DREAM I find myself alone in a room. I hear musical chimes—a sort of music-box tune—and I look around to see where the sound is coming from.

"I'm in a bedroom. Heavy curtains close off the windows, and it's quite dark, but I can sense that the furnishings are entirely antique—late Victorian, I think. There's a large four-poster bed, with its curtains drawn. Beside the bed is a small night table upon which a candle is burning. It is from here that the music seems to be coming.

"I walk across the room toward the bed, and as I stand beside it I see a gold watch resting on the night table next to the candlestick. The music-box tune is coming from the watch, I realize. It's one of those old pocket-watch affairs with a case that opens. The case is open now, and I see that the watch's hands are almost at midnight. I sense that on the inside of the watchcase there will be a picture, and I pick up the watch to see whose picture it is.

"The picture is obscured with a red smear. It's fresh blood.

"I look up in sudden fear. From the bed, a hand is pulling aside the curtain.

"That's when I wake up."

"Bravo!" applauded someone.

Lisette frowned momentarily, then realized that the comment was directed toward another of the chattering groups crowded into the gallery. She sipped her champagne; she must be a bit tight, or she'd never have started talking about the dreams.

"What do you think, Dr Magnus?"

It was the gala reopening of Covent Garden. The venerable fruit, flower and vegetable market, preserved from the demolition crew, had been renovated into an airy mall of expensive shops and galleries: "London's new shopping experience." Lisette thought it an unhappy hybrid of born-again Victorian exhibition hall and trendy "shoppes." Let the dead past bury its dead. She wondered what they might make of the old Billingsgate fish market, should SAVE win its fight to preserve that landmark, as now seemed unlikely.

"Is this dream, then, a recurrent one, Miss Seyrig?"

She tried to read interest or skepticism in Dr Magnus' pale blue eyes. They told her nothing.

"Recurrent enough."

To make me mention it to Danielle, she finished in her thoughts. Danielle Borland shared a flat—she'd stopped terming it an apartment even in her mind—with her in a row of terrace houses in Bloomsbury, within an easy walk of London University. The gallery was Maitland Reddin's project; Danielle was another. Whether Maitland really thought to make a business of it, or only intended to showcase his many friends' not always evident talents was not open to discussion. His gallery in Knightsbridge was certainly successful, if that meant anything.

"How often is that?" Dr Magnus touched his glass to his blonde-bearded lips. He was drinking only Perrier water, and, at that, was using his glass for little more than to gesture.

"I don't know. Maybe half a dozen times since I can remember. And then, that many again since I came to London."

"You're a student at London University, I believe Danielle said?"

"That's right. In art. I'm over here on fellowship."

Danielle had modelled for an occasional session—Lisette now was certain it was solely from a desire to display her body rather than due to any financial need—and when a muttered profanity at a dropped brush disclosed a common American heritage, the two *émigrés* had rallied at a pub afterward to exchange news and views. Lisette's bed-sit near the Museum was impossible, and Danielle's roommate had just skipped to the Continent with two months' owing. By closing time it was settled.

"How's your glass?"

Danielle, finding them in the crowd, shook her head in mock dismay and refilled Lisette's glass before she could cover it with her hand.

"And you, Dr Magnus?"

"Quite well, thank you."

"Danielle, let me give you a hand?" Maitland had charmed the two of them into acting as hostesses for his opening.

"Nonsense, darling. When you see me starting to pant with the heat, then call up the reserves. Until then, do keep Dr Magnus from straying away to the other parties."

Danielle swirled off with her champagne bottle and her smile. The gallery, christened "Such Things May Be" after Richard Burton (*not* Liz Taylor's ex, Danielle kept explaining, and got laughs each time), was ajostle with friends and well-wishers—as were most of the shops tonight: private parties with evening dress and champagne, only a scattering of displaced tourists, gaping and photographing. She and Danielle were both wearing slit-to-thigh

crepe de Chine evening gowns and could have passed for sisters:
Lisette blonde, green-eyed, with a dust of freckles; Danielle light
brunette, hazel-eyed, acclimated to the extensive facial makeup
London women favored; both tall without seeming coltish, and
close enough of a size to wear each other's clothes.

"It must be distressing to have the same nightmare over and
again," Dr Magnus prompted her.

"There have been others as well. Some recurrent, some not.
Similar in that I wake up feeling like I've been through the sets
of some old Hammer film."   -

"I gather you were not actually troubled with such nightmares
until recently?"

"Not really. Being in London seems to have triggered them. I
suppose it's repressed anxieties over being in a strange city." It was
bad enough that she'd been taking some of Danielle's pills in order
to seek dreamless sleep.

"Is this, then, your first time in London, Miss Seyrig?"

"It is." She added, to seem less the typical American student:
"Although my family was English."

"Your parents?"

"My mother's parents were both from London. They emigrated
to the States just after World War 1."

"Then this must have been rather a bit like coming home for
you."

"Not really. I'm the first of our family to go overseas. And I have
no memory of Mother's parents. Grandmother Keswicke died the
morning I was born." Something Mother never was able to work
through emotionally, Lisette added to herself.

"And have you consulted a physician concerning these nightmares?"

"I'm afraid your National Health Service is a bit more than I
can cope with." Lisette grimaced at the memory of the night she
had tried to explain to a Pakistani intern why she wanted sleeping
medications.

She suddenly hoped her words hadn't offended Dr Magnus, but
then, he scarcely looked the type who would approve of socialized
medicine. Urbane, perfectly at ease in formal evening attire, he
reminded her somewhat of a blonde-bearded Peter Cushing. Enter
Christopher Lee, in black cape, she mused, glancing toward the
door. For that matter, she wasn't at all certain just what sort of
doctor Dr Magnus might be. Danielle had insisted she talk with
him, very likely had insisted that Maitland invite him to the private
opening: "The man has such *insight*! And he's written a number of

books on dreams and the subconscious—and not just rehashes of Freudian silliness!"

"Are you going to be staying in London for some time, Miss Seyrig?"

"At least until the end of the year."

"Too long a time to wait to see whether these bad dreams will go away once you're back home in San Francisco, don't you agree? It can't be very pleasant for you, and you really should look after yourself."

Lisette made no answer. *She* hadn't told Dr Magnus she was from San Francisco. So then, Danielle had already talked to him about her.

. Dr Magnus smoothly produced his card, discreetly offered it to her. "I should be most happy to explore this further with you on a professional level, should you so wish."

"I don't really think it's worth . . ."

"Of course it is, my dear. Why otherwise would we be talking? Perhaps next Tuesday afternoon? Is there a convenient time?"

Lisette slipped his card into her handbag. If nothing else, perhaps he could supply her with some barbs or something. "Three?"

"Three it is, then."

II

The passageway was poorly lighted, and Lisette felt a vague sense of dread as she hurried along it, holding the hem of her nightgown away from the gritty filth beneath her bare feet. Peeling scabs of wallpaper blotched the leprous plaster, and, when she held the candle close, the gouges and scratches that patterned the walls with insane graffiti seemed disquietingly nonrandom. Against the mottled plaster, her figure threw a double shadow: distorted, one crouching forward, the other following.

A full-length mirror panelled one segment of the passageway, and Lisette paused to study her reflection. Her face appeared frightened, her blonde hair in disorder. She wondered at her nightgown—pale, silken, billowing, of an antique mode—not remembering how she came to be wearing it. Nor could she think how it was that she had come to this place.

Her reflection puzzled her. Her hair seemed longer than it should be, trailing down across her breasts. Her finely chiselled features, prominent jawline, straight nose—her face, except the expression, was not hers: lips fuller, more sensual, redder than her lip-gloss, glinted; teeth fine and white. Her green eyes, intense beneath level brows, cat-cruel, yearning.

Lisette released the hem of her gown, raised her fingers to her reflection in wonder. Her fingers passed through the glass, touched the face beyond.

Not a mirror. A doorway. Of a crypt.

The mirror-image fingers that rose to her face twisted in her hair, pulled her face forward. Glass-cold lips bruised her own. The dank breath of the tomb flowed into her mouth.

Dragging herself from the embrace, Lisette felt a scream rip from her throat . . .

. . . And Danielle was shaking her awake.

III

The business card read *Dr Ingmar Magnus*, followed simply by *Consultations* and a Kensington address. Not Harley Street, at any rate. Lisette considered it for the hundredth time, watching for street names on the corners of buildings as she walked down Kensington Church Street from the Notting Hill Gate station. No clue as to what type of doctor, nor what sort of consultations; wonderfully vague, and just the thing to circumvent licensing laws, no doubt.

Danielle had lent her one of his books to read; *The Self Reborn*, put out by one of those miniscule scholarly publishers clustered about the British Museum. Lisette found it a bewildering *mélange* of occult philosophy and lunatic-fringe theory—all evidently having something to do with reincarnation—and gave it up after the first chapter. She had decided not to keep the appointment, until her nightmare Sunday night had given force to Danielle's insistence.

Lisette wore a loose silk blouse above French designer jeans and ankle-strap sandal-toe high heels. The early summer heat wave now threatened rain, and she would have to run for it if the grey skies made good. She turned into Holland Street, passed the recently closed Equinox bookshop, where Danielle had purchased various works by Aleister Crowley. A series of back streets—she consulted her map of Central London—brought her to a modestly respectable row of nineteenth-century brick houses, now done over into offices and flats. She checked the number on the brass plaque with her card, sucked in her breath and entered.

Lisette hadn't known what to expect. She wouldn't have been surprised, knowing some of Danielle's friends, to have been greeted with clouds of incense, Eastern music, robed initiates. Instead she found a disappointingly mundane waiting room, rather small but expensively furnished, where a pretty Eurasian receptionist took her name and spoke into an intercom. Lisette noted that there was no one else—patients? clients?—in the waiting room. She glanced at her watch and noticed she was several minutes late.

"Please do come in, Miss Seyrig." Dr Magnus stepped out of his office and ushered her inside. Lisette had seen a psychiatrist briefly a few years before, at her parents' demand, and Dr Magnus's office suggested the same—from the tasteful, relaxed decor, the shelves of scholarly books, down to the traditional psychoanalyst's couch. She took a chair beside the modern, rather carefully arranged desk, and Dr Magnus seated himself comfortably in the leather swivel chair behind it.

"I almost didn't come," Lisette began, somewhat aggressively.

"I'm very pleased that you did decide to come." Dr Magnus smiled reassuringly. "It doesn't require a trained eye to see that something is troubling you. When the unconscious tries to speak to us, it is foolhardy to attempt to ignore its message."

"Meaning that I may be cracking up?"

"I'm sure that must concern you, my dear. However, very often dreams such as yours are evidence of the emergence of a new level of self-awareness—sort of growing pains of the psyche, if you will—and not to be considered a negative experience by any means. They distress you only because you do not understand them—even as a child kept in ignorance through sexual repression is frightened by the changes of puberty. With your cooperation, I hope to help you come to understand the changes of your growing self-awareness, for it is only through a complete realization of one's self that one can achieve personal fulfillment and thereby true inner peace."

"I'm afraid I can't afford to undergo analysis just now."

"Let me begin by emphasizing to you that I am not suggesting psychoanalysis; I do not in the least consider you to be neurotic, Miss Seyrig. What I strongly urge is an *exploration* of your unconsciousness—a discovery of your whole self. My task is only to guide you along the course of your self-discovery, and for this privilege I charge no fee."

"I hadn't realized the National Health Service was this inclusive."

Dr Magnus laughed easily. "It isn't, of course. My work is supported by a private foundation. There are many others who wish to learn certain truths of our existence, to seek answers where mundane science has not yet so much as realized there are questions. In that regard I am simply another paid researcher, and the results of my investigations are made available to those who share with us this yearning to see beyond the stultifying boundaries of modern science."

He indicated the book-lined wall behind his desk. Much of one shelf appeared to contain books with his own name prominent upon their spines.

"Do you intend to write a book about me?" Lisette meant to put more of a note of protest in her voice.

"It is possible that I may wish to record some of what we discover together, my dear. But only with scrupulous discretion, and, needless to say, only with your complete permission."

"My dreams." Lisette remembered the book of his that she had tried to read. "Do you consider them to be evidence of some previous incarnation?"   "Perhaps. We can't be certain until we explore them further. Does the idea of reincarnation smack too much of the occult to your liking, Miss Seyrig? Perhaps we should speak in more fashionable terms of Jungian archetypes, genetic memory or mental telepathy. The fact that the phenomenon has so many designations is ample proof that dreams of a previous existence are a very real part of the unconscious mind. It is undeniable that many people have experienced, in dreams or under hypnosis, memories that cannot possibly arise from their personal experience. Whether you believe that the immortal soul leaves the physical body at death to be reborn in the living embryo, or prefer to attribute it to inherited memories engraved upon DNA, or whatever explanation—this is a very real phenomenon and has been observed throughout history.

"As a rule, these memories of past existence are entirely buried within the unconscious. Almost everyone has experienced *déjà vu*. Subjects under hypnosis have spoken in languages and archaic dialects of which their conscious mind has no knowledge, have recounted in detail memories of previous lives. In some cases these submerged memories burst forth as dreams; in these instances, the memory is usually one of some emotionally laden experience, something too potent to remain buried. I believe that this is the case with your nightmares—the fact that they are recurrent being evidence of some profound significance in the events they recall."

Lisette wished for a cigarette; she'd all but stopped buying cigarettes with British prices, and from the absence of ashtrays here. Dr Magnus was a nonsmoker.

"But why have these nightmares only lately become a problem?"

"I think I can explain that easily enough. Your forebears were from London. The dreams became a problem after you arrived in London. While it is usually difficult to define any relationship between the subject and the remembered existence, the timing and the force of your dream regressions would seem to indicate that you may be the reincarnation of someone—an ancestress, perhaps—who lived here in London during this past century."

"In that case, the nightmares should go away when I return to the States."

"Not necessarily. Once a doorway to the unconscious is opened, it is not so easily closed again. Moreover, you say that you had experienced these dreams on rare occasions prior to your coming here. I would suggest that what you are experiencing is a natural process—a submerged part of your self is seeking expression, and it would be unwise to deny this shadow stranger within you. I might further argue that your presence here in London is hardly coincidence—that your decision to study here was determined by that part of you who emerges in these dreams."

Lisette decided she wasn't ready to accept such implications just now. "What do you propose?"

Dr Magnus folded his hands as neatly as a bishop at prayer. "Have you ever undergone hypnosis?"

"No." She wished she hadn't made that sound like two syllables.

"It has proved to be extraordinarily efficacious in a great number of cases such as your own, my dear. Please do try to put from your mind the ridiculous trappings and absurd mumbo-jumbo with which the popular imagination connotes hypnotism. Hypnosis is no more than a technique through which we may release the entirety of the unconscious mind to free expression, unrestricted by the countless artificial barriers that make us strangers to ourselves."

"You want to hypnotize me?" The British inflection came to her, turning her statement into both question and protest.

"With your fullest cooperation, of course. I think it best. Through regressive hypnosis we can explore the significance of these dreams that trouble you, discover the shadow stranger within your self. Remember—this is a part of *you* that cries out for conscious expression. It is only through the full realization of one's identity, of one's total self, that true inner tranquillity may be achieved. Know thyself, and you will find peace."

"Know myself?"

"Precisely. You must put aside this false sense of guilt, Miss Seyrig. You are not possessed by some alien and hostile force. These dreams, these memories of another existence—this is *you*."

IV

"Some bloody weirdo made a pass at me this afternoon," Lisette confided.

"On the tube, was it?" Danielle stood on her toes, groping along the top of their bookshelf. Freshly showered, she was wearing only a lace-trimmed teddy—cami-knickers, they called them in the shops here—and her straining thigh muscles shaped her buttocks nicely.

"In Kensington, actually. After I had left Dr Magnus's office." Lisette was lounging in an old satin slip she'd found at a stall in Church Street. They were drinking Bristol Cream out of brandy snifters. It was an intimate sort of evening they loved to share together, when not in the company of Danielle's various friends.

"I was walking down Holland Street, and there was this seedy-looking creep all dressed out in punk regalia, pressing his face against the door where that Equinox bookshop used to be. I made the mistake of glancing at him as I passed, and he must have seen my reflection in the glass, because he spun right around, looked straight at me, and said: 'Darling! What a lovely surprise to see you!'"

Lisette sipped her sherry. "Well. I gave him my hardest stare, and would you believe the creep just stood there smiling like he knew me, and so I yelled, 'Piss off!' in my loudest American accent, and he just froze there with his mouth hanging open."

"Here it is," Danielle announced. "I'd shelved it beside Roland Franklyn's *We Pass from View*—that's another you ought to read. I must remember someday to return it to that cute Liverpool writer who lent it to me."

She settled cozily beside Lisette on the couch, handed her a somewhat smudged paperback, and resumed her glass of sherry. The book was entitled *More Stately Mansions: Evidences of the Infinite* by Dr Ingmar Magnus, and bore an affectionate inscription from the author to Danielle. "This is the first. The later printings had two of his studies deleted; I can't imagine why. But these are the sort of sessions he was describing to you."

"He wants to put *me* in one of his books," Lisette told her with an extravagant leer. "Can a woman trust a man who writes such ardent inscriptions to place her under hypnosis?"

"Dr Magnus is a perfect gentleman," Danielle assured her, somewhat huffily. "He's a distinguished scholar and is thoroughly dedicated to his research. And besides, I've let him hypnotize me on a few occasions."

"I didn't know that. Whatever for?"

"Dr Magnus is always seeking suitable subjects. I was fascinated by his work, and when I met him at a party I offered to undergo hypnosis."

"What happened?"

Danielle seemed envious. "Nothing worth writing about, I'm afraid. He said I was either too thoroughly integrated, or that my previous lives were too deeply buried. That's often the case, he says, which is why absolute proof of reincarnation is so difficult to demonstrate. After a few sessions I decided I couldn't spare the time to try further."

"But what was it like?"

"As adventurous as taking a nap. No caped Svengali staring into my eyes. No lambent girasol ring. No swirling lights. Quite dull, actually. Dr Magnus simply lulls you to sleep."

"Sounds safe enough. So long as I don't get molested walking back from his office."

Playfully, Danielle stroked her hair. "You hardly look the punk rock type. You haven't chopped off your hair with garden shears and dyed the stubble green. And not a single safety pin through your cheek."

"Actually I suppose he may not have been a punk rocker. Seemed a bit too old, and he wasn't garish enough. It's just that he was wearing a lot of black leather, and he had gold earrings and some sort of medallion."

"In front of the Equinox, did you say? How curious."

"Well, I think I gave him a good start. I glanced in a window to see whether he was trying to follow me, but he was just standing there looking stunned."

"*Might* have been an honest mistake. Remember the old fellow at Midge and Fiona's party who kept insisting he knew you?"

"And who was pissed out of his skull. Otherwise he might have been able to come up with a more original line."

Lisette paged through *More Stately Mansions* while Danielle selected a Tangerine Dream album from the stack and placed it on her stereo at low volume. The music seemed in keeping with the grey drizzle of the night outside and the coziness within their sitting room. Seeing she was busy reading, Danielle poured sherry for them both and stood studying the bookshelves—a hodgepodge of occult and metaphysical topics stuffed together with art books and recent paperbacks in no particular order. Wedged between Aleister Crowley's *Magick in Theory and Practice* and *How I Discovered My Infinite Self* by "An Initiate," was Dr Magnus's most recent book, *The Shadow*

Stranger. She pulled it down, and Dr Magnus stared thoughtfully from the back of the dust jacket.

"Do you believe in reincarnation?" Lisette asked her.

"I do. Or rather, I do some of the time." Danielle stood behind the couch and bent over Lisette's shoulder to see where she was reading. "Midge Vaughn assures me that in a previous incarnation I was hanged for witchcraft."

"Midge should be grateful she's living in the twentieth century."

"Oh, Midge says we were sisters in the same coven and were hanged together; that's the reason for our close affinity."

"I'll bet Midge says that to all the girls."

"Oh, I like Midge." Danielle sipped her sherry and considered the rows of spines. "Did you say that man was wearing a medallion? Was it a swastika or that sort of thing?"

"No. It was something like a star in a circle. And he wore rings on every finger."

"Wait! Kind of greasy black hair slicked back from a widow's peak to straight over his collar in back? Eyebrows curled up into points like they've been waxed?"

"That's it."

"Ah, Mephisto!"

"Do you know him, then?"

"Not really. I've just seen him a time or two at the Equinox and a few other places. He reminds me of some ham actor playing Mephistopheles. Midge spoke to him once when we were by there, but I gather he's not part of her particular coven. Probably hadn't heard that the Equinox had closed. Never impressed me as a masher; very likely he actually did mistake you for someone."

"Well, they do say that everyone has a double. I wonder if mine is walking somewhere about London, being mistaken for me?"

"And no doubt giving some unsuspecting classmate of yours a resounding slap on the face."

"What if I met her suddenly?"

"Met your double—your *Doppelgänger*? Remember William Wilson? Disaster, darling—*disaster!*"

V

There really wasn't much to it; no production at all. Lisette felt nervous, a bit silly and perhaps a touch cheated.

"I want you to relax," Dr Magnus told her. "All you have to do is just relax."

That's what her gynecologist always said, too. Lisette thought with a sudden tenseness. She lay on her back on Dr Magnus's analyst's couch: her head on a comfortable cushion, legs stretched primly out on the leather upholstery (she'd deliberately worn jeans again), fingers clenched damply over her tummy. A white gown instead of jeans, and I'll be ready for my coffin, she mused uncomfortably.

"Fine. That's it. You're doing fine, Lisette. Very fine. Just relax. Yes, just relax, just like that. Fine, that's it. Relax."

Dr Magnus's voice was a quiet monotone, monotonously repeating soothing encouragements. He spoke to her tirelessly, patiently, slowly dissolving her anxiety.

"You feel sleepy, Lisette. Relaxed and sleepy. Your breathing is slow and relaxed, slow and relaxed. Think about your breathing now, Lisette. Think how slow and sleepy and deep each breath comes. You're breathing deeper, and you're feeling sleepier. Relax and sleep, Lisette, breathe and sleep. Breathe and sleep . . ."

She *was* thinking about her breathing. She counted the breaths; the slow monotonous syllables of Dr Magnus's voice seemed to blend into her breathing like a quiet, tuneless lullaby. She *was* sleepy, for that matter, and it was very pleasant to relax here, listening to that dim, droning murmur while he talked on and on. How much longer until the end of the lecture . . .

"You are asleep now, Lisette. You are asleep, yet you can still hear my voice. Now you are falling deeper, deeper, deeper into a pleasant, relaxed sleep, Lisette. Deeper and deeper asleep. Can you still hear my voice?"

"Yes."

"You are asleep, Lisette. In a deep, deep sleep. You will remain in this deep sleep until I shall count to three. As I count to three, you will slowly arise from your sleep until you are fully awake once again. Do you understand?"

"Yes."

"But when you hear me say the word *amber*, you will again fall into a deep, deep sleep, Lisette, just as you are asleep now. Do you understand?"

"Yes."

"Listen to me as I count, Lisette. One. Two. Three."

Lisette opened her eyes. For a moment her expression was blank, then a sudden confusion. She looked at Dr Magnus seated beside her, then smiled ruefully. "I was asleep, I'm afraid. Or was I . . .?"

"You did splendidly, Miss Seyrig." Dr Magnus beamed reassurance. "You passed into a simple hypnotic state, and as you can see now, there was no more cause for concern than in catching an afternoon nap."

"But I'm sure I just dropped off." Lisette glanced at her watch. Her appointment had been for three, and it was now almost four o'clock.

"Why not just settle back and rest some more, Miss Seyrig. That's it, relax again. All you need is to rest a bit, just a pleasant rest."

Her wrist fell back onto the cushions, as her eyes fell shut.

"Amber."

Dr Magnus studied her calm features for a moment. "You are asleep now, Lisette. Can you hear me?"

"Yes."

"I want you to relax, Lisette. I want you to fall deeper, deeper, deeper into sleep. Deep, deep sleep. Far, far, far into sleep."

He listened to her breathing, then suggested: "You are thinking of your childhood now, Lisette. You are a little girl, not even in school yet. Something is making you very happy. You remember how happy you are. Why are you so happy?"

Lisette made a childish giggle. "It's my birthday party, and Ollie the Clown came to play with us."

"And how old are you today?"

"I'm five." Her right hand twitched, extended fingers and thumb.

"Go deeper now, Lisette. I want you to reach farther back. Far, far back into your memories. Go back to a time before you were a child in San Francisco. Far, farther back, Lisette. I want you to go back to the time of your dreams."

He studied her face. She remained in a deep hypnotic trance, but her expression registered sudden anxiousness. It was as if she lay in normal sleep—reacting to some intense nightmare. She moaned.

"Deeper, Lisette. Don't be afraid to remember. Let your mind flow back to another time."

Her features still showed distress, but she seemed less agitated as his voice urged her deeper.

"Where are you?"

"I'm . . . I'm not certain." Her voice came in a well-bred English accent. "It's quite dark. Only a few candles are burning. I'm frightened."

"Go back to a happy moment," Dr Magnus urged her, as her tone grew sharp with fear. "You are happy now. Something very pleasant and wonderful is happening to you."

Anxiety drained from her features. Her cheeks flushed; she smiled pleasurably.

"Where are you now?"

"I'm dancing. It's a grand ball to celebrate Her Majesty's Diamond Jubilee, and I've never seen such a throng. I'm certain Charles means to propose to me tonight, but he's ever so shy, and now he's simply fuming that Captain Stapledon has the next two dances. He's so dashing in his uniform. Everyone is watching us together."

"What is your name?"

"Elisabeth Beresford."

"Where do you live, Miss Beresford?"

"We have a house in Chelsea. . . ."

Her expression abruptly changed. "It's dark again. I'm all alone. I can't see myself, although surely the candles shed sufficient light. There's something there in the candlelight. I'm moving closer."

"One."

"It's an open coffin." Fear edged her voice.

"Two."

"*God in Heaven!*"

"Three."

VI

"We," Danielle announced grandly, "are invited to a party."

She produced an engraved card from her bag, presented it to Lisette, then went to hang up her damp raincoat.

"Bloody English summer weather!" Lisette heard her from the kitchen. "Is there any more coffee made? Oh, fantastic!"

She reappeared with a cup of coffee and an opened box of cookies—Lisette couldn't get used to calling them biscuits. "Want some?"

"No, thanks. Bad for my figure."

"And coffee on an empty tummy is bad for the nerves," Danielle said pointedly.

"*Who* is Beth Garrington?" Lisette studied the invitation.

"Um." Danielle tried to wash down a mouthful of crumbs with too-hot coffee. "Some friend of Midge's. Midge dropped by the gallery this afternoon and gave me the invitation. A costume revel. Rock stars to royalty among the guests. Midge promises that it will be super fun; said the last party Beth threw was unbridled debauchery—there was cocaine being passed around in an antique snuff box for the guests. Can you imagine that much coke!"

"And how did Midge manage the invitation?"

"I gather the discerning Ms. Garrington had admired several of my drawings that Maitland has on display—yea, even unto so far as to purchase one. Midge told her that she knew me and that we two were ornaments for any debauchery."

"The invitation is in both our names."

"Midge *likes* you."

"Midge despises me. She's jealous as a cat."

"Then she must have told our depraved hostess what a lovely couple we make. Besides, Midge is jealous of everyone—even dear Maitland, whose interest in me very obviously is not of the flesh. But don't fret about Midge—English women are naturally bitchy toward 'foreign' women. They're oh-so proper and fashionable, but they never shave their legs. That's why I love mah fellow Americans."

Danielle kissed her chastely on top of her head, powdering Lisette's hair with biscuit crumbs. "And I'm cold and wet and dying for a shower. How about you?"

"A masquerade?" Lisette wondered. "What sort of costume? Not something that we'll have to trot off to one of those rental places for, surely?"

"From what Midge suggests, anything goes so long as it's wild. Just create something divinely decadent, and we're sure to knock them dead." Danielle had seen *Cabaret* half a dozen times. "It's to be in some back alley stately old home in Maida Vale, so there's no danger that the tenants downstairs will call the cops."

When Lisette remained silent, Danielle gave her a playful nudge. "Darling, it's a party we're invited to, not a funeral. What is it—didn't your session with Dr Magnus go well?"

"I suppose it did." Lisette smiled without conviction. "I really can't say; all I did was doze off. Dr Magnus seemed quite excited about it, though. I found it all . . . well, just a little bit scary."

"I thought you said you just dropped off. *What* was scary?"

"It's hard to put into words. It's like when you're starting to have a bad trip on acid: there's nothing wrong that you can explain, but somehow your mind is telling you to be afraid."

Danielle sat down beside her and squeezed her arm about her shoulders. "That sounds to me like Dr Magnus is getting somewhere. I felt just the same sort of free anxiety the first time I underwent analysis. It's a good sign, darling. It means you're beginning to understand all those troubled secrets the ego keeps locked away."

"Perhaps the ego keeps them locked away for some perfectly good reason."

"Meaning hidden sexual conflicts, I suppose." Danielle's fingers gently massaged Lisette's shoulders and neck. "Oh, Lisette. You mustn't be shy about getting to know yourself. *I* think it's exciting."

Lisette curled up against her, resting her cheek against Danielle's breast while the other girl's fingers soothed the tension from her muscles. She supposed she was overreacting. After all, the nightmares were what distressed her so; Dr Magnus seemed completely confident that he could free her from them.

"Which of your drawings did our prospective hostess buy?" Lisette asked, changing the subject.

"Oh, didn't I tell you?" Danielle lifted up her chin. "It was that charcoal study I did of you."

Lisette closed the shower curtains as she stepped into the tub. It was one of those long, narrow, deep tubs beloved of English bathrooms that always made her think of a coffin for two. A Rube Goldberg plumbing arrangement connected the hot and cold faucets, and from the common spout was affixed a rubber hose with a shower head which one might either hang from a hook on the wall or hold in hand. Danielle had replaced the ordinary shower head with a shower massage when she moved in, but she left the previous tenant's shaving mirror—a bevelled glass oval in a heavily enameled antique frame—hanging on the wall above the hook.

Lisette glanced at her face in the steamed-over mirror. "I shouldn't have let you display that at the gallery."

"But why not?" Danielle was shampooing, and lather blinded her as she turned about. "Maitland thinks it's one of my best."

Lisette reached around her for the shower attachment. "It seems a bit personal somehow. All those people looking at me. It's an invasion of privacy."

"But it's thoroughly modest, darling. Not like some topless billboard in Soho."

The drawing was a charcoal and pencil study of Lisette, done in what Danielle described as her David Hamilton phase. In sitting for it, Lisette had piled her hair in a high chignon and dressed in an antique cotton camisole and drawers with lace insertions that she'd found at a shop in Westbourne Grove. Danielle called it *Dark Rose*. Lisette had thought it made her look fat.

Danielle grasped blindly for the shower massage, and Lisette placed it in her hand. "It just seems a bit too personal to have some total stranger owning my picture." Shampoo coursed like seafoam over Danielle's breasts. Lisette kissed the foam.

"Ah, but soon she won't be a total stranger," Danielle reminded her, her voice muffled by the pulsing shower spray.

Lisette felt Danielle's nipples harden beneath her lips. The brunette still pressed her eyes tightly shut against the force of the shower, but the other hand cupped Lisette's head encouragingly. Lisette gently moved her kisses downward along the other girl's slippery belly, kneeling as she did so. Danielle murmured, and when Lisette's tongue probed her drenched curls, she shifted her legs to let her knees rest beneath the blonde girl's shoulders. The shower massage dropped from her fingers.

Lisette made love to her with a passion that surprised her—spontaneous, suddenly fierce, unlike their usual tenderness together. Her lips and tongue pressed into Danielle almost ravenously, her own ecstasy even more intense than that which she was drawing from Danielle. Danielle gasped and clung to the shower rail with one hand, her other fist clenched upon the curtain, sobbing as a long orgasm shuddered through her.

"Please, darling!" Danielle finally managed to beg. "My legs are too wobbly to hold me up any longer!"

She drew away. Lisette raised her face.

"Oh!"

Lisette rose to her feet with drugged movements. Her wide eyes at last registered Danielle's startled expression. She touched her lips and turned to look in the bathroom mirror.

"I'm sorry," Danielle put her arm about her shoulder. "I must have started my period. I didn't realize . . ."

Lisette stared at the blood-smeared face in the fogged shaving mirror.

Danielle caught her as she started to slump.

VII

She was conscious of the cold rain that pelted her face, washing from her nostrils the too-sweet smell of decaying flowers. Slowly she opened her eyes onto darkness and mist. Rain fell steadily, spiritlessly, glueing her white gown to her drenched flesh. She had been walking in her sleep again.

Wakefulness seemed forever in coming to her, so that only by slow degrees did she become aware of herself, of her surroundings. For a moment she felt as if she were a chess-piece arrayed upon a board in a darkened room. All about her, stone monuments crowded together, their weathered surfaces streaming with moisture. She felt neither fear nor surprise that she stood in a cemetery.

She pressed her bare arms together across her breasts. Water ran over her pale skin as smoothly as upon the marble tomb-stones, and though her flesh felt as cold as the drenched marble, she did not feel chilled. She stood barefoot, her hair clinging to her shoulders above the low-necked cotton gown that was all she wore.

Automatically, her steps carried her through the darkness, as if following a familiar path through the maze of glistening stone. She knew where she was: this was Highgate Cemetery. She could not recall how she knew that, since she had no memory of ever having been to this place before. No more could she think how she knew her steps were taking her deeper into the cemetery instead of toward the gate.

A splash of color trickled onto her breast, staining its paleness as the rain dissolved it into a red rose above her heart.

She opened her mouth to scream, and a great bubble of unswallowed blood spewed from her lips.

"Elisabeth! Elisabeth!"

"Lisette! Lisette!"

Whose voice called her?

"Lisette! You can wake up now, Lisette."

Dr Magnus's face peered into her own. Was there sudden concern behind that urbane mask?

"You're awake now, Miss Seyrig. Everything is all right."

Lisette stared back at him for a moment, uncertain of her reality, as if suddenly awakened from some profound nightmare.

"I . . . I thought I was dead." Her eyes still held her fear.

Dr Magnus smiled to reassure her. "Somnambulism, my dear. You remembered an episode of sleepwalking from a former life. Tell me, have you yourself ever walked in your sleep?"

Lisette pressed her hands to her face, abruptly examined her fingers. "I don't know. I mean, I don't think so."

She sat up, searched in her bag for her compact. She paused for a moment before opening the mirror.

"Dr Magnus, I don't think I care to continue these sessions." She stared at her reflection in fascination, not touching her makeup, and when she snapped the case shut, the frightened strain began to relax from her face. She wished she had a cigarette.

Dr Magnus sighed and pressed his fingertips together, leaning back in his chair; watched her fidget with her clothing as she sat nervously on the edge of the couch.

"Do you really wish to terminate our exploration? We have, after all, made excellent progress during these last few sessions."

"Have we?"

"We have, indeed. You have consistently remembered incidents from the life of one Elisabeth Beresford, a young English lady living in London at the close of the last century. To the best of your knowledge of your family history, she is not an ancestress."

Dr Magnus leaned forward, seeking to impart his enthusiasm. "Don't you see how important this is? If Elisabeth Beresford was not your ancestress, then there can be no question of genetic memory being involved. The only explanation must therefore be reincarnation—proof of the immortality of the soul. To establish this I must first confirm the existence of Elisabeth Beresford, and from that demonstrate that no familial bond exists between the two of you. We simply must explore this further."

"Must we? I meant, what progress have we made toward helping me, Dr Magnus? It's all very good for you to be able to confirm your theories of reincarnation, but that doesn't do anything for me. If anything, the nightmares have grown more disturbing since we began these sessions."

"Then perhaps we dare not stop."

"What do you mean?" Lisette wondered what he might do if she suddenly bolted from the room.

"I mean that the nightmares will grow worse regardless of whether you decide to terminate our sessions. Your unconscious self is struggling to tell you some significant message from a previous existence. It will continue to do so no matter how stubbornly you will yourself not to listen. My task is to help you listen to this voice, to understand the message it must impart to you—and with this understanding and self-awareness, you will experience inner peace. Without my help . . . Well, to be perfectly frank, Miss Seyrig, you are in some danger of a complete emotional breakdown."

Lisette slumped back against the couch. She felt on the edge of panic and wished Danielle were here to support her.

"Why are my memories always nightmares?" Her voice shook, and she spoke slowly to control it.

"But they aren't always frightening memories, my dear. It's just that the memory of some extremely traumatic experience often seeks to come to the fore. You would expect some tremendously emotional laden memory to be a potent one."

"Is Elisabeth Beresford . . . dead?"

"Assuming she was approximately twenty years of age at the time of Queen Victoria's Diamond Jubilee, she would have been past one hundred today. Besides, Miss Seyrig, her soul has been born again as your own. It must therefore follow . . ."

"Dr Magnus. I don't *want* to know how Elisabeth Beresford died."

"Of course," Dr Magnus told her gently. "Isn't that quite obvious?"

VIII

"For a wonder, it's forgot to rain tonight."

"Thank god for small favors," Lisette commented, thinking July in London had far more to do with monsoons than the romantic city of fogs celebrated in song. "All we need is to get these rained on."

She and Danielle bounced about on the back seat of the black Austin taxi, as their driver democratically seemed as willing to challenge lorries as pedestrians for right-of-way on the Edgeware Road. Feeling a bit self-conscious, Lisette tugged at the hem of her patent leather trench coat. They had decided to wear brightly embroidered Chinese silk lounging pyjamas that they'd found at one of the vintage clothing shops off the Portobello Road—gauzy enough for stares, but only a demure trouser-leg showing beneath their coats. "We're going to a masquerade party," Lisette had felt obliged to explain to the driver. Her concern was needless, as he hadn't given them a second glance. Either he was used to the current Chinese look in fashion, or else a few seasons of picking up couples at discos and punk rock clubs had inured him to any sort of costume.

The taxi turned into a series of side streets off Maida Vale and eventually made a neat U-turn that seemed almost an automotive pirouette. The frenetic beat of a new wave rock group clattered past the gate of an enclosed courtyard: something Mews—the iron plaque on the brick wall was too rusted to decipher in the dark—but from the lights and noise it must be the right address. A number of expensive-looking cars—Lisette recognized a Rolls or two and at least one Ferrari—were among those crowded against the curb. They squeezed their way past them and made for the source of the revelry, a brick-fronted town-house of three or more storeys set at the back of the courtyard.

The door was opened by a girl in an abbreviated maid's costume. She checked their invitation while a similarly clad girl took their coats, and a third invited them to select from an assortment of masks and indicated where they might change. Lisette and Danielle chose sequined domino masks that matched the dangling scarves they wore tied low across their brows.

Danielle withdrew an ebony cigarette holder from her bag and considered their reflections with approval. "Divinely decadent," she drawled, gesturing with her black-lacquered nails. "All that time for my eyes, and just to cover them with a mask. Perhaps later—when it's cock's-crow and all unmask . . . Forward, darling."

Lisette kept at her side, feeling a bit lost and out of place. When they passed before a light, it was evident that they wore nothing beneath the silk pyjamas, and Lisette was grateful for the strategic brocade. As they came upon others of the newly arriving guests, she decided there was no danger of outraging anyone's modesty here. As Midge had promised, anything goes so long as it's wild, and while their costumes might pass for street wear, many of the guests needed avail themselves of the changing rooms upstairs.

A muscular young man clad only in a leather loincloth and a sword belt with broadsword descended the stairs leading a buxom girl by a chain affixed to her wrists; aside from her manacles, she wore a few scraps of leather. A couple in punk rock gear spat at them in passing; the girl was wearing a set of panties with dangling razor blades for tassels and a pair of black latex tights that might have been spray paint. Two girls in vintage Christian Dior New Look evening gowns ogled the seminude swordsman from the landing above; Lisette noted their pronounced shoulders and Adam's apples and felt a twinge of jealousy that hormones and surgery could let them show a better cleavage than she could.

· A new wave group called the Needle was performing in a large first-floor room—Lisette supposed it was an actual ballroom, although the house's original tenants would have considered tonight's ball a *danse macabre*. Despite the fact that the decibel level was well past the threshold of pain, most of the guests were congregated here, with smaller, quieter parties gravitating into other rooms. Here, about half were dancing, the rest standing about trying to talk. Marijuana smoke was barely discernible within the harsh haze of British cigarettes.

"There's Midge and Fiona," Danielle shouted in Lisette's ear. She waved energetically and steered a course through the dancers.

Midge was wearing an elaborate medieval gown—a heavily brocaded affair that ran from the floor to midway across her nipples. Her blonde hair was piled high in some sort of conical headpiece, complete with flowing scarf. Fiona waited upon her in a page boy's costume.

"Are you just getting here?" Midge asked, running a deprecative glance down Lisette's costume. "There's champagne over on the sideboard. Wait, I'll summon one of the cute little French maids."

Lisette caught two glasses from a passing tray and presented one to Danielle. It was impossible to converse, but then she hadn't anything to talk about with Midge, and Fiona was no more than a shadow.

"Where's our hostess?" Danielle asked.

"Not down yet," Midge managed to shout. "Beth always waits to make a grand entrance at her little do's. You won't miss her."

"Speaking of entrances . . ." Lisette commented, nodding toward the couple who were just coming onto the dance floor. The woman wore a Nazi SS officer's hat, jackboots, black trousers and braces across her bare chest. She was astride the back of her male companion, who wore a saddle and bridle in addition to a few other bits of leather harness.

"I can't decide whether that's kinky or just tacky," Lisette said.

"Not like your little sorority teas back home, is it?" Midge smiled.

"Is there any coke about?" Danielle interposed quickly.

"There was a short while ago. Try the library—that's the room just down from where everyone's changing."

Lisette downed her champagne and grabbed a refill before following Danielle upstairs. A man in fish-net tights, motorcycle boots and a vest comprised mostly of chain and bits of Nazi medals caught at her arm and seemed to want to dance. Instead of a mask, he wore about a pound of eye shadow and black lipstick. She shouted an inaudible excuse, held a finger to her nostril and sniffed, and darted after Danielle.

"That was Eddie Teeth, lead singer for the Trepans, whom you just cut," Danielle told her. "Why didn't he grab *me!*"

"You'll get your chance," Lisette told her. "I think he's following us."

Danielle dragged her to a halt halfway up the stairs.

"Got toot right here, loves." Eddie Teeth flipped the silver spoon and phial that dangled amidst the chains on his vest.

"Couldn't take the noise in there any longer," Lisette explained.

"Needle's shit." Eddie Teeth wrapped an arm about either waist and propelled them up the stairs. "You gashes sisters? I can dig incest."

The library was pleasantly crowded—Lisette decided she didn't want to be cornered with Eddie Teeth. A dozen or more guests stood about, sniffing and conversing energetically. Seated at a table, two of the ubiquitous maids busily cut lines onto mirrors and set them out for the guests, whose number remained more or less constant as people wandered in and left. A cigarette box offered tightly rolled joints.

"That's Thai." Eddie Teeth groped for a handful of the joints, stuck one in each girl's mouth, the rest inside his vest. Danielle giggled and fitted hers to her cigarette holder. Unfastening a silver tube from his vest, he snorted two thick lines from one of the mirrors. "Toot your eyeballs out, loves," he invited them.

One of the maids collected the mirror when they had finished and replaced it with another—a dozen lines of cocaine neatly arranged across its surface. Industriously she began to work a chunk of rock through a sifter to replenish the empty mirror. Lisette watched in fascination. This finally brought home to her the wealth this party represented: all the rest simply seemed to her like something out of a movie, but dealing out coke to more than a hundred guests was an extravagance she could relate to.

"Danielle Borland, isn't it?"

A man dressed as Mephistopheles bowed before them. "Adrian Tregannet. We've met at one of Midge Vaughn's parties, you may recall."

Danielle stared at the face below the domino mask. "Oh, yes. Lisette, it's Mephisto himself."

"Then this is Miss Seyrig, the subject of your charcoal drawing that Beth so admires." Mephisto caught Lisette's hand and bent his lips to it. "Beth is so much looking forward to meeting you both."

Lisette retrieved her hand. "Aren't you the . . ."

"The rude fellow who accosted you in Kensington some days ago," Tregannet finished apologetically. "Yes, I'm afraid so. But you really must forgive me for my forwardness. I actually did mistake you for a very dear friend of mine, you see. Won't you let me make amends over a glass of champagne?"

"Certainly." Lisette decided that she had had quite enough of Eddie Teeth, and Danielle was quite capable of fending for herself if she grew tired of having her breasts squeezed by a famous pop star.

Tregannet quickly returned with two glasses of champagne. Lisette finished another two lines and smiled appreciatively as she accepted a glass. Danielle was trying to shotgun Eddie Teeth through her cigarette holder, and Lisette thought it a good chance to slip away.

"Your roommate is tremendously talented," Tregannet suggested. "Of course, she chose so charming a subject for her drawing."

Slick as snake oil, Lisette thought, letting him take her arm. "How very nice of you to say so. However, I really feel a bit embarrassed to think that some stranger owns a portrait of me in my underwear."

"Utterly chaste, my dear—as chaste as the *Dark Rose* of its title. Beth chose to hang it in her boudoir, so I hardly think it is on public display. I suspect from your garments in the drawing that you must share Beth's appreciation for the dress and manners of this past century."

Which is something I'd never suspect of our hostess, judging from this party, Lisette considered. "I'm quite looking forward to meeting

her. I assume then that Ms. is a bit too modern for one of such quiet
tastes. Is it Miss or Mrs Garrington?"

"Ah, I hadn't meant to suggest an impression of a genteel dowager.
Beth is entirely of your generation—a few years older than yourself,
perhaps. Although I find Ms. too suggestive of American slang, I'm
sure Beth would not object. However, there's no occasion for such
formality here."

"You seem to know her well, Mr Tregannet."

"It is an old family. I know her aunt, Julia Weatherford, quite well
through our mutual interest in the occult. Perhaps you, too . . .?"

"Not really; Danielle is the one you should chat with about that.
My field is art. I'm over here on fellowship at London University."
She watched Danielle and Eddie Teeth toddle off for the ballroom
and jealously decided that Danielle's taste in her acquaintances left
much to be desired. "Could I have some more champagne?"

"To be sure. I won't be a moment."

Lisette snorted a few more lines while she waited. A young man
dressed as an Edwardian dandy offered her his snuff box and gravely
demonstrated its use. Lisette was struggling with a sneezing fit when
Tregannet returned.

"You needn't have gone to all the bother," she told him. "These
little French maids are dashing about with trays of champagne."

"But those glasses have lost the proper chill," Tregannet explained.
"To your very good health."

"Cheers." Lisette felt lightheaded, and promised herself to go easy
for a while. "Does Beth live here with her aunt, then?"

"Her aunt lives on the Continent; I don't believe she's visited
London for several years. Beth moved in about ten years ago. Theirs
is not a large family, but they are not without wealth, as you can
observe. They travel a great deal as well, and it's fortunate that
Beth happened to be in London during your stay here. Incidently,
just how long will you be staying in London?"

"About a year is all." Lisette finished her champagne. "Then it's
back to my dear, dull family in San Francisco."

"Then there's no one here in London . . .?"

"Decidedly not, Mr Tregannet. And now if you'll excuse me, I
think I'll find the ladies'."

Cocaine might well be the champagne of drugs, but cocaine
and champagne didn't seem to mix well, Lisette mused, turning
the bathroom over to the next frantic guest. Her head felt really
buzzy, and she thought she might do better if she found a bedroom
somewhere and lay down for a moment. But then she'd most likely
wake up and find some man on top of her, judging from this lot. She

decided she'd lay off the champagne and have just a line or two to shake off the feeling of having been sandbagged.

The crowd in the study had changed during her absence. Just now it was dominated by a group of guests dressed in costumes from *The Rocky Horror Show*, now closing out its long run at the Comedy Theatre in Piccadilly. Lisette had grown bored with the fad the film version had generated in the States, and pushed her way past the group as they vigorously danced the Time Warp and bellowed out songs from the show.

"'Give yourself over to absolute pleasure,'" someone sang in her ear as she industriously snorted a line from the mirror. "'Erotic nightmares beyond any measure,'" the song continued.

Lisette finished a second line, and decided she had had enough. She straightened from the table and broke for the doorway. The tall transvestite dressed as Frankie barred her way with a dramatic gesture, singing ardently: "'Don't dream it—be it!'"

Lisette blew him a kiss and ducked around him. She wished she could find a quiet place to collect her thoughts. Maybe she should find Danielle first—if she could handle the ballroom that long.

The dance floor was far more crowded than when they'd come in. At least all these jostling bodies seemed to absorb some of the decibels from the blaring banks of amplifiers and speakers. Lisette looked in vain for Danielle amidst the dancers, succeeding only in getting champagne sloshed on her back. She caught sight of Midge, recognizable above the mob by her conical medieval headdress, and pushed her way toward her.

Midge was being fed caviar on bits of toast by Fiona while she talked with an older woman who looked like the pictures Lisette had seen of Marlene Dietrich dressed in men's formal evening wear.

"Have you seen Danielle?" Lisette asked her.

"Why, not recently, darling," Midge smiled, licking caviar from her lips with the tip of her tongue. "I believe she and that rock singer were headed upstairs for a bit more privacy. I'm sure she'll come collect you once they're finished."

"Midge, you're a cunt," Lisette told her through her sweetest smile. She turned away and made for the doorway, trying not to ruin her exit by staggering. Screw Danielle—she needed to have some fresh air.

A crowd had gathered at the foot of the stairway, and she had to push through the doorway to escape the ballroom. Behind her, the Needle mercifully took a break. "She's coming down!" Lisette heard someone whisper breathlessly. The inchoate babel of the party fell to a sudden lull that made Lisette shiver.

At the top of the stairway stood a tall woman, enveloped in a black velvet cloak from her throat to her ankles. Her blonde hair was piled high in a complex variation of the once-fashionable French twist. Strings of garnets entwined in her hair and edged the close-fitting black mask that covered the upper half of her face. For a hushed interval she stood there, gazing imperiously down upon her guests.

Adrian Tregannet leapt to the foot of the stairway. He signed to a pair of maids, who stepped forward to either side of their mistress.

"Milords and miladies!" he announced with a sweeping bow. "Let us pay honor to our bewitching mistress whose feast we celebrate tonight! I give you the lamia who haunted Adam's dreams—Lilith!"

The maids smoothly swept the cloak from their mistress' shoulders. From the multitude at her feet came an audible intake of breath. Beth Garrington was attired in a strapless corselette of gleaming black leather, laced tightly about her waist. The rest of her costume consisted only of knee-length, stiletto-heeled tight boots, above-the-elbow gloves, and a spiked collar around her throat—all of black leather that contrasted starkly against her white skin and blonde hair. At first Lisette thought she wore a bull-whip coiled about her body as well, but then the coils moved, and she realized that it was an enormous black snake.

"Lilith!" came the shout, chanted in a tone of awe. "Lilith!"

Acknowledging their worship with a sinuous gesture, Beth Garrington descended the staircase. The serpent coiled from gloved arm to gloved arm, entwining her cinched waist; its eyes considered the revellers imperturbably. Champagne glasses lifted in a toast to Lilith, and the chattering voice of the party once more began to fill the house.

Tregannet touched Beth's elbow as she greeted her guests at the foot of the stairway. He whispered into her ear, and she smiled graciously and moved away with him.

Lisette clung to the staircase newel, watching them approach. Her head was spinning, and she desperately needed to lie down in some fresh air, but she couldn't trust her legs to carry her outside. She stared into the eyes of the serpent, hypnotized by its flickering tongue.

The room seemed to surge in and out of focus. The masks of the guests seemed to leer and gloat with the awareness of some secret jest; the dancers in their fantastic costumes became a grotesque horde of satyrs and wanton demons, writhing about the ballroom in some witches' sabbat of obscene mass copulation. As in a nightmare, Lisette willed her legs to turn and run, realized that her body was no longer obedient to her will.

"Beth, here's someone you've been dying to meet," Lisette heard Tregannet say. "Beth Garrington, allow me to present Lisette Seyrig."

The lips beneath the black mask curved in a pleasurable smile. Lisette gazed into the eyes behind the mask, and discovered that she could no longer feel her body. She thought she heard Danielle cry out her name.

The eyes remained in her vision long after she slid down the newel and collapsed upon the floor.

IX

The Catherine Wheel was a pub on Kensington Church Street. They served good pub lunches there, and Lisette liked to stop in before walking down Holland Street for her sessions with Dr Magnus. Since today was her final such session, it seemed appropriate that they should end the evening here.

"While I dislike repeating myself," Dr Magnus spoke earnestly. "I really do think we should continue."

Lisette drew on a cigarette and shook her head decisively. "No way, Dr Magnus. My nerves are shot to hell. I mean, look—when I freak out at a costume party and have to be carted home to bed by my roommate! It was like when I was a kid and got hold of some bad acid: the whole world was some bizarre and sinister freak show for weeks. Once I got my head back on, I said: No more acid."

"That was rather a notorious circle you were travelling in. Further, you were, if I understand you correctly, overindulging a bit that evening."

A few glasses of champagne and a little toot never did anything before but make me a bit giggly and talkative." Lisette sipped her half of lager; she'd never developed a taste for English bitter, and at least the lager was chilled. They sat across from each other at a table the size of a hubcap; she in the corner of a padded bench against the wall, he at a chair set out into the room, pressed in by a wall of standing bodies. A foot away from her on the padded bench, three young men huddled about a similar table, talking animatedly. For all that, she and Dr Magnus might have been all alone in the room. Lisette wondered if the psychologist who had coined the faddish concept of "space" had been inspired in a crowded English pub.

"It isn't just that I fainted at the party. It isn't just the night-mares." She paused to find words. "It's just that everything somehow seems to be drifting out of focus, out of control. It's . . . well, it's frightening."

"Precisely why we must continue."

"Precisely why we must not." Lisette sighed. They'd covered this ground already. It had been a moment of weakness when she agreed to allow Dr Magnus to buy her a drink afterward instead of heading back to the flat. Still, he had been so distressed when she told him she was terminating their sessions.

"I've tried to cooperate with you as best I could, and I'm certain you are entirely sincere in your desire to help me." Well, she wasn't all *that* certain, but no point in going into that. "However, the fact remains that since we began these sessions, my nerves have gone to hell. You say they'd be worse without the sessions. I say the sessions have made them worse, and maybe there's no connection at all—it's just that my nerves have gotten worse, so now I'm going to trust my intuition and try life without these sessions. Fair enough?"

Dr Magnus gazed uncomfortably at his barely tasted glass of sherry. "While I fully understand your rationale, I must in all conscience beg you to reconsider, Lisette. You are running risks that . . ."

"Look. If the nightmares go away, then terrific. If they don't, I can always pack up and head back to San Francisco. That way I'll be clear of whatever it is about London that disagrees with me, and if not, I'll see my psychiatrist back home."

"Very well, then." Dr Magnus squeezed her hand. "However, please bear in mind that I remain eager to continue our sessions at any time, should you change your mind."

"That's fair enough, too. And very kind of you."

Dr Magnus lifted his glass of sherry to the light. Pensively, he remarked: "Amber."

X

"Lisette?"

Danielle locked the front door behind her and hung up her inadequate umbrella in the hallway. She considered her face in the mirror and grimaced at the mess of her hair. "Lisette? Are you here?"

No answer, and her rain things were not in the hallway. Either she was having a late session with Dr Magnus, or else she'd wisely decided to duck under cover until this bloody rain let up. After she'd had to carry Lisette home in a taxi when she passed out at the party. Danielle was starting to feel real concern over her state of health.

Danielle kicked off her damp shoes as she entered the living room. The curtains were drawn against the greyness outside, and she switched on a lamp to brighten the flat a bit. Her dress clung to her like a clammy fish-skin; she shivered, and thought about a cup of coffee. If Lisette hadn't returned yet, there wouldn't be any brewed. She'd have a warm shower instead, and after that she'd see to the coffee—if Lisette hadn't returned to set a pot going in the meantime.

"Lisette?" Their bedroom was empty. Danielle turned on the overhead light. Christ, it was gloomy! So much for long English summer evenings—with all the rain, she couldn't remember when she'd last seen the sun. She struggled out of her damp dress, spread it flat across her bed with the vague hope that it might not wrinkle too badly, then tossed her bra and tights onto a chair.

Slipping into her bathrobe, Danielle padded back into the living room. Still no sign of Lisette, and it was past nine. Perhaps she'd stopped off at a pub. Crossing to the stereo, Danielle placed the new Blondie album on the turntable and turned up the volume. Let the neighbors complain—at least this would help dispel the evening's gloom.

She cursed the delay needed to adjust the shower temperature to satisfaction, then climbed into the tub. The hot spray felt good, and she stood under it contentedly for several minutes—initially revitalized, then lulled into a delicious sense of relaxation. Through the rush of the spray, she could hear the muffled beat of the stereo. As she reached for the shampoo, she began to move her body with the rhythm.

The shower curtain billowed as the bathroom door opened. Danielle risked a soapy squint around the curtain—she knew the flat was securely locked, but after seeing *Psycho* . . . It was only Lisette, already undressed, her long blonde hair falling over her breasts.

"Didn't hear you come in with the stereo going," Danielle greeted her. "Come on in before you catch cold."

Danielle resumed lathering her hair as the shower curtain parted and the other girl stepped into the tub behind her. Her eyes squeezed shut against the soap, she felt Lisette's breasts thrust against her back, her flat belly press against her buttocks. Lisette's hands came around her to cup her breasts gently.

At least Lisette had gotten over her silly tiff about Eddie Teeth. She'd explained to Lisette that she'd ditched that greasy slob when he'd tried to dry hump her on the dance floor, but how do you reason with a silly thing who faints at the sight of a snake?

"Jesus, you're chilled to the bone!" Danielle complained with a shiver. "Better stand under the shower and get warm. Did you get caught in the rain?"

The other girl's fingers continued to caress her breasts, and instead of answering, her lips teased the nape of Danielle's neck. Danielle made a delighted sound deep in her throat, letting the spray rinse the lather from her hair and over their embraced bodies. Languidly she turned about to face her lover, closing her arms about Lisette's shoulders for support.

Lisette's kisses held each taut nipple for a moment, teasing them almost painfully. Danielle pressed the other girl's face to her breasts, sighed as her kisses nibbled upward to her throat. She felt weak with arousal, and only Lisette's strength held her upright in the tub. Her lover's lips upon her throat tormented her beyond enduring; Danielle gasped and lifted Lisette's face to meet her own.

Her mouth was open to receive Lisette's red-lipped kiss, and it opened wider as Danielle stared into the eyes of her lover. Her first emotion was one of wonder.

"You're not Lisette!"

It was nearly midnight when Lisette unlocked the door to their flat and quietly let herself in. Only a few lights were on, and there was no sign of Danielle—either she had gone out, or, more likely, had gone to bed.

Lisette hung up her raincoat and wearily pulled off her shoes. She'd barely caught the last train. She must have been crazy to let Dr Magnus talk her into returning to his office for another session that late, but then he was quite right: as serious as her problems were, she really did need all the help he could give her. She felt a warm sense of gratitude to Dr Magnus for being there when she so needed his help.

The turntable had stopped, but a light on the amplifier indicated that the power was still on. Lisette cut it off and closed the lid over the turntable. She felt too tired to listen to an album just now.

She became aware that the shower was running. In that case, Danielle hadn't gone to bed. She supposed she really ought to apologize to her for letting Midge's bitch lies get under her skin. After all, she had ruined the party for Danielle; poor Danielle had had to get her to bed and had left the party without ever getting to meet Beth Garrington, and she was the one Beth had invited in the first place.

"Danielle? I'm back." Lisette called through the bathroom door. "Do you want anything?"

No answer. Lisette looked into their bedroom, just in case Danielle had invited a friend over. No, the beds were still made up; Danielle's clothes were spread out by themselves.

"Danielle?" Lisette raised her voice. Perhaps she couldn't hear over the noise of the shower. "Danielle?" Surely she was all right.

Lisette's feet felt damp. She looked down. A puddle of water was seeping beneath the door. Danielle must not have the shower curtains closed properly.

"Danielle! You're flooding us!"

Lisette opened the door and peered cautiously within. The curtain was closed, right enough. A thin spray still reached through a gap, and the shower had been running long enough for the puddle to spread. It occurred to Lisette that she should see Danielle's silhouette against the translucent shower curtain.

"Danielle!" She began to grow alarmed. "Danielle! Are you all right?"

She pattered across the wet tiles and drew aside the curtain. Danielle lay in the bottom of the tub, the spray falling on her upturned smile, her flesh paler than the porcelain of the tub.

XI

It was early afternoon when they finally allowed her to return to the flat. Had she been able to think of another place to go, she probably would have gone there. Instead, Lisette wearily slumped onto the couch, too spent to pour herself the drink she desperately wanted.

Somehow she had managed to phone the police, through her hysteria make them understand where she was. Once the squad car arrived, she had no further need to act out of her own initiative; she simply was carried along in the rush of police investigation. It wasn't until they were questioning her at New Scotland Yard that she realized she herself was not entirely free from suspicion.

The victim had bled to death, the medical examiner ruled, her blood washed down the tub drain. A safety razor used for shaving legs had been opened, its blade removed. There were razor incisions along both wrists, directed lengthwise, into the radial artery, as opposed to the shallow, crosswise cuts utilized by suicides unfamiliar with human anatomy. There was, in addition, an incision in the left side of the throat. It was either a very determined suicide, or a skillfully concealed murder. In view of the absence of any signs of forced entry or of a struggle, more likely the former. The victim's roommate did admit to a recent quarrel. Laboratory tests would indicate whether the victim might have been drugged or rendered unconscious through a blow. After that, the inquest would decide.

Lisette had explained that she had spent the evening with Dr Magnus. The fact that she was receiving emotional therapy, as they interpreted it, caused several mental notes to be made. Efforts to reach Dr Magnus by telephone proved unsuccessful, but his secretary did confirm that Miss Seyrig had shown up for her appointment the previous afternoon. Dr Magnus would get in touch with them as soon as he returned to his office. No, she did not know why he had cancelled today's appointments, but it was not unusual for Dr Magnus to dash off suddenly when essential research demanded immediate attention.

After a while they let Lisette make phone calls. She phoned her parents, then wished she hadn't. It was still the night before in California, and it was like turning back the hands of time to no avail. They urged her to take the next flight home, but of course it wasn't all that simple, and it just wasn't feasible for either of them to fly over on a second's notice, since after all there really was nothing they could do. She phoned Maitland Reddin, who was stunned at the news and offered to help in any way he could, but Lisette couldn't think of any way. She phoned Midge Vaughn, who hung up on her. She phoned Dr Magnus, who still couldn't be reached. Mercifully, the police took care of phoning Danielle's next of kin.

A physician at New Scotland Yard had spoken with her briefly and had given her some pills—a sedative to ease her into sleep after her ordeal. They had driven her back to the flat after impressing upon her the need to be present at the inquest. She must not be concerned should any hypothetical assailant yet be lurking about, inasmuch as the flat would be under surveillance.

Lisette stared dully about the flat, still unable to comprehend what had happened. The police had been thorough—measuring, dusting for fingerprints, leaving things in a mess. Bleakly, Lisette tried to convince herself that this was only another nightmare, that in a moment Danielle would pop in and find her asleep on the couch. Christ, what was she going to do with all of Danielle's things? Danielle's mother was remarried and living in Colorado; her father was an executive in a New York investment corporation. Evidently he had made arrangements to have the body shipped back to the States.

"Oh, Danielle." Lisette was too stunned for tears. Perhaps she should check into a hotel for now. No, she couldn't bear being all alone with her thoughts in a strange place. How strange to realize now that she really had no close friends in London other than Danielle—and what friends she did have were mostly people she'd met through Danielle.

She'd left word with Dr Magnus's secretary for him to call her once he came in. Perhaps she should call there once again, just in case Dr Magnus had missed her message. Lisette couldn't think what good Dr Magnus could do, but he was such an understanding person, and she felt much better whenever she spoke with him.

She considered the bottle of pills in her bag. Perhaps it would be best to take a couple of them and sleep around the clock. She felt too drained just now to have energy enough to think.

The phone began to ring. Lisette stared at it for a moment without comprehension, then lunged up from the couch to answer it.

"Is this Lisette Seyrig?"

It was a woman's voice—one Lisette didn't recognize. "Yes. Who's calling, please?"

"This is Beth Garrington, Lisette. I hope I'm not disturbing you."

"That's quite all right."

"You poor dear! Maitland Redding phoned to tell me of the tragedy. I can't tell you how shocked I am. Danielle seemed such a dear from our brief contact, and she had such a great talent."

"Thank you. I'm sorry you weren't able to know her better." Lisette sensed guilt and embarrassment at the memory of that brief contact.

"Darling, you can't be thinking about staying in that flat alone. Is there someone there with you?"

"No, there isn't. That's all right. I'll be fine."

"Don't be silly. Listen, I have enough empty bedrooms in this old barn to open a hotel. Why don't you just pack a few things and come straight over?"

"That's very kind of you, but I really couldn't."

"Nonsense! It's no good for you to be there all by yourself. Strange as this may sound, but when I'm not throwing one of these invitational riots, this is a quiet little backwater and things are dull as church. I'd love the company, and it will do you a world of good to get away."

"You're really very kind to invite me, but I . . ."

"Please, Lisette—be reasonable. I have guest rooms here already made up, and I'll send the car around to pick you up. All you need do is say yes and toss a few things into your bag. After a good night's sleep, you'll feel much more like coping with things tomorrow."

When Lisette didn't immediately reply, Beth added carefully: "Besides, Lisette. I understand the police haven't ruled out the possibility of murder. In that event, unless poor Danielle simply forgot to lock up, there is a chance that whoever did this has a key to your flat."

"The police said they'd watch the house."

"He might also be someone you both know and trust, someone Danielle invited in."

Lisette stared wildly at the sinister shadows that lengthened about the flat. Her refuge had been violated. Even familiar objects seemed tainted and alien. She fought back tears. "I don't know what to think." She realized she'd been clutching the receiver for a long, silent interval.

"Poor dear! There's nothing you need think about! Now listen. I'm at my solicitor's tidying up some property matters for Aunt Julia. I'll phone right now to have my car sent around for you. It'll be there by the time you pack your toothbrush and pyjamas, and whisk you straight off to bucolic Maida Vale. The maids will plump up your pillows for you, and you can have a nice nap before I get home for dinner. Poor darling, I'll bet you haven't eaten a thing. Now, say you'll come."

"Thank you. It's awfully good of you. Of course I will."

"Then it's done. Don't worry about a thing, Lisette. I'll see you this evening."

XII

Dr Magnus hunched forward on the narrow seat of the taxi, wearily massaging his forehead and temples. It might not help his mental fatigue, but maybe the reduced muscle tension would ease his headache. He glanced at his watch. Getting on past ten. He'd had no sleep last night, and it didn't look as if he'd be getting much tonight. If only those girls would answer their phone!

It didn't help matters that his conscience plagued him. He had broken a sacred trust. He should never have made use of posthypnotic suggestion last night to persuade Lisette to return for a further session. It went against all principles, but there had been no other course: the girl was adamant, and he had to know—he was so close to establishing final proof. If only for one final session of regressive hypnosis . . .

Afterward he had spent a sleepless night, too excited for rest, at work in his study trying to reconcile the conflicting elements of

Lisette's released memories with the historical data his research had so far compiled. By morning he had been able to pull together just enough facts to deepen the mystery. He had phoned his secretary at home to cancel all his appointments, and had spent the day at the tedious labor of delving through dusty municipal records and newspaper files, working feverishly as the past reluctantly yielded one bewildering clue after another.

By now Dr Magnus was exhausted, hungry and none too clean, but he had managed to establish proof of his theories. He was not elated. In doing so he had uncovered another secret, something undreamt of in his philosophies. He began to hope that his life work was in error.

"Here's the address, sir."

"Thank you, driver." Dr Magnus awoke from his grim revery and saw that he had reached his destination. Quickly, he paid the driver and hurried up the walk to Lisette's flat. Only a few lights were on, and he rang the bell urgently—a helpless sense of foreboding making his movements clumsy.

"Just one moment, sir!"

Dr Magnus jerked about at the voice. Two men in plain clothes approached him briskly from the pavement.

"Stand easy! We're police."

"Is something the matter, officers?" Obviously, something was.

"Might we ask what your business here is, sir?"

"Certainly. I'm a friend of Miss Borland and Miss Seyrig. I haven't been able to reach them by phone, and as I have some rather urgent matters to discuss with Miss Seyrig, I thought perhaps I might try reaching her here at her flat." He realized he was far too nervous.

"Might we see some identification, sir?"

"Is there anything wrong, officers?" Magnus repeated, producing his wallet.

"Dr Ingmar Magnus." The taller of the pair regarded him quizzically. "I take it you don't keep up with the news, Dr Magnus."

"Just what is this about!"

"I'm Inspector Bradley, Dr Magnus, and this is Detective Sergeant Wharton. CID. We've been wanting to ask you a few questions, sir, if you'll just come with us."

It was totally dark when Lisette awoke from troubled sleep. She stared wide-eyed into the darkness for a moment, wondering where she was. Slowly memory supplanted the vague images of her dream.

Switching on a lamp beside her bed, Lisette frowned at her watch. It was close to midnight. She had overslept.

Beth's Rolls had come for her almost before she had had time hastily to pack her overnight bag. Once at the house in Maida Vale, a maid—wearing a more conventional uniform than those at her last visit—had shown her to a spacious guest room on the top floor. Lisette had taken a sedative pill and gratefully collapsed onto the bed. She'd planned to catch a short nap, then meet her hostess for dinner. Instead she had slept for almost ten solid hours. Beth must be convinced she was a hopeless twit after this.

As so often happens after an overextended nap, Lisette now felt restless. She wished she'd thought to bring a book. The house was completely silent. Surely it was too late to ring for a maid. No doubt Beth had meant to let her sleep through until morning, and by now would have retired herself. Perhaps she should take another pill and go back to sleep herself.

On the other hand, Beth Garrington hardly seemed the type to make it an early night. She might well still be awake, perhaps watching television where the noise wouldn't disturb her guest. In any event, Lisette didn't want to go back to sleep just yet.

She climbed out of bed, realizing that she'd only half undressed before falling asleep. Pulling off bra and panties, Lisette slipped into the antique nightdress of ribbons and lace she'd brought along. She hadn't thought to pack slippers or a robe, but it was a warm night, and the white cotton gown was modest enough for a peek into the hall.

There was a ribbon of light edging the door of the room at the far end of the hall. The rest of the hallway lay in darkness. Lisette stepped quietly from her room. Since Beth hadn't mentioned other guests, and the servants' quarters were elsewhere, presumably the light was coming from her hostess's bedroom and indicated she might still be awake. Lisette decided she really should make the effort to meet her hostess while in a conscious state.

She heard a faint sound of music as she tiptoed down the hallway. The door to the room was ajar, and the music came from within. She was in luck; Beth must still be up. At the doorway she knocked softly.

"Beth? Are you awake? It's Lisette."

There was no answer, but the door swung open at her touch.

Lisette started to call out again, but her voice froze in her throat. She recognized the tune she heard, and she knew this room. When she entered the bedroom, she could no more alter her actions than she could control the course of her dreams.

It was a large bedroom, entirely furnished in the mode of the late Victorian period. The windows were curtained, and the room's only light came from a candle upon a night table beside the huge four-poster bed. An antique gold pocket watch lay upon the night table also, and the watch was chiming an old music-box tune.

Lisette crossed the room, praying that this was no more than another vivid recurrence of her nightmare. She reached the night table and saw that the watch's hands pointed toward midnight. The chimes stopped. She picked up the watch and examined the picture that she knew would be inside the watchcase.

The picture was a photograph of herself.

Lisette let the watch clatter onto the table, stared in terror at the four-poster bed.

From within, a hand drew back the bed curtains.

Lisette wished she could scream, could awaken.

Sweeping aside the curtains, the occupant of the bed sat up and gazed at her.

And Lisette stared back at herself.

"Can't you drive a bit faster than this?"

Inspector Bradley resisted the urge to wink at Detective Sergeant Wharton. "Sit back, Dr Magnus. We'll be there in good time. I trust you'll have rehearsed some apologies for when we disrupt a peaceful household in the middle of the night."

"I only pray such apologies will be necessary," Dr Magnus said, continuing to sit forward as if that would inspire the driver to go faster.

It hadn't been easy, Dr Magnus reflected. He dare not tell them the truth. He suspected that Bradley had agreed to making a late night call on Beth Garrington more to check out his alibi than from any credence he gave to Magnus's improvised tale.

Buried all day in frenzied research, Dr Magnus hadn't listened to the news, had ignored the tawdry London tabloids with their lurid headlines: "Naked Beauty Slashed in Tub" "Nude Model Slain in Bath" "Party Girl Suicide or Ripper's Victim?" The shock of learning of Danielle's death was seconded by the shock of discovering that he was one of the "important leads" police were following.

It had taken all his powers of persuasion to convince them to release him—or, at least, to accompany him to the house in Maida Vale. Ironically, he and Lisette were the only ones who could account for each other's presence elsewhere at the time of Danielle's death. While the CID might have been sceptical as to the nature of their late night session at Dr Magnus's office, there were a few corroborating details. A barman at the Catherine Wheel had remembered the distinguished gent with the beard leaving after his lady friend had dropped off of a sudden. The cleaning lady had heard voices and left his office undisturbed. This much they'd already checked, in verifying Lisette's whereabouts that night. Half a dozen harassed records clerks could testify as to Dr Magnus's presence for today.

Dr Magnus grimly reviewed the results of his research. There was an Elisabeth Beresford, born in London in 1879, of a well-to-do family who lived in Cheyne Row on the Chelsea Embankment. Elisabeth Beresford married a Captain Donald Stapledon in 1899 and moved to India with her husband. She returned to London, evidently suffering from consumption contracted while abroad, and died in 1900. She was buried in Highgate Cemetery. That much Dr Magnus had initially learned with some difficulty. From that basis he had pressed on for additional corroborating details, both from Lisette's released memories and from research into records of the period.

It had been particularly difficult to trace the subsequent branches of the family—something he must do in order to establish that Elisabeth Beresford could not have been an ancestress of Lisette Seyrig. And it disturbed him that he had been unable to locate Elisabeth Stapledon née Beresford's tomb in Highgate Cemetery.

Last night he had pushed Lisette as relentlessly as he dared. Out of her resurfacing visions of horror he finally found a clue. These were not images from nightmare, not symbolic representations of buried fears. They were literal memories.

Because of the sensation involved and the considerable station of the families concerned, public records had discreetly avoided reference to the tragedy, as had the better newspapers. The yellow journals were less reticent, and here Dr Magnus began to know fear.

Elisabeth Stapledon had been buried alive.

At her final wishes, the body had not been embalmed. The papers suggested that this was a clear premonition of her fate, and quoted passages from Edgar Allan Poe. Captain Stapledon paid an evening visit to his wife's tomb and discovered her wandering in a dazed condition about the graves. This was more than a month after her entombment.

The newspapers were full of pseudo-scientific theories, spiritualist explanations and long accounts of Indian mystics who had remained in a state of suspended animation for weeks on end. No one seems to have explained exactly how Elisabeth Stapledon escaped from both coffin and crypt, but it was supposed that desperate strength had wrenched loose the screws, while providentially the crypt had not been properly locked after a previous visit.

Husband and wife understandably went abroad immediately afterward, in order to escape publicity and for Elisabeth Stapledon to recover from her ordeal. This she very quickly did, but evidently the shock was more than Captain Stapledon could endure. He died in 1902, and his wife returned to London soon after, inheriting his extensive fortune and properties, including their house in Maida Vale. When she later inherited her own family's estate—her sole brother fell in the Boer War—she was a lady of great wealth.

Elisabeth Stapledon became one of the most notorious hostesses of the Edwardian era and on until the close of the First World War. Her beauty was considered remarkable, and men marvelled while her rivals bemoaned that she scarcely seemed to age with the passing years. After the War she left London to travel about the exotic East. In 1924 news came of her death in India.

Her estate passed to her daughter, Jane Stapledon, born abroad in 1901. While Elisabeth Stapledon made occasional references to her daughter, Jane was raised and educated in Europe and never seemed to have come to London until her arrival in 1925. Some had suggested that the mother had wished to keep her daughter pure from her own Bohemian life style, but when Jane Stapledon appeared, it seemed more likely that her mother's motives for her seclusion had been born of jealousy. Jane Stapledon had all her mother's beauty—indeed, her older admirers vowed she was the very image of Elisabeth in her youth. She also had inherited her mother's taste for wild living; with a new circle of friends from her own age group, she took up where her mother had left off. The newspapers were particularly scandalized by her association with Aleister Crowley and others of his circle. Although her dissipations bridged the years of Flaming Youth to the Lost Generation, even her enemies had to admit she carried her years extremely well. In 1943 Jane Stapledon was missing and presumed dead after an air raid levelled and burned a section of London where she had gone to dine with friends.

Papers in the hands of her solicitor left her estate to a daughter living in America, Julia Weatherford, born in Miami in 1934. Evidently her mother had enjoyed a typical whirlwind resort romance with an American millionaire while wintering in Florida. Their marriage was a secret one, annulled following Julia's birth, and her daughter had been left with her former husband. Julia Weatherford arrived from the States early in 1946. Any doubts as to the authenticity of her claim were instantly banished, for she was the very picture of her mother in her younger days. Julia again seemed to have the family's wild streak, and she carried on the tradition of wild parties and bizarre acquaintances through the Beat Generation to the Flower Children. Her older friends thought it amazing that Julia in a minidress might easily be mistaken as being of the same age group as her young, pot-smoking, hippie friends. But it may have been that at last her youth began to fade, because since 1967 Julia Weatherford had been living more or less in seclusion in Europe, occasionally visited by her niece.

Her niece, Beth Garrington, born in 1950, was the orphaned daughter of Julia's American half-sister and a wealthy young Englishman from Julia's collection. After her parents' death in a plane crash in 1970, Beth had become her aunt's *protégée*, and carried on the mad life in London. It was apparent that Beth Garrington would inherit her aunt's property as well. It was also apparent that she was the spitting image of her Aunt Julia when the latter was her age. It would be most interesting to see the two of them together. And that, of course, no one had ever done.

At first Dr Magnus had been unwilling to accept the truth of the dread secret he had uncovered. And yet, with the knowledge of Lisette's released memories, he knew there could be no other conclusion.

It was astonishing how thoroughly a woman who thrived on notoriety could avoid having her photographs published. After all, changing fashions and new hair styles, careful adjustments with cosmetics, could only do so much, and while the mind's eye had an inaccurate memory, a camera lens did not. Dr Magnus did succeed in finding a few photographs through persistent research. Given a good theatrical costume and makeup crew, they all might have been taken of the same woman on the same day.

They might also all have been taken of Lisette Seyrig.

However, Dr Magnus knew that it *would* be possible to see Beth Garrington and Lisette Seyrig together.

And he prayed he would be in time to prevent this.

With this knowledge tormenting his thoughts, it was a miracle that Dr Magnus had held onto sanity well enough to persuade New Scotland Yard to make this late night drive to Maida Vale—desperate, in view of what he knew to be true. He had suffered a shock as severe as any that night when they told him at last where Lisette had gone.

"She's quite all right. She's staying with a friend."

"Might I ask where?"

"A chauffered Rolls picked her up. We checked registration, and it belongs to a Miss Elisabeth Garrington in Maida Vale."

Dr Magnus had been frantic then, had demanded that they take him there instantly. A telephone call informed them that Miss Seyrig was sleeping under sedation and could not be disturbed; she would return his call in the morning.

Controlling his panic, Dr Magnus had managed to contrive a disjointed tangle of half-truths and plausible lies—anything to convince them to get over to the Garrington house as quickly as possible. They already knew he was one of those occult kooks. Very well, he assured them that Beth Garrington was involved in a secret society of drug fiends and satanists (all true enough), that Danielle and Lisette had been lured to their most recent orgy for unspeakable purposes. Lisette had been secretly drugged, but Danielle had escaped to carry her roommate home before they could be used for whatever depraved rites awaited them—perhaps ritual sacrifice. Danielle had been murdered—either to shut her up or as part of the ritual—and now they had Lisette in their clutches as well.

All very melodramatic, but enough of it was true. Inspector Bradley knew of the sex and drugs orgies that took place there, but there was firm pressure from higher up to look the other way. Further, he knew enough about some of the more bizzare cult groups in London to consider that ritual murder was quite feasible, given the proper combination of sick minds and illegal drugs. And while it hadn't been made public, the medical examiner was of the opinion that the slashes to the Borland girl's throat and wrists had been an attempt to disguise the fact that she had already bled to death from two deep punctures through the jugular vein.

A demented killer, obviously. A ritual murder? You couldn't discount it just yet. Inspector Bradley had ordered a car.

"Who are you, Lisette Seyrig, that you wear my face?"

Beth Garrington rose sinuously from her bed. She was dressed in an off-the-shoulder nightgown of antique lace, much the same as that which Lisette wore. Her green eyes—the eyes behind the mask that had so shaken Lisette when last they'd met—held her in their spell.

"When first faithful Adrian swore he'd seen my double, I thought his brain had begun to reel with final madness. But after he followed you to your little gallery and brought me there to see your portrait, I knew I had encountered something beyond even my experience."

Lisette stood frozen with dread fascination as her nightmare came to life. Her twin paced about her, appraising her coolly as a serpent considers its hypnotized victim.

"Who are you, Lisette Seyrig, that yours is the face I have seen in my dreams, the face that haunted my nightmares as I lay dying, the face that I thought was my own?"

Lisette forced her lips to speak. "*Who* are you?"

"My name? I change that whenever it becomes prudent for me to do so. Tonight I am Beth Garrington. Long ago I was Elisabeth Beresford."

"How can this be possible?" Lisette hoped she was dealing with a madwoman, but knew her hope was false.

"A spirit came to me in my dreams and slowly stole away my mortal life, in return giving me eternal life. You understand what I say, even though your reason insists that such things cannot be."

She unfastened Lisette's gown and let it fall to the floor, then did the same with her own. Standing face to face, their nude bodies seemed one a reflection of the other.

Elisabeth took Lisette's face in her hands and kissed her full on the lips. The kiss was a long one; her breath was cold in Lisette's mouth. When Elisabeth released her lips and gazed longingly into her eyes, Lisette saw the pointed fangs that now curved downward from her upper jaw.

"Will you cry out, I wonder? If so, let it be in ecstasy and not in fear. I shan't drain you and discard you as I did your silly friend. No, Lisette, my new-found sister. I shall take your life in tiny kisses from night to night—kisses that you will long for with your entire being. And in the end you shall pass over to serve me as my willing chattel—as have the few others I have chosen over the years."

Lisette trembled beneath her touch, powerless to break away. From the buried depths of her unconscious mind, understanding slowly emerged. She did not resist when Elisabeth led her to the bed and lay down beside her on the silken sheets. Lisette was past knowing fear.

Elisabeth stretched her naked body upon Lisette's warmer flesh, lying between her thighs as would a lover. Her cool fingers caressed Lisette; her kisses teased a path from her belly across her breasts and to the hollow of her throat.

Elisabeth paused and gazed into Lisette's eyes. Her fangs gleamed with a reflection of the inhuman lust in her expression.

"And now I give you a kiss sweeter than any passion your mortal brain dare imagine, Lisette Seyrig—even as once I first received such a kiss from a dream-spirit whose eyes stared into mine from my own face. Why have you haunted my dreams, Lisette Seyrig?"

Lisette returned her gaze silently, without emotion. Nor did she flinch when Elisabeth's lips closed tightly against her throat, and the only sound was a barely perceptible tearing, like the bursting of a maidenhead, and the soft movement of suctioning lips.

Elisabeth suddenly broke away with an inarticulate cry of pain. Her lips smeared with scarlet, she stared down at Lisette in bewildered fear. Lisette, blood streaming from the wound on her throat, stared back at her with a smile of unholy hatred.

"*What* are you, Lisette Seyrig?"

"I am Elisabeth Beresford." Lisette's tone was implacable. "In another lifetime you drove my soul from my body and stole my flesh for your own. Now I have come back to reclaim that which once was mine."

Elisabeth sought to leap away, but Lisette's arms embraced her with sudden, terrible strength—pulling their naked bodies together in a horrid imitation of two lovers at the moment of ecstasy.

The scream that echoed into the night was not one of ecstasy.

At the sound of the scream—afterward they never agreed whether it was two voices together or only one—Inspector Bradley ceased listening to the maid's outraged protests and burst past her into the house.

"Upstairs! On the double!" He ordered needlessly. Already Dr Magnus had lunged past him and was sprinting up the stairway.

"I think it came from the next floor up! Check inside all the rooms!" Later he cursed himself for not posting a man at the door, for by the time he was again able to think rationally, there was no trace of the servants.

In the master bedroom at the end of the third-floor hallway, they found two bodies behind the curtains of the big four-poster bed. One had only just been murdered; her nude body was drenched in the blood from her torn throat—seemingly far too much blood for one body. The other body was a desiccated corpse, obviously dead for a great many years. The dead girl's limbs obscenely embraced the mouldering cadaver that lay atop her, and her teeth, in final spasm, were locked in the lich's throat. As they gaped in horror, clumps of hair and bits of dried skin could be seen to drop away.

Detective Sergeant Wharton looked away and vomited on the floor.

"I owe you a sincere apology, Dr Magnus." Inspector Bradley's face was grim. "You were right. Ritual murder by a gang of sick degenerates. Detective Sergeant! Leave off that, and put out an all-points bulletin for Beth Garrington. And round up anyone else you find here! Move, man!"

"If only I'd understood in time," Dr Magnus muttered. He was obviously to the point of collapse.

"No, *I* should have listened to you sooner," Bradley growled. "We might have been in time to prevent this. The devils must have fled down some servants' stairway when they heard us burst in. I confess I've bungled this badly."

"She was a vampire, you see," Dr Magnus told him dully, groping to explain. "A vampire loses its soul when it becomes one of the undead. But the soul is deathless; it lives on even when its previous incarnation has become a soulless demon. Elisabeth Beresford's soul lived on, until Elisabeth Beresford found reincarnation, in Lisette Seyrig. Don't you see? Elisabeth Beresford met her own reincarnation, and that meant destruction for them both."

Inspector Bradley had been only half listening. "Dr Magnus, you've done all you can. I think you should go down to the car with Detective Sergeant Wharton now and rest until the ambulance arrives."

"But you must see that I was right!" Dr Magnus pleaded. Madness danced in his eyes. "If the soul is immortal and infinite, then time has no meaning for the soul. Elisabeth Beresford was haunting herself."

Basil Copper

Doctor Porthos

Basil Copper has been described as "Britain's leading purveyor of the macabre" and by the Los Angeles Herald-Tribune *as "the best writer in the genre since H.P. Lovecraft."*

Since selling his first story to The Pan Book of Horror Stories *in 1964, Copper has written more than eighty books, including the non-fiction volume,* The Vampire, *and his work has been anthologised widely and adapted for television and radio.*

In 1991, his story 'The Recompensing of Albano Pizar' was dramatised on the BBC Radio 4 series Fear on Four *under the title 'Invitation to the Vaults', and after a ten year delay, his magnum opus of the supernatural,* The Black Death, *was recently published in America.*

'Doctor Porthos' is another vampire story with a surprising twist at the end. It was bought by Universal for the 1970s television series Rod Serling's Night Gallery, *but unlike another Copper story, 'Camera Obscura', it was never filmed.*

I

NERVOUS DEBILITY, THE doctor says. And yet Angelina has never been ill in her life. Nervous debility! Something far more powerful is involved here; I am left wondering if I should not call in specialist advice. Yet we are so remote and Dr Porthos is well spoken of by the local people. Why on earth did we ever come to this house? Angelina was perfectly well until then. It is extraordinary to think that two months can have wrought such a change in my wife.

In the town she was lively and vivacious; yet now I can hardly bear to look at her without profound emotion. Her cheeks are sunken and pale, her eyes dark and tired, her bloom quite gone at twenty-five. Could it be something in the air of the house? It seems barely possible. But in that case Dr Porthos' ministrations should have proved effective. But so far all his skills have been powerless to produce any change for the better. If it had not been for the terms of my uncle's will we would never have come at all.

Friends may call it cupidity, the world may think what it chooses, but the plain truth is that I needed the money. My own health is far from robust and long hours in the family business—ours is an honoured and well-established counting house—had made it perfectly clear to me that I must seek some other mode of life. And yet I could not afford to retire; the terms of my uncle's will, as retailed to me by the family solicitor, afforded the perfect solution.

An annuity—a handsome annuity to put it bluntly—but with the proviso that my wife and I should reside in the old man's house for a period of not less than five years from the date the terms of the will became effective. I hesitated long; both my wife and I were fond of town life and my uncle's estate was in a remote area, where living for the country people was primitive and amenities few. As I had understood it from the solicitor, the house itself had not even the benefit of gas-lighting; in summer it was not so bad but the long months of winter would be melancholy indeed with only the glimmer of candles and the pale sheen of oil lamps to relieve the gloom of the lonely old place.

I debated with Angelina and then set off one week-end alone for a tour of the estate. I had cabled ahead and after a long and cold railway journey which itself occupied most of the day, I was met at my destination by a horse and chaise. The next part of my pilgrimage occupied nearly four hours and I was dismayed on seeing into what a wild and remote region my uncle had chosen to penetrate in order to select a dwelling.

The night was dark but the moon occasionally burst its veiling of cloud to reveal in feeble detail the contours of rock and hill and tree; the chaise jolted and lurched over an unmade road, which was deeply rutted by the wheels of the few vehicles which had torn up the surface in their passing over many months. My solicitor had wired to an old friend, Dr Porthos, to whose good offices I owed my mode of transport, and he had promised to greet me on arrival at the village nearest the estate.

Sure enough, he came out from under the great porch of the timbered hostelry as our carriage grated into the inn-yard. He was a tall, spare man, with square pince-nez which sat firmly on his thin nose; he wore a many-pleated cape like an ostler and the green top hat, worn rakishly over one eye gave him a somewhat dissipated look. He greeted me effusively but there was something about the man which did not endear him to me.

There was nothing that one could isolate. It was just his general manner; perhaps the coldness of his hand which struck my palm with the clamminess of a fish. Then too, his eyes had a most disconcerting way of looking over the tops of his glasses; they were a filmy grey and their piercing glance seemed to root one to the spot. To my dismay I learned that I was not yet at my destination. The estate was still some way off, said the doctor, and we would have to stay the night at the inn. My ill-temper at his remarks was soon dispelled by the roaring fire and the good food with which he plied me; there were few travellers at this time of year and we were the only ones taking dinner in the vast oak-panelled dining room.

The doctor had been my uncle's medical attendant and though it was many years since I had seen my relative I was curious to know what sort of person he had been.

"The Baron was a great man in these parts," said Porthos. His genial manner emboldened me to ask a question to which I had long been awaiting an answer.

"Of what did my uncle die?" I asked.

Firelight flickered through the gleaming redness of Dr Porthos' wineglass and tinged his face with amber as he replied simply, "Of a lacking of richness in the blood. A fatal quality in his immediate line, I might say."

I pondered for a moment. "Why do you think he chose me as his heir?" I added.

Dr Porthos' answer was straight and clear and given without hesitation.

"You were a different branch of the family," he said.."New blood, my dear sir. The Baron was most particular on that account. He wanted to carry on the great tradition."

He cut off any further questions by rising abruptly. "Those were the Baron's own words as he lay dying. And now we must retire as we still have a fair journey before us in the morning."

II

Dr Porthos' words come back to me in my present trouble. "Blood, new blood . . ." What if this be concerned with those dark legends the local people tell about the house? One hardly knows what to think in this atmosphere. My inspection of the house with Dr Porthos confirmed my worst fears; sagging lintels, mouldering cornices, worm-eaten panelling. The only servitors a middle-aged couple, husband and wife, who have been caretakers here since the Baron's death; the local people sullen and unco-operative, so Porthos says. Certainly, the small hamlet a mile or so from the mansion had every door and window shut as we clattered past and not a soul was stirring. The house has a Gothic beauty, I suppose, viewed from a distance; it is of no great age, being largely re-built on the remains of an older pile destroyed by fire. The restorer—whether he be my uncle or some older resident I have not bothered to discover—had the fancy of adding turrets, a draw-bridge with castellated towers and a moated surround. Our footsteps echoed mournfully over this as we turned to inspect the grounds.

I was surprised to see marble statuary and worn obelisks, all tumbled and awry, as though the uneasy dead were bursting from the soil, protruding over an ancient moss-grown wall adjoining the courtyard of the house.

Dr Porthos smiled sardonically.

"The old family burial ground," he explained. "Your uncle is interred here. He said he likes to be near the house."

III

Well, it is done; we came not two months since and then began the profound and melancholy change of which I have already spoken. Not just the atmosphere—though the very stones of the house seem steeped in evil whispers—but the surroundings, the dark, unmoving trees, even the furniture, seem to exude something inimical to life as we knew it; as it is still known to those fortunate enough to dwell in towns.

A poisonous mist rises from the moat at dusk; it seems to doubly emphasize our isolation. The presence of Angelina's own maid and a handyman who was in my father's employ before me, do little to dispel the ambiance of this place. Even their sturdy matter of factness seems affected by a miasma that wells from the pores of the building. It has become so manifest of late that I even welcome the daily visits of Dr Porthos, despite the fact that I suspect him to be the author of our troubles.

They began a week after our arrival when Angelina failed to awake by my side as usual; I shook her to arouse her and my screams must have awakened the maid. I think I fainted then and came to myself in the great morning room; the bed had been awash with blood, which stained the sheets and pillows around my dear wife's head; Porthos' curious grey eyes had a steely look in them which I had never seen before. He administered a powerful medicine and had then turned to attend to me.

Whatever had attacked Angelina had teeth like the sharpest canine, Porthos said; he had found two distinct punctures in Angelina's throat, sufficient to account for the quantities of blood. Indeed, there had been so much of it that my own hands and linen were stained with it where I had touched her; I think it was this which had made me cry so violently. Porthos had announced that he would sit up by the patient that night.

Angelina was still asleep, as I discovered when I tiptoed in later. Porthos had administered a sleeping draught and had advised me to take the same, to settle my nerves, but I declined. I said I would wait up with him. The doctor had some theory about rats or other nocturnal creatures and sat long in the library looking through some of the Baron's old books on natural history. The man's attitude puzzles me; what sort of creature would attack Angelina in her own bedroom? Looking at Porthos' strange eyes, my old fears are beginning to return, bringing with them new ones.

IV

There have been three more attacks, extending over a fortnight. My darling grows visibly weaker, though Porthos has been to the nearest town for more powerful drugs and other remedies. I am in purgatory; I have not known such dark hours in my life until now. Yet Angelina herself insists that we should stay to see this grotesque nightmare through. The first evening of our vigil both Porthos and I slept; and in the morning the result was as the night before. Considerable emissions of blood and the bandage covering the wound had been removed to allow the creature access to the punctures. I hardly dare conjecture what manner of beast could have done this.

I was quite worn out and on the evening of the next day I agreed to Porthos' suggestion that I should take a sleeping draught. Nothing happened for several nights and Angelina began to recover; then the terror struck again. And so it will go on, my reeling senses tell me. I daren't trust Porthos and on the other hand I cannot accuse him before the members of my household. We are isolated here and any mistake I make might be fatal.

On the last occasion I almost had him. I woke at dawn and found Porthos stretched on the bed, his long, dark form quivering, his hands at Angelina's throat. I struck at him, for I did not know who it was, being half asleep, and he turned, his grey eyes glowing in the dim room. He had a hypodermic syringe half full of blood in his hand. I am afraid I dashed it to the floor and shattered it beneath my heel.

In my own heart I am convinced I have caught this creature which has been plaguing us, but how to prove it? Dr Porthos is staying in the house now; I dare not sleep and continually refuse the potions he urgently presses upon me. How long before he destroys me as well as Angelina? Was man ever in such an appalling situation since the world began?

I sit and watch Porthos, who stares at me sideways with those curious eyes, his inexpressive face seeming to hint that he can afford to watch and wait and that his time is coming; my pale wife, in her few intervals of consciousness sits and fearfully watches both of us. Yet I cannot even confide in her for she would think me mad. I try to calm my racing brain. Sometimes I think I shall go insane altogether, the nights are so long. God help me.

V

It is over. The crisis has come and gone. I have laid the mad demon which has us in thrall. I caught him at it. Porthos writhed as I got my hands at his throat. I would have killed him at his foul work, the syringe glinted in his hand. Now he has slipped aside, eluded me for the moment. My cries brought in the servants who have my express instructions to hunt him down. He shall not escape me this time. I pace the corridors of this worm-eaten mansion and when I have cornered him I shall destroy him. Angelina shall live! And my hands will perform the healing work of his destruction . . . But now I must rest. Already it is dawn again. I will sit in this chair by the pillar, where I can watch the hall. I sleep.

VI

Later. I awake to pain and cold. I am lying on earth. Something slippery trickles over my hand. I open my eyes. I draw my hand across my mouth. It comes away scarlet. I can see more clearly now. Angelina is here too. She looks terrified but somehow sad and composed. She is holding the arm of Dr Porthos.

He is poised above me, his face looking satanic in the dim light of the crypt beneath the house. He whirls a mallet while shriek after shriek disturbs the silence of this place. Dear Christ, the stake is against MY BREAST!

Bram Stoker

Dracula's Guest

Abraham Stoker (1847–1912) will always be remembered as the author of Dracula, *the most famous and influential vampire novel ever written. Born in Dublin, and employed as a civil servant, Stoker's first love was always the theatre. In 1877 he moved to London and became the manager of the greatest actor-producer of his age, Henry Irving.*

Although he had written the occasional short story, it was during this period that Stoker really began to concentrate on his fiction, publishing Dracula *in 1897. Unfortunately, the novels that followed—*The Mystery of the Sea, The Jewel of the Seven Stars, The Lady of the Shroud, *and* The Lair of the White Worm*—never achieved the same success.*

'Dracula's Guest' is a self-contained chapter that was originally part of Stoker's manuscript for Dracula *but was omitted because of the length of the published book. It first appeared in a posthumous collection entitled* Dracula's Guest and Other Weird Stories *(1914), which also included other such excellent tales as 'The Judge's House', 'The Burial of the Rats' and 'The Squaw'. On September 14th, 1927, a special souvenir edition of 1,000 numbered copies was issued on the occasion of the 250th London performance of the play* Dracula. *When the members of the audience opened their mystery packet they found between the covers of the book a black bat, powered by elastic, which flew out as the volume was opened.*

Dracula *has of course been the influence for countless movies, and the atmospheric story that follows was also credited as the basis for* Dracula's Daughter *(1936), Universal's belated sequel to the 1930 original starring* Bela Lugosi.

WHEN WE STARTED for our drive the sun was shining brightly on Munich, and the air was full of the joyousness of early summer. Just as we were about to depart, Herr Delbrück (the maître d'hôtel of the Quatre Saisons, where I was staying) came down, bareheaded, to the carriage and, after wishing me a pleasant drive, said to the coachman, still holding his hand on the handle of the carriage door:

"Remember you are back by nightfall. The sky looks bright but there is a shiver in the north wind that says there may be a sudden storm. But I am sure you will not be late." Here he smiled, and added, "for you know what night it is."

Johann answered with an emphatic, "ja, mein Herr," and, touching his hat, drove off quickly. When we had cleared the town, I said, after signalling to him to stop:

"Tell me, Johann, what is to-night?"

He crossed himself, as he answered laconically:

"Walpurgis Nacht." Then he took out his watch, a great, old-fashioned German silver thing as big as a turnip, and looked at it, with his eyebrows gathered together and a little impatient shrug of his shoulders. I realised that this was his way of respectfully protesting against the unnecessary delay, and sank back in the carriage, merely motioning him to proceed. He started off rapidly, as if to make up for lost time. Every now and then the horses seemed to throw up their heads and sniff the air suspiciously. On such occasions I often looked round in alarm. The road was pretty bleak, for we were traversing a sort of high, wind-swept plateau. As we drove, I saw a road that looked but little used, and which seemed to dip through a little, winding valley. It looked so inviting that, even at the risk of offending him, I called Johann to stop—and when he had pulled up, I told him I would like to drive down that road. He made all sorts of excuses, and frequently crossed himself as he spoke. This somewhat piqued my curiosity, so I asked him various questions. He answered fencingly, and repeatedly looked at his watch in protest. Finally I said:

"Well, Johann, I want to go down this road. I shall not ask you to come unless you like; but tell me why you do not like to go, that is all I ask." For answer he seemed to throw himself off the box, so quickly did he reach the ground. Then he stretched out his hands appealingly to me, and implored me not to go. There was just enough of English mixed with the German for me to understand the drift of his talk. He seemed always just about to tell me something—the very idea of which evidently frightened him—but each time he pulled himself up, saying, as he crossed himself:

"Walpurgis Nacht!"

I tried to argue with him, but it was difficult to argue with a man when I did not know his language. The advantage certainly rested with him, for although he began to speak in English, of a very crude and broken kind, he always got excited and broke into his native tongue—and every time he did so, he looked at his watch. Then the horses became restless and sniffed the air. At this he grew very pale, and, looking around in a frightened way, he suddenly jumped forward, took them by the bridles and led them on some twenty feet. I followed, and asked why he had done this. For answer he crossed himself, pointed to the spot we had left and drew his carriage in the direction of the other road, indicating a cross, and said, first in German, then in English: "Buried him—him what killed themselves."

I remembered the old custom of burying suicides at cross-roads: "Ah! I see, a suicide. How interesting!" But for the life of me I could not make out why the horses were frightened.

Whilst we were talking, we heard a sort of sound between a yelp and a bark. It was far away; but the horses got very restless, and it took Johann all his time to quiet them. He was pale, and said: "It sounds like a wolf—but yet there are no wolves here now."

"No?" I said, questioning him; "isn't it long since the wolves were so near the city?"

"Long, long," he answered, "in the spring and summer; but with the snow the wolves have been here not so long."

Whilst he was petting the horses and trying to quiet them, dark clouds drifted rapidly across the sky. The sunshine passed away, and a breath of cold wind seemed to drift past us. It was only a breath, however, and more in the nature of a warning than a fact, for the sun came out brightly again. Johann looked under his lifted hand at the horizon and said:

"The storm of snow, he comes before long time."

Then he looked at his watch again, and, straightway holding his reins firmly—for the horses were still pawing the ground restlessly and shaking their heads—he climbed to his box as though the time had come for proceeding on our journey.

I felt a little obstinate and did not at once get into the carriage.

"Tell me," I said, "about this place where the road leads," and I pointed down.

Again he crossed himself and mumbled a prayer, before he answered: "It is unholy."

"What is unholy?" I enquired.

"The village."

"Then there is a village?"

"No, no. No one lives there hundreds of years."

My curiosity was piqued: "But you said there was a village."

"There was."

"Where is it now?"

Whereupon he burst out into a long story in German and English, so mixed up that I could not quite understand exactly what he said, but roughly I gathered that long ago, hundreds of years, men had died there and been buried in their graves; and sounds were heard under the clay, and when the graves were opened, men and women were found rosy with life, and their mouths red with blood. And so, in haste to save their lives (aye, and their souls!—and here he crossed himself) those who were left fled away to other places, where the living lived, and the dead were dead and not—not something. He was evidently afraid to speak the last words. As he proceeded with his narration, he grew more and more excited. It seemed as if his imagination had got hold of him, and he ended in a perfect paroxysm of fear—white-faced, perspiring, trembling and looking round him, as if expecting that some dreadful presence would manifest itself there in the bright sunshine on the open plain. Finally, in an agony of desperation, he cried:

"Walpurgis Nacht!" and pointed to the carriage for me to get in. All my English blood rose at this, and, standing back, I said:

"You are afraid, Johann—you are afraid. Go home; I shall return alone; the walk will do me good." The carriage door was open. I took from the seat my oak walking-stick—which I always carry on my holiday excursions—and closed the door, pointing back to Munich, and said, "Go home, Johann—Walpurgis Nacht doesn't concern Englishmen."

The horses were now more restive than ever, and Johann was trying to hold them in, while excitedly imploring me not to do anything so foolish. I pitied the poor fellow, he was so deeply in earnest; but all the same I could not help laughing. His English was quite gone now. In his anxiety he had forgotten that his only means of making me understand was to talk my language, so he jabbered away in his native German. It began to be a little tedious. After giving the direction, "Home!" I turned to go down the cross-road into the valley.

With a despairing gesture, Johann turned his horses towards

Munich. I leaned on my stick and looked after him. He went slowly along the road for a while: then there came over the crest of the hill a man tall and thin. I could see so much in the distance. When he drew near the horses, they began to jump and kick about, then to scream with terror. Johann could not hold them in; they bolted down the road, running away madly. I watched them out of sight, then looked for the stranger, but I found that he, too, was gone.

With a light heart I turned down the side road through the deepening valley to which Johann had objected. There was not the slightest reason, that I could see, for his objection; and I daresay I tramped for a couple of hours without thinking of time or distance, and certainly without seeing a person or a house. So far as the place was concerned, it was desolation itself. But I did not notice this particularly till, on turning a bend in the road, I came upon a scattered fringe of wood; then I recognised that I had been impressed unconsciously by the desolation of the region through which I had passed.

I sat down to rest myself, and began to look around. It struck me that it was considerably colder than it had been at the commence-ment of my walk—a sort of sighing sound seemed to be around me, with, now and then, high overhead, a sort of muffled roar. Looking upwards I noticed that great thick clouds were drifting rapidly across the sky from North to South at a great height. There were signs of coming storm in some lofty stratum of the air. I was a little chilly, and, thinking that it was the sitting still after the exercise of walking, I resumed my journey.

The ground I passed over was now much more picturesque. There were no striking objects that the eye might single out; but in all there was a charm of beauty. I took little heed of time and it was only when the deepening twilight forced itself upon me that I began to think of how I should find my way home. The brightness of the day had gone. The air was cold, and the drifting of clouds high overhead was more marked. They were accompanied by a sort of far-away rushing sound, through which seemed to come at intervals that mysterious cry which the driver had said came from a wolf. For a while I hesitated. I had said I would see the deserted village, so on I went, and presently came on a wide stretch of open country, shut in by hills all around. Their sides were covered with trees which spread down to the plain, dotting, in clumps, the gentler slopes and hollows which showed here and there. I followed with my eye the winding of the road, and saw that it curved close to one of the densest of these clumps and was lost behind it.

As I looked there came a cold shiver in the air, and the snow began to fall. I thought of the miles and miles of bleak country I had passed, and then hurried on to seek the shelter of the wood in front. Darker and darker grew the sky, and faster and heavier fell the snow, till the earth before and around me was a glistening white carpet the further edge of which was lost in misty vagueness. The road was here but crude, and when on the level its boundaries were not so marked as when it passed through the cuttings, and in a little while I found that I must have strayed from it, for I missed underfoot the hard surface, and my feet sank deeper in the grass and moss. Then the wind grew stronger and blew with ever increasing force, till I was fain to run before it. The air became icy cold, and in spite of my exercise I began to suffer. The snow was now falling so thickly and whirling around me in such rapid eddies that I could hardly keep my eyes open. Every now and then the heavens were torn asunder by vivid lightning, and in the flashes I could see ahead of me a great mass of trees, chiefly yew and cypress and heavily coated with snow.

I was soon amongst the shelter of the trees, and there, in comparative silence, I could hear the rush of the wind high overhead. Presently the blackness of the storm had become merged in the darkness of the night. By-and-by the storm seemed to be passing away: it now only came in fierce puffs or blasts. At such moments the weird sound of the wolf appeared to be echoed by many similar sounds around me.

Now and again, through the black mass of drifting cloud, came a straggling ray of moonlight, which lit up the expanse, and showed me that I was at the edge of a dense mass of cypress and yew trees. As the snow had ceased to fall, I walked out from the shelter and began to investigate more closely. It appeared to me that, amongst so many old foundations as I had passed, there might be still standing a house in which, though in ruins, I could find some sort of shelter for a while. As I skirted the edge of the copse, I found that a low wall encircled it and following this I presently found an opening. Here the cypresses formed an alley leading up to a square mass of some kind of building. Just as I caught sight of this, however, the drifting clouds obscured the moon, and I passed up the path in darkness. The wind must have grown colder, for I felt myself shiver as I walked; but there was hope of shelter, and I groped my way blindly on.

I stopped, for there was a sudden stillness. The storm had passed; and in sympathy with nature's silence, my heart seemed to cease to beat. But this was only momentarily; for suddenly the moonlight broke through the clouds, showing me that I was in a graveyard, and that the square object before me was a great massive tomb of marble, as white as the snow that lay on and all around it. With the moonlight

there came a fierce sigh of the storm, which appeared to resume its
course with a long, low howl, as of many dogs or wolves. I was awed
and shocked, and felt the cold perceptibly grow upon me till it seemed
to grip me by the heart. Then while the flood of moonlight still fell
on the marble tomb, the storm gave further evidence of renewing,
as though it was returning on its track. Impelled by some sort of
fascination, I approached the sepulchre to see what it was, and why
such a thing stood alone in such a place. I walked around it, and
read, over the Doric door, in German—

COUNTESS DOLINGEN OF GRATZ
IN STYRIA
SOUGHT AND FOUND DEATH
1801

On the top of the tomb, seemingly driven through the solid
marble—for the structure was composed of a few vast blocks of
stone—was a great iron spike or stake. On going to the back I saw,
graven in great Russian letters:

"The dead travel fast."

There was something so weird and uncanny about the whole thing
that it gave me a turn and made me feel quite faint. I began to wish,
for the first time, that I had taken Johann's advice. Here a thought
struck me, which came under almost mysterious circumstances and
with a terrible shock. This was Walpurgis Night!

Walpurgis Night, when, according to the belief of millions of
people, the devil was abroad—when the graves were opened and
the dead came forth and walked. When all evil things of earth and
air and water held revel. This very place the driver had specially
shunned. This was the depopulated village of centuries ago. This
was where the suicide lay; and this was the place where I was
alone—unmanned, shivering with cold in a shroud of snow with
a wild storm gathering again upon me! It took all my philosophy,
all the religion I had been taught, all my courage, not to collapse
in a paroxysm of fright.

And now a perfect tornado burst upon me. The ground shook as
though thousands of horses thundered across it; and this time the
storm bore on its icy wings, not snow, but great hailstones which
drove with such violence that they might have come from the thongs
of Balearic slingers—hailstones that beat down leaf and branch and

made the shelter of the cypresses of no more avail than though their stems were standing corn. At the first I had rushed to the nearest tree; but I was soon fain to leave it and seek the only spot that seemed to afford refuge, the deep Doric doorway of the marble tomb. There, crouching against the massive bronze door, I gained a certain amount of protection from the beating of the hailstones, for now they only drove against me as they ricocheted from the ground and the side of the marble.

As I leaned against the door, it moved slightly and opened inwards. The shelter of even a tomb was welcome in that pitiless tempest, and I was about to enter it when there came a flash of forked lightning that lit up the whole expanse of the heavens. In the instant, as I am a living man, I saw, as my eyes were turned into the darkness of the tomb, a beautiful woman, with rounded cheeks and red lips, seemingly sleeping on a bier. As the thunder broke overhead, I was grasped as by the hand of a giant and hurled out into the storm. The whole thing was so sudden that, before I could realise the shock, moral as well as physical, I found the hailstones beating me down. At the same time I had a strange dominating feeling that I was not alone. I looked towards the tomb. Just then there came another blinding flash which seemed to strike the iron stake that surmounted the tomb and to pour through to the earth, blasting and crumbling the marble, as in a burst of flame. The dead woman rose for a moment of agony, while she was lapped in the flame, and her bitter scream of pain was drowned in the thundercrash. The last thing I heard was this mingling of dreadful sound, as again I was seized in the giant-grasp and dragged away, while the hailstones beat on me, and the air around seemed reverberant with the howling of wolves. The last sight that I remembered was a vague, white, moving mass, as if all the graves around me had sent out the phantoms of their sheeted dead, and that they were closing in on me through the white cloudiness of the driving hail.

Gradually there came a sort of vague beginning of consciousness; then a sense of weariness that was dreadful. For a time I remembered nothing; but slowly my senses returned. My feet seemed positively racked with pain, yet I could not move them. They seemed to be numbed. There was an icy feeling at the back of my neck and all down my spine, and my ears, like my feet, were dead, yet in torment; but there was in my breast a sense of warmth which was, by comparison, delicious. It was as a nightmare—a physical nightmare, if one may use such an expression; for some heavy weight on my chest made it difficult for me to breathe.

This period of semi-lethargy seemed to remain a long time, and as it faded away I must have slept or swooned. Then came a sort of loathing, like the first stage of sea-sickness, and a wild desire to be free from something—I knew not what. A vast stillness enveloped me, as though all the world were asleep or dead—only broken by the low panting as of some animal close to me. I felt a warm rasping at my throat, then came a consciousness of the awful truth, which chilled me to the heart and sent the blood surging up through my brain. Some great animal was lying on me and now licking my throat. I feared to stir, for some instinct of prudence bade me lie still; but the brute seemed to realize that there was now some change in me, for it raised its head. Through my eyelashes I saw above me the two great flaming eyes of a gigantic wolf. Its sharp white teeth gleamed in the gaping red mouth, and I could feel its hot breath fierce and acrid upon me.

For another spell of time I remembered no more. Then I became conscious of a low growl, followed by a yelp, renewed again and again. Then seemingly very far away, I heard a "Holloa! holloa!" as of many voices calling in unison. Cautiously I raised my head and looked in the direction whence the sound came; but the cemetery blocked my view. The wolf still continued to yelp in a strange way, and a red glare began to move round the grove of cypresses, as though following the sound. As the voices drew closer, the wolf yelped faster and louder. I feared to make either sound or motion. Nearer came the red glow, over the white pall which stretched into the darkness around me. Then all at once from beyond the trees there came at a trot a troop of horsemen bearing torches. The wolf rose from my breast and made for the cemetery. I saw one of the horsemen (soldiers by their caps and their long military cloaks) raise his carbine and take aim. A companion knocked up his arm, and I heard the ball whizz over my head. He had evidently taken my body for that of the wolf. Another sighted the animal as it slunk away, and a shot followed. Then, at a gallop, the troop rode forward—some towards me, others following the wolf as it disappeared amongst the snow-clad cypresses.

As they drew nearer I tried to move, but was powerless, although I could see and hear all that went on around me. Two or three of the soldiers jumped from their horses and knelt beside me. One of them raised my head, and placed his hand over my heart.

"Good news, comrades!" he cried. "His heart still beats!"

Then some brandy was poured down my throat; it put vigour into me, and I was able to open my eyes fully and look around. Lights and shadows were moving among the trees, and I heard men call to one another. They drew together, uttering frightened exclamations; and the lights flashed as the others came pouring out of the cemetery pell-mell, like men possessed. When the further ones came close to us, those who were around me asked them eagerly;

"Well, have you found him?"

The reply rang out hurriedly:

"No! no! Come away quick—quick! This is no place to stay, and on this of all nights!"

"What was it?" was the question, asked in all manner of keys. The answer came variously and all indefinitely as though the men were moved by some common impulse to speak, yet were restrained by some common fear from giving their thoughts.

"It-it-indeed!" gibbered one, whose wits had plainly given out for the moment.

"A wolf—and yet not a wolf!" another put in shudderingly.

"No use trying for him without the sacred bullet," a third remarked in a more ordinary manner.

"Serve us right for coming out on this night! Truly we have earned our thousand marks!" were the ejaculations of a fourth.

"There was blood on the broken marble," another said after a pause—"the lightning never brought that there. And for him—is he safe? Look at his throat! See, comrades, the wolf has been lying on him and keeping his blood warm."

The officer looked at my throat and replied:

"He is all right; the skin is not pierced. What does it all mean? We should never have found him but for the yelping of the wolf."

"What became of it?" asked the man who was holding up my head, and who seemed the least panic-stricken of the party, for his hands were steady and without tremor. On his sleeve was the chevron of a petty officer.

"It went to its home," answered the man, whose long face was pallid, and who actually shook with terror as he glanced around him fearfully. "There are graves enough there in which it may lie. Come, comrades—come quickly! Let us leave this cursed spot."

The officer raised me to a sitting posture, as he uttered a word of command; then several men placed me upon a horse. He sprang to the saddle behind me, took me in his arms, gave the word to advance; and, turning our faces away from the cypresses, we rode away in swift, military order.

As yet my tongue refused its office, and I was perforce silent. I must have fallen asleep; for the next thing I remembered was finding myself standing up, supported by a soldier on each side of me. It was almost broad daylight, and to the north a red streak of sunlight was reflected, like a path of blood, over the waste of snow. The officer was telling the men to say nothing of what they had seen, except that they found an English stranger, guarded by a large dog.

"Dog! that was no dog," cut in the man who had exhibited such fear. "I think I know a wolf when I seen one."

The young officer answered calmly: "I said a dog."

"Dog!" reiterated the other ironically. It was evident that his courage was rising with the sun; and, pointing to me, he said, "Look at his throat. Is that the work of a dog, master?"

Instinctively I raised my hand to my throat, and as I touched it I cried out in pain. The men crowded round to look, some stooping down from their saddles; and again there came the calm voice of the young officer:

"A dog, as I said. If aught else were said we should only be laughed at."

I was then mounted behind a trooper, and we rode on into the suburbs of Munich. Here we came across a stray carriage, into which I was lifted, and it was driven off to the Quatre Saisons—the young officer accompanying me, whilst a trooper followed with his horse, and the others rode off to their barracks.

When we arrived, Herr Delbrück rushed so quickly down the steps to meet me, that it was apparent he had been watching within. Taking me by both hands he solicitously led me in. The officer saluted me and was turning to withdraw, when I recognized his purpose, and insisted that he should come to my rooms. Over a glass of wine I warmly thanked him and his brave comrades for saving me. He replied simply that he was more than glad, and that Herr Delbrück had at the first taken steps to make all the searching party pleased; at which ambiguous utterance the maître d'hôtel smiled, while the officer pleaded duty and withdrew.

"But Herr Delbrück," I enquired, "how and why was it that the soldiers searched for me?"

He shrugged his shoulders, as if in depreciation of his own deed, as he replied:

"I was so fortunate as to obtain leave from the commander of the regiment in which I served, to ask for volunteers."

"But how did you know I was lost?" I asked.

"The driver came hither with the remains of his carriage, which had been upset when the horses ran away."

"But surely you would not send a search-party of soldiers merely on this account?"

"Oh, no!" he answered; "but even before the coachman arrived, I had this telegram from the Boyar whose guest you are," and he took from his pocket a telegram which he handed to me, and I read:

BISTRITZ.

"Be careful of my guest—his safety is most precious to me. Should aught happen to him, or if he be missed, spare nothing to find him and ensure his safety. He is English and therefore adventurous. There are often dangers from snow and wolves at night. Lose not a moment if you suspect harm to him. I answer your zeal with my fortune.—Dracula."

As I held the telegram in my hand, the room seemed to whirl around me; and, if the attentive maître d'hôtel had not caught me, I think I should have fallen. There was something so strange in all this, something so weird and impossible to imagine, that there grew on me a sense of my being in some way the sport of opposite forces—the mere vague idea of which seemed in a way to paralyse me. I was certainly under some form of mysterious protection. From a distant country had come, in the very nick of time, a message that took me out of the danger of the snow-sleep and the jaws of the wolf.

Dennis Etchison

It Only Comes Out at Night

"I don't think I've ever written a vampire story" said Dennis Etchison, and he might be right. However, 'It Only Comes Out at Night' (as the title indicates) could be a vampire story, and as it's one of my favourite pieces of fiction by one of America's foremost short story writers, I decided to include it here anyway.

Etchison made his first professional sale in 1961, since when he has been published in a wide variety of magazines and anthologies. His short fiction has been collected in The Dark Country, Red Dreams *and* The Blood Kiss, *he's written several film and television scripts, five novels (three under a pseudonym), and edited a handful of anthologies. A new novel and anthology are forthcoming.*

IF YOU LEAVE L.A. by way of San Bernardino, headed for Route 66 and points east, you must cross the Mojave Desert.

Even after Needles and the border, however, there is no relief; the dry air only thins further as the long, relentless climb continues in earnest. Flagstaff is still almost two hundred miles, and Winslow, Gallup and Albuquerque are too many hours away to think of making without food, rest and, mercifully, sleep.

It is like this: the car runs hot, hotter than it ever has before, the plies of the tires expand and contract until the sidewalls begin to shimmy slightly as they spin on over the miserable Arizona roads, giving up a faint odor like burning hair from between the treads, as the windshield colors over with essence of honeybee, wasp, dragonfly, mayfly, June bug, ladybug and the like, and the radiator, clotted with the bodies of countless kamikaze insects, hisses like a moribund lizard in the sun. . . .

All of which means, of course, that if you are traveling that way between May and September, you move by night.

Only by night.

For there are, after all, dawn check-in motels, Do Not Disturb signs for bungalow doorknobs; there are diners for mid-afternoon breakfasts, coffee by the carton; there are 24-hour filling stations bright as dreams—Whiting Brothers, Conoco, Terrible Herbst—their flags as unfamiliar as their names, with ice machines, soda machines, candy machines; and there are the sudden, unexpected Rest Areas, just off the highway, with brick bathrooms and showers and electrical outlets, constructed especially for those who are weary, out of money, behind schedule. . . .

So McClay had had to learn, the hard way.

He slid his hands to the bottom of the steering wheel and peered ahead into the darkness, trying to relax. But the wheel stuck to his fingers like warm candy. Off somewhere to his left, the horizon flickered with pearly luminescence, then faded again to black. This time he did not bother to look. Sometimes, though, he wondered just how far away the lightning was striking; not once during the night had the sound of its thunder reached him here in the car.

In the back seat, his wife moaned.

The trip out had turned all but unbearable for her. Four days it had taken, instead of the expected two-and-a-half; he made a great effort not to think of it, but the memory hung over the car like a thunderhead.

It had been a blur, a fever dream. Once, on the second day, he had been passed by a churning bus, its silver sides blinding him until he noticed a Mexican woman in one of the window seats. She was not looking at him. She was holding a swooning infant to the glass, squeezing water onto its head from a plastic baby bottle to keep it from passing out.

McClay sighed and fingered the buttons on the car radio.

He knew he would get nothing from the AM or FM bands, not out here, but he clicked it on anyway. He left the volume and tone controls down, so as not to wake Evvie. Then he punched the seldom-used middle button, the shortwave band, and raised the

gain carefully until he could barely hear the radio over the hum
of the tires.

Static.

Slowly he swept the tuner across the bandwidth, but there was
only white noise. It reminded him a little of the summer rain
yesterday, starting back, the way it had sounded bouncing off the
windows.

He was about to give up when he caught a voice, crackling, drifting
in and out. He worked the knob like a safecracker, zeroing in on
the signal.

A few bars of music. A tone, then the voice again. ". . . Greenwich
Mean Time." Then the station ID.

It was the Voice of America Overseas Broadcast.

He grunted disconsolately and killed it.

His wife stirred.

"Why'd you turn it off" she murmured. "I was listening to that.
Good. Program."

"Take it easy," he said, "easy, you're still asleep. We'll be
stopping soon."

". . . Only comes out at night," he heard her say, and then she
was lost again in the blankets.

He pressed the glove compartment, took out one of the Automobile
Club guides. It was already clipped open. McClay flipped on the
overhead light and drove with one hand, reading over—for the
hundredth time?—the list of motels that lay ahead. He knew the
list by heart, but seeing the names again reassured him somehow.
Besides, it helped to break the monotony.

It was the kind of place you never expect to find in the middle of
a long night, a bright place with buildings (a building, at least)
and cars, other cars drawn off the highway to be together in the
protective circle of light.

A Rest Area.

He would have spotted it without the sign. Elevated sodium vapor
lighting bathed the scene in an almost peach-colored glow, strikingly
different from the cold blue-white sentinels of the Interstate Highway. He had seen other Rest Area signs on the way out, probably
even this one. But in daylight the signs had meant nothing more to
him than FRONTAGE ROAD or BUSINESS DISTRICT NEXT
RIGHT. He wondered if it was the peculiar warmth of light that
made the small island of blacktop appear so inviting.

McClay decelerated, downshifted and left Interstate 40.

The car dipped and bumped, and he was aware of the new

level of sound from the engine as it geared down for the first time
in hours.

He eased in next to a Pontiac Firebird, toed the emergency brake
and cut the ignition.

He allowed his eyes to close and his head to sink back into the
headrest. At last.

The first thing he noticed was the quiet.

It was deafening. His ears literally began to ring, with the
high-pitched whine of a late-night TV test pattern.

The second thing he noticed was a tingling at the tip of his
tongue.

It brought to mind a picture of a snake's tongue. Picking up
electricity from the air, he thought.

The third was the rustling awake of his wife, in back.

She pulled herself up. "Are we sleeping now? Why are the
lights . . .?"

He saw the outline of her head in the mirror. "It's just a rest stop,
hon. I—the car needs a break." Well, it was true, wasn't it? "You
want the rest room? There's one back there, see it?"

"Oh my God."

"What's the matter now?"

"Leg's asleep. Listen, are we or are we not going to get a— "

"There's a motel coming up." He didn't say that they wouldn't
hit the one he had marked in the book for another couple of hours;
he didn't want to argue. He knew she needed the rest—he needed
it too, didn't he? "Think I'll have some more of that coffee, though,"
he said.

"Isn't any more," she yawned.

The door slammed.

Now he was able to recognize the ringing in his ears for what it
was: the sound of his own blood. It almost succeeded in replacing
the steady drone of the car.

He twisted around, fishing over the back of the seat for the
ice chest.

There should be a couple of Cokes left, at least.

His fingers brushed the basket next to the chest, riffling the edges
of maps and tour books, by now reshuffled haphazardly over the
first-aid kit he had packed himself (tourniquet, forceps, scissors,
ammonia inhalants, Merthiolate, triangular bandage, compress,
adhesive bandages, tannic acid) and the fire extinguisher, the extra
carton of cigarettes, the remainder of a half-gallon of drinking
water, the thermos (which Evvie said was empty, and why would
she lie?).

He popped the top of a can.

Through the side window he saw Evvie disappearing around the corner of the building. She was wrapped to the gills in her blanket.

He opened the door and slid out, his back aching.

He stood there blankly, the unnatural light washing over him.

He took a long, sweet pull from the can. Then he started walking.

The Firebird was empty.

And the next car, and the next.

Each car he passed looked like the one before it, which seemed crazy until he realized that it must be the work of the light. It cast an even, eerie tan over the baked metal tops, like orange sunlight through air thick with suspended particles. Even the windshields appeared to be filmed over with a thin layer of settled dust. It made him think of country roads, sundowns.

He walked on.

He heard his footsteps echo with surprising clarity, resounding down the staggered line of parked vehicles. Finally it dawned on him (and now he knew how tired he really was) that the cars must actually have people in them—sleeping people. Of course. Well hell, he thought, watching his step, I wouldn't want to wake anyone. The poor devils.

Besides the sound of his footsteps, there was only the distant *swish* of an occasional, very occasional car on the highway; from here, even that was only a distant hush, growing and then subsiding like waves on a nearby shore.

He reached the end of the line, turned back.

Out of the corner of his eye he saw, or thought he saw, a movement by the building.

It would be Evvie, shuffling back.

He heard the car door slam.

He recalled something he had seen in one the tourist towns in New Mexico: circling the park—in Taos, that was where they had been—he had glimpsed an ageless Indian, wrapped in typical blanket, ducking out of sight into the doorway of a gift shop; with the blanket over his head that way, the Indian had somehow resembled an Arab, or so it had seemed to him at the time.

He heard another car door slam.

That was the same day—was it only last week?—that she had noticed the locals driving with their headlights on (in honor of something or other, some regional election, perhaps: "'My face speaks for itself,' drawled Herman J. 'Fashio' Trujillo, Candidate for Sheriff"); she had insisted at first that it must be a funeral procession, though for whom she could not guess.

McClay came to the car, stretched a last time, and crawled back in.

Evvie was bundled safely again in the back seat.

He lit a quick cigarette, expecting to hear her voice any second, complaining, demanding that he roll down the windows, at least, and so forth. But, as it turned out, he was able to sit undisturbed as he smoked it down almost to the filter.

Paguate. Bluewater. Thoreau.

He blinked.

Klagetoh. Joseph City. Ash Fork.

He blinked and tried to focus his eyes from the taillights a half mile ahead to the bug-spattered glass, then back again.

Petrified Forest National Park.

He blinked, refocusing. But it did no good.

A twitch started on the side of his face, close by the corner of his eye.

Rehoboth.

He strained at a road sign, the names and mileages, but instead a seemingly endless list of past and future shops and detours shimmered before his mind's eye.

I've had it, he thought. Now, suddenly, it was catching up with him, the hours of repressed fatigue; he felt a rushing out of something from his chest. No way to make that motel—hell, I can't even remember the name of it now. Check the book. But it doesn't matter. The eyes. *Can't control my eyes anymore.*

(He had already begun to hallucinate things like tree trunks and cows and Mack trucks speeding toward him on the highway. The cow had been straddling the broken line; in the last few minutes its lowing, deep and regular, had become almost inviting.)

Well, he could try for *any* motel. Whatever turned up next.

But how much farther would that be?

He ground his teeth together, feeling the pulsing at his temples. He struggled to remember the last sign.

The next town. It might be a mile. Five miles. Fifty.

Think! He said it, he thought it, he didn't know which.

If he could just pull over, pull over right now and lie down for a few minutes—

He seemed to see clear ground ahead. No rocks, no ditch. The shoulder, just ahead.

Without thinking he dropped into neutral and coasted, aiming for it.

The car glided to a stop.

God, he thought.

He forced himself to turn, reach into the back seat.

The lid to the chest was already off. He dipped his fingers into the ice and retrieved two half-melted cubes, lifted them into the front seat and began rubbing them over his forehead.

He let his eyes close, seeing dull lights fire as he daubed at the lids, the rest of his face, the forehead again. As he slipped the ice into his mouth and chewed, it broke apart as easily as snow.

He took a deep breath. He opened his eyes again.

At that moment a huge tanker roared past, slamming an aftershock of air into the side of the car. The car rocked like a boat at sea.

No. It was no good.

So. So he could always turn back, couldn't he? And why not? The Rest Area was only twenty, twenty-five minutes behind him. (Was that all?) He could pull out and hang a U and turn back, just like that. And then sleep. It would be safer there. With luck, Evvie wouldn't even know. An hour's rest, maybe two; that was all he would need.

Unless—was there another Rest Area ahead?

How soon?

He knew that the second wind he felt now wouldn't last, not for more than a few minutes. No, it wasn't worth the chance.

He glanced in the rearview mirror.

Evvie was still down, a lumpen mound of blanket and hair.

Above her body, beyond the rear window, the raised headlights of another monstrous truck, closing ground fast.

He made the decision.

He slid into first and swung out in a wide arc, well ahead of the blast of the truck, and worked up to fourth gear. He was thinking about the warm, friendly lights he had left behind.

He angled in next to the Firebird and cut the lights.

He started to reach for a pillow from the back, but why bother? It would probably wake Evvie, anyway.

He wadded up his jacket, jammed it against the passenger armrest, and lay down.

First he crossed his arms over his chest. Then behind his head. Then he gripped his hands between his knees. Then he was on his back again, his hands at his sides, his feet cramped against the opposite door.

His eyes were wide open.

He lay there, watching chain lightning flash on the horizon.

Finally he let out a breath that sounded like all the breaths he had ever taken going out at once, and drew himself up.

He got out and walked over to the rest room.

Inside, white tiles and bare lights. His eyes felt raw, peeled. Finished, he washed his hands but not his face; that would only make sleep more difficult.

Outside again and feeling desperately out of synch, he listened to his shoes falling hollowly on the cement.

"Next week we've got to get organized . . ."

He said this, he was sure, because he heard his voice coming back to him, though with a peculiar empty resonance. Well, this time tomorrow night he would be home. As unlikely as that seemed now.

He stopped, bent for a drink from the water fountain.

The footsteps did not stop.

Now wait, he thought, I'm pretty far gone, but—

He swallowed, his ears popping.

The footsteps stopped.

Hell, he thought, I've been pushing too hard. We. She. No, it was my fault, my plan this time. To drive nights, sleep days. Just so. As long as you *can* sleep.

Easy, take it easy.

He started walking again, around the corner and back to the lot.

At the corner, he thought he saw something move at the edge of his vision.

He turned quickly to the right, in time for a fleeting glimpse of something—someone—hurrying out of sight into the shadows.

Well, the other side of the building housed the women's rest room. Maybe it was Evvie.

He glanced toward the car, but it was blocked from view.

He walked on.

Now the parking area resembled an oasis lit by firelight. Or a western camp, the cars rimming the lot on three sides in the manner of wagons gathered against the night.

Strength in numbers, he thought.

Again, each car he passed looked at first like every other. It was the flat light, of course. And of course they were the same cars he had seen a half-hour ago. And the light still gave them a dusty, abandoned look.

He touched a fender.

It *was* dusty.

But why shouldn't it be? His own car had probably taken on quite a layer of grime after so long on these roads.

He touched the next car, the next.

Each was so dirty that he could have carved his name without scratching the paint.

He had an image of himself passing this way again—God forbid—a year from now, say, and finding the same cars parked here. The *same* ones.

What if, he wondered tiredly, what if some of these cars had been abandoned? Overheated, exploded, broken down one fine midday and left here by owners who simply never returned? Who would ever know? Did the Highway Patrol, did anyone bother to check? Would an automobile be preserved here for months, years by the elements, like a snakeskin shed beside the highway?

It was a thought, anyway.

His head was buzzing.

He leaned back and inhaled deeply, as deeply as he could at this altitude.

But he did hear something. A faint tapping. It reminded him of running feet, until he noticed the lamp overhead:

There were hundreds of moths beating against the high fixture, their soft bodies tapping as they struck and circled and returned again and again to the lens; the light made their wings translucent.

He took another deep breath and went on to his car.

He could hear it ticking, cooling down, before he got there. Idly he rested a hand on the hood. Warm, of course. The tires? He touched the left front. It was taut, hot as a loaf from the oven. When he took his hand away, the color of the rubber came off on his palm like burned skin.

He reached for the door handle.

A moth fluttered down onto the fender. He flicked it off, his finger leaving a streak on the enamel.

He looked closer and saw a wavy, mottled pattern covering his unwashed car, and then he remembered. The rain, yesterday afternoon. The rain had left blotches in the dust, marking the finish as if with dirty fingerprints.

He glanced over at the next car.

It, too, had the imprint of dried raindrops—but, close up, he saw that the marks were superimposed in layers, over and over again.

The Firebird had been through a great many rains.

He touched the hood.

Cold.

He removed his hand, and a dead moth clung to his thumb. He tried to brush it off on the hood, but other moth bodies stuck in its place. Then he saw countless shriveled, mummified moths pasted over the hood and top like peeling chips of paint. His fingers were coated with the powder from their wings.

He looked up.

High above, backed by banks of roiling cumulous clouds, the swarm of moths vibrated about the bright, protective light.

So the Firebird had been here a very long time.

He wanted to forget it, to let it go. He wanted to get back in the car. He wanted to lie down, lock it out, everything. He wanted to go to sleep and wake up in Los Angeles.

He couldn't.

He inched around the Firebird until he was facing the line of cars. He hesitated a beat, then started moving.

A LeSabre.

A Cougar.

A Chevy van.

A Corvair.

A Ford.

A Mustang.

And every one was overlaid with grit.

He paused by the Mustang. Once—how long ago?—it had been a luminous candy-apple red; probably belonged to a teenager. Now the windshield was opaque, the body dulled to a peculiar shade he could not quite place.

Feeling like a voyeur at a drive-in movie theater, McClay crept to the driver's window.

Dimly he perceived two large outlines in the front seat.

He raised his hand.

Wait.

What if there were two people sitting there on the other side of the window, watching him?

He put it out of his mind. Using three fingers, he cut a swath through the scum on the glass and pressed close.

The shapes were there. Two headrests.

He started to pull away.

And happened to glance into the back seat.

He saw a long, uneven form.

A leg, the back of a thigh. Blonde hair, streaked with shadows. The collar of a coat.

And, delicate and silvery, a spider web, spun between the hair and collar.

He jumped back.

His leg struck the old Ford. He spun around, his arms straight. The blood was pounding in his ears.

He rubbed out a spot on the window of the Ford and scanned the inside.

The figure of a man, slumped on the front seat.

The man's head lay on a jacket. No, it was not a jacket. It was a large, formless stain. In the filtered light, McClay could see that it had dried to a dark brown.

It came from the man's mouth.

No, not from the mouth.

The throat had a long, thin slash across it, reaching nearly to the ear.

He stood there stiffly, his back almost arched, his eyes jerking, trying to close, trying not to close. The lot, the even light reflecting thinly from each windshield, the Corvair, the van, the Cougar, the LeSabre, the suggestion of a shape within each one.

The pulse in his ears muffled and finally blotted out the distant gearing of a truck up on the highway, the death-rattle of the moths against the seductive lights.

He reeled.

He seemed to be hearing again the breaking open of doors and the scurrying of padded feet across paved spaces.

He remembered the first time. He remembered the sound of a second door slamming in a place where no new car but his own had arrived.

Or—had it been the door to his car slamming a second time, after Evvie had gotten back in?

If so, how? Why?

And there had been the sight of someone moving, trying to slip away.

And for some reason now he remembered the Indian in the tourist town, slipping out of sight in the doorway of that gift shop. He held his eyelids down until he saw the shop again, the window full of kachinas and tin gods and tapestries woven in a secret language.

At last he remembered it clearly: the Indian had not been entering the store. *He had been stealing away.*

McClay did not understand what it meant, but he opened his eyes, as if for the first time in centuries, and began to run toward his car.

If I could only catch my goddamn breath, he thought.

He tried to hold on. He tried not to think of her, of what might have happened the first time, of what he may have been carrying in the back seat ever since.

He had to find out.

He fought his way back to the car, against a rising tide of fear he could not stem.

He told himself to think of other things, of things he knew he could control: mileages and motel bills, time zones and weather reports, spare tires and flares and tubeless repair tools, hydraulic jack and Windex and paper towels and tire iron and socket wrench and waffle cushion and traveler's checks and credit cards and Dopp Kit (toothbrush and paste, deodorant, shaver, safety blade, brushless cream) and sunglasses and Sight Savers and tear-gas pen and fiber-tip pens and portable radio and alkaline batteries and fire extinguisher and desert water bag and tire guage and motor oil and his moneybelt with identification sealed in plastic—

In the back of his car, under the quilt, nothing moved, not even when he finally lost his control and his mind in a thick, warm scream.

Peter Tremayne

Dracula's Chair

Peter Tremayne is the pseudonym of historian and Celticist, Peter Berresford Ellis, who has published numerous works on Celtic history and cultures including A Dictionary of Irish Mythology, *paperbacked by the Oxford University Press, and the companion volume,* A Dictionary of Celtic Mythology.

As Tremayne, he has published twenty-five books in the horror and heroic fantasy genre, often concentrating on tales based on themes from Celtic mythology, such as the recent Island of Shadows.

Although only a score of his short stories have appeared, they have been well received on both sides of the Atlantic and translated into a dozen European languages. "Peter Tremayne weaves no less engrossing tales than Edgar Allan Poe" said the Asbury Park Press.

'Dracula's Chair' was only his third short story. It was originally written as an epilogue to his novel The Revenge of Dracula *(1979), the second volume in his Dracula trilogy which also includes* Dracula Unborn *(1977, USA:* Bloodright*) and* Dracula, My Love *(1980). He decided to omit it on the grounds that it was "artistic overkill".*

MAYBE THIS IS an hallucination. Perhaps I am mad. How else can this be explained?

I sit here alone and helpless! So utterly alone! Alone in an age which is not mine, in a body which is not mine. Oh God! I am slowly being killed—or worse! Yet what is worse than death? That terrifying limbo that is the borderland of Hell, that state that is neither the restful sleep of death nor the perplexities of life but is the nightmare of undeath.

He is draining me of life and yet, *yet is it me who is the victim?* How can I tell him that the person he thinks I am, the person whose body my mind inhabits, is no longer in that body? How can I tell him that *I* am in the body of his victim? *I* . . . a person from another time, another age, another place!

God help me! He is draining me of life and I cannot prevent him!

When did this nightmare begin? An age away. I suppose it began when my wife and I saw the chair.

We were driving back to London one hot July Sunday afternoon, having been picnicking in Essex. We were returning about mid-afternoon down the A11, through the village of Newport, when my wife suddenly called upon me to pull over and stop.

"I've just seen the most exquisite chair in the window of an antique shop."

I was somewhat annoyed because I wanted to get home early that evening to see a vintage Humphrey Bogart film on the television, one I'd never seen before even though I have been a Bogart fan for years.

"What's the point?" I muttered grumpily, getting out of the car and trailing after her. "The shop's shut anyway."

But the shop wasn't shut. Passing trade on a Sunday from Londoners was apparently very lucrative and most antique shops in the area opened during the afternoons.

The chair stood like a lone sentinel in the window. It was square in shape, a wooden straight-backed chair with sturdy arms. It was of a plain and simple design, dark oak wood yet with none of the ornate woodwork that is commonly associated with such items. The seat was upholstered in a faded tapestry work which was obviously the original. It was a very unattractive upholstery for it was in a faded black with a number of once white exotic dragon's heads. The same upholstery was reflected in a piece which provided a narrow back rest—a strip a foot deep thrust across the middle of the frame. My impression of the chair was hardly "exquisite"—it was a squat, ugly and aggressive piece. Certainly it did not seem worth the £100 price ticket which was attached by string to one arm.

My wife had contrary ideas. It was, she felt, exactly the right piece to fill a corner in my study and provide a spare chair for extra guests. It could, she assured me, easily be re-upholstered to fit in with our general colour scheme of greens and golds. What was wanted, she said, was a functional chair and this was it. She was adamant and so I resigned myself to a minimum of grumbling, one eye on my watch to ensure I would not miss the Bogart film. The transaction was concluded fairly quickly by comparison with my wife's usual standard of detailed questioning and examination. Perhaps the vendor was rather more loquacious than the average antique dealer.

"It's a very nice chair," said the dealer with summoned enthusiasm. "It's a Victorian piece of eastern European origin. Look, on the back you can actually see a date of manufacture and the place of origin." He pointed to the back of the chair where, carved into the wood with small letters was the word "Bistritz" and the date "1887." The dealer smiled in the surety of knowledge. "That makes it Romanian in origin. Actually, I purchased the piece from the old Purfleet Art Gallery."

"The Purfleet Art Gallery?" said I, thinking it time to make some contribution to the conservation. "Isn't that the old gallery and museum over which there were some protests a few months ago?"

"Yes, do you know the place? Purfleet in Essex? The gallery was housed in an ancient building, a manor house called Carfax, which was said to date back to medieval times. The old gallery had been there since the late Victorian period but had to close through lack of government subsidies, and the building is being carved up into apartments."

I nodded, feeling I had, perhaps, made too much of a contribution.

The antique dealer went on obliviously.

"When the gallery closed, a lot of its *objets d'art* were auctioned and I bought this chair. According to the auctioneer's catalogue it had been in the old house when the gallery first opened and had belonged to the previous owner. He was said to have been a foreign nobleman . . . probably a Romanian by the workmanship of the chair."

Finally, having had her fears assuaged over matters of woodworm, methods of upholstery and the like, the purchase was concluded by my wife. The chair was strapped to the roofrack of my car and we headed homewards.

The next day was Monday. My wife, who is in research, had gone to her office while I spent the morning in my study doodling on pieces of paper and vainly waiting for a new plot to mature for the television soap-opera that I was scripting at the time. At mid-day my wife telephoned to remind me to check around for some price quotations for re-upholstering our purchase. I had forgotten all about the chair, still strapped to the roofrack of my car. Feeling a little guilty, I went down to the garage and untied it, carrying it up to my study and placing it in the alloted corner with a critical eye. I confess, I did not like the thing; it was so square and seemed to somehow challenge me. It is hard to define what I mean but you have, I suppose, seen certain types of people with thrust out jaws, square and aggressive? Well, the chair gave the same impression.

After a while, perhaps in response to its challenge, I decided to sit down in the chair, and as I sat, a sudden coldness spread up my spine and a weird feeling of unease came over me. So strong was it that I immediately jumped up. I stood there looking down at the chair and feeling a trifle self-conscious. I laughed nervously. Ridiculous! What would my friend Philip, who was a psychiatrist, say to such behaviour? I did not like the chair but there was no need to create physical illusions around my distaste.

I sat down again and, as expected, the cold feelings of unease were gone—a mere shadow in my mind. In fact, I was surprised at the comfort of the chair. I sat well back, arms and hands resting on the wooden arm rests, head leaning against the back, legs spread out. It was extremely comfortable.

So comfortable was it that a feeling of deep relaxation came over me, and with the relaxation came the desire to have a cat-nap. I must confess, I tend to enjoy a ten minute nap just after lunch. It relaxes me and stimulates the mind. I sat back, closed my drooping eyelids and gently let myself drift, drift

It was dark when I awoke.

For an instant I struggled with the remnants of my dreams. Then my mind cleared and I looked about me. My first thought was the question—how long had I slept? I could see the dark hue of early evening through the tall windows. Then I started *for there were no tall windows in my study nor anywhere in our house!*

Blinking my eyes rapidly to focus them in the darkened room, I abruptly perceived that I was not in my study, nor was I in any room that I had even seen before. I tried to rise in my surprise and found that I could not move—some sluggish feeling in my body prevented me from coordinating my limbs. My mind had clarity and will but below my neck my whole body seemed numb. And so I just sat there, staring wildly at the unfamiliar room in a cold sweat of fear and panic. I tried to blink away the nightmare, tried to rationalize.

I could move my head around and doing so I found that I

was sitting in the same chair—that accursed chair! Yet it seemed strangely newer than I remembered it. I thought, perhaps it was a trick of the light. But I discovered that around my legs was tucked a woolen blanket while the top half of me was clad in a pajama jacket over which was a velvet smoking jacket, a garment that I knew I had never owned. My eyes wandered around the room from object to unfamiliar object, each unfamiliar item causing the terror to mount in my veins, now surging with adrenalin. I was in a lounge filled with some fine pieces of Victoriana. The chair in which I sat now stood before an open hearth in which a few coals faintly glimmered. In one corner stood a lean, tall grandfather clock, whose steady tick-tock added to the oppressiveness of the scene. There was, so far as I could see, nothing modern in the room at all.

But for me the greatest horror was the strange paralysis which kept me anchored in that chair. I tried to move until the sweat poured from my face with the effort. I even tried to shout, opening my mouth wide to emit strange choking-like noises. What in God's name had happened to me?

Suddenly a door opened. Into the room came a young girl of about seventeen holding aloft one of those old brass oil lamps, the sort you see converted into electric lamps these days by "trendy" people. Yet this was no converted lamp but a lamp from which a flame spluttered and emitted the odour of burning paraffin. And the girl! She wore a long black dress with a high button collar, with a white linen apron over it. Her fair hair was tucked inside a small white cap set at a jaunty angle on her head. In fact, she looked like a serving maid straight out of those Victorian drama serials we get so often on the television these days. She came forward and placed the lamp on a table near me, and then started, seeing my eyes wide open and upon her. I tried to speak to her, to demand, to exhort some explanation, to ask what the meaning of this trickery was, but only a strangled gasp came from my throat.

The girl was clearly frightened and bobbed what was supposed to be a curtsy in my direction before turning to the door.

"Ma'am! Ma'am!" her strong Cockney accent made the word sound like "Mum!" "Master's awake, ma'am. What'll I do?"

Another figure moved into the room, tall, graceful, wearing an elegant Victorian dress hung low at the shoulders, and leaving very little of her bust to the imagination. A black ribbon with a cameo was fastened to her pale throat. Her raven black hair was done up in a bun at the back of her head. Her face was small, heart-shaped, and pretty. The lips were naturally red though a trifle sullen for her features. The eyes were deep green and seemed a little sad. She came towards me, bent over me and gave a wan smile. There was a strange, almost unnatural pallor to her complexion.

"That's all, Fanny," she said. "I'll see to him now."

"Yes, ma'am," the girl bobbed another curtsy and was gone through the door.

"Poor Upton," whispered the woman before me. "Poor Upton. I wish I knew whether you hurt at all? No one seems to know from what strange malady you suffer."

She stood back and sighed sorrowfully and deeply.

"It's time for your medication."

She picked up a bottle and a spoon, pouring a bitter smelling amber liquid which she forced down my throat. I felt a numbing bitterness searing down my gullet.

"Poor Upton," she sighed again. "It's bitter I know but the doctor says it will take away any pain."

I tried to speak; tried to tell her that I was not Upton, that I did not want her medicine, that I wanted this play-acting to cease. I succeeded only in gnashing my teeth and making inarticulate cries like some wild beast at bay. The woman took a step backwards, her eyes widening in fright. Then she seemed to regain her composure.

"Come, Upton," she chidded. "This won't do at all. Try to relax."

The girl, Fanny, reappeared.

"Doctor Seward is here, ma'am."

A stocky man in a brown tweed suit, looking like some character out of a Dickens novel, stepped into the room and bowed over the woman's profferred hand.

"John," smiled the woman. "I'm so glad you've come."

"How are you, Clara," smiled the man. "You look a trifle weary, a little pale."

"I'm alright, John. But I worry about Upton."

The man turned to me.

"Yes, how is the patient? I swear he looks a little more alert today."

The woman, Clara, spread her hands and shrugged.

"To me he seems little better, John. Even when he seems more alert physically he can only growl like a beast. I try my best but I fear . . . I fear that . . ."

The man called John patted her hand and gestured her to silence. Then he came and bent over me with a friendly smile.

"Strange," he murmured. "Indeed, a strange affliction. And yet . . . yet I do detect a more intelligent gleam in the eyes today. Hello, old friend, do you know me. It's John . . . John Seward? Do you recognise me?"

He leaned close to my face, so close I could smell the scent of oranges on his breath.

I struggled to break the paralysis which gripped me and only succeeded in issuing a number of snarls and grunts. The man drew back.

"Upon my word, Clara, has he been violent at all?"

"Not really, John. He does excite himself so with visitors. But perhaps it is his way of trying to communicate with us."

The man grunted and nodded.

"Well, the only remedy for pain is to keep dosing him with the laudanum as I prescribed it. I think he is a little better. However, I shall call again tomorrow to see if there is a significant improvement. If not, I will ask your permission to consult a specialist, perhaps a doctor from Harley Street. There are a number of factors that still puzzle me—the anaemia, the apparent lack of red blood corpuscles or hemoglobin. His paleness and languor. And these strange wounds on his neck do not seem to be healing at all."

The woman bit her lip and lowered her voice.

"You may be frank with me, John. You have known Upton and me for some years now. I am resigned to the fact that there can only be a worsening of his condition. I do fear for his life."

The man glanced at me nervously.

"Should you talk like this in front of him?"

The woman sighed. "He cannot understand, of that I am sure. Poor Upton. Just to think that a few short days ago he was so full of life, so active, and now this strange disease has cut him down . . ."

The man nodded.

"You have been a veritable goddess, Clara, charity herself, nursing him constantly day and night. I shall look in again tomorrow, but if there is no improvement I shall seek permission to call in a specialist."

Clara lowered her head as if in resignation.

The man turned to me and forced a smile.

"So long, old fellow . . ."

I tried to call, desperately tried to plead for help. Then he was gone.

The minutes dragged into hours as the woman, Clara, who was supposed to be my wife, sat gazing into the fire, while I sat pinioned in my accursed chair opposite to her. How long we sat thus I do not truly know. From time to time I felt her gaze, sad and thoughtful, upon me. Then I became aware, somewhere in the house, of a clock commencing to strike. A few seconds later it was followed by the resonant and hollow sounds of the grandfather clock. Without raising my head I counted slowly to twelve. Midnight.

The woman Clara abruptly sprung from her chair and stood upright before the fire.

As I looked up she seemed to change slightly—it is hard to explain. Her face seemed to grow coarser, more bloated. Her tongue, a red glistening object, darted nervously over her lips making them moist and of a deeper red than before, contrasting starkly to the sharp whiteness of her teeth. A strange lustre began to sparkle in her eyes. She raised a languid hand and began to massage her neck slowly, sensually.

Then, abruptly, she laughed—a low voluptuous chuckle that made the hairs on my neck bristle.

She gazed down at me with a wanton expression, a lascivious smile.

"Poor Upton," her tone was a gloating caress. "He'll be coming soon. You'll like that won't you? Yet why he takes you first, I cannot understand. Why *you*? Am I not full of the warmth of life—does not warm, rich young blood flow in my veins? Why *you*?"

She made an obscene, seductive gesture with her body.

The way she crooned, the saliva trickling from a corner of those red—oh, so red—lips, made my heart beat faster yet at the same time, the blood seemed to deny its very warmth and pump like some ice-cold liquid in my veins.

What new nightmare was this?

How *he* appeared I do not know.

One minute there was just the woman and myself in the room. Then he was standing there.

A tall man, apparently elderly although his pale face held no aging of the skin, only the long white moustache which drooped over his otherwise clean-shaven face gave the impression of age. His face was strong—extremely strong, aquiline with a high-bridged nose and peculiarly arched nostrils. His forehead was loftily domed and hair grew scantily round the temples but profusely elsewhere. The eyebrows were massive and nearly met across the bridge of the nose.

It was his mouth which captured my attention—a mouth set in the long pale face, fixed and cruel looking, with teeth that protruded over the remarkably ruddy lips whose redness had the effect of highlighting his white skin and giving the impression of an extraordinary pallor. And where the teeth protruded over the lips, they were white and sharp.

His eyes seemed a ghastly red in the glow of the flickering fire.

The woman, Clara, took a step toward him, hands out as if imploring, a glad cry on her red wanton lips, her breasts heaving as if with some wild ectasy.

"My Lord," she cried, "you have come!"

The tall man ignored her. His red eyes were upon mine, seeming to devour me.

The woman raised a hand to massage her throat.

"Lord, take me first! Take me now!"

The tall man took a stride towards me, drawing back an arm and pushing her roughly aside.

"It is he that I shall take first," he said sibilantly, with a strange accent to his English. "You shall wait your turn which shall be in a little while."

The woman made to protest but he stopped her with an upraised hand.

"Dare you question me?" he said mildly. "Have no fear. You shall be my bountiful wine press in a while. But first I shall slake my thirst with him."

He towered over me as I remained helpless in that chair, that accursed chair. A smile edged his face.

"Is it not just?" whispered the tall man. "Is it not just that having thwarted me, you Upton Welsford, now become everything that you abhorred and feared?"

And while part of my mind was witnessing this obscene hallucination, another part of it began to experience a strange excitement—almost a sexual excitement as the man lowered his face to mine . . . closer came those awful red eyes to gaze deep into my soul. His mouth was open slightly, I could smell a vile reek of corruption. There was a deliberate voluptuousness about his movements that was both thrilling and appalling—he licked his lips like some animal, the scarlet tongue flickering over the white sharp teeth.

Lower came his head, lower, until it passed from my sight and I could hear the churning sound of his tongue against his teeth and could feel his hot breath on my neck. The skin of my throat began to tingle. Then I felt the soft shivering touch of his cold lips on my throat, the hard indent of two sharp white teeth!

For a while, how long I could not measure, I seemed to fall into a languorous ectasy.

Then he was standing above me, smiling down sardonically, a trickle of blood on his chin. My blood!

"There is one more night to feast with him," he said softly. "One night more and then, Upton Welford, you shall be my brother."

The woman exclaimed in anger.

"But you promised! You promised! When am I to be called?"

The tall man turned and laughed.

"Aye, I promised, my slender vine. You already bear my mark. You belong to me. You shall be one with me, never fear. Immortality will soon be yours and we shall share in the drinking. You will provide me with the wine of life. Have patience, for the greatest wines are long in the savouring. I shall return."

Then to my horror the man was gone. Simply gone, as if he had dissolved into elemental dust.

For some time I sat in horror staring at the woman who seemed to have retreated into a strange trance. Then the grandfather clock began to chime and the woman started, as if waking from a deep sleep. She stared in amazement at the clock and then towards the window where the faint light of early dawn was beginning to show.

"Good Lord, Upton," she exclaimed, "we seemed to have been up all night. I must have fallen asleep, I'm sorry."

She shook herself.

"I've had a strange dream. Ah well, no matter. I'd better get you up to bed. I'll go and wake poor Fanny to help me."

She smiled softly at me as she left the room; there was no trace of the wanton seductress left on her delicate features.

She left me sitting alone, alone in my prison of a chair.

I sit here alone and helpless. So utterly alone! Alone in an age which is not mine, in a body which is not mine. Oh God! I am slowly being killed—or worse! Yet what is worse than death? That terrifying limbo that is the borderland of Hell, that state that is neither the restful sleep of death nor the perplexities of life but is the nightmare of undeath.

And where is this person . . . the Upton Welsford whose body I now inhabit? Where is he? Has he, by some great effort of will, exchanged his body with mine? Is he even now awakening from that cat-nap sometime in the future? Awakening in my body, in my study, to resume my life? Is he doing even as I have done? What does it all mean?

Maybe this is an hallucination. Perhaps I am mad. How else can all this be explained?

Melanie Tem

The Better Half

Melanie Tem's first novel, the dark fantasy Prodigal, *was published by Abyss in 1991 and her second,* Blood Moon, *recently appeared from The Women's Press.*

Her short stories can be found in Isaac Asimov's Science Fiction Magazine, Women of Darkness, Women of the West, Skin of the Soul, Final Shadows, Copper Star, Cold Shocks, Dark Voices 3: The Pan Book of Horror *and* Fantasy Tales. *Roadkill Press published her story* Daddy's Side *as a limited edition chapbook, while collaborations with her husband Steve Rasnic Tem recently appeared in* The Ultimate Dracula *and* The Ultimate Frankenstein.

'The Better Half' is one of those vampire stories that takes an oblique look at the theme. It is no less disturbing a piece of fiction for that . . .

KELLY OPENED THE door before I'd even come close to her house. The opening and closing of the red door in the white house startled me, like a mouth baring teeth. I stopped where I was, halfway down the block. Kelly was wearing a yellow dress and something white around her shoulders. She stepped farther out onto the porch and shaded her eyes against the high July sun.

For some reason, I didn't want her to see me just yet. I stepped behind a thick lilac bush dotted with the hard purplish nubs of spent flowers. A small brown dog in the yard across the street yapped twice at me, then gave it up and went back to its spot in the shade.

I hadn't seen Kelly in fifteen years. I'd thought I'd forgotten her, but I'd have known her anywhere. In college we'd been very close for awhile. Now that I was older and more careful, I'd have expected not to understand the ardor I'd felt for her then; it distressed me that I understood it perfectly, even felt a pulse of it again, like hot blood. Watching her from a distance and through the purple and green filtering of the lilac bush, I found myself a little afraid of her.

Later I learned that it was not Kelly I had reason to fear. But my father had died in the spring, and I was afraid of everything. Afraid of loving. Afraid of not loving. Afraid of coming home or rounding a corner and discovering something terrible that I, by my presence, could have stopped. I cowered behind the lilac bush and wished I could make myself invisible. I wondered why she'd called. I wondered savagely why I'd come. I thought about retreating along the hot bright sidewalk away from her house. I could hardly keep myself from rushing headlong to her.

Slowly I approached her. It was obvious that she still hadn't seen me; she was looking the other way. Looking for me. I was, purposely, a few minutes late. Then she turned, and I knew with a chill that something was terribly wrong.

It wasn't just that she looked alien, although she was elegantly dressed on a Saturday morning in a neighborhood where a business suit on a weekday was an oddity. It wasn't just that I felt invaded, although her house was around the corner from the diner where Daddy and I had often had breakfast, the park where we'd walked sometimes, the apartment where we'd lived. It was more than that. There was something wrong with *her*. I stopped again and stared.

It was mid-July and high noon. Hot green light through the porch awning flooded her face, the same heavy brows, high cheekbones, slightly aquiline nose. She looked sick. The spots of color high on her cheeks could have been paint or fever. She was breathing hard. Even from here I could see that she was shivering violently. And around her shoulders, in the noonday summer heat, was a white fur jacket.

I have told myself that at that point I nearly left, but I don't think that's true. I stood there looking at her across the neat green of the Kentucky bluegrass in her north Denver lawn. Sprinklers were on, making rainbows. I was drawn to her as I'd always been. Something was wrong, and I was about to be drenched in it, too.

She saw me and smiled, a weak and heart-wrenching grimace.

I wished desperately that I'd never come but the impulse toward self-preservation, like others throughout my life, came too late.

"Brenda! Hello!"

I opened the waist-high, filigreed, wrought-iron gate, turned to latch it carefully behind me, turned again to walk between even rows of pinwheel petunias. "Kelly," I said, with an effort holding out my hand. "It's good to see you."

Her hand was icy cold. I still vividly recall the shock of touching it, the momentary disorientation of having to remind myself that the temperature was nearly a hundred degrees. She leaned toward me over the porch railing, and a tiny hot breeze stirred the half-dozen windchimes that hung from the eave, making a sweet cacophony. Healthy plants hung thick around her, almost obscuring her face. I could smell both her honeysuckle perfume and the faint sickly odor of her breath. She was smiling cordially; her lips were pale pink, almost colorless, against the yellow-white of her teeth. There were dark circles under her eyes. For a moment I had the terrifying fantasy that she would tumble off the porch into my arms, and that when she hit she would weigh no more than the truncated melodies from the sway of the chimes.

Her voice was much as I remembered it: husky, controlled, well-modulated. But I thought I'd heard it break, as though the two words she'd spoken had been almost too much for her. She took a deep breath, encircled my wrist with the thin icy fingers of her other hand, and said, "Come in."

I had last seen Kelly at her wedding. I'd watched the ceremony from a gauzy distance, wondering how she could bring herself to do such a thing and whether I'd ever get the chance; my father had already been sick and my mother, of course, long gone. Then I had passed through a long reception line to have her press my hand and kiss my cheek as though she'd never seen me before. Or never would again.

Ron, her new husband, had bent to kiss me, too, and I'd made a point to cough at the silly musk of his aftershave. He was tall and very fair, with baby-soft stubble on his cheeks and upper lip. His big pawlike hands cupped my shoulders as he gazed earnestly down at me. "I love her, Brenda." He could have been reciting the Boy Scout pledge. "Already she's my better half."

Later I repeated that comment to my friends; we all laughed and rolled our eyes. Ron was always terribly sincere. He could be making an offhand remark about the weather or the cafeteria food, and from his tone and delivery you'd think he was issuing a proclamation to limit worldwide nuclear arms proliferation.

Ron was *simple*. Often you could tell he'd missed the punchline of a joke, especially if it was off-color; he'd chuckle good-naturedly anyway. He had a hard time keeping up with our rapid Eastern chatter, but he'd look from one speaker to the next like an alert puppy, as if he were following right along. He was such an easy target that few of us resisted the temptation to make fun of him.

Kelly, who was brilliant, got him through school. At first she literally wrote his papers for him; he was a poli sci major and she took languages, so it meant double studying for her, but she didn't seem to pull any more all-nighters than the rest of us. Gradually he learned to write first drafts, which she then edited meticulously; you'd see them huddled at a table in the library, Kelly looking grim, Ron looking earnest and genial and bewildered.

She taught him everything. How to write a simple sentence. How to study for an exam. How to read a paragraph from beginning to end and catch the drift. How to eat without grossing everybody out. How to behave during fraternity rush. At a time when the entire Greek system was the object of much derision on our liberal little campus, Ron became a proud and busy Delt; senior year he was elected president, and Kelly, demure in gold chiffon, clung to his arm.

We gossiped that she taught him everything he knew about sex, too. That first year, before the mores and the rules loosened to allow men and women in each other's rooms, everybody made out in the courtyard of the freshman women's dorm. Because Kelly said they had too much work to do, they weren't there as often as some of the rest of us; for a while that winter and spring, I spent most of my waking hours, and a few asleep, in the courtyard with a handsome and knowledgeable young man from New Jersey named Jan.

But Ron and Kelly were there often enough for us to observe them and comment on their form. His back would be hard against the wall and his arms stiffly down around her waist. She'd be stretched up to nuzzle in his neck—or, we speculated unkindly, to whisper instructions. At first, if you said hello on your way past—and we would, just to be perverse—Ron's innate politeness would have him nodding and passing the time of day. Kelly didn't acknowledge anything but Ron; she was totally absorbed in him. Before long, he had also learned to ignore us, or to seem to.

Kelly was moody, intense, determined. Absolutely focused. I knew her before she met Ron; they assigned us as roommates freshman year. There was something about her—besides our age, the sense that we were standing on a frontier—that made me tell her things I hadn't told anybody, hadn't even thought of before. And made me listen to her self-revelations with bated breath, as though I were witness to the birth of fine music or ferreting out the inkling of a mystery.

In those days Kelly was already fascinated by women who had died for something they believed in, like Joan of Arc about whom she read in lyrical French, or for something they were and couldn't help, like Anne Frank whose diary she read in deceptively robust German. I didn't understand the words—I was a sociology major—but I knew the stories, and I loved the way Kelly looked and sounded when she read. When she stopped, there would be a rapturous silence, and then one or both of us would breathe, "Oh, that was *beautiful!*"

After she met Ron, things between Kelly and me changed. At first all she talked about was him, and I understood that; I talked about Jan a lot, too. But gradually she quit talking to me at all, and when she listened it was politely, her pen poised over the essay whose editing I had interrupted.

Ron seemed as open and expansive and featureless as the prairies of his native Nebraska. I was convinced she was wasting her life. He wasn't good enough for her. I could not imagine what she saw in him.

Unless it was the unlimited opportunity to play puppeteer, sculptor, inventor. I said that to her one night when we were both lying awake, trying not to be disturbed by the party down the hall. She was my best friend, and I thought I owed it to her to tell her what I thought.

"What is it between you and Ron anyway?" I demanded, somewhat abruptly. We'd been complaining desultorily to each other about the noise and making derogatory comments about *some people's* study habits, and in my own ears I sounded suddenly angry and hurt, which was not what I'd intended. But I went on anyway. "What is this, a role-reversed Pygmalion, or what?"

She was silent for such a long time that I thought either she'd fallen asleep or she was completely ignoring me this time. I was just about to pose my challenge again, maybe even get out of bed and cross the room and shake her by the shoulders until she paid attention to me, when she answered calmly. "There are worse things."

"Kelly, you're beautiful and brilliant. You could have any man on this campus. Ron is just so *ordinary*."

"Ron is good for me, Brenda. I don't expect you to understand." But then she assuaged my hurt feelings by trying to explain. "He takes me out of myself."

That was the last time Kelly and I talked about anything important. It was practically the last time we talked at all. For the rest of freshman year I might have had a single room, except for intimate, hurtful evidence of her—stockings hung like empty skin on the closet doorknob to dry, bottles of perfume and makeup like a string of amulets across her nightstand—all of it carefully on her side of the room. The next year she roomed with a sorority sister, somebody whom I didn't know and whom I didn't think Kelly knew very well, either.

I was surprised and a little offended to get a wedding invitation. I told myself I had no obligation to go. I went anyway, and cried, and pressed her hand. To this day I'm not sure she knew who I was when I went through the reception line. I spent most of the reception making conversation with Kelly's parents, a gaunt pale woman who looked very much like Kelly and a tall fair robust man. They were proud of their daughter; Ron was a fine young man who would go far in this world. Her father was jocular and verbose; he danced with all the young women, several times with me. Her mother barely said a word, seldom got out of her chair; her smile was like the winter sun.

At the time I didn't know that I'd noticed all that about Kelly's parents. I hadn't thought about them in years, probably had never thought about them directly. But the impressions were all there, ready for the taking. If I'd just paid attention, I might have been warned.

And then I don't know what I would have done.

Since college, Kelly and I had barely kept in touch. For a while I had kept approximate track of her through mutual friends and the alumni newsletter. I moved out West because the dry climate might be better for Daddy's health, got a graduate degree in planning and a job with the Aurora city government. Left Daddy alone too much, then hired a stranger to nurse him so I could live my own life. As if there was such a thing.

From sporadic Christmas cards, I knew that Kelly and her family had lived in various parts of Europe; Ron was an attorney specializing in international law and a high-ranking officer in the military, and his job had something to do with intelligence, maybe the CIA. I knew that they had two sons. In every communication, no matter how brief, Kelly mentioned that she had never worked a day outside the home, that when Ron was away she sometimes went for days without talking to an adult, that her languages were getting rusty except for the language of the country she happened to be living in at the time. It seemed to me that even her English was awkward, childlike, although it was hard to tell from the few sentences she wrote.

Last year I'd received a copy of a form Christmas letter, run off on pale green paper with wreaths along the margin, ostensibly composed by Ron. It was so eloquent and interesting and grammatically sophisticated that at first I was a little shocked. Then I decided—with distaste, but also with a measure of relief that should have been a clue if I'd been paying attention—that Kelly must still be ghost-writing.

For some reason, I'd kept that letter, though as far as I could remember I hadn't answered it. After Kelly's call, I'd pulled it out and re-read it. The letter described the family's travels in the Alps; though it read like a travel brochure, the prose was competent and there were vivid images. It outlined the boys' many activities and commented, "Without Kelly, of course, none of this would be possible." It mentioned that Kelly had been ill lately, tired: "The gray wet winters of northern Europe really don't agree with her. We're hoping that some of her sparkle will return when we move back home."

I'd thought there was nothing significant in that slick, chatty, green-edged letter. I'd been wrong.

Kelly's house was very orderly and close and clean. She led me down a short hallway lined with murky photographs of people I didn't think I knew, into a living room where a fire crackled in a plain brick fireplace and not a speck of ash marred the dappled marble surface of the hearth. Heavy maroon drapes were pulled shut floor to ceiling, and all the lights were on; the room was stifling.

Startled and confused, I paused in the arched doorway while Kelly went on ahead of me. I saw her pull the white fur jacket closer around her, as if she were cold.

"We haven't lived here very long," she said over her shoulder. She was apologizing, but I didn't know what for.

"It's nice," I said, and followed her into the nightlike, winterlike room.

She gestured toward a rocker-recliner. "Make yourself at home."

I sat down. Though the chair was across the room, the part of my body which faced the fire grew hot in a matter of seconds, and I had started to sweat. Kelly pulled an ottoman nearly onto the hearth and huddled onto it hugging her knees.

I was quickly discomfited by the silence between us, through which I could hear her labored breathing and the spitting of the fire. "How long have you lived here?" I asked, to have something to say.

"Just a few months. Since the first of April." So she knew it was summer.

"How long will you be here?" I knew it was sounding like an interrogation, but I desperately needed to ground myself in time and space. That was not a new impulse, though I hadn't been so acutely aware of it before. I was shaking, and the heat was making my head swim. It seemed to me that I had been floating for a long time.

I understand now, of course, how misguided it was to look to Kelly for ballast. She had almost no weight herself by that time, no substance of her own, so she couldn't have held anybody down.

Abruptly, as often happened to me when I was invaded by even a hint of strong emotion—fear, pleasure, grief—I could feel the slight weight of my father's body in my arms, the web of his baby-fine hair across my lips. I closed my eyes against the pain and curled my arms into my chest as though to keep from dropping him.

Almost tonelessly Kelly asked, "What's wrong, Brenda?" and I realized I'd covered my face with my empty hands.

"You remind me of somebody," I said. That surprised me. I wasn't even sure what it meant. Self-stimulating like an autistic child, I was rocking furiously in the cumbersome chair. I forced myself to press my palms flat against its nubby arms, stopping the motion. "Somebody else who left me," I added.

She didn't ask me what I meant. She didn't defend against my interpretation of what had happened between us. She just cocked her head in a quizzical gesture so familiar to me that I caught my breath, although I wouldn't have guessed that I remembered anything significant about her.

Absently she picked two bits of lint off the brown carpet, which had looked spotless to me, and deposited them into her other palm, closing her fingers protectively. I noticed her silver-pink nails. I noticed that her mauve stockings were opaque, thicker than standard nylons, and that the stylish high-heeled boots she wore were fur-lined. I wanted to go sit beside her, have her hug me to warm us both. I was sweating profusely.

I think I was on the verge of telling her about my father. I think I might have said things to her that I hadn't yet said to myself. I'm still haunted by the suspicion that, if I'd spoken up at that moment, subsequent events might have turned out very differently. The thought makes my blood run cold.

But I didn't say anything, for at that moment Kelly's sons came home. I flinched as I heard a screen door slam, heard children's voices laughing and squabbling. It was as if their liveliness tore at something.

Daddy died while I was out. He hadn't wanted me to go, though he would never have said so. He hadn't liked the man, any man, I was with. When I came home—earlier than I'd intended though not early enough, determined not to see that man again—I'd found my father dead on the floor. If I'd been there I could have saved him, or at least held him while he died. I owed him. He gave me life.

Struggling to stay in focus when the boys burst in, I kept my eyes on Kelly. The transformation was remarkable. Many times after that I saw it happen to her, and I was always astounded, but that first time was like witnessing a miracle, or the results of a spectacular compact with the devil.

She filled out like an inflatable doll. Color flooded into her cheeks. Her shoulders squared and she sat up straight. By the time her boys found us and rushed into the living room, bringing with them like sirens their light and fresh air and energy, she was holding out her arms to them and beaming and the white fur jacket had slipped from her shoulders onto the hearth behind her, where I thought it might burn.

I stayed at Kelly's house for a long time that first day, though I hadn't intended to. When Kelly introduced me as an old friend from college, Joshua, the younger child, stared at me solemn-eyed and demanded, "Do you know my daddy, too?" I admitted that I did, or used to. He nodded. He was very serious.

We had a picnic lunch outside on the patio. I watched the children splash in the sprinkler and bounce on the backyard trampoline, watched Kelly bask like a chameleon in the sunshine. She was a nervous hostess. She fluttered and fussed to make sure the boys and I were served, persistently inquired whether the lemonade was sweet enough and whether the sandwiches had too much mayonnaise, was visibly worried whenever any of us stopped eating. She herself didn't eat at all, as if she wasn't entitled to. She didn't swat at flies or fan herself or complain about the heat. She hardly talked to me; her interactions with the children were impatient. She watched us eat and play, and the look on her face was near-panic, as if she couldn't be sure she was getting it right.

I was restless. I wasn't used to sitting still for so long without something to occupy me—television, a newspaper, knitting. At one point I got up and went over to join the boys. I tossed the new yellow frisbee, spotted Clay on the tramp, squirted Joshua with the sprinkler. I was clumsy and they didn't like it; my intrusion altered the rhythms of their play. "Quit it!" Josh shrieked when the water hit him, and Clay simply slid off the end of the trampoline and stalked away when he discovered I'd taken up position at the side.

Somewhat aimlessly, I strolled around the yard. Red and salmon late roses climbed the privacy fence; I touched their petals and thorns, bent to sniff their fragrance. "Ron likes roses," Kelly said from behind me, and I jumped; I hadn't realized how close she was. "That's why we planted all those bushes. They're hard to take care of, though. I'm still learning. Ron buys me books."

"They're beautiful," I said.

"They're a lot of care. He's never here to do any of it. It's part of my job."

Clay appeared at my elbow. He was carrying a framed and glass-covered family portrait big enough that he had to hold it with both hands.

"Clay!" his mother remonstrated, much more sharply than I'd have expected from her. "Don't drop that!"

"I'll put it back," he said lightly, dismissing her. "See," he said earnestly to me. "That's my dad."

I didn't know what I was supposed to say, what acknowledgement would be satisfactory. I looked at him, at his brother across the yard, at the portrait. It had been taken several years ago; the boys looked much younger. Kelly was pale and lovely, clinging to her husband's arm even though the photographer had no doubt posed her standing up straight. The uniformed man at the hub of the family grouping was taller, ruddier, and possessed of much more presence than I remembered. "You look like him." I finally said to Clay. "You both do." He grinned and nodded and took the heavy picture back into the house.

I sat on the kids' swing and watched a gray bird sitting in the apple tree. It was the wrong time of the season, between blossom and fruit, to tell whether there would be a good crop; I wondered idly whether Kelly made applesauce, whether Ron and the boys liked apple pie. "My dad put up those swings for us!" Joshua shouted from the wading pool, sounding angry. I took the lemonade pitcher inside for more ice, although no one who lived there had suggested it.

Being alone in Kelly's kitchen gave me a sense of just-missed intimacy. I guessed that she spent a good deal of time here, cooking and cleaning, but there seemed to be nothing personal about her in the room. I looked around.

The pictures on the wall above the microwave were standard, square, factory-painted representations of vegetables, a tomato and a carrot and an ear of corn, pleasant enough. On the single-shelf spice rack above the dishwasher were two red-and-white cans and two undistinguished glass bottles: cinnamon, onion powder, salt, and pepper. Nothing idiosyncratic or identifying. No dishes soaked in the sink; no meat was thawing on the counter for dinner.

I remember thinking that, if I looked through the cupboards and drawers and into the back shelves of the refrigerator, I'd surely find something about Kelly, but I couldn't quite bring myself to make such a deliberate search. Now, of course, I know that there wouldn't have been anything anyway. No favorite snacks of hers secreted away. No dishes that meant anything special to her. No special recipes. In the freezer I'd probably have found fudgsicles for Clay and Eskimo Pies for Josh, and no doubt there was a six-pack of Coors Lite on the top shelf of the refrigerator for Ron. But, no matter how deeply I looked or how broadly I interpreted, I wouldn't have found anything personal about Kelly, except in what she'd made sure was there for the others.

I set the pitcher on the counter and moved so that I was standing in the middle of the floor with my hands at my sides and my eyes closed. I held my breath. It was like being trapped in a flotation tank. I could hear the boys squealing and shouting outside, the hum of a lawnmower farther away and the ticking of a clock nearby, but the sounds were outside of me, not touching. I could smell whiffs and layers of homey kitchen odors—coffee, cinnamon, onions—but I had never been fed in this room.

I opened my eyes and was dizzy. Without knowing it, I had turned, so that now I was facing a little alcove that opened off the main kitchen. A breakfast nook, maybe, or a pantry. I rounded the multicolored plexiglas partition and caught my breath.

The place was a shrine. On all three walls, from the waist-high wainscoting nearly to the ceiling, were photographs of Ron and Clay and Joshua. Black-and-white photos on a plain white background, unlike the busy kitchen wallpaper in the rest of the room. Pictures of them singly and in various combinations: Ron in uniform, looking stoic and sensible; Clay doing a flip on the trampoline; Joshua in his Cub Scout uniform; the three of them in a formal pose, each boy with his hand on his father's shoulder; the boys by a Christmas tree. I counted; there were forty-three photographs.

I couldn't bring myself to go into the alcove. I think I was afraid I'd hear voices. And there was not a single likeness of Kelly anywhere on the open white walls.

Later, a grim and wonderful thought occurred to me: it would have been virtually impossible for a detective to find out anything useful about Kelly. Or for a voodoo practitioner to fashion an efficacious doll. There was little essence of her left. There were few details. By the end, it would have been easy to say that she had no soul.

For the rest of that summer and into the fall, I spent a great deal of time at Kelly's house. It started with lunch on Saturdays, always a picnic lunch with the boys on the patio, sandwiches and lemonade and chips. She never let me bring anything; she seemed to take offense when I tried to insist.

"Why don't you and I go somewhere for lunch, Kelly? Get a sitter for the boys or take them to the pool or something."

"The pool isn't safe. I don't like the kind of kids who go there."

Kelly and I never seemed to be alone together. Her sons were always there, in the same room or within earshot or about to rush in and demand something of her. I chafed. I didn't much like the boys anyway; I found them mouthy and rude, to me but especially to their mother, and altogether too high-spirited for my taste.

"It's nice to see a mother spend as much time with her kids as you do," I said once, lying, trying to understand, trying to get her to talk to me about something.

"We've always been—close," she said, a little hesitantly. "They both nursed until they were almost two. Sometimes Josh will still try to nip my breast. In play, you know."

A little taken aback, I said, "You seem to enjoy their company." I didn't know whether that was true or not.

She shrugged and laughed a little. "I think I've inherited my father's attitudes toward children. They'd be fine if you could teach them and train them and mold them into what you want. Otherwise, they're mostly irritating." She laughed again and shivered, hugged herself, passed a hand over her eyes. "But I don't have to *like* my kids in order to be a good mother, do I?"

For a long time, I didn't see Ron. He was always at work when I was there, and, no matter how late I stayed, he worked later.

"Come with me to see this movie. I've been wanting to see it for a long time, and it's about to leave town, and I don't want to go alone."

"There's a movie that the boys want to see. One of those Kung fu things. I promised I'd take them this weekend."

Kelly's roses faded, and the marigolds and petunias and then chrysanthemums came into their own. The apple tree bore nicely, tiny fruit clustered all on the south side of the tree because, Kelly speculated, the blossoms on the north side had been frozen early in the spring. That distressed her enormously; her eyes shone with tears when she talked about it. The boys went back to school.

"Now you have lots of free time. Let's go to the art museum one morning next week. I can take a few hours off."

"Oh, Brenda, the work around here is endless. Really. I have fall housecleaning to do. I'm redecorating Clay's room. There must be a dozen layers of wallpaper on those walls. My first responsibility is to Ron and the children. You're welcome to come here, though. I could fix you lunch."

One crisp Wednesday in late September I had a meeting over on her side of town, and I didn't have to be back at the office until my two o'clock staff meeting. Impulsively, I turned off onto a side street toward her house.

I had never been to Kelly's house on a weekday before. I had never dropped in on her unexpectedly. I had seldom dropped in on anybody unexpectedly; I liked to have time to prepare, and was keenly aware of the differences between people in private and people when they met the world, even the small and confusd part of the world represented by me. My heart was skittering uneasily, and I felt a little feverish, chilled, though the sun was warm and the sky brilliant. The houses and trees and fence rows along these old blocks had taken on that sharp-edged qualilty that autumn sometimes imparts to a city; every brick seemed outlined, every flower and leaf a jewel.

I parked by the side of her house, across the street. I opened and shut the gate as quietly as I could. I stood for a while on her porch, listening to the windchimes, catching stray rainbows from the lopsided paper leaf Josh had made in school and hung in the front window. She had moved the plants inside for the winter, and the porch seemed bare. Finally I pushed the button for the doorbell and waited. A few cars went by behind me. I touched the doorbell button again, listened for any sound inside the house, could hear none.

When I tried the door, it opened easily. I went in quickly and shut the door behind me, thinking to keep out the light and dust. I was nearly through the front hall and to the kitchen before I called her name.

"In here, Brenda," she answered, as though she'd been expecting me. I stopped for a moment, bewildered; maybe I'd somehow forgotten that I had called ahead, or maybe we'd had plans for today that I hadn't written in my appointment book.

"Where?"

"In here."

I found her, finally, in the master bedroom. She was in bed, under the covers; she wore a scarf and a stocking cap on her head, mittens on the hands that pulled the covers up to her chin.

Around her neck I could see the collar of the white fur jacket. Her teeth were chattering, and her skin was so pale that it was almost green. I stood in the doorway and stared. The shaft of light through the blinded window looked wintry. "Kelly, what's wrong? Are you sick?" It was a question I could have asked months before; now it seemed impossible to avoid.

"I'm *cold*," she said weakly. "I—don't seem to have any energy."

"Should I call somebody?"

"No, it's all right. Usually if I stay in bed all day I'm all right by the time the boys get home from school."

"How often does this happen?"

"Oh, I don't know. Every other day or so now, I guess."

I had advanced into the room, stood by the side of the bed. I was reluctant to touch her. I now know that the contagion had nothing to do with physical contact with Kelly, that I was safer alone in that house with her than I've been at any time since. But that morning all I knew was cold fear, and alarm for my friend, and an intense, exhilarating curiosity. "Where's Ron?" I demanded. "Is he still out of town? Does he know about this?"

"He came home late last night," she told me, and I had no way of appreciating the significance of what she'd said.

"What shall I do? Should I call him at work? Or call a doctor?"

"No." With a great sigh and much tremulous effort, she lifted her feet over the side of the bed and sat up. I could feel her dizziness; I put my hand flat against the wall and lowered my head to let it clear. Kelly stood up. "Take me out somewhere," she said. "I'm hungry. Let's go to lunch."

Without my help, she made it out of the house, down the walk, and into the car. The sun had been shining in the passenger window, so it would be warm for her there. There was definitely a fall chill in the air, I decided, as I found myself shivering a little. "Where do you want to go?" I asked her.

"Someplace fast."

In Denver I have always been delighted, personally and professionally, by contrasts, one of which is the proximity of quiet residential neighborhoods like Kelly's to bustling commercial strips. We were five minutes from half a dozen fast-food places. Kelly said she didn't care which one, so I drove somewhat randomly and found the one with the least-crowded parking lot. She wanted to go inside.

The place was bright, warm, cacophonous. I saw Kelly wrap herself more tightly in the fur jacket, saw people glance at her and then glance away. She went to find a seat, as far away from the windows and the doors as she could, and I ordered for both of us, not knowing what she wanted, taking a chance. There was a very long line. When I finally got to her, she was staring with a stricken look on her face at the middle-aged woman in the ridiculous uniform who was clearing the tables and sweeping the floor. "I talked to her," Kelly whispered as I set the laden tray down. "She has a master's degree."

"In what?" I asked, making conversation. It seemed important to keep her engaged, though I didn't know what she was talking about. "Here's your shake. I hope chocolate's all right. They were out of strawberry."

When she didn't answer right away I looked at her more closely. The expression of horror on her face made my stomach turn. Her eyes were bloodshot and bulging. She was breathing heavily through her mouth. Her gloved hands on the tabletop were clawed, as if trying to find in the formica something to cling to. "That could be me a few years from now," she said hoarsely. "Working in a fast-food place, for a little extra money and something to do. Alone. That could be me."

"Don't be silly," I snapped. "You have a lot more going for you than that woman does."

Suddenly she was shrieking at me. "How do you know that? How can you know? I've let everybody down! Everybody! All my teachers and professors who said I had so much potential! My father! Everybody! You don't know what you're talking about!" Then, to my own horror, she struggled to her feet and hobbled out the door. For a moment, I really thought she'd disappeared, vanished somehow into the air that wasn't much thinner than she was. I told myself that was crazy and followed her.

The lunchtime crowd had filled in behind Kelly and was all of a piece again. I pushed through it and through the door, which framed the busy street scene as though it were a poor photograph, flat and without meaning to me until I entered it. I looked around. Kelly had collapsed on the hot sidewalk against the building. Her knees were drawn up, her head was down so that the stringy dark hair fell over her face, the collar of the jacket stood up around her ears. Two women in shorts and halter tops crouched beside her. I hurried, as though to save her from them, although, of course, by then Kelly wasn't the one who needed protecting.

* * *

I met Ron at the hospital. From the ambulance stretcher, in a flat high voice that almost seemed part of the siren, Kelly had told me how to reach him. I hadn't wanted to; I hadn't wanted him with us. By the time I made it through all the layers and synapses of the bureaucracy he worked in and heard his official voice on the other end of the line, I was furious. But I hadn't missed anything; Kelly was still waiting in the emergency room, slumped in a chair. Ron did not sound especially alarmed; I told myself it was his training. He said he'd be there in fifteen minutes, and he was.

They had just taken Kelly to be examined when he got there. I was standing at the counter looking after her, feeling bereft; they wouldn't let me go back behind the curtain with her, and she was too weak to ask for me. When the tall blond uniformed man strode by me, I didn't try to speak to him, and no one else did either. I doubt that Kelly asked for him, or gave permission, or even recognized him when he came. None of that was necessary. He was her husband. She was part of him. He had the right.

My father and I had been bound like that, too. If I'd asserted the right to be part of him, welcomed and treasured it, I could have been. Instead, I'd thought it was necessary for me to grow up, to separate. And so I'd lost him. Lost us both, I thought then, for without him I had no idea who I was.

I felt Ron's presence approaching me before I opened my eyes and saw him. "She's unconscious," he said. "They don't know yet what's wrong. You don't look very good yourself. Come and sit down."

I didn't let him touch me then, but I preceded him to a pair of orange plastic bucket chairs attached to a metal bar against the wall. We were then sitting squarely side-by-side, and the chairs didn't move; I didn't make the effort to face him. He was friendly and solemn, as befitted the occasion. He took my hand in both of his, swallowing it. "Brenda," he said; he made my name sound far more significant than I'd ever thought it was, and—despite myself, despite the circumstances, despite what I'd have mistakenly called my better judgment—something inside me stirred gratefully. "It's nice to see you again after all these years. I'm sorry our reunion turned out to be like this. Kelly has talked a great deal about you over the past few months."

I nodded. I didn't know what to say.

"What happened?" Ron asked. He let go of my hand and it was cold. I put both hands in my pockets.

"She—collapsed," I told him. The more I told him, the angrier I became, and the closer to the kind of emptying, wracking sobs I'd been so afraid of. Now I know there's nothing to fear in being emptied; Kelly simply hadn't taken it far enough. To the end, some part of her fought it. I don't fight at all anymore.

"What do you mean? Tell me what happened. The details." He was moving in, assuming command. It crossed my mind to resist him, but from the instant he'd walked into the room I'd felt exhausted.

"I dropped by to see her. I was in the neighbourhood. When I got there she was sick. She asked me to take her out to lunch. So we— "

"Out?" His blond eyebrows rose and then furrowed disapprovingly. "Out of the house? With you?"

I mustered a little indignation. "What's wrong with that?"

"It's—unusual, that's all. Go on."

I told him the rest of what I knew. It seemed to take an enormous amount of time to say it all, though I wouldn't have thought I had that much to say. I stumbled over words. There were long silences. Ron listened attentively. At one point he rested his hand on my shoulder in a comradely way, and I was too tired and disoriented to pull free. When I finished, he nodded, and then someone came for him from behind the curtains and lights, and I was left alone again, knowing I hadn't said enough.

Kelly never came home from the hospital. She died without regaining consciousness. Many times since then I've wondered what she would have said to me if she'd awakened, what advice she would have given, what warning, how she would have passed the torch.

I wasn't there when she died. Ron was. He called me early the next morning to tell me. He sounded drained; his voice was flat and thin. "Oh, Ron," I said, foolishly, and then waited for him to tell me what to do.

"I'd like you to come over," he said. "The boys are having a hard time."

I haven't left since. I haven't been back to my apartment even to pick up my things; none of my former possessions seems worth retrieval. I had no animals to feed, no plants to water, no books or clothes or furniture or photographs that mean anything to me now.

Kelly kept her house orderly. From the first day, I could find things. The boys' schedules were predictable, although very busy; names and phone numbers of their friends' parents, Scout leaders, piano teachers were on a laminated list on the kitchen bulletin board. In her half of the master bedroom closet, I found clothes of various sizes, and the larger ones, from before she lost so much weight, fit fine.

The first week I took personal leave from work. Since then I've been calling in sick, when I think of it; most recently I haven't called in at all and, of course, they don't know where I am.

Ron is away a good deal. The work he does is important and mysterious; I don't know exactly what it is, but I'm proud to be able to help him do it.

But he was home that first week, and we got used to each other. "You're very different from the man I knew in college," I told him. We were sitting in the darkened living room. We'd been talking about Kelly. We'd both been crying.

He was sitting beside me on the couch. I saw him nod and slightly smile. "Kelly used to say I'd developed my potential beyond her wildest dreams," he admitted, "and she'd lost hers."

I felt a flash of anger against her. She was dead. "She had a choice," I pointed out. "Nobody forced her to do anything. She could have done other things with her life."

"Don't be too sure of that," he said, sharply. His tone surprised and hurt me. I glanced at him through the shadows, saw him lean forward to set his drink on the coffee table. He took my empty glass from my hands and put it down, too, then swiftly lowered his face to my neck.

There was a small pain and, afterwards, a small stinging wound. When he was finished he stood up, wiped his mouth with his breast pocket handkerchief, and went upstairs to bed. I sat up for a long time, amazed, touched, frightened. No longer lonely. No longer having decisions to be made or protection to construct. That first night, that first time, I did not feel tired or cold; the sickness has since begun, but the exhilaration has heightened, too.

Ron says he loves me. He says he and the boys need me, couldn't get along without me. I like to hear that. I know what he means.

M. R. James

An Episode of Cathedral History

Montague Rhodes James (1862–1936) is widely regarded as the author of "some of the most alarming and unforgettable ghost stories in the English language". A serious child, he developed a life-long interest in medieval books and antiques at an early age. He was educated at Eton and later King's College, Cambridge, and in 1905 he became Provost of King's and was Vice-Chancellor of the University from 1913–15, before returning to Eton as Provost in 1918.

Most of his stories were written for friends or college magazines, and include such subtle chillers as 'Lost Hearts', 'Canon Alberic's Scrap-Book', 'The Mezzotint', 'Casting the Runes', 'Count Magnus' and the classic 'Oh, Whistle, and I'll Come to You, My Lad'. His first collection was Ghost Stories of an Antiquary *(1904), followed by* More Ghost Stories of an Antiquary, A Thin Ghost and Others, A Warning to the Curious *and* The Collected Ghost Stories.

'An Episode of Cathedral History' originally appeared in the Cambridge Review *before being included in James's third collection, published in 1919. Although it remains one of his less well-known tales, told in the author's usual understated style, James's wild-looking vampire is still a truly unnerving creation.*

THERE WAS ONCE a learned gentleman who was deputed to examine and report upon the archives of the Cathedral of Southminster. The examination of these records demanded a very considerable expenditure of time: hence it became advisable for him to engage lodgings in the city: for though the Cathedral body were profuse in their offers of hospitality, Mr Lake felt that he would prefer to be master of his day. This was recognised as reasonable. The Dean eventually wrote advising Mr Lake, if he were not already suited, to communicate with Mr Worby, the principal Verger, who occupied a house convenient to the church and was prepared to take in a quiet lodger for three or four weeks. Such an arrangement was precisely what Mr Lake desired. Terms were easily agreed upon, and early in December, like another Mr Datchery (as he remarked to himself), the investigator found himself in the occupation of a very comfortable room in an ancient and "cathedraly" house.

One so familiar with the customs of Cathedral churches, and treated with such obvious consideration by the Dean and Chapter of this Cathedral in particular, could not fail to command the respect of the Head Verger. Mr Worby even acquiesced in certain modifications of statements he had been accustomed to offer for years to parties of visitors. Mr Lake, on his part, found the Verger a very cheery companion, and took advantage of any occasion that presented itself for enjoying his conversation when the day's work was over.

One evening, about nine o'clock, Mr Worby knocked at his lodger's door. "I've occasion," he said, "to go across to the Cathedral, Mr Lake, and I think I made you a promise when I did so next I would give you the opportunity to see what it looked like at night time. It's quite fine and dry outside, if you care to come."

"To be sure I will; very much obliged to you, Mr Worby, for thinking of it, but let me get my coat."

"Here it is, sir, and I've another lantern here that you'll find advisable for the steps, as there's no moon."

"Anyone might think we were Jasper and Durdles, over again, mightn't they?" said Lake, as they crossed the close, for he had ascertained that the Verger had read *Edwin Drood*.

"Well, so they might," said Mr Worby, with a short laugh, "though I don't know whether we ought to take it as a compliment. Odd ways, I often think, they had at that Cathedral, don't it seem so to you, sir? Full choral matins at seven o'clock in the morning all the year round. Wouldn't suit our boys' voices nowadays, and I think there's one or two of the men would be applying for a rise if the Chapter was to bring it in—particular the altos."

They were now at the south-west door. As Mr Worby was unlocking it, Lake said, "Did you ever find anybody locked in here by accident?"

"Twice I did. One was a drunk sailor; however he got in I don't know. I s'pose he went to sleep in the service, but by the time I got to him he was praying fit to bring the roof in. Lor'! what a noise that man did make! said it was the first time he'd been inside a church for ten years, and blest if ever he'd try it again. The other was an old sheep: them boys it was, up to their games. That was the last time they tried it on, though. There, sir, now you see what we look like; our late Dean used now and again to bring parties in, but he preferred a moonlight night, and there was a piece of verse he'd say to 'em, relating to a Scotch cathedral, I understand; but I don't know; I almost think the effect's better when it's all dark-like. Seems to add to the size and height. Now if you won't mind stopping somewhere in the nave while I go up into the choir where my business lays, you'll see what I mean."

Accordingly Lake waited, leaning against a pillar, and watched the light wavering along the length of the church, and up the steps into the choir, until it was intercepted by some screen or other furniture, which only allowed the reflection to be seen on the piers and roof. Not many minutes had passed before Worby reappeared at the door of the choir and by waving his lantern signalled to Lake to rejoin him.

"I suppose it *is* Worby, and not a substitute," thought Lake to himself, as he walked up the nave. There was, in fact, nothing untoward. Worby showed him the papers which he had come to fetch out of the Dean's stall, and asked him what he thought of the spectacle: Lake agreed that it was well worth seeing. "I suppose," he said, as they walked towards the altar-steps together, "that you're too much used to going about here at night to feel nervous—but you must get a start every now and then, don't you, when a book falls down or a door swings to?"

"No, Mr Lake, I can't say I think much about noises, not nowadays: I'm much more afraid of finding an escape of gas or a burst in the stove pipes than anything else. Still there have been times, years ago. Did you notice that plain altar-tomb there—fifteenth century we say it is, I don't know if you agree to that? Well, if you didn't look at it, just come back and give it a glance, if you'd be so good." It was on the north side of the choir, and rather awkwardly placed: only about three feet from the enclosing stone screen. Quite plain, as the Verger had said, but for some ordinary stone panelling. A metal cross of some size on the northern side (that next to the screen) was the solitary feature of any interest.

Lake agreed that it was not earlier than the Perpendicular period: "But," he said, "unless it's the tomb of some remarkable person, you'll forgive me for saying that I don't think it's particularly noteworthy."

"Well, I can't say as it is the tomb of anybody noted in 'istory," said Worby, who had a dry smile on his face, "for we don't own any record whatsoever of who it was put up to. For all that, if you've half an hour to spare, sir, when we get back to the house, Mr Lake, I could tell you a tale about that tomb. I won't begin on it now; it strikes cold here, and we don't want to be dawdling about all night."

"Of course I should like to hear it immensely."

"Very well, sir, you shall. Now if I might put a question to you," he went on, as they passed down the choir aisle, "in our little local guide—and not only there, but in the little book on our Cathedral in the series—you'll find it stated that this portion of the building was erected previous to the twelfth century. Now of course I should be glad enough to take that view, but—mind the step, sir—but, I put it to you—does the lay of the stone 'ere in this portion of the wall"—which he tapped with his key—"does it to your eye carry the flavour of what you might call Saxon masonry? No, I thought not; no more it does to me: now, if you'll believe me, I've said as much to those men—one's the librarian of our Free Library here, and the other came down from London on purpose—fifty times, if I have once, but I might just as well have talked to that bit of stonework. But there it is, I suppose everyone's got their opinions."

The discussion of this peculiar trait of human nature occupied Mr Worby almost up to the moment when he and Lake re-entered the former's house. The condition of the fire in Lake's sitting-room led to a suggestion from Mr Worby that they should finish the evening in his own parlour. We find them accordingly settled there some short time afterwards.

Mr Worby made his story a long one, and I will not undertake to tell it wholly in his own words, or in his own order. Lake committed the substance of it to paper immediately after hearing it, together with some few passages of the narrative which had fixed themselves *verbatim* in his mind; I shall probably find it expedient to condense Lake's record to some extent.

Mr Worby was born, it appeared, about the year 1828. His father before him had been connected with the Cathedral, and likewise his grandfather. One or both had been choristers, and in later life both had done work as mason and carpenter respectively about the fabric. Worby himself, though possessed, as he frankly acknowledged, of an indifferent voice, had been drafted into the choir at about ten years of age.

It was in 1840 that the wave of the Gothic revival smote the Cathedral of Southminster. "There was a lot of lovely stuff went then, sir," said Worby, with a sigh. "My father couldn't hardly believe it when he got his orders to clear out the choir. There was a new dean just come in—Dean Burscough it was—and my father had been 'prenticed to a good firm of joiners in the city, and knew what good work was when he saw it. Crool it was, he used to say: all that beautiful wainscot oak, as good as the day it was put up, and garlands-like of foliage and fruit, and lovely old gilding work on the coats of arms and the organ pipes. All went to the timber yard—every bit except some little pieces worked up in the Lady Chapel, and 'ere in this overmantel. Well—I may be mistook, but I say our choir never looked as well since. Still there was a lot found out about the history of the church, and no doubt but what it did stand in need of repair. There was very few winters passed but what we'd lose a pinnacle." Mr Lake expressed his concurrence with Worby's views of restoration, but owns to a fear about this point lest the story proper should never be reached. Possibly this was perceptible in his manner.

Worby hastened to reassure him, "Not but what I could carry on about that topic for hours at a time, and do so when I see my opportunity. But Dean Burscough he was very set on the Gothic period, and nothing would serve him but everything must be made agreeable to that. And one morning after service he appointed for my father to meet him in the choir, and he came back after he'd taken off his robes in the vestry, and he'd got a roll of paper with him, and the verger that was then brought in a table, and they begun spreading it out on the table with prayer books to keep it down, and my father helped 'em, and he saw it was a picture of the inside of a choir in a Cathedral; and the Dean—he was a quick-spoken gentleman—he says, 'Well, Worby, what do you think of that?' 'Why,' says my father, 'I don't think I 'ave the pleasure of knowing that view. Would that be Hereford Cathedral, Mr Dean?' 'No, Worby,' says the Dean, 'that's Southminster Cathedral as we hope to see it before many years.' 'Indeed, sir,' says my father, and that was all he did say—leastways to the Dean—but he used to tell me he felt really faint in himself when he looked round our choir as I can remember it, all comfortable and furnished-like, and then see this nasty little dry picter, as he called it, drawn out by some London architect.

Well, there I am again. But you'll see what I mean if you look at this old view."

Worby reached down a framed print from the wall. "Well, the long and the short of it was that the Dean he handed over to my father a copy of an order of the Chapter that he was to clear out every bit of the choir—make a clean sweep—ready for the new work that was being designed up in town, and he was to put it in hand as soon as ever he could get the breakers together. Now then, sir, if you look at that view, you'll see where the pulpit used to stand: that's what I want you to notice, if you please." It was, indeed, easily seen; an unusually large structure of timber with a domed sounding-board, standing at the east end of the stalls on the north side of the choir, facing the bishop's throne. Worby proceeded to explain that during the alterations, services were held in the nave, the members of the choir being thereby disappointed of an anticipated holiday, and the organist in particular incurring the suspicion of having wilfully damaged the mechanism of the temporary organ that was hired at considerable expense from London.

The work of demolition began with the choir screens and organ loft, and proceeded gradually eastwards, disclosing, as Worby said, many interesting features of older work. While this was going on the members of the Chapter were, naturally, in and about the choir a great deal, and it soon became apparent to the elder Worby—who could not help overhearing some of their talk—that, on the part of the senior Canons especially, there must have been a good deal of disagreement before the policy now being carried out had been adopted. Some were of opinion that they should catch their deaths of cold in the return-stalls, unprotected by a screen from the draughts in the nave: others objected to being exposed to the view of persons in the choir aisles, especially, they said, during the sermons, when they found it helpful to listen in a posture which was liable to misconstruction. The strongest opposition, however, came from the oldest of the body, who up to the last moment objected to the removal of the pulpit. "You ought not to touch it, Mr Dean," he said with great emphasis one morning, when the two were standing before it: "you don't know what mischief you may do." "Mischief? it's not a work of any particular merit, Canon." "Don't call me Canon," said the old man with great asperity, "that is, for thirty years I've been known as Dr Ayloff, and I shall be obliged, Mr Dean, if you would kindly humour me in that matter. And as to the pulpit (which I've preached from for thirty years, though I don't insist on that), all I'll say is, I *know* you're doing wrong in moving it." "But what sense could there be, my dear Doctor, in leaving it where it is, when we're fitting up the rest of the choir in a totally different *style*? What reason could be given—apart from the look of the thing?" "Reason! reason!" said old Dr Ayloff; "if you young men—if I may say so without any disrespect, Mr Dean—if you'd only listen to reason a little, and not be always asking for it, we should get on better. But there, I've said my say." The old gentleman hobbled off, and as it proved, never entered the Cathedral again. The season—it was a hot summer—turned sickly on a sudden. Dr Ayloff was one of the first to go, with some affection of the muscles of the thorax, which took him painfully at night. And at many services the number of choirmen and boys was very thin.

Meanwhile the pulpit had been done away with. In fact, the sounding-board (part of which still exists as a table in a summer-house in the palace garden) was taken down within an hour or two of Dr Ayloff's protest. The removal of the base—not effected without considerable trouble—disclosed to view, greatly to the exultation of the restoring party, an altar-tomb—the tomb, of course, to which Worby had attracted Lake's attention that same evening. Much fruitless research was expended in attempts to identify the occupant; from that day to this he has never had a name put to him. The structure had been most carefully boxed in under the pulpit-base, so that such slight ornament as it possessed was not defaced; only on the north side of it there was what looked like an injury; a gap between two of the slabs composing the side. It might be two or three inches across. Palmer, the mason, was directed to fill it up in a week's time, when he came to do some other small jobs near that part of the choir.

The season was undoubtedly a very trying one. Whether the church was built on a site that had once been a marsh, as was suggested, or for whatever reason, the residents in its immediate neighbourhood had, many of them, but little enjoyment of the exquisite sunny days and the calm nights of August and September. To several of the older people—Dr Ayloff, among others, as we have seen—the summer proved downright fatal, but even among the younger, few escaped either a sojourn in bed for a matter of weeks, or at the least, a brooding sense of oppression, accompanied by hateful nightmares. Gradually there formulated itself a suspicion—which grew into a conviction—that the alterations in the Cathedral had something to say in the matter. The widow of a former old verger, a pensioner of the Chapter of Southminster, was visited by dreams, which she retailed to her friends, of a shape that slipped out of the little door of the south transept as the dark fell in, and flitted—taking a fresh direction every night—about the Close, disappearing for a while in house after house, and finally emerging again when the night sky was paling. She could see nothing of it, she said, but that it was a moving form: only she had an impression that when it returned to the church, as it seemed to do in the end of the dream, it turned its head: and then, she could not tell why, but she thought it had red eyes. Worby remembered hearing the old lady tell this dream at a tea-party in the house of the chapter clerk. Its recurrence might, perhaps, he said, be taken as a symptom of approaching illness; at any rate before the end of September the old lady was in her grave.

The interest excited by the restoration of this great church was not confined to its own county. One day that summer an F.S.A., of some celebrity, visited the place. His business was to write an account of the discoveries that had been made, for the Society of Antiquaries, and his wife, who accompanied him, was to make a series of illustrative drawings for his report. In the morning she employed herself in making a general sketch of the choir; in the afternoon she devoted herself to details. She first drew the newly-exposed altar-tomb, and when that was finished, she called her husband's attention to a beautiful piece of diaper-ornament on the screen just behind it, which had, like the tomb itself, been completely concealed by the pulpit. Of course, he said, an illustration of that must be made; so she seated herself on the tomb and began a careful drawing which occupied her till dusk.

Her husband had by this time finished his work of measuring and description, and they agreed that it was time to be getting back to their hotel. "You may as well brush my skirt, Frank," said the lady, "it must have got covered with dust, I'm sure." He obeyed dutifully; but, after a moment, he said, "I don't know whether you value this dress particularly, my dear, but I'm inclined to think it's seen its best days. There's a great bit of it gone." "Gone? Where?" said she. "I don't know where it's gone, but it's off at the bottom edge behind here." She pulled it hastily into sight, and was horrified to find a jagged tear extending some way into the substance of the stuff; very much, she said, as if a dog had rent it away. The dress was, in any case, hopelessly spoilt, to her great vexation, and though they looked everywhere, the missing piece could not be found. There were many ways, they concluded, in which the injury might have come about, for the choir was full of old bits of woodwork with nails sticking out of them. Finally, they could only suppose that one of these had caused the mischief, and that the workmen, who had been about all day, had carried off that particular piece with the fragment of dress still attached to it.

It was about this time, Worby thought, that his little dog began to wear an anxious expression when the hour for it to be put into the shed in the back yard approached. (For his mother had ordained that it must not sleep in the house.) One evening, he said, when he was just going to pick it up and carry it out, it looked at him "like a Christian, and waved its 'and, and, I was going to say—well, you know 'ow they do carry on sometimes, and the end of it was I put it under my coat, and 'uddled it upstairs—and I'm afraid I as good as deceived my poor mother on the subject. After that the dog acted very artful with 'iding itself under the bed for half an hour or more before bedtime came, and we worked it so as my mother never found out what we'd done." Of course Worby was glad of its company anyhow, but more particularly when the nuisance that is still remembered in Southminster as "the crying" set in.

"Night after night," said Worby, "that dog seemed to know it was coming; he'd creep out, he would, and snuggle into the bed and cuddle right up to me shivering, and when the crying come he'd be like a wild thing, shoving his head under my arm, and I was fully near as bad. Six or seven times we'd hear it, not more, and when he'd dror out his 'ed again I'd know it was over for that night. What was it like, sir? Well, I never heard but one thing that seemed to hit it off. I happened to be playing about in the Close, and there was two of the Canons met and said 'Good morning' one to another. 'Sleep well last night?' says one—it was Mr Henslow that one, and Mr Lyall was the other. 'Can't say I did,' says Mr Lyall, 'rather too much of Isaiah xxxiv.14 for me.' 'xxxiv.14,' says Mr Henslow, 'what's that?' 'You call yourself a Bible reader!' says Mr Lyall. (Mr Henslow, you must know, he was one of what used to be termed Simeon's lot—pretty much what we should call the Evangelical party.) 'You go and look it up.' I wanted to know what he was getting at myself, and so off I ran home and got out my own Bible, and there it was: 'the satyr shall cry to his fellow.' Well, I thought, is that what we've been listening to these past nights? and I tell you it made me look over my shoulder a time or two. Of course I'd asked my father and mother about what it could be before that, but they both said it was most likely cats: but they spoke very short, and I could see they was troubled. My word! that was a noise—'ungry-like, as if it was calling after someone that wouldn't come. If ever you felt you wanted company, it would be when you was waiting for it to begin again. I believe two or three nights there was men put on to watch in different parts of the Close; but they all used to get together in one corner, the nearest they could to the High Street, and nothing came of it.

"Well, the next thing was this. Me and another of the boys—he's in business in the city now as a grocer, like his father before him—we'd gone up in the choir after morning service was over, and we heard old Palmer the mason bellowing to some of his men. So we went up nearer, because we knew he was a rusty old chap and there might be some fun going. It appears Palmer 'd told this man to stop up the chink in that old tomb. Well, there was this man keeping on saying he'd done it the best he could, and there was Palmer carrying on like all possessed about it. 'Call that making a job of it?' he says. 'If you had your rights you'd get the sack for this. What do you suppose I pay you your wages for? What do you suppose I'm going to say to the Dean and Chapter when they come round, as come they may do any time, and see where you've been bungling about covering the 'ole place with mess and plaster and Lord knows what?' 'Well, master, I done the best I could,' says the man; 'I don't know no more than what you do 'ow it come to fall out this way. I tamped it right in the 'ole,' he says, 'and now it's fell out,' he says, 'I never see.'

"'Fell out!' says old Palmer, 'why it's nowhere near the place. Blowed out, you mean'; and he picked up a bit of plaster, and so did I, that was laying up against the screen, three or four feet off, and not dry yet; and old Palmer he looked at it curious-like, and then he turned round on me and he says, 'Now then, you boys, have you been up to some of your games here?' 'No,' I says, 'I haven't, Mr Palmer; there's none of us been about here till just this minute'; and while I was talking the other boy, Evans, he got looking in through the chink, and I heard him draw in his breath, and he came away sharp and up to us, and says he, 'I believe there's something in there. I saw something shiny.' 'What! I dare say!' says old Palmer; 'well, I ain't got time to stop about there. You, William, you go off and get some more stuff and make a job of it this time; if not, there'll be trouble in my yard,' he says.

"So the man he went off, and Palmer too, and us boys stopped behind, and I says to Evans, 'Did you really see anything in there?' 'Yes,' he says, 'I did indeed.' So then I says, 'Let's shove something in and stir it up.' And we tried several of the bits of wood that was laying about, but they were all too big. Then Evans he had a sheet of music he'd brought with him, an anthem or a service, I forget which it is now, and he rolled it up small and shoved it in the chink; two or three times he did it, and nothing happened. 'Give it to me, boy,' I said, and I had a try. No, nothing happened. Then, I don't know why I thought of it, I'm sure, but I stooped down just opposite the chink and put my two fingers in my mouth and whistled—you know the way—and at that I seemed to think I heard something stirring, and

I says to Evans, 'Come away,' I says; 'I don't like this,' 'Oh, rot,' he says, 'give me that roll,' and he took it and shoved it in. And I don't think ever I see anyone go so pale as he did. 'I say, Worby,' he says, 'it's caught, or else someone's got hold of it.' 'Pull it out or leave it,' I says. 'Come and let's get off.' So he gave a good pull, and it came away. Leastways most of it did, but the end was gone. Torn off it was, and Evans looked at it for a second and then he gave a sort of a croak and let it drop, and we both made off out of there as quick as ever we could. When we got outside Evans says to me, 'Did you see the end of that paper?' 'No,' I says, 'only it was torn.' 'Yes, it was,' he says, 'but it was wet too, and black!' Well, partly because of the fright we had, and partly because that music was wanted in a day or two, and we knew there'd be a set-out about it with the organist, we didn't say nothing to anyone else, and I suppose the workmen they swept up the bit that was left along with the rest of the rubbish. But Evans, if you were to ask him this very day about it, he'd stick to it he saw that paper wet and black at the end where it was torn."

After that the boys gave the choir a wide berth, so that Worby was not sure what was the result of the mason's renewed mending of the tomb. Only he made out from fragments of conversation dropped by the workmen passing through the choir that some difficulty had been met with, and that the governor—Mr Palmer to wit—had tried his own hand at the job. A little later, he happened to see Mr Palmer himself knocking at the door of the Deanery and being admitted by the butler. A day or so after that, he gathered from a remark his father let fall at breakfast, that something a little out of the common was to be done in the Cathedral after morning service on the morrow. "And I'd just as soon it was today," his father added; "I don't see the use of running risks." "'Father,' I says, 'what are you going to do in the Cathedral tomorrow?' And he turned on me as savage as I ever see him—he was a wonderful good-tempered man as a general thing, my poor father was. 'My lad,' he says, 'I'll trouble you not to go picking up your elders' and betters' talk: it's not manners and it's not straight. What I'm going to do or not going to do in the Cathedral tomorrow is none of your business: and if I catch sight of you hanging about the place tomorrow after your work's done, I'll send you home with a flea in your ear. Now you mind that.' Of course I said I was very sorry and that, and equally of course I went off and laid my plans with Evans. We knew there was a stair up in the corner of the transept which you can get up to the triforium, and in them days the door to it was pretty well always open, and even if it wasn't we knew the key usually laid under a bit of matting hard by. So we made up our minds we'd be putting away music and that, next morning while the rest of the boys was clearing off, and then slip up the stairs and watch from the triforium if there was any signs of work going on.

"Well, that same night I dropped off asleep as sound as a boy does, and all of a sudden the dog woke me up, coming into the bed, and thought I, now we're going to get it sharp, for he seemed more frightened than usual. After about five minutes sure enough came this cry. I can't give you no idea what it was like; and so near too—nearer than I'd heard it yet—and a funny thing, Mr Lake, you know what a place this Close is for an echo, and particular if you stand this side of it. Well, this crying never made no sign of an echo at all. But, as I said, it was dreadful near this night; and on the top of the start I got with hearing it, I got another fright; for I heard something rustling outside in the passage. Now to be sure I thought I was done; but I noticed the dog seemed to perk up a bit, and next there was someone whispered outside the door, and I very near laughed out loud, for I knew it was my father and mother that had got out of bed with the noise. 'Whatever is it?' says my mother. 'Hush! I don't know,' says my father, excited-like, 'don't disturb the boy. I hope he didn't hear nothing.'

"So, me knowing they were just outside, it made me bolder, and I slipped out of bed across to my little window—giving on the Close—but the dog he bored right down to the bottom of the bed—and I looked out. First go off I couldn't see anything. Then right down in the shadow under a buttress I made out what I shall always say was two spots of red—a dull red it was—nothing like a lamp or a fire, but just so as you could pick 'em out of the black shadow. I hadn't but just sighted 'em when it seemed we wasn't the only people that had been disturbed, because I see a window in a house on the left-hand side become lighted up, and the light moving. I just turned my head to make sure of it, and then looked back into the shadow for those two red things, and they were gone, and for all I peered about and stared, there was not a sign more of them. Then come my last fright that night—something come against my bare leg—but that was all right: that was my little dog had come out of bed, and prancing about making a great to-do, only holding his tongue, and me seeing he was quite in spirits again, I took him back to bed and we slept the night out!

"Next morning I made out to tell my mother I'd had the dog in my room, and I was surprised, after all she'd said about it before, how quiet she took it. 'Did you?' she says. 'Well, by good rights you ought to go without your breakfast for doing such a thing behind my back: but I don't know as there's any great harm done, only another time you ask my permission, do you hear?' A bit after that I said something to my father about having heard cats again. '*Cats*' he says; and he looked over at my poor mother, and she coughed and he says, "Oh! ah! yes, cats. I believe I heard 'em myself."

"That was a funny morning altogether: nothing seemed to go right. The organist he stopped in bed, and the minor Canon he forgot it was the 19th day and waited for the *Venite*; and after a bit the deputy he set off playing the chant for evensong, which was a minor; and then the Decani boys were laughing so much they couldn't sing, and when it came to the anthem the solo boy he got took with the giggles, and made out his nose was bleeding, and shoved the book at me what hadn't practised the verse and wasn't much of a singer if I had known it. Well, things was rougher, you see, fifty years ago, and I got a nip from the counter-tenor behind me that I' remembered".

"So we got through somehow, and neither the men nor the boys weren't by way of waiting to see whether the Canon in residence—Mr Henslow it was—would come to the vestries and fine 'em, but I don't believe he did: for one thing I fancy he'd read the wrong lesson for the first time in his life, and knew it. Anyhow, Evans and me didn't find no difficulty in slipping up the stairs as I told you, and when we got up we laid ourselves down flat on our stomachs where we could just stretch our heads out over the old tomb, and we hadn't but just done so when we heard the verger that was then, first shutting the iron porch-gates and locking the south-west door, and then the transept door, so we knew there was something up, and they meant to keep the public out for a bit.

"Next thing was, the Dean and the Canon come in by their door on the north, and then I see my father, and old Palmer, and a couple of their best men, and Palmer stood a talking for a bit with the Dean in the middle of the choir. He had a coil of rope and the men had crows. All of 'em looked a bit nervous. So there they stood talking, and at last I heard the Dean say, 'Well, I've no time to waste, Palmer. If you think this'll satisfy Southminster people, I'll permit it to be done; but I must say this, that never in the whole course of my life have I heard such arrant nonsense from a practical man as I have from you. Don't you agree with me, Henslow?' As far as I could hear Mr Henslow said something like 'Oh well! we're told, aren't we, Mr Dean, not to judge others?' And the Dean he gave a kind of sniff, and walked straight up to the tomb, and took his stand behind it with his back to the screen, and the others they come edging up rather gingerly. Henslow, he stopped on the south side and scratched on his chin, he did. Then the Dean spoke up: 'Palmer,' he says, 'which can you do easiest, get the slab off the top, or shift one of the side slabs?'"

"Old Palmer and his men they pottered about a bit looking round the edge of the top slab and sounding the sides on the south and east and west and everywhere but the north. Henslow said something about it being better to have a try at the south side, because there was more light and more room to move about in. Then my father, who'd been 'awatching of them, went round to the north side, and knelt down and felt the slab by the chink, and he got up and dusted his knees and says to the Dean: 'Beg pardon, Mr Dean, but I think if Mr Palmer'll try this here slab he'll find it'll come out easy enough. Seems to me one of the men could prise it out with his crow by means of this chink.' 'Ah! thank you, Worby,' says the Dean; 'that's a good suggestion. Palmer, let one of your men do that, will you?'"

"So the man come round, and put his bar in and bore on it, and just that minute when they were all bending over, and we boys got our heads well over the edge of the triforium, there came a most fearful crash down at the west end of the choir, as if a whole stack of big timber had fallen down a flight of stairs. Well, you can't expect me to tell you everything that happened all in a minute. Of course there was a terrible commotion. I heard the slab fall out, and the crowbar on the floor, and I heard the Dean say, 'Good God!'"

"When I looked down again I saw the Dean tumbled over on the floor, the men was making off down the choir, Henslow was just going to help the Dean up, Palmer was going to stop the men (as he said afterwards) and my father was sitting on the altar step with his face in his hands. The Dean he was very cross. 'I wish to goodness you'd look where you're coming to, Henslow,' he says. 'Why you should all take to your heels when a stick of wood tumbles down I cannot imagine'; and all Henslow could do, explaining he was right away on the other side of the tomb, would not satisfy him."

"Then Palmer came back and reported there was nothing to account for this noise and nothing seemingly fallen down, and when the Dean finished feeling of himself they gathered round—except my father, he sat where he was—and someone lighted up a bit of candle and they looked into the tomb. 'Nothing there,' says the Dean, 'what did I tell you? Stay! here's something. What's this? a bit of music paper, and a piece of torn stuff—part of a dress it looks like. Both quite modern—no interest whatever. Another time perhaps you'll take the advice of an educated man'—or something like that, and off he went, limping a bit, and out through the north door, only as he went he called back angry to Palmer for leaving the door standing open. Palmer called out 'Very sorry, sir,' but he shrugged his shoulders, and Henslow says, 'I fancy Mr Dean's mistaken. I closed the door behind me, but he's a little upset.' Then Palmer says, 'Why, where's Worby?' and they saw him sitting on the step and went up to him. He was recovering himself, it seemed, and wiping his forehead, and Palmer helped him up on to his legs, as I was glad to see."

"They were too far off for me to hear what they said, but my father pointed to the north door in the aisle, and Palmer and Henslow both of them looked very surprised and scared. After a bit, my father and Henslow went out of the church, and the others made what haste they could to put the slab back and plaster it in. And about as the clock struck twelve the Cathedral was opened again and us boys made the best of our way home.

"I was in a great taking to know what it was had given my poor father such a turn, and when I got in and found him sitting in his chair taking a glass of spirits, and my mother standing looking anxious at him, I couldn't keep from bursting out and making confession where I'd been. But he didn't seem to take on, not in the way of losing his temper. 'You was there, was you? Well, did you see it?' 'I saw everything, father,' I said, 'except when the noise came.' 'Did you see what it was knocked the Dean over?' he says, 'that what come out of the monument? You didn't? Well, that's a mercy.' 'Why, what was it, father?' I said. 'Come, you must have seen it,' he says. '*Didn't* you see? A thing like a man, all over hair, and two great eyes to it?'

"Well, that was all I could get out of him that time, and later on he seemed as if he was ashamed of being so frightened, and he used to put me off when I asked him about it. But years after when I was got to be a grown man, we had more talk now and again on the matter, and he always said the same thing. 'Black it was,' he'd say, 'and a mass of hair, and two legs, and the light caught on its eyes.'

"Well, that's the tale of that tomb, Mr Lake; it's one we don't tell to our visitors, and I should be obliged to you not to make any use of it till I'm out of the way. I doubt Mr Evans'll feel the same as I do, if you ask him."

This proved to be the case. But over twenty years have passed by, and the grass is growing over both Worby and Evans; so Mr Lake felt no difficulty about communicating his notes—taken in 1890—to me. He accompanied them with a sketch of the tomb and a copy of the short inscription on the metal cross which was affixed at the expense of Dr Lyall to the centre of the northern side. It was from the Vulgate of Isaiah xxiv., and consisted merely of the three words—

IBI CUBAVIT LAMIA.

Manly Wade Wellman

Chastel

Manly Wade Wellman was one of the most prolific contributors to the pulp magazines of the 1930s and '40s, with stories appearing regularly in such titles as Weird Tales, Wonder Stories *and* Astounding Stories. *During his long career he wrote more than seventy-five books and over two hundred short stories, ranging from comic books, mystery novels, juveniles, county histories and works on the American Civil War.*

However, his first love was always the field of science fiction, fantasy and horror, and he twice won the World Fantasy Award before his death in 1986. Some of Wellman's finest supernatural fiction can be found in the collections Who Fears the Devil? *(filmed in 1972),* Worse Things Waiting, Lonely Vigils *and* The Valley So Low.

In 'Chastel', two of Wellman's best-known characters, Lee Cobbett and Judge Keith Hilary Pursuivant, join forces to battle an age-old seductress. The author revealed that the novella was based on fact: "The Connecticut setting for a vampire outbreak harks back to long-ago Connecticut papers, which told of such things apparently happening. It's in the books cited here. Incidentally, both the poems I quote are actual ones. I've puzzled over the one from Grant's odd book, have never seen it anywhere else, and have never found anyone who had heard of it. Like Pursuivant here, I give myself to wonder if it isn't a fake antique, like Clerk Saunders' better known vampire poem to be found in Montague Summers."

"THEN YOU WON'T let Count Dracula rest in his tomb?" inquired Lee Cobbett, his square face creasing with a grin.

Five of them sat in the parlor of Judge Keith Hilary Pursuivant's hotel suite on Central Park West. The Judge lounged in an armchair, a wineglass in his big old hand. On this, his eighty-seventh birthday, his blue eyes were clear, penetrating. His once tawny hair and mustache had gone blizzard-white, but both grew thick, and his square face showed rosy. In his tailored blue leisure suit, he still looked powerfully deep-chested and broad-shouldered.

Blocky Lee Cobbett wore jacket and slacks almost as brown as his face. Next to him sat Laurel Parcher, small and young and cinnamon-haired. The others were natty Phil Drumm the summer theater producer, and Isobel Arrington from a wire press service. She was blond, expensively dressed, she smoked a dark cigarette with a white tip. Her pen scribbled swiftly.

"Dracula's as much alive as Sherlock Holmes," argued Drumm. "All the revivals of the play, all the films— "

"Your musical should wake the dead, anyway," said Cobbett, drinking. "What's your main number, Phil? 'Garlic Time?' 'Gory, Gory Hallelujah?'"

"Let's have Christian charity here, Lee," Pursuivant came to Drumm's rescue. "Anyway, Miss Arrington came to interview me. Pour her some wine and let me try to answer her questions."

"I'm interested in Mr Cobbett's remarks," said Isobel Arrington, her voice deliberately throaty. "He's an authority on the supernatural."

"Well, perhaps," admitted Cobbett, "and Miss Parcher has had some experiences. But Judge Pursuivant is the true authority, the author of Vampiricon."

"I've read it, in paperback," said Isobel Arrington. "Phil, it mentions a vampire belief up in Connecticut, where you're having your show. What's that town again?"

"Deslow," he told her. "We're making a wonderful old stone barn into a theater. I've invited Lee and Miss Parcher to visit."

She looked at Drumm. "Is Deslow a resort town?"

"Not yet, but maybe the show will bring tourists. In Deslow, up to now, peace and quiet is the chief business. If you drop your shoe, everybody in town will think somebody's blowing the safe."

"Deslow's not far from Jewett City," observed Pursuivant. "There were vampires there about a century and a quarter ago. A family named Ray was afflicted. And to the east, in Rhode Island, there was a lively vampire folklore in recent years."

"Let's leave Rhode Island to H. P. Lovecraft's imitators," suggested Cobbett. "What do you call your show, Phil?"

"*The Land Beyond the Forest*," said Drumm. "We're casting it now. Using locals in bit parts. But we have Gonda Chastel to play Dracula's countess."

"I never knew that Dracula had a countess," said Laurel Parcher.

"There was a stage star named Chastel, long ago when I was young," said Pursuivant. "Just the one name—Chastel."

"Gonda's her daughter, and a year or so ago Gonda came to live in Deslow," Drumm told them. "Her mother's buried there. Gonda has invested in our production."

"Is that why she has a part in it?" asked Isobel Arrington.

"She has a part in it because she's beautiful and gifted," replied Drumm, rather stuffily. "Old people say she's the very picture of her mother. Speaking of pictures, here are some to prove it."

He offered two glossy prints to Isobel Arrington, who murmured "Very sweet," and passed them to Laurel Parcher. Cobbett leaned to see.

One picture seemed copied from an older one. It showed a woman who stood with unconscious stateliness, in a gracefully draped robe with a tiara binding her rich flow of dark hair. The other picture was of a woman in fashionable evening dress, her hair ordered in modern fashion, with a face strikingly like that of the woman in the other photograph.

"Oh, she's lovely," said Laurel. "Isn't she, Lee?"

"Isn't she?" echoed Drumm.

"Magnificent," said Cobbett, handing the pictures to Pursuivant, who studied them gravely.

"Chastel was in Richmond, just after the First World War," he said slowly. "A dazzling Lady Macbeth. I was in love with her. Everyone was."

"Did you tell her you loved her?" asked Laurel.

"Yes. We had supper together, twice. Then she went ahead with her tour, and I sailed to England and studied at Oxford. I never saw her again, but she's more or less why I never married."

Silence a moment. Then: "*The Land Beyond the Forest*," Laurel repeated. "Isn't there a book called that?"

"There is indeed, my child," said the Judge. "By Emily de Laszowska Gerard. About Transylvania, where Dracula came from."

"That's why we use the title, that's what Transylvania means," put in Drumm. "It's all right, the book's out of copyright. But I'm surprised to find someone who's heard of it."

"I'll protect your guilty secret, Phil," promised Isobel Arrington. "What's over there in your window, Judge?"

Pursuivant turned to look. "Whatever it is," he said, "it's not Peter Pan."

Cobbett sprang up and ran toward the half-draped window. A silhouette with head and shoulders hung in the June night. He had a glimpse of a face, rich-mouthed, with bright eyes. Then it was gone. Laurel had hurried up behind him. He hoisted the window sash and leaned out.

Nothing. The street was fourteen stories down. The lights of moving cars crawled distantly. The wall below was course after course of dull brick, with recesses of other windows to right and left, below, above. Cobbett studied the wall, his hands braced on the sill.

"Be careful, Lee," Laurel's voice besought him.

He came back to face the others. "Nobody out there," he said evenly. "Nobody could have been. It's just a wall—nothing to hang to. Even that sill would be tricky to stand on."

"But I saw something, and so did Judge Pursuivant," said Isobel Arrington, the cigarette trembling in her fingers.

"So did I," said Cobbett. "Didn't you, Laurel?"

"Only a face."

Isobel Arrington was calm again. "If it's a trick, Phil, you played a good one. But don't expect me to put it in my story."

Drumm shook his head nervously. "I didn't play any trick, I swear."

"Don't try this on old friends," she jabbed at him. "First those pictures, then whatever was up against the glass. I'll use the pictures, but I won't write that a weird vision presided over this birthday party."

"How about a drink all around?" suggested Pursuivant.

He poured for them. Isobel Arrington wrote down answers to more questions, then said she must go. Drumm rose to escort her. "You'll be at Deslow tomorrow, Lee?" he asked.

"And Laurel, too. You said we could find quarters there."

"The Mapletree's a good auto court," said Drumm. "I've already reserved cabins for the two of you."

"On the spur of the moment," said Pursuivant suddenly, "I think I'll come along, if there's space for me."

"I'll check it out for you, Judge," said Drumm.

He departed with Isobel Arrington. Cobbett spoke to Pursuivant. "Isn't that rather offhand?" he asked. "Deciding to come with us?"

"I was thinking about Chastel." Pursuivant smiled gently. "About making a pilgrimage to her grave."

"We'll drive up about nine tomorrow morning."

"I'll be ready, Lee."

Cobbett and Laurel, too, went out. They walked down a flight of stairs to the floor below, where both their rooms were located. "Do you think Phil Drumm rigged up that illusion for us?" asked Cobbett.

"If he did, he used the face of that actress, Chastel."

He glanced keenly at her. "You saw that."

"I thought I did, and so did you."

They kissed goodnight at the door to her room.

Pursuivant was ready next morning when Cobbett knocked. He had only one suitcase and a thick, brown-blotched malacca cane, banded with silver below its curved handle.

"I'm taking only a few necessaries, I'll buy socks and such things in Deslow if we stay more than a couple of days," he said. "No, don't carry it for me, I'm quite capable."

When they reached the hotel garage, Laurel was putting her luggage in the trunk of Cobbett's black sedan. Judge Pursuivant declined the front seat beside Cobbett, held the door for Laurel to get in, and sat in the rear. They rolled out into bright June sunlight.

Cobbett drove them east on Interstate 95, mile after mile along the Connecticut shore, past service stations, markets, sandwich shops. Now and then they glimpsed Long Island Sound to the right. At toll gates, Cobbett threw quarters into hoppers and drove on.

"New Rochelle to Port Chester," Laurel half chanted, "Norwalk, Bridgeport, Stratford— "

"Where, in 1851, devils plagued a minister's home," put in Pursuivant.

"The names make a poem," said Laurel.

"You can get that effect by reading any timetable," said Cobbett. "We miss a couple of good names—Mystic and Giants Neck, though they aren't far off from our route. And Griswold—that means Gray Woods—where the Judge's book says Horace Ray was born."

"There's no Griswold on the Connecticut map anymore," said the Judge.

"Vanished?" said Laurel. "Maybe it appears at just a certain time of the day, along about sundown."

She laughed, but the Judge was grave.

"Here we'll pass by New Haven," he said. "I was at Yale here, seventy years ago."

They rolled across the Connecticut River between Old Saybrook and Old Lyme. Outside New London, Cobbett turned them north on State Highway 82 and, near Jewett City, took a two-lane road that brought them into Deslow, not long after noon.

There were pleasant clapboard cottages among elm trees and flower beds. Main Street had bright shops with, farther along, the belfry of a sturdy old church. Cobbett drove them to a sign saying MAPLETREE COURT. A row of cabins faced along a cement-floored colonnade, their fronts painted white with blue doors and window frames. In the office, Phil Drumm stood at the desk, talking to the plump proprietress.

"Welcome home," he greeted them. "Judge, I was asking Mrs Simpson here to reserve you a cabin."

"At the far end of the row, sir," the lady said. "I'd have put you next to your two friends, but so many theater folks have already moved in."

"Long ago I learned to be happy with any shelter," the Judge assured her.

They saw Laurel to her cabin and put her suitcases inside, then walked to the farthest cabin where Pursuivant would stay. Finally Drumm followed Cobbett to the space next to Laurel's. Inside, Cobbett produced a fifth of bourbon from his briefcase. Drumm trotted away to fetch ice. Pursuivant came to join them.

"It's good of you to look after us," Cobbett said to Drumm above his glass.

"Oh, I'll get my own back," Drumm assured him. "The Judge and you, distinguished folklore experts—I'll have you in all the papers."

"Whatever you like," said Cobbett. "Let's have lunch, as soon as Laurel is freshened up."

The four ate crab cakes and flounder at a little restaurant while Drumm talked about *The Land Beyond the Forest*. He had signed the minor film star Caspar Merrick to play Dracula. "He has a fine baritone singing voice," said Drumm. "He'll be at afternoon rehearsal."

"And Gonda Chastel?" inquired Pursuivant, buttering a roll.

"She'll be there tonight." Drumm sounded happy about that. "This afternoon's mostly for bits and chorus numbers. I'm directing as well as producing." They finished their lunch, and Drumm rose. "If you're not tired, come see our theater."

It was only a short walk through town to the converted barn. Cobbett judged it had been built in Colonial times, with a recent roof of composition tile, but with walls of stubborn, brown-gray New England stone. Across a narrow side street stood the old white church, with a hedge-bordered cemetery.

"Quaint, that old burying ground," commented Drumm. "Nobody's spaded under there now, there's a modern cemetery on the far side, but Chastel's tomb is there. Quite a picturesque one."

"I'd like to see it," said Pursuivant, leaning on his silver-banded cane.

The barn's interior was set with rows of folding chairs, enough for several hundred spectators. On a stage at the far end, workmen moved here and there under lights. Drumm led his guests up steps at the side.

High in the loft, catwalks zigzagged and a dark curtain hung like a broad guillotine blade. Drumm pointed out canvas flats, painted to resemble grim castle walls. Pursuivant nodded and questioned.

"I'm no authority on what you might find in Transylvania," he said, "but this looks convincing."

A man walked from the wings toward them. "Hello, Caspar," Drumm greeted him. "I want you to meet Judge Pursuivant and Lee Cobbett. And Miss Laurel Parcher, of course." He gestured the introductions. "This is Mr Caspar Merrick, our Count Dracula."

Merrick was elegantly tall, handsome, with carefully groomed black hair. Sweepingly he bowed above Laurel's hand and smiled at them all. "Judge Pursuivant's writings I know, of course," he said richly. "I read what I can about vampires, inasmuch as I'm to be one."

"Places for the Delusion number!" called a stage manager.

Cobbett, Pursuivant and Laurel went down the steps and sat on chairs. Eight men and eight girls hurried into view, dressed in knockabout summer clothes. Someone struck chords on a piano, Drumm gestured importantly, and the chorus sang. Merritt, coming downstage, took solo on a verse. All joined in the refrain. Then Drumm made them sing it over again.

After that, two comedians made much of confusing the words vampire and empire. Cobbett found it tedious. He excused himself to his companions and strolled out and across to the old, tree-crowded churchyard.

The gravestones bore interesting epitaphs: not only the familiar PAUSE O STRANGER PASSING BY/ AS YOU ARE NOW SO ONCE WAS I, and A BUD ON EARTH TO BLOOM IN HEAVEN, but several of more originality. One bewailed a man who, since he had been lost at sea, could hardly have been there at all. Another bore, beneath a bat-winged face, the declaration DEATH PAYS ALL DEBTS and the date 1907, which Cobbett associated with a financial panic.

Toward the center of the graveyard, under a drooping willow, stood a shedlike structure of heavy granite blocks. Cobbett picked his way to the door of heavy grillwork, which was fastened with a rusty padlock the size of a sardine can. On the lintel were strongly carved letters: CHASTEL.

Here, then, was the tomb of the stage beauty Pursuivant remembered so romantically. Cobbett peered through the bars.

It was murkily dusty in there. The floor was coarsely flagged, and among sooty shadows at the rear stood a sort of stone chest that must contain the body. Cobbett turned and went back to the theater. Inside, piano music rang wildly and the people of the chorus desperately rehearsed what must be meant for a folk dance.

"Oh, it's exciting," said Laurel as Cobbett sat down beside her. "Where have you been?"

"Visiting the tomb of Chastel."

"Chastel?" echoed Pursuivant. "I must see that tomb."

Songs and dance ensembles went on. In the midst of them, a brisk reporter from Hartford appeared, to interview Pursuivant and Cobbett. At last Drumm resoundingly dismissed the players on stage and joined his guests.

"Principals rehearse at eight o'clock," he announced. "Gonda Chastel will be here, she'll want to meet you. Could I count on you then?"

"Count on me, at least," said Pursuivant. "Just now, I feel like resting before dinner, and so, I think, does Laurel here."

"Yes, I'd like to lie down for a little," said Laurel.

"Why don't we all meet for dinner at the place where we had lunch?" said Cobbett. "You come too, Phil."

"Thanks, I have a date with some backers from New London."

It was half-past five when they went out.

Cobbett went to his quarters, stretched out on the bed, and gave himself to thought.

He hadn't come to Deslow because of this musical interpretation of the Dracula legend. Laurel had come because he was coming, and Pursuivant on a sudden impulse that might have been more than a wish to visit the grave of Chastel. But Cobbett was here because this, he knew, had been vampire country, maybe still was vampire country.

He remembered the story in Pursuivant's book about vampires at Jewett City, as reported in the Norwich *Courier* for 1854. Horace Ray, from the now vanished town of Griswold, had died of a "wasting disease." Thereafter his oldest son, then his second son had also gone to their graves. When a third son sickened, friends and relatives dug up Horace Ray and the two dead brothers and burned the bodies in a roaring fire. The surviving son got well. And something like that had happened in Exeter, near Providence in Rhode Island. Very well, why organize and present the Dracula musical here in Deslow, so near those places?

Cobbett had met Phil Drumm in the South the year before, knew him for a brilliant if erratic producer, who relished tales of devils and the dead who walk by night. Drumm might have known enough stage magic to have rigged that seeming appearance at Pursuivant's window in New York. That is, if indeed it was only a seeming appearance, not a real face. Might it have been real, a manifestation of the unreal? Cobbett had seen enough of what people dismissed as unreal, impossible, to wonder.

A soft knock came at the door. It was Laurel. She wore green slacks, a green jacket, and she smiled, as always, at sight of Cobbett's face. They sought Pursuivant's cabin. A note on the door said: MEET ME AT THE CAFÉ.

When they entered there, Pursuivant hailed them from the kitchen door. "Dinner's ready," he hailed them. "I've been supervising in person, and I paid well for the privilege."

A waiter brought a laden tray. He arranged platters of red-drenched spaghetti and bowls of salad on a table. Pursuivant himself sprinkled Parmesan cheese. "No salt or pepper," he warned. "I seasoned it myself, and you can take my word it's exactly right."

Cobbett poured red wine into glasses. Laurel took a forkful of spaghetti. "Delicious," she cried. "What's in it, Judge?"

"Not only ground beef and tomatoes and onions and garlic," replied Pursuivant. "I added marjoram and green pepper and chile and thyme and bay leaf and oregano and parsley and a couple of other important ingredients. And I also minced in some Italian sausage."

Cobbett, too, ate with enthusiastic appetite. "I won't order any dessert," he declared. "I want to keep the taste of this in my mouth."

"There's more in the kitchen for dessert if you want it," the Judge assured him. "But here, I have a couple of keepsakes for you."

He handed each of them a small, silvery object. Cobbett examined his. It was smoothly wrapped in foil. He wondered if it was a nutmeat.

"You have pockets, I perceive," the Judge said. "Put those into them. And don't open them, or my wish for you won't come true."

When they had finished eating, a full moon had begun to rise in the darkening sky. They headed for the theater.

A number of visitors sat in the chairs and the stage lights looked bright. Drumm stood beside the piano, talking to two plump men in summer business suits. As Pursuivant and the others came down the aisle, Drumm eagerly beckoned them and introduced them to his companions, the financial backers with whom he had taken dinner.

"We're very much interested," said one. "This vampire legend intrigues anyone, if you forget that a vampire's motivation is simply nourishment."

"No, something more than that," offered Pursuivant. "A social motivation."

"Social motivation," repeated the other backer.

"A vampire wants company of its own kind. A victim infected becomes a vampire, too, and an associate. Otherwise the original vampire would be a disconsolate loner."

"There's a lot in what you say," said Drumm, impressed.

After that there was financial talk, something in which Cobbett could not intelligently join. Then someone else approached, and both the backers stared.

It was a tall, supremely graceful woman with red-lighted black hair in a bun at her nape, a woman of impressive figure and assurance. She wore a sweeping blue dress, fitted to her slim waist, with a frill-edged neckline. Her arms were bare and white and sweetly turned, with jeweled bracelets on them. Drumm almost ran to bring her close to the group.

"Gonda Chastel," he said, half-prayerfully. "Gonda, you'll want to meet these people."

The two backers stuttered admiringly at her. Pursuivant bowed and Laurel smiled. Gonda Chastel gave Cobbett her slim, cool hand. "You know so much about this thing we're trying to do here," she said, in a voice like cream.

Drumm watched them. His face looked plaintive.

"Judge Pursuivant has taught me a lot, Miss Chastel," said Cobbett. "He'll tell you that once he knew your mother."

"I remember her, not very clearly," said Gonda Chastel. "She died when I was just a little thing, thirty years ago. And I followed her here, now I make my home here."

"You look very like her," said Pursuivant.

"I'm proud to be like my mother in any way," she smiled at them. She could be overwhelming, Cobbett told himself.

"And Miss Parcher," went on Gonda Chastel, turning toward Laurel. "What a little presence she is. She should be in our show—I don't know what part, but she should." She smiled dazzlingly. "Now then, Phil wants me on stage."

"Knock-at-the-door number, Gonda," said Drumm.

Gracefully she mounted the steps. The piano sounded, and she sang. It was the best song, felt Cobbett, that he had heard so far in the rehearsals. "Are they seeking for a shelter from the night?" Gonda Chastel sang richly. Caspar Merritt entered, to join in a recitative. Then the chorus streamed on, singing somewhat shrilly.

Pursuivant and Laurel had sat down. Cobbett strode back up the aisle and out under a moon that rained silver-blue light.

He found his way to the churchyard. The trees that had offered pleasant afternoon shade now made a dubious darkness. He walked underneath branches that seemed to lower like hovering wings as he approached the tomb structure at the center.

The barred door that had been massively locked now stood open. He peered into the gloom within. After a moment he stepped across the threshold upon the flagged floor.

He had to grope, with one hand upon the rough wall. At last he almost stumbled upon the great stone chest at the rear.

It, too, was flung open, its lid heaved back against the wall.

There was, of course, complete darkness within it. He flicked on his cigar lighter. The flame showed him the inside of the stone coffer, solidly made and about ten feet long. Its sides of gray marble were snugly fitted. Inside lay a coffin of rich dark wood with silver fittings and here, yet again, was an open lid.

Bending close to the smudged silk lining, Cobbett seemed to catch an odor of stuffy sharpness, like dried herbs. He snapped off his light and frowned in the dark. Then he groped back to the door, emerged into the open, and headed for the theater again.

"Mr Cobbett," said the beautiful voice of Gonda Chastel.

She stood at the graveyard's edge, beside a sagging willow. She was almost as tall as he. Her eyes glowed in the moonlight.

"You came to find the truth about my mother," she half-accused.

"I was bound to try," he replied. "Ever since I saw a certain face at a certain window of a certain New York hotel."

She stepped back from him. "You know that she's a— "

"A vampire," Cobbett finished for her. "Yes."

"I beg you to be helpful—merciful." But there was no supplication in her voice. "I already realized, long ago. That's why I live in little Deslow. I want to find a way to give her rest. Night after night, I wonder how."

"I understand that," said Cobbett.

Gonda Chastel breathed deeply. "You know all about these things. I think there's something about you that could daunt a vampire."

"If so, I don't know what it is," said Cobbett truthfully.

"Make me a solemn promise. That you won't return to her tomb, that you won't tell others what you and I know about her. I—I want to think how we two together can do something for her."

"If you wish, I'll say nothing," he promised.

Her hand clutched his.

"The cast took a five-minute break, it must be time to go to work again," she said, suddenly bright. "Let's go back and help the thing along."

They went.

Inside, the performers were gathering on stage. Drumm stared unhappily as Gonda Chastel and Cobbett came down the aisle. Cobbett sat with Laurel and Pursuivant and listened to the rehearsal.

Adaptation from Bram Stoker's novel was free, to say the least. Dracula's eerie plottings were much hampered by his having a countess, a walking dead beauty who strove to become a spirit of good. There were some songs, in interesting minor keys. There was a dance, in which men and women leaped like kangaroos. Finally Drumm called a halt, and the performers trooped wearily to the wings.

Gonda Chastel lingered, talking to Laurel. "I wonder, my dear, if you haven't had acting experience," she said.

"Only in school entertainments down South, when I was little."

"Phil," said Gonda Chastel, "Miss Parcher is a good type, has good presence. There ought to be something for her in the show."

"You're very kind, but I'm afraid that's impossible," said Laurel, smiling.

"You may change your mind, Miss Parcher. Will you and your friends come to my house for a nightcap?"

"Thank you," said Pursuivant. "We have some notes to make, and we must make them together."

"Until tomorrow evening, then Mr Cobbett, we'll remember our agreement."

She went away toward the back of the stage. Pursuivant and Laurel walked out. Drumm hurried up the aisle and caught Cobbett's elbow.

"I saw you," he said harshly. "Saw you both as you came in."

"And we saw you, Phil. What's this about?"

"She likes you." It was half an accusation. "Fawns on you, almost."

Cobbett grinned and twitched his arm free. "What's the matter, Phil, are you in love with her?"

"Yes, God damn it, I am. I'm in love with her. She knows it but she won't let me come to her house. And you—the first time she meets you, she invites you."

"Easy does it, Phil," said Cobbett. "If it'll do you any good, I'm in love with someone else, and that takes just about all my spare time."

He hurried out to overtake his companions.

Pursuivant swung his cane almost jauntily as they returned through the moonlight to the auto court.

"What notes are you talking about, Judge?" asked Cobbett.

"I'll tell you at my quarters. What do you think of the show?"

"Perhaps I'll like it better after they've rehearsed more," said Laurel. "I don't follow it at present."

"Here and there, it strikes me as limp," added Cobbett.

They sat down in the Judge's cabin. He poured them drinks. "Now," he said, "there are certain things to recognize here. Things I more or less expected to find."

"A mystery, Judge?" asked Laurel.

"Not so much that, if I expected to find them. How far are we from Jewett City?"

"Twelve or fifteen miles as the crow flies," estimated Cobbett. "And Jewett City is where that vampire family, the Rays, lived and died."

"Died twice, you might say," nodded Pursuivant, stroking his white mustache. "Back about a century and a quarter ago. And here's what might be a matter of Ray family history. I've been thinking about Chastel, whom once I greatly admired. About her full name."

"But she had only one name, didn't she?" asked Laurel.

"On the stage she used one name, yes. So did Bernhardt, so did Duse, so later did Garbo. But all of them had full names. Now, before we went to dinner, I made two telephone calls to theatrical historians I know. To learn Chastel's full name."

"And she had a full name," prompted Cobbett.

"Indeed she did. Her full name was Chastel Ray."

Cobbett and Laurel looked at him in deep silence.

"Not apt to be just coincidence," elaborated Pursuivant. "Now then, I gave you some keepsakes today."

"Here's mine," said Cobbett, pulling the foil-wrapped bit from his shirt pocket.

"And I have mine here," said Laurel, her hand at her throat. "In a little locket I have on this chain."

"Keep it there," Pursuivant urged her. "Wear it around your neck at all times. Lee, have yours always on your person. Those are garlic cloves, and you know what they're good for. You can also guess why I cut up a lot of garlic in our spaghetti for dinner."

"You think there's a vampire here," offered Laurel.

"A specific vampire." The Judge took a deep breath into his broad chest. "Chastel. Chastel Ray."

"I believe it, too," declared Cobbett tonelessly, and Laurel nodded. Cobbett looked at the watch on his wrist.

"It's past one in the morning," he said. "Perhaps we'd all be better off if we had some sleep."

They said their good nights and Laurel and Cobbett walked to where their two doors stood side by side. Laurel put her key into the lock, but did not turn it at once. She peered across the moonlit street.

"Who's that over there?" she whispered. "Maybe I ought to say, what's that?"

Cobbett looked. "Nothing, you're just nervous. Good night, dear."

She went in and shut the door. Cobbett quickly crossed the street.

"Mr Cobbett," said the voice of Gonda Chastel.

"I wondered what you wanted, so late at night," he said, walking close to her.

She had undone her dark hair and let it flow to her shoulders. She was, Cobbett thought, as beautiful a woman as he had ever seen.

"I wanted to be sure about you," she said. "That you'd respect your promise to me, not to go into the churchyard."

"I keep my promises, Miss Chastel."

He felt a deep, hushed silence all around them. Not even the leaves rustled in the trees.

"I had hoped you wouldn't venture even this far," she went on. "You and your friends are new in town, you might tempt her specially." Her eyes burned at him. "You know I don't mean that as a compliment."

She turned to walk away. He fell into step beside her. "But you're not afraid of her," he said.

"Of my own mother?"

"She was a Ray," said Cobbett. "Each Ray sapped the blood of his kinsmen. Judge Pursuivant told me all about it."

Again the gaze of her dark, brilliant eyes. "Nothing like that has ever happened between my mother and me." She stopped, and so did he. Her slim, strong hand took him by the wrist.

"You're wise and brave," she said. "I think you may have come here for a good purpose, not just about the show."

"I try to have good purposes."

The light of the moon soaked through the overhead branches as they walked on. "Will you come to my house?" she invited.

"I'll walk to the churchyard," replied Cobbett. "I said I wouldn't go into it, but I can stand at the edge."

"Don't go in."

"I've promised that I wouldn't, Miss Chastel."

She walked back the way they had come. He followed the street on under silent elms until he reached the border of the churchyard. Moonlight flecked and spattered the tombstones. Deep shadows lay like pools. He had a sense of being watched from within.

As he gazed, he saw movement among the graves. He could not define it, but it was there. He glimpsed, or fancied he glimpsed, a head, indistinct in outline as though swathed in dark fabric. Then another. Another. They huddled in a group, as though to gaze at him.

"I wish you'd go back to your quarters," said Gonda Chastel beside him. She had drifted after him, silent as a shadow herself.

"Miss Chastel," he said, "tell me something if you can. Whatever happened to the town or village of Griswold?"

"Griswold?" she echoed. "What's Griswold? That means gray woods."

"Your ancestor, or your relative, Horace Ray, came from Griswold to die in Jewett City. And I've told you that I knew your mother was born a Ray."

Her shining eyes seemed to flood upon him. "I didn't know that," she said.

He gazed into the churchyard, at those hints of furtive movement.

"The hands of the dead reach out for the living," murmured Gonda Chastel.

"Reach out for me?" he asked.

"Perhaps for both of us. Just now, we may be the only living souls awake in Deslow." She gazed at him again. "But you're able to defend yourself, somehow."

"What makes you think that?" he inquired, aware of the clove of garlic in his shirt pocket.

"Because they—in the churchyard there—they watch, but they hold away from you. You don't invite them."

"Nor do you, apparently," said Cobbett.

"I hope you're not trying to make fun of me," she said, her voice barely audible.

"On my soul, I'm not."

"On your soul," she repeated. "Good night, Mr Cobbett."

Again she moved away, tall and proud and graceful. He watched her out of sight. Then he headed back toward the motor court.

Nothing moved in the empty street. Only one or two lights shone here and there in closed shops. He thought he heard a soft rustle behind him, but did not look back.

As he reached his own door, he heard Laurel scream behind hers.

Judge Pursuivant sat in his cubicle, his jacket off, studying a worn little brown book. Skinner, said letters on the spine, and *Myths and Legends of Our Own Land*. He had read the passage so often that he could almost repeat it from memory:

"To lay this monster he must be taken up and burned; at least his heart must be; and he must be disinterred in the daytime when he is asleep and unaware."

There were other ways, reflected Pursuivant.

It must be very late by now, rather it must be early. But he had no intention of going to sleep. Not when stirs of motion sounded outside, along the concrete walkway in front of his cabin. Did motion stand still, just beyond the door there? Pursuivant's great, veined hand touched the front of his shirt, beneath which a bag of garlic hung like an amulet. Garlic—was that enough? He himself was fond of garlic, judiciously employed in sauces and salads. But then, he could see himself in the mirror of the bureau yonder, could see his broad old face with its white sweep of mustache like a wreath of snow on a sill. It was a clear image of a face, not a calm face just then, but a determined one. Pursuivant smiled at it, with a glimpse of even teeth that were still his own.

He flicked up his shirt cuff and looked at his watch. Half past one, about. In June, even with daylight savings time, dawn would come early. Dawn sent vampires back to the tombs that were their melancholy refuges, "asleep and unaware," as Skinner had specified.

Putting the book aside, he poured himself a small drink of bourbon, dropped in cubes of ice and a trickle of water, and sipped. He had drunk several times during that day, when on most days he partook of only a single highball, by advice of his doctor; but just now he was grateful for the pungent, walnutty taste of the liquor. It was one of earth's natural things, a good companion when not abused. From the table he took a folder of scribbled notes. He looked at jottings from the works of Montague Summers.

These offered the proposition that a plague of vampires usually stemmed from a single source of infection, a king or queen vampire whose feasts of blood drove victims to their graves, to rise in their turn. If the original vampires were found and destroyed, the others relaxed to rest as normally dead bodies. Bram Stoker had followed the same gospel when he wrote *Dracula*, and doubtless Bram Stoker had known. Pursuivant looked at another page, this time a poem copied from James Grant's curious *Mysteries of All Nations*. It was a ballad in archaic language, that dealt with baleful happenings in "The Towne of Peste"—Budapest?

> It was the Corpses that our Churchyardes filled
> That did at midnight lumberr up our Stayres;
> They suck'd our Bloud, the gorie Banquet swilled,
> And harried everie Soule with hydeous Feares . . .

Several verses down:

> They barr'd with Boltes of Iron the Churchyard-pale
> To keep them out; but all this wold not doe;
> For when a Dead-Man has learn'd to draw a naile,
> He can also burst an iron Bolte in two.

Many times Pursuivant had tried to trace the author of that verse. He wondered if it was not something quaintly confected not long before 1880, when Grant published his work. At any rate, the Judge felt that he knew what it meant, the experience that it remembered.

He put aside the notes, too, and picked up his spotted walking stick. Clamping the balance of it firmly in his left hand, he twisted the handle with his right and pulled. Out of the hollow shank slid a pale, bright blade, keen and lean and edged on both front and back.

Pursuivant permitted himself a smile above it. This was one of his most cherished possessions, this silver weapon said to have been forged a thousand years ago by St Dunstan. Bending, he spelled out the runic writing upon it:

Sic pereant omnes inimici tui, Domine

That was the end of the fiercely triumphant song of Deborah in the Book of Judges: So perish all thine enemies, O Lord. Whether the work of St Dunstan or not, the metal was silver, the writing was a warrior's prayer. Silver and writing had proved their strength against evil in the past.

Then, outside, a loud, tremulous cry of mortal terror.

Pursuivant sprang out of his chair on the instant. Blade in hand, he fairly ripped his door open and ran out. He saw Cobbett in front of Laurel's door, wrenching at the knob, and hurried there like a man half his age.

"Open up, Laurel," he heard Cobbett call. "It's Lee out here!"

The door gave inward as Pursuivant reached it, and he and Cobbett pressed into the lighted room.

Laurel half-crouched in the middle of the floor. Her trembling hand pointed to a rear window. "She tried to come in," Laurel stammered.

"There's nothing at that window," said Cobbett, but even as he spoke, there was. A face, pale as tallow, crowded against the glass. They saw wide, staring eyes, a mouth that opened and squirmed. Teeth twinkled sharply.

Cobbett started forward, but Pursuivant caught him by the shoulder. "Let me," he said, advancing toward the window, the point of his blade lifted.

The face at the window writhed convulsively as the silver weapon came against the pane with a clink. The mouth opened as though to shout, but no sound came. The face fell back and vanished from their sight.

"I've seen that face before," said Cobbett hoarsely.

"Yes," said Pursuivant. "At my hotel window. And since."

He dropped the point of the blade to the floor. Outside came a whirring rush of sound, like feet, many of them.

"We ought to wake up the people at the office," said Cobbett.

"I doubt if anyone in this little town could be wakened," Pursuivant told him evenly. "I have it in mind that every living soul, except the three of us, is sound asleep. Entranced."

"But out there— " Laurel gestured at the door, where something seemed to be pressing.

"I said, every living soul," Pursuivant looked from her to Cobbett. "Living," he repeated.

He paced across the floor, and with his point scratched a perpendicular line upon it. Across this he carefully drove a horizontal line, making a cross. The pushing abruptly ceased.

"There it is, at the window again," breathed Laurel.

Pursuivant took long steps back to where the face hovered, with black hair streaming about it. He scraped the glass with his silver blade, up and down, then across, making lines upon it. The face drew away. He moved to mark similar crosses on the other windows.

"You see," he said, quietly triumphant, "the force of old, old charms."

He sat down in a chair, heavily. His face was weary, but he looked at Laurel and smiled.

"It might help if we managed to pity those poor things out there," he said.

"Pity?" she almost cried out.

"Yes," he said, and quoted:

> "'. . . Think how sad it must be
> To thirst always for a scorned elixir,
> The salt of quotidian blood.'"

"I know that," volunteered Cobbett. "It's from a poem by Richard Wilbur, a damned unhappy poet."

"Quotidian," repeated Laurel to herself.

"That means something that keeps coming back, that returns daily," Cobbett said.

"It's a term used to refer to a recurrent fever," added Pursuivant.

Laurel and Cobbett sat down together on the bed.

"I would say that for the time being we're safe here," declared Pursuivant. "Not at ease, but at least safe. At dawn, danger will go to sleep and we can open the door."

"But why are we safe, and nobody else?" Laurel cried out. "Why are we awake, with everyone else in this town asleep and helpless?"

"Apparently because we all of us wear garlic," replied Pursuivant patiently, "and because we ate garlic, plenty of it, at dinnertime. And because there are crosses—crude, but unmistakable—wherever something might try to come in. I won't ask you to be calm, but I'll ask you to be resolute."

"I'm resolute," said Cobbett between clenched teeth. "I'm ready to go out there and face them."

"If you did that, even with the garlic," said Pursuivant, "you'd last about as long as a pint of whiskey in a five-handed poker game. No, Lee, relax as much as you can, and let's talk."

They talked, while outside strange presences could be felt rather than heard. Their talk was of anything and everything but where they were and why. Cobbett remembered strange things he had encountered, in towns, among mountains, along desolate roads, and what he had been able to do about them. Pursuivant told of a vampire he had known and defeated in upstate New York, of a werewolf in his own Southern countryside. Laurel, at Cobbett's urging, sang songs, old songs, from her own rustic home place. Her voice was sweet. When she sang "Round is the Ring," faces came and hung like smudges outside the cross-scored windows. She saw, and sang again, an old Appalachian carol called "Mary She Heared a Knock in the Night." The faces drifted away again. And the hours, too, drifted away, one by one.

"There's a horde of vampires on the night street here, then." Cobbett at last brought up the subject of their problem.

"And they lull the people of Deslow to sleep, to be helpless victims," agreed Pursuivant. "About this show, *The Land Beyond the Forest*, mightn't it be welcomed as a chance to spread the infection? Even a townful of sleepers couldn't feed a growing community of blood drinkers."

"If we could deal with the source, the original infection— " began Cobbett.

"The mistress of them, the queen," said Pursuivant. "Yes. The one whose walking by night rouses them all. If she could be destroyed, they'd all die properly."

He glanced at the front window. The moonlight had a touch of slaty gray.

"Almost morning," he pronounced. "Time for a visit to her tomb."

"I gave my promise I wouldn't go there," said Cobbett.

"But I didn't promise," said Pursuivant, rising. "You stay here with Laurel."

His silver blade in hand, he stepped out into darkness from which the moon had all but dropped away. Overhead, stars were fading out. Dawn was at hand.

He sensed a flutter of movement on the far side of the street, an almost inaudible gibbering of sound. Steadily he walked across. He saw nothing along the sidewalk there, heard nothing. Resolutely he tramped to the churchyard, his weapon poised. More grayness had come to dilute the dark.

He pushed his way through the hedge of shrubs, stepped in upon the grass, and paused at the side of a grave. Above it hung an eddy of soft mist, no larger than the swirl of water draining from a sink. As Pursuivant watched, it seemed to soak into the earth and disappear. That, he said to himself, is what a soul looks like when it seeks to regain its coffin.

On he walked, step by weary, purposeful step, toward the central crypt. A ray of the early sun, stealing between heavily leafed boughs, made his way more visible. In this dawn, he would find what he would find. He knew that.

The crypt's door of open bars was held shut by its heavy padlock. He examined that lock closely. After a moment, he slid the point of his blade into the rusted keyhole and judiciously pressed this way, then that, and back again the first way. The spring creakily relaxed and he dragged the door open. Holding his breath, he entered.

The lid of the great stone vault was closed down. He took hold of the edge and heaved. The lid was heavy, but rose with a complaining grate of the hinges. Inside he saw a dark, closed coffin. He lifted the lid of that, too.

She lay there, calm-faced, the eyes half shut as though dozing.

"Chastel," said Pursuivant to her. "Not Gonda. Chastel."

The eyelids fluttered. That was all, but he knew that she heard what he said.

"Now you can rest," he said. "Rest in peace, really in peace."

He set the point of his silver blade at the swell of her left breast. Leaning both his broad hands upon the curved handle, he drove downward with all his strength.

She made a faint squeak of sound.

Blood sprang up as he cleared his weapon. More light shone in. He could see a dark moisture fading from the blade, like evaporating dew.

In the coffin, Chastel's proud shape shrivelled, darkened. Quickly he slammed the coffin shut, then lowered the lid of the vault into place and went quickly out. He pushed the door shut again and fastened the stubborn old lock. As he walked back through the churchyard among the graves, a bird twittered over his head. More distantly, he heard the hum of a car's motor. The town was waking up.

In the growing radiance, he walked back across the street. By now, his steps were the steps of an old man, old and very tired.

Inside Laurel's cabin, Laurel and Cobbett were stirring instant coffee into hot water in plastic cups. They questioned the Judge with their tired eyes.

"She's finished," he said shortly.

"What will you tell Gonda?" asked Cobbett.

"Chastel was Gonda."

"But— "

"She was Gonda," said Pursuivant again, sitting down. "Chastel died. The infection wakened her out of her tomb, and she told people she was Gonda, and naturally they believed her." He sagged wearily. "Now that she's finished and at rest, those others—the ones she had bled, who also rose at night—will rest, too."

Laurel took a sip of coffee. Above the cup, her face was pale.

"Why do you say Chastel was Gonda?" she asked the Judge. "How can you know that?"

"I wondered from the very beginning. I was utterly sure just now."

"Sure?" said Laurel. "How can you be sure?"

Pursuivant smiled at her, the very faintest of smiles.

"My dear, don't you think a man always recognizes a woman he has loved?"

He seemed to recover his characteristic defiant vigor. He rose and went to the door and put his hand on the knob. "Now, if you'll just excuse me for a while."

"Don't you think we'd better hurry and leave?" Cobbett asked him. "Before people miss her and ask questions?"

"Not at all," said Pursuivant, his voice strong again. "If we're gone, they'll ask questions about us, too, possibly embarrassing questions. No, we'll stay. We'll eat a good breakfast, or at least pretend to eat it. And we'll be as surprised as the rest of them about the disappearance of their leading lady."

"I'll do my best," vowed Laurel.

"I know you will, my child," said Pursuivant, and went out the door.

Howard Waldrop

Der Untergang Des Abendlandesmenschen

*Howard Waldrop's stories are filled with images from contemporary American
culture: rock 'n' roll music, bad science fiction movies and real-life characters
have all found their way into his uniquely comic/tragic fiction.*

*Born in 1946 in Houston, Mississipi, Waldrop has lived in Texas since he
was four years old. He won a Nebula Award for his story 'The Ugly Chicken'
(1980) and his books include the novels* The Texas-Israeli War: 1999, *
written with Jake Saunders, and* Them Bones, *along with such collections
as* Howard Who?, All About Strange Monsters of the Recent Past,
and Night of the Cooters and More Neat Stories. *His latest novel is
titled* The Moon World.

The following story is typical Waldrop . . .

THEY RODE THROUGH the flickering landscape to the tune of organ
music.

Broncho Billy, short like an old sailor, and William S., tall and
rangy as a windblown pine. Their faces, their horses, the landscape
all darkened and became light; were at first indistinct then sharp
and clear as they rode across one ridge and down into the valley
beyond.

Ahead of them, in much darker shades, was the city of Bremen, Germany.

Except for organ and piano music, it was quiet in most of Europe.
In the vaults below the Opera, in the City of Lights, Erik the phantom played the *Toccata and Fugue* while the sewers ran blackly by.

In Berlin, Cesare the somnambulist slept. His mentor Caligari lectured at the University, and waited for his chance to send the monster through the streets.
Also in Berlin, Dr Mabuse was dead and could no longer control the underworld.
But in Bremen . . .
In Bremen, something walked the night.

To the cities of china eggs and dolls, in the time of sawdust bread and the price of six million marks for a postage stamp, came Broncho Billy and William S. They had ridden hard for two days and nights, and the horses were heavily lathered.
They reined in, and tied their mounts to a streetlamp on the Wilhelmstrasse.
"What say we get a drink, William S.?" asked the shorter cowboy. "All this damn flickering gives me a headache."
William S. struck a pose three feet away from him, turned his head left and right, and stepped up to the doors of the *gasthaus* before them.
With his high-pointed hat and checked shirt, William S. looked like a weatherbeaten scarecrow, or a child's version of Abraham Lincoln before the beard. His eyes were like shiny glass, through which some inner hellfires showed.
Broncho Billy hitched up his pants. He wore Levis, which on him looked too large, a dark vest, lighter shirt, big leather chaps with three tassles at hip, knee and calf. His hat seemed three sizes too big.
Inside the tavern, things were murky grey, black and stark white. And always, the flickering.
They sat down at a table and watched the clientele. Ex-soldiers, in the remnants of uniforms, seven years after the Great War had ended. The unemployed, spending their last few coins on beer. The air was thick with grey smoke from pipes and cheap cigarettes.
Not too many people had noticed the entrance of William S. and Broncho Billy.
Two had.

* * *

"Quirt!" said an American captain, his hand on his drinking buddy, a sergeant.

"What?" asked the sergeant, his hand on the barmaid.

"Look who's here!"

The sergeant peered toward the haze of flickering grey smoke where the cowboys sat.

"Damn!" he said.

"Want to go over and chat with 'em?" asked the captain.

"&%*$%@no!" cursed the sergeant. "This ain't our %&*!*$ing picture."

"I suppose you're right," said the captain, and returned to his wine.

"You must remember, my friend," said William S. after the waiter brought them beer, "that there can be no rest in the pursuit of evil."

"Yeah, but hell, William S., this is a long way from home."

William S. lit a match, put it to a briar pipe containing his favorite shag tobacco. He puffed on it a few moments, then regarded his companion across his tankard.

"My dear Broncho Billy," he said. "No place is too far to go in order to thwart the forces of darkness. This is something Dr Helioglabulus could not handle by himself, else he should not have summoned us."

"Yeah, but William S., my butt's sore as a rizen after two days in the saddle. I think we should bunk down before we see this doctor fellow."

"Ah, that's where you're wrong, my friend," said the tall, hawk-nosed cowboy. "Evil never sleeps. Men must."

"Well, I'm a man," said Broncho Billy. "I say, let's sleep."

Just then, Doctor Helioglabulus entered the tavern.

He was dressed as a Tyrolean mountain guide, in *lederhosen* and feathered cap, climbing boots and suspenders. He carried with him an alpenstock, which made a large *clunk* each time it touched the floor.

He walked through the flickering darkness and smoke and stood in front of the table with the two cowboys.

William S. had risen.

"Dr— " he began.

"Eulenspigel," said the other, an admonitory finger to his lips.

Broncho Billy rolled his eyes heavenward.

"Dr Eulenspigel, I'd like you to meet my associate and chronicler, Mr Broncho Billy."

The doctor clicked his heels together.

"Have a chair," said Broncho Billy, pushing one out from under the table with his boot. He tipped his hat up off his eyes.

The doctor, in his comic opera outfit, sat.

"Helioglabulus," whispered William S., "whatever are you up to?"

"I had to come incognito. There are . . . others who should not learn of my presence here."

Broncho Billy looked from one to the other and rolled his eyes again.

"Then the game is afoot?" asked William S., his eyes more alight than ever.

"Game such as man has never before seen," said the doctor.

"I see," said William S., his eyes narrowing as he drew on his pipe. "Moriarty?"

"Much more evil."

"More evil?" asked the cowboy, his fingertips pressed together. "I cannot imagine such."

"Neither could I, up until a week ago," said Helioglabulus. "Since then, the city has experienced wholesale terrors. Rats run the streets at night, invade houses. This tavern will be deserted by nightfall. The people lock their doors and say prayers, even in this age. They are reverting to the old superstitions."

"They have just cause?" asked William S.

"A week ago, a ship pulled into the pier. On board was—one man!" He paused for dramatic effect. Broncho Billy was unimpressed. The doctor continued. "The crew, the passengers were gone. Only the captain was aboard, lashed to the wheel. And he was—drained of blood!"

Broncho Billy became interested.

"You mean," asked William S., bending over his beer, "that we are dealing with—the undead?"

"I am afraid so," said Dr Helioglabulus, twisting his mustaches.

"Then we shall need the proper armaments," said the taller cowboy.

"I have them," said the doctor, taking cartridge boxes from his backpack.

"Good!" said William S. "Broncho Billy, you have your revolver?"

"What!? Whatta ya mean, 'do you have your revolver?' Just what do you mean? Have you ever seen me without my guns, William S.? Are you losing your mind?"

"Sorry, Billy," said William S., looking properly abashed.

"Take these," said Helioglabulus.

Broncho Billy broke open his two Peace-makers, dumped the .45 shells on the table. William S. unlimbered his two Navy .36s and pushed the recoil rod down in the cylinders. He punched each cartridge out onto the table-top.

Billy started to load up his pistols, then took a closer look at the shells; held one up and examined it.

"Goddam, William S.," he yelled. "Wooden bullets! Wooden bullets?"

Helioglabulus was trying to wave him to silence. The tall cowboy tried to put his hand on the other.

Everyone in the beer hall had heard him. There was a deafening silence, all the patrons turned toward their table.

"Damn," said Broncho Billy. "You can't shoot a wooden bullet fifteen feet and expect it to hit the broad side of a corncrib. What the hell we gonna shoot wooden bullets at?"

The tavern began to empty, people rushing from the place, looking back in terror. All except five men at a far table.

"I am afraid, my dear Broncho Billy," said William S., "that you have frightened the patrons, and warned the evil ones of our presence."

Broncho Billy looked around.

"You mean those guys over there?" he nodded toward the other table. "Hell, William S., we both took on twelve men one time."

Dr Helioglabulus sighed. "No, no, you don't understand. Those men over there are harmless; crackpot revolutionists. William and I are speaking of *nosferatu* . . ."

Broncho Billy continued to stare at him.

". . . the undead . . ."

No response.

". . . er, ah, vampires . . ."

"You mean," asked Billy, "like Theda Bara?"

"Not vamps, my dear friend," said the hawknosed wrangler. "Vampires. Those who rise from the dead and suck the blood of the living."

"Oh," said Broncho Billy. Then he looked at the cartridges. "These kill 'em?"

"Theoretically," said Helioglabulus.

"Meaning you don't know?"

The doctor nodded.

"In that case," said Broncho Bill, "we go halfies." He began to load his .45s with one regular bullet, then a wooden one, then another standard.

William S. had already filled his with wooden slugs.

"Excellent," said Helioglabulus. "Now, put these over your hatbands. I hope you never have to get close enough for them to be effective."

What he handed them were silver hatbands. Stamped on the shiny surface of the bands was a series of crosses. They slipped them on their heads, settling them on their hatbrims.

"What next?" asked Broncho Billy.

"Why, we wait for nightfall, for the *nosferatu* to strike!" said the doctor.

"Did you hear them, Hermann?" asked Joseph.

"Sure. You think we ought to do the same?"

"Where would we find someone to make wooden bullets for pistols such as ours?" asked Joseph.

The five men sitting at the table looked toward the doctor and the two cowboys. All five were dressed in the remnants of uniforms belonging to the War. The one addressed as Hermann still wore the Knight's Cross on the faded splendor of his dress jacket.

"Martin," said Hermann. "Do you know where we can get wooden bullets?"

"I'm sure we could find someone to make them for the automatics," he answered. "Ernst, go to Wartman's, see about them."

Ernst stood, then slapped the table. "Every time I hear the word vampire, I reach for my Browning!" he said.

They all laughed. Martin, Hermann, Joseph, Ernst most of all. Even Adolf laughed a little.

Soon after dark, someone ran into the place, white of face. "The vampire!" he yelled, pointing vaguely toward the street, and fell out.

Broncho Billy and William S. jumped up. Helioglabulus stopped them. "I'm too old, and will only hold you up," he said. "I shall try to catch up later. Remember . . . the crosses. The bullets in the heart!"

As they rushed out past the other table, Ernst, who had left an hour earlier, returned with two boxes.

"Quick, Joseph!" he said as the two cowboys went through the door. "Follow them! We'll be right behind. Your pistol!"

Joseph turned, threw a Browning automatic pistol back to Hermann, then went out the doors as hoofbeats clattered in the street.

The other four began to load their pistols from the boxes of cartridges.

The two cowboys rode toward the commotion.

"Yee-haw!" yelled Broncho Billy. They galloped down the well-paved streets, their horses' hooves striking sparks from the cobbles.

They passed the police and others running towards the sounds of screams and dying. Members of the Free Corps, ex-soldiers and students, swarmed the streets in their uniforms. Torches burned against the flickering black night skies.

The city was trying to overcome the *nosferatu* by force.

Broncho Billy and William S. charged toward the fighting. In the center of a square stood a coach, all covered in black crepe. The driver, a plump, cadaverous man, held the reins to four black horses. The four were rearing high in their traces, their hooves menacing the crowd.

But it was not the horses which kept the mob back.

Crawling out of a second story hotel window was a vision from a nightmare. Bald, with pointed ears, teeth like a rat, beady eyes bright in the flickering night, the vampire climbed from a bedroom to the balcony. The front of his frock coat was covered with blood, its face and arms were smeared. A man's hand stuck halfway out the window, and the curtains were spattered black.

The *nosferatu* jumped to the ground, and the crowd parted as he leaped from the hotel steps to the waiting carriage. Then the driver cracked his whip over the horses—there was no sound—and the team charged, tumbling people like leaves before the night wind.

The carriage seemed to float to the two cowboys who rode after it. There was no sound of hoofbeats ahead, no noise from the harness, no creak of axles. It was as if they followed the wind itself through the night-time streets of Bremen.

They sped down the flickering main roads. Once, when Broncho Billy glanced behind him, he thought he saw motorcycle headlights following. But he devoted most of his attention to the fleeing coach.

William S. rode beside him. They gained on the closed carriage.

Broncho Billy drew his left-handed pistol (he was ambidexterous) and fired at the broad back of the driver. He heard the splintery clatter of the wooden bullet as it ricocheted off the coach. Then the carriage turned ahead of them.

He was almost smashed against a garden wall by the headlong plunge of his mount, then he recovered, leaning far over in the saddle, as if his horse were a sailboat and he a sailor heeling against the wind.

Then he and William S. were closing with the hearse on a long broad stretch of the avenue. They pulled even with the driver.

And for the first time, the hackles rose on Broncho Billy's neck as he rode beside the black-crepe coach. There was no sound but him, his horse, their gallop. He saw the black-garbed driver crack the long whip, heard no *snap*, heard no horses, heard no wheels.

His heart in his throat, he watched William S. pull even on the other side. The driver turned that way, snapped his whip toward the taller cowboy. Broncho Billy saw his friend's hat fly away, cut in two.

Billy took careful aim and shot the lead horse in the head, twice. It dropped like a ton of cement, and the air was filled with a vicious, soundless image: four horses, the driver, the carriage, he, his mount and William S. all flying through the air in a tangle. Then the side of the coach caught him and the incessant flickering went out.

He must have awakened a few seconds later. His horse was atop him, but he didn't think anything was broken. He pushed himself out from under it.

The driver was staggering up from the flinders of the coach— strange, thought Broncho Billy, now I hear the sounds of the wheels turning, the screams of the dying horses. The driver pulled a knife. He started toward the cowboy.

Broncho Billy found his right-hand pistol, still in its holster. He pulled it, fired directly into the heart of the fat man. The driver folded from the recoil, then stood again.

Billy pulled the trigger.

The driver dropped as the wooden bullet turned his heart to giblets.

Broncho Billy took all the regular ammo out of his pistol and began to cram the wooden ones in.

As he did, motorcycles came screaming to a stop beside him, and the five men from the tavern climbed from them or their sidecars.

He looked around for William S. but could not see him. Then he heard the shooting from the rooftop above the street—twelve shots, quick as summer thunder.

One of William S.'s revolvers dropped four stories and hit the ground beside him.

The Germans were already up the stairs ahead of Broncho Billy as he ran.

When the carriage had crashed into them, William S. had been thrown clear. He jumped up in time to see the vampire run into the doorway of the residential block across the way. He tore after while the driver pulled himself from the wreckage and Broncho Billy was crawling from under his horse.

Up the stairs he ran. He could now hear the pounding feet of the living dead man ahead, unlike the silence before the wreck. A flickering murky hallway was before him, and he saw the door at the far end close.

William S. smashed into it, rolled. He heard the scrape of teeth behind him, and saw the rat-like face snap shut inches away. He came up, his pistols leveled at the vampire.

The bald-headed thing grabbed the open door, pulled it before him.

William S. stood, feet braced, a foot from the door and began to fire into it. His Colt .36s inches in front of his face, he fired again and again into the wooden door, watching chunks and splinters shear away. He heard the vampire squeal, like a rat trapped behind a trash can, but still he fired until both pistols clicked dry.

The door swung slowly awry, pieces of it hanging.

The *nosferatu* grinned, and carefully pushed the door closed. It hissed and crouched.

William S. reached up for his hat.

And remembered that the driver had knocked it off his head before the collision.

The thing leaped.

One of his pistols was knocked over the parapet.

Then he was fighting for his life.

The five Germans, yelling to each other, slammed into the doorway at the end of the hall. From beyond, they heard the sounds of scuffling, labored breathing, the rip and tear of cloth.

Broncho Billy charged up behind them.

"The door! It's jammed," said one.

"His hat!" yelled Broncho Billy. "He lost his hat!"

"Hat?" asked the one called Joseph in English. "Why his hat?" The others shouldered against the gapped door. Through it, they saw flashes of movement and the flickering night sky.

"Crosses!" yelled Broncho Billy. "Like this!" He pointed to his hatband.

"Ah!" said Joseph. "Crosses."

He pulled something from the one called Adolf, who hung back a little, threw it through the hole in the door.

"*Cruzen!*" yelled Joseph.

"The cross!" screamed Broncho Billy. "William S.! The cross!"
The sound of scuffling stopped.
Joseph tossed his pistol through the opening.
They continued to bang on the door.

The thing had its talons on his throat when the yelling began. The vampire was strangling him. Little circles were swimming in his sight. He was down beneath the monster. It smelled of old dirt, raw meat, of death. Its rat-eyes were bright with hate.

Then he heard the yell "A cross!" and something fluttered at the edge of his vision. He let go one hand from the vampire and grabbed it up.

It felt like cloth. He shoved it at the thing's face.

Hands let go.

William S. held the cloth before him as his breath came back in a rush. He staggered up, and the *nosferatu* put its hands over its face. He pushed toward it.

Then the Browning Automatic pistol landed beside his foot, and he heard noises at the door behind him.

Holding the cloth, he picked up the pistol.

The vampire hissed like a radiator.

William S. aimed and fired. The pistol was fully automatic.

The wooden bullets opened the vampire like a zipper coming off.

The door crashed outward, the five Germans and Broncho Billy rushed through.

William S. held to the doorframe and caught his breath. A crowd was gathering below, at the site of the wrecked hearse and the dead horses. Torchlights wobbled their reflections on the houses across the road. It looked like something from Dante.

Helioglabulus came onto the roof, took one look at the vampire and ran his alpenstock, handle first, into its ruined chest.

"Just to make sure," he said.

Broncho Billy was clapping him on the back. "Shore thought you'd gone to the last roundup," he said.

The five Germans were busy with the vampire's corpse.

William S. looked at the piece of cloth still clenched tightly in his own hand. He opened it. It was an armband.

On its red cloth was a white circle with a twisted black cross.

Like the decorations the Indians used on their blankets, only in reverse.

He looked at the Germans. Four of them wore the armbands; the fifth, wearing an old corporal's uniform, had a torn sleeve.

They were slipping a yellow armband over the arm of the vampire's coat. When they finished, they picked the thing up and carried it to the roof edge. It looked like a spitted pig.

The yellow armband had two interlocking triangles, like the device on the chest of the costumes William S. had worn when he played *Ben-Hur* on Broadway. The Star of David.

The crowd below screamed as the corpse fell toward them.

There were shouts, then.

The unemployed, the war-wounded, the young, the bitter, the disillusioned. Then the shouting stopped . . . and they began to chant.

The five Germans stood on the parapet, looking down at the milling people. They talked among themselves.

Broncho Billy held William S. until he caught his breath.

They heard the crowds disperse, fill in again, break, drift off, reform, reassemble, grow larger.

"Well, pard," said Broncho Billy. "Let's mosey over to a hotel and get some shut-eye."

"That would be nice," said William S.

Helioglabulus joined them.

"We should go by the back way," he said.

"I don't like the way this crowd is actin'," said Broncho Billy.

William S. walked to the parapet, looked out over the city.

Under the dark flickering sky, there were other lights. Here and there, synagogues began to flicker.

And then to burn.

E. F. Benson

The Room in the Tower

Edward Frederic Benson (1867–1940) showed an early interest in the classics and archaeology. He was the Mayor of Rye from 1934–37 and was awarded the MBE. His first book was the bestselling society novel Dodo, *published in 1893, and he is still remembered for his series of sophisticated Mapp and Lucia comedies.*

But whereas many of his general works have become dated, Benson's horror fiction retains much of its original impact. His macabre novels include The Judgement Books, The Image in the Sand, The Angel of Pain, Colin I *and* Colin II, The Inheritor *and* Raven's Brood. *However, Benson excelled in the short story form, and among his classic tales are 'Caterpillars', 'The Horror Horn' and two other vampire stories, 'Mrs Amworth' and 'And No Bird Sings'. His short fiction is collected in* The Room in the Tower and Other Stories, Visible and Invisible, Spook Stories, More Spook Stories, The Horror Horn *and* The Flint Knife.

'The Room in the Tower' is one of Benson's best stories, in which the protagonist is plunged into a chillingly prophetic dreamscape and an encounter with the undead.

IT IS PROBABLE that everybody who is at all a constant dreamer has had at least one experience of an event or a sequence of circumstances which have come to his mind in sleep being subsequently realized in the material world. But, in my opinion, so far from this being a strange thing, it would be far odder if this fulfilment did not occasionally happen, since our dreams are, as a rule, concerned with people whom we know and places with which we are familiar, such as might very naturally occur in the awake and daylit world. True, these dreams are often broken into by some absurd and fantastic incident, which puts them out of court in regard to their subsequent fulfilment, but on the mere calculation of chances, it does not appear in the least unlikely that a dream imagined by anyone who dreams constantly should occasionally come true. Not long ago, for instance, I experienced such a fulfilment of a dream which seems to me in no way remarkable and to have no kind of physical significance. The manner of it was as follows.

A certain friend of mine, living abroad, is amiable enough to write to me about once in a fortnight. Thus, when fourteen days or thereabouts have elapsed since I last heard from him, my mind, probably, either consciously or subconsciously, is expectant of a letter from him. One night last week I dreamed that as I was going upstairs to dress for dinner I heard, as I often heard, the sound of the postman's knock on my front door, and diverted my direction downstairs instead. There, among other correspondence, was a letter from him. Thereafter the fantastic entered, for on opening it I found inside the ace of diamonds, and scribbled across it in his well-known handwriting, "I am sending you this for safe custody, as you know it is running an unreasonable risk to keep aces in Italy." The next evening I was just preparing to go upstairs to dress when I heard the postman's knock, and did precisely as I had done in my dream. There, among other letters, was one from my friend. Only it did not contain the ace of diamonds. Had it done so, I should have attached more weight to the matter, which, as it stands, seems to me a perfectly ordinary coincidence. No doubt I consciously or subconsciously expected a letter from him, and this suggested to me my dream. Similarly, the fact that my friend had not written to me for a fortnight suggested to him that he should do so. But occasionally it is not so easy to find such an explanation, and for the following story I can find no explanation at all. It came out of the dark, and into the dark it has gone again.

All my life I have been a habitual dreamer: the nights are few, that is to say, when I do not find on awaking in the morning that some mental experience has been mine, and sometimes, all night long, apparently, a series of the most dazzling adventures befall me. Almost without exception these adventures are pleasant, though often merely trivial. It is of an exception that I am going to speak.

It was when I was about sixteen that a certain dream first came to me, and this is how it befell. It opened with my being set down at the door of a big red-brick house, where, I understood, I was going to stay. The servant who opened the door told me that tea was going on in the garden, and led me through a low dark-panelled hall, with a large open fireplace, on to a cheerful green lawn set round with flower beds. There were grouped about the tea-table a small party of people, but they were all strangers to me except one, who was a school-fellow called Jack Stone, clearly the son of the house, and he introduced me to his mother and father and a couple of sisters. I was, I remember, somewhat astonished to find myself here, for the boy in question was scarcely known to me, and I rather disliked what I knew of him; moreover, he had left school nearly a year before. The afternoon was very hot, and an intolerable oppression reigned. On the far side of the lawn ran a red-brick wall, with an iron gate in its centre, outside which stood a walnut tree. We sat in the shadow of the house opposite a row of long windows inside which I could see a table with cloth laid, glimmering with glass and silver. This garden front of the house was very long, and at one end of it stood a tower of three stories, which looked to me much older than the rest of the building.

Before long, Mrs Stone, who, like the rest of the party, had sat in absolute silence, said to me, "Jack will show you your room: I have given you the room in the tower."

Quite inexplicably my heart sank at her words. I felt as if I had known that I should have the room in the tower, and that it contained something dreadful and significant. Jack instantly got up, and I understood that I had to follow him. In silence we passed through the hall, and mounted a great oak staircase with many corners, and arrived at a small landing with two doors set in it. He pushed one of these open for me to enter, and without coming in himself, closed it behind me. Then I knew that my conjecture had been right: there was something awful in the room, and with the terror of nightmare growing swiftly and enveloping me, I awoke in a spasm of terror.

Now that dream or variations on it occurred to me intermittently for fifteen years. Most often it came in exactly this form, the arrival, the tea laid out on the lawn, the deadly silence succeeded by that one deadly sentence, the mounting with Jack Stone up to the room in the tower where horror dwelt, and it always came to a close in the nightmare of terror at that which was in the room, though I never saw what it was. At other times I experienced variations on this same theme. Occasionally, for instance, we would be sitting at dinner in the dining-room, into the windows of which I had looked on the first night when the dream of this house visited me, but wherever we were, there was the same silence, the same sense of dreadful oppression and foreboding. And the silence I knew would always be broken by Mrs Stone saying to me, "Jack will show you your room: I have given you the room in the tower." Upon which (this was invariable) I had to follow him up the oak staircase with many corners, and enter the place that I dreaded more and more each time that I visited it in sleep. Or, again, I would find myself playing cards still in silence in a drawing-room lit with immense chandeliers, that gave a blinding illumination. What the game was I have no idea; what I remember, with a sense of miserable anticipation, was that soon Mrs Stone would get up and say to me, "Jack will show you your room: I have given you the room in the tower." This drawing-room where we played cards was next to the dining-room, and, as I have said, was always brilliantly illuminated, whereas the rest of the house was full of dusk and shadows. And yet, how often, in spite of those bouquets of lights, have I not pored over the cards that were dealt me, scarcely able for some reason to see them. Their designs, too, were strange: there were no red suits, but all were black, and among them there were certain cards which were black all over. I hated and dreaded those.

As this dream continued to recur, I got to know the greater part of the house. There was a smoking-room beyond the drawing-room, at the end of a passage with a green baize door. It was always very dark there, and as often as I went there I passed somebody whom I could not see in the doorway coming out. Curious developments, too, took place in the characters that peopled the dream as might happen to living persons. Mrs Stone, for instance, who, when I first saw her, had been black haired, became grey, and instead of rising briskly, as she had done when she said, "Jack will show you your room: I have given you the room in the tower," got up very feebly, as if the strength was leaving her limbs. Jack also grew up, and became a rather ill-looking young man, with a brown moustache, while one of the sisters ceased to appear, and I understood she was married.

Then it so happened that I was not visited by this dream for six months or more, and I began to hope, in such inexplicable dread did I hold it, that it had passed away for good. But one night after this interval I again found myself being shown out on to the lawn for tea, and Mrs Stone was not there, while the others were all dressed in black. At once I guessed the reason, and my heart leaped at the thought that perhaps this time I should not have to sleep in the room in the tower, and though we usually all sat in silence, on this occasion the sense of relief made me talk and laugh as I had never yet done. But even then matters were not altogether comfortable, for no one else spoke, but they all looked secretly at each other. And soon the foolish stream of my talk ran dry, and gradually an apprehension worse than anything I had previously known gained on me as the light slowly faded.

Suddenly a voice which I knew well broke the stillness, the voice of Mrs Stone, saying, "Jack will show you your room: I have given you the room in the tower." It seemed to come from near the gate in the red-brick wall that bounded the lawn, and looking up, I saw that the grass outside was sown thick with gravestones. A curious greyish light shone from them, and I could read the lettering on the grave nearest me, and it was, "In evil memory of Julia Stone." And as usual Jack got up, and again I followed him through the hall and up the staircase with many corners. On this occasion it was darker than usual, and when I passed into the room in the tower I could only just see the furniture, the position of which was already familiar to me. Also there was a dreadful odour of decay in the room, and I woke screaming.

The dream, with such variations and developments as I have mentioned, went on at intervals for fifteen years. Sometimes I would dream it two or three nights in succession; once, as I have said, there was an intermission of six months, but taking a reasonable average, I should say that I dreamed it quite as often as once in a month. It had, as is plain, something of nightmare about it, since it always ended in the same appalling terror, which so far from getting less, seemed to me to gather fresh fear every time that I experienced it. There was, too, a strange and dreadful consistency about it. The characters in it, as I have mentioned, got regularly older, death and marriage visited this silent family, and I never in the dream, after Mrs Stone had died, set eyes on her again. But it was always her voice that told me that the room in the tower was prepared for me, and whether we had tea out on the lawn, or the scene was laid in one of the rooms overlooking it, I could always see her gravestone standing just outside the iron gate. It was the same, too, with the married daughter; usually she was not present, but once or twice she returned again, in company with a man, whom I took to be her husband. He, too, like the rest of them, was always silent. But, owing to the constant repetition of the dream, I had ceased to attach, in my waking hours, any significance to it. I never met Jack Stone again during all those years, nor did I ever see a house that resembled this dark house of my dream. And then something happened.

I had been in London in this year, up till the end of July, and during the first week in August went down to stay with a friend in a house he had taken for the summer months, in the Ashdown Forest district of Sussex. I left London early, for John Clinton was to meet me at Forest Row Station, and we were going to spend the day golfing, and go to his house in the evening. He had his motor with him, and we set off, about five of the afternoon, after a thoroughly delightful day, for the drive, the distance being some ten miles. As it was still so early we did not have tea at the club house, but waited till we should get home. As we drove, the weather, which up till then had been, though hot, deliciously fresh, seemed to me to alter in quality, and become very stagnant and oppressive, and I felt that indefinable sense of ominous apprehension that I am accustomed to before thunder. John, however, did not share my views, attributing my loss of lightness to the fact that I had lost both my matches. Events proved, however, that I was right, though I do not think that the thunderstorm that broke that night was the sole cause of my depression.

Our way lay through deep high-banked lanes, and before we had gone very far I fell asleep, and was only awakened by the stopping of the motor. And with a sudden thrill, partly of fear but chiefly of curiosity, I found myself standing in the doorway of my house of dream. We went, I half wondering whether or not I was dreaming still, through a low oak-panelled hall, and out on to the lawn, where tea was laid in the shadow of the house. It was set in flower beds, a red-brick wall, with a gate in it, bounded one side, and out beyond that was a space of rough grass with a walnut tree. The façade of the house was very long, and at one end stood a three-storeyed tower, markedly older than the rest.

Here for the moment all resemblance to the repeated dream ceased. There was no silent and somehow terrible family, but a large assembly of exceedingly cheerful persons, all of whom were known to me. And in spite of the horror with which the dream itself had always filled me, I felt nothing of it now that the scene of it was thus reproduced before me. But I felt the intensest curiosity as to what was going to happen.

Tea pursued its cheerful course, and before long Mrs Clinton got up. And at that moment I think I knew what she was going to say. She spoke to me, and what she said was:

"Jack will show you your room: I have given you the room in the tower."

At that, for half a second, the horror of the dream took hold of me again. But it quickly passed, and again I felt nothing more than the most intense curiosity. It was not very long before it was amply satisfied.

John turned to me.

"Right up at the top of the house," he said, "but I think you'll be comfortable. We're absolutely full up. Would you like to go and see it now? By Jove, I believe that you are right, and that we are going to have a thunderstorm. How dark it has become."

I got up and followed him. We passed through the hall, and up the perfectly familiar staircase. Then he opened the door, and I went in. And at that moment sheer unreasoning terror again possessed me. I did not know for certain what I feared: I simply feared. Then like a sudden recollection, when one remembers a name which has long escaped the memory, I knew what I feared. I feared Mrs Stone, whose grave with the sinister inscription, "In evil memory," I had so often seen in my dream, just beyond the lawn which lay below my window. And then once more the fear passed so completely that I wondered what there was to fear, and I found myself sober and quiet and sane, in the room in the tower, the name of which I had so often heard in my dreams, and the scene of which was so familiar.

I looked round it with a certain sense of proprietorship, and found that nothing had been changed from the dreaming nights in which I knew it so well. Just to the left of the door was the bed, lengthways along the wall, with the head of it in the angle. In a line with it was the fireplace and a small bookcase; opposite the door the outer wall was pierced by two lattice-paned windows, between which stood the dressing-table, while ranged along the fourth wall was the washing-stand and a big cupboard. My luggage had already been unpacked, for the furniture of dressing and undressing lay orderly on the washstand and toilet-table, while my dinner clothes were spread out on the coverlet of the bed. And then, with a sudden start of unexplained dismay, I saw that there were two rather conspicuous objects which I had not seen before in my dreams: one a life-sized oil-painting of Mrs Stone, the other a black-and-white sketch of Jack Stone, representing him as he had appeared to me only a week before in the last of the series of these repeated dreams, a rather secret and evil-looking man of about thirty. His picture hung between the windows, looking straight across the room to the other portrait, which hung at the side of the bed. At that I looked next, and as I looked I felt once more the horror of nightmare seize me.

It represented Mrs Stone as I had seen her last in my dreams: old and withered and white haired. But in spite of the evident feebleness of body, a dreadful exuberance and vitality shone through the envelope of flesh, an exuberance wholly malign, a vitality that foamed and frothed with unimaginable evil. Evil beamed from the narrow, leering eyes; it laughed in the demon-like mouth. The whole face was instinct with some secret and appalling mirth; the hands, clasped together on the knee, seemed shaking with suppressed and nameless glee. Then I saw also that it was signed in the left-hand bottom corner, and wondering who the artist could be, I looked more closely, and read the inscription, "Julia Stone by Julia Stone."

There came a tap at the door, and John Clinton entered.

"Got everything you want?" he asked.

"Rather more than I want," said I, pointing to the picture.

He laughed.

"Hard-featured old lady," he said. "By herself, too, I remember. Anyhow, she can't have flattered herself much."

"But don't you see?" said I. "It's scarcely a human face at all. It's the face of some witch, of some devil."

He looked at it more closely.

"Yes; it isn't very pleasant," he said. "Scarcely a bedside manner, eh? Yes; I can imagine getting the nightmare if I went to sleep with that close by my bed. I'll have it taken down if you like."

"I really wish you would," I said.

He rang the bell, and with the help of a servant we detached the picture and carried it out on to the landing, and put it with its face to the wall.

"By Jove, the old lady is a weight," said John, mopping his forehead. "I wonder if she had something on her mind."

The extraordinary weight of the picture had struck me too. I was about to reply when I caught sight of my own hand. There was blood on it, in considerable quantities, covering the whole palm.

"I've cut myself somehow," said I.

John gave a little startled exclamation.

"Why, I have too," he said.

Simultaneously the footman took out his handkerchief and wiped his hand with it. I saw that there was blood also on his handkerchief.

John and I went back into the tower room and washed the blood off; but neither on his hand nor on mine was there the slightest trace of a scratch or cut. It seemed to me that, having ascertained this, we both, by a sort of tacit consent, did not allude to it again. Something in my case had dimly occurred to me that I did not wish to think about. It was but a conjecture, but I fancied that I knew the same thing had occurred to him.

The heat and the oppression of the air, for the storm we had expected was still undischarged, increased very much after dinner, and for some time most of the party, among whom were John Clinton and myself, sat outside on the path bounding the lawn, where we had had tea. The night was absolutely dark, and no twinkle of star or moon ray could penetrate the pall of cloud that overset the sky. By degrees our assembly thinned, the women went up to bed, men dispersed to the smoking or billiard room, and by eleven o'clock my host and I were the only two left. All the evening I thought that he had something on his mind, and as soon as we were alone he spoke.

"The man who helped us with the picture had blood on his hand, too, did you notice?" he said. " I asked him just now if he had cut himself, and he said he supposed he had, but that he could find no mark of it. Now where did that blood come from?"

By dint of telling myself that I was not going to think about it, I had succeeded in not doing so, and I did not want, especially just at bedtime, to be reminded of it.

"I don't know," said I, "and I don't really care so long as the picture of Mrs Julia Stone is not by my bed."

He got up.

"But it's odd," he said. "Ha! Now you'll see another odd thing."

A dog of his, an Irish terrier by breed, had come out of the house as we talked. The door behind us into the hall was open, and a bright oblong of light shone across the lawn to the iron gate which led on to the rough grass outside, where the walnut tree stood. I saw that the dog had all his hackles up, bristling with rage and fright; his lips were curled back from his teeth, as if he were ready to spring at something, and he was growling to himself. He took not the slightest notice of his master or me, but stiffly and tensely walked across the grass to the iron gate. There he stood for a moment, looking through the bars and still growling. Then all of a sudden his courage seemed to desert him: he gave one long howl, and scuttled back to the house with a curious crouching sort of movement.

"He does that half-a-dozen times a day," said John. "He sees something which he both hates and fears."

I walked to the gate and looked over it. Something was moving on the grass outside, and soon a sound which I could not instantly identify came to my ears. Then I remembered what it was: it was the purring of a cat. I lit a match, and saw the purrer, a big blue Persian, walking round and round in a little circle just outside the gate, stepping high and ecstatically, with tail carried aloft like a banner. Its eyes were bright and shining, and every now and then it put its head down and sniffed at the grass.

I laughed.

"The end of that mystery, I am afraid," I said. "Here's a large cat having Walpurgis night all alone."

"Yes, that Darius," said John. "He spends half the day and all night there. But that's not the end of the dog mystery, for Toby and he are the best of friends, but the beginning of the cat mystery. What's the cat doing there? And why is Darius pleased, while Toby is terror-stricken?"

At that moment I remembered the rather horrible detail of my dreams when I saw through the gate, just where the cat was now, the white tombstone with the sinister inscription. But before I could answer the rain began, as suddenly and heavily as if a tap had been turned on, and simultaneously the big cat squeezed through the bars of the gate, and came leaping across the lawn to the house for shelter. Then it sat in the doorway, looking out eagerly into the dark. It spat and struck at John with its paw, as he pushed it in, in order to close the door.

Somehow, with the portrait of Julia Stone in the passage outside, the room in the tower had absolutely no alarm for me, and as I went to bed, feeling very sleepy and heavy, I had nothing more than interest for the curious incident about our bleeding hands, and the conduct of the cat and dog. The last thing I looked at before I put out my light was the square empty space by my bed where the portrait had been. Here the paper was of its original full tint of dark red: over the rest of the walls it had faded. Then I blew out my candle and instantly fell asleep.

My awaking was equally instantaneous, and I sat bolt upright in bed under the impression that some bright light had been flashed in my face, though it was now absolutely pitch dark. I knew exactly where I was, in the room which I had dreaded in dreams, but no horror that I ever felt when asleep approached the fear that now invaded and froze my brain. Immediately after a peal of thunder crackled just above the house, but the probability that it was only a flash of lightning which awoke me gave no reassurance to my galloping heart. Something I knew was in the room with me, and instinctively I put out my right hand, which was nearest the wall, to keep it away. And my hand touched the edge of a picture-frame hanging close to me.

I sprang out of bed, upsetting the small table that stood by it, and I heard my watch, candle, and matches clatter on to the floor. But for the moment there was no need of light, for a blinding flash leaped out of the clouds, and showed me that by my bed again hung the picture of Mrs Stone. And instantly the room went into blackness again. But in that flash I saw another thing also, namely a figure that leaned over the end of my bed, watching me. It was dressed in some close-clinging white garment, spotted and stained with mould, and the face was that of the portrait.

Overhead the thunder cracked and roared, and when it ceased and the deathly stillness succeeded, I heard the rustle of movement coming nearer me, and, more horrible yet, perceived an odour of corruption and decay. And then a hand was laid on the side of my neck, and close beside my ear I heard quick-taken eager breathing. Yet I knew that this thing, though it could be perceived by touch, by smell, by eye and by ear, was still not of this earth, but something that had passed out of the body and had power to make itself manifest. Then a voice, already familiar to me, spoke.

"I knew you would come to the room in the tower," it said. "I have been long waiting for you. At last you have come. To-night I shall feast; before long we will feast together."

And the quick breathing came closer to me; I could feel it on my neck.

At that the terror, which I think had paralysed me for the moment, gave way to the wild instinct of self-preservation. I hit wildly with both arms, kicking out at the same moment, and heard a little animal-squeal, and something soft dropped with a thud beside me. I took a couple of steps forward, nearly tripping up over whatever it was that lay there, and by the merest good luck found the handle of the door. In another second I ran out on the landing, and had banged the door behind me. Almost at the same moment I heard a door open somewhere below, and John Clinton, candle in hand, came running upstairs.

"What is it?" he said. "I slept just below you, and heard a noise as if—Good heavens, there's blood on your shoulder."

I stood there, so he told me afterwards, swaying from side to side, white as a sheet, with the mark on my shoulder as if a hand covered with blood had been laid there.

"It's in there," I said, pointing. "She, you know. The portrait is in there too, hanging up on the place we took it from."

At that he laughed.

"My dear fellow, this is a mere nightmare," he said.

He pushed by me, and opened the door, I standing there simply inert with terror, unable to stop him, unable to move.

"Phew! What an awful smell!" he said.

Then there was silence; he had passed out of my sight behind the open door. Next moment he came out again, as white as myself, and instantly shut it.

"Yes, the portrait's there," he said, "and on the floor is a thing—a thing spotted with earth, like what they bury people in. Come away, quick, come away."

How I got downstairs I hardly know. An awful shuddering and nausea of the spirit rather than of the flesh had seized me, and more than once he had to place my feet upon the steps, while every now and then he cast glances of terror and apprehension up the stairs. But in time we came to his dressing-room on the floor below, and there I told him what I have here described.

The sequel can be made short; indeed, some of my readers have perhaps already guessed what it was, if they remember that inexplicable affair of the churchyard at West Fawley, some eight years ago, where an attempt was made three times to bury the body of a certain woman who had committed suicide. On each occasion the coffin was found in the course of a few days again protruding from the ground. After the third attempt, in order that the thing should not be talked about, the body was buried elsewhere in unconsecrated ground. Where it was buried was just outside the iron gate of the garden belonging to the house where this woman had lived. She had committed suicide in a room at the top of the tower in that house. Her name was Julia Stone.

Subsequently the body was again secretly dug up, and the coffin was found to be full of blood.

Graham Masterton

Laird of Dunain

Graham Masterton was born in Edinburgh, and a recent return to Scotland inspired this story, which was specially written for this anthology.

A former editor of Mayfair *and* Penthouse, *and still one of the world's best-selling writers of sexual "how-to" books, Masterton began his career in horror in 1974 with the* The Manitou *(filmed in 1978), and he has written two dozen horror novels since then, culminating in* Manitou 3.

His recent books include The Hymn, *a neo-Nazi story of opera and spontaneous combustion;* Walkers, *a tale of Druids and homicidal lunatics, and* Black Angel, *which he describes as being about "a ritual killer whose activities make Hannibal Lecter look about as threatening as Pee-Wee Herman."*

At 45, Masterton is still an enfant terrible *of horror fiction: his story 'Pig's Dinner' in* The Mammoth Book of Terror *put a lot of readers off their bacon, while his contribution to the short story magazine* Frightners *resulted in the banning of the very first issue throughout the UK.*

He points out that, "'Laird of Dunain' is less grisly, but should still send a deep shiver of anxiety through those who value the colour of their corpuscles."

"The tailor fell thro' the bed, thimbles an' a'
"The blankets were thin and the sheets they were sma'
"The tailor fell thro' the bed, thimbles an' a'

* * *

OUT ONTO THE lawns in the first gilded mists of morning came the Laird of Dunain in kilt and sporran and thick oatmeal-coloured sweater, his face pale and bony and aesthetic, his beard red as a burning flame, his hair as wild as a thistle-patch.

Archetypal Scotsman; the kind of Scotsman you saw on tins of shortbread or bottles of single malt whisky. Except that he looked so drawn and gaunt. Except that he looked so spiritually hungry.

It was the first time that Claire had seen him since her arrival, and she reached over and tapped Duncan's arm with the end of her paintbrush and said, "Look, there he is! Doesn't he look *fantastic*?"

All nine members of the painting class turned to stare at the laird as he fastidiously patrolled the shingle path that ran along the back of Dunain Castle. At first, however, he appeared not to notice them, keeping his hands behind his back and his head aloof, as if he were breathing in the fine summer air, and surveying his lands, and thinking the kind of things that Highland lairds were supposed to think, like how many stags to cull, and how to persuade the Highlands Development Board to provide him with mains electricity.

"I wonder if he'd sit for us?" asked Margot, a rotund frizzy-haired girl from Liverpool. Margot had confessed to Claire that she had taken up painting because the smocks hid her hips.

"We could try asking him," Claire suggested—Claire with her straight dark bob and her serious, well structured face. Her husband, her *former* husband, had always said that she looked "like a sensual schoolmistress." Her painting smock and her Alice-band and her moon-round spectacles only heightened the impression.

"He's so *romantic*," said Margot. "Like Rob Roy. Or Bonnie Prince Charlie."

Duncan sorted through his box of watercolours until he found the half-burned nip-end of a cigarette. He lit it with a plastic lighter with a scratched transfer of a topless girl on it. "The trouble with painting in Scotland," he said, "is that *everything* looks so fucking romantic. You put your heart and your soul into painting Glenmoriston, and you end up with something that looks like a Woolworth's dinner-mat."

"I'd still like him to sit for us," said Margot.

The painting class had arranged their easels on the sloping south lawn of Dunain Castle, just above the stone-walled herb gardens. Beyond the herb gardens the grounds sloped grassy and gentle to the banks of the Caledonian Canal, where it cut its way between the north-eastern end of Loch Ness and the city of Inverness itself, and out to the Moray Firth. All through yesterday, the sailing-ships of the Tall Ships Race had been gliding through the canal, and they had appeared to be sailing surrealistically through fields and hedges, like ships in a dream, or a nightmare.

Mr Morrissey called out, "Pay particular attention to the light; because it's golden and very even just now; but it'll change."

Mr Morrissey (bald, round-shouldered, speedy, fussy) was their course-instructor; the man who had greeted them when they first arrived at Dunain Castle, and who had showed them their rooms ("You'll *adore* this, Mrs Bright . . . such a view of the garden . . .") and who was now conducting their lessons in landscape-painting. In his way, he was very good. He sketched austerely; he painted monochromatically. He wouldn't tolerate sentimentality.

"You've not come to Scotland to reproduce The Monarch of the Glen," he had told them, when he had collected them from the station at Inverness. "You're here to paint life, and landscape, in light of unparalleled clarity."

Claire returned to her charcoal-sketching but she could see (out of the corner of her eye) that the Laird of Dunain was slowly making his way across the lawns. For some reason, she felt excited, and began to sketch more quickly and more erratically. Before she knew it, the Laird was standing only two or three feet away from her, his hands still clasped behind his back. His aura was prickly and electric, almost as if he were already running his thick ginger beard up her inner thighs.

"Well, well," he remarked, at last, in a strong Inverness accent. "You have all of the makings, I'd say. You're not one of Gordon's usual giglets."

Claire blushed, and found that she couldn't carry on sketching. Margot giggled.

"Hech," said the Laird, "I wasn't flethering. You're good."

"Not really," said Claire. "I've only been painting for seven months."

The Laird stood closer. Claire could smell tweed and tobacco and heather and something else, something cloying and sweet, which she had never smelled before.

"You're good," he repeated. "You can draw well; and I'll lay money that ye can paint well. Mr Morrissey!"

Mr Morrissey looked up and his face was very white.

"Mr Morrissey, do you have any objection if I fetch this unback'd filly away from the class?"

Mr Morrissey looked dubious. "It's supposed to be landscape, this morning."

"Aye, but a wee bit of portraiture won't harm her now, will it? And I'm dying to have my portrait painted."

Very reluctantly, Mr Morrissey said, "No, I suppose it won't harm."

"That's settled, then," the Laird declared; and immediately began to fold up Claire's easel and tidy up her box of watercolours.

"Just a minute— " said Claire, almost laughing at his impertinence.

The Laird of Dunain stared at her with eyes that were green like emeralds crushed with a pestle-and-mortar. "I'm sorry," he said. "You don't *object*, do you?"

Claire couldn't stop herself from smiling. "No," she said. "I don't object."

"Well, then," said the Laird of Dunain, and led the way back to the castle.

"Hmph," said Margot, indignantly.

He posed in a dim upper room with dark oak paneling all around, and a high ceiling. The principal light came from a leaded clerestory window, falling almost like a spotlight. The Laird of Dunain sat on a large iron-bound trunk, his head held high, and managed to remain completely motionless while Claire began to sketch.

"You'll have come here looking for something else, apart from painting and drawing," he said, after a while.

Claire's charcoal-twig was quickly outlining his left shoulder. "Oh, yes?" she said. She couldn't think what he meant.

"You'll have come here looking for peace of mind, won't you, and a way to sort everything out?"

She thought, briefly, of Alan, and of Susan, and of doors slamming. She thought of walking for miles through Shepherd's Bush, in the pouring April rain.

"That's what art's all about it, isn't it?" she retorted. "Sorting things out."

The Laird of Dunain smiled obliquely. "That's what my father used to say. In fact, my father believed it quite implicitly."

There was something about his tone of voice that stopped Claire from sketching for a moment. Something very serious; something *suggestive*; as if he were trying to tell her that his words had more than one meaning.

"I shall have to carry on with this tomorrow," she said.

The Laird of Dunain nodded. "That's all right. We have all the time in the world."

The next day, while the rest of the class took a minibus to Fort Augustus to paint the downstepping locks of the Caledonian Canal,

Claire sat with the Laird of Dunain in his high gloomy room and started to paint his portrait. She used designer's colours, in preference to oils, because they were quicker; and she sensed that there was something mercurial in the Laird of Dunain which she wouldn't be capable of catching with oils.

"You're a very good sitter," she said, halfway through the morning. "Don't you want to take a break? Perhaps I could make some coffee."

The Laird of Dunain didn't break his rigid pose, even by an inch. "I'd rather get it finished, if you don't mind."

She carried on painting, squeezing out a half a tube of red. She was finding it difficult to give his face any colour. Normally, for faces, she used little more than a palette of yellow ochre, terra verte, alizarin crimson and cobalt blue. But no matter how much red she mixed into her colours, his face always seemed anemic—almost deathly.

"I'm finding it hard to get your flesh-tones right," she confessed, as the clock in the downstairs hallway struck two.

The Laird of Dunain nodded. "They always said of the Dunains of Dunain that they were a bloodless family. Mind you, I think we proved them wrong at Culloden. That was the day that the Laird of Dunain was caught and cornered by half-a-dozen of the Duke of Cumberland's soldiers, and cut about so bad that he stained a quarter of an acre with his own blood."

"That sounds awful," said Claire, squeezing out more alizarin crimson.

"It was a long time ago," replied the Laird of Dunain. "The sixteenth day of April, 1746. Almost two hundred and fifty years ago; and whose memory can span such a time?"

"You make it sound like yesterday," said Claire, busily mixing.

The Laird of Dunain turned his head away for the very first time that day. "On that day, when he lay bleeding, the laird swore that he would have his revenge on the English for every drop of blood that he had let. He would have it back, he said, a thousandfold; and then a thousandfold more.

"They never discovered his body, you know, although there were plenty of tales in the glens that it was hurried away by Dunains and Macduffs. That was partly the reason that the Duke of Cumberland pursued the Highlanders with such savagery. He made his own promise that he would never return to England until he had seen for himself the body of Dunain of Dunain, and fed it to the dogs."

"Savage times," Claire remarked. She sat back. The laird's face was still appallingly white, even though she had mixed his skin-tones with almost two whole tubes of crimson. She couldn't understand it. She ran her hand back through her hair and said, "I'll have to come back to this tomorrow."

"Of course," said the Laird of Dunain.

On her way to supper, she met Margot in the oak-panelled corridor. Margot was unexpectedly bustling and fierce. "You didn't come with us yesterday and you didn't come with us today. Today we sketched sheep."

"I've been— " Claire began, inclining her head toward the Laird of Dunain's apartments.

"Oh, yes," said Margot. "I thought as much. We *all* thought as much." And then she went off, with wig-wagging bottom.

Claire was amazed. But then she suddenly thought: *she's jealous. She's really jealous.*

All the next day while the Laird of Dunain sat composed and motionless in front of her, Claire struggled with her portrait. She used six tubes of light red and eight tubes of alizarin crimson, and still his face appeared as starkly white as ever.

She began to grow more and more desperate, but she refused to give up. In a strange way that she couldn't really understand, her painting was like a battlefield on which she and the Laird of Dunain were fighting a silent, deadly struggle. Perhaps she was doing nothing more than struggling with Alan, and all of the men who had treated her with such contempt.

Halfway through the afternoon, the light in the clerestory window gradually died, and it began to rain. She could hear the raindrops pattering on the roof and the gutters quietly gurgling.

"Are you sure you can see well enough?" asked the laird.

"I can see," she replied, doggedly squeezing out another glistening fat worm of red gouache.

"You could always give up," he said. His voice sounded almost sly.

"I can *see*," Claire insisted. "And I'll finish this bloody portrait if it kills me."

She picked up her scalpel to open the cellophane wrapping around another box of designers' colours.

"I'm sorry I'm such an awkward subject," smiled the laird. He sounded as if it quite amused him, to be awkward.

"Art always has to be a challenge," Claire retorted. She was still struggling to open the new box of paints. Without warning, there was a devastating bellow of thunder, so close to the castle roof that

Clair felt the rafters shake. Her hand slipped on the box and the scalpel sliced into the top of her finger.

"Ow!" she cried, dropping the box and squeezing her finger. Blood dripped onto the painting, one quick drop after another.

"Is anything wrong?" asked the laird, although he didn't make any attempt to move from his seat on the iron-bound trunk.

Claire winced, watching the blood well up. She was about to tell him that she had cut herself and that she wouldn't be able to continue painting when she saw that her blood had mingled with the wet paint on the laird's face *and had suffused it with an unnaturally healthy flush.*

"You've not hurt yourself, have you?" asked the laird.

"Oh, no," said Claire. She squeezed out more blood, and began to mix it with her paintbrush. Gradually the laird's face began to look rosier, and much more alive. "I'm fine, I'm absolutely fine." Thinking to herself: *now I've got you, you sly bastard. Now I'll show you how well I can paint. I'll catch you here for ever and ever; the way that I saw you; the way that I want you to be.*

The laird held his pose and said nothing, but watched her with a curious expression of satisfaction and contentedness, like a man who has tasted a particularly fine wine.

That night, in her room overlooking the grounds, Claire dreamed of men in ragged cloaks and feathered bonnets; men with gaunt faces and hollow eyes. She dreamed of smoke and blood and screaming. She heard a sharp, aggressive rattle of drums—drums that pursued her through one dream and into another.

When she woke up, it was still only five o'clock in the morning, and raining, and the window-catch was rattling and rattling in time to the drums in her dreams.

She dressed in jeans and a blue plaid blouse, and then she quiet-footedly climbed the stairs to the room where she was painting the laird's portrait. Somehow she knew what she was going to find, but she was still shocked.

The portrait was as white-faced as it had been before she had mixed the paint with her own blood. Whiter, if anything. His whole expression seemed to have changed, too, to a glare of silent emaciated fury.

Claire stared at the portrait in horror and fascination. Then, slowly, she sat down, and opened up her paintbox, and began to mix a flesh tone. Flake white, red and yellow ochre. When it was ready, she picked up her scalpel, and held her wrist over her palette. She hesitated for only a moment. The Laird of Dunain was glaring at her too angrily; too resentfully. She wasn't going to let a man like him get the better of her.

She slit her wrist in a long diagonal, and blood instantly pumped from her artery onto the palette, almost drowning the watercolours in rich and sticky red.

When the palette was flooded with blood, she bound her paint-rag around her wrist as tightly as she could, and gripped it with her teeth while she knotted it. Trembling, breathless, she began to mix blood and gouache, and then she began to paint.

She worked with her brush for almost an hour, but as fast as she applied the mixture of blood and paint, the faster it seemed to drain from the laird's chalk-white face.

At last—almost hysterical with frustration—she sat back and dropped her brush. The laird stared back at her—mocking, accusing, belittling her talent and her womanhood. Just like Alan. Just like every other man. You gave them everything and they still treated you with complete contempt.

But not this time. Not this time. She stood up, and unbuttoned her blouse, so that she confronted the portrait of the Laird of Dunain bare-breasted. Then she picked up her scalpel in her fist, so that the point pricked the plump pale flesh just below her navel.

"*The sleepy bit lassie, she dreaded nae ill; the weather was cauld and the lassie lay still. She thought that the tailor could do her no ill.*"

She cut into her stomach. Her hand was shaking but she was calm and deliberate. She cut through skin and layers of white fat and deeper still, until her intestines exhaled a deep sweet breath. She was disappointed by the lack of blood. She had imagined that she would bleed like a pig. Instead, her wound simply glistened, and yellowish fluid flowed.

"*There's somebody weary wi' lying her lane; there's some that are dowie, I trow wad be fain . . . to see that bit tailor come skippin' again.*"

Claire sliced upward, right up to her breastbone, and the scalpel was so sharp that it became lodged in her rib. She tugged it out, and the tugging sensation was worse than the pain. She wanted the blood, but she hadn't thought that it would hurt so much. The pain was as devastating as the thunderclap had been, overwhelming. She thought about screaming but she wasn't sure that it would do any good; and she had forgotten how.

With bloodied hands she reached inside her sliced-open stomach and grasped all the hot slippery heavy things she found there. She heaved them out, all over her painting of the Laird of Dunain, and wiped them around, and wiped them around, until the art-board was smothered in blood, and the portrait of the laird was almost completely obscured.

Then she pitched sideways, knocking her head against the oak-boarded floor. The light from the clerestory window brightened and faded, brightened and faded, and then faded away forever.

They took her to the Riverside Medical Centre but she was already dead. Massive trauma, loss of blood. Duncan stood in the car-park furiously smoking a cigarette and clutching himself. Margot sat on the leatherette seats in the waiting-room and wept.

They drove back to Dunain Castle. The laird was standing on the back lawn, watching the light play across the valley.

"She's dead, then?" he said, as Margot came marching up to him. "A grousome thing, no doubt about it."

Margot didn't know what to say to him. She could only stand in front of him and quake with anger. He seemed so self-satisfied, so calm, so pleased; his eyes green like emeralds, but flecked with red.

"Look," said the Laird of Dunain, pointing up to the birds that were circling overhead. "The hoodie-craws. They always know when there's a death."

Margot stormed up to the room where—only two hours ago—she had found Claire dying. It was bright as a church. And there on its board was the portrait of the Laird of Dunain, shining and clean, without a single smear of blood on it. The smiling, triumphant, rosy-cheeked Laird of Dunain.

"Self-opinionated chauvinist sod," she said, and she seized the art-board and ripped it in half, top to bottom. Out of temper. Out of enraged feminism. But, more than anything else, out of jealousy. Why had *she* never met a man that she would kill herself for?

And out in the garden, on the sloping lawns, the painting class heard a scream. It was a scream so echoing and terrible that they could scarcely believe that it had been uttered by one man.

In front of their eyes, the Laird of Dunain literally burst apart. His face exploded, his jawbone dropped out, his chest came bursting through his sweater in a crush of ribs and a bucketful of blood. There was so much blood that it sprayed up the walls of Dunain Castle, and ran down the windows.

They sat, open-mouthed, their paintbrushes poised, while he dropped onto the gravel path, and twitched, and lay still, while blood ran down everywhere, and the hoodie-craws circled and cried and cried again, because they always knew when there was a death.

"*Gie me the groat again, canny young man; the day it is short and the night it is lang; the dearest siller that ever I wan.*

"*The tailor fell thro' the bed, thimbles an' a'.*"

F. Paul Wilson

Midnight Mass

Over two million copies of F. Paul Wilson's books are in print in America, and he is the author of such bestselling novels as The Keep *(filmed in 1983),* The Tomb, The Touch, Reborn *and* Reprisal, *while his short fiction has been collected in* Soft & Others. *The Spring 1992* Weird Tales *honoured him with a special F. Paul Wilson issue.*

The following short novel was originally published as an individual booklet. A fast-moving thriller, with echoes of Richard Matheson's I Am Legend *and Stephen King's* Salem's Lot, *Wilson comes up with a new twist on the theme while keeping his undead strictly in the traditional vein . . .*

I

IT HAD BEEN almost a full minute since he'd slammed the brass knocker against the heavy oak door. That should have been proof enough. After all, wasn't the knocker in the shape of a cross? But no, they had to squint through their peephole and peer through the sidelights that framed the door.

Rabbi Zev Wolpin sighed and resigned himself to the scrutiny. He couldn't blame people for being cautious, but this seemed a bit overly so. The sun was in the west and shining full on his back; he was all but silhouetted in it. What more did they want?

I should maybe take off my clothes and dance naked?

He gave a mental shrug and savored the damp sea air. At least it was cool here. He'd bicycled from Lakewood, which was only ten miles inland from this same ocean but at least twenty degrees warmer. The bulk of the huge Tudor retreat house stood between him and the Atlantic, but the ocean's briny scent and rhythmic rumble were everywhere.

Spring Lake. An Irish Catholic seaside resort since before the turn of the century. He looked around at its carefully restored Victorian houses, the huge mansions arrayed here along the beach front, the smaller homes set in neat rows running straight back from the ocean. Many of them were still occupied. Not like Lakewood. Lakewood was an empty shell.

Not such a bad place for a retreat, he thought. He wondered how many houses like this the Catholic Church owned.

A series of clicks and clacks drew his attention back to the door as numerous bolts were pulled in rapid succession. The door swung inward revealing a nervous-looking young man in a long black cassock. As he looked at Zev his mouth twisted and he rubbed the back of his wrist across it to hide a smile.

"And what should be so funny?" Zev asked.

"I'm sorry. It's just— "

"I know," Zev said, waving off any explanation as he glanced down at the wooden cross slung on a cord around his neck. "I know."

A bearded Jew in a baggy black serge suit wearing a yarmulke and a cross. Hilarious, no?

So, *nu?* This was what the times demanded, this was what it had come to if he wanted to survive. And Zev did want to survive. Someone had to live to carry on the traditions of the Talmud and the Torah, even if there were hardly any Jews left alive in the world.

Zev stood on the sunny porch, waiting. The priest watched him in silence.

Finally Zev said, "Well, may a wandering Jew come in?"

"I won't stop you," the priest said, "but surely you don't expect me to invite you."

Ah, yes. Another precaution. The vampire couldn't cross the threshold of a home unless he was invited in, so don't invite. A good habit to cultivate, he supposed.

He stepped inside and the priest immediately closed the door behind him, relatching all the locks one by one. When he turned around Zev held out his hand.

"Rabbi Zev Wolpin, Father. I thank you for allowing me in."

"Brother Christopher, sir," he said, smiling and shaking Zev's hand. His suspicions seemed to have been completely allayed. "I'm not a priest yet. We can't offer you much here, but— "

"Oh, I won't be staying long. I just came to talk to Father Joseph Cahill."

Brother Christopher frowned. "Father Cahill isn't here at the moment."

"When will he be back?"

"I—I'm not sure. You see— "

"Father Cahill is on another bender," said a stentorian voice behind Zev.

He turned to see an elderly priest facing him from the far end of the foyer. White-haired, heavy set, wearing a black cassock.

"I'm Rabbi Wolpin."

"Father Adams," the priest said, stepping forward and extending his hand.

As they shook Zev said, "Did you say he was on 'another' bender? I never knew Father Cahill to be much of a drinker."

"Apparently there was a lot we never knew about Father Cahill," the priest said stiffly.

"If you're referring to that nastiness last year," Zev said, feeling the old anger rise in him, "I for one never believed it for a minute. I'm surprised anyone gave it the slightest credence."

"The veracity of the accusation was irrelevant in the final analysis. The damage to Father Cahill's reputation was a *fait accompli*. Father Palmeri was forced to request his removal for the good of St Anthony's parish."

Zev was sure that sort of attitude had something to do with Father Joe being on "another bender."

"Where can I find Father Cahill?"

"He's in town somewhere, I suppose, making a spectacle of himself. If there's any way you can talk some sense into him, please do. Not only is he killing himself with drink but he's become quite an embarrassment to the priesthood and to the Church."

Which bothers you more? Zev wanted to ask but held his tongue.

"I'll try."

He waited for Brother Christopher to undo all the locks, then stepped toward the sunlight.

"Try Morton's down on Seventy-one," the younger man whispered as Zev passed.

Zev rode his bicycle south on 71. It was almost strange to see people on the streets. Not many, but more than he'd ever see in Lakewood again. Yet he knew that as the vampires consolidated their grip on the world and infiltrated the Catholic communities, there'd be fewer and fewer day people here as well.

He thought he remembered passing a place named Morton's on his way to Spring Lake. And then up ahead he saw it, by the railroad track crossing, a white stucco one-story box of a building with "Morton's Liquors" painted in big black letters along the side.

Father Adams' words echoed back to him: . . . *on another bender* . . .

Zev pushed his bicycle to the front door and tried the knob. Locked up tight. A look inside showed a litter of trash and empty shelves. The windows were barred; the back door was steel and locked as securely as the front. So where was Father Joe?

Then he spotted the basement window at ground level by the overflowing trash dumpster. It wasn't latched. Zev went down on his knees and pushed it open.

Cool, damp, musty air wafted against his face as he peered into the Stygian blackness. It occurred to him that he might be asking for trouble by sticking his head inside, but he had to give it a try. If Father Cahill wasn't here, Zev would begin the return trek to Lakewood and write this whole trip off as wasted effort.

"Father Joe?" he called. "Father Cahill?"

"That you again, Chris?" said a slightly slurred voice. "Go home, will you? I'll be all right. I'll be back later."

"It's me, Joe. Zev. From Lakewood."

He heard shoes scraping on the floor and then a familiar face appeared in the shaft of light from the window.

"Well I'll be damned. It *is* you! Thought you were Brother Chris come to drag me back to the retreat house. Gets scared I'm gonna get stuck out after dark. So how ya doin', Reb? Glad to see you're still alive. Come on in!"

Zev saw that Father Cahill's eyes were glassy and he swayed ever so slightly, like a skyscraper in the wind. He wore faded jeans and a black Bruce Springsteen *Tunnel of Love* Tour sweatshirt.

Zev's heart twisted at the sight of his friend in such condition. Such a mensch like Father Joe shouldn't be acting like a *shikker*. Maybe it was a mistake coming here. Zev didn't like seeing him like this.

"I don't have that much time, Joe. I came to tell you— "

"Get your bearded ass down here and have a drink or I'll come up and drag you down."

"All right," Zev said. "I'll come in but I won't have a drink."

He hid his bike behind the dumpster, then squeezed through the window. Father Joe helped him to the floor. They embraced, slapping each other on the back. Father Joe was a taller man, a giant from Zev's perspective. At six-four he was ten inches taller, at thirty-five he was a quarter-century younger; he had a muscular frame, thick brown hair, and—on better days—clear blue eyes.

"You're grayer, Zev, and you've lost weight."

"Kosher food is not so easily come by these days."

"All kinds of food is getting scarce." He touched the cross slung from Zev's neck and smiled. "Nice touch. Goes well with your zizith."

Zev fingered the fringe protruding from under his shirt. Old habits didn't die easily.

"Actually, I've grown rather fond of it."

"So what can I pour you?" the priest said, waving an arm at the crates of liquor stacked around him. "My own private reserve. Name your poison."

"I don't want a drink."

"Come on, Reb. I've got some nice hundred-proof Stoly here. You've got to have at least *one* drink— "

"Why? Because you think maybe you shouldn't drink alone?"

Father Joe smiled. "Touché."

"All right," Zev said. "*Bissel.* I'll have *one* drink on the condition that you *don't* have one. Because I wish to talk to you."

The priest considered that a moment, then reached for the vodka bottle.

"Deal."

He poured a generous amount into a paper cup and handed it over. Zev took a sip. He was not a drinker and when he did imbibe he preferred his vodka ice cold from a freezer. But this was tasty. Father Cahill sat back on a crate of Jack Daniel's and folded his arms.

"*Nu?*" the priest said with a Jackie Mason shrug.

Zev had to laugh. "Joe, I still say that somewhere in your family tree is Jewish blood."

For a moment he felt light, almost happy. When was the last time he had laughed? Probably more than a year now, probably at their table near the back of Horovitz's deli, shortly before the St Anthony's nastiness began, well before the vampires came.

Zev thought of the day they'd met. He'd been standing at the counter at Horovitz's waiting for Yussel to wrap up the stuffed derma he had ordered when this young giant walked in. He towered over the other rabbis in the place, looked as Irish as Paddy's pig, and wore a Roman collar. He said he'd heard this was the only place on the whole Jersey Shore where you could get a decent corned beef sandwich. He ordered one and cheerfully warned that it better be good. Yussel asked him what could he know about good corned beef and the priest replied that he grew up in Bensonhurst. Well, about half the people in Horovitz's on that day—and on any other day for that matter—grew up in Bensonhurst and before you knew it they were all asking him if he knew such-and-such a store and so-and-so's deli.

Zev then informed the priest—with all due respect to Yussel Horovitz behind the counter—that the best corned beef sandwich in the world was to be had at Shmuel Rosenberg's Jerusalem Deli in Bensonhurst. Father Cahill said he'd been there and agreed one hundred per cent.

Yussel served him his sandwich then. As he took a huge bite out of the corned beef on rye, the normal *tummel* of a deli at lunchtime died away until Horovitz's was as quiet as a *shoul* on Sunday morning. Everyone watched him chew, watched him swallow. Then they waited. Suddenly his face broke into this big Irish grin.

"I'm afraid I'm going to have to change my vote," he said. "Horovitz's of Lakewood makes the best corned beef sandwich in the world."

Amid cheers and warm laughter, Zev led Father Cahill to the rear table that would become theirs and sat with this canny and charming gentile who had so easily won over a roomful of strangers and provided such a *mechaieh* for Yussel. He learned that the young priest was the new assistant to Father Palmeri, the pastor at St Anthony's Catholic church at the northern end of Lakewood. Father Palmeri had been there for years but Zev had never so much as seen his face. He asked Father Cahill—who wanted to be called Joe—about life in Brooklyn these days and they talked for an hour.

During the following months they would run into each other so often at Horovitz's that they decided to meet regularly for lunch, on Mondays and Thursdays. They did so for years, discussing religion—Oy, the religious discussions!—politics, economics, philosophy, life in general. During those lunchtimes they solved most of the world's problems. Zev was sure they'd have solved them all if the scandal at St Anthony's hadn't resulted in Father Joe's removal from the parish.

But that was in another time, another world. The world before the vampires took over.

Zev shook his head as he considered the current state of Father Joe in the dusty basement of Morton's Liquors.

"It's about the vampires, Joe," he said, taking another sip of the Stoly. "They've taken over St Anthony's."

Father Joe snorted and shrugged.

"They're in the majority now, Zev, remember? They've taken over

everything. Why should St Anthony's be different from any other
parish in the world?"

"I didn't mean the parish. I meant the church."

The priest's eyes widened slightly. "The church? They've taken
over the building itself?"

"Every night," Zev said. "Every night they are there."

"That's a holy place. How do they manage that?"

"They've desecrated the altar, destroyed all the crosses. St
Anthony's is no longer a holy place."

"Too bad," Father Joe said, looking down and shaking his head
sadly. "It was a fine old church." He looked up again, at Zev. "How
do you know about what's going on at St Anthony's? It's not exactly
in your neighborhood."

"A neighborhood I don't exactly have any more."

Father Joe reached over and gripped his shoulder with a huge
hand.

"I'm sorry, Zev. I heard how your people got hit pretty hard over
there. Sitting ducks, huh? I'm really sorry."

Sitting ducks. An appropriate description. Oh, they'd been smart,
those bloodsuckers. They knew their easiest targets. Whenever they
swooped into an area they singled out Jews as their first victims, and
among Jews they picked the Orthodox first of the first. Smart. Where
else would they be less likely to run up against a cross? It worked for
them in Brooklyn, and so when they came south into New Jersey,
spreading like a plague, they headed straight for the town with one
of the largest collections of yeshivas in North America.

But after the Bensonhurst holocaust the people in the Lakewood
communities did not take quite so long to figure out what was
happening. The Reformed and Conservative synagogues started
handing out crosses at Shabbes—too late for many but it saved
a few. Did the Orthodox congregations follow suit? No. They hid
in their homes and shules and yeshivas and read and prayed.

And were liquidated.

A cross, a crucifix—they held power over the vampires, drove
them away. His fellow rabbis did not want to accept that simple fact
because they could not face its devastating ramifications. To hold up
a cross was to negate two thousand years of Jewish history, it was to
say that the Messiah had come and they had missed him.

Did it say that? Zev didn't know. Argue about it later. Right now,
people were dying. But the rabbis had to argue it now. And as they
argued, their people were slaughtered like cattle.

How Zev railed at them, how he pleaded with them! Blind,
stubborn fools! If a fire was consuming your house, would you

refuse to throw water on it just because you'd always been taught
not to believe in water? Zev had arrived at the rabbinical council
wearing a cross and had been thrown out—literally sent hurtling
through the front door. But at least he had managed to save a few
of his own people. Too few.

He remembered his fellow Orthodox rabbis, though. All the ones
who had refused to face the reality of the vampires' fear of crosses,
who had forbidden their students and their congregations to wear
crosses, who had watched those same students and congregations
die en masse only to rise again and come for them. And soon those
very same rabbis were roaming their own community, hunting the
survivors, preying on other yeshivas, other congregations, until
the entire community was liquidated and incorporated into the
brotherhood of the vampire. The great fear had come to pass:
they'd been assimilated.

The rabbis could have saved themselves, could have saved their
people, but they would not bend to the reality of what was happening
around them. Which, when Zev thought about it, was not at all out
of character. Hadn't they spent generations learning to turn away
from the rest of the world?

Those early days of anarchic slaughter were over. Now that the
vampires held the ruling hand, the blood-letting had become more
organized. But the damage to Zev's people had been done—and
it was irreparable. Hitler would have been proud. His Nazi "final
solution" was an afternoon picnic compared to the work of the
vampires. They did in months what Hitler's Reich could not do
in all the years of the Second World War.

There's only a few of us now. So few and so scattered. A final
Diaspora.

For a moment Zev was almost overwhelmed by grief, but he
pushed it down, locked it back into that place where he kept his
sorrows, and thought of how fortunate it was for his wife Chana that
she died of natural causes before the horror began. Her soul had been
too gentle to weather what had happened to their community.

"Not as sorry as I, Joe," Zev said, dragging himself back to the
present. "But since my neighbourhood is gone, and since I have
hardly any friends left, I use the daylight hours to wander. So call
me the Wandering Jew. And in my wanderings I meet some of your
old parishioners."

The priest's face hardened. His voice became acid.

"Do you, now? And how fares the remnant of my devoted flock?"

"They've lost all hope, Joe. They wish you were back."

He laughed. "Sure they do! Just like they rallied behind me when my name and honor were being dragged through the muck last year. Yeah, they want me back. I'll bet!"

"Such anger, Joe. It doesn't become you."

"Bullshit. That was the old Joe Cahill, the naive turkey who believed all his faithful parishioners would back him up. But no. Palmeri tells the bishop the heat is getting too much for him, the bishop removes me, and the people I dedicated my life to all stand by in silence as I'm railroaded out of my parish."

"It's hard for the commonfolk to buck a bishop."

"Maybe. But I can't forget how they stood quietly by while I was stripped of my position, my dignity, my integrity, of everything I wanted to be . . ."

Zev thought Joe's voice was going to break. He was about to reach out to him when the priest coughed and squared his shoulders.

"Meanwhile, I'm a pariah over here in the retreat house. A goddam leper. Some of them actually believe— " He broke off in a growl. "Ah, what's the use? It's over and done. Most of the parish is dead anyway, I suppose. And if I'd stayed there I'd probably be dead too. So maybe it worked out for the best. And who gives a shit anyway."

He reached for the bottle of Glenlivet next to him.

"No-no!" Zev said. "You promised!"

Father Joe drew his hand back and crossed his arms across his chest.

"Talk on, oh, bearded one. I'm listening."

Father Joe had certainly changed for the worse. Morose, bitter, apathetic, self-pitying. Zev was beginning to wonder how he could have called this man a friend.

"They've taken over your church, desecrated it. Each night they further defile it with butchery and blasphemy. Doesn't that mean anything to you?"

"It's Palmeri's parish. I've been benched. Let him take care of it."

"Father Palmeri is their leader."

"He should be. He's their pastor."

"No. He leads the vampires in the obscenities they perform in the church."

Father Joe stiffened and the glassiness cleared from his eyes.

"Palmeri? He's one of them?"

Zev nodded. "More than that. He's the local leader. He orchestrates their rituals."

Zev saw rage flare in the priest's eyes, saw his hands ball into fists, and for a moment he thought the old Father Joe was going to burst through.

Come on, Joe. Show me that old fire.

But then he slumped back onto the crate.

"Is that all you came to tell me?"

Zev hid his disappointment and nodded. "Yes."

"Good." He grabbed the scotch bottle. "Because I need a drink."

Zev wanted to leave, yet he had to stay, had to probe a little bit deeper and see how much of his old friend was left, and how much had been replaced by this new, bitter, alien Joe Cahill. Maybe there was still hope. So they talked on.

Suddenly he noticed it was dark.

"Gevalt!" Zev said. "I didn't notice the time!"

Father Joe seemed surprised too. He ran to the window and peered out.

"Damn! Sun's gone down!" He turned to Zev. "Lakewood's out of the question for you, Reb. Even the retreat house is too far to risk now. Looks like we're stuck here for the night."

"We'll be safe?"

He shrugged. "Why not? As far as I can tell I'm the only one who's been in here for months, and only in the daytime. Be pretty odd if one of those human leeches should decide to wander in here tonight."

"I hope so."

"Don't worry. We're okay if we don't attract attention. I've got a flashlight if we need it, but we're better off sitting here in the dark and shooting the breeze till sunrise." Father Joe smiled and picked up a huge silver cross, at least a foot in length, from atop one of the crates. "Besides, we're armed. And frankly, I can think of worse places to spend the night."

He stepped over to the case of Glenlivet and opened a fresh bottle. His capacity for alcohol was enormous.

Zev could think of worse places too. In fact he had spent a number of nights in much worse places since the holocaust. He decided to put the time to good use.

"So, Joe. Maybe I should tell you some more about what's happening in Lakewood."

After a few hours their talk died of fatigue. Father Joe gave Zev the flashlight to hold and stretched out across a couple of crates to sleep. Zev tried to get comfortable enough to doze but found sleep impossible. So he listened to his friend snore in the darkness of the cellar.

Poor Joe. Such anger in the man. But more than that—hurt. He felt betrayed, wronged. And with good reason. But with everything falling apart as it was, the wrong done to him would never be righted. He should forget about it already and go on with his life, but apparently he couldn't. Such a shame. He needed something to pull him out of his funk. Zev had thought news of what had happened to his old parish might rouse him, but it seemed only to make him want to drink more. Father Joe Cahill, he feared, was a hopeless case.

Zev closed his eyes and tried to rest. It was hard to get comfortable with the cross dangling in front of him so he took it off but laid it within easy reach. He was drifting toward a doze when he heard a noise outside. By the dumpster. Metal on metal.

My bicycle!

He slipped to the floor and tiptoed over to where Father Joe slept. He shook his shoulder and whispered.

"Someone's found my bicycle!"

The priest snorted but remained sleeping. A louder clatter outside made Zev turn, and as he moved his elbow struck a bottle. He grabbed for it in the darkness but missed. The sound of smashing glass echoed through the basement like a cannon shot. As the odor of scotch whiskey replaced the musty ambiance, Zev listened for further sounds from outside. None came.

Maybe it had been an animal. He remembered how raccoons used to raid his garbage at home . . . when he'd had a home . . . when he'd had garbage . . .

Zev stepped to the window and looked out. Probably an animal. He pulled the window open a few inches and felt cool night air wash across his face. He pulled the flashlight from his coat pocket and aimed it through the opening.

Zev almost dropped the light as the beam illuminated a pale, snarling demonic face, baring its fangs and hissing. He fell back as the thing's head and shoulders lunged through the window, its curved fingers clawing at him, missing. Then it launched itself the rest of the way through, hurtling toward Zev.

He tried to dodge but he was too slow. The impact knocked the flashlight from his grasp and it went rolling across the floor. Zev cried out as he went down under the snarling thing. Its ferocity was overpowering, irresistible. It straddled him and lashed at him, batting his fending arms aside, its clawed fingers tearing at his collar to free his throat, stretching his neck to expose the vulnerable flesh, its foul breath gagging him as it bent its fangs toward him. Zev screamed out his helplessness.

II

Father Joe awoke to the cries of a terrified voice.

He shook his head to clear it and instantly regretted the move. His head weighed at least two hundred pounds, and his mouth was stuffed with foul-tasting cotton. Why did he keep doing this to himself? Not only did it leave him feeling lousy, it gave him bad dreams. Like now.

Another terrified shout, only a few feet away.

He looked toward the sound. In the faint light from the flashlight rolling across the floor he saw Zev on his back, fighting for his life against—

Damn! This was no dream! One of those bloodsuckers had got in here!

He leaped over to where the creature was lowering its fangs toward Zev's throat. He grabbed it by the back of the neck and lifted it clear of the floor. It was surprisingly heavy but that didn't slow him. Joe could feel the anger rising in him, surging into his muscles.

"Rotten piece of filth!"

He swung the vampire by its neck and let it fly against the cinderblock wall. It impacted with what should have been bone-crushing force, but it bounced off, rolled on the floor, and regained its feet in one motion, ready to attack again. Strong as he was, Joe knew he was no match for a vampire's power. He turned, grabbed his big silver crucifix, and charged the creature.

"Hungry? Eat this!"

As the creature bared its fangs and hissed at him, Joe shoved the long lower end of the cross into its open mouth. Blue-white light flickered along the silver length of the crucifix, reflecting in the creature's startled, agonized eyes as its flesh sizzled and crackled. The vampire let out a strangled cry and tried to turn away but Joe wasn't through with it yet. He was literally seeing red as rage poured out of a hidden well and swirled through him. He rammed the cross deeper down the thing's gullet. Light flashed deep in its throat, illuminating the pale tissues from within. It tried to grab the cross and pull it out but the flesh of its fingers burned and smoked wherever they came in contact with the cross.

Finally Joe stepped back and let the thing squirm and scrabble up the wall and out the window into the night. Then he turned to Zev. If anything had happened—

"Hey, Reb!" he said, kneeling beside the older man. "You all right?"

"Yes," Zev said, struggling to his feet. "Thanks to you."

Joe slumped onto a crate, momentarily weak as his rage dissipated. *This is not what I'm about*, he thought. But it had felt so damn good to let it loose on that vampire. Too good. And that worried him.

I'm falling apart . . . like everything else in the world.

"That was too close," he said to Zev, giving the older man's shoulder a fond squeeze.

"Too close for that vampire for sure," Zev said, replacing his yarmulke. "And would you please remind me, Father Joe, that in the future if ever I should maybe get my blood sucked and become a vampire that I should stay far away from you."

Joe laughed for the first time in too long. It felt good.

They climbed out at first light. Joe stretched his cramped muscles in the fresh air while Zev checked on his hidden bicycle.

"Oy," Zev said as he pulled it from behind the dumpster. The front wheel had been bent so far out of shape that half the spokes were broken. "Look what he did. Looks like I'll be walking back to Lakewood."

But Joe was less interested in the bike than in the whereabouts of their visitor from last night. He knew it couldn't have got far. And it hadn't. They found the vampire—or rather what was left of it—on the far side of the dumpster: a rotting, twisted corpse, blackened to a crisp and steaming in the morning sunlight. The silver crucifix still protruded from between its teeth.

Joe approached and gingerly yanked his cross free of the foul remains.

"Looks like you've sucked your last pint of blood," he said and immediately felt foolish.

Who was he putting on the macho act for? Zev certainly wasn't going to buy it. Too out of character. But then, what *was* his character these days? He used to be a parish priest. Now he was a nothing. A less than nothing.

He straightened up and turned to Zev.

"Come on back to the retreat house, Reb. I'll buy you breakfast."

But as Joe turned and began walking away, Zev stayed and stared down at the corpse.

"They say they don't wander far from where they spent their lives," Zev said. "Which means it's unlikely this fellow was Jewish if he lived around here. Probably Catholic. Irish Catholic, I'd imagine."

Joe stopped and turned. He stared at his long shadow. The hazy rising sun at his back cast a huge hulking shape before him, with a dark cross in one shadow hand and a smudge of amber light where it poured through the unopened bottle of Scotch in the other.

"What are you getting at?" he said.

"The Kaddish would probably not be so appropriate so I'm just wondering if maybe someone should give him the last rites or whatever it is you people do when one of you dies."

"He wasn't one of us," Joe said, feeling the bitterness rise in him. "He wasn't even human."

"Ah, but he used to be before he was killed and became one of them. So maybe now he could use a little help."

Joe didn't like the way this was going. He sensed he was being maneuvered.

"He doesn't deserve it," he said and knew in that instant he'd been trapped.

"I thought even the worst sinner deserved it," Zev said.

Joe knew when he was beaten. Zev was right. He shoved the cross and bottle into Zev's hands—a bit roughly, perhaps—then went and knelt by the twisted cadaver. He administered a form of the final sacrament. When he was through he returned to Zev and snatched back his belongings.

"You're a better man than I am, Gunga Din," he said as he passed.

"You act as if they're responsible for what they do after they become vampires," Zev said as he hurried along beside him, panting as he matched Joe's pace.

"Aren't they?"

"No."

"You're sure of that?"

"Well, not exactly. But they certainly aren't human anymore, so maybe we shouldn't hold them accountable on human terms."

Zev's reasoning tone flashed Joe back to the conversations they used to have in Horovitz's deli.

"But Zev, we know there's some of the old personality left. I mean, they stay in their home towns, usually in the basements of their old houses. They go after people they knew when they were alive. They're not just dumb predators, Zev. They've got the old consciousness they had when they were alive. Why can't they rise above it? Why can't they . . . resist?"

"I don't know. To tell the truth, the question has never occurred to me. A fascinating concept: an undead refusing to feed. Leave it to Father Joe to come up with something like that. We should discuss this on the trip back to Lakewood."

Joe had to smile. So *that* was what this was all about.

"I'm not going back to Lakewood."

"Fine. Then we'll discuss it now. Maybe the urge to feed is too strong to overcome."

"Maybe. And maybe they just don't try hard enough."

"This is a hard line you're taking, my friend."

"I'm a hard-line kind of guy."

"Well, you've become one."

Joe gave him a sharp look. "You don't know what I've become."

Zev shrugged. "Maybe true, maybe not. But do you truly think you'd be able to resist?"

"Damn straight."

Joe didn't know whether he was serious or not. Maybe he was just mentally preparing himself for the day when he might actually find himself in that situation.

"Interesting," Zev said as they climbed the front steps of the retreat house. "Well, I'd better be going. I've a long walk ahead of me. A long, *lonely* walk all the way back to Lakewood. A long, lonely, possibly *dangerous* walk back for a poor old man who— "

"All right, Zev! All *right*!" Joe said, biting back a laugh. "I get the point. You want me to go back to Lakewood. Why?"

"I just want the company," Zev said with pure innocence.

"No, really. What's going on in that Talmudic mind of yours? What are you cooking?"

"Nothing, Father Joe. Nothing at all."

Joe stared at him. Damn it all if his interest wasn't piqued. What was Zev up to? And what the hell? Why not go? He had nothing better to do.

"All right, Zev. You win. I'll come back to Lakewood with you. But just for today. Just to keep you company. And I'm not going anywhere near St Anthony's, okay? Understood?"

"Understood, Joe. Perfectly understood."

"Good. Now wipe that smile off your face and we'll get something to eat."

III

Under the climbing sun they walked south along the deserted beach, barefooting through the wet sand at the edge of the surf. Zev had never done this. He liked the feel of the sand between his toes, the coolness of the water as it sloshed over his ankles.

"Know what day it is?" Father Joe said. He had his sneakers slung over his shoulder. "Believe it or not, it's the Fourth of July."

"Oh, yes. Your Independence Day. We never made much of secular holidays. Too many religious ones to observe. Why should I not believe it's this date?"

Father Joe shook his head in dismay. "This is Manasquan Beach. You know what this place used to look like on the Fourth before the vampires took over? Wall-to-wall bodies."

"Really? I guess maybe sun-bathing is not the fad it used to be."

"Ah, Zev! Still the master of the understatement. I'll say one thing, though: the beach is cleaner than I've ever seen it. No beer cans or hypodermics." He pointed ahead. "But what's that up there?"

As they approached the spot, Zev saw a pair of naked bodies stretched out on the sand, one male, one female, both young and short-haired. Their skin was bronzed and glistened in the sun. The man lifted his head and stared at them. A blue crucifix was tattooed in the center of his forehead. He reached into the knapsack beside him and withdrew a huge, gleaming, nickel-plated revolver.

"Just keep walking," he said.

"Will do," Father Joe said. "Just passing through."

As they passed the couple, Zev noticed a similar tattoo on the girl's forehead. He noticed the rest of her too. He felt an almost-forgotten stirring deep inside him.

"A very popular tattoo," he said.

"Clever idea. That's one cross you can't drop or lose. Probably won't help you in the dark, but if there's a light on it might give you an edge."

They turned west and made their way inland, finding Route 70 and following it into Ocean County via the Brielle Bridge.

"I remember nightmare traffic jams right here every summer," Father Joe said as they trod the bridge's empty span. "Never thought I'd miss traffic jams."

They cut over to Route 88 and followed it all the way into Lakewood. Along the way they found a few people out and about in Bricktown and picking berries in Ocean County Park, but in the heart of Lakewood . . .

"A real ghost town," the priest said as they walked Forest Avenue's deserted length.

"Ghosts," Zev said, nodding sadly. It had been a long walk and he was tired. "Yes. Full of ghosts."

In his mind's eye he saw the shades of his fallen brother rabbis and all the yeshiva students, beards, black suits, black hats, crisscrossing back and forth at a determined pace on weekdays, strolling with their wives on Shabbes, their children trailing behind like ducklings.

Gone. All gone. Victims of the vampires. Vampires themselves now, most of them. It made him sick at heart to think of those good, gentle men, women, and children curled up in their basements now to avoid the light of day, venturing out in the dark to feed on others, spreading the disease . . .

He fingered the cross slung from his neck. *If only they had listened*!

"I know a place near St Anthony's where we can hide," he told the priest.

"You've traveled enough today, Reb. And I told you, I don't care about St Anthony's."

"Stay the night, Joe," Zev said, gripping the young priest's arm. He'd coaxed him this far; he couldn't let him get away now. "See what Father Palmeri's done."

"If he's one of them he's not a priest anymore. Don't call him Father."

"*They* still call him Father."

"Who?"

"The vampires."

Zev watched Father Joe's jaw muscles bunch.

Joe said, "Maybe I'll just take a quick trip over to St Anthony's myself— "

"No. It's different here. The area is thick with them—maybe twenty times as many as in Spring Lake. They'll get you if your timing isn't just right. I'll take you."

"You need rest, pal."

Father Joe's expression showed genuine concern. Zev was detecting increasingly softer emotions in the man since their reunion last night. A good sign perhaps?

"And rest I'll get when we get to where I'm taking you."

IV

Father Joe Cahill watched the moon rise over his old church and wondered at the wisdom of coming back. The casual decision made this morning in the full light of day seemed reckless and foolhardy now at the approach of midnight.

But there was no turning back. He'd followed Zev to the second floor of this two-story office building across the street from St Anthony's, and here they'd waited for dark. Must have been a law office once. The place had been vandalized, the windows broken, the furniture trashed, but there was an old Temple University Law School degree on the wall, and the couch was still in one piece. So while Zev caught some Z's, Joe sat and sipped a little of his scotch and did some heavy thinking.

Mostly he thought about his drinking. He'd done too much of

that lately, he knew; so much so that he was afraid to stop cold. So he was taking just a touch now, barely enough to take the edge off. He'd finish the rest later, after he came back from that church over there.

He'd stared at St Anthony's since they'd arrived. It too had been extensively vandalized. Once it had been a beautiful little stone church, a miniature cathedral, really; very Gothic with all its pointed arches, steep roofs, crocketed spires, and multifoil stained glass windows. Now the windows were smashed, the crosses which had topped the steeple and each gable were gone, and anything resembling a cross in its granite exterior had been defaced beyond recognition.

As he'd known it would, the sight of St Anthony's brought back memories of Gloria Sullivan, the young, pretty church volunteer whose husband worked for United Chemical International in New York, commuting in every day and trekking off overseas a little too often. Joe and Gloria had seen a lot of each other around the church offices and had become good friends. But Gloria had somehow got the idea that what they had went beyond friendship, so she showed up at the rectory one night when Joe was there alone. He tried to explain that as attractive as she was, she was not for him. He had taken certain vows and meant to stick by them. He did his best to let her down easy but she'd been hurt. And angry.

That might have been that, but then her six-year-old son Kevin had come home from altar boy practice with a story about a priest making him pull down his pants and touching him. Kevin was never clear on who the priest had been, but Gloria Sullivan was. Obviously it had been Father Cahill—any man who could turn down the heartfelt offer of her love and her body had to be either a queer or worse. And a child molester was worse.

She took it to the police and to the papers.

Joe groaned softly at the memory of how swiftly his life had become hell. But he had been determined to weather the storm, sure that the real culprit eventually would be revealed. He had no proof—still didn't—but if one of the priests at St Anthony's was a pederast, he knew it wasn't him. That left Father Alberto Palmeri, St Anthony's fifty-five-year-old pastor. Before Joe could get to the truth, however, Father Palmeri requested that Father Cahill be removed from the parish, and the bishop complied. Joe had left under a cloud that had followed him to the retreat house in the next county and hovered over him till this day. The only place he'd found even brief respite from the impotent anger and bitterness that roiled under his skin and soured his gut every minute of every day was in the bottle—and that was sure as hell a dead end.

So why had he agreed to come back here? To torture himself? Or to get a look at Palmeri and see how low he had sunk?

Maybe that was it. Maybe seeing Palmeri wallowing in his true element would give him the impetus to put the whole St Anthony's incident behind him and rejoin what was left of the human race— which needed him now more than ever.

And maybe it wouldn't.

Getting back on track was a nice thought, but over the past few months Joe had found it increasingly difficult to give much of a damn about anyone or anything.

Except maybe Zev. He'd stuck by Joe through the worst of it, defending him to anyone who would listen. But an endorsement from an Orthodox rabbi had meant diddly in St Anthony's. And yesterday Zev had biked all the way to Spring Lake to see him. Old Zev was all right.

And he'd been right about the number of vampires here too. Lakewood was *crawling* with the things. Fascinated and repelled, Joe had watched the streets fill with them shortly after sundown.

But what had disturbed him more were the creatures who'd come out *before* sundown.

The humans. Live ones.

The collaborators.

If there was anything lower, anything that deserved true death more than the vampires themselves, it was the still-living humans who worked for them.

Someone touched his shoulder and he jumped. It was Zev. He was holding something out to him. Joe took it and held it up in the moonlight: a tiny crescent moon dangling from a chain on a ring.

"What's this?"

"An earring. The local Vichy wear them."

"Vichy? Like the Vichy French?"

"Yes. Very good. I'm glad to see that you're not as culturally illiterate as the rest of your generation. Vichy humans—that's what I call the collaborators. These earrings identify them to the local nest of vampires. They are spared."

"Where'd you get them?"

Zev's face was hidden in the shadows. "Their previous owners . . . lost them. Put it on."

"My ear's not pierced."

A gnarled hand moved into the moonlight. Joe saw a long needle clasped between the thumb and index finger.

"That I can fix," Zev said.

"Maybe you shouldn't see this," Zev whispered as they crouched in the deep shadows on St Anthony's western flank.

Joe squinted at him in the darkness, puzzled.

"You lay a guilt trip on me to get me here, now you're having second thoughts?"

"It is horrible like I can't tell you."

Joe thought about that. There was enough horror in the world outside St Anthony's. What purpose did it serve to see what was going on inside?

Because it used to be my church.

Even though he'd only been an associate pastor, never fully in charge, and even though he'd been unceremoniously yanked from the post, St Anthony's had been his first parish. He was here. He might as well know what they were doing inside.

"Show me."

Zev led him to a pile of rubble under a smashed stained glass window. He pointed up to where faint light flickered from inside.

"Look in there."

"You're not coming?"

"Once was enough, thank you."

Joe climbed as carefully, as quietly as he could, all the while becoming increasingly aware of a growing stench like putrid, rotting meat. It was coming from inside, wafting through the broken window. Steeling himself, he straightened up and peered over the sill.

For a moment he was disoriented, like someone peering out the window of a city apartment and seeing the rolling hills of a Kansas farm. This could not be the interior of St Anthony's.

In the flickering light of hundreds of sacramental candles he saw that the walls were bare, stripped of all their ornaments, of the plaques for the stations of the cross; the dark wood along the wall was scarred and gouged wherever there had been anything remotely resembling a cross. The floor too was mostly bare, the pews ripped from their neat rows and hacked to pieces, their splintered remains piled high at the rear under the choir balcony.

And the giant crucifix that had dominated the space behind the altar—only a portion of it remained. The cross-pieces on each side had been sawed off and so now an armless, life-size Christ hung upside down against the rear wall of the sanctuary.

Joe took in all that in a flash, then his attention was drawn to the unholy congregation that peopled St Anthony's this night. The collaborators—the Vichy humans, as Zev called them—made up the periphery of the group. They looked like normal, everyday people but each was wearing a crescent moon earring.

But the others, the group gathered in the sanctuary—Joe felt his hackles rise at the sight of them. They surrounded the altar in a tight knot. Their pale, bestial faces, bereft of the slightest trace of human warmth, compassion, or decency, were turned upward. His gorge rose when he saw the object of their rapt attention.

A naked teenage boy—his hands tied behind his back, was suspended over the altar by his ankles. He was sobbing and choking, his eyes wide and vacant with shock, his mind all but gone. The skin had been flayed from his forehead—apparently the Vichy had found an expedient solution to the cross tattoo—and blood ran in a slow stream down his abdomen and chest from his freshly truncated genitals. And beside him, standing atop the altar, a bloody-mouthed creature dressed in a long cassock. Joe recognized the thin shoulders, the graying hair trailing from the balding crown, but was shocked at the crimson vulpine grin he flashed to the things clustered below him.

"Now," said the creature in a lightly accented voice Joe had heard hundreds of times from St Anthony's pulpit.

Father Alberto Palmeri.

And from the group a hand reached up with a straight razor and drew it across the boy's throat. As the blood flowed down over his face, those below squeezed and struggled forward like hatchling vultures to catch the falling drops and scarlet trickles in their open mouths.

Joe fell away from the window and vomited. He felt Zev grab his arm and lead him away. He was vaguely aware of crossing the street and heading toward the ruined legal office.

                                    V

"Why in God's name did you want me to see that?"

Zev looked across the office toward the source of the words. He could see a vague outline where Father Joe sat on the floor, his back against the wall, the open bottle of scotch in his hand. The priest had taken one drink since their return, no more.

"I thought you should know what they were doing to your church."

"So you've said. But what's the reason behind that one?"

Zev shrugged in the darkness. "I'd heard you weren't doing well, that even before everything else began falling apart, you had already fallen apart. So when I felt it safe to get away, I came to see you. Just as I expected, I found a man who was angry at everything and letting it eat up his *guderim*. I thought maybe it would be good to give that man something very specific to be angry at."

"You bastard!" Father Joe whispered. "Who gave you the right?"

"Friendship gave me the right, Joe. I should hear that you are rotting away and do nothing? I have no congregation of my own anymore so I turned my attention on you. Always I was a somewhat meddlesome rabbi."

"Still are. Out to save my soul, ay?"

"We rabbis don't save souls. Guide them maybe, hopefully give them direction. But only you can save your soul, Joe."

Silence hung in the air for awhile. Suddenly the crescent-moon earring Zev had given Father Joe landed in the puddle of moonlight on the floor between them.

"Why do they do it?" the priest said. "The Vichy—why do they collaborate?"

"The first were quite unwilling, believe me. They cooperated because their wives and children were held hostage by the vampires. But before too long the dregs of humanity began to slither out from under their rocks and offer their services in exchange for the immortality of vampirism."

"Why bother working for them? Why not just bare your throat to the nearest bloodsucker?"

"That's what I thought at first," Zev said. "But as I witnessed the Lakewood holocaust I detected the vampires' pattern. They can choose who joins their ranks, so after they've fully infiltrated a population, they change their tactics. You see, they don't want too many of their kind concentrated in one area. It's like too many carnivores in one forest—when the herds of prey are wiped out, the predators starve. So they start to employ a different style of killing. For only when the vampire draws the life's blood from the throat with its fangs does the victim become one of them. Anyone drained as in the manner of that boy in the church tonight dies a true death. He's as dead now as someone run over by a truck. He will not rise tomorrow night."

"I get it," Father Joe said. "The Vichy trade their daylight services and dirty work to the vampires now for immortality later on."

"Correct."

There was no humor in the soft laugh that echoed across the room from Father Joe.

"Swell. I never cease to be amazed at our fellow human beings. Their capacity for good is exceeded only by their ability to debase themselves."

"Hopelessness does strange things, Joe. The vampires know that. So they rob us of hope. That's how they beat us. They transform our friends and neighbors and leaders into their own, leaving us feeling alone, completely cut off. Some of us can't take the despair and kill ourselves."

"Hopelessness," Joe said. "A potent weapon."

After a long silence, Zev said, "So what are you going to do now, Father Joe?"

Another bitter laugh from across the room.

"I suppose this is the place where I declare that I've found new purpose in life and will now go forth into the world as a fearless vampire killer."

"Such a thing would be nice."

"Well screw that. I'm only going as far as across the street."

"To St Anthony's?"

Zev saw Father Joe take a swig from the Scotch bottle and then screw the cap on tight.

"Yeah. To see if there's anything I can do over there."

"Father Palmeri and his nest might not like that."

"I told you, don't call him Father. And screw *him*. Nobody can do what he's done and get away with it. I'm taking my church back."

In the dark, behind his beard, Zev smiled.

VI

Joe stayed up the rest of the night and let Zev sleep. The old guy needed his rest. Sleep would have been impossible for Joe anyway. He was too wired. He sat up and watched St Anthony's.

They left before first light, dark shapes drifting out the front doors and down the stone steps like parishioners leaving a predawn service. Joe felt his back teeth grind as he scanned the group for Palmeri, but he couldn't make him out in the dimness. By the time the sun began to peek over the rooftops and through the trees to the east, the street outside was deserted.

He woke Zev and together they approached the church. The heavy oak and iron front doors, each forming half of a pointed arch, were closed. He pulled them open and fastened the hooks to keep them open. Then he walked through the vestibule and into the nave.

Even though he was ready for it, the stench backed him up a few steps. When his stomach settled, he forced himself ahead, treading a path between the two piles of shattered and splintered pews. Zev walked beside him, a handkerchief pressed over his mouth.

Last night he had thought the place a shambles. He saw now that it was worse. The light of day poked into all the corners, revealing everything that had been hidden by the warm glow of the candles. Half a dozen rotting corpses hung from the ceiling—he hadn't noticed them last night—and others were sprawled on the floor against the walls. Some of the bodies were in pieces. Behind the chancel rail a headless female torso was draped over the front of the pulpit. To the left stood the statue of Mary. Someone had fitted her with foam rubber breasts and a huge dildo. And at the rear of the sanctuary was the armless Christ hanging head down on the upright of his cross.

"My church," he whispered as he moved along the path that had once been the center aisle, the aisle brides used to walk down with their fathers. "Look what they've done to my church!"

Joe approached the huge block of the altar. Once it had been backed against the far wall of the sanctuary, but he'd had it moved to the front so that he could celebrate Mass facing his parishioners. Solid Carrara marble, but you'd never know it now. So caked with dried blood, semen, and feces it could have been made of styrofoam.

His revulsion was fading, melting away in the growing heat of his rage, drawing the nausea with it. He had intended to clean up the place but there was so much to be done, too much for two men. It was hopeless.

"Fadda Joe?"

He spun at the sound of the strange voice. A thin figure stood uncertainly in the open doorway. A man of about fifty edged forward timidly.

"Fadda Joe, izat you?"

Joe recognized him now. Carl Edwards. A twitchy little man who used to help pass the collection basket at 10:30 Mass on Sundays. A transplantee from Jersey City—hardly anyone around here was originally from around here. His face was sunken, his eyes feverish as he stared at Joe.

"Yes, Carl. It's me."

"Oh, tank God!" He ran forward and dropped to his knees before Joe. He began to sob. "You come back! Tank God, you come back!"

Joe pulled him to his feet.

"Come on now, Carl. Get a grip."

"You come back ta save us, ain'tcha? God sent ya here to punish him, din't He?"

"Punish whom?"

"Fadda Palmeri! He's one a dem! He's da woist a alla dem! He— "

"I know," Joe said. "I know."

"Oh, it's so good to have ya back, Fadda Joe! We ain't knowed what to do since da suckers took ova. We been prayin fa someone like youse an now ya here. It's a freakin' miracle!"

Joe wanted to ask Carl where he and all these people who seemed to think they needed him now had been when he was being railroaded out of the parish. But that was ancient history.

"Not a miracle, Carl," Joe said, glancing at Zev. "Rabbi Wolpin brought me back." As Carl and Zev shook hands, Joe said, "And I'm just passing through."

"Passing t'rough? No. Dat can't be! Ya gotta stay!"

Joe saw the light of hope fading in the little man's eyes. Something twisted within him, tugging him.

"What can I do here, Carl? I'm just one man."

"I'll help! I'll do whatever ya want! Jes tell me!"

"Will you help me clean up?"

Carl looked around and seemed to see the cadavers for the first time. He cringed and turned a few shades paler.

"Yeah . . . sure. Anyting."

Joe looked at Zev. "Well? What do you think?"

Zev shrugged. "I should tell you what to do? My parish it's not."

"Not mine either."

Zev jutted his beard at Carl. "I think maybe he'd tell you differently."

Joe did a slow turn. The vaulted nave was utterly silent except for the buzzing of the flies around the cadavers.

A massive clean-up job. But if they worked all day they could make a decent dent in it. And then—

And then what?

Joe didn't know. He was playing this by ear. He'd wait and see what the night brought.

"Can you get us some food, Carl? I'd sell my soul for a cup of coffee."

Carl gave him a strange look.

"Just a figure of speech, Carl. We'll need some food if we're going to keep working."

The man's eyes lit again.

"Dat means ya staying?"

"For a while."

"I'll getcha some food," he said excitedly as he ran for the door. "An' coffee. I know someone who's still got coffee. She'll part wit' some of it for Fadda Joe." He stopped at the door and turned. "Ay, an' Fadda, I neva believed any a dem tings dat was said aboutcha. Neva."

Joe tried but he couldn't hold it back.

"It would have meant a lot to have heard that from you last year, Carl."

The man lowered his eyes. "Yeah. I guess it woulda. But I'll make it up to ya, Fadda. I will. You can take dat to da bank."

Then he was out the door and gone. Joe turned to Zev and saw the old man rolling up his sleeves.

"*Nu?*" Zev said. "The bodies. Before we do anything else, I think maybe we should move the bodies."

VII

By early afternoon, Zev was exhausted. The heat and the heavy work had taken their toll. He had to stop and rest. He sat on the chancel rail and looked around. Nearly eight hours work and they'd barely scratched the surface. But the place did look and smell better.

Removing the flyblown corpses and scattered body parts had been the worst of it. A foul, gut-roiling task that had taken most of the morning. They'd carried the corpses out to the small graveyard behind the church and left them there. Those people deserved a decent burial but there was no time for it today.

Once the corpses were gone, Father Joe had torn the defilements from the statue of Mary and then they'd turned their attention to the huge crucifix. It took a while but they finally found Christ's plaster arms in the pile of ruined pews. They were still nailed to the sawn-off cross-piece of the crucifix. While Zev and Father Joe worked at jury-rigging a series of braces to reattach the arms, Carl found a mop and bucket and began the long, slow process of washing the fouled floor of the nave.

Now the crucifix was intact again—the life-size plaster Jesus had his arms reattached and was once again nailed to his refurbished cross. Father Joe and Carl had restored him to his former position of dominance. The poor man was upright again, hanging over the center of the sanctuary in all his tortured splendor.

A grisly sight. Zev could never understand the Catholic attachment to these gruesome statues. But if the vampires loathed them, then Zev was for them all the way.

His stomach rumbled with hunger. At least they'd had a good breakfast. Carl had returned from his food run this morning with bread, cheese, and two thermoses of hot coffee. He wished now they'd saved some. Maybe there was a crust of bread left in the sack. He headed back to the vestibule to check and found an aluminium pot and a paper bag sitting by the door. The pot was full of beef stew and the sack contained three cans of Pepsi.

He poked his head out the doors but no one was in sight on the street outside. It had been that way all day—he'd spy a figure or two peeking in the front doors; they'd hover there for a moment as if to confirm that what they had heard was true, then they'd scurry away. He looked at the meal that had been left. A group of the locals must have donated from their hoard of canned stew and precious soft drinks to fix this. Zev was touched.

He called Father Joe and Carl.

"Tastes like Dinty Moore," Father Joe said around a mouthful of the stew.

"It is," Carl said. "I recognize da little potatoes. Da ladies of the parish must really be excited about youse comin' back to break inta deir canned goods like dis."

They were feasting in the sacristy, the small room off the sanctuary where the priests had kept their vestments—a clerical Green Room, so to speak. Zev found the stew palatable but much too salty. He wasn't about to complain, though.

"I don't believe I've ever had anything like this before."

"I'd be real surprised if you had," said Father Joe. "I doubt very much that something that calls itself Dinty Moore is kosher."

Zev smiled but inside he was suddenly filled with a great sadness. Kosher . . . how meaningless now seemed all the observances which he had allowed to rule and circumscribe his life. Such a fierce proponent of strict dietary laws he'd been in the days before the Lakewood holocaust. But those days were gone, just as the Lakewood community was gone. And Zev was a changed man. If he hadn't changed, if he were still observing, he couldn't sit here and sup with these two men. He'd have to be elsewhere, eating special classes of specially prepared foods off separate sets of dishes. But really, wasn't division what holding to the dietary laws in modern times was all about? They served a purpose beyond mere observance of tradition. They placed another wall between observant Jews and outsiders, keeping them separate even from other Jews who didn't observe.

Zev forced himself to take a big bite of the stew. Time to break down all the walls between people . . . while there was still enough time and people left alive to make it matter.

"You okay, Zev?" Father Joe asked.

Zev nodded silently, afraid to speak for fear of sobbing. Despite all its anachronisms, he missed his life in the good old days of last year. Gone. It was all gone. The rich traditions, the culture, the friends, the prayers. He felt adrift—in time and in space. Nowhere was home.

"You sure?" The young priest seemed genuinely concerned.

"Yes, I'm okay. As okay as you could expect me to feel after spending the better part of the day repairing a crucifix and eating non-kosher food. And let me tell you, that's not so okay."

He put his bowl aside and straightened from his chair.

"Come on, already. Let's get back to work. There's much yet to do."

VIII

"Sun's almost down," Carl said.

Joe straightened from scrubbing the altar and stared west through one of the smashed windows. The sun was out of sight behind the houses there.

"You can go now, Carl," he said to the little man. "Thanks for your help."

"Where youse gonna go, Fadda?"

"I'll be staying right here."

Carl's prominent Adam's apple bobbed convulsively as he swallowed.

"Yeah? Well den, I'm staying too. I tol' ya I'd make it up ta ya, din't I? An besides, I don't tink the suckas'll like da new, improved St Ant'ny's too much when dey come back tonight, d'you? I don't even tink dey'll get t'rough da doors."

Joe smiled at the man and looked around. Luckily it was July when the days were long. They'd had time to make a difference here. The floors were clean, the crucifix was restored and back in its proper position, as were most of the Stations of the Cross plaques. Zev had found them under the pews and had taken the ones not shattered beyond recognition and rehung them on the walls. Lots of new crosses littered those walls. Carl had found a hammer and nails and had made dozens of them from the remains of the pews.

"No. I don't think they'll like the new decor one bit. But there's something you can get us if you can, Carl. Guns. Pistols, rifles, shotguns, anything that shoots."

Carl nodded slowly. "I know a few guys who can help in dat department."

"And some wine. A little red wine if anybody's saved some."

"You got it."

He hurried off.

"You're planning Custer's last stand, maybe?" Zev said from where he was tacking the last of Carl's crude crosses to the east wall.

"More like the Alamo."

"Same result," Zev said with one of his shrugs.

Joe turned back to scrubbing the altar. He'd been at it for over an hour now. He was drenched with sweat and knew he smelled like a bear, but he couldn't stop until it was clean.

An hour later he was forced to give up. No use. It wouldn't come clean. The vampires must have done something to the blood and foulness to make the mixture seep into the surface of the marble like it had.

He sat on the floor with his back against the altar and rested. He didn't like resting because it gave him time to think. And when he started to think he realized that the odds were pretty high against his seeing tomorrow morning.

At least he'd die well fed. Their secret supplier had left them a dinner of fresh fried chicken by the front doors. Even the memory of it made his mouth water. Apparently someone was *really* glad he was back.

To tell the truth, though, as miserable as he'd been, he wasn't ready to die. Not tonight, not any night. He wasn't looking for an Alamo or a Little Big Horn. All he wanted to do was hold off the vampires till dawn. Keep them out of St Anthony's for one night. That was all. That would be a statement—*his* statement. If he found an opportunity to ram a stake through Palmeri's rotten heart, so much the better, but he wasn't counting on that. One night. Just to let them know they couldn't have their way everywhere with everybody whenever they felt like it. He had surprise on his side tonight, so maybe it would work. One night. Then he'd be on his way.

"What the fuck have you *done*?"

Joe looked up at the shout. A burly, long-haired man in jeans and a flannel shirt stood in the vestibule staring at the partially restored nave. As he approached, Joe noticed his crescent moon earring.

A Vichy.

Joe balled his fists but didn't move.

"Hey, I'm talking to you, mister. Are you responsible for this?" When all he got from Joe was a cold stare, he turned to Zev.

"Hey, you! Jew! What the hell do you think *you're* doing?" He started toward Zev. "You get those fucking crosses off— "

"Touch him and I'll break you in half," Joe said in a low voice. The Vichy skidded to a halt and stared at him.

"Hey, asshole! Are you crazy? Do you know what Father Palmeri will do to you when he arrives?"

"*Father* Palmeri? Why do you still call him that?"

"It's what he wants to be called. And he's going to call you *dog meat* when he gets here!"

Joe pulled himself to his feet and looked down at the Vichy. The man took two steps back. Suddenly he didn't seem so sure of himself.

"Tell him I'll be waiting. Tell him Father Cahill is back."

"You're a priest? You don't look like one."

"Shut up and listen. Tell him Father Joe Cahill is back—and he's pissed. Tell him that. Now get out of here while you still can."

The man turned and hurried out into the growing darkness. Joe turned to Zev and found him grinning through his beard.

"'Father Joe Cahill is back—and he's pissed.' I like that."

"We'll make it into a bumper sticker. Meanwhile let's close those doors. The criminal element is starting to wander in. I'll see if we can find some more candles. It's getting dark in here."

IX

He wore the night like a tuxedo.

Dressed in a fresh cassock, Father Alberto Palmeri turned off County Line Road and strolled toward St Anthony's. The night was lovely, especially when you owned it. And he owned the night in this area of Lakewood now. He loved the night. He felt at one with it, attuned to its harmonies and its discords. The darkness made him feel so alive. Strange to have to lose your life before you could really feel alive. But this was it. He'd found his niche, his métier.

Such a shame it had taken him so long. All those years trying to deny his appetites, trying to be a member of the other side, cursing himself when he allowed his appetites to win, as he had with increasing frequency toward the end of his mortal life. He should have given in to them completely long ago.

It had taken undeath to free him.

And to think he had been afraid of undeath, had cowered in fear each night in the cellar of the church, surrounded by crosses. Fortunately he had not been as safe as he'd thought and one of the beings he now called brother was able to slip in on him in the dark while he dozed. He saw now that he had lost nothing but his blood by that encounter.

And in trade he'd gained a world.

For now it was his world, at least this little corner of it, one in which he was completely free to indulge himself in any way he wished. Except for the blood. He had no choice about the blood. That was a new appetite, stronger than all the rest, one that would not be denied. But he did not mind the new appetite in the least. He'd found interesting ways to sate it.

Up ahead he spotted dear, defiled St Anthony's. He wondered what his servants had prepared for him tonight. They were quite imaginative. They'd yet to bore him.

But as he drew nearer the church, Palmeri slowed. His skin prickled. The building had changed. Something was very wrong there, wrong inside. Something amiss with the light that beamed from the windows. This wasn't the old familiar candlelight, this was something else, something more. Something that made his insides tremble.

Figures raced up the street toward him. Live ones. His night vision picked out the earrings and familiar faces of some of his servants. As they neared he sensed the warmth of the blood coursing just beneath their skins. The hunger rose in him and he fought the urge to rip into one of their throats. He couldn't allow himself that pleasure. He had to keep the servants dangling, keep them working for him and the nest. They needed the services of the indentured living to remove whatever obstacles the cattle might put in their way.

"Father! Father!" they cried.

He loved it when they called him Father, loved being one of the undead and dressing like one of the enemy.

"Yes, my children. What sort of victim do you have for us tonight?"

"No victim, father—trouble!"

The edges of Palmeri's vision darkened with rage as he heard of the young priest and the Jew who had dared to try to turn St Anthony's into a holy place again. When he heard the name of the priest, he nearly exploded.

"Cahill? Joseph Cahill is back in my church?"

"He was cleaning the altar!" one of the servants said.

Palmeri strode toward the church with the servants trailing behind. He knew that neither Cahill nor the Pope himself could clean that altar. Palmeri had desecrated it himself; he had learned how to do that when he became nest leader. But what else had the young pup dared to do?

Whatever it was, it would be undone. *Now!*

Palmeri strode up the steps and pulled the right door open— and screamed in agony.

The light! The *light!* The LIGHT! White agony lanced through Palmeri's eyes and seared his brain like two hot pokers. He retched and threw his arms across his face as he staggered back into the cool, comforting darkness.

It took a few minutes for the pain to drain off, for the nausea to pass, for vision to return.

He'd never understand it. He'd spent his entire life in the presence of crosses and crucifixes, surrounded by them. And yet as soon as he'd become undead, he was unable to bear the sight of one. As a matter of fact, since he'd become undead, he'd never even *see* one. A cross was no longer an object. It was a light, a light so excruciatingly bright, so blazingly white that it was sheer agony to look at it. As a child in Naples he'd been told by his mother not to look at the sun, but when there'd been talk of an eclipse, he'd stared directly into its eye. The pain of looking at a cross was a hundred, no, a thousand times worse than that. And the bigger the cross or crucifix, the worse the pain.

He'd experienced monumental pain upon looking into St Anthony's tonight. That could only mean that Joseph, that young bastard, had refurbished the giant crucifix. It was the only possible explanation.

He swung on his servants.

"Get in there! Get that crucifix down!"

"They've got guns!"

"Then get help. But get it *down!*"

"We'll get guns too! We can— "

"*No!* I want him! I want that priest alive! I want him for myself! Anyone who kills him will suffer a very painful, very long and lingering true death! Is that clear?"

It was clear. They scurried away without answering.

Palmeri went to gather the other members of the nest.

X

Dressed in a cassock and a surplice, Joe came out of the sacristy and approached the altar. He noticed Zev keeping watch at one of the windows. He didn't tell him how ridiculous he looked carrying the shotgun Carl had brought back. He held it so gingerly, like it was full of nitroglycerine and would explode if he jiggled it.

Zev turned, and smiled when he saw him.

"*Now* you look like the old Father Joe we all used to know."

Joe gave him a little bow and proceeded toward the altar.

All right: He had everything he needed. He had the Missal they'd found in among the pew debris earlier today. He had the wine; Carl had brought back about four ounces of sour red babarone. He'd found a smudged surplice and a dusty cassock on the floor of one of the closets in the sacristy, and he wore them now. No hosts, though. A crust of bread left over from breakfast would have to do. No chalice, either. If he'd known he was going to be saying Mass he'd have come prepared. As a last resort he'd used the can opener in the rectory to remove the top from one of the Pepsi cans from lunch. Quite a stretch from the gold chalice he'd used since his ordination, but probably more in line with what Jesus had used at that first Mass—the Last Supper.

He was uncomfortable with the idea of weapons in St Anthony's but he saw no alternative. He and Zev knew nothing about guns, and Carl knew little more; they'd probably do more damage to themselves than to the Vichy if they tried to use them. But maybe the sight of them would make the Vichy hesitate, slow them down. All he needed was a little time here, enough to get to the consecration.

This is going to be the most unusual Mass in history, he thought.

But he was going to get through it if it killed him. And that was a real possibility. This might well be his last Mass. But he wasn't afraid. He was too excited to be afraid. He'd had a slug of the Scotch—just enough to ward off the DTs—but it had done nothing to quell the buzz of the adrenalin humming along every nerve in his body.

He spread everything out on the white tablecloth he'd taken from the rectory and used to cover the filthy altar. He looked at Carl.

"Ready?"

Carl nodded and stuck the .38 caliber pistol he'd been examining in his belt.

"Been a while, Fadda. We did it in Latin when I was a kid but I tink I can swing it."

"Just do your best and don't worry about any mistakes."

Some Mass. A defiled altar, a crust for a host, a Pepsi can for a chalice, a fifty-year-old, pistol-packing altar boy, and a congregation consisting of a lone, shotgun-carrying Orthodox Jew.

Joe looked heavenward.

You do understand, don't you, Lord, that this was arranged on short notice?

Time to begin.

He read the Gospel but dispensed with the homily. He tried to remember the Mass as it used to be said, to fit in better with Carl's outdated responses. As he was starting the Offertory the front doors flew open and a group of men entered—ten of them, all with crescent moons dangling from their ears. Out of the corner of his eye he saw Zev move away from the window toward the altar, pointing his shotgun at them.

As soon as they entered the nave and got past the broken pews, the Vichy fanned out toward the sides. They began pulling down the Stations of the Cross, ripping Carl's makeshift crosses from the walls and tearing them apart. Carl looked up at Joe from where he knelt, his eyes questioning, his hand reaching for the pistol in his belt.

Joe shook his head and kept up with the Offertory.

When all the little crosses were down, the Vichy swarmed behind the altar. Joe chanced a quick glance over his shoulder and saw them begin their attack on the newly repaired crucifix.

"Zev!" Carl said in a low voice, cocking his head toward the Vichy. "Stop 'em!"

Zev worked the pump on the shotgun. The sound echoed through the church. Joe heard the activity behind him come to a sudden halt He braced himself for the shot . . .

But it never came.

He looked at Zev. The old man met his gaze and sadly shook his head. He couldn't do it. To the accompaniment of the sound of renewed activity and derisive laughter behind him, Joe gave Zev a tiny nod of reassurance and understanding, then hurried the Mass toward the Consecration.

As he held the crust of bread aloft, he started at the sound of the life-sized crucifix crashing to the floor, cringed as he heard the freshly buttressed arms and crosspiece being torn away again.

As he held the wine aloft in the Pepsi can, the swaggering, grinning Vichy surrounded the altar and brazenly tore the cross from around his neck. Zev and Carl put up a struggle to keep theirs but were overpowered.

And then Joe's skin began to crawl as a new group entered the nave. There had to be at least forty of them, all of them vampires.

And Palmeri was leading them.

XI

Palmeri hid his hesitancy as he approached the altar. The crucifix and its intolerable whiteness were gone, yet something was not right. Something repellent here, something that urged him to flee. What?

Perhaps it was just the residual effect of the crucifix and all the crosses they had used to line the walls. That had to be it. The unsettling aftertaste would fade as the night wore on. Oh, yes. His nightbrothers and sisters from the nest would see to that.

He focused his attention on the man behind the altar and laughed when he realized what he held in his hands.

"Pepsi, Joseph? You're trying to consecrate Pepsi?" He turned to his nest siblings. "Do you see this, my brothers and sisters? Is this the man we are to fear? And look who he has with him! An old Jew and a parish hanger-on!"

He heard their hissing laughter as they fanned out around him, sweeping toward the altar in a wide phalanx. The Jew and Carl—he recognized Carl and wondered how he'd avoided capture for so long—retreated to the other side of the altar where they flanked Joseph. And Joseph . . . Joseph's handsome Irish face so pale and drawn, his mouth drawn into such a tight, grim line. He looked scared to death. And well he should be.

Palmeri put down his rage at Joseph's audacity. He was glad he had returned. He'd always hated the young priest for his easy manner with people, for the way the parishioners had flocked to him with their problems despite the fact that he had nowhere near the experience of their older and wiser pastor. But that was over now. That world was gone, replaced by a nightworld—Palmeri's world. And no one would be flocking to Father Joe for anything when Palmeri was through with him. "Father Joe"—how he'd hated it when way the parishioners had started calling him that. Well, their Father Joe would provide superior entertainment tonight. This was going to be *fun*.

"Joseph, Joseph, Joseph," he said as he stopped and smiled at the young priest across the altar. "This futile gesture is so typical of your arrogance."

But Joseph only stared back at him, his expression a mixture of defiance and repugnance. And that only fueled Palmeri's rage.

"Do I repel you, Joseph? Does my new form offend your precious shanty-Irish sensibilities? Does my undeath disgust you?"

"You managed to do all that while you were still alive, Alberto."

Palmeri allowed himself to smile. Joseph probably thought he was putting on a brave front, but the tremor in his voice betrayed his fear.

"Always good with the quick retort, weren't you, Joseph. Always thinking you were better than me, always putting yourself above me."

"Not much of a climb where a child molester is concerned."

Palmeri's anger mounted.

"So superior. So self-righteous. What about _your_ appetites, Joseph? The secret ones? What are they? Do you always hold them in check? Are you so far above the rest of us that you never give in to an improper impulse? I'll bet you think that even if we made you one of us you could resist the blood hunger."

He saw by the startled look in Joseph's face that he had struck a nerve. He stepped closer, almost touching the altar.

"You do, don't you? You really think you could resist it! Well, we shall see about that, Joseph. By dawn you'll be drained—we'll each take a turn at you—and when the sun rises you'll have to hide from its light. When the night comes you'll be one of us. And then all the rules will be off. The night will be yours. You'll be able to do anything and everything you've ever wanted. But the blood hunger will be on you too. You won't be sipping your god's blood, as you've done so often, but _human_ blood. You'll thirst for hot, human blood, Joseph. And you'll have to sate that thirst. There'll be no choice. And I want to be there when you do, Joseph. I want to be there to laugh in your face as you suck up the crimson nectar, and keep on laughing every night as the red hunger lures you into infinity."

And it _would_ happen. Palmeri knew it as sure as he felt his own thirst. He hungered for the moment when he could rub dear Joseph's face in the muck of his own despair.

"I was about to finish saying Mass," Joseph said coolly. "Do you mind if I finish?"

Palmeri couldn't help laughing this time.

"Did you really think this charade would work? Did you really think you could celebrate Mass on _this_?"

He reached out and snatched the tablecloth from the altar, sending the Missal and the piece of bread to the floor and exposing the fouled surface of the marble.

"Did you really think you could effect the Transubstantiation here? Do you really believe any of that garbage? That the bread and wine actually take on the substance of— " he tried to say the name but it wouldn't form "—the Son's body and blood?"

One of the nest brothers, Frederick, stepped forward and leaned over the altar, smiling.

"Transubstantiation?" he said in his most unctuous voice, pulling the Pepsi can from Joseph's hands. "Does that mean that this is the blood of the Son?"

A whisper of warning slithered through Palmeri's mind. Something about the can, something about the way he found it difficult to bring its outline into focus . . .

"Brother Frederick, maybe you should— "

Frederick's grin broadened. "I've always wanted to sup on the blood of a deity."

The nest members hissed their laughter as Frederick raised the can and drank.

Palmeri was jolted by the explosion of intolerable brightness that burst from Fredrick's mouth. The inside of his skull glowed beneath his scalp and shafts of pure white light shot from his ears, nose, eyes—every orifice in his head. The glow spread as it flowed down through his throat and chest and into his abdominal cavity, silhouetting his ribs before melting through his skin. Frederick was liquefying where he stood, his flesh steaming, softening, running like glowing molten lava.

No! This couldn't be happening! Not now when he had Joseph in his grasp!

Then the can fell from Frederick's dissolving fingers and landed on the altar top. Its contents splashed across the fouled surface, releasing another detonation of brilliance, this one more devastating than the first. The glare spread rapidly, extending over the upper surface and running down the sides, moving like a living thing, engulfing the entire altar, making it glow like a corpuscle of fire torn from the heart of the sun itself.

And with the light came blast-furnace heat that drove Palmeri back, back, back until he had to turn and follow the rest of his nest in a mad, headlong rush from St Anthony's into the cool, welcoming safety of the outer darkness.

XII

As the vampires fled into the night, their Vichy toadies behind them, Zev stared in horrid fascination at the puddle of putrescence that was all that remained of the vampire Palmeri had called Frederick. He glanced at Carl and caught the look of dazed wonderment on his face. Zev touched the top of the altar—clean, shiny, every whorl of the marble surface clearly visible.

There was fearsome power here. Incalculable power. But instead of elating him, the realization only depressed him. How long had this been going on? Did it happen at every Mass? Why had he spent his entire life ignorant of this?

He turned to Father Joe.

"What happened?"

"I—I don't know."

"A miracle!" Carl said, running his palm over the altar top.

"A miracle and a meltdown," Father Joe said. He picked up the empty Pepsi can and looked into it. "You know, you go through the seminary, through your ordination, through countless Masses *believing* in the Transubtantiation. But after all these years . . . to actually *know* . . ."

Zev saw him rub his finger along the inside of the can and taste it. He grimaced.

"What's wrong?" Zev asked.

"Still tastes like sour barbarone . . . with a hint of Pepsi."

"Doesn't matter what it tastes like. As far as Palmeri and his friends are concerned, it's the real thing."

"No," said the priest with a small smile. "That's Coke."

And then they started laughing. It wasn't that funny, but Zev found himself roaring along with other two. It was more a release of tension than anything else. His sides hurt. He had to lean against the altar to support himself.

It took the return of the Vichy to cure the laughter. They charged in carrying a heavy fire blanket. This time Father Joe did not stand by passively as they invaded his church. He stepped around the altar and met them head on.

He was great and terrible as he confronted them. His giant stature and raised fists cowed them for a few heartbeats. But then they must have remembered that they outnumbered him twelve to one and charged him. He swung a massive fist and caught the lead Vichy square on the jaw. The blow lifted him off his feet and he landed against another. Both went down.

Zev dropped to one knee and reached for the shotgun. He would use it this time, he would shoot these vermin, he swore it!

But then someone landed on his back and drove him to the floor. As he tried to get up he saw Father Joe, surrounded, swinging his fists, laying the Vichy out every time he connected. But there were too many. As the priest went down under the press of them, a heavy boot thudded against the side of Zev's head. He sank into darkness.

XIII

. . . a throbbing in his head, stinging pain in his cheek, and a voice, sibilant yet harsh . . .

". . . now, Joseph. Come on. Wake up. I don't want you to miss this!"

Palmeri's sallow features swam into view, hovering over him, grinning like a skull. Joe tried to move but found his wrists and arms tied. His right hand throbbed, felt twice its normal size; he must have broken it on a Vichy jaw. He lifted his head and saw that he was tied spread-eagle on the altar, and that the altar had been covered with the fire blanket.

"Melodramatic, I admit," Palmeri said, "but fitting, don't you think? I mean, you and I used to sacrifice our god symbolically here every weekday and multiple times on Sundays, so why shouldn't this serve as _your_ sacrificial altar?"

Joe shut his eyes against a wave of nausea. This couldn't be happening.

"Thought you'd won, didn't you?" When Joe wouldn't answer him, Palmeri went on. "And even if you'd chased me out of here for good, what would you have accomplished? The world is ours now, Joseph. Feeders and cattle—that is the hierarchy. We are the feeders. And tonight you'll join us. But _he_ won't. _Voila!_"

He stepped aside and made a flourish toward the balcony. Joe searched the dim, candlelit space of the nave, not sure what he was supposed to see. Then he picked out Zev's form and he groaned. The old man's feet were lashed to the balcony rail; he hung upside down, his reddened face and frightened eyes turned his way. Joe fell back and strained at the ropes but they wouldn't budge.

"Let him go!"

"What? And let all that good rich Jewish blood go to waste? Why, these people are the Chosen of God! They're a delicacy!"

"Bastard!"

If he could just get his hands on Palmeri, just for a minute.

"Tut-tut, Joseph. Not in the house of the Lord. The Jew should have been smart and run away like Carl."

Carl got away? Good. The poor guy would probably hate himself, call himself a coward the rest of his life, but he'd done what he could. Better to live on than get strung up like Zev.

We're even, Carl.

"But don't worry about your rabbi. None of us will lay a fang on him. He hasn't earned the right to join us. We'll use the razor to bleed him. And when he's dead, he'll be dead for keeps. But not you, Joseph. Oh no, not you." His smile broadened. "You're mine."

Joe wanted to spit in Palmeri's face—not so much as an act of defiance as to hide the waves of terror surging through him—but there was no saliva to be had in his parched mouth. The thought of being undead made him weak. To spend eternity like . . . he looked at the rapt faces of Palmeri's fellow vampires as they clustered under Zev's suspended form . . . like *them?*

He *wouldn't* be like them! He wouldn't allow it!

But what if there was no choice? What if becoming undead toppled a lifetime's worth of moral constraints, cut all the tethers on his human hungers, negated all his mortal concepts of how a life should be lived? Honor, justice, integrity, truth, decency, fairness, love—what if they became meaningless words instead of the footings for his life?

A thought struck him.

"A deal, Alberto," he said.

"You're hardly in a bargaining position, Joseph."

"I'm not? Answer me this: Do the undead ever kill each other? I mean, has one of them ever driven a stake through another's heart?"

"No. Of course not."

"Are you sure? You'd better be sure before you go through with your plans tonight. Because if I'm forced to become one of you, I'll be crossing over with just one thought in mind: to find you. And when I do I won't stake your heart, I'll stake your arms and legs to the pilings of the Point Pleasant boardwalk where you can watch the sun rise and feel it slowly crisp your skin to charcoal."

Palmeri's smile wavered. "Impossible. You'll be different. You'll want to thank me. You'll wonder why you ever resisted."

"You'd better sure of that, Alberto . . . for your sake. Because I'll have all eternity to track you down. And I'll find you, Alberto. I swear it on my own grave. Think on that."

"Do you think an empty threat is going to cow me?"

"We'll find out how empty it is, won't we? But here's the deal: Let Zev go and I'll let you be."

"You care that much for an old Jew?"

"He's something you never knew in life, and never will know: he's a friend." *And he gave me back my soul.*

Palmeri leaned closer. His foul, nauseous breath wafted against Joe's face.

"A friend? How can you be friends with a dead man?" With that he straightened and turned toward the balcony. "Do him! *Now!*"

As Joe shouted out frantic pleas and protests, one of the vampires climbed up the rubble toward Zev. Zev did not struggle. Joe saw him close his eyes, waiting. As the vampire reached out with the straight razor, Joe bit back a sob of grief and rage and helplessness. He was about to squeeze his own eyes shut when he saw a flame arc through the air from one of the windows. It struck the floor with a crash of glass and a *wooomp!* of exploding flame.

Joe had only heard of such things, but he immediately realized that he had just seen his first Molotov cocktail in action. The splattering gasoline caught the clothes of a nearby vampire who began running in circles, screaming as it beat at its flaming clothes. But its cries were drowned by the roar of other voices, a hundred or more. Joe looked around and saw people—men, women, teenagers—climbing in the windows, charging through the front doors. The women held crosses on high while the men wielded long wooden pikes—broom, rake, and shovel handles whittled to sharp points. Joe recognized most of the faces from the Sunday Masses he had said here for years.

St Anthony's parishioners were back to reclaim their church.

"Yes!" he shouted, not sure of whether to laugh or cry. But when he saw the rage in Palmeri's face, he laughed. "Too bad, Alberto!"

Palmeri made a lunge at his throat but cringed away as a woman with an upheld crucifix and a man with a pike charged the altar—Carl and a woman Joe recognized as Mary O'Hare.

"Told ya I wun't letcha down, din't I, Fadda?" Carl said, grinning and pulling out a red Swiss Army knife. He began sawing at the rope around Joe's right wrist. "Din't I?"

"That you did, Carl. I don't think I've ever been so glad to see anyone in my entire life. But how—?"

"I told 'em. I run t'rough da parish, goin' house ta house. I told 'em dat Fadda Joe was in trouble an' dat we let him down before but we shoun't let him down again. He come back fa us, now we gotta go back fa him. Simple as dat. And den *dey* started runnin' house ta house, an afore ya knowed it, we had ourselfs a little army. We come ta kick ass, Fadda, if you'll excuse da expression."

"Kick all the ass you can, Carl."

Joe glanced at Mary O'Hare's terror-glazed eyes as she swiveled around, looking this way and that; he saw how the crucifix trembled in her hand. She wasn't going to kick too much ass in her state, but she was *here*, dear God, she was here for him and for St Anthony's despite the terror that so obviously filled her. His heart swelled with love for these people and pride in their courage.

As soon as his arms were free, Joe sat up and took the knife from
Carl. As he sawed at his leg ropes, he looked around the church.

The oldest and youngest members of the parishioner army were
stationed at the windows and doors where they held crosses aloft,
cutting off the vampires' escape, while all across the nave—chaos.
Screams, cries, and an occasional shot echoed through St Anthony's.
The vampires were outnumbered three to one and seemed blinded
and confused by all the crosses around them. Despite their super-
human strength, it appeared that some were indeed getting their
asses kicked. A number were already writhing on the floor, impaled
on pikes. As Joe watched, he saw a pair of the women, crucifixes
held before them, backing a vampire into a corner. As it cowered
there with its arms across its face, one of the men charged in with
a sharpened rake handle held like a lance and ran it through.

But a number of parishioners lay in inert, bloody heaps on the
floor, proof that the vampires and the Vichy were claiming their
share of victims too.

Joe freed his feet and hopped off the altar. He looked around
for Palmeri—he *wanted* Palmeri—but the vampire priest had lost
himself in the melée. Joe glanced up at the balcony and saw that
Zev was still hanging there, struggling to free himself. He started
across the nave to help him.

XIV

Zev hated that he should be hung up here like a salami in a deli
window. He tried again to pull his upper body up far enough
to reach his leg ropes but he couldn't get close. He had never
been one for exercise; doing a sit-up flat on the floor would have
been difficult, so what made him think he could do the equivalent
maneuver hanging upside down by his feet? He dropped back,
exhausted, and felt the blood rush to his head again. His vision
swam, his ears pounded, he felt like the skin of his face was going
to burst open. Much more of this and he'd have a stroke or worse
maybe.

He watched the upside-down battle below and was glad to see the
vampires getting the worst of it. These people—seeing Carl among
them, Zev assumed they were part of St Anthony's parish—were
ferocious, almost savage in their attacks on the vampires. Months'
worth of pent-up rage and fear was being released upon their
tormentors in a single burst. It was almost frightening.

Suddenly he felt a hand on his foot. Someone was untying his

knots. Thank you, Lord. Soon he would be on his feet again. As the
cords came loose he decided he should at least attempt to participate
in his own rescue.

Once more, Zev thought. *Once more I'll try.*

With a grunt he levered himself up, straining, stretching to grasp
something, anything. A hand came out of the darkness and he
reached for it. But Zev's relief turned to horror when he felt the
cold clamminess of the thing that clutched him, that pulled him
up and over the balcony rail with inhuman strength. His bowels
threatened to evacuate when Palmeri's grinning face loomed not six
inches from his own.

"It's not over yet, Jew," he said softly, his foul breath clogging
Zev's nose and throat. "Not by a long shot!"

He felt Palmeri's free hand ram into his belly and grip his belt at
the buckle, then the other hand grab a handful of his shirt at the
neck. Before he could struggle or cry out, he was lifted free of the
floor and hoisted over the balcony rail.

And the demon's voice was in his ear.

"Joseph called you a friend, Jew. Let's see if he really meant it."

XV

Joe was half way across the floor of the nave when he heard Palmeri's
voice echo above the madness.

"Stop them, Joseph! Stop them now or I drop your friend!"

Joe looked up and froze. Palmeri stood at the balcony rail, leaning
over it, his eyes averted from the nave and all its newly arrived
crosses. At the end of his outstretched arms was Zev, suspended in
mid-air over the splintered remains of the pews, over a particularly
large and ragged spire of wood that pointed directly at the middle
of Zev's back. Zev's frightened eyes were flashing between Joe and
the giant spike below.

Around him Joe heard the sounds of the melée drop a notch,
then drop another as all eyes were drawn to the tableau on the
balcony.

"A human can die impaled on a wooden stake just as well as a
vampire!" Palmeri cried. "And just as quickly if it goes through his
heart. But it can take hours of agony if it rips through his gut."

St Anthony's grew silent as the fighting stopped and each faction
backed away to a different side of the church, leaving Joe alone in
the middle.

"What do you want, Alberto?"

"First I want all those crosses put away so that I can see!"

Joe looked to his right where his parishioners stood.

"Put them away," he told them. When a murmur of dissent arose, he added, "Don't put them down, just out of sight. Please."

Slowly, one by one at first, then in groups, the crosses and crucifixes were placed behind backs or tucked out of sight within coats.

To his left, the vampires hissed their relief and the Vichy cheered. The sound was like hot needles being forced under Joe's fingernails. Above, Palmeri turned his face to Joe and smiled.

"That's better."

"What do you want?" Joe asked, knowing with a sick crawling in his gut exactly what the answer would be.

"A trade," Palmeri said.

"Me for him, I suppose?" Joe said.

Palmeri's smile broadened. "Of course."

"No, Joe!" Zev cried.

Palmeri shook the old man roughly. Joe heard him say, "Quiet, Jew, or I'll snap your spine!" Then he looked down at Joe again. "The other thing is to tell your rabble to let my people go." He laughed and shook Zev again. "Hear that, Jew? A Biblical reference—Old Testament, no less!"

"All right," Joe said without hesitation.

The parishioners on his right gasped as one and cries of "No!" and "You can't!" filled St Anthony's. A particularly loud voice nearby shouted, "He's only a lousy kike!"

Joe wheeled on the man and recognized Gene Harrington, a carpenter. He jerked a thumb back over his shoulder at the vampires and their servants.

"You sound like you'd be more at home with them, Gene."

Harrington backed up a step and looked at his feet.

"Sorry, Father," he said in a voice that hovered on the verge of a sob. "But we just got you back!"

"I'll be all right," Joe said softly.

And he meant it. Deep inside he had a feeling that he would come through this, that if he could trade himself for Zev and face Palmeri one-on-one, he could come out the victor, or at least battle him to a draw. Now that he was no longer tied up like some sacrificial lamb, now that he was free, with full use of his arms and legs again, he could not imagine dying at the hands of the likes of Palmeri.

Besides, one of the parishioners had given him a tiny crucifix. He had it closed in the palm of his hand.

But he had to get Zev out of danger first. That above all else. He looked up at Palmeri.

"All right, Alberto. I'm on my way up."

"Wait!" Palmeri said. "Someone search him."

Joe gritted his teeth as one of the Vichy, a blubbery, unwashed slob, came forward and searched his pockets. Joe thought he might get away with the crucifix but at the last moment he was made to open his hands. The Vichy grinned in Joe's face as he snatched the tiny cross from his palm and shoved it into his pocket.

"He's clean now!" the slob said and gave Joe a shove toward the vestibule.

Joe hesitated. He was walking into the snake pit unarmed now. A glance at his parishioners told him he couldn't very well turn back now.

He continued on his way, clenching and unclenching his tense, sweaty fists as he walked. He still had a chance of coming out of this alive. He was too angry to die. He prayed that when he got within reach of the ex-priest the smoldering rage at how he had framed him when he'd been pastor, at what he'd done to St Anthony's since then would explode and give him the strength to tear Palmeri to pieces.

"No!" Zev shouted from above. "Forget about me! You've started something here and you've got to see it through!"

Joe ignored his friend.

"Coming, Alberto."

Father Joe's coming, Alberto. And he's pissed. Royally *pissed.*

XVI

Zev craned his neck around, watching Father Joe disappear beneath the balcony.

"Joe! Come back!"

Palmeri shook him again.

"Give it up, old Jew. Joseph never listened to anyone and he's not listening to you. He still believes in faith and virtue and honesty, in the power of goodness and truth over what he perceives as evil. He'll come up here ready to sacrifice himself for you, yet sure in his heart that he's going to win in the end. But he's wrong."

"No!" Zev said.

But in his heart he knew that Palmeri was right. How could Joe stand up against a creature with Palmeri's strength, who could hold Zev in the air like this for so long? Didn't his arms ever tire?

"Yes!" Palmeri hissed. "He's going to lose and we're going to win. We'll win for the same reason we'll always win. We don't let anything as silly and transient as sentiment stand in our way. If we'd been winning below and situations were reversed—if Joseph were holding one of my nest brothers over that wooden spike below—do you think I'd pause for a moment? For a second? Never! That's why this whole exercise by Joseph and these people is futile."

Futile . . . Zev thought. Like much of his life, it seemed. Like all of his future. Joe would die tonight and Zev would live on, a cross-wearing Jew, with the traditions of his past sacked and in flames, and nothing in his future but a vast, empty, limitless plain to wander alone.

There was a sound on the balcony stairs and Palmeri turned his head.

"Ah, Joseph," he said.

Zev couldn't see the priest but he shouted anyway.

"Go back Joe! Don't let him trick you!"

"Speaking of tricks," Palmeri said, leaning further over the balcony rail as an extra warning to Joe, "I hope you're not going to try anything foolish."

"No," said Joe's tired voice from somewhere behind Palmeri. "No tricks. Pull him in and let him go."

Zev could not let this happen. And suddenly he knew what he had to do. He twisted his body and grabbed the front of Palmeri's cassock while bringing his legs up and bracing his feet against one of the uprights of the brass balcony rail. As Palmeri turned his startled face toward him, Zev put all his strength into his legs for one convulsive backward push against the railing, pulling Palmeri with him. The vampire priest was overbalanced. Even his enormous strength could not help him once his feet came free of the floor. Zev saw his undead eyes widen with terror as his lower body slipped over the railing. As they fell free, Zev wrapped his arms around Palmeri and clutched his cold and surprisingly thin body tight against him.

"What goes through this old Jew goes through you!" he shouted into the vampire's ear.

For an instant he saw Joe's horrified face appear over the balcony's receding edge, heard Joe's faraway shout of "*No!*" mingle with Palmeri's nearer scream of the same word, then there was a spine-cracking jar and a tearing, wrenching pain beyond all comprehension in his chest. In an eyeblink he felt the sharp spire of wood rip through him and into Palmeri.

And then he felt no more.

As roaring blackness closed in he wondered if he'd done it, if this last desperate, foolish act had succeeded. He didn't want to die without finding out. He wanted to know—

But then he knew no more.

XVII

Joe shouted incoherently as he hung over the rail and watched Zev's fall, gagged as he saw the bloody point of the pew remnant burst through the back of Palmeri's cassock directly below him. He saw Palmeri squirm and flop around like a speared fish, then go limp atop Zev's already inert form.

As cheers mixed with cries of horror and the sounds of renewed battle rose from the nave, Joe turned away from the balcony rail and dropped to his knees.

"Zev!" he cried aloud! "Good God, Zev!"

Forcing himself to his feet, he stumbled down the back stairs, through the vestibule, and into the nave. The vampires and the Vichy were on the run, as cowed and demoralized by their leader's death as the parishioners were buoyed by it. Slowly, steadily, they were falling before the relentless onslaught. But Joe paid them scant attention. He fought his way to where Zev lay impaled beneath Palmeri's already rotting corpse. He looked for a sign of life in his old friend's glazing eyes, a hint of a pulse in his throat under his beard, but there was nothing.

"Oh, Zev, you shouldn't have. You shouldn't have."

Suddenly he was surrounded by a cheering throng of St Anthony's parishioners.

"We did it, Fadda Joe!" Carl cried, his face and hands splattered with blood. "We killed 'em all! We got our church back!"

"Thanks to this man here," Joe said, pointing to Zev.

"No!" someone shouted. "Thanks to *you!*"

Amid the cheers, Joe shook his head and said nothing. Let them celebrate. They deserved it. They'd reclaimed a small piece of the planet as their own, a toe-hold and nothing more. A small victory of minimal significance in the war, but a victory nonetheless. They had their church back, at least for tonight. And they intended to keep it.

Good. But there would be one change. If they wanted their Father Joe to stick around they were going to have to agree to rename the church.

St Zev's.

Joe liked the sound of that.

Nancy Holder

Blood Gothic

Nancy Holder sold her first book, a young adult romance, in 1981, and she wrote romances for five years under various pseudonyms. Seven of her novels placed on the Waldenbooks Romance Bestseller list, and she received several awards from Romantic Times.

More recently, Warner Books published her mainstream thriller Rough Cut, *and her short fiction has appeared in a wide range of magazines and anthologies, including several volumes of Charles L. Grant's* Shadows *series,* Doom City *and* Women of Darkness *(the wonderfully-titled 'Cannibal Cats Come Out Tonight').*

Holder's contribution to this volume could best be summed up as a dark romance . . .

SHE WANTED TO have a vampire lover. She wanted it so badly that she kept waiting for it to happen. One night, soon, she would awaken to wings flapping against the window and then take to wearing velvet ribbons and cameo lockets around her delicate, pale neck. She knew it.

She immersed herself in the world of her vampire lover: she devoured Gothic romances, consumed late-night horror movies. Visions of satin capes and eyes of fire shielded her from the harshness of the daylight, from mortality and the vain and meaningless

struggles of the world of the sun. Days as a kindergarten teacher
and evenings with some overly eager, casual acquaintance could
not pull her from her secret existence: always a ticking portion of
her brain planned, proceeded, waited.

She spent her meager earnings on dark antiques and intricate
clothes. Her wardrobe was crammed with white negligees and
ruffled underthings. No crosses and no mirrors, particularly not
in her bedroom. White tapered candles stood in pewter sconces,
and she would read late into the night by their smoky flickerings,
she scented and ruffled, hair combed loosely about her shoulders.
She glanced at the window often.

She resented lovers—though she took them, thrilling to the fullness of life in them, the blood and the life—who insisted upon staying
all night, burning their breakfast toast and making bitter coffee. Her
kitchen, of course, held nothing but fresh ingredients and copper and
ironware; to her chagrin, she could not do without ovens or stoves or
refrigerators. Alone, she carried candles and bathed in cool water.

She waited, prepared. And at long last, her vampire lover began
to come to her in dreams. They floated across the moors, glided
through the fields of heather. He carried her to his crumbling castle,
undressing her, pulling off her diaphanous gown, caressing her lovely
body until, in the height of passion, he bit into her arched neck,
drawing the life out of her and replacing it with eternal damnation
and eternal love.

She awoke from these dreams drenched in sweat and feeling
exhausted. The kindergarten children would find her unusually
quiet and self-absorbed, and it frightened them when she rubbed
her spotless neck and smiled wistfully. *Soon and soon and soon*, her
veins chanted, in prayer and anticipation. *Soon.*

The children were her only regret. She would not miss her inquisitive relatives and friends, the ones who frowned and studied her as
if she were a portrait of someone they knew they were supposed to
recognize. Those, who urged her to drop by for an hour, to come with
them to films, to accompany them to the seashore. Those, who were
connected to her—or thought they were—by the mere gesturing of
the long and milky hands of Fate. Who sought to distract her from her
one true passion; who sought to discover the secret of that passion.
For, true to the sacredness of her vigil for her vampire lover, she had
never spoken of him to a single earthly, earthbound soul. It would
be beyond them, she knew. They would not comprehend a bond of
such intentioned sacrifice.

But she would regret the children. Never would a child of their
love coo and murmur in the darkness; never would his proud and

noble features soften at the sight of the mother and her child of his loins. It was her single sorrow.

Her vacation was coming. June hovered like the mist and the children squirmed in anticipation. Their own true lives would begin in June. She empathized with the shining eyes and smiling faces, knowing their wait was as agonizing as her own. Silently, as the days closed in, she bade each of them a tender farewell, holding them as they threw their little arms around her neck and pressed fervent summertime kisses on her cheeks.

She booked her passage to London on a ship. Then to Romania, Bulgaria, Transylvania. The hereditary seat of her beloved; the fierce, violent backdrop of her dreams. Her suitcases opened themselves to her long, full skirts and her brooches and lockets. She peered into her hand mirror as she packed it. "I am getting pale," she thought, and the idea both terrified and delighted her.

She became paler, thinner, more exhausted as her trip wore on. After recovering from the disappointment of the raucous, modern cruise ship, she raced across the Continent to find refuge in the creaky trains and taverns she had so yearned for. Her heart thrilled as she meandered past the black silhouettes of ruined fortresses and ancient manor houses. She sat for hours in the mists, praying for the howling wolf to find her, for the bat to come and join her.

She took to drinking wine in bed, deep, rich, blood-red burgundy that glowed in the candlelight. She melted into the landscape within days, and cringed as if from the crucifix itself when flickers of her past life, her American, false existence, invaded her serenity. She did not keep a diary; she did not count the days as her summer slipped away from her. She only rejoiced that she grew weaker.

It was when she was counting out the coins for a Gypsy shawl that she realized she had no time left. Tomorrow she must make for Frankfurt and from there fly back to New York. The shopkeeper nudged her, inquiring if she were ill, and she left with her treasure, trembling.

She flung herself on her own rented bed. "This will not do. This will not do." She pleaded with the darkness. "You must come for me tonight. I have done everything for you, my beloved, loved you above all else. You must save me." She sobbed until she ached.

She skipped her last meal of veal and paprika and sat quietly in her room. The innkeeper brought her yet another bottle of burgundy and after she assured him that she was quite all right, just a little tired, he wished his guest a pleasant trip home.

The night wore on; though her book was open before her, her eyes were riveted to the windows, her hands clenched around the wineglass as she sipped steadily, like a creature feeding. Oh, to feel him against her veins, emptying her and filling her!

Soon and soon and soon . . .

Then, all at once, it happened. The windows rattled, flapped inward. A great shadow, a curtain of ebony, fell across the bed, and the room began to whirl, faster, faster still; and she was consumed with a bitter, deathly chill. She heard, rather than saw, the wineglass crash to the floor, and struggled to keep her eyes open as she was overwhelmed, engulfed, taken.

"Is it you?" she managed to whisper through teeth that rattled with delight and cold and terror. "Is it finally to be?"

Freezing hands touched her everywhere: her face, her breasts, the desperate offering of her arched neck. Frozen and strong and never-dying. Sinking, she smiled in a rictus of mortal dread and exultation. Eternal damnation, eternal love. Her vampire lover had come for her at last.

When her eyes opened again, she let out a howl and shrank against the searing brilliance of the sun. Hastily, they closed the curtains and quickly told her where she was: home again, where everything was warm and pleasant and she was safe from the disease that had nearly killed her.

She had been ill before she had left the States. By the time she had reached Transylvania, her anemia had been acute. Had she never noticed her own pallor, her lassitude?

Anemia. Her smile was a secret on her white lips. So they thought, but he *had* come for her, again and again. In her dreams. And on that night, he had meant to take her finally to his castle forever, to crown her the best-beloved one, his love of the moors and the mists.

She had but to wait, and he would finish the deed.

Soon and soon and soon.

She let them fret over her, wrapping her in blankets in the last days of summer. She endured the forced cheer of her relatives, allowed them to feed her rich food and drink in hopes of restoring her.

But her stomach could no longer hold the nourishment of their kind; they wrung their hands and talked of stronger measures when it became clear that she was wasting away.

At the urging of the doctor, she took walks. Small ones at first, on painfully thin feet. Swathed in wool, cowering behind sunglasses, she took tiny steps like an old woman. As she moved through the summer hours, her neck burned with an ungovernable pain that would not cease until she rested in the shadows. Her stomach lurched at the sight of grocery-store windows. But at the butcher's, she paused, and licked her lips at the sight of the raw, bloody meat.

But she did not go to him. She grew neither worse nor better.

"I am trapped," she whispered to the night as she stared into the flames of a candle by her bed. "I am disappearing between your world and mine, my beloved. Help me. Come for me." She rubbed her neck, which ached and throbbed but showed no outward signs of his devotion. Her throat was parched, bone-dry, but water did not quench her thirst.

At long last, she dreamed again. Her vampire lover came for her as before, joyous in their reunion. They soared above the crooked trees at the foothills, streamed like black banners above the mountain crags to his castle. He could not touch her enough, worship her enough, and they were wild in their abandon as he carried her in her diaphanous gown to the gates of his fortress.

But at the entrance, he shook his head with sorrow and could not let her pass into the black realm with him. His fiery tears seared her neck, and she thrilled to the touch of the mark even as she cried out for him as he left her, fading into the vapors with a look of entreaty in his dark, flashing eyes.

Something was missing; he required a boon of her before he could bind her against his heart. A thing that she must give to him . . .

She walked in the sunlight, enfeebled, cowering. She thirsted, hungered, yearned. Still she dreamed of him, and still he could not take the last of her unto himself.

Days and nights and days. Her steps took her finally to the schoolyard, where once, only months before, she had embraced and kissed the children, thinking never to see them again. They were all there, who had kissed her cheeks so eagerly. Their silvery laughter was like the tinkling of bells as dust motes from their games and antics whirled around their feet. How free they seemed to her who was so troubled, how content and at peace.

The children.

She shambled forward, eyes widening behind the shields of smoky glass.

He required something of her first.

Her one regret. Her only sorrow.

She thirsted. The burns on her neck pulsated with pain.

Tears of gratitude welled in her eyes for the revelation that had not come too late. Weeping, she pushed open the gate of the schoolyard and reached out a skeleton-limb to a child standing apart from the rest, engrossed in a solitary game of cat's cradle. Tawny-headed, ruddy-cheeked, filled with the blood and the life.

For him, as a token of their love.

"My little one, do you remember me?" she said softly.

The boy turned. And smiled back uncertainly in innocence and trust.

Then she came for him, swooped down on him like a great, winged thing, with eyes that burned through the glasses, teeth that flashed, once, twice . . .

soon and soon and soon.

Les Daniels

Yellow Fog

Les Daniels has been a freelance writer, composer, film buff and musician. His first book was Comix: A History of Comic Books in America *(1971), and 1991 saw the publication of* Marvel, *his huge history of Marvel Comics. He also wrote the non-fiction study* Living in Fear: A History of Horror in the Mass Media *and edited the anthologies* Dying of Fright: Masterpieces of the Macabre *and* Thirteen Tales of Terror *(with Diane Thompson).*

His short fiction has been published in Cutting Edge, Book of the Dead, Borderlands, The Seaharp Hotel, After the Darkness *and* Dark Voices 4: The Pan Book of Horror, *while his articles have appeared in various newspapers,* Shock Xpress, Horror: 100 Best Books, Supernatural Fiction Writers: Fantasy & Horror *and* World Fantasy Convention Program Books.

In 1978 Daniels introduced his enigmatic vampire-hero Don Sebastian de Villanueva in his debut novel, The Black Castle. *He has since resurrected the character in a series of superior horror novels:* The Silver Skull, Citizen Vampire, Yellow Fog *(an expanded version of the short novel that appears here) and* No Blood Spilled. *A sixth Sebastian novel, entitled* White Demon, *is forthcoming.*

I. Black Plumes

THE BOY ON the steps had been told to look unhappy, and he was doing his best, but he found it hard to mourn for a corpse he had never known, especially when the old man's death was making him money. Still, a job was a job, and Syd had no desire to lose this one. He stifled a smirk and glanced across the black-draped door toward his partner, but the sight of the old fellow with his fancy dress and his watery eyes was more than Syd could bear. He knew he must look just as foolish himself, wearing a top hat festooned with black crepe and carrying a long wand draped with more of the same, yet he felt a laugh rising in his chest that he barely succeeded in changing into a cough before it reached his lips. The crepe rustled, and Syd's partner altered his expression for an instant from dignified melancholy to threatening wrath. Mr Callender had paid Entwistle and Son a substantial sum for a proper funeral, and that meant that the mutes would remain mute.

Syd stiffened, hoping that the procession would arrive soon to relieve him of his post. His nose itched, and his left foot seemed to have gone numb. After a whole morning standing on duty in front of Callender's house, Syd was beginning to look to the long march to All Souls as a positive pleasure. It would at least mean a bit of exercise, and it would bring Syd closer to the time when he would finally be able to make a little profit out of the business. There was no pay in being apprenticed to an undertaker, even if it was Entwistle and Son. Just the Son now, actually, thought Syd, and it didn't look like he could expect to live much longer himself, except that he couldn't bear the thought of dying and letting anybody else bury him. Entwistle and Son was the best there was, and the hearse Syd saw turning the corner from Kensington High Street proved it.

Six matched black horses drew the hearse, their heads crowned with bobbing black plumes of dyed peacock feathers, their backs covered with hangings of black velvet. The low, black hearse, its glass sides etched in floral patterns, bore the oaken coffin upon a bed of lilies, under a canopy of more swaying black plumes. The driver proceeded at a measured pace to accommodate the mutes who trudged with downcast eyes beside the slowly rolling gilt-edged wheels. Behind them came the first mourning coach, and then the second; when the procession drew up before the house Syd was startled to see that there were no more. It seemed incredible that such an expensive funeral should have so few mourners; Syd could hardly believe that a man rich enough to afford Entwistle's best should have had so few friends.

The Son himself stepped from the second coach, the crepe on his hat fluttering across his face in the brisk autumn breeze. Syd snapped to attention like the soldiers he had seen outside Buckingham Palace guarding the Queen, and stared straight ahead as the undertaker glided up the steps with the black cloth alternately masking and unmasking his pale and furrowed face. Syd had learned long ago not to fear the dead, but he still feared the man who tended them, and he did not look to the side when he heard the sound of the brass door knocker. Shuffling steps approached the door, and the latch clicked.

"Mr Callender, please," said Mr Entwistle.

"Mr Callender asks that you wait for him outside," came the reply. The door closed quietly.

Syd stood so rigidly that he was starting to tremble as Mr Entwistle made his way stiffly down the steps and toward the second coach. Syd's feelings were a mixture of shock and delight; he saw that the expression on the face of his fellow mute was now genuinely grief-stricken. It was a revelation to discover a household too grand to receive Mr Entwistle, and Syd was far too impressed to do anything but stare when the door opened again to let the funeral party out.

There was a fat butler, a young gentleman with sandy side-whiskers, and a little lady with gray hair, but what Syd noticed was the one who stood behind them in the shadows. Her skin was fair, her eyes were of the lightest blue, and her hair was a blonde that was nearly white. There was next to no color in her, and she was as beautiful as a statue. All of them were dressed in black, and the little lady had the younger one by the arm.

"There's no need for you to come, Felicia," she said. "It's not the sort of thing a young lady ought to see."

"And yet you're going, Aunt Penelope."

"I'm no longer a young lady, and we can't send Mr Callender off alone on such a sad errand."

"But surely my place is with Reginald, Aunt Penelope."

"You've done more than enough for him already, and if he loves you he wouldn't dream of exposing you to such an ordeal. Beside, you're needed here to keep an eye on the servants, or there won't be much left of the feast by the time we return."

Neither the butler nor his master made any comment on this or anything else, but when the older woman said "I'll hear no more about it," the young gentleman took her arm and the butler closed the door behind them. Syd, whose only concern had been the pale angel who stayed behind, recollected himself and returned to his job, escorting Reginald Callender and the angel's Aunt Penelope to the first mourning coach. One of the horses stirred despite its blinders as they passed; everything else was still but Aunt Penelope's tongue.

"A gray day is just as well for a funeral, I think. It's appropriately solemn, but not really unpleasant. The day we buried poor Felicia's parents, the rain was so heavy it was almost a storm, and the child was crying so much on top of it, I don't think I've ever been so wet in all my born days. I really think it affected her, too. She's always been so delicate. A sunny day's not right, either, though. I remember burying a cousin when the day was so fine that it spoiled the whole occasion. It just wasn't fitting. No, I think a gray day is best."

She gestured decisively with her fan of black plumes and waited for Syd to open the carriage door.

"Uncle William chose the day, not I," said Reginald Callender as he helped Aunt Penelope up the step.

"Nonsense! If your Uncle William had his choice, this day never would have come at all. He would much rather have spent his fortune than left it all to you, Mr Callender. Not that you'll need it, with such a wealthy wife soon to be yours. It is a fine thing, though, is it not, to see two family fortunes joined along with their heirs?"

"No doubt," replied Callender as the door shut behind them and he took his seat beside his fiancee's aunt. His head throbbed already and he realized that burying his uncle would be more of an ordeal than whatever grief he felt would warrant. Last night he had taken too much whiskey, to calm his nerves and muffle his tactless conviction that he was, in his hour of bereavement, the luckiest man alive. What more could a man wish but riches and a beautiful wife, except to be free of the headache and a chattering woman who seemed to dote on death?

"It's a tragedy, the funeral party being so small, don't you think? Of course everything has been done in the very height of fashion, but it seems a shame that nobody's here to enjoy it."

"My uncle survived all his partners by some years, and I am his last living relative, as you know. The last of the Callenders. There is simply no one left to mourn him."

"And Felicia looked so lovely in that black silk! She can't keep wearing it, you know; she's not really in mourning, but it was so dear that it certainly should be seen. I took her to Jay's in Regent Street, you know. They make a specialty of mourning, and they furnished both of us for your uncle's funeral."

"Very handsomely, to be sure," murmured Callender, laying a

hand beside his head in a gesture that he hoped would suggest intelligent interest while still providing him with the opportunity to massage an aching temple. The motion of the coach was beginning to make him slightly sick.

"Of course I've had dresses from Jay's before; so many of one's friends and family seem to die as the years pass. I think the widow's weeds are most attractive, but a woman can't be a widow before she's a wife, can she?"

Callender might have answered, but Aunt Penelope had turned from him to gaze out of the coach at the streets of London. "I see you have chosen to travel by way of the park," she said. "Very wise, I'm sure. I thought you might have chosen the shorter route instead, where we should hardly have been seen at all."

"It was my uncle's wish," said Callender. "He left instructions for his funeral with his solicitor, Mr Frobisher."

"What a clever man! I never thought of such a thing, but I must certainly make plans for my own passing at the first possible moment. Of course I have no fortune to compensate my heirs for the expense. . . ."

"I am sure that Felicia will be happy to accommodate you," sighed Callender.

"Do you think so? Yes, I suppose she will. Such a generous girl, and such a spiritual nature. Her thoughts are always with the angels."

Callender wished fervently that Aunt Penelope could be with the angels too. He closed his eyes and thought of Felicia. Just a moment's peace would be enough to bring him sleep.

"Then Kensal Green was your uncle's choice as well?"

"I beg your pardon?" said Callender, pulling himself back to consciousness.

"Kensal Green, I said. All Souls Cemetery. It's certainly where I would choose to rest in peace. I visit there sometimes, and I still think it's the loveliest cemetery in London, even if there are a few that have opened since. The first of anything is often the best, don't you think? And of course anything would be better than one of the old churchyards. You must have heard the stories about the pestilence bred in those awful places, and about the way the skeletons were dug up and stored in sheds to make way for more graves? It's enough to make a body shudder."

Callender looked up to see if she were shuddering, and almost thought he saw her waving at a passerby, but he could not be certain. Although thoroughly dismayed by her enjoyment of the proceedings, he decided to resign himself. He had little choice in any case, and a day of pleasure for his beloved's maiden aunt was a small enough additional tax on the life of happiness that lay before him. He settled back in his seat as the coach rolled on.

Felicia Lamb closed her book and sat for a moment staring into space. Critics had attacked the novel and its unknown author, Ellis Bell, and Felicia admitted to herself that she had sometimes been dismayed by the savagery of its setting and the brutishness of its characters. Yet something in the story had compelled her interest: the idea of an immortal love that transcended even death. Such a passion both fascinated and frightened her; half of her longed for something like it, but she realized that destiny had decided to provide her with a much more practical match. Reginald Callender had his virtues, as her Aunt Penelope was frequently at pain to point out, but she could hardly imagine anyone accusing him of a supernatural longing. Perhaps it was just as well, Felicia thought. She knew that she was inclined toward morbidity, as certainly her father's sister was, so it was possible that her fiance had been sent to help keep her feet firmly planted on the ground.

She sighed and placed the last volume of *Wuthering Heights* on the highly polished surface of a table in the center of the drawing room. What light from the afternoon sky pressed through the heavy curtains was weak and dismal; the pendulum of the clock in the corner seemed to push the hours on toward darkness. Surely it was late enough for Reginald and Aunt Penelope to have returned. Against her will Felicia pictured a terrible accident that might at one blow deprive her of the only two people whose lives touched her own. She realized it was a foolish fancy, yet she had lost both her parents at once a dozen years ago, and knew all too well that such things were possible. She had more faith in the next world than she had in her chances for happiness in this.

She gazed up at the portrait of Reginald's Uncle William that hung magisterially over the mantel, and she wondered where he was now. The round, ruddy face and the thick body were, of course, in a coffin under six feet of earth, but where was William Callender himself? And where were her mother and father? The spirits of the dead haunted her without ever appearing as phantoms; perhaps she would have been less troubled by them if they had. She longed for Reginald to return and pull her away from such brooding, even though she always half resented him when he did.

"Shall I light the fire, Miss?"

A ghost would have startled her less than the voice did, but she realized in an instant that it was only the butler. And while she doubted that flames could eliminate the chill she felt within her, a cheery fire would at least be welcome to anyone returning from a long funeral on a raw autumn day.

"Thank you, Booth. I think Mr Callender would appreciate it." She heard his knees creak as he bent before the picture of his late master, and she felt a twinge of regret that she had not tended to the matter herself; it would have been much easier for her than it was for the old man. Her guilt propelled her from the room to supervise the preparations for the funeral feast, but she was not really needed for that, either.

"Is everything ready, Alice?" she asked the pretty, dark-haired maid. The girl, whose black uniform had lost its white ruffles to the dignity of the day, gave Felicia a curtsey and a small smile.

"Oh yes, Miss, thank you. Mr Entwistle's people took care of everything themselves, and it's very nice, I'm sure."

The sideboard was covered with food: a ham, a roast of beef, bread, pies, cakes, and bottles of sherry and port. There was enough to feed dozens of people, though only three were to be served.

"So much?" asked Felicia without stopping to consider the propriety of conversing with the servants on matters of form.

"Oh, yes, Miss. I asked them if there might be some mistake, but the gentleman assured me it was all called for in Mr Callender's will. May I serve you something, Miss?"

"Thank you, no," answered Felicia, who had never felt less hungry in her life. "I'll wait for the others, Alice. Do I hear them coming in now?"

"I'll go see, Miss," said the maid as she scurried off.

A moment later Felicia was joined by her Aunt Penelope, her eyes bright beneath her black bonnet as she surveyed the lavish meal spread out before her. "Well," she said, "this is very handsomely done, Felicia. And so it should be, I say. Weddings and funerals are important occasions. Will you pour me a glass of sherry, dear? Just a small one."

Aunt Penelope popped a small cake into her mouth as Reginald Callender strode into the room and reached for a bottle of port. He filled a glass and swallowed it at once.

"A lovely funeral, Mr Callender," said Aunt Penelope. "And the mausoleum was very splendid indeed. Did your uncle make provisions for you to join him there when you are called?"

Callender made no reply except to pour himself another drink. He collected himself enough to offer a glass to Felicia, but she refused it and seated herself on a small, straight-backed chair in a corner.

"I don't think I approve of closed coffins, however," said Aunt Penelope.

Callender's face turned suddenly hard. "Surely you saw enough of my uncle when he was lying in state, didn't you?"

"Oh, to be sure, Mr Callender. I meant no criticism. Sometimes, I suppose, the last look may be too painful to endure. Would you be kind enough to slice me some of that ham? Thank you. And how have you spent the day, Felicia?"

"In thinking of those who have gone before us, Aunt."

"Oh? And what were your conclusions, dear?"

"Only that there is much to know, and we know very little of it," said Felicia.

"Perhaps you will be wiser tomorrow evening, after our visit to Mr Newcastle."

Felicia's eyes widened, and she glanced anxiously back and forth between her aunt and her fiance.

"Newcastle? And who, pray tell, is Mr Newcastle, that you should visit him at night?" demanded Callender, brandishing the carving knife as he passed a plate of ham to Aunt Penelope.

"Why the spirit medium, of course," she said as she took the plate. "We passed his house on the way to Kensal Green."

Felicia sank back farther into her corner under Callender's accusing stare. "The spirit medium!" he roared, then turned to Aunt Penelope. "Is this some of your nonsense?"

"It is my own idea, Reginald," Felicia said quietly.

"I positively forbid it."

"You will forbid me nothing before I become your wife. You know how I long to know what lies behind this life. Why should you want to deny me?"

"Because it's all fraud and nonsense and superstition. How can an intelligent girl like you believe in such antiquated fancies in this day and age? This is 1847, and we are in an age of progress when such things should be cast aside once and for all."

"We progress in many things, Reginald; and why should not the knowledge of what lies beyond the veil be one of them? You must have heard of what Mr David Home has achieved, and I am told that Mr Newcastle's gifts are even more remarkable. I am certain that there are persons with the ability to see things that are invisible to us."

"What they see that's invisible to you is that you are a gullible woman with too much money. What's dead is dead, Felicia, and best forgotten."

She rose from her chair and clasped her hands together earnestly. "But the dead do live on, Reginald. How can you doubt it? Aren't you a Christian?"

Callender hacked viciously at the ham. "Yes, I'm a Christian. Church of England every Sunday, and money in the plate. But what do you think the Reverend Mr Fisher would say if he knew you were raising spooks? And what do you really know about this fellow Newcastle? Must be a lunatic. It isn't safe, and I ask you again to forget this folly."

"I have promised to act as my niece's chaperone," volunteered Aunt Penelope as she helped herself to more sherry. "And in exchange she has agreed to accompany me to the Dead Room at Madame Tussaud's. Neither of us is quite brave enough to indulge her fancy alone, but we do intend to have our curiosity satisfied, Mr Callender."

"What? The place *Punch* calls The Chamber of Horrors? That's a fine place for a sensitive girl, I must say, but at least I suppose it's harmless. But this master of goblins is quite another matter. He's either a charlatan or a madman, and the fact that you are two helpless females instead of one does nothing to reassure me. I'll wager he wants more than a few shillings for admission too, eh?"

Aunt Penelope moved to her niece's side and put a hand on her shoulder which Felicia took gratefully.

"We shall not be dissuaded," said Aunt Penelope.

Callender smiled ruefully. "Then I suppose I must accompany you," he said.

"Oh, Reginald, will you?" Felicia asked eagerly. "Please come with us. I hope to speak with my mother and father again, and perhaps Mr Newcastle will let you commune with your Uncle William."

"I trust my Uncle William is happy where he is, Felicia, and I would not wish to drag him down again to the clay, even if I believed I could. Let him rest in peace, I say."

He put his arms around Felicia and led her across the room to a love seat as far removed as possible from the food that the dead man had ordered. "Can you not forget the dead?" he asked her. "We are among the living now, and whatever questions we have to ask of our forebears will be answered in due time. Until then, it is our duty to live our lives as best we can. Will you live for me instead of these idle dreams?"

Felicia's fingers stroked his face, but her eyes remained distant, "How can we know what we should do," she demanded, "when we do not know what lies ahead of us? How much pleasure can we take here, when we know it is only a school for the lessons we shall learn?"

"We may have been born to die," said Callender, "but that is only part of it. The pleasures offered to us here are not our enemies. We are young and wealthy, Felicia. We are blessed. Let us not spurn fate's favors."

"He's right, you know," said Aunt Penelope as she cut into a pie. "We shall be quit of this world soon enough without denying it. But still, Mr Callender, we shall make our visits."

"And if you must," he said, "I shall be with you."

He might have said more, but the butler interrupted him.

"Yes, Booth?" he murmured as the old man bent down to whisper in his ear. Callender rose, bowed to the ladies, and hurried out into the hall.

And there in the twilight stood the gaunt form of Mr Entwistle. "I know how these things are, sir," he said, "and I would not wish to keep you waiting." He handed Callender a few small objects tied in a handkerchief. "His rings, his pins, and his watch," he said.

Callender cringed, but thanked the undertaker nonetheless.

"I understand entirely," said Mr Entwistle. "It is not all uncommon for young gentlemen to experience a temporary embarrassment while waiting for the reading of the will. You may be sure that your uncle's estate will compensate us for our trouble." He bowed and slithered back into the gathering darkness.

Reginald Callender stood with his uncle's jewelry in his hand and a wave of disgust pouring over him. While Felicia worried about souls, he was forced to concern himself with the problem of raising enough money to keep the household in order. It was hardly gentlemanly behavior; in fact, it was almost like robbing the dead. Still, his uncle's adornments had been visible in the open coffin, yet had been rescued from the grave. Supported since childhood by the investments of his mother's brother, Callender truly had no notion of supporting himself except to sell what came to hand. It was only a temporary aberration, he told himself; soon the estate would make him rich.

Still, he was angry with himself, and more angry with Felicia for concerning herself with spirits when he was so desperate for material comfort. He saw the maid hurrying across the hallway and called out to her.

"Alice," he said. "come here for a moment."

The girl came slowly toward him.

"Are you happy with your position here?"

"Oh, yes sir," said Alice.

"And were you happy with my uncle?"

Alice blushed and nodded.

"Then we shall continue the same arrangement now that I am master?"

"Just as you say, sir," said Alice.

"Very well. My visitors will be leaving soon. I shall expect you later this evening, Alice. Everything will be as it was before. I will expect you at ten. And bring my uncle's riding crop."

II. The Resurrection Men

The boy with the crowbar strapped to his leg ordered another pint of beer. He rarely drank the stuff, because it cost too much and he had no head for it anyway, but tonight he felt as jumpy as a cat, and certain of enough money to buy a whole barrel if he liked. And anyway, he told himself, it would be Syd's fault if he got drunk. They had agreed to meet an hour ago in this pub, "The World Turned Upside Down," and since Syd was so late, it became necessary to keep buying beer. Henry could hardly expect to stay inside without spending money, and even at that there had been a few jokes about his age, but Henry Donahue was unconcerned. He was fifteen, after all, and old enough to drink all he could hold, and old enough to rob a grave. Still, he wished Syd would hurry.

Henry had picked the place himself, even though he had never been inside before, partly for its proximity to Kensal Green and partly because he had always liked its sign. Whether the globe on it was really upside down he could not have said, but something in the idea appealed to him. And things were quiet enough inside, which he supposed was good, though he would have preferred enough of a crowd to make him feel a bit less conspicuous. He was looking around the dim room, convinced that all the other patrons were watching him, when he saw the door open and Syd's sharp, pimply face peer in. Henry gulped down the last of his drink and walked briskly toward the door. Syd was half way inside, but Henry pushed him out again.

"Let me come in for a minute, will you?" protested Syd.

"You're late enough without dawdling here any longer, don't you think?"

"I know, I know, but I'm cold enough already, aren't I? Is it my fault if I couldn't get away?"

"It'll be your fault if we're any later, Syd. I can't be out all night, you know."

"You smell like you already have been, mate. A fine thing, drinking on the job. You won't be much good for picking locks now, will you?"

Henry grabbed Syd's arm to quiet him. A lamplighter was shuffling down the empty street toward them, the yellow fog of London dimming the light of the small hand-lamp he carried. The two boys leaned against the building with feigned unconcern, Henry gazing at the sign while Syd read the words guaranteeing the availability of Courage and Company's Entire and wondered how much of it Henry had consumed. The old man climbed up his ladder, turned the gas cock, applied his lamp, and scrambled down again, leaving the entrance to the public house only a little brighter than it had been before. The boys waited until his footsteps had died away.

"You were really scared of him, weren't you?" sneered Syd. "Maybe you should run home now and forget all this, Henry."

"I'm not scared of anything. But there's no point in letting anyone know what we're up to, is there? Burke and Hare were hanged, weren't they?"

"They were murderers, you dunce, and we're not even stealing bodies. There's no market for 'em anymore, is there? All we're doing is relieving the old gent of some jewelry that he'll never miss. It would be a crime to let it rot with him, wouldn't it?"

"Not a crime you can be charged with," Henry said.

"Well, if you don't want the money, mate, you run along."

But Henry was already walking toward the cemetery, pulling his cap down over his shaggy red hair and turning his collar up against the cold and the eyes of passersby.

"You're sure he's got all this stuff on him, are you, Syd?"

"I saw it, didn't I? There's not much else to do when you work for an undertaker but look at the bodies. Just like there's not much for an apprentice locksmith to do but learn how to open things. I've just been waiting to meet a partner like you, Henry. We're in business now, you know, and we have splendid prospects."

The closer they got to Kensal Green the more unhappy Henry was. The houses were thinning out here, the lights were farther apart, and the fog filled the empty spaces. Henry began to feel as if he were lost somewhere out in the countryside, and would have happily turned back at once except for a certain reluctance to disgrace himself in front of Syd: it was easier to face corpses than to admit to a boy a year older than himself that he wanted nothing more out of life than to be back in his bed in a garret.

Henry watched his feet slip over the damp cobblestones; they were almost all he could see. The dark was bad enough, but the fog was worse. "We'll never find it," Henry said.

"What do you mean, we'll never find it? We're here!"

Henry looked up and saw something like a temple looming through the mist. There were columns and walls and fences, and it looked to

him less like a churchyard than the Bank of England. The gigantic
gates were clearly locked, and he could perceive nothing behind
them but another wall of impenetrable fog.

"I don't want to open those gates," he said. "Someone might come
along."

"Don't worry," Syd insisted. "We'll just climb the wall."

"What's the use?" said Henry. "We can't find anything in there.
The fog."

"I know where it is, don't I? How many times have I been here,
eh? It's my job. Just give me a leg up. Come on, over here."

Henry almost ran away, but he didn't. Instead he hurried toward
the sound of Syd's voice, and was almost relieved to be touching
someone else, even if it was his partner in a crime that he would
have willingly abandoned. At least he was not alone. He squatted,
close to the ground where the air was a little clearer, and made his
hands into a cradle for Syd's foot.

Syd scrambled up, and Henry thought for an instant that he had
broken a wrist. He grunted, and then lost Syd in the fog. "Where
are you? Are you up?" A hand dropped down to him.

"Here. Grab it. Come on. Get off the street!"

Henry grabbed onto Syd's wrist and felt himself hauled up
against the wall, scraping and squirming until he reached the
top. "You're up?" said Syd. "Then drop down," and suddenly
Henry was alone again.

He looked into the opaque night, shivered at the thought of an
observer, and dropped into the darkness. He landed on Syd, and
both of them tumbled on the wet grass of All Soul's Cemetery.

"That's fine. You'll kill us both."

"Are we in? Where are we, Syd?"

"Kensal Green, my boy. We're in. Follow me."

"Wait a minute, Syd! Where are you? You can't know where we're
going."

"I tell you I know this place like I know my mother, even if I
haven't seen her for years."

"Give us your hand then, will you? I'm lost."

"Take hold then. You'll hold a prettier hand than this one, once
we're done."

Henry hung onto Syd, wandering through a sea of fog that might
have been Heaven or Hell. From time to time a monument loomed
up, a spire or an angel or a slab. Some of them were huge. He let
Syd drag him through the clouds. It was so cold that his nose began
to run, and all at once he was hungry. "We'll never find it, Syd. Let's
go home."

"No. We'll never find it?"

Something loomed in the fog. Henry blinked twice and then sat down. "It's big enough," he said.

"The lock is small."

A gray box squatted in the yellow fog. A stone box, its roof pointed, with pillars beside the door. Two figures made of marble stood on either side of the door; they looked to Henry like women in nightshirts. He couldn't see much, but what he saw was enough.

Syd knocked on the door while Henry shuddered. "Mr Callender's residence?"

"Don't do that, Syd."

"No? Think he'll wake up, do you? Don't worry, I threw his guts away myself. If he did rise up, he'd fall right over."

"That's not funny."

"Don't laugh, then. Just open the door."

"I can't."

"You haven't even tried yet. You're terrified, that's what's wrong with you."

"I can't see, can I? How do you expect me to work?"

"I got a bunch of Lucifers, and I told you what the lock is like. Just work. The sooner you start, the sooner we'll be out of here."

Syd lit a match, and the way it colored his eyes was enough to send Henry toward the lock. He reached in his pocket and produced several instruments.

"I'd love to know how to work those."

"I'll teach you. Then you can do this by yourself."

"Don't be like that. Just a few more minutes, and we'll be rich men, Henry. You take care of the lock, and I'll take care of the body, all right?"

"Splendid," muttered Henry, his stiff fingers fumbling. He heard something snap, then wished he hadn't. Syd pushed him toward the metal door, and it fell away before them into hideous blackness. Henry twitched and looked toward the sky, but all he saw was the name "Callender" carved in the marble over his head. He lost his balance and sprawled against a wet wall as Syd shoved him into the house of the dead. The stink of dying flowers turned his stomach. He sat down in a corner and watched Syd strike another match and light a candle with it. The light flickered around stone walls like slabs. Henry looked outside and glimpsed a shadow. "There's something out there, Syd."

"Ghosts."

"Don't be smart, I saw a dog."

"Then shut the door and he won't see us."

"Too late for that," he said, but he pushed the iron door back.

Immediately he felt trapped. He hurriedly caught the edge of the door before it could swing shut, pulled the crowbar out from under the leg of his jagged trousers, and braced it against the jamb. The opening allayed his fear slightly, even when he saw wisps of fog drift through it, but Syd was not pleased with his handiwork.

"What do you think you're doing with that, then? Have you been walking stiff-legged all night so we could have a doorstop? Give it here."

Henry handed it over reluctantly, unhappy to be farther from the exit and closer to the sinister oblong of stone that brooded in the center of the small, dark room. Syd stuck the candle to the floor with its drippings, then turned to the sarcophagus and began to pry off its lid. Henry backed away at the hideous sound of scraping, grating stone and put one foot outside the tomb, relieved to find that they were not already imprisoned by some uncanny force. Syd pushed and grunted against the ponderous weight while Henry prayed that he would fail to move it.

"You could help," gasped Syd.

"A bargain's a bargain. The lock was my job, and the body's yours."

"It's only another box in there. It won't hurt you."

"I know it won't, since I'm not going near it."

"All right, then!" Syd threw himself furiously on the bar and the stone slab tilted ominously. For an instant he hung counterbalanced in the air; then the lid screeched and fell to the floor with a crash that sounded to Henry like the end of the world. And at the same instant Syd dropped on the other side and snuffed out the candle. The echoing tomb was black.

"Oh my God," whispered Henry.

"He's not likely to be much help to you when you're on a job like this one, is he, mate?"

Something shuffled in the dark, and another of Syd's matches burst into flame, making his face as red as a painted devil's, but no less reassuring to Henry for that. He was amazed to discover that he had not run away, then realized that he had been too startled to move. Syd lit the broken candle and handed it to him. "Hold this," he said.

"I don't want to look."

"Of course you do. I'll bet that's half of why you came."

Henry didn't answer, but neither did he turn away when Syd approached the oaken coffin in its bed of stone. The candle flame shimmered in his shaking hand, and he knew without a doubt that

when the coffin opened a hideously mouldering corpse would rise
from its depths and drag him straight to Hell. He thought he heard
a dog howl somewhere outside. He closed his eyes. Wood croaked,
and then he heard Syd groan. The groan rose into a wail.

"We've been robbed!"

"What?" Henry opened his eyes, and for an instant saw nothing
but Syd's red, furious face.

"Look for yourself! It must have been old Entwistle, the grasping,
bloody bastard. He's taken it all. The rings, the watch, the stickpin,
too. There's nothing left but the damn body!"

Unwilling to believe his ears, Henry moved with the light until
he could see into the coffin. He quickly checked the pale fingers and
the black cravat. Nothing gleamed on them. He began to curse, then
realized that he was staring into the face of a dead man.

It was not as bad as he had imagined. Just a plump old boy
with rosy cheeks, really nothing to be afraid of; he looked as if he
were taking a nap. It was only when Henry's nostrils caught the
mingled odors of flowers, chemicals, and death that his stomach
began to heave.

And then the iron door behind him crashed open.

Henry screamed, dropped the candle, and spun toward the sound.
Silhouetted against the foggy night stood the gigantic figure of a man,
his outstretched arms barring the way out of the tomb. Henry's mind
went blank, his fanciful fear of the corpse forgotten in the sudden and
very real conviction that he was doomed. The blood drained out of
his face as he saw himself on the gallows, and he could hold on to
only one idea: I'm caught, I'm caught, I'm caught. He hardly heard
the low, calm voice of the figure at the door.

"Have you found what you seek?"

Henry was amazed to hear Syd's brassy answer.

"Nah, there's nothing here. Somebody's stripped him bare."

Another match flared. Syd's hand was steady, his expression
insolent. "Bring that candle over here, will you, Henry?"

Henry was startled into action, almost believing that Syd's bold-
ness might somehow set them free. Not even a second flame showed
much of the dark intruder's face as he spoke again.

"These dead are mine."

"And welcome to 'em," answered Syd, moving back toward the
doorway with the crowbar held behind his back. Henry followed
him like a sonambulist, but stopped dead when he saw the tall
man's face. The skin was pale under long, stringy black hair; the
lips were hidden by a drooping black mustache; the eyes seemed
no more than dark hollows, the left bisected by a scar that ran from

brow to chin. The countenance was so expressionless that it might
have been a mask.

"It's not the caretaker," Henry heard himself saying, "it's that
spirit reader from across the way."

"That's torn it," said Syd, and he swung for the man's head
with the crowbar. The blow never landed. Henry stood frozen and
watched a long white hand shoot out to grasp Syd's wrist while
another attached itself to its face, the fingers scrabbling like a pale
spider. The man opened his arms in a gesture that seemed almost
hospitable, and Syd's hand came off at the wrist in a shower of blood
while the flesh of his face was ripped from the bones.

Henry dropped the candle again and dove for the darkness where
the door had been.

He tumbled to the ground in a blind panic and crawled through
the yellow fog. He thought about God. He ran.

A tree stopped him. It bloodied his nose and broke two fingers,
but he got up and ran again.

A low tombstone caught him just below the kneecap. He rolled
in the wet grass and whimpered. Then he arose and limped away.

He couldn't see where he was going, but he didn't stop until the
agony of his broken leg compelled him to. He rested under a marble
angel and waited for death to come.

It came on black wings.

III. The Spiritualist

The house near the cemetery where he had buried his Uncle William
was so nondescript that Reginald Callender scarcely remembered
having passed it twice before. He was almost disappointed. He had
expected something either gaudy or else picturesquely dilapidated
and sinister, but Mr Sebastian Newcastle's dwelling was an unpretentious house of good English brick, perhaps fifty years old. The
tall cypresses surrounding it had a slightly funereal air, but that was
all. Every window was dark but one, which glowed faintly through
the fog.

Callender had accompanied Felicia and her Aunt Penelope despite
his misgivings; he was not a man to tolerate argument from a
woman, especially one he expected to have as his bride, and he
was deeply suspicious of Felicia's interest in this spirit medium,
who was certainly a charlatan and probably a criminal who prayed
on the sentiments of bereaved ladies. And the fact that the man he
already thought of as his enemy was so unpretentious in his tastes

gave Callender pause. Subtlety always irritated him.

He helped Aunt Penelope out of the coach, and then Felicia, listening with approval when she told the driver to wait. Soon he would be giving orders to her servants himself, but until his uncle's estate could be settled he had so little cash on hand that he had been obliged to dismiss his own coachman, although he could hardly get along without the household servants, especially Alice. She would have to go soon enough, he told himself, but a glance at Felicia told him that the sacrifice would be worthwhile. Sometimes he wondered why it was necessary to wed a lady in order to bed her, but that was the way of the world, and meanwhile there were willing wenches in it.

A shapeless shadow flitted across the window as they approached the house, one of the ladies on each of his arms, and the look of it somehow sickened him, but they did not seem to have noticed. He opened his mouth to begin again his arguments about the foolish recklessness of the business they were embarked upon, but thought better of it. He had already decided to show them, and that was why he was here. The old woman was simply a sensation seeker, and would be just as happy to discover that the spiritualist was a fraud, but Felicia was something of a fanatic on the subject, and that would never do. Still, this night's work should settle that, and another night's work, after the wedding, would provide her with a new interest in life. Determined to take matters in his own hand, Callender rapped on the door with a gloved fist.

While he waited impatiently, Felicia reached past him and pulled on a narrow, rattling chain that he had never noticed. "The bell," she explained. "He may not hear you knocking from upstairs."

"No lights upstairs," said Callender. "Besides, I saw someone move down here, unless it was one of his confederates."

"Mr Newcastle has no need of confederates, nor has he any need of light."

Aunt Penelope, thrilled into temporary silence by her approach to the land that lies beyond death, gave a little squeal when the door in front of them abruptly opened.

A tall man stood on the threshold with a silver candlestick in his hand, a single flame illuminating a lean, pale face that was shadowed by black hair and a long mustache. Callender was startled for a moment by the scar, then dismissed it as an effective theatrical touch and spent most of the next few minutes trying to decide if it were real. The man, who was quite clearly Newcastle rather than a servant, stepped back silently and ushered them into an empty hall with a dusty carpet of no determinable pattern.

At the end of the hallway was a double door, and beyond that a room that seemed unnaturally dark even after their host had brightened it with his lone candle. Callender saw that both the floor and the ceiling had been painted black, and that black velvet draperies completely covered the walls. A small round table sat there surrounded by four high-backed wooden chairs; all of them appeared to have been made of ebony. The medium set his candlestick in the center of the table and stood quietly waiting for his visitors to follow him into the gloomy chamber. His clothing was a black as Callender's mourning, so that only his white face and hands were distinctly visible, apparently floating disembodied in the air. When the ladies entered with their dark cloaks and bonnets the effect was much the same, and Callender had no reason to believe that he looked any different. The illusion was disconcerting.

The two women sat down across from one another, but Mr Reginald Callender remained on his feet, squinting into the shadows where Sebastian Newcastle's eyes were hidden. He expected the spiritualist to flinch before his penetrating stare, but the fellow was imperturbable, and ultimately it was Callender who turned away in what he told himself was pure disdain. A mounting sense of irritation caused him to break the long silence at last.

"Well! Bring on your spooks sir, or must we pay you for them first?"

"Reginald!" Felicia's voice was harsher than he had ever heard it sound, and before he knew what had happened he was seated beside her, feeling very much like a chastened schoolboy and wondering for the first time if married life might be something less than pleasant. Aunt Penelope suppressed a nervous giggle. Callender had a deep desire to lash out at someone, but had difficulty deciding who it should be. Sebastian Newcastle sat down across the table from him.

"There will be no charge for your visit, Mr Callender, since I do not expect you to enjoy it."

"I don't know, I've always enjoyed conjuring tricks, but you won't find me as easy to fool as some of your visitors."

"Miss Lamb and her aunt are hardly fools, Mr Callender, even if they do seek to be still wiser than they are. And have you never wondered what waits beyond the grave?"

"We have churches to tell us that, and not for money."

"Your churches are far richer than I am, and likely to remain so."

"Well, Mr Newcastle, you'll have a chance to change that tonight. Here's ten guineas." Callender reached into his waistcoat pocket and placed the money on the table. He could ill afford to lose it. "If I see anything here that I cannot explain, that belongs to you." He pointed emphatically to the cash and noticed to his amazement that it was gone. "By God!" he said. "These are very materialistic spirits, sir."

"You will find that they have returned the money to your pocket, Mr Callender."

Callender felt for the money and almost forgot himself enough to curse.

"Is it there?" asked Aunt Penelope.

"I think Reginald's face answers that question for him," observed Felicia coldly. "Really, Reginald, we have not come here to insult our host, but to learn from him. Do be quiet, if only to please me. Mr Newcastle has promised to summon my parents tonight."

"Your parents were killed in a railway accident twelve years ago, Felicia, and if your father had not been one of the chief stockholders in that railway, this man would have no interest in him or in you."

"He will certainly have no interest if you will not give him the peace he needs to pierce the veil."

Callender reminded himself again that he had determined to hold his tongue, and realized ruefully that he should have done so. Even Aunt Penelope had said almost nothing.

"Silence is an aid to concentration," Newcastle said evenly.

Callender nodded almost imperceptibly, and was delighted to find himself rewarded at once when Felicia took his hand. He was more than a little startled, though, when Aunt Penelope did the same, and then he surmised that this was common behavior at a seance. Still, it took all his willpower to refrain from comment when he saw his fiancée's delicate fingers in the pale clutch of the man with the dark eyes.

The four of them sat quietly in the black room, Callender never taking his eyes from the medium who gradually sank back in his chair and allowed his head to slump forward. He looked like an old man dozing after a heavy dinner, reminding Callender of his Uncle William. After a few minutes the atmosphere grew chilly, and Callender was almost convinced that he could feel a damp breeze waft past him, although he could see no way it could have come into the room. Still, it was enough to make him look around uncomfortably, taking his eyes off the medium just long enough for something strange to happen.

For a moment Callender thought the man might be on fire. Vague tendrils of smoke seemed to be rising from his head, but they looked more like mist than smoke, and they wove patterns in the air that did not seem natural. Callender turned to his right and his left, but the two women holding his hands were not dismayed, and seemed to be regarding the display with intelligent approval. The medium groaned, and now his head was almost hidden by shifting fingers of mist. He seemed to be dissolving into the darkness. Callender started involuntarily and had half risen from his chair when a blast of frigid wind roared at him from across the table. The candle flame went out.

He felt Felicia's grip on his fingers increase till it was almost painful, and a certain unexpected weakness in his knees compelled him to sink down into his seat again. Nothing was visible except the writhing cloud of mist which seemed to glow with its own faint luminescence. He tried to convince himself that it was some sort of trick with chemicals, but he was not happy looking at it, especially when it began to coalesce into features which were not those of Sebastian Newcastle.

It was the face of a woman, its mouth working feebly as if it did not have the strength to speak. A sound came from somewhere that was like whispering, or the scurrying of rats. The face shifted and flickered, and sometimes it seemed to be a man with a full beard. Now there were two whispers, one lower than the other, and Callender began to believe that he could hear what they were saying. It was one word, repeated over and over again: "Felicia."

Callender knew that his hands were trembling, and hoped the women would not notice. The light of the glowing mist was gleaming in Felicia's eyes as she leaned forward across the table, and Callender was dismayed by the eagerness with which she seemed to welcome this horror, whether it was fraudulent or not. He hoped it was an illusion, for he had no wish to think it real, yet it infuriated him to realize that he could be frightened by a humbug. He closed his eyes, but the sound of the whispering, wavering voices was even more disturbing when he was blind to their source. He would have preferred to leave.

"Felicia," whispered the sibilant chorus. "Beware, daughter. Beware of false friends. There is one here whom you must not trust."

"Who is it?" asked Felicia breathlessly. She and her aunt stared into the shifting mist."

"It is the man," the voices cried.

"Which man?"

"The man who tells you these damned lies!" shouted Callender. He pushed back his chair and pulled his hands free while the floating faces burst into brilliant light and disappeared into impenetrable darkness. He fumbled for a match while Aunt Penelope screamed.

Callender struck a light on the side of the table and applied it at once to the candle. The two women stood behind him, clutched in one another's arms, and an indistinct figure sat slumped in the medium's chair. Callender waited for another trick, fearful that the flame would be extinguished again, but there was only silence in the black room. The body of Sebastian Newcastle was ominously still.

"Is he dead?" asked Aunt Penelope.

"I hope so," muttered Callender. He walked briskly to the figure in the chair and grasped it roughly by the hair to pull its hanging head up into the light. The features that rose up to meet him were those of his Uncle William.

The waxy eyelids were closed, but the full lips moved. "Dead," said Uncle William.

Aunt Penelope gasped and swayed into the arms of her niece, who hurried the fainting woman from the room with brisk efficiency, while Callender stood as if paralyzed and stared into the face of a familiar corpse. His fingers slipped slowly from its head, and its lips twisted themselves into a comfortable grin. When the eyes opened they were William Callender's: he might have been alive again.

"Surprised, are you my boy? Well, there will be more surprises in store for you soon. Wait till you talk to old Frobisher tomorrow about my will!"

Callender was hardly listening, although he would have cause to remember those words soon enough. Whatever it was in the chair seemed so relaxed and genial that it convinced him more than an army of phantoms could have done. "Is it really you?" he asked.

"Of course it's me!"

"Back from the dead?"

"Not so far to come, really. Takes time to travel on, you know. Especially for someone like me, who's not what you could call spiritually advanced. But this Newcastle is a very clever fellow, and he's helping me along. Don't trifle with him, my boy."

Callender had almost forgotten that he was speaking to a ghost. Everything was very natural, and full of the ordinary irritations of talking with his uncle. "The man is a threat to Felicia," insisted the irate nephew. "Even the spirits of her parents told her so."

"Oh, no, my dear boy. They were talking about you."

"Me? Why should she beware of me?"

"You're not so spiritually advanced yourself, are you, Reginald? Much too interested in the pleasures of the flesh, of course, and very bad tempered on top of it. And possessive, of course. I'm sure you'd make the poor girl miserable. And I'm sorry to say you're really no more than a fortune hunter. You really should be more careful. Look."

Uncle William pointed to the door, and Reginald Callender turned to find Felicia standing there. Evidently she had heard everything. Callender felt a hot flush roar up his throat as he whirled to confront his uncle, but the figure in the chair was Sebastian Newcastle, smiling with his sharp teeth and holding a pack of cards in one hand. "Will you have your fortune told before you go, Mr Callender? No? Then I bid you a good evening." And with that the medium glided out of the chair and through the black velvet curtains that covered the walls.

Callender hurried to his fiancée's side. "Did you see him? Did you see Uncle William?"

Felicia nodded. "And so did Aunt Penelope. I had to help her out to the carriage, but she swears she never had such a stimulating evening in her life."

"And did you hear what he said?"

"Only what Mr Newcastle said to you. And since he has retired I believe we should follow his example."

Callender wondered for the first time but not the last if it was possible that she was mocking him. Yet he was confused enough to take her arm and walk halfway down the hall with her before he pulled away.

"He's a fraud, I tell you, and I can prove it." He hurried back into the black room, devoid of a strategy but determined to redeem himself. He glared around at emptiness and then rushed to a wall. "All tricks," he told himself. "The curtains!"

He grasped two fistfuls of midnight velvet and pulled them apart, peering fiercely through them, ready for almost any sight but the one that confronted him. There was no machinery, no hidden door. There was not even a wall. There was only the night, an ebony void where clouds of yellow fog obscured the stars. Callender swayed, keeping his feet only because he held onto the curtains. For a moment he felt like a man lying on his back and staring up at the sky. His head reeled.

Then he turned on his heel and walked stiffly out of the house to the carriage where the women waited.

IV. The Inheritance

Callender would have wasted no time in visiting his uncle's solicitor in any case, but the ghostly warning he had received was so alarming that he was awake and dressed and in the offices of Frobisher and Jarndyce long before the hour of noon. He tried to convince himself that what he had seen had been a dream, or a trick, or perhaps the result of mesmerism, which reportedly had the power to make a man see anything, but certainly the previous evening's entertainment was enough to make an heir curious about the terms of the will that would determine his future.

Rising early proved to be a fruitless gesture, however, since Callender was not expected until afternoon, and Clarence Frobisher had chosen to spend the morning in Chancery. A clerk had left the heir apparent to cool his heels in Frobisher's dusty chambers with no company and no entertainment except a shelf of leather bound law books. More than once Callender toyed with the idea of nipping out for a quick one, but missing his man would have been intolerable, and truth to tell, he had an almost superstitious conviction that fortune would favor him if he remained sober until the momentous meeting had been concluded.

Nothing prevented him from dozing, however, and his brain was as foggy as the streets of London when he opened one eye suspiciously and discovered the solicitor making his stately entrance, marred only by a cough which may have been intended to wake his client.

Clarence Frobisher, as Callender had had occasion to observe before, was a man with a very dry manner and an equally wet face. His voice was rasping and sandy; his attitude was distant and aloof; but his brow was perpetually dabbled with perspiration, his rheumy eyes seemed always on the verge of tears, and a soiled handkerchief was never far from his dripping nose. Callender had never liked Frobisher, but he was prepared to overlook the solicitor's personal shortcomings in exchange for the speedy delivery of Uncle William's estate.

Frobisher nodded and adjusted his rusty black suit as he lowered himself into an old horse-hair chair behind his heavy mahogany desk, its surface littered with papers and broken bits of sealing wax. He glanced at a document, reached for a quill pen, then seemed to recollect himself and peered at Callender over his gold eyeglasses.

"Mr Callender?"

"I've come about my Uncle William's estate."

"Well, sir. You are prompt. More than prompt, I might say."

"There is no difficulty with the will, I hope?"

"Difficulty?"

"No changes?"

"Changes? Certainly not."

Reginald Callender, now a man of property, allowed himself the luxury of a sigh. Yet something continued to nag at him. Perhaps it was the expression on Frobisher's moist lips. Had it been anyone else, he would have suspected the man was smiling.

"Then I am still the sole heir?"

"Sole heir? Yes, in a manner of speaking. There are other considerations. My fee, for one."

"Well," said Callender expansively, "I hope you will be handsomely paid."

"I have seen to that. Your uncle settled with me when the will was drawn."

"Nothing else, then?"

"The funeral arrangements were the first order of business, according to your uncle's orders. He wished no expense to be spared. There is a substantial bill from Entwistle and Son, but this is a pittance compared to the cost of the marble mausoleum."

Callender, who had not even considered this, felt thousands slipping through his fingers. "But of course the estate is large enough to pay for this," he suggested nervously.

"Precisely."

"And there is nothing else?"

"Nothing."

Something in this last exchange made Callender feel hollow inside. He could not shake off the feeling that Frobisher was toying with him. He watched the handkerchief working and wondered if the solicitor was laughing behind it.

"When I say nothing else," Callender began, "I mean no other claims against my uncle's fortune."

"Precisely."

"And when you say the estate is precisely large enough . . ."

"I am speaking as plainly as I can, Mr Callender."

Frobisher blew his nose and made a choking, wheezing sound.

"Then be plainer still, or be damned, sir! How much is left for me? Speak!"

Frobisher pocketed his handkerchief and picked up a sheet of paper. He glanced at it, blinked, and handed it to Callender. "What is left for you," he said, and paused to clear his throat, "is precisely nothing."

Callender looked at the desk, studying the grain of the wood. He found the pattern oddly intriguing; it held his attention totally for some time, long enough in fact for the solicitor to become somewhat alarmed.

"Mr Callender?"

"What?"

"A glass of port, perhaps?"

Callender laughed for an instant, and watched as the solicitor stepped to a sideboard and poured the wine. It struck him as really very decent of the old boy. He could hardly think of anything else except that he would be grateful for the drink, and when he gulped it down, it did restore him to a semblance of sanity. Then all at once his thoughts were racing so fast that he was almost dizzy.

"Nothing left?" he asked. "What became of it all?"

"He spent it."

"All of it? But he was worth a bloody fortune!"

"So he was, Mr Callender. Not even the bad investments he made in India could have made a pauper of him—or should I say of you? There's still some accounting to be made in regard to that, but I doubt if you will see enough from the colonies to stand you a good dinner."

"And the rest of it?"

"As I have said. It is more common than you might suppose for an elderly man of affairs to awake one day and realize that his hours with us are numbered, and that the money he has struggled to accumulate has brought him very little in the way of pleasure. Faced with the choices of delighting you or delighting himself, your uncle unhesitatingly decided on the latter course. You might say that he went out in a blaze of glory. Women, of course, and quite a bit of gambling as well. I suppose if he had won he would have been obliged to leave you something. . . ."

"But to have spent so much," Callender began.

"He became quite a generous man in his last days. Quite a bit was spent on diamonds, and I personally arranged the gift of a handsome residence to one of his favorite mistresses. He also gave substantial sums to some of the household servants, the only stipulation being that they remain in service until the day after he was laid to rest. There was a man named Booth, and a housemaid; I think her name was Alice. They should be gone by now."

Callender thought back to the empty house which he had hardly noticed in his eagerness to visit Frobisher and Jarndyce. "I should have whipped her harder," he muttered.

"I beg your pardon?"

"Nothing. At least there's still the house."

"Mortgaged to the hilt, I'm afraid. I think he meant for you to have it, but he surprised his doctors and himself by living longer than he anticipated, and his funds were very low. Still, you might realize something if you can sell it before the inevitable foreclosure. And there might be a bit left over from the Indian disaster; I believe your uncle's representative is on a ship bound for England now. A Mr Nigel Stone."

"Cousin Nigel! That idiot! No wonder everything was lost."

Frobisher consulted another document. "I understand that you were offered the post, but preferred to remain in London at your uncle's expense. Is my information incorrect?"

Callender pushed himself up from his chair and strode toward the door. He threw it open, then turned for a parting shot. "Of course I'll contest the will," he said.

"And I would be happy to represent you, but I do advise against it, since you are in fact the sole beneficiary. The problem is that the whole estate was spent before your turn came. To spend what little you have left on legal fees would be ill-advised."

"I suppose that advice is free, is it?" Callender looked around desperately. "I believe the old bastard did this just to spite me."

"I would hardly put it as bluntly as that," suggested Frobisher. "Mr Callender! You have forgotten your stick."

Callender whirled in the doorway and stormed back into the room to retrieve his ebony walking stick. He was tempted to smash it across Frobisher's desk, but managed to stop himself in time with the realization that he could hardly afford to replace it.

Reginald Callender retreated to the nearest public house and drank three glasses of neat gin in quick succession, but even that was not enough to keep his hand from trembling. He left the place and began to walk toward the house where Sally lived, trusting that the time the journey took would enable him to collect his thoughts.

In a sense Sally Wood was his mistress, though he was hardly fool enough to imagine that he was the only man who shared her favors. It was a considerable source of pride to him, however, to reflect that he was almost certainly the only one of her lovers who had never been obliged to pay her. She liked him, apparently; it pleased Callender to believe that was because he was more distinguished than most of the men she met at the music hall. Still, it was at least possible that his stature as the nephew of a wealthy and elderly gentleman had something to do with Sally's attitude; Callender wondered what she would say if she were to learn that he was destitute. Not that he would tell her, of course, but providing her with little presents or even the occasional meal might become a problem very soon. The real difficulty, though, lay with Felicia; the panic with which he contemplated keeping his poverty from her was what drove him on toward Sally's door.

Callender possessed a key to her lodging house, but after ascending the dark stairs he felt it advisable to pause at the door to her room before entering. He listened stealthily, always conscious of the occasion when he had intruded on a scene he would have chosen not to witness, yet there was no sound from inside but a woman's voice humming a snatch of song. Callender knocked. There was a rustling from within, and then the door opened to reveal Sally, undressed except for a black corset trimmed with red silk. A hairbrush backed with mother-of-pearl was in her hand.

"Reggie! Hello, dear."

Callender's brief touch of irritation at her use of the detested pet name was soon smothered in the warmth of her embrace. Enveloped in a cloud of perfume, he maneuvered Sally back across the threshold and shut the door behind him, then kissed her ravenously while his hands crawled over her exposed flesh. After a few moments she pushed him away, gasping and laughing at the same time. "A girl needs air, you know," she said, "and a lady likes to be spoken to first."

She sent him a smile over her shoulder, then sat down at a dressing table covered with pots of paint and powder. For the time Callender was content to lounge against the wall and watch as she brushed her gleaming chestnut hair. Sally was such a contrast to Felicia: ruddy rather than pale, voluptuous rather than slender, and distinctly physical rather than spiritual. It puzzled him that somehow he was not satisfied with Sally, who seemed to offer him everything he wanted, yet he was convinced with no proof to speak of that having his way with his fiancee would be a more stimulating experience than any that Sally could provide. It hardly mattered, though; Felicia's fortune in itself was sufficient to make her a much more suitable companion. A glance around the room was sufficient to convince Callender of that.

The cheerful disarray which might be charming in a mistress would be utterly unsuitable in a wife. The floor was dusty, the bed unmade, and every article of furniture was covered with piles of hastily discarded clothing. The general effect would have been the same, he thought, if there were an explosion in a dressmaker's shop.

A pamphlet half covered by a crumpled sheet caught his attention; he picked it up and straightened the wrinkled cover, embellished by a crude drawing of a cloaked, skeletal figure looming over a sleeping woman. Bats and gravestones decorated the lurid title: *Varney the Vampire, or The Feast of Blood.*

"Reading penny dreadfuls, Sally?"

"A girl gets bored sometimes. And it's a good story."

"It's rubbish."

"That's as may be, but it's exciting. It's about a gent who's dead, but he comes back at night and drinks people's blood. Sneaks right into their rooms, he does, and drains 'em dry while they sleep. He bites their throats." Sally touched her own throat to emphasize the point.

"Sounds deucedly unpleasant to me," observed Callender, flipping through the pages looking for more illustrations.

"And then they turn into vampires themselves, after he's done with them."

"He also seems to go about sticking logs into people," said Callender as he found a particularly lurid drawing.

"Oh, no Reggie. That's what they have to do to kill the vampires for good and all. Pound a stick of wood right into their hearts, they do." Sally laid a dramatic hand on her own substantial bosom.

"You don't believe this nonsense, do you?"

"I don't know about that, but it's something to think about, isn't it? Besides, I like the way it makes me feel. All goose pimply."

"Then I advise you to light a fire."

"Would you do it, Reggie dear? I've got my hands full."

"Getting ready to go out?"

"In a bit, dear. Why?"

"Because I know a better way to warm you up." Callender tossed the pamphlet back onto the bed and walked purposefully toward the dressing table. He buried his face in Sally's curly, perfumed hair and clutched one of her breasts in each of his hands. She arched her back, closed her eyes, and smiled as she felt his breath on her face.

"Go into a public for a drain of gin, did you?"

"Anything wrong with that?" asked Callender as he fumbled with her corset.

"You might have brought some with you."

"Aren't I intoxicating enough?"

"That you are, Reggie. It's wonderful to have a wealthy lover. Makes a girl feel special."

Callender tore at his cravat. "You'd love me without that, wouldn't you?"

"Of course I would. And I was sorry to hear about your uncle." She pushed his clumsy hands away and quickly undressed herself.

And before long they were on her bed, the forgotten copy of *Varney the Vampire* crushed beneath their thrashing bodies.

V. The Dead Room

The parade of kings stood still and a common man marched past. He was a guide, dressed in a uniform that made him look like a soldier, and he announced each crowned head of Europe in a hoarse voice that Callender found increasingly irritating. He was thoroughly sick of the officious little man and his apparently endless procession of wax effigies; his dislike of these soft statues and their false finery had begun before he had even entered Madame Tussaud's, when he had been informed that, due to the flammable nature of the exhibits, he would be obliged to throw away the last of his Uncle William's imported cigars.

And nothing before or after this affront to Callender had been calculated to soothe his temper. The expedition to Madame Tussaud's exhibition in Baker Street had begun disastrously when the cab Callender hired had arrived at Felicia Lamb's residence only to find her absent. Aunt Penelope, however, had been obtrusively present, coquettishly claiming Callender as her escort with the explanation that Mr Newcastle, the medium, had taken Felicia into his coach a quarter of an hour ago. Callender's initial indignation had rapidly given way to a feeling close to panic; he could not quite suppress the unreasonable fear that his fiancee had been abducted and he would never see her again. The journey to the wax museum, orchestrated by Aunt Penelope's incessant chatter, had been excruciating.

The upshot, which surprised him by irritating him, had been nothing at all. Felicia, eyes downcast demurely, had stood in the gaslit lobby of the Baker Street Bazaar, and she had been holding Sebastian Newcastle's long, thin arm. This apparent intimacy, combined with the anti-climax of it all, left Callender fuming, and as Aunt Penelope pulled him toward the exhibition, he thought he saw Felicia smile gratefully at her. Apparently Newcastle had paid for all their tickets, and there was nothing that Callender could reasonably be expected to do about that.

Callender's tour of the wax museum had become a nightmare long before he reached the chamber of horrors. He hardly noticed the exhibits, but he did not miss a single one of the glances exchanged by his fiancee and Sebastian Newcastle. They seemed to be hanging back deliberately, engaged in private conversation, while Callender was pushed forward by the press of the crowd and by Aunt Penelope,

a woman he would willingly have strangled. Callender's face was
hot, and his cravat was choking him: was it possible that Felicia was
deliberately snubbing him? He was so intent on the couple behind
him that he nearly knocked over the guide when the procession suddenly came to a halt in front of a door barred by a red velvet rope.

"This concludes the tour of the exhibition," announced the little
man in the blue uniform. "The general exhibition, that is. But behind
me, ladies and gentlemen, behind this rope, behind this door, there
stands The Dead Room. Or, as some have been generous to call it,
Madame Tussaud's Chamber of Horrors. Those of you who have
purchased tickets for this special display may follow me now, but
I caution you that this is a room filled with effigies of evil and
engines of extermination. Here are the most notorious murderers and
malefactors of history and of the present day, together with authentic
devices of torture and execution, including the very guillotine that
killed the King of France. In addition, you will see replicas of
the severed heads of the King and his Queen Marie Antoinette,
along with those of such notables as Mister Robespierre, all of
them authentic impressions taken immediately after decapitation
by the fair hands of Madame Tussaud when she was but a young
girl, more than half a century ago. This is not an exhibit for the
faint-hearted, ladies and gentlemen, but you have been warned,
and those of you who are willing to brave The Dead Room will
now please follow me."

Callender watched in some surprise as the crowd melted away;
whether they were prudent or merely parsimonious, the British
public did not seem inclined, at least on this night, to feast on
horrors. In fact, there were finally only four customers, and they
were all of Callender's party, although of course it was really Aunt
Penelope's, a point she emphasized with a little cry of excitement
as the portal to the Chamber of Horrors opened to admit her.

The room was dark, deliberately, thought Callender, and his first
impression was of a crowd of men waiting in the shadows. As his
eyes became accustomed to the lack of light, he realized that the
figures had been grouped like prisoners waiting for sentence in the
dock. And he noticed that there were women scattered among the
men; an ancient woman in a gray gown particularly caught his eye.
In general, though, they seemed to be a nondescript lot, and only
statues anyway.

"So this is the celebrated Dead Room," boomed Callender, conscious that Felicia was following him. "It doesn't look that frightening. I'd gladly take the hundred guineas to spend the night among
these frozen fiends."

"Sorry, sir," replied the smiling guide. "Dame Rumor offered that reward, not Madame Tussaud, who has no wish for visitors after we close our doors at night at ten o'clock. The only living human being allowed to spend the night among these figures is Madame Tussaud herself."

"Would you really have done it, Reginald?" gasped Aunt Penelope, and Callender was conscious of a certain satisfaction, even though he would have preferred to elicit a response from Felicia. He risked a glance backward, and was pleased to see her pale blue eyes upon him.

"Of course the story of the reward is a lie," he said. "There's nothing here to scare a school-boy. Who are those two fellows?" He gestured with his stick at a pair of shaggy ruffians bedecked in caps and ragged scarves.

"Well, sir, you're taking them out of order, but since there are so few of you tonight I don't suppose it matters. Those are Burke and Hare. Ghouls, graverobbers and murderers, who stole bodies for a doctor's dissecting lessons, then turned to killing when the supply of fresh corpses ran short. Burke was executed in 1829, on his partner's evidence. They stole dignity from the dead and breath from the living. A most despicable pair, and one of our most popular groupings."

The story, which reminded Callender of something in his own past, did not really amuse him. "Of course this sort of thing is far behind us," he observed, "now that we provide our medical schools with the specimens they need."

"Yet still there are vermin who would rob the dead," said Sebastian Newcastle. Callender's hand moved involuntarily toward the pocket of his waistcoat, and toward his Uncle William's watch. He wondered again how much power the medium might possess, then shook off his suspicions together with his memories of the seance. That vision had been the result of hypnotism, or fatigue, or perhaps of some drug, but it certainly had nothing to do with the supernatural.

"Surely no man could be so contemptible," murmured Felicia, and again Callender felt a flush of shame. Could they know? He remembered a line from an old play his uncle had dragged him to see, about conscience creating cowards, and he kept his peace. Yet it disturbed him to realize that neither Sebastian Newcastle nor Felicia Lamb had spoken a word to him, outside of perfunctory greetings, until the subject of rifling corpses had arisen. He looked desperately for a diversion, and found one he could hardly have hoped for, when Felicia's Aunt Penelope began to scream.

His eyes followed her pointing finger, then widened in shock when he saw what she had seen first. It was the old woman in gray, half hidden among the murderers. She rose. Her wrinkled face turned toward the dim gaslight, and her eyes gleamed as a small smile twisted her wizened features. A gigantic shadow rose behind her as she stood, and Callender stumbled backward as Aunt Penelope collapsed into his arms. They both would have fallen to the floor but for the cold, rigid bulk of Mr Newcastle. Callender felt Newcastle's hand close on his flailing wrist, and suddenly he was less afraid of a walking effigy than he was of the icy presence behind him. He saw in flashes the cold face of Newcastle, the rigid and contemptuous countenance of Felicia, and the wrinkled features of the old woman that glided toward him. All of them were pale.

"Madame Tussaud!" said the guide, scuttling back in a broad gesture that was equally composed of bowing and cringing. "I didn't expect you here!"

"You all but announced me, Joseph. And where else would a crone like me find her friends except among the dead? You may leave early tonight, Joseph; I shall be hostess to our guests. There is one among them who interests me."

Joseph virtually fled, and Callender whipped his head around from the disappearing form, expecting to find the eyes of the old waxworker focused on him, but he saw at once that Madame Tussaud was blinking intently at Sebastian Newcastle.

"Have we not met, sir?"

"I hardly think I could have encountered Madame without remembering her."

"You are gracious, but are you truthful?"

Madame Tussaud's English, however fluent, still betrayed her French upbringing, and there was something foreign in Newcastle's speech as well, but Callender could not identify it.

"You have a memorable face, I think," said the old woman.

"Now you flatter me," said Newcastle.

"That was hardly my intention, but your scar, if I may be so blunt, is all but unforgettable."

"I apologize if it affronts you."

"No, sir. It is I who should beg you pardon, but I think I remember you. One who has lived eighty-seven years, as I have, has seen much. And it seems to me that I recollect a man with a face like yours, or at least talk of him. But that was so many years ago that the man could hardly have been you."

Sebastian Newcastle contented himself with a bow. The Dead Room was so dark, and their faces so indistinct, that Callender could hardly tell what the two of them were thinking. More than anything, he was aware of the way Felicia's eyes shifted back and forth between the two. What really shocked him, though, was the sudden recovery of Aunt Penelope, who pulled herself out of his arms and demanded to know whether the two of them were acquainted or not.

"There were stories in Paris, when the Revolution raged," said Madame Tussaud, "about a magician, one who had found a way to keep himself alive forever."

"No doubt there were many such stories in a time of turmoil," said Newcastle.

"Of course," agreed Madame Tussaud. "And the man I speak of would have been older then than I am by now. This was more than fifty years ago. It can be no more than a coincidence."

"Men say that there are such things," said Newcastle.

"He was a Spaniard," said Madame Tussaud, "and I would have given much to model him in wax, but that is all behind us now. Will you look at my relics of the Revolution? I paid dearly for them."

"How so?" asked Felicia. Fascinated by the exchange between the others, Callender had almost forgotten her.

"With the blood on my hands, young lady, and with memories that will last as long as this old body holds them. I was apprenticed to my uncle, and the leaders of the Revolution ordered me to make impressions in wax of heads fresh from the basket of the executioner. Fresh from the blade of that!"

Madame Tussaud thrust her arm out dramatically. Her trembling finger pointed toward a looming silhouette of wooden beams and ropes. Even in the dim light, the slanted steel blade at the top gleamed dully.

"The guillotine," gasped Aunt Penelope.

She swayed toward it slowly, like a woman in a trance, and stared up at the sharp edge as if she expected it to shudder down and smash into its base at her approach. She lowered her eyes gradually, then bent over to examine the displays at the foot of the guillotine. She looked to Callender like a housekeeper examining the choice cuts in a butcher shop.

The waxy heads stared up reproachfully, their indignation three-fold: bad enough to have been cut off, worse yet to have been captured in wax, but unsupportable to be displayed to gawkers at a penny apiece. Aunt Penelope seemed to wilt under their gaze. She made a strange sound.

"I don't feel well at all," she said. "I think I should go home."

"We should all go," said Callender.

"No, no, my boy, I wouldn't think of it. Mr Newcastle is Madame Tussaud's old friend. You take me, and let the others stay." Aunt

Penelope began to sway toward Callender's arms again, a habit which was becoming increasingly annoying.

"It's very good of you, Reginald," added Felicia with sweet finality. "I shall be quite safe here with Mr Newcastle."

Callender was sorely tempted to disagree, but he sensed the futility of argument. There was very little choice for anyone who wanted to look like a gentleman except to carry the old fool out and find her a cab. He tried to maintain his composure while he backed clumsily out of The Dead Room and the three who stayed behind smiled at him; he might not have succeeded if he had seen Aunt Penelope winking at her niece.

"Evidently age brings wisdom even to a woman such as she," Newcastle remarked.

"She's such a dear, really, even if she does rattle on sometimes. She knew how much I wanted to remain a little longer, and Reginald would have been bound to cause a scene of some sort."

"Then you wish to see more of my handiwork?" asked Madame Tussaud.

"No," Felicia replied at once. "I mean yes, of course, but, I really wanted to hear more about the gentleman you spoke of, the one who was so like Mr Newcastle."

"He might have been an ancestor, perhaps," suggested the man with the scar.

"And are such wounds as this passed on from father to son?" asked the old woman. She reached up and caressed Newcastle's cheek. "I could wish to make a model of such a face."

"For your Dead Room, Madame?" Newcastle asked.

"Mr Newcastle is no stranger to the dead," Felicia said. "He speaks to them. He is a spiritualist." She felt that she had to say something, even though a mixture of common courtesy and uncommon fear kept her from posing the question she longed to ask. There was some sort of understanding between these two, and she was impatient to share it. "This gentleman from Paris," she said at last. "Do you remember his name?"

"He was a Spanish nobleman . . . Don Sebastian . . . can you help me, Mr Newcastle?"

"I believe I can. Of course I have made a study of such things. His name was Don Sebastian de Villanueva, but I also recall that any claim he had to immortality was false. Was he not reported dead?"

The old woman thought for a moment. "A girl was found, driven quite out of her wits, who said she saw him shatter like glass, or vanish in a puff of smoke, or some such thing, so I suppose he is dead. Then again, a master of the black arts might be capable of such tricks, if he found it convenient to disappear for a time. . . ."

"Quite so," said Sebastian Newcastle, and Felicia Lamb shivered. From somewhere nearby she heard the tolling of a bell.

"The hour grows late," said Madame Tussaud, "and I am an old woman. I must ask you to leave me alone among my friends."

"Indeed, Miss Lamb," said Newcastle. He drew a silver watch from his waistcoat and glanced at its face. The watch was shaped like a skull. "The time is late, the museum is closed, and a man in my position must never be accused of keeping a young lady out till an indecent hour. We must take our leave. Goodnight, Madame."

The waxworker curtseyed, the medium bowed, and Felicia felt herself being hurried from The Dead Room, but as soon as she was through the door, Newcastle paused.

"Please wait here. I must return for a few seconds. I neglected to pay our guide for our tour."

Madame Tussaud was waiting for him in the shadows by the guillotine. "Don Sebastian," she said.

"Madame," he replied. "I trust you to keep my secret."

"You can hardly expect to keep it much longer from that girl, you know."

"It matters little. She will become a disciple. She wishes it."

"And has she said as much?"

"She need not speak for me to know."

"And have you many such disciples after half a century in London?"

"None," said Don Sebastian. He gazed at the wax figures around him. "But I have my dead, like you, and also those who will pay to see them. A small income, but my needs are simple."

"I think you need something that you cannot buy with gold, do you not?"

"Gold will buy more than than you think, sometimes. And when it will not, I feed as lightly as I can, so that my prey knows nothing more than a few days of weakness, soon forgotten. And I never drink from the same fountain twice. I rarely forget myself enough to dine too heavily, and if I do, well, there is a remedy for that."

"A physic made of wood, perhaps?"

"You are wise, Madame."

The old woman shuffled over to a rocking chair that sat in a corner. "If eighty-seven years have not made me wise, sir, then what can I hope for?"

"I had forgotten myself, Madame. Twice I have been driven back into the world of spirits, and so my years on earth have been scarcely more than yours."

"And did you never find peace?"

"Once, when an ancient world came to an end, its gods took me to their paradise, but after some centuries a spell of my own devising drew me back to earth again, to your Paris. And since I know how many less pleasant realms there are where spirits dwell, I am content to remain here."

The old woman settled back in her chair. "Then I wish you good night, sir, and bon voyage."

"I have forgotten one thing," said Don Sebastian. He raised his arm, and a shower of golden guineas streamed from his empty hand into the basket that contained the wax remains of Marie Antoinette.

"Very prettily done sir," said Madame Tussaud, "but I hope you have not damaged that head!"

"I would not dream of such a thing, Madame. You are an artist!"

VI. A Visitor from India

Reginald Callender sat in his uncle's study with the last bottle of his uncle's brandy on the desk in front of him. He still thought of what little was left here as his uncle's, since he himself had inherited nothing. And most of what remained in the house was gone now, sold to a furniture dealer to raise a bit of ready money. Callender had no head for business, just enough to know he had been cheated, but he hardly cared anymore. The laborers who came to loot the house had left him his bed, and the trappings of this one room where he had hidden while they gutted his birthright.

He had no idea what time it was. The thick velvet curtains kept out the sun, and he had already pawned his uncle's watch along with everything else pilfered from the coffin. His crime, if it was one, had brought him discouragingly little. He poured himself another drink. The glass was dirty, and the bottle was dusty from its sleep in the cellar. He wondered how such things could be cleaned. This, along with such mysteries as the cooking of food or the washing of clothes, were as enigmatic to him as the secret of what lay beyond the grave. He could only smoke and swear, drink and dream, but even two of these required money he did not possess.

And his dreams, infuriatingly enough, were of Sally Wood. He cursed himself for this. Now, if ever, his self interest demanded that he devote himself to dancing attendance upon Felicia Lamb, who clearly held his fate in her small hands. Yet it was Sally's heavy-lidded, full-lipped face that rose before him in the gloom, offering him not so much her beauty, and certainly not her love, but rather the sense of power that surged through him when he held her moaning in his arms. She could make him feel like a man again, and not the quivering, drink-soaked wretch he was becoming while he watched his fiancee and his fortune slip away. Still, to see her might be to risk everything: better to have another drink instead.

His trembling hand nearly dropped the bottle when he heard a heavy pounding from somewhere in the house. He sat frozen in his chair, baffled and suspicious, until the sound came again and he realized it was someone knocking loudly on the front door. He attempted to ignore it, but the visitor was so insistent that Callender finally dragged himself to his unsteady feet and went out into the hall. Stripped of its furnishings, the empty house reminded him of Sebastian Newcastle's, and it was the scarred and sinister medium that Callender half expected to greet on the doorstep.

Instead, it was a stranger, a beefy, red-faced man with graying hair and clothing that was not only a decade out of fashion, but seemed to have been cut to suit a man slimmer by several stone. He carried a small travelling bag in his left hand, and looked ready to knock again with his right when Callender pulled open the heavy oak door.

The two men peered at each other through a foggy gray that Callender dimly recognized as dusk, and at last the stranger spoke.

"Reggie?"

Callender, who was still at least sober enough to know his own name, did not find this an edifying remark.

"I know who I am, sir, damn your eyes, but who in blazes are you?"

"Don't you know me?"

"I've said as much, blast you! Go away!"

The man in the fog looked genuinely hurt. "But it's your cousin!" he said. "Nigel! Nigel Stone!"

Callender swayed in the doorway and blinked at his visitor. "Stone? From India?"

"That's right, and home at last. How's Uncle William?"

"Dead."

"Dead? Oh dear. Sorry."

"Yes," said Callender. "You'd better come in."

Callender swayed in the doorway and stepped unsteadily back inside. His cousin followed him into what Callender now realized was almost impenetrable blackness. Nigel Stone paused for a minute trying to get his bearings.

"My dear fellow! The place has been stripped bare!"

"Yes. Yes. It was the servants."

"Servants?"

"Yes. Servants. While I was at the funeral, they and their confederates stole all they could and carted it away."

"Good Lord. Beastly things, servants. Some of the brown fellows where I was would rob you blind if you didn't keep an eye on them. A blind eye, eh? Almost a joke."

"It's not funny to me, cousin."

"No. Of course not. Sorry."

"You'd better follow me into the study. This way."

The first thing Stone saw in the room was a brandy bottle flanked by two candles, stuck in their own grease to the surface of a massive desk. Callender sat down in a chair behind it and picked up his glass. In his haste to get his own seat, he neglected the courtesy of offering one to his cousin.

"Tell me, Cousin Nigel, how is business in India?"

"Not so good, I'm afraid. That's why Uncle William summoned me."

"Oh? Just how bad is it?"

"Bloody damned bad, if you want to know, my dear fellow. Haven't a farthing."

"Nothing left at all?" asked Callender. His eyes glistened in the candlelight as he drained his glass.

"Oh, there's a few boxes of textiles that I had shipped back with me. They should be here in the morning, but that was all I could save. It took the last penny to pay my passage home. No, I'm a liar. I still have half a crown. See?"

"You idiot!" Callender leaped out of his chair and lunged across the desk. He grasped Stone by the collar and hauled him forward, snuffing out a candle and sending the bottle smashing to the floor. Stone was too startled to do more than grunt at first, but when his cousin began to slam him against the desk, the older man broke free and pushed his drunken assailant across the room. Callender fell to the floor and lay there sobbing, both arms crossed over his face.

His cousin stood leaning on the desk, breathing heavily and wishing desperately for a drink from the broken bottle. "Empty anyway," he muttered. "Look here, Reggie! Are you all right?"

He moved hesitantly toward the quivering form on the carpet. "It wasn't my fault, really. It's conditions. You don't know what it's like

there. Rebellion, robberies, and murder. The whole country's filled
with madmen and fanatics. I was lucky to escape with my life!"

Callender sat up so suddenly that his cousin started back. "What
is your life to me?" he wailed. "It's money that I need!"

"Really? What do you mean, old fellow? You must be rolling in
the stuff. You're his heir, ain't you? I'm sure he didn't leave me
anything, after all I've lost!"

Callender looked at Stone oddly. "What? His heir? Yes, of course
I'm his heir." He laughed harshly. "But the money . . . the money
isn't here yet. It's all tied up with those damned lawyers, and it may
be weeks before I see any of it. You can see what a state I'm in."

"You really don't look well, my dear fellow," said Stone, helping
Callender back to his chair. "I'm sorry to hear this, you know. Bit
of trouble for both of us. I was really hoping, well, that I might be
able to stay here for a while, just till I can get myself back on my
feet, as it were. . . . I can lend you half a crown. . . ."

· The two cousins laughed together, Stone with genuine mirth,
Callender with a wheezing bitterness that ended with an offer
of sorts. "I suppose you can stay, cousin, if you're willing to
rough it."

"Rough it? I've done nothing else for ten years. We'll do fine
together, eh? And buck up! It's only a matter of days."

"Days?" Callender asked sharply. "What day is this? What is
the time?"

"Eh? It's Thursday, isn't it? And the last clock I passed said just
after six, as near as I could see it through this damned fog."

"Thursday at six! Damn! I'm to dine with my fiancee in an
hour."

"Your fiancee! Well, you are a fortunate fellow. And to think that
I should find you in such a state." Stone paused and subjected his
cousin to careful scrutiny. "You know, old fellow, you're really in
no condition to meet a lady, or even a constable. You need a wash
and a shave at least."

"Shave?" barked Callender. "With this hand? I might as well cut
my throat and be done with it." The fingers he held before Stone's
face were visibly trembling.

"I see. A case of the shakes. Well, we'll have to think of something
else. I think I could do a bit of barbering, and I have a razor right
here in my bag. You have some water? And a log for the fire. We
must cheer you up, cuz. I mean to dance at your wedding."

"If there is a wedding."

"What? Something wrong?"

"Much. I'm half afraid I'm losing her. That damned spiritualist!"

"Eh? Someone out to lure her away from you? We can't have that."

"It hasn't come to that, I think," said Callender. "At least not yet. But he has some kind of hold on her, filling her head with stories of spooks, and spirits, and other worlds. I don't know how to fight it, but I feel he's changing her."

Nigel Stone's face was suddenly grimmer than Callender had imagined it could be. "That's a bad business," Stone said. "Very bad, fooling about with spirits."

"And what would you know about it?" sneered Callender.

"I didn't spend ten years in India for nothing, cuz. I may not have made any money, but at least I learned a thing or two. The whole country is rife with superstition, and what might be more than superstition. Men go mad believing in ghosts and demons there. They kill each other and they kill themselves, and some fall under spells that are unspeakable."

"Rubbish."

"And I tell you it's not rubbish! These things can happen, cuz, and even if they don't, just thinking about them can do the worst sort of harm to body and soul. We must do something for this girl before it's too late."

"You do it, then," said Callender. "She only laughs at me when I try." He paused, and contemplated Stone with new interest. "You look like you could do with a good dinner."

"I could indeed."

"Then come along with me tonight, will you? See if you can scare this nonsense out of Felicia before it injures her. I always end up trapped with her accursed aunt anyway."

"Has she an aunt?"

"Yes, a spinster, and about your age, cousin, but don't even think of it. No man could bear her. You stick to the niece. And as for now, do you remember where Uncle William's wine cellar is?"

"Downstairs somewhere, isn't it?"

"That's the idea. Fetch us a bottle of port, will you? Then it will be soon enough for the fire, and the water, and the razor, don't you think?"

"As you say." Nigel Stone hesitated for a moment at the thought of the wine, since Callender clearly had no need of it, but he decided he could stand a drop himself, and that this was justification enough for a descent into the cellar. With one backward glance he started out on his first task as the unpaid valet of the impoverished cousin he hoped would soon be a rich relative.

*　　*　　*

In the midst of what might have been a pleasant dinner, Stone tried to convince himself that the drop he had shared with his cousin really could not have made much difference. For Reginald Callender, helping himself to every decanter in sight, was as drunk as the lord he undoubtedly wished himself to be, and his increasingly erratic behavior interfered at least a bit with Stone's delight in the food, the drink, and the company.

Stone found the girl, Felicia Lamb, as pretty as a picture but not much more animated. Her aunt Penelope, however, was a lively, bird-like little woman who not only kept his plate and his glass filled, but had the courtesy if not the good taste to hang on his every word. For a man long cut off from polite society, such a dinner partner was a positive delight, and the luxury of her surroundings fulfilled the hopes that he had held for his Uncle William's house. Stone grew expansive, but he also remembered his promise to his cousin.

"I understand you take an interest in spiritualism," he said to Felicia.

"I do," she replied evenly.

"Did it never occur to you that it might be dangerous?"

"Dangerous? You betray your kinship with Mr Callender, sir. I refuse to accept the idea that my search for wisdom is a threat to me."

"No? You could be right, I suppose. I wouldn't want to contradict a lady, but some of the things I saw in India would be enough to make a man cautious. Or even a woman."

"Do tell us about it, Mr Stone," purred Aunt Penelope. "I'm sure it's fascinating."

"Yes," interrupted Callender. "And informative, too. You listen to this, Felicia." His fiancee stiffened noticeably while he clumsily poured himself another brandy, spilling as much on the tablecloth as he did into his glass.

"Well," Stone began uncomfortably, "I don't want to make too much of this. Some of what goes on there is just tomfoolery, I reckon, like the fellows who send ropes into the air and then climb up 'em. No harm in that unless the rope breaks, eh?" He laughed, but only Aunt Penelope joined him. "I think it's just a trick anyway. What I mean to say is that some of 'em start out like that and then go on to do things that might hurt them badly. They think some of their gods or spirits are watching over them, so they feel free to walk on burning coals or lie down on beds of iron spikes. I've seen it! And they seem to be unharmed, too, but what if something went wrong, eh? What if the spirits weren't there when the fellow decided to take a nap? What then?"

"I'm sure I'm not interested in spikes, Mr Stone," Felicia said.

"No, my dear young lady, I'm sure you're not. But neither were these chaps, once upon a time. Do you see what I'm driving at? Nobody's born thinking of such things, but they're led into them by degrees."

"He's right, Felicia," said Callender. His speech was slurred, and she did not deign to reply.

"Then these things are really true?" asked Aunt Penelope.

"Damned if I know. Oh, pardon me. My point, though, is that it doesn't really matter if they're true or not, as long as people believe in 'em. Take the Thugs, for instance."

"Thugs?" asked Aunt Penelope. "Are they some sort of monster?"

"They're only men, but I suppose you could call 'em monsters too. They're a cult of murderers, men, women, and children. Whole families of 'em, whole villages, maybe even whole cities, all mad from believing in the spirits of the dead and some goddess of the dead that wants them to kill. They prey on travellers. Wiped out a whole caravan I would have been on if I hadn't been ill, just as if the earth had swallowed 'em up. Lord Bentinck hanged a lot of these Thugs, I've heard, but there are more, you may be sure of it. That's what thinking too much about the dead can do!"

"I only wish to learn of the secrets of the dead," said Felicia, "not to add to their number."

"The dead know nothing!" roared Callender. "Learn from me! Life!"

"Really, Reginald," said Felicia coolly. "And shall I learn by example?"

"Example? And what's the dead's example? Lie down and die yourself, I suppose?" Callender, drunk and angry, was half way up from his seat when Aunt Penelope tactfully interrupted.

"Please, Mr Callender. Let us hear Mr Stone out. And you be still, too, Felicia. It's not polite to argue with a guest, especially one who has travelled half way around the world to give us the benefit of his experience. Do tell us more, Mr Stone."

"Thank you, dear lady. What I mean to say is that if there are spirits, and you call them up, you can't tell what you'll get. If there are spirits, there must be wicked ones, don't you think? In India, they tell tales of an evil spirit. It's called a Baital, or a Vetala, or some such thing. It gets into corpses somehow, and makes them move about, and it draws the life out of every living thing it touches. Would you like to call up one of those? Could you put it down again?"

"It sounds like a vampire," Felicia suggested.

"Vampire? Oh, you mean that old book by Lord Byron. Read it when I was a lad. Quite made my hair stand on end. I suppose it's the same sort of thing."

"Please forgive me for contradicting you," said Felicia with excessive sweetness, "But *The Vampyre* was written by Lord Byron's physician, Dr Polidori. I know a gentleman who met them both."

"Really? No doubt you're right. Not much of a literary man myself."

"She reads too much," mumbled Callender, but he was ignored.

"And take the ghouls," continued Stone.

"What?" demanded Callender.

"Ghouls. Not the kind we have here, not grave robbers exactly. The Indian ghouls are creatures who tear open graves and, well, they feast on what they find there."

"How horrible." Aunt Penelope shuddered cheerfully.

"Isn't it? Of course, we eat dead things ourselves, don't we? I hope the sheep who provided this excellent mutton has gone to its reward, eh?"

"Oh, Mr Stone," laughed Aunt Penelope. "You're a wicked, wicked man."

"What's all this talk of robbing graves?" Reginald Callender was on his feet, a brimming glass of brandy in his hand. "You see what she does?" he shouted. "She turns us all into ghouls!" He whirled to face Felicia, and the brandy splashed over the front of her gown.

"Damn!" shouted Callender. He snatched up a napkin and applied it vigorously to her bodice.

"Your hands, sir!" cried Felicia.

"Mr Callender!" gasped Aunt Penelope.

"My word!" said Nigel Stone.

Felicia Lamb jumped up and gathered her skirts around her. "I believe it's time that we were all in bed," she announced. Her ordinarily pale face was flushed a hot pink.

"Fine!" roared Callender. "Let's all go together!"

Felicia, her head held high, swept from the room. Callender laughed harshly and sat back into his chair, barely conscious of his surroundings.

"Oh dear," said Aunt Penelope.

"Time to go home, old fellow," said Stone, pulling the comatose Callender to his feet. "My apologies, Miss Penelope. He took our uncle's death very hard."

"Goodnight, Mr Stone. I hope you will call on us again."

"Nothing would please me more," said Stone, grunting over the weight of his burden as he backed toward the door. "Good night."

Almost before he knew it, Nigel Stone was in the street. He might as well have been at sea. The thick, yellow fog made London look like a spirit world, one in which the misty glow of the street lamps revealed nothing but their own iridescence. His cousin was on his feet, but not much more. They had walked to dinner from Uncle William's house, and Stone knew that it could not be far away, but he was a bit worse for the wine himself, and not really sure of his bearings.

He longed for a cab, and he wondered how lost he was. Callender said "Sally" several times, but this only confused his cousin more.

Helping Callender across an intersection, Nigel Stone heard a horse snorting, and he dragged his burden back to a spot only a few feet from Felicia Lamb's house. Later, he convinced himself that he hadn't spoken to the driver because he realized they hadn't the money to hire a ride. What really decided him, though, before he even thought of his purse, was the sinister look of the driver. He was gaunt and pale, with dark hollows for eyes, and down the left side of his face ran a horrible scar.

VII. The Bride of Death

Felicia Lamb heard the old clock downstairs strike midnight before she thought it safe to rise from her curtained bed and begin to dress. It took her some time to prepare herself, but she was determined to do everything with exquisite care, for this was to be her ultimate rendezvous with the unknown.

She held neither lamp or candle when she slowly pulled open the door of her bed chamber and slipped out into the dark hall, but she had lived in this house all her life, and had no need of light to show her the way. Her only fear was that she might be detected, and that her aunt or even the servants might try to protect her from what could be considered danger, but which she knew she had desired from the day of her birth. So that she could be sure of silence, her feet were bare.

She tiptoed quickly down the carpeted staircase, her hand resting heavily on the bannister so that her tread would be light, then walked confidently through the hallway toward the door that led to the world beyond the home of her father and mother. She felt for the bolt, moved it with a practiced hand, and opened the door. Yellow fog drifted in to meet her and she stepped out into its embrace. She pulled the iron key from her bosom and locked the house behind her so that all within it might be safe. Then she stepped out into the shrouded street, wrapping her hooded cloak around her.

The coach was where she was told it would be waiting. Neither she nor the driver spoke a word, and the hooves of the horses had been muffled. There was hardly a sound to disturb the sleep of London as the coach rolled unerringly through the impenetrable mist.

Felicia still held the key clutched tightly in her fingers, but when her conveyance had rounded several corners, she threw her key into the gutter. It would never be recognized, and she did not intend to use it again.

She sat back quietly and waited to reach her destination, not even bothering to glance out the windows until the horses came to a smooth stop. She alighted without a moment's hesitation and stood almost blinded in thick clouds that might have been born in heaven or hell. A figure materialized beside her, almost as if it had drawn its substance from the fog; it guided her through a doorway and into darkness. Something shut behind her.

The two moved forward together, through a passageway which held at its end a globe of luminescence. Felicia felt that she was in a dream. The light resolved itself into a glowing ball of crystal, resting on an ebony table with chairs at either end, and casting its pale yellow light on an all-encompassing shroud of black velvet curtains. She was in the consulting room of Sebastian Newcastle, and he stood at her side.

He moved away from her and seated himself at the far end of the table, his face aglow in sickly light. "Will you not remove your cloak and sit with me, Miss Lamb?"

Felicia did neither. She was suddenly hesitant, suspicious. "Is this what you have promised me?" she said. "Only another seance?"

"Might it not be better so? There is much you could learn as you are, and much more that you may not wish to know."

"Then you have lied to me, sir?"

The light before Sebastian Newcastle's face flickered and dimmed. "Will you not wait, Felicia? What you seek comes soon enough, and lasts forever."

"Another seance, then? Will you call upon the dead for me? Will you call the shade of anyone I name?"

"I shall do what I can."

"Then call for me the spirit of a wizard. A master of the darkness, one who mastered death and reckoned not the price. Call for me the spirit of your double, Don Sebastian de Villanueva. Can you do it, Mr Sebastian Newcastle? Do you dare?"

"I can. But do you dare to let me?"

"Have I not asked it of you?"

"You have," he said. "You have asked too often to be denied. And yet the blame will be all mine."

"I absolve you," said Felicia Lamb.

"Spoken like the angel you so fervently desire to be," Sebastian said. His voice was almost brutal. "Will you do me the courtesy to sit down?"

"You can hardly hope to frighten me with gruff tones when we have come so far," Felicia said.

"No. Nothing will frighten you but what you cannot change. And when that terror comes, will you be brave enough to bear it, or brave enough to put an end to it?"

"Surely I shall be one or the other," she replied as she seated herself at the table. "Shall we begin?"

"I warn you because I care for you," Sebastian said.

"I believe it," she said. "Now show me who it is that cares for me so much."

She reached out for his cold hand, but he drew back. He did not speak. He crossed his arms before his face, and the light in the crystal was snuffed out in an instant. The black room was entombed in ebony.

Felicia stared ahead, her hand at her heart, more frightened than she would have admitted under torture. Something was about to happen, and she had longed for it, but she was half afraid that she would be ravished and murdered in the dark. Was that what she had demanded?

She hoped for a vision, but instead she heard a voice. It might have been human, indeed it must have been human, but the low, echoing, senseless syllables sounded more like an animal in agony. It ended in a note that was a hollow song of pain.

Sebastian's face appeared abruptly in the gloom. The flesh glowed with the pale blue light of putrescence, and the flame of decay grew brighter until the features burned away and left only a gleaming silver skull beneath. It spoke to her.

"What is worse than death, my love? Flee from it!"

The mouth that moved was full of unnaturally sharp teeth that gleamed like swords. The skull screamed, and then burst into flame. A dull and rusted blade dropped from the ceiling and sundered the skull from whatever held it erect. The flashes of fire turned cold blue as it rolled across the table toward Felicia; the hollow sockets where its eyes had been bubbled up with globes of glistening jelly, while locks of black and silky hair sprouted from the burnished surface of the silver skull.

The head fell upon her breast, and all at once Sebastian was in her arms. The black room was alive with silver.

"I am the one you seek," he said. "Turn away."

Felicia pulled away from him and stood, leaving him on his knees, his head bent over the arms of the ebony chair. He turned toward her, relieved to think that she would run from all that he could offer her. She took a deep breath, then pulled the dark hood from her face and the dark cloak from her body.

"I am the one you seek," she said. "Would you deny my desire, and your own?"

She wore a white wedding gown, its silk scarcely paler than her own ivory flesh.

The gown had been her mother's, forty years ago, when fashion was more graceful and less refined. Her arms were bare, her shoulders were bare, and her breasts were almost bare as well, the silk gathered beneath them and flowing down in delicate folds that brushed against the ebony floor. Felicia would never have dared to dress in such a manner if it had not been her wedding night, but now she exulted in her shamelessness. The glow around her turned the silk, her skin, her pale eyes, and her ashen hair to silver.

The black figure of Sebastian glided toward her.

"Destiny," he murmured.

He grasped her almost cruelly. She felt his cold breath upon her throat, his cold fingers in her flowing hair. She arched her back and exposed her white neck, but Sebastian pulled her forward and turned away from her.

He would not look at her as he spoke.

"I have become what I am, a creature of the night who feeds on blood, because I would not die. Why should you, a young woman with years of life before her, spurn the most precious gift in all creation?"

"Because I would know more of its creator." She reached out to touch his shoulder.

"If you care nothing for yourself, think of your friends. Think of your family."

"I have no friends," Felicia said. "As for my family, those I love most have gone before me. As for Aunt Penelope, I think she will be content with my fortune."

"And the young man?"

"You have seen what he is. I wish to God that I had seen it sooner."

"Then is there nothing for you in this world?"

"Nothing but to be rid of it."

"Then at least die a true death," Sebastian said, "and I will guide your spirit as I do those others you have seen, those who are lost. Take poison, cut your throat, jump from a tower, do anything but take this curse upon yourself. For many centuries I have carried it alone, and it is better so."

"You have not renounced your fate. In truth, I think you relish it. You love to be the lord of life and death, to stand between them and cast a cold eye on both. Is it because I am a woman that you think I do not know my own desires? Do you think that I am not as brave as you? Could it not be that I have been sent to end your loneliness forever?"

Sebastian whirled to confront her, his face a mask of fury. "Loneliness? Why need I be lonely when I have companions such as this to comfort me?"

The glowing curtains rippled in the black and silver room behind Sebastian. A shape appeared behind them: aimless, clumsy, menacing, and unutterably sad. A faltering white hand emerged through the drapes, and despite herself Felicia gasped. What shuffled into the room had been a boy. His shaggy hair was red, but his slack-jawed face was almost gray, and his eyes were those of an idiot. His lips were drooling, and his teeth were sharp. He limped toward Sebastian, one leg twisted and broken.

"Please, sir," he muttered.

"My God, Sebastian," Felicia said. "What is this?"

"A grave robber. He said his name was Henry Donahue. I found him and another at their work, and killed the first one outright, but by the time I caught young Donahue again, my fury and my bloodlust were so great that I slaked my thirst on him. And here he is, one of the living dead, and quite mad. I should have destroyed him, and surely I must, but now I am happy to have been delayed. Gaze on him. Is this what you wish to become?"

At the sound of her voice, the dead boy had turned toward Felicia. He dragged his shattered leg across the black carpet, his eyes fastened on her throat. Felicia felt suddenly naked and defenseless.

"Please, miss," said the boy.

He touched her.

Suddenly his hands were reaching for her throat, his dirty little teeth gnashing at the air as she tried to push him away. There was a strange strength in his small fingers. Felicia screamed.

The boy had her half sprawled on the ebony table when Sebastian yanked him back by his red hair and threw him across the room. Half of his scalp stayed in Sebastian's hand, and his head was a raw but bloodless wound as he implacably scuttled over the floor to reach the woman he wanted.

Sebastian pounced on him again, caught his twisted leg, and dragged the snarling creature through the velvet curtains and out of the room.

Felicia was alone, heart pounding, her breath coming in frantic gasps. She was terrified, and yet exhilarated too. She struggled down from the table top and collapsed into an ebony chair. From somewhere in the recesses of the house came a high pitched wail of agony that rose to a crescendo and then stopped abruptly. Felicia knew she would never see the boy again.

She waited.

When Sebastian returned to her, his hair hung over his face and his clothes were torn. His hands were spotted with blood. He looked at them and then at Felicia.

"There was little enough in him," Sebastian said. "He had been starved. Now you see what I would save you from."

Felicia trembled, but she remained where she was. "Between you and this boy is as much difference as there must have been in life," she said. "I will not be like him."

"Go!" shouted Sebastian, but even as he did he advanced upon her, his mouth twisting uncontrollably.

Felicia gritted her teeth and clutched the arms of the ebony chair with all her might. She held her head high, and felt the pulses throbbing in her long white neck as Sebastian overwhelmed her.

Then they were on the carpet, her carefully coiffed pale hair spilled upon its darkness, her gown in disarray, her body throbbing with delight and dread. She felt an ecstasy of fear, stunned more by the desires of her flesh than by the small, sweet sting she felt as he sank into her and life flowed between them. She rocked and moaned beneath the body of the man she loved. She took life and love and death and made them one.

And when it was over, Sebastian arose alone. She lay at ease, her limbs sprawled in graceful carelessness, her face marked by abandon hardly tinged by shock. She was pale as a marble statue, colored with a few drops of virgin's blood. She was at peace, but Sebastian knew that she would rise full of dark desire when the next sun set.

Even his tears, when they came, were tinged with her bright blood.

VIII. The Final Note

Nigel Stone paced through the empty rooms of the echoing house he shared with his cousin. He had been in the place for less than a day, but already its atmosphere oppressed him. He knew that Callender was upstairs somewhere sleeping off what must have been an appalling headache, yet somehow the mansion seemed utterly deserted, a fit abode for ghosts rather than men. Out of sheer desperation, Stone was tempted to drop off himself, on the settee in the study that had served him as a bed, but he fought the temptation, though there was little enough for a man to do in London when he had no money and no friends. It wasn't even a fit day for a stroll around the old town, unfortunately; a heavy rain had been falling for most of the afternoon, interrupted from time to time by distant growls of thunder and dim glimmerings of lightning.

Still, Stone decided that a storm would be more stimulating than wandering through a house that seemed half haunted. He headed for the door, threw it open, and stared out into the street. The rain rattled down and splashed in the gutters; wind blew some of it into Stone's face. Across the way a man scrambled for shelter, and his antics made Stone feel very satisfied to be indoors after all. And yet something in the power of the elements made him feel strong and alive; he remembered how he had run shouting through storms when he had been a boy.

As he looked out on nature's fury, Stone saw a coach round a corner and pull up in front of the doorway that sheltered him. The horses steamed and shivered in the downpour. Stone felt a trifle foolish to be standing there, but would have been even more ashamed to duck back inside like a frightened child, especially when the coachman ducked down from his perch, his high hat dripping, and scrambled up the steps to meet him. Stone did his best to act like a prosperous householder.

"Mr Nigel Stone?" asked the coachman.

"What? Me?" stammered Stone. "Yes, of course it's me. What can I do for you, my good man?"

"A message for you from a lady, sir. She said to wait for an answer." He pulled a piece of paper from somewhere inside his soaking coat and handed it to Stone. The wet ink was already beginning to blur.

My Dear Mr Stone,
  Please come at once, and if you can, come without Mr Callender.
My niece Felicia vanished last night, and I fear for her safety. I
believe I can rely on you, and no one else.

A drop of rain turned the signature to a gray smudge, but there could
be no doubt about the name. Stone felt pleasure at the summons,
and then a twinge of shame that he should take such delight in the
misfortune of a young woman.

"I'll come at once," he said.

"Then come with me, sir. I'll wait here while you get your
greatcoat."

"No need for that," mumbled Stone. He was embarrassed to
confess that he owned no such garment, but not quite desperate
enough to pilfer his cousin's; he hoped the coachman would take his
scanty costume as a sign of dedication rather than desperation. A
blast of thunder ripped the sky apart as he hurried down the steps.

The same thunder woke Reginald Callender at last. He cursed,
and sat up so quickly that he wrenched his back. His sheets were
soaked with his own sweat, and they had begun to stink. He itched
all over, and he started to tremble as soon as he awoke. And when
he heard the rain, he was seized with a wild desire to run naked into
London and wash himself clean, but he had just enough judgement
left to realize this might not be wise.

Callender huddled under his quilts and pulled damp pillows over
his head, trying without much success to shut out the world. Now
that he was conscious again, he could not bear to lie awake alone
with his own thoughts. Visions of doom hounded him in his own
bed. He could not stay there.

He crawled out into the clammy air and began to shiver. He called
for the servants, even though he knew that they were gone. Then he
called for his cousin Nigel, but there was no reply. He felt utterly
abandoned.

The house was too big for him. He had a sudden, unreasoning
fear of being a small speck in a vast space. It was unbearable.

He pulled on such clothes as he could find, and took a pull
from the bottle beside the bed. He thanked heaven for his uncle's
cellar, which was still his even if the house would soon be sold
for debts, and he dreaded the day when the wine would run
dry. He drank again, and heard the rain battering against his
window.

He hardly cared for the weather, though, when his mind was in
such an uproar. There was a need in him to escape from these walls

and from his memories. Compared to them, a thunderstorm was a small thing.

A song rang through his head, a tantalizing tune that meant nothing yet said much. Against it as a counterpoint rang heavy sounds of resentment and recrimination, memories of an evening when he had said and done much that might not be forgiven. Much wiser, he thought, to follow the notes of the sweeter, shallower song, and to forget the rest. He felt in his pockets, found a few shillings, then staggered down the staircase and out the door to stand under the streaming skies. He had no cash for a cab, but he knew the way to The Glass Slipper.

His journey was a vision. Water fell in curtains before him, and it rose in glistening fountains at every curb. Rainbows formed in every gaslight, and phantoms in the fog. His way was weary, but he was too tired to rest. From time to time the whirling wheels that passed him covered him in water, but it was no more to him than paint on lips that were already scarlet. Drenched and deranged, Reginald Callender made his way through forgotten streets until he reached his remembered goal.

The glass globes over the flickering flames at the entrance to The Glass Slipper seemed to Callender like stars in the heavens. He stepped over cigars, mud, and orange peels to reach the arch where a shilling brought him his way into the saloon bar.

"Buy us a bottle of fizz?" Callender pushed the drab out of his way and proceeded up into the balcony. This had always been a disorderly house, but now it struck him as the true home of chaos. Each face he saw was a twisted demon shape, and each voice a mockery. He was vaguely aware that some spurned him for the unshaven, sodden wretch he had become, but it mattered little when he knew he was so close to Sally Wood.

"Give your orders, gentlemen, please!" The harsh voice cut through the tobacco fumes, the smell of stale beer and cheap perfume. In another life Callender would have ignored the summons, but now that he was destitute he felt compelled to buy a glass of beer. A girl with plump arms and a vacant face offered to sell him sweets from a glass jar, but she backed away when she saw his expression. The orchestra struck up a tinny tune, and it was one Callender recognized. The gods were with him after all. It was Sally's song.

> Some girls place a price upon their maidenhood,
> Defend it, never spend it till the price is good.
> They wouldn't give a gent a tumble if they could.
> They couldn't if they would,

> *They wouldn't if they could,*
> *But everybody knows Sally Wood.*

And there she was, in a gaudy red dress, strutting saucily across the stage. She bawled out her litany, her skirts hiked up to her garters, and Callender dreamed of what lay beyond them. He wondered how many men shared the same dreams, perhaps even the same memories, and he hated them all.

Someone clapped him on the back and handed him a glass of brandy; he didn't even notice who it was. When Sally hit her final note and made a low curtsey in her low-cut dress, he stood stock still and stared while every other man in The Glass Slipper gave vent to boisterous shouts and applause. He did not move as Sally leaped from the stage, wove her way expertly through the orchestra, pushed through the crowd with a few playful slaps, and hurried up to the balcony bar. She passed within a few feet of Callender on her way to the spot where a man with a leathery face and gray sidewhiskers was standing. There was a bottle of champagne beside him on the bar, and he poured Sally a glass as she approached, her face flushed and her chestnut hair flowing.

Callender awoke from his paralysis and stumbled toward Sally. She turned when he grasped her arm.

"Reggie!" she said, and then she laughed. "You do look a sight!"

"It's the rain."

"You'd better go home, dear, or you'll catch your death. I'll talk to you another night."

She turned her back on him.

"Sally! You'll talk to me now!" He reached out for her again, but the stranger put himself between them.

"You can see that the lady is occupied," he said. His tone was the one that Callender had been accustomed to use when talking to servants. Callender tried to push him away, but the man was like an oak.

Callender took a swing at the man, who ducked back without hesitation and then put a bony fist in his opponent's face.

Callender was surprised to find himself sitting on the floor. His nose and mouth felt hot and wet. There was laughter all around him.

He was trying to decide what to do when he had another shock: he saw Sally slap her escort's face. This brought another roar from the crowd, which burst into wilder applause than it had ever granted one of her songs when Sally knelt down beside the stricken Callender and took him in her arms.

"Come on, Reggie," she said. "You're all right."

"Sally?" He didn't know what else to say.

"That's right, dear. You come along with me. Can't have my husband murdered, can I?"

Her words hardly registered as she helped him to his feet and out of The Glass Slipper.

The rain was still falling, and Callender lifted his face toward it to wash away the blood. He hardly looked where he was walking, but he was conscious enough to remember that her lodgings were just around the corner from the music hall. He dragged his boots through a puddle like a child, and he found a kind of pleasure in it. He had begun to love the storm. When the thunder rumbled, he made the same sort of noise himself. Sally just looked at him and smiled.

She led him up two flights of stairs and into her disordered room, as full of jumble as his own dwelling was barren, then sat him down on an unmade bed covered with clothes. He saw a pamphlet, half hidden by a dress, and picked it up.

"Still reading penny dreadfuls, Sal?"

"Oh, you mean the vampire. You should take that along, Reggie. I'm finished with that bit, and it's awfully good."

Callender shrugged and stuffed the thing into his pocket. His mind was fuddled, but somewhere in it was the glimmer of an idea. There was something else, too, something he wanted to remember.

"Look here. What was that you said to me back at the Slipper, eh?"

"What do you mean, dear? Take off your coat. It's wet."

"Leave me alone. I want to be wet."

"Have it your own way, then," said Sally, peeling off her gown and posing before him in her corset. "I just wanted to get you warm."

"Warm, is it? And what did you say to me back there about a husband?"

She sat beside him and ran her tongue across his lips. "Only that a girl has to take care of her intended, Reggie."

He looked at her blearily. "You must be mad," he said.

"Not half, I'm not. You promised to marry me, right here in this very bed, and I mean to hold you to it, Mr Reggie Callender."

"Dreaming," he said.

"What?"

"One of us is dreaming. Whatever made you think that I would marry you?"

"You did, dear. When your uncle died, you said, and you were wealthy in your own right, you said you'd make an honest woman

of me. And now he's dead, ain't he? I can see you took it hard, with
your kind heart, but that will pass, and then we'll be wed. You do
love me, don't you dear? There's nobody else?"

He fumbled at her, more out of habit than passion. "Of course
there's nobody else," he said.

"No?" Sally pushed him down on the bed and slapped him harder
than she had the man in The Glass Slipper. "And what about Miss
Felicia Lamb?"

Callender was too stunned to reply.

"You think I'm stupid, don't you? You thought I didn't know
about her! What do you take me for?"

Callender just sat on the bed and looked across the room.

"Here," said Sally. "Have some gin." She pulled a bottle from a
pile of dresses in a corner and gave it to Callender. He uncorked it
and poured half of it down his throat.

"That's right," said Sally. "Get yourself used to the idea. You
thought I was just a silly girl. That's what you think of all of us,
ain't it? And that's why we do what we can to protect ourselves.
You recollect a girl named Alice? Your uncle's maid. We were
good friends, Alice and me. She told me all about you. Now I
don't begrudge you your bit of fun, Reggie. I've had mine. We'll
forget Alice, even if she has seen more of your uncle's money than
ever I did. But I won't let you marry this Felicia Lamb."

Callender took another pull on the bottle and put his head in
his hands. The liquor burned against his bleeding gums. This was
hardly the evening he had planned.

"I saw her once, you know," Sally said. "A blueblood virgin with
big eyes and a tiny mouth. She's no woman for a man like you. I'll
bet she wouldn't even raise her skirt to piss!"

It was Callender's turn to slap Sally. Then he picked up his hat
and his stick and shuffled toward the door. "She is the woman I
love," he said.

"Love, is it?" shouted Sally. "See how much love you find there
after today, Mr Callender! She'll have nothing to do with you now!
You're mine! Do you think I spent two years on my back for the
pure pleasure of it?" She rushed to follow him, shouting in his ear.

Callender summoned up a drunken dignity. "There is nothing you
can do to prevent this marriage," he said. "You and I shall not meet
again."

"I've stopped you already," Sally screamed. "I sent her a note,
that's what I did. A letter telling her what you had been to me.
She'll have read it by now, and that'll be an end to any love
between you!"

Callender staggered back against the door. To have lost two fortunes in so short a time was more than he could bear. Without thinking, without even wishing to, he slammed his ebony walking stick into Sally's face.

She seemed bewildered, and she made a whimpering sound. He saw by the candlelight that he had turned her right eye into red pulp.

She put her hand to her face, and something came away in it. She dropped to her knees and began to wail.

Callender was horrified. He stooped to help her, but she pushed him away and crawled across the floor. She began to scream.

It was intolerable. He hit her again, this time on the top of her head, but it only made her screams louder.

He struck her twice more. The stick broke, and Sally slumped to the floor. The screaming stopped.

Callender ran down the stairs and into the street. In an alley, in the rain, he vomited again and again. At first he thought it would kill him, but when he was done his head began to clear. The storm was lifting, and the gleams of lightning seemed to come from miles away.

He was almost home when he realized that he was holding only half a stick. He gazed at the jagged stump in disbelief. He tried to convince himself that he had dropped the other half somewhere in the street, but he felt a sick certainty that it was lying beside Sally Wood. Could it be used to identify him? Callender had heard of the detective inspectors newly appointed to Scotland Yard, and of the tricks they could play in catching criminals of every kind. He could not take the chance of leaving anything behind.

The journey back was agonizing. He wanted nothing less than to visit Sally Wood again, yet speed seemed imperative since he knew her corpse would be discovered eventually. He had to be there and gone again before it was. He could not bear to think of what would happen if he were caught with her corpse, yet he could not think of anything else. He wanted a drink. He was half tempted to hurry home for one, yet all the while his feet were carrying him back to The Glass Slipper. His thoughts were so agitated that he found himself there before he was quite prepared.

Several loungers stood outside, and the faint sound of music came from within. It was as if nothing had happened. Could it be that they didn't know?

The thought froze Callender for an instant, and then he backed into the shadows of an alley. For the first time in his life he was afraid to be seen. Yet it was madness to remain here, a few feet from his crime but doing nothing to conceal it. He pulled down his hat and turned up his collar as if seeking protection from the rain, then stepped casually out into the street and walked briskly round the corner.

He looked up at Sally's solitary window, where a light still burned. There was no hue and cry, no sign of anything but sleep. He pushed the street door open cautiously, thanking whatever power might protect him that he had neglected to close anything behind him in his hurry to be gone. He crept up the stairs, his ear cocked for the slightest sound. The house was as still, he thought wryly, as a tomb.

And so it remained until he reached Sally's door. The sound he heard behind it gave him a chill the rain could not. He knew it must be his imagination, some symptom of a guilty conscience, but he would have sworn he recognized the melody of the song Sally had performed at The Glass Slipper not more than an hour ago. Someone seemed to be humming it.

Could this be a ghost? Another trick of that damned spiritualist? He didn't believe it. He couldn't. It had to be a trick of his own mind. A small thing, really, and he needed the rest of that stick.

He opened the door.

What he saw was worse than what he feared. It was Sally, her face awash with blood and her pretty hair matted down with it. She was crawling on her hands and knees around the room, singing her song as best she could through lips that dribbled blood. She had not died at all, but clearly she should have.

Sally knocked over a table, but still she sang her song. Callender realized that he had damaged her beyond repair. She had no idea that he was in the room.

His mouth twitched uncontrollably as he raised his boot and brought it down with all his weight on the back of Sally's neck. He heard the spine snap.

He needed the last of the gin he took from her.

He picked up the second half of his walking stick and hurried home to his bed, where he spent the next three days attempting to convince himself that he had never left it.

IX. The Heiress

Three men dressed in blue gathered in front of a tall brick house near the gates of All Souls Cemetery. Their high hats held sturdy metal frames, and their knee-length coats had buttons made of brass. In each man's belt was a wooden staff; one of them used his to knock on the door.

They waited in the darkness and the damp. One of them shivered in the cold. "There's no one here," he said. "We should have come by day."

"And so we have, some of us, but we had no answer then, anymore than we have now."

"We could break down the door."

"We're only seeking information from a gentleman. The people have little enough use for Scotland Yard without us making a name for ourselves as housebreakers."

"Then knock again."

"I'll give the orders here," said the man with the staff, but he used it again anyway.

A light appeared in one of the windows.

"We've roused someone."

"Be still, will you?"

The door opened slowly and silently; a tall man with a black mustache appeared on the threshold, a black candle in his hand. Its flickering light gleamed unpleasantly on a long scar than ran down the left side of his face.

"Good evening, sir. I hope we have not disturbed you."

"I have been sleeping, constable. What brings you here?"

"A woman, sir. Miss Felicia Lamb."

"I do not see her with you."

"No sir. She's not to be seen anywhere, and that's what concerns us. Are you Mr Newcastle, sir?"

"I am."

"Well, sir, we've been informed that Miss Lamb was a frequent visitor here, and since she's vanished, we take it upon ourselves to make inquiries. We'd be most appreciative of any help."

"I see. Tell me, constable, how long has she been missing?"

"Just three days. It's Sunday, and she was last seen on Thursday night, at a dinner party."

"It has been longer than that since I have seen Miss Lamb, constable. Have you spoken to the people who dined with her?"

"Two of them sir. Her aunt, who mentioned you to us, and a friend of the family, a Mr Nigel Stone. The third would be her betrothed, a Mr Callender. We have visited him several times but found nobody home."

"Perhaps they have run away together."

"Yes. We thought of that. But why should they elope when they were already pledged?"

"From what I have seen of Mr Callender, he is a most headstrong young man."

"So we have been told. You know him, sir?"

"We have met twice. And even on such short acquaintance, I could not form a high opinion of his character."

"As you say, sir. We've had reports that he'd been drinking heavily."

"Just so. Is there more that I can do for you, constable? Would you care to search for Miss Lamb within?"

Sebastian Newcastle stepped aside and gestured into the black recesses of his home.

The three men from Scotland Yard looked into the darkness and then at each other.

"Well, sir," said their leader. "Since you've been good enough to offer, it follows that we needn't bother you tonight. Clearly you have nothing to hide."

"Then may I bid you goodnight, gentlemen? The hour is late."

"Just so, sir. Thanks for your trouble, and good night to you."

Sebastian shut the door and stood for a few moments with nothing to keep him company but the small flame of his candle. When he knew that the men had gone, he turned into the dark depths of the house and called for Felicia, but he knew before he spoke that there would be no answer. She could not be constrained at night; she wandered, ever weaker, through the valley of stones where the dead slept.

Sebastian went out into the night. He dissolved into an iridescent fog before the gates and drifted into All Souls, part of the thick mist that made the land look like a forgotten sea whose turbulence hid all but the wreckage of tortured trees and abandoned monuments. The landscape was more like a limbo for unhappy spirits than a part of the green earth.

He found Felicia sitting on a monument, her pale arms wrapped around the marble figure of an angel, her pale eyes staring off into the fog.

"Three men came to look for you," he said.

"And did three men leave?"

"Since they came from Scotland Yard, it seemed unwise to detain any of them."

"Police," Felicia said. "Have I destroyed your sanctuary here, Sebastian?"

"Perhaps, but that matters little when I see you as you are."

"I am as I wished to be."

"And was it worth it, then, to see life and death as two sides of the same coin, and to hold that coin in your own hand?"

"I have learned much," Felicia said.

"You have learned more than you bargained for. The price of that coin is blood."

Felicia hugged herself and looked down at the ground. "I cannot, Sebastian," she said.

"And yet you must," he said, "and most assuredly you will. The lives of others must become your life, and their blood your own. It is your fate, and none may resist it."

"I shall. I swear it. You know what I am now, better than any other could, but whatever I have become, I am still innocent of blood. I shall not stain my soul with it."

Sebastian turned away from her. She rose and took his arm. "I meant no reproach to you," she said.

"Then I must reproach myself. As you have said, I know what will become of you. You will grow weaker, and the thirst will grow stronger, until at length you will be transformed into the thirst. You saw how long I could resist you, for all my wish to do so."

"You did what I desired you to do," Felicia said.

"I would have done it anyway!"

Sebastian took her beautiful pale face into his cold hands. "You came to me as my bride," he said, "and I have been alone too long. Now I must see to it that you survive."

"Is there no other way?"

"If you can resist the thirst, then it will doom you. Your body will become too frail to move, but still it will contain your soul. Your spirit will never be free to seek the worlds beyond our own. It will be trapped in a lifeless husk, and you will be truly damned."

She gazed deeply into his dark eyes, then stiffened in his arms at the sound of a human voice nearby.

A lantern gleamed dully through the yellow fog.

"Three men," she said, long before she could see them.

"The constables," Sebastian said.

"Then let us greet them and be done with this." She laughed loudly and bitterly.

Three dark figures emerged from the mist, clustering around their light as if they feared to lose it.

"Mr Newcastle," one of them said.

Sebastian bowed slightly but made no reply.

"And Miss Felicia Lamb?"

"And what is that to you?" Felicia snapped.

"Your aunt said you were lost, Miss."

"And now I am found."

"Just so, Miss. But look where we've found you. In a graveyard, at night, and with nothing to cover you but a nightgown."

"This is my mother's wedding dress."

"Oh, I see. A wedding dress, is it? A runaway heiress and a foreign gentleman. You weren't quite honest with us, were you, Mr Newcastle?"

"Sometimes a gentleman must keep his tongue, constable," Felicia said. "Though you seem to know nothing of that."

"No, Miss, I'm no gentleman, right enough. Just a rough fellow trying to do his job. Still, I offer our protection if you ask for it. This is no fit place for a young lady, and no fit company if I'm any judge."

"You may never live to be a judge," Sebastian said. He cast his eye on the lantern in the constable's hand. At once its faint flame turned a blazing red; the metal was too hot to hold. The man screamed in anguish as he dropped the light; suddenly there was only blackness and the smell of burning flesh.

"There is danger in the dark," Sebastian said as he moved forward. He felt Felicia's grip on his shoulder and saw her pale eyes imploring him to stop. Together they watched the three men scramble away through the tombstones and the trees. At last there was silence.

"There will be danger from them," Sebastian finally said. "We might have feasted, and now we must flee. Was it wise for you to stop me?"

"I stopped you because I wanted nothing more than to let you go. To join you, in fact. The one on the right, the young one. I wanted him."

"He was yours, Felicia. He can be yours in a moment."

"No, Sebastian. It must not be. I cannot do what you have done. I never thought of it. I only dreamed of death, and peace, and freedom. I wanted knowledge, not the power to destroy."

"There is more to know," Sebastian said, "and time enough to know it, but only if you will take life."

She pulled back from him, and leaned against a marble slab engraved with the name of one long dead. She had never seemed more beautiful to him, and never more beloved, than when she renounced all that he could offer her.

"You have thrown away the mortal life that you were born to live," he said. "If you throw away this second chance, there will be nothing left for you but an eternity of emptiness."

"Would that be so different from what you endure?"

"At least I still exist. I walk the earth. What could be more precious?"

"Then this is all your magic offers you? The chance to walk the earth like other men?"

"Other men die," Sebastian said.

Felicia reached out to him, took one step forward, and then sank to her knees. "Help me," she murmured.

He looked down at her compassionately. "You must not kneel to me," he said, "or any man."

"I did not do it willingly," she said. "I cannot stand."

"You must have blood, and you must have it now."

"No," she said. "Too late. No blood. No life."

She sank into the damp grass. Sebastian hovered over her; he tried to raise her to her feet. He kissed her; he shouted at her.

Nothing mattered. She could not be awakened.

Sebastian swept her up in his arms and moved toward his house, but he realized at once that men would be waiting for him there. He turned back toward the stones, toward the tombs he had guarded for half a century, but there was no consolation in them. He searched her face for some faint flicker of life and saw nothing but cold perfection. Yet he knew that her soul was trapped within her corpse, and would remain there until time stopped.

He put her to rest in a tomb and raged through the night. Dogs howled, marble shattered like glass, and three men who trembled in the night fog came to the decision that their investigations might be best conducted in the light of day.

X. The Wine Cellar

Reginald Callender awoke to the sound of a distant and insistent banging. It came from far enough away so that it drifted slowly into his consciousness, becoming part of his dreams before it ended them. He was striking something again and again with his cane.

Then he was staring at the ceiling. His head throbbed with each repeated blow on the door downstairs, but Callender only cursed quietly and waited for the noise to stop. He wondered what day it was, and even if it were day at all. He raised one crusted eyelid and saw a stray shaft of sunlight break through the drawn curtains. Then he went back to sleep.

The next time he was disturbed, there was no putting it off. Someone had him by the shoulders, and was shaking him more savagely than the aftermath of drink could ever do. A splash of cold water hit him in the face. Callender shouted, sputtered, and looked up into the ruddy face of his cousin.

"God damn you, sir," Callender roared. "Have you gone completely mad?"

"You call me mad, do you? It's Monday morning. Where have you been for four days, eh? Do you know what's happened to the girl you're going to marry?"

"What? Sally?"

"Who's Sally? What are you talking about? I mean Miss Lamb!"

"Felicia. Of course. I went to see her . . . when was it? But the servants said that she was not at home to me."

"She wasn't at home to anyone, my dear fellow. She has been missing for the best part of a week."

Callender pulled himself into a sitting position. "How long has she been gone?"

"Since last Thursday. The night we had dinner at her house. The night I came to visit you."

"It's been a short enough visit, then, hasn't it? Where have you been ever since? And where's that bottle? My head!"

Callender felt under his bed and came up with what he sought.

"I thought you'd finished all the brandy," Stone said.

"So I did. But there's plenty of port. And now there's cause to celebrate as well. Felicia could never have read that letter, could she?"

"Letter? What letter?"

"A note from someone who wanted to drive us apart. Hasn't anyone seen it?"

"Who cares for letters at a time like this?" demanded Stone.

"No, of course not." Callender took a drink of wine. "And you say Felicia's gone?"

"Well, we did have some word of her."

"We?"

Stone's face turned a bit redder. "I've been with her aunt. Miss Penelope. She's terribly concerned, of course."

"Oh? You've been busy. The wealthy niece is missing, and all at once you're lodging in an elegant house with her spinster aunt."

"I'm doing what should have been done by you," Stone replied defensively. "Have you been locked in this empty house for all these days?"

"Of course I've been here," said Callender. "Where else would I have been?"

"That's what I decided, finally, even though those fellows from Scotland Yard were here more than once and said there wasn't a soul about."

Callender nearly dropped his bottle, and after he caught it he took a long drink. "Scotland Yard?"

"We naturally called them in when we couldn't find the girl, and they just as naturally sought to make inquiries of the man she's going to marry. I think they were a bit suspicious of you until they got some information."

"Thank God for that," said Callender. He sagged back on the bed. "Then I'm not suspected."

"Of course not! Look here, cousin, what's wrong with you? You don't seem to care what's happened to Felicia. Don't you want to hear what's become of her? She's been seen."

Stone paced indignantly across the room while Callender attempted to collect his thoughts. "Then she's safe?" he asked.

"I suppose you could say that, according to the law, but if you ask me I'd say she was in mortal danger. She was seen with that man Newcastle."

Callender leaped from the bed, still half dressed in trousers and a soiled shirt. "Newcastle!" he shouted. He grasped his cousin by the collar and stared wildly into his eyes. "What has he done with her?"

"I don't know, I'm sure," said Stone as he disengaged himself. "But the constables said she was wearing what she called a wedding gown."

"Didn't they stop her? Didn't they take her away with them? My God!"

"Well. They said there was no law against a girl getting married if she had a mind, or taking a walk with her husband in the night air, if it came to that. Even if it was in a graveyard. And I think he did something to frighten them."

Callender snatched up a coat that had been thrown over a chair and began to rummage through its pockets. Half of a broken walking stick rattled to the floor, but he ignored it. At last he found a bedraggled little book and waved it at his cousin with an air of triumph. He sat down heavily in the chair and began turning pages with intense concentration. "He's done for me," he muttered. "And now I'll do for him."

"Look here, Reggie," began Stone.

"Be quiet, you fool! Can't you see I'm reading?"

"I can see I'm no use here," said Stone, more baffled than ever when he saw his cousin reach down for the broken stick and clutch it triumphantly. "I'll let myself out. When you come to your senses, if you do, perhaps you'll do something to help us save Miss Lamb."

He strode from the room, and was halfway down the stairs when he heard Stone raving at him, or at the world.

"Save her? I'll save her! I'm the only one who can! I'm the only one who knows how!"

Nigel Stone never looked back. He locked the front door behind him and stepped out into the afternoon, the first he had seen with even a touch of sun since his arrival in London. He was content to take it as an omen. Elopements there might be, or even abductions, and madness certainly, but what did they matter? He was on his way to meet Miss Penelope Lamb, and for his own part he was happy.

A few minutes later, Reginald Callender came out of the same door and squinted into the same sunlight. His hair was disheveled, his cravat awry, his gait unsteady. He tried to hail a cab, but the first two drivers merely glanced at him and then passed by. A third pulled to a stop a few yards down the street, and Callender staggered after him. The cabman looked down from his perch.

"Let's see the color of your money before you climb aboard," he said.

Callender was obliged to go through his pockets once again. He pulled out Sally's penny dreadful, one half of a broken stick and then the other. A small flask completed the catalog of his possessions.

"Looks like you'll be walking," said the cabman as he trotted off.

Callender hurled *Varney the Vampire* after the retreating cab. "I don't need this anymore," he screamed. "And I don't need you!"

He was suddenly aware that he had attracted the attention of several passersby, and that he was standing in the middle of a tranquil street wailing like a fishwife. He recognized a neighbor who had been accustomed to tip his hat but now looked ostentatiously away. Callender saw the two sharp sticks and the flask that he had been waving in the air. He thrust them back into his coat and hurried away.

It was a long walk to All Souls Cemetery.

Callender's mind raced faster than his feet could carry him, but his thoughts ran in circles. He had lost everything: his fortune, his mistress, his bride, and her fortune too. The list ran through his mind like a litany, so that he began to suspect that he was losing his senses as well. In fact, he thought that he might welcome it if he could go completely mad, when his only alternative was to live in a world where he was besieged by devils.

At least he knew who was to blame. Newcastle had even produced his uncle's ghost, and by this time Callender was more than willing to believe that somehow the spiritualist had plundered his uncle's estate as well. But Newcastle wasn't a spiritualist, of course. He was a vampire.

The explanation seemed so simple to Callender now. Hadn't he heard Felicia holding forth on vampires just before she disappeared? Still, the one he really had to thank was Sally Wood, whose lurid little books on the subject had revealed not only the cause of his troubles, but a remedy for them. And if not a remedy, then at least revenge. Callender felt a twinge of pity when he thought of Sally now; he wished he could have killed her quickly.

His next killing would have to be quick whether he wished it or not. As he approached Newcastle's house, he saw that the sun was low in the sky behind the trees of All Souls. Could it really be that the dead would rise soon?

He hurried toward Sebastian Newcastle's house, but what he saw there disturbed him even more than the setting sun. Before the entrance stood a man dressed in a long blue coat with brass buttons. Clearly the house was under the surveillance of Scotland Yard.

Callender hesitated. His plan had been to ransack the place, find Newcastle's undead corpse, and bury his broken cane in it, but this would hardly be possible under the circumstances. He might get some information from the constable on guard, but he hardly liked the idea of presenting himself to the law when he was a murderer himself. Should he risk it, or should he run?

His mouth was dry. He found the flask in his pocket and drained most of the port; the rest of it spilled down the front of his coat. The drink gave him courage enough to approach the house, and find out what he needed to know. He made an effort to regain his dignity, walking very carefully as he approached the lair of his nemesis. He decided as he took the last few steps that aggression might be more effective than supplication.

"What's going on here?" he said. "Where's Mr Newcastle?"

"That's what we'd like to know, sir. What's your business with him?"

"He's eloped with my fiancee. Is that business enough?"

"Are you Mr Callender? We've been wanting to talk to you. What do you know about all this?"

"Nothing but what I've been told. I quarreled with Miss Lamb, about nothing really, and now I hear this man has spirited her away. Have you any word of her?"

"No more than that, sir. She was seen with him once, in that graveyard yonder, but only then, and only for a moment."

"And have you searched the house?" demanded Callender.

"From top to bottom, sir."

"Are you certain? This is a strange house, you know," said Callender. "One night when I was here, the very walls seemed to dissolve into a fog."

"Indeed, sir! I've had nights like that myself. You seem to be having one now, if I may say so, and it ain't even night yet."

Callender ran the back of his hand over his dry lips. "How would you feel?" he asked. "What would you do? If I find this man Newcastle, I'll kill him."

"Well, sir, as to that, if a man ran off with my old woman, I'd buy him a drink! Eh? We mustn't take these things too serious." The constable paused, and squinted at Callender as if seeing him for the first time. "You wouldn't kill a lady, would you, sir?"

Callender swallowed hard. "Whatever do you mean?" he stammered. "Of course not!"

"Sometimes gentlemen lose their heads, in a manner of speaking. And Miss Lamb can't be found, you know."

"You're a fool," said Callender, turning on his heel.

"That's as may be, sir," the constable shouted at Callender's retreating back. "Will we find you at home, if something should turn up?"

Callender hurried off without bothering to reply. He could hardly have controlled himself for another second, especially when the talk of killing women started. The man seemed to be an ignorant commoner, but who could tell?

As he passed the cemetery once again, Callender noticed that the gates were open. He paused before them and peered in. This was where Felicia had been only a few hours before. If she and Newcastle were not in the house, might they not still be here? Callender entered All Souls.

The place was peaceful in the twilight, almost like a park with its green grass and gently rolling hills. Birds sang in the trees and perched on figures of white marble. This was like a city of the dead, and Callender hardly knew which way to turn in it. Rows of effigies and headstones stretched in every direction; in the distance lay clusters of white mausoleums.

Almost helplessly, he moved along the streets of marble toward his Uncle William's tomb. There his torment had started; perhaps it would end there, too. He had a vision, half inspired by Sally's cheap fiction, of rushing to that pale edifice and finding Felicia imprisoned there, the victim of a villain he could vanquish with one blow of his ebony stick. He longed to be a hero almost as much as he longed for another drink. He prayed to be free of his nightmare.

When he reached his goal, however, he found an avenging angel posed before it. Sitting in front of his uncle's final resting place was another man dressed in blue. His left hand was wrapped in bandages.

"Mr Callender," he said. "Paying your last respects?"

"I don't know you," said Callender as he backed away.

"We should be better acquainted, then. What brings you here this evening?"

It took Callender some time to find his tongue. "I'm told Miss Lamb was seen here," he finally said.

"At this very spot? Who told you that? None of my men, I'll warrant you."

"This is the only spot I know," said Callender. "My uncle is interred behind you."

"I see. And does he lie alone?"

"Is there someone else?" gasped Callender. "Felicia? Newcastle?"

"Neither of those, sir," said the chief constable.

"Then where are they?"

"We don't know yet." The chief constable stood up. "But we do know there are two bodies in that tomb that don't belong there, both of them horribly mutilated. The bodies of two young boys. What do you make of that, Mr Callender, sir?"

Callender backed away, almost convinced that this was another of his drunken dreams. The man from Scotland Yard just stared at him. Callender wheeled around and ran.

Running suited him, Callender decided. His lungs rasped, his heart thumped, and his stomach churned, but he was leaving everything behind him. When he glanced back, the immobile man in blue had dwindled to a tiny figure, no more threatening than a toy soldier.

Still, under darkening skies, Callender ran. He ran past monuments and mausoleums, through iron gates, then down streets where living men and women walked who scattered at the sight of him. He tumbled into the gutter once, and when he rose he was face to face with a lamp-lighter on his rounds. "So soon?" screamed Callender as he raced on.

He knew that he must be home before night fell.

He could hardly believe his good fortune when he reached the ugly, empty house that was his sanctuary. He fumbled for his key, and howled in agony when it was nowhere to be found. In panic, he pounded on the door, then to his amazement felt it open for him. Dimly he recalled that he had never had his key, and never locked the house. He slammed his door on the sunset and turned the bolt behind him. He was safe.

Callender sank to his knees in the dark hallway. He was ruined, and he acknowledged it. He wandered through the hollow rooms while the last rays of the day died outside. He was on the verge of tears, and he hated himself for that. The tears might have been for Felicia Lamb, or for Sally Wood, or even for his Uncle William, but all these had betrayed him. Callender wept for himself.

It made no difference.

He beat his hands against bare walls; he cursed the universe. It did not care.

At length his desolation brought him to himself, which was all that he had left to him. It was not enough. He could at least have a bottle to keep him company.

In the last week he had learned the way to the wine cellar. He thought he might take residence there, among the dusty bottles and the crates of cloth his cousin had brought back from India. He could make a bed for himself in the worthless textiles, and the wine would be close at hand. The idea pleased him. He made his way through the kitchen, and the pantry, where he found the stub of a candle to light his way.

The dark stairs were old friends to him, and the dark vault that he had reached was refuge. He found the shelves where the old port rested, and picked the best vintage left to him. He broke the top off the bottle and poured the rich, red liquid down his throat. He had to spit out a chip of glass, but at least it had only cut his lip.

He sat down in the dust and looked around. He drank again, but at the same time he noticed that something had been disturbed. One of the heavy boxes from India had been removed from the pile and set in the middle of the cellar. Its lid was loose.

Callender approached it cautiously. He left the candle on the floor, to keep both hands free. And as soon as he touched the top of the box, it clattered to the stones below.

There seemed to be nothing more inside than bolts of dyed cotton, but Callender was dissatisfied. He pulled the colored cloth aside. Beneath it was the face of Sebastian Newcastle.

Callender was too stunned to relish the sight, but only for a moment. He had found the lair of the vampire in the foundations of his own house. Felicia might be anywhere, in any state, but at least her betrayer had betrayed himself. Callender chuckled at a clever ruse that had gone awry. No doubt the vampire had imagined himself ingeniously concealed; he had not realized that Callender's thirst was as ravenous as his own. Callender tossed more cotton to the floor, and saw Sebastian Newcastle naked to the waist. The sight of this nude seducer drove him into a frenzy.

There were shadows all around him, and Callender knew that the sun had set. He knew the monster might leap up and devour him. He pulled half of the broken cane out of his coat; one end was needle sharp. He needed something to strike the fatal blow, and he needed it at once. The heavy butt end of the wine bottle would do.

Callender felt his own heart beating wildly, and this helped him to select the precise spot where he should strike. He placed the jagged point against the cold smooth skin. He smashed the shaft down with the heavy glass.

The ebony ripped through the yielding flesh, and a high pitched wail was forced from the corpse's lips, startling Callender into striking again and again. Each blow produced a delicate moan that made his skin crawl. The death agonies were uncanny. Something was wrong.

The vampire's body began to shake. It thrashed from side to side, then crumbled like a hollow shell. Pieces of flesh dropped away. A glass eye rolled across the cellar. The skin shattered. Something was breaking free.

Shards of Sebastian flew in all directions, and others settled into the box. Most of his face came to rest beside the other face beneath it.

Felicia Lamb lay among wax fragments, the sharp shaft of Callender's broken cane embedded in her breast.

Callender wondered why she didn't bleed. He had no way of knowing that there was not a drop of blood inside her. She was as white as a marble statue. Her golden hair, unleashed as he had never seen it, spread round her head like a halo. And all about her were parts of a waxen man, the remnants of Newcastle's last cruel joke.

Callender thought he saw Felicia's lashes flutter, her lips part, her fingers reaching toward her shattered heart. Then she was still, garbed in a gown of pure white silk. She looked like a sleeping angel.

His candle flared for an instant.

Callender laughed. He could hardly help himself. He picked up the bits of wax and smashed them underfoot. He found another bottle and broke its neck, drinking from sharp glass that sliced into his lips.

He heard footsteps overhead, and knowing that they came for him, he laughed again.

They found him there, his mouth dribbling blood, beside the punctured corpse of his beloved. The sound of his incoherent voice had drawn them to him.

There were three men in blue, one of them holding a lantern in his bandaged hand. Behind them came Nigel Stone, apologetically brandishing a key. The light sent shadows shimmering all over the wine cellar.

"Mr Callender," said the chief constable. "What have you been doing to Miss Lamb?"

XI. The Conscientious Cousin

Mr and Mrs Nigel Stone sat side by side on a horsehair settee and shared a bottle of fine old sherry.

Their wedding might have been a hasty one, but, as Mrs Stone observed, a hasty wedding was better than none at all. And furthermore, their union served to disperse the sadness that might have blighted both their lives.

"To think that I have married a hero!" chirped Mrs Stone.

"Not really," murmured Mr Stone. "I only let the fellows in to capture him."

"But you might have been killed!" she said.

"I suppose so. He did have another half of that stick in his coat."

"I have found a brave man and inherited a fortune in the same week," said Mrs Stone. "Was any woman ever so blessed?"

"Oh, I don't know," said Mr Stone. "I've come home from years in the wilderness, and right away I've found a charming bride. Surely I'm the lucky one."

The bride and groom exchanged chaste kisses.

"Did you hear that Madame Tussaud will be putting poor Felicia and your cousin on display?" asked Mrs Stone. "They will be part of a large addition to The Dead Room. It pleases me to think that the poor girl won't be forgotten."

"Indeed," said Mr Stone.

"Would it be in bad taste for us to visit the display?"

"Just as you think best, Penelope."

Mrs Stone took a thoughtful sip of sherry. "And what of Mr Newcastle?" she asked. "Has he been found?"

"Not a trace of him, I'm afraid." said Mr Stone. "The police think Reggie might have done away with him as well, and of course that's what the fool said he'd done when he shoved that stick into Felicia's heart."

"Yes," said Mrs Stone. "Was there much blood?"

"What? I really didn't like to look at her, to tell you the truth. She seemed quite clean, though, really, but poor old Reggie had blood all over his mouth."

"And had he really lost his mind?"

"What other explanation could there be for such unchivalrous behavior?" Mr Stone filled both their glasses. "I wonder if they'll keep him in the madhouse or just take him out and hang him. I wish there were more I could do for him somehow."

"I hardly think you need concern yourself, after his barbaric treatment of my niece."

"As you say, Penelope. At least I did him one good turn."

"And what was that?"

"A small thing, really. I went back to the house the day after all that happened, and I found a packing crate in the hallway."

"A packing crate?"

"Yes, and quite a large one. It was sealed, and the labels were on it, so I took it on myself to have it sent on, though heaven knows what business Reggie could have in India."

"India?"

"It was addressed to some fellow in Calcutta. I don't remember who it was, but it looked to me like some sort of Spanish name."

"A Spanish name?" said Mrs Stone. "Oh, dear!"

Steve Rasnic Tem

Vintage Domestic

Steve Rasnic Tem lives with his wife, writer Melanie Tem, in a supposedly haunted Victorian house in Denver, Colorado.

One of the most prolific authors currently working in the anthology and small press markets, recent appearances have included Fantasy Tales 4, Pulphouse 7, Psycho-Paths 2, New Crimes 3, Best New Horror *and* Best New Horror 2, The Year's Best Fantasy and Horror, In Dreams, Tales of the Wandering Jew, The Dedalus Book of Femmes Fatales, Snow White Blood Red, Gauntlet 3 *and the chapbook* Absenses: Charlie Goode's Ghosts.

His short fiction was collected by publisher Denoel in France under the title Ombres sur la route, *and his novel* Excavation *appeared in 1987.*

The powerful story that follows is original to this collection . . .

SHE USED TO tell him that they'd have the house forever. One day their children would live there. When Jack grew too old to walk, or to feed himself, she would take care of him in this house. She would feed him right from her own mouth, with a kiss. He'd always counted on her keeping this promise.

But as her condition worsened, as the changes accelerated, he realized that this was a promise she could not keep. The roles were to be reversed, and it was to be he who fed his lifetime lover with a kiss full of raw meat and blood. Sweet, domestic vintage.

Early in their marriage his wife had told him that there was this history of depression in her family. That's the way members of the family always talked about it: the sadness, the melancholy, the long slow condition. Before he understood what this meant he hadn't taken it that seriously, because at the time she never seemed depressed. Once their two oldest reached the teen years, however, she became sad, and slow to move, her eyes dark stones in the clay mask of her face, and she stopped telling him about her family's history of depression. When he asked her about the old story, she acted as if she didn't know what he was talking about.

At some point during her rapid deterioration someone had labeled his family "possibly dysfunctional." Follow-up visits from teachers and social workers had removed "possibly" from his family's thickening file. Studies and follow-up studies had been completed, detailed reports and addenda analyzing his children's behavior and the family dynamics. He had fought them all the way, and perhaps they had tired of the issue, because they finally gave up on their investigations. His family had weathered their accusations. He had protected his wife and children, fulfilled his obligations. Finally people left them alone, but they could not see that something sacred was occurring in this house.

The house grew old quickly. But not as quickly as his wife and children.

"You're so damned cheerful all the time," she said to him. "It makes me sick."

At one time that might have been a joke. Looking into her gray eyes at this moment, he knew it was not. "I'm maintaining," he said. "That's all." He thought maybe her vision was failing her. He was sure it had been months since he'd last smiled. He bent over her with the tea, then passed her a cracker. She stretched her neck and tried to catch his lips in her teeth. He expected a laugh but it didn't come.

"You love me?" she asked, her voice flat and dusty. He put the cracker in his mouth and let her take it from his lips. He could hear his teenage daughters in the next room moaning from the bed. They'd been there two months already, maybe more.

She reached up with a brittle touch across his cheek. "They take after me, you know?" And then she *did* smile, then opened her mouth around a dry cough of a laugh.

Downstairs their seven-year-old son made loud motorcycle noises with moist lips and tongue. Thank God he takes after his father, he thought, and would have laughed if he could. Beneath him his sweet wife moaned, her lips cracked and peeling. A white tongue flickered like the corner of a starched handkerchief.

He bit down hard into the tender scar on the inside of his mouth. He ground one tooth, two, through the tentative pain. When he tasted salt he began to suck, mixing the salt and iron taste with a saliva that had become remarkable in its quantity, until the frothy red cocktail was formed.

He bent over her lips with this beverage kiss and allowed her tongue to meet his, her razor teeth still held back in supplication. In this way he fed her when she could no longer feed herself, when she could not move, when she could not hunt, when in their house tall curtains of dust floated gently around them.

"The girls," she said, once her handkerchief tongue was soaked and her pale lips glistened pinkly.

But still he could not go into his daughters' bedroom, and had to listen to them moan their hunger like pale and hairless, motherless rats.

"Tell me again, Jack," his wife whispered wetly from the bed. "Tell me again how wonderful life is." These were among the last words she would ever use with him.

The young man at the front door wore the blue uniform of the delivery service. Overripe brown sacks filled each of his arms, blending into his fat cheeks as if part of them. He smiled all the time. Jack smiled a hungry smile back.

"Your groceries, sir." Behind him were the stirrings of dry skin against cloth, insect legs, pleadings too starved and faint to be heard clearly.

As the young man handed the sacks over to him, Jack's fingertips brushed the pale backs of the man's hands. He imagined he could feel the heat there, the youthful coursing through veins, feeding pale tissues, warming otherwise cold meat.

Sometimes he took his daughters hunting, if they were strong enough, but so far he had been able to limit them to slugs, worms, insects, small animals. He wondered how long he could hold them to that when the stores kept sending them tender young delivery boys. He wondered how long it would be before his daughters were as immobile as his wife, and begged him to bring them something more. Somewhere behind him there was a tiny gasp, the rising pressure of tears which could not fall.

Some evenings he would sit up talking to his family long into the night. They did not always respond precisely to his confessions of loneliness, of dreams which did not include them, and he wondered if it was because of the doors that separated them from him.

Sometimes he would go to the closet doors and open them. Where his wife stood, folded back against the wall with the coats and robes. Where his daughters leaned one against the other like ancient, lesbian mops. *Kiss us*, the dry whisper came from somewhere within the pale flaps of their faces. Jack still loved them desperately, but he could not do what they asked.

His youngest, his only son, had taken to his bed.

Jack brought his daughters mice and roaches he had killed himself. They sucked on them like sugar candy until most of the color was gone, and then they spat them out.

Months ago they had stopped having their periods. The last few times had been pale pink and runny. and Jack had cried for them, then cleaned them up with old burlap sacks.

His son disappeared from his bed one evening. Jack found him standing in the closet, his eyes full of moths, his hands stiffened into hooks.

Later his son would disappear from time to time, sometimes showing up in one of the other closets, clutching at mother or sisters, sometimes curled up inside the empty toy box (the boy had no more use for toys, having his own body to play with—sometimes he'd chew a finger into odd shapes).

Jack continued to feed his wife from his own mouth. Sometimes his mouth was so raw he could not tear any more skin off the insides. Then he'd bite through a rat or a bird himself, holding its rank warmth in his cheeks until he could deliver the meal. She returned his kisses greedily, always wanting more than he could provide. But he had spoiled her. She would not feed any other way.

His son became a good hunter, and sometimes Jack would hear him feeding on the other side of the closet door. Pets began disappearing from the neighborhood, and Jack stopped answering the door even for delivery boys.

His daughters became despondent and refused to eat. When he opened their closet door they tried to disguise themselves as abandoned brooms. Finally Jack had to hold them one at a time, forcing his blood smeared tongue past their splintered lips into the dry cisterns of their mouths so that they might leech nourishment. Once he'd overcome their initial resistance they scraped his tongue clean, then threatened to carve it down to the root, but Jack always knew the exact moment to pull out.

Sometimes he wondered if they still considered him a good father, an adequate husband. He tried singing his children lullabies, reciting poetry to his wife. They nodded their full heads of dust in the gale of his breath, but said nothing.

When the food delivery boys no longer came he saved a portion of his kills for himself. And whenever possible he swallowed his own bloody wet kisses, and tried to remember the feel of his wife's hands on his face, back when her skin was soft and her breath was sweet.

In the houses around him, he knew a hundred hearts beat, desperately chasing life's apprehensions through a racecourse of veins. He tried to ignore the hunger brought on by such thinking. He tried to picture his neighbors' faces, but could not.

His family became so light he could carry them about the house without effort. If he hadn't heard their close whispers, he might have thought them a few old towels thrown across his shoulder. Sometimes he would set them down and forget them, later rushing around in panic to find where they'd been mislaid.

The lighter, the thinner they became, the more blood they seemed to require. When his mouth became too sore to chew he would apply razor blades to the scar tissue, slicing through new white skin into the thicker layers beneath, finally into muscle so that the blood would fill his mouth to spilling before he could get his mouth completely over theirs. Blood stained their thin chests with a rough crimson bib.

And still they grew thinner, their bones growing fibrous, pulpy before beginning to dissolve altogether. He made long rips in his forearms, his thighs, his calves, and held his wife and children up to drink there. The blood soaked through the tissues of their flesh, through the translucent fibres of their hair, washing through their skin until in the dusty shadows of the house they looked vaguely tanned.

But almost as quickly they were pale again, and thin as a distant memory.

He took to slicing off hunks of thigh muscle, severing fingertips, toes. His family ate for months off the bloody bits, their small rat teeth nibbling listlessly. They had ceased using words of any kind long ago, so they could not express their thanks. But Jack didn't mind. This was the family he'd always dreamed of. The look of appreciation in their colorless eyes was thanks enough.

At first he tore his clothes to rags to staunch the blood, but even the rags eventually fell apart. One day seeing his son sucking up the last bit of red from a torn twist of cloth he decided to forego the last vestiges of his modesty and throw the ragged clothes away. After that time he would walk about the dreary old house naked, wearing only the paperthin bodies of his family wrapped around him, their mouths fixed tightly to his oozing wounds.

This went on for months, wearing his family constantly, their feeding so regular and persistent it seemed to alter the very rhythm of his heart. He would wake up in the middle of the night to the soft sucking noise their lips and teeth made against his flesh. He would awaken a few hours later and the first thing he would see was the stupored look in their eyes as they gazed up at him in adoration. He was pleased to see that such constant nourishment fattened them and brought color to their skin so that eventually they fell off his body from the sheer weight of them.

Wriggling about his feet at first, they eventually decided to explore the house on their own. Obviously, they felt far healthier than before.

Again they did not thank him, but what did a good husband and father need of thanks?

They soon grew thin again, soft, transparent.

After a year he had not seen them again. Although occasionally he might swear to a face hidden within the upholstery, an eye rolling past a furniture leg, a dry mouth praying silently among the house plants filmed in a dark, furry dust.

After five years even the garbled whispering had stopped. He continued to watch over the house, intent on his obligation. And after preparing a blood kiss in the pale vacancy of his mouth, he was content to drink it himself.

Kim Newman

Red Reign

Kim Newman is a prolific writer, editor, broadcaster and film critic whose novels and short fiction have fast gained him a cult reputation and regular appearances in the "Year's Best" anthologies.

In 1990, Newman won the Horror Writers of America Bram Stoker Award for Horror: 100 Best Books *(with Stephen Jones), and the following year he picked up the British Science Fiction Award for his story 'The Original Dr Shade'. His other non-fiction works include* Ghastly Beyond Belief *(with Neil Gaiman),* Nightmare Movies *and* Wild West Movies. *As well as editing the music anthology* In Dreams *(with Paul J. McAuley) and writing a series of gaming novelisations and a downmarket horror novel under the byline of "Jack Yeovil", his novels include* The Night Mayor, Bad Dreams *and* Jago, *and he plans to expand "Red Reign" for future book publication under the title* Anno Dracula.

In the meantime, experience Newman's typically bizarre alternate Victorian society, where vampires hold sway. And while you are along for the ride, see how many references from movies, literature and history you can spot in this fanciful short novel, being published here for the very first time.

I
Dr Seward's Diary
(Kept in phonograph.)

8 SEPTEMBER, 1888. *Tonight's was easier than last week's. Perhaps, with
practice, everything becomes easier. If never easy. Never . . . easy.*

I'm sorry

*It is hard to keep one's thoughts in order, and this apparatus is unforgiving
of digressions. I cannot ink over hasty words, terminate unthought-out thoughts,
tear out a spoiled page. I must be concise. After all, I have had medical training.
This record may be of importance to posterity.*

Very well.

*Subject: female, apparently in her twenties. Recently dead, I would say. Pro-
fession: obvious. Location: Hanbury Street, Whitechapel. Near the Salvation
Army mission. Time: shortly before five in the morning. The fog was thick as
mud, which is the best for my nightwork. In this year, fog is welcome. The
less one can see of what London has become, the better.*

*She gave her name as Lulu. She was not English. From her accent, I
would judge her German or Austrian by birth. A pretty thing, distinctive.
Shiny black hair cut short and lacquered, in an almost Chinese style. In
the fog and with the poor light of the street, her red lips seemed quite
black. Like all of them, she smiled too easily, disclosing sharp little pearl-
chip teeth. A cloud of cheap perfume, sickly sweet scent to cover the reek
of decay.*

*The streets are filthy in Whitechapel, open sewers of vice and foulness. The
dead are everywhere.*

*She laughed musically, the sound like something wrung from a mechanism,
and beckoned me over, loosening the ragged feathers around her throat. Lulu's
laugh reminded me of Lucy. Lucy when she was alive, not the leech-thing we
finished in Kingstead Cemetery.*

*Three years ago, when only Van Helsing believed . . . The world has changed
since then. Thanks to the Prince Consort.*

*Van Helsing would have understood my nightwork. When he was alive. And
the others. A family, we were. My friend Arthur Holmwood, the Texan Morris,
the clerk Harker, his wife. And the Dutch doctor, mangling the language and
tutting over his impedimenta. Only I am left of the family. Alive. I must continue
to fight . . .*

*I learned from last week's in Buck's Row—Polly Nicholls, the newspapers
say her name was, Polly or Mary Ann—to do it quickly and precisely. Throat.
Heart. Tripes. Then get the head off. That finishes the things. Clean silver,
and a clean conscience. Van Helsing, blinkered by folklore and symbolism, spoke*

always of the heart, but any of the major organs will do. The kidneys are easiest to get to.

I had made my preparations carefully. For half an hour, I sat in my office, allowing myself to become aware of the pain in my right hand. The madman is dead—truly dead—but Renfield left his jaw-marks, semi-circles of deep indentations, scabbed over many times but never right again. With Nicholls, my mind was still dull from the laudanum I take for the pain, and I was not as precise as I might have been. Learning to be left-handed hasn't helped either. I missed the major artery, and the thing had time to screech before I could saw through the neck. I am afraid I lost control, and became a butcher when I should be a surgeon, a deliverer.

Lulu went better. She clung as tenaciously to life, but I think there was an acceptance of my gift. She was relieved, at the last, to have her soul cleansed by silver. It is hard to come by. Now, the coinage is all gold or copper. I kept back a store of sovereigns while the money was changing, and found a tradesman who would execute my commission. I've had the surgical instruments since my days at the Purfleet asylum. Now the blades are plated, a core of steel strength inside killing silver. Before venturing out into the fog, I unlocked my private cabinet and spent some time looking at the shine of the silver. This time, I selected the postmortem scalpel. It is fitting, I think, to employ a tool intended for rooting around in the bodies of the dead.

Lulu invited me into a doorway to do her business, and wriggled her skirts up over slim white legs. I took the time to open her blouse, to get her collar and feathers away from her unmarked throat. She asked about my lumpily-gloved hand, and I told her it was an old wound. She smiled and I drew my silver edge across her neck, pressing firmly with my thumb, cutting deep into pristine deadflesh.

I held her up with my body, shielding my work from any passersby, and slipped the scalpel through her ribs into her heart. I felt her whole body shudder, and then fall lifeless. But I know how resilient the dead can be, and took care to finish the job, exposing as well as puncturing the heart, cutting a few of the tubes in the belly, taking out the kidneys and part of the uterus, then enlarging the throat wound until the head came loose. Having exposed the vertebrae, I worried the head back and forth until the neckbones parted.

There was little blood in her. She must not have fed tonight.

II

She rested in her tiny office at Toynbee Hall. It was as safe a place as any to pass the few days each month when lassitude came over her and she shared the sleep of the dead. Up high in the building, the room had only a tiny skylight and the door could be secured from the inside. It served its purpose, just as coffins and crypts served for those of the Prince Consort's bloodlike.

She heard hammering. Insistent, repeated blows. Noise reached into her dark fog. Meat and bone pounding against wood.

In her dreams, Genevieve had been back in her warm girlhood. When she had been her father's daughter, not Chandagnac's get. Before she had been turned, before the Dark Kiss had made her what she had become.

Her tongue felt sleep-filmed teeth. Her eyes opened, and she tried to focus on the dingy glass of the skylight. The sun was not yet down.

In her dreams, the hammering had been a mallet striking the end of a snapped-in-half quarterstaff. The English captain had finished her father-in-darkness like a butterfly, pinning Chandagnac to the bloodied earth. Those had been barbarous times.

In an instant, dreams were washed away and she was awake, as if a gallon of icy water had been dashed into her face.

"Mademoiselle Dieudonné," a voice sounded. "Open up."

She sat up, the sheet falling away from her body. She slept on the floor, on a blanket laid over the rough planks.

"There's been another murder."

Genevieve took a Chinese silk robe from a hook by the door, and drew it around herself. It was not what etiquette recommended she wear while entertaining a gentleman caller, but it would have to do. Etiquette, so important a few short years ago, meant less and less. They were sleeping in coffins lined with earth in Mayfair, and drinking from their servants' necks, and so the correct form of address for a Bishop was hardly a major consideration this year.

She slid back the bolts, and the hammering stopped. She had traces of fog still in her head. Outside, the afternoon was dying. She would not be at her best until night was around her again. She pulled open her door, and saw a small new-born, with a long coat around him like a cloak and a bowler hat in his hand, standing in the corridor outside.

"Inspector Lestrade," she said, allowing the detective in. His jagged, irregular teeth stuck awkwardly out of his mouth, unconcealed by the scraggly moustache he had been cultivating. The sparse whiskers only made him look more like a rat than he had done when he was alive. He wore smoked glasses, but crimson points behind the lenses suggested active eyes.

The Scotland Yard man took off his hat, and set it down upon her desk.

"Last night," he began, hurriedly, "in Hanbury Street. It was butchery, plain and simple."

"Last night?"

"I'm sorry," he drew breath, making an allowance for her recent sleep. "It's the eighth now. Of September."

"I've been asleep three days."

"I thought it best to rouse you. Feelings are running high. The warm are getting restless, and the new-borns."

"You were quite right," she said. She rubbed sleep-gum from her eyes, and tried to clear her head. Even the last shards of sunlight, filtered through the grimy square of glass above, were icicles jammed into her forehead.

"When the sun is set," Lestrade was saying, "there'll be pandemonium on the streets. It could be another Bloody Sunday. Some say Van Helsing has come back."

"The Prince Consort would love that."

Lestrade shook his head. "It's just a rumour. Van Helsing is dead. His head is still on a spike outside the Palace."

"You've checked?"

"The Palace is always under guard. The Prince Consort has his Carpathians about him. Our kind cannot be too careful. We have many enemies."

"Our kind?"

"The Un-Dead."

Genevieve almost laughed. "I'm not your kind, Inspector. You are of the bloodline of Vlad Tepes, I am of the bloodline of Chandagnac. We are at best cousins."

The detective shrugged and snorted at the same time. Bloodline meant nothing to the vampires of London, Genevieve knew. Even at a third, a tenth or a twentieth remove, they all had the Prince Consort as father-in-darkness.

"Has the news travelled?"

"Fast," the detective told her. "The evening editions all carry the story. It'll be all over London by now. There are those among the warm who do not love us, Mademoiselle Dieudonné. They are rejoicing. And when the new-borns come out, there could be a panic. I've requested troops, but Commissioner Warren is leery of sending in the army. After that business last year . . ."

A group of warm insurrectionists, preaching sedition against the Crown, had rioted in Trafalgar Square. Someone declared a Republic, and tried to rally the anti-monarchist forces. Sir Charles Warren, the Commissioner of Scotland Yard, had called in the army, and a new-born lieutenant had ordered his men, a mixture of vampires and the living, to fire upon the demonstrators. The Revolution had nearly started then. If it had not been for the intervention of the Queen herself, the Empire could have exploded like a barrel of gunpowder.

"And what, pray, can I do," Genevieve asked, "to serve the purpose of the Prince Consort?"

Lestrade chewed his moustache, teeth glistening, flecks of froth on his lips.

"You may be needed, Mademoiselle. The hall is being overrun. Some don't want to be out on the streets with this murderer about. Some are spreading panic and sedition, firing up vigilante mobs. You have some influence . . ."

"I do, don't I?"

"I wish . . . I would humbly request . . . you would use your influence to calm the situation. Before any disaster occurs. Before any more are unnecessarily killed."

Genevieve was not above enjoying the taste of power. She slipped off her robe, shocking the detective with her nakedness. Death and rebirth had not shaken the prejudices of his time out of him. While Lestrade tried to shrink behind his smoked glasses, she swiftly dressed, fastening the seeming hundreds of small catches and buttons with neat movements of sharp-tipped fingers. After all these years, it was as if the costume of her warm days, as intricate and cumbersome as a full suit of armour, had returned to plague her again. As a new-born, she had, with relief, worn the simple tunics and trews made acceptable if not fashionable by the Maid of Orleans, vowing never again to let herself be sewed into breath-stopping formal dress.

The Inspector was too pale to blush properly, but penny-sized red patches appeared on his cheeks and he huffed involuntarily. Lestrade, like many new-borns, treated her as if she were the age of her face. She had been sixteen in 1432 when Chandagnac gave her the Dark Kiss. She was older, by a decade or more, than the Prince Consort. While he was a new-born, nailing Turks' turbans to their skulls and lowering his countrymen onto sharpened posts, she had been a full vampire, continuing the bloodline of her father-in-darkness, learning the skills that now made her among the longest-lived of her kind. With four and a half centuries behind her, it was hard not to be irritated when the fresh-risen dead, still barely cooled, patronised her.

"This murderer must be found, and stopped," Lestrade said. "Before he kills again."

"Indubitably," Genevieve agreed. "It sounds like a problem for your old associate, the consulting detective."

She could sense, with the sharpened perceptions that told her night was falling, the chilling of the Inspector's heart.

"Mr Holmes is not available, Mademoiselle. He has his differences with the current government."

"You mean he has been removed—like so many of our finest minds—to those pens on the Sussex Downs. What are the newspapers calling them, concentration camps?"

"I regret his lack of vision . . ."

"Where is he? Devil's Dyke?"

Lestrade nodded, almost ashamed. There was a lot of the man left inside. Many new-borns clung to their warm lives as if nothing had changed. Genevieve wondered how long they would last before they grew like the bitch vampires the Prince Consort brought from the land beyond the mountains, an appetite on legs, mindlessly preying.

Genevieve finished with her cuffs, and turned to Lestrade, arms lightly out. That was a habit born of four hundred and fifty years without mirrors, always seeking an opinion on how she looked. The detective nodded grudging approval, and she was ready to face the world. She pulled a hooded cloak around her shoulders.

In the corridor outside her room, gaslamps were already lit. Beyond the row of windows, the hanging fog was purging itself of the last blood of the dying sun.

One window was open, letting in cold night air. Genevieve could taste life in it. She would have to feed soon, within two or three days. It was always that way after her sleep.

"I have to be at the inquest," Lestrade said. "It might be best if you came."

"Very well, but I must talk with the director first. Someone will have to take care of my duties."

They were on the stairs. Already, the building was coming to life. No matter how London had changed with the coming of the Prince Consort, Toynbee Hall was still required. The poor and destitute needed shelter, food, medical attention, education. The new-borns, potentially immortal destitutes, were hardly better off than their warm brothers and sisters. Sometimes, Genevieve felt like Sisyphus, forever rolling a rock uphill, always losing a yard for every foot gained.

On the first-floor landing, Lilly sat, rag-doll in her lap. One of her arms was withered, leathery membrane bunched in folds beneath it, the drab dress cut away to allow freedom of movement. The little girl smiled at Genevieve, teeth sharp but uneven, patches of dark fur on her neck and forehead. New-borns could not change their shape properly. But that didn't prevent them from trying, and mostly ending up in as bad a shape as Lilly, or worse . . .

The door of the director's office stood open. Genevieve stroked Lilly's hair, and went in, rapping a knuckle on the plaque as she passed. The director looked up from his desk, shutting a ledger he had been studying. He was a young man, still warm, but his face was deeply lined, and his hair was streaked grey. Many who had lived through the last few years looked like him, older than their years. He nodded, acknowledging the policeman.

"Jack," she said, "Inspector Lestrade wants me to attend an inquest. Can you spare me?"

"There's been another," the director said, making a statement not asking a question.

"A new-born," said Lestrade. "In Hanbury Street."

"Very well, Genevieve. Druitt can take your rounds if he's back from his regular jaunt. We weren't, ah, expecting you for a night or two yet anyway."

"Thank you."

"That's quite all right. Come and see me when you get back. Inspector Lestrade, good evening."

"Dr Seward," Lestrade said, putting on his hat, "good night."

III

"What's to be done?" shouted a new-born in a peaked cap. "What's to stop this fiend murdering more of our women?"

Wynne Baxter, an old man of Gladstonian appearance, was angrily trying to keep control of the inquest. Unlike a high court judge, he had no gavel and so was forced to slap his wooden desk with an open fist.

"Any further interruptions," Baxter began, glaring, "and I shall be forced to clear the public from this court."

The new-born, a surly rough who must have looked hungry even when warm, slumped back into his chair. He was surrounded by a similar crew. They had long scarves, ragged coats, pockets distended by books, heavy boots and thin beards. Genevieve knew the type. Whitechapel had all manner of Republican, anarchist, socialist and insurrectionist factions.

"Thank you," said the coroner, rearranging his notes. New-borns did not like positions where someone warm had the authority. But a lifetime of cringing when official old men frowned on them left habits. Baxter was a familiar type too, resisting the Dark

Kiss, wearing his wrinkles and bald pate as badges of humanity.

Dr Llewellyn, the local practitioner—well known at Toynbee Hall—who had done the preliminary examination of the body, had already given his testimony. It boiled down to the simple facts that Lulu Schön—a German girl, recently arrived in London and even more recently turned—had been heart-stabbed, disembowelled and decapitated. It had taken much desk-banging to quieten the outrage that followed the revelation of the method of murder.

Now, Baxter was hearing evidence from Dr Henry Jekyll, a scientific researcher. "Whenever a vampire's killed," Lestrade explained, "Jekyll comes creeping round. Something rum about him, if you get my drift . . ."

Genevieve thought the man, who was giving a detailed and anatomically precise description of the atrocities, a little stuffy, but listened with interest—more interest than expressed by the yawning newspaper reporters in the front row—to what he was saying.

". . . we have not learned enough about the precise changes in the human body that accompany the so-called transformation from normal life to the state of vampirism," Jekyll said. "Precise information is hard to come by, and superstition hangs like a London fog over the whole subject. My studies have been checked by official indifference, even hostility. We could all benefit from more research work. Perhaps the divisions which lead to tragic incidents like the death of this girl could then be erased from our society."

The anarchists were grumbling again. Without divisions, their cause would have no purpose.

"Too much of what we believe about vampirism is rooted in folklore," Jekyll continued. "The stake through the heart, the silver scythe to remove the head. The vampire *corpus* is remarkably resilient, but any major breach of the vital organs seems to produce true death, as here."

"Would you venture to suggest that the murderer was familiar with the workings of the human body, whether of a vampire or not?"

"Yes, your honour. The extent of the injuries betokens a certain frenzy of enthusiasm, but the actual wounds—one might almost say incisions—have been wrought with some skill."

"He's a bleedin' doctor," shouted the chief anarchist.

The court exploded into an uproar, again. The anarchists, who were about half-and-half warm and new-borns, stamped their feet and yelled, while others—a gaggle of haggard mainly un-dead women in colourful dresses who were presumably associates of the deceased, a scattering of well-dressed medical men, some of

Lestrade's uniformed juniors, a sprinkling of sensation-seekers, press-men, clergymen and social reformers—just talked loudly among themselves. Baxter hurt his hand hitting his desk.

Genevieve noticed a man standing at the back of the courtroom, observing the clamour with cool interest. Well-dressed, with a cloak and top hat, he might have been a sensation-seeker but for a certain air of purpose. He was not a vampire, but—unlike the coroner, or even Dr Jekyll—he showed no signs of being disturbed to be among so many of the un-dead. He leant on a black cane.

"Who is that?" she asked Lestrade.

"Charles Beauregard," the new-born detective said, curling a lip. "Have you heard of the Diogenes Club?"

She shook her head.

"When they say 'high places', that's where they mean. Important people are taking an interest in this case. And Beauregard is their catspaw."

The coroner had order again. A clerk had nipped out of the room and returned with six more constables, all new-borns, and they were lining the walls like a guard. The anarchists were brooding again, their purpose obviously to cause just enough trouble to be an irritant but not enough to get their names noted.

"If I might be permitted to address the implied question raised by the gentleman in the second row," Jekyll asked, eliciting a nod from the coroner, "a knowledge of the position of the major organs does not necessarily betoken medical education. If you are not interested in preserving life, a butcher can have out a pair of kidneys as neatly as a surgeon. You need only a steady hand and a sharp knife, and there are plenty of those in Whitechapel."

"Do you have an opinion as to the instrument used by the murderer?"

"A blade of some sort, obviously. Silvered."

The word brought a collective gasp.

"Steel or iron would not have done such damage," Jekyll continued. "Vampire physiology is such that any wounds inflicted with ordinary weapons heal almost immediately. Tissue and bone regenerate, just as a lizard may grow a new tail. Silver has a counteractive effect on this process. Only a silver knife could do such permanent, fatal harm to a vampire."

Beauregard nodded. "You are familiar with the case of Mary Ann Nicholls?"

Jekyll nodded.

"Have you drawn any conclusions from a comparison of these two incidents?"

"Indeed. These two killings were undoubtably the work of the same individual. A left-handed man of above average height, with more than normal physical strength . . ."

"Mr Holmes would've been able to tell his mother's maiden name from a fleck of cigar ash," Lestrade muttered to Genevieve.

". . . I would add that, considering the case from an alienist's point of view, it is my belief that the murderer is not himself a vampire."

The anarchist was on his feet, but the coroner's extra constables were around him before he could even shout.

Smiling to himself at his subjugation of the court, Baxter made a note of the last point and thanked Dr Jekyll.

The man Beauregard, Genevieve noticed, was gone. The coroner began his elaborate summing-up of the situation, before delivering the verdict of "murder by person or persons unknown", adding that the murderer of Lulu Schön was judged to be the same man who had murdered, one week earlier, Mary Ann Nicholls.

Reporters began asking questions, all at once.

IV

Beauregard strolled in the fog, trying to digest the information he had gleaned from the inquest. He would have to make a full report later, and so he wanted the facts ordered in his mind.

Somewhere nearby, a street organ ground into the night. The air was "Take a Pair of Crimson Eyes", from Gilbert and Sullivan's *The Vampyres of Venice: or: A Maid, a Shade and a Blade*. That seemed apt. The maid—so to speak—and the blade were obviously part of the case, and the shade was the murderer, obscured by fog and blood.

Despite Dr Jekyll's testimony, Beauregard had been toying with the notion that the crimes to date were the work of different men, ritual killings like *thuggee* stranglings, acts of revolt against the new masters. Such incidents were not uncommon. But these murders were different, the work of a madman not an insurrectionist. Of course, that would not prevent street-corner ranters like those who had interrupted the inquest from claiming these pathetic eviscerations as victories.

A vampire whore in Flower and Dean Street offered to make him immortal for an ounce or two of his blood. He flipped her a copper coin, and went on his way. He wondered how long he would have the strength to resist. At thirty-five, he was already aware that he was slowing. At fifty, at sixty, would his resolve to stay warm seem ridiculous, perverse? Sinful, even? Was refusing vampirism the moral equivalent of suicide? His father had been fifty-eight when he died.

Vampires needed the warm, to feed and succour them, to keep the country running through the days. There were already vampires—here in the East End, if not in the salons of Mayfair—starving as the poor always had done. How long before the "desperate measures" Lord Henry Wotton was always advocating in parliament—the penning-up of still more warm, not just criminals but any simply healthy specimens, to serve as cattle for the vampires of breeding who were essential to the governance of the country—were seriously considered. Stories crept back from Devil's Dyke that made Beauregard's heart turn to ice. Already the definition of "criminal" had extended to include too many good men and women who were simply unable to come to an accommodation with the new regime.

It took him a while to find a cab. After dark, Whitechapel was coming to life. Public houses and music halls were lit up, people crammed inside, laughing and shouting. And the streets were busy. Traders were selling sheet music, phials of "human" blood, scissors, Royal souvenirs. Chestnuts roasted in a barrel-fire on Half Moon Street were sold to new-born and warm alike. Vampires did not need to eat, but apparently the habit was hard to lose. Crowds took note of his clothes and mainly kept out of his way. Beauregard was conscious of the watch in his waistcoat and the wallet in his inside breast pocket. There were nimble fingers all around, and sharp nailed claws. Blood was not all the new-borns wanted. He swung his cane purposefully, warding off evil.

At length, he found a hansom and offered the cabbie three shillings to take him to Cheyne Walk, Chelsea. The man touched his whip to the brim of his bowler, and Beauregard slipped inside. The interior was upholstered in red, like the plush coffins displayed in the shops along Oxford Street. It seemed altogether too luxurious a conveyance for this quarter of the city, and Beauregard wondered whether it had brought a distinguished visitor or two from the West End, in search of amorous adventures. There were houses all over the district, catering to every taste. Women and boys, warm and vampire, were freely available for a few shillings. Drabs like Polly Nicholls and Lulu Schön could be had for coppers or a squirt of blood. It was possible that the murderer was not from Whitechapel, that he was just another toff pursuing his peculiar pleasures. In Whitechapel, they said, you could get anything, either by paying for it or taking it.

His duties, in what they called the Great Game, had taken him to worse places. He had spent weeks as a one-eyed beggar in

Afghanistan, dogging the movements of a Russian envoy suspected
of stirring up the hill-tribes. During the Boer Rebellion, he had
endeavoured to negotiate a treaty with the Amahagger, whose idea
of an evening's entertainment was baking the heads of captives in
pots. And, for a month, he had been entertained in the perfumed
dungeons of an imaginative Chinese mandarin. However, it had been
something of a surprise to return, after years abroad in the discreet
service of Her Majesty, to find London itself transformed into a city
more strange, dangerous and bizarre than any in his experience. It
was no longer the heart of Empire, just a sponge absorbing the blood
of the Queen's domain until it burst.

The cab's wheels rattled against the cobbles, lulling him like the
soft crash of waves under a ship.

While Beauregard had been away, the Prince Consort had taken
London. He had wooed and won the Queen, persuading her to
abandon her widow's black, then he had introduced vampirism to
the British Isles, and reshaped the greatest Empire on the globe
to suit his own desires. Charles Beauregard still served his Queen.
He had promised death would not interfere with his loyalty to her
person, but when he had made that vow he had thought he meant
his own death.

The Prince Consort, who had taken for himself the additional
title of Lord Protector, ruled Great Britain now, his get executing
his wishes and whims. A vampire, Lord Ruthven, was Prime Minister, and another, Sir Francis Varney, Viceroy of India. An elite
Carpathian guard, gussied up in comic opera uniforms, patrolled the
grounds of Buckingham Palace, and caroused throughout the West
End like sacred terrors. The army, the navy, the diplomatic corps,
the police and the Church of England all were in the Prince Consort's
thrall, new-borns promoted over the warm at every opportunity.
Beauregard had been told, by his new-born colleague Adamant, that
his own chances for advancement within the Diogenes Club—perhaps the least well-known arm of the British government—would
be increased a hundredfold were he to accept the Dark Kiss.

While the business of the kingdom continued much as it always
had done, there were other changes: people vanished from public
and private life, camps such as Devil's Dyke springing up in remote
areas of the country, and the apparatus of a government—secret
police, sudden arrests, casual executions—he associated not with
the Queen but with the Tsars and Taiping. There were Republican
bands playing Robin Hood in the wilds of Scotland and Ireland,
and cross-waving curates were always trying to brand new-born
provincial mayors with the mark of Cain.

Something irritated him. He had grown used to trusting his occasional feelings of irritation. On several occasions, they had been the saving of his life.

The cab was in the Commercial Road, heading East, not West. He could smell the docks. Beauregard resolved to see this out. It was an interesting development, and he had hopes that the cabbie did not merely intend to murder and rob him.

He eased aside the catch in the head of his cane, and slid a few inches of shining steel out of the body of the stick. The sword would draw freely if he needed it. Still, it was only steel. He wondered whether silver might not have been wiser.

V

At the Whitechapel Police Station, Lestrade introduced her to Inspector Abberline, who was in charge of the continuing murder investigation. Having handled the Nicholls case, without any notable results, he was now saddled with Lulu Schön, and any more yet to come. Jekyll's testimony confirmed what Genevieve had already intuited. These horrors would not stop of their own accord. The man with the silver knife would keep at his work until he was caught or killed.

Lestrade and Abberline went off together, to have a huddle. Abberline was warm, and elaborately—without realising it?—came up with other things to do with his hands whenever the possibility of pressing flesh with a vampire was raised. He lit his pipe and listened as Lestrade ticked off points on his fingers. Genevieve looked around the reception room, which was already busy.

Outside the station, there were several groups of interested parties. A Christian Crusade band, flying the cross of St George, were supporting a preacher, who was calling down God's Justice on vampirekind, upholding the Whitechapel Murderer as a true instrument of the Will of Christ. They were being heckled by a few professional insurrectionists, some of the crew she had seen at the inquest, and ridiculed by a knot of painted new-born women, who offered expensive kisses and changed lives. Genevieve understood that many new-borns paid to become some street tart's get, seeking vampirism as a way out of their warmth.

A sergeant was turning out some of the station's regulars. Genevieve recognised most of them. There were plenty—warm and vampire—who spent their lives shuffling between the holding cells and Toynbee Hall, in the constant search for a bed and a free meal.

"Miss Dee," said a woman, recognising her, "Miss Dee . . ."

"Cathy," she said, acknowledging the new-born, "are you being well treated?"

"Loverly, miss, loverly," she said, simpering at the sergeant, "it's an 'ome from 'ome."

Cathy Eddowes looked hardly better as a vampire than she must have done when warm. Gin and too many nights outdoors had raddled her, and the red shine in her eyes and on her hair didn't outweigh the mottled skin under her heavy rouge. Like many in Whitechapel, Cathy still exchanged her body for drink. Her customers' blood was probably as high in its alcohol content as the gin to which she used to be devoted.

The new-born primped her hair, arranging a red ribbon that kept her tight curls away from her wide face. There was a running sore on the back of her hand.

"Let me look at that, Cathy."

Genevieve had seen marks like these. New-borns had to be careful. They were stronger, more lasting than the warm. But too much of their diet was tainted. And disease was still a danger. The Dark Kiss did something strange—something Dr Jekyll would probably find of great interest—to any diseases a person happened to carry over from warm life to their undead state.

"Do you have many of these sores?"

Cathy shook her head, but Genevieve knew she meant yes.

A clear fluid was weeping from the red patch on the back of the new-born's hand, and there were damp marks on Cathy's tight bodice, suggesting more patches. She wore her scarf in an unnatural fashion, covering her neck and upper breasts. Genevieve peeled the wool away, and smelled the pungent discharge that glistened on Cathy's skin.

Genevieve looked into the woman's eyes, and saw fear. Cathy Eddowes knew something was wrong, but was superstitiously afraid of finding out what it was.

"Cathy, you must call in at the Hall tonight. See Mr Druitt, or, better yet, Dr Seward. Something can be done for your condition. I promise you."

"I'll be all right, love."

"Not unless you get some treatment, Cathy."

Cathy tried to laugh, and tottered out onto the streets. One of her boot heels was gone, so she had a music hall limp. She held up her head, wrapping her scarf around her like a duchess's fur stole, and wiggled provocatively past the Christian Crusade speaker, slipping into the fog.

"Dead in a year," said the sergeant, a red-eyed new-born with a snoutlike protrusion in the centre of his face.

"Not if I can help it."

VI

The cab took him to Limehouse, somewhere near the Basin. It was not a part of the city he knew well, although he had been here in Her Majesty's Service several times. The door was opened for him, and a pair of red eyes glittered in the dark beyond.

"Sorry for the inconvenience, Beauregard," purred a silky voice, male but not entirely masculine, "but I hope you'll understand. It's a sticky wicket . . ."

Beauregard stepped down, and found himself in a yard off one of the warren of streets near the docks. There were people all around. The one who had spoken was an Englishman, a vampire with a good coat and soft hat, face in darkness. His posture studied in its langour, he was an athlete at rest and Beauregard would not have liked to go four rounds with him. The others were Chinese, pig-tailed and bowed, hands in their sleeves. Most were warm, but the massive fellow by the cab-door was a new-born, naked to the waist to show off his dragon tattoos and his vampire indifference to the autumn chill.

The Englishman stepped forward, and moonlight caught his youthful face. He had pretty eyelashes, like a woman's, and Beauregard recognised him.

"I saw you get six sixes from six balls in '85," he said. "Gentlemen and Players, the MCC."

The sportsman shrugged modestly. "You play what's chucked at you, I always say."

Beauregard had heard the new-born's name in the Diogenes Club, tentatively linked with a series of daring jewel robberies. He supposed the sportsman's involvement in this evident kidnapping confirmed that he was indeed the author of those criminal feats.

"This way," said the amateur cracksman, indicating a wet stretch of stone wall. The new-born Chinese pressed a brick, and a section of the wall tilted upwards, forming a hatch-like door. "Duck down or you'll bash your bean. Deuce small, these chinks."

Beauregard followed the new-born, who could see in the dark better than he, and was in turn followed by some of the Chinese. They went down a passageway that sloped sharply, and he realised they must be below street level. Everything was damp and glistening, suggesting these underground chambers must be close to the river.

Doors were opened, and Beauregard was ushered into a dimly-lit drawing room, richly furnished. He noticed there were no windows, just *chinoiserie* screens. The centrepiece was a large desk, behind which sat an ancient Chinaman, his long, hard fingernails like knifepoints on his blotter. There were others in the room, in comfortable armchairs arranged in a half-circle about the desk.

One man turned his head, red cigar-end making a Devil's mask of his face. He was a vampire, but the Chinaman was not.

"Mr Beauregard," began the Celestial, "so kind of you to join our wretched and unworthy selves."

"So kind of you to invite me."

The Chinaman clapped his hands, and nodded to a dead-faced servant, a Burmese.

"Take our visitor's hat, cloak and *cane*."

Beauregard was relieved of his burdens. When the Burmese was close enough, Beauregard observed the singular earring, and the ritual tattooing about his neck.

"A Dacoit?" he inquired.

"Very observant."

"I have some experience of the world of secret societies."

"Indeed you have, Mr Beauregard. Our paths have crossed three times: in Egypt, in the Kashmir, and in Shansi Province. You caused me some little inconvenience."

Beauregard realised to whom he was talking. "My apologies, doctor."

The Chinaman leaned forward, his face emerging into the light, his fingernails clacking as he brushed away Beauregard's apologies. "Think nothing of it. Those were trivial matters, of no import beyond the ordinary."

They called this man the "Devil Doctor" or "the Lord of Strange Deaths", and he was reputed to be one of the Council of Seven, the ruling body of the Si–Fan, a *tong* whose influence extended from China to all the quarters of the Earth. One of Beauregard's superiors—now in exile in France—reckoned the Celestial among the three most dangerous men in the world.

The amateur cracksman turned up the gaslight, and faces became clear, dark corners of the room were dispelled.

"Business," snorted a military-looking vampire, "time is money, remember . . ."

"A thousand pardons, Colonel Moran. In the East, things are

different. Here, we must bow to your Western ways, hurry and bustle, haste and industry."

The cigar-smoker stood up, unbending a lanky figure from which hung a frock coat marked around the pockets with chalk. The Colonel deferred to him, and stepped back, eyes falling. The smoker's head oscillated from side to side like a lizard's, eyeteeth protruding over his lower lip.

"My associate is a businessman," he explained between puffs, "our cricketing friend is a dilettante, Griffin over there is a scientist, Sikes is continuing his family business, I am a mathematician, but you, my dear doctor, are an artist."

"The Professor flatters me."

Beauregard had heard of the Professor too. "With two of the three most dangerous men in the world in one room, I have to ask myself where the third might be?"

"I see our names and positions are not unknwon to you, Mr Beauregard," said the Chinaman. "Dr Nikola is unavailable for our little gathering. I believe he may be found investigating some sunken ships off the coast of Tasmania. He no longer concerns us. He has his own interests."

Beauregard looked at the others in the meeting, those still unaccounted for. Griffin, whom the Professor had mentioned, was an albino who seemed to fade into the background like a chameleon. Sikes was a pig-faced man, warm, short, barrel-chested and brutal. With a loud check jacket and cheap oil on his hair, he looked out of place in such a distinguished gathering. Alone in the company, he was the image of a criminal.

"Professor, if you would care to explain . . ."

"Thank you, doctor," replied the man they called "The Napoleon of Crime". "Mr Beauregard, as you are aware, none of us in this room—and I include you among our number—has what we might call common cause. We pursue our own furrows, and if they happen to intersect . . . well, that is often unfortunate. Lately, the world has changed, but whatever personal metamorphoses we might have welcomed, our calling has remained essentially the same. We are a shadow community, and we always have been. To a great extent, we have come to an accommodation. We pit our wits against each other, but when the sun comes up, we draw a line, we let well enough alone. It grieves me greatly to have to say this, but that line seems not to be holding . . ."

"There was police raids all over the East End," Sikes interrupted. "Years of bloody work overturned in a single day. 'Ouses smashed. Gambling, opium, girls: nuffin' sacred. Our business 'as been bought

and paid for, and the filthy peelers done us dirty when they went back
on the deal."

"I have nothing to do with the police," Beauregard said.

"Do not think us naive," said the Professor. "Like all the members
of the Diogenes Club, you have no official position at all. But what
is official and what is effective are separate things."

"This persecution of our interests will continue," the Celestial
said, "so long as the Whitechapel Murderer is at liberty."

Beauregard nodded. "I suppose so. There's always a chance the
killer will be turned up by the raids."

"He's not one of us," snorted Colonel Moran.

"'E's a ravin' nutter, that's what 'e is. Listen, none of us is 'zactly
squeamish—know what I mean?—but this bloke is takin' it too
far. If an 'ore makes trouble, you takes a razor to 'er face not 'er
bleedin' froat."

"There's never been any suggestion, so far as I know, that any of
you were involved in the murders."

"That's not the point, Mr Beauregard," the Professor continued.
"Our shadow empire is like a spiderweb. It extends throughout
the world, but it is concentrated here, in this city. It is thick and
complicated and surprisingly delicate. If enough threads are severed,
it will fall. And threads are being severed left and right. We have all
suffered since Mary Ann Nicholls was killed, and the inconvenience
was redoubled tonight. Each time this murderer strikes at the public,
he stabs at us also."

"My 'ores don't wanna go on the streets wiv 'im out there. It's
'urtin' me pockets."

"I'm sure the police will catch the man. There's a reward of fifty
pounds for information."

"And we have posted a reward of a thousand guineas, but nothing
has come of it."

"Mr Beauregard," said the Chinaman. "We should like to add our
humble efforts to those of the most excellent police. We pledge that
any knowledge which comes into our possession—as knowledge on
so many matters so often does—shall be passed directly to you. In
return, we ask that the personal interest in this matter, which we
know the Diogenes Club has required you take, be persecuted with
the utmost vigour."

Beauregard tried not to show it, but he was deeply shocked that
the innermost workings of the Diogenes Club were somehow known
to the Lord of Strange Deaths. And yet the insidious Chinaman
evidently knew in detail of the briefing he had been given only hours
earlier.

"This bounder is letting the side down," the amateur cracksman said, "and it would be best if he stripped his whites and went back to the bally pavilion."

"We've put up a thousand guineas for information," the Colonel said, "and two thousand for his rotten head."

"Do we have an understanding, Mr Beauregard?"

"Yes, Professor."

The new-born smiled a thin smile, fangs scraping his thin underlip. One murderer meant very little to these men, but a loose cannon of crime was an inconvenience they would not brook.

"A cab will take you to Cheyne Walk," the Celestial explained, a smile crinkling his eyes and lifting his thin moustaches. "This meeting is at an end. Serve our purpose, and you will be rewarded. Fail us, and the consequences will be . . . not so pleasant."

With a wave, Beauregard was dismissed.

As the amateur cracksman took him back through the passage, Beauregard wondered just how many Devils he would have to ally himself with in order to discharge his duty to the Crown.

His hat, cloak and cane were waiting for him inside the cab.

"Toodle-oo," said the cricketer, red eyes shining, "see you at Lords."

VII

When the sun came up, the new-borns scurried to their coffins and corners. Genevieve trailed alone through the streets, never thinking to be afraid of the shrinking shadows, wandering back to Toynbee Hall. Like the Prince Consort, she was old enough not to shrivel in the sun as the more sensitive new-borns did, but she felt the energy that had come with the blood of the warm girl seep away as the first light of dawn filtered orange through the swirling fog. She passed a warm policeman on the Commercial Road, and nodded a greeting to him. He turned away, and kept on his beat. There were more policemen in Whitechapel even at this hour than there would be in six weeks' time at the Lord Mayor's Parade.

In the last week and a half, she had spent more time on the Ripper than on her work. Druitt was pulling double shifts, juggling the limited number of places at the Hall to deal with the most needy first. She had been seconded to a Committee for Public Safety, and had been to so many meetings that even now words still rung in her ears as music rings in the ears of those who sit too near the orchestra. The socialists George Bernard Shaw and Beatrice Webb

had been making speeches all over the city, using the murders to
bring attention to the conditions of the East End. Toynbee Hall
was momentarily the recipient of enough charitable donations to
make Druitt propose that it would be a good idea to sponsor the
Ripper's activities as a means of raising funds, a suggestion that
did not amuse the serious-minded Jack Seward. Neither Shaw nor
Webb were vampires themselves, and Shaw at least had been linked,
Genevieve understood, with one of the Republican factions.

A poster up on the wall of an ostler's yard promised the latest
reward for information leading to the capture of Jack the Ripper. It
bore a photographic representation of the letter the Central News
Agency had received, covered in a spidery red scrawl. Nobody had
recognised the handwriting yet, and Genevieve guessed that tracing
the prankster with the red ink would get the police no nearer the
Whitechapel Murderer than they already were. Which was to say,
not very near at all.

Rival groups of warm and new-born vigilantes had roamed the
streets with billy-clubs and razors, scrapping with each other and
setting upon dubiously innocent passersby. Since the last killing,
the street girls had started complaining less about the danger of
the murderer and more about the lack of custom noticable since
the vigilantes started harassing anyone who came to Whitechapel
looking for a woman. Genevieve heard that the whores of Soho and
Covent Garden were doing record business, and record gloating.

A lunatic—almost certainly not the killer—had written to the
Central News Agency, wittering on in scarlet. "I am down on
whores and leeches and shan't quit ripping them till I get buckled
. . . I saved some of the proper red stuff in a ginger beer bottle to
write with but it went thick like glue and I can't use it. Red ink
is fit enough I hope, ha ha . . . My knife is silver and sharp and I
want to get to work straight away if I can." The anonymous crank's
letter had been signed "yours truly, Jack the Ripper", and the name
had stuck.

Genevieve had heard Jack was a leather-aproned shoemaker, a
Polish Jew carrying out ritual killings, a foreign sailor, a degenerate
from the West End, the ghost of Abraham Van Helsing or Charley
Peace. He was a policeman, a doctor, a midwife, a priest. With
each rumour, more innocent people were thrown to the mob. A
shoemaker named Pizer had been locked up in the police cells
for his own protection when someone took it into their heads to
write "Jack's Shack" on his shopfront. After a Christian Crusade
speaker argued that the killer could walk unhindered about the area
killing at will because he was a policeman, a vampire constable was

dragged into a yard off Coke Street and impaled on a length of picket fence.

Genevieve passed the doorway where Lilly slept. The new-born child, who might grow old but never become an adult, was curling up for the day with some scraps of blanket that had been given to her at the Hall. Genevieve noticed the girl's half-shapeshifted arm was worse, useless wing sprouting from hip to armpit. Changing was a trick the Prince Consort kept to himself, and there were too many imperfect freaks about. Lilly had a cat nestled against her face, its neck in her mouth. The animal was still barely alive.

Abberline and Lestrade had questioned dozens, but made no arrests. There were always rival groups of protesters outside the police station. Genevieve heard rumours that psychic mediums like Lees and Carnacki had been called for. Sir Charles Warren had been forced to explain himself in private to the Prime Minister, and Ruthven would have the Commissioner's resignation if there was no action soon. Any number of consulting detectives—Sexton Blake, Martin Hewitt, Max Carados, August Van Dusen—had prowled Whitechapel, hoping to turn something up. Even the venerable Hawkshaw had come out of retirement. But with their acknowledged master in Devil's Dyke, the enthusiasm of the detective community had ebbed considerably, and no solutions were forthcoming. The Queen, young again and plump, had expressed concern about "these ghastly murders", but nothing had been heard from the Prince Consort, to whom Genevieve assumed the lives of a few streetwalkers, vampire or not, were of as much importance as those of beetles.

Gradually, as she came to realise just how powerless she was to affect the behaviour of this unknown maniac, she also sensed just how important this case was becoming. Everyone involved seemed to begin their arguments by declaring that it was about more than just two dead vampire whores. It was about D'Israeli's "two nations", it was about the regrettable spread of vampirism among the lower orders, it was about the fragile equilibrium of the transformed kingdom. The murders were mere sparks, but the British Empire was a tinderbox.

She spent a lot of time with whores—she had been an outcast long enough to feel a certain identification with them—and shared their fears. Tonight, nearing dawn, she had found a warm girl in Mrs Warren's house off Raven Row and bled her, out of need not pleasure. After so many years, she should be used to her predator's life, but the Prince Consort had turned everything topsy-turvy and she was ashamed again, not of what she must do to prolong her existence, but of the things vampirekind, those of the bloodline of Vlad Tepes, did around her. The warm girl had been bitten several times, and was pale and fragile. Eventually, she would turn. Nobody's get, she would have to find her own way in the darkness, and doubtless end up as raddled as Cathy Eddowes or as truly dead as Polly Nicholls.

Her head was fuzzy from the gin her warm girl had drunk. The whole city seemed sick. Dawn shot the fog full of blood.

VIII

September 28, 1888. Today, I went to Kingstead to lay the annual wreath. It is three years, to the day, since Lucy's death. Her destruction, rather. The tomb bears the date of her first death, and only I—or so I thought—remember the date of Van Helsing's expedition. The Prince Consort and Lord Protector, after all, is hardly likely to make it a national holiday. Then, we trailed along with the old Dutchman, not really believing what he had told us of Lucy. My load of grief at her death had been more than enough to bear, without being told that she had risen from her coffin and was the dark woman who had taken to biting children on Hampstead Heath.

I still dream of Lucy, too much. Once, I had hoped to take her for my wife. But Arthur's charms—not to mention his title and his wealth—prevailed. Her lips, her pale skin, her hair, her eyes. Many times have my dreams of Lucy been responsible for my noctural emissions. Wet kisses and wet dreams . . .

Lucy was the first in England of the Prince Consort's get, and the first to be destroyed. I only regret now that it was Arthur Holmwood—Lord Godalming—who did the honours, driving the wooden stake into her heart, setting her free of her unwelcome condition. I helped decapitate the hissing corpse, and filled her mouth with garlic. If only Van Helsing had been as quick to lead us to the second new-born, the third, the tenth, the hundredth. There was a point, I suppose, when Dracula could have been driven from these shores, could have been hounded back to his Transylvanian fastness, could have been properly dispatched with wood and silver and steel. But I don't know when that could have been.

I have chosen to work in Whitechapel because it is the ugliest part of the Prince Consort's realm. Here, the superficialities which some say make his rule tolerable are at their thinnest. With vampire sluts on every corner, baying for blood, and befuddled or dead men littering the cramped streets, it is possible to see the true, worm-eaten face of what has been wrought. It is hard to keep my control among so many of the leeches, but my vocation is strong. Once, I was a doctor, a specialist in mental disorders. Now, I am a vampire killer. My duty is to cut out the corrupt heart of the city.

The fog that shrouds London in autumn has got thicker since Dracula came. I understand all manner of vermin—rats, wild dogs, cats—have thrived, and some quarters of the city have even seen a resurgence of the mediaeval diseases they carry. It is as if the Prince Consort were a bubbling sinkhole, disgorging filth from where he sits, grinning his wolf's grin as it seeps throughout his kingdom. The fog means there is less and less distinction between day and night. In Whitechapel, many days, the sun truly does not shine. That excites the new-borns. We've been seeing more and more go half-mad in the daytime, muddy light burning out their brains.

The rest of the city is more sedate, but no better. On the way to Kingstead, I stopped off at an inn in Hampstead for a pork pie and a pint of beer. In the gloom of the afternoon, gentlefolk paraded themselves on the Heath, skins pale, eyes shining red. It is quite the thing, I understand, to follow fashions set by the Queen, and vampirism—although resisted for several years—has now become more than acceptable. Prim, pretty girls in bonnets, ivory-dagger teeth artfully concealed by Japanese fans, flock to the Heath on sunless afternoons, thick black parasols held high. There is no difference, really, between them and the blood-sucking whores of the Ten Bells and the Vlad IV in Whitechapel.

The gates of Kingstead hung open, unattended. Since dying became unfashionable, churchyards have fallen into disuse. Most churches are empty too, although the court has its tame archbishops, trying desperately to reconcile Anglicanism with vampirism. When he was truly alive, the Prince Consort slaughtered thousands in the defence of the faith, and he still fancies himself a Christian. Entering the graveyard, I could not help but remember . . . Lucy's "sickness", her funeral, Van Helsing's diagnosis, the cure. We destroyed a thing, not the girl I had loved. Cutting through her neck, I found a calling.

My hand hurt damnably, a throbbing lump of tissue. I know I should seek treatment, but I think I need my pain. It gives me resolve.

At the start of it, some new-borns had taken to opening the tombs of their dead relatives, hoping by some strange osmosis to return them to vampire life. I had to watch my step to avoid the chasm-like holes left in the ground by these fruitless endeavours. The fog was thin up here, a muslin curtain.

It was something of a shock to see a figure outside the Westenra tomb. A young woman, slim and dark, in a velvet-collared coat, a straw hat with a dead bird on it perched on her tightly-bound hair.

Hearing my approach, she turned and I caught the glint of red eyes.

With the light behind her, it could have been Lucy.

"Sir?" she said, startled by my interruption. "Who might that be?"

The voice was Irish, uneducated, light. It was not Lucy.

I left my hat on, but nodded. There was something familiar about the new-born.

"Why," she said, "'tis Dr Seward, from the Toynbee."

A shaft of late sun speared through the fog, and the vampire flinched. I saw her face.

"Kelly, isn't it?"

"Marie, sir," she said, recovering her composure, remembering to simper, to smile, to ingratiate. "Come to pay your respects?"

I nodded, and laid my wreath. She had put her own at the door of the tomb, a penny posy now dwarfed by my shilling tribute.

"Did you know the young miss?"

"I did."

Arthur had beat me out with Lucy, as he beat me out with his hammer and stake. Lord Godalming was a vampire himself now, a sharp-faced blade and the ornament of any society gathering. Eventually, I must take my silver to his treacherous dead heart.

"She was a beauty," Kelly said. "Beautiful."

I could not conceive of any connection in life between my Lucy and this broad-boned drab. Mary Kelly—our records say Mary Jane, but she sometimes styles herself Marie Jeanette—is fresher than most, but she's just another whore, really. Like Nicholls, and Schön . . .

"She turned me," Kelly explained. "Found me on the Heath one night when I was walking home from the house of a gentleman, an' delivered me into my new life."

I looked more closely at Kelly. If she was Lucy's get, she bore out the theory I have heard that a vampire's progeny come to resemble their parent-in-darkness. There was definitely something of Lucy's delicacy about her red little mouth and her white little teeth.

"I'm her get, as she was the Prince Consort's. That makes me almost royalty. The Queen is my aunt-in-darkness."

Kelly giggled, fangs shining.

My hand was dipped in fire in my pocket, a tight fist at the centre of a ball of pain.

Kelly came close to me, so close I could whiff the rot on her breath under her perfume, and stroked the collar of my coat.

"That's good material, sir."

She kissed my neck, quick as a snake, and my heart spasmed. Even now, I cannot explain or excuse the feelings that came over me.

"I could turn you, warm sir, make royalty of you . . ."

My body was rigid as she moved against me, pressing forward with her hips, her hands slipping around my shoulders, my back.

I shook my head.

"Tis your loss, sir."

She stood away. Blood pounded in my temples, my heart raced like a Wessex Cup winner. I was nauseated by the thing's presence. Had my scalpel been in my pocket, I would have ripped—hideous word, courtesy of the unknown jester

who gave me my "trade name"—her heart out. But there were other emotions.
She looked so like Lucy, so like the Lucy who bothers my dreams.

I tried to speak, but just croaked. Kelly understood. She must be experienced.

The leech turned and smiled, slipping near me again.

"Somethin' else, sir."

I nodded, and, slowly, she began to loosen my clothes. She took my hand
out of my pocket, and cooed over the wound, licking the bled-through bandage
with shudders of pleasure. I looked about.

"We won't be disturbed here, doctor, sir . . ."

"Jack," I muttered.

"Jack," she said, pleased with the sound.

(Who is the letter-writer? Jack or John is a common name. He can't know.
If he knew, I would not still be alive.)

In the lea of Lucy's tomb, I rutted with the foul creature, tears on my face,
a dreadful burning inside me. Her flesh was cool and white. Afterwards, she
took me into her mouth and—with exquisite, torturous care—bled me slightly.
I offered her coin, but my blood was enough for her. She looked at me with
tenderness, almost with pity, before she left. If only I had had my scalpel.

Now, I am jittery, nervous. It has been too long since I last struck.
Whitechapel has become dangerous. There have been people snooping around
all the time, seeing the Ripper in every shadow.

My scalpel is on my desk, shining silver. Sharp as a whisper.

They say that I am mad. They do not understand my purpose.

Returning from Kingstead, I admitted something to myself. When I dream
of Lucy, I do not dream of her as she was when she was alive, when I loved
her. I dream of Lucy as a vampire.

It is nearly midnight. I must go out.

IX

The city was on fire!

As Genevieve understood it, the Ripper had struck twice last
night. In Duffield Yard, off Berner Street, the murderer had cut a
new-born whore's throat, but been disturbed by a passerby named
Diemschutz and fled before he could finish his job. Within the hour,
he had cornered Catherine Eddowes—Cathy!—in Mitre Square,
and done a thorough dissection, going so far as to clip the ears and
carry off some of the internal organs.

A double event!

She had spent the evening at the Hall. The director had put her in
charge of the shift, since Druitt was off on some business of his own.

Lilly was dying, and Genevieve had been with her. The girl's human body was immortal, but the animal she had tried to become was taking over, and that animal was dead. As Lilly's tissue transformed into leathery dead flesh, the girl was dying by inches. Genevieve wished for a silver knife like the Ripper's, to make the merciful cut. One of the warm nurses had given Lilly a little blood, but it was no use. Genevieve talked to the girl, sang the songs of her own long-ago childhood, but she did not know if Lilly could even hear.

An hour before dawn, the news had come. One of the pimps, arm laid open to the bone by someone's razor, was brought in, and the crowd with him had five different versions of the story. Jack the Ripper was caught, and was being held at the police station, his identity concealed because he was one of the Royal Family. Jack had gutted a dozen in full view, and eluded pursuers by leaping over a twenty-foot wall, escaping thanks to springs on his boots. Jack's face was a silver skull, his arms bloodied scythes, his breath purging fire.

Jack had killed. Again. Twice.

A police constable told her the bare facts. She had been shocked to hear about Cathy. The other woman she didn't think she had met.

"He's takin' them two at a time," the constable had said, "you almost have to admire him, the Devil."

Now, with the sun up, Genevieve was nearly dozing. She was tired of keeping things together, with Druitt and Seward away. A crowd of whores had been around, mainly in hysterical tears, begging for money to escape from the death-trap of Whitechapel. Actually, the district had been a death-trap long before the Ripper silvered his knives.

Noisily, Lilly died.

Genevieve wrapped the tiny corpse in a sheet. It was already starting to rot, and would have to be removed before the stink became too bad to bear. Whenever anyone she knew died, another grain of ice clung to her heart. She could see how easy it was to become a monster of callousness. A few more centuries, and she could be a match for Vlad Tepes, caring for nothing but power and hot blood in her throat.

There was a commotion—*another* commotion—downstairs in the receiving rooms. Genevieve had been expecting more injuries to come in during the day. After the murders, there would be street brawls, vigilante victims, maybe even a lynching in the American style . . .

Four uniformed policemen were in the hallway, something heavy slung in an oilcloth between them. Lestrade was pacing nervously, clothes in disarray. The coppers had had to fight their way through hostile crowds. "It's as if he's laughin' at us," the constable had said, "stirring' them all up against us."

"Mademoiselle Dieudonné, clear a private room."

"Inspector . . ."

"Don't argue, just do it. One of them's still alive."

She understood at once, and checked her charts. Immediately, she realised she knew there was an empty room.

They followed her upstairs, grunting under their awkward burden, and she let them into Lilly's room. She shifted the tiny bundle from the bed, and the policemen manoeuvered the woman onto it, pulling away the oilcloth.

"Mademoiselle Dieudonné, meet Long Liz Stride."

The new-born was tall and thin, rouge smeared on her sunken cheeks, her hair a tatty grey. She wore a cotton shift, dyed red from neckline to waist. Her throat was opened to the bone, cut from ear to ear like a clown's smile.

She was gurgling, her cut pipes trying to mesh.

"Jackie Boy didn't have enough time for his usual," Lestrade explained. "Saved it up for Cathy Eddowes. Warm bastard"

Liz Stride tried to yell, but couldn't call up air from her lungs into her throat. A draught whispered through her wound. Her teeth were gone, but for four sharp incisors. Her limbs convulsed like galvanised frogs' legs. Two of the coppers had to hold her down. Her hands shook like trees in a storm.

"She won't last," Genevieve told him. "She's too far gone."

Another vampire might have survived such a wound—she had herself lived through worse—but Liz Stride was a new-born, and had been turned too late in life. She had been dying for years, poisoning herself with rough gin, taking too many hard knocks.

"She doesn't have to last, she just has to give a statement."

Genevieve was not sure that was a realistic hope.

"Inspector, I don't know if she *can* talk. I think her vocal cords have been severed."

Lestrade chewed his moustache. Liz Stride was his first chance at the Ripper, and he didn't want to let it go.

The door was pushed in, and people crowded through. Lestrade turned to shout "out" at them, but swallowed his command.

"Mr Beauregard, sir," he said.

The tall, well-dressed man Genevieve had seen at Lulu Schön's inquest came into the room, with Dr Seward in his wake. There were more people—nurses, attendants—in the corridor.

"Inspector," the tall man said. "May I . . ."

"Always a pleasure to help the Diogenes Club, Mr Beauregard," Lestrade said, in a tone which suggested it was rather more of a pleasure to pour caustic soda into one's own eyes.

Beauregard slid through the constables with an elegant movement, polite but forceful. He flicked his cloak over his shoulders, to give his arms freedom of movement.

"Good God," he said. "Can nothing be done for this poor wretch?"

Genevieve was strangely impressed. Beauregard was the first person who had said anything to suggest he thought Liz Stride was worth doing anything for, rather than someone whom something ought to be done about.

"It's too late," Genevieve explained. "She's trying to renew herself, but her injuries are too great, her reserves of strength too meagre . . ."

The torn flesh around Liz Stride's open throat swarmed, but failed to knit. Her convulsions were more regular now.

"Dr Seward?" Beauregard said, asking for a second opinion.

The director approached the bucking, thrashing woman. Genevieve saw again that he had a distaste—almost always held tightly in check—for vampires.

"Mademoiselle Dieudonné is right, I'm afraid. Poor creature. I have some silver salts upstairs. We could ease her passing. It would be the kindest course."

"Not until she gives us answers," Lestrade interrupted.

"For heaven's sake, man," Beauregard countered. "She's a human being, not a clue."

Seward touched Liz Stride's forehead, and looked into her eyes, which were red marbles. He shook his head.

Suddenly, the wounded new-born was possessed with a surge of strength. She threw off the constable who was holding down her shoulders, and lunged for the director, her jaws opening as wide as a cobra's.

Genevieve pushed Seward out of the way, and ducked to avoid Liz Stride's slashing talons.

"She's changing," someone shouted.

It was true. Liz Stride reared up, her backbone curving, her limbs drawing in. A wolfish snout grew out of her face, and swathes of hair ran over her exposed skin.

Seward crab-walked backwards to the wall. Lestrade called his men out of danger. Beauregard was reaching under his cloak for something.

Liz Stride was trying to become a wolf or a dog. But that was a hard trick—like her father-in-darkness before her, Genevieve could not shapeshift—and it took immense concentration and a strong sense of one's own self. Not the resources available to a gin-soaked mind, or to a newborn in mortal pain.

"Hell Fire," someone said.

Liz Stride's lower jaw stuck out like an alligator's, growing too large to fix properly to her skull. Her right leg and arm shrivelled, while her left side bloated, slabs of muscle forming around the bone. Her bloody clothes tore.

The wound in her throat mended over, and reformed, new yellow teeth shining at the edges of the cut. A taloned foot lashed out, and tore into a warm constable's uniformed chest. Blood gushed.

The half-creature was yelping screeches out of its neck-hole. She leaped, pushing through policemen, and landed in a clump, scrabbling across the floor, a powerfully-razored hand reaching for Seward.

"Aside," Beauregard ordered.

The man from the Diogenes Club held a revolver. He thumb-cocked the gun, and took a careful aim.

Liz Stride turned, and looked up at the barrel.

"That's useless," Genevieve protested.

Liz Stride sprung into the air.

Beauregard pulled the trigger. His shot took Liz Stride in the heart, and slammed her back against the wall. She fell, lifeless, onto Seward, body turning back into what it had been, and then into rotten meat.

Genevieve looked a question at Beauregard.

"Silver bullet," he explained, without pride.

Seward stood up, wiping the blood from his face. He was shaking, barely repressing his disgust.

"Well, you've finished the Ripper's business, and that's a fact," Lestrade muttered.

"I'm not complainin'," said Watkins, the gash-chested warm constable.

Genevieve bent over the corpse, and confirmed Liz Stride's death. Suddenly, with a last convulsion, her arm—still wolfish—leaped out, and her claws fastened in Seward's trousers-cuff.

X

"I think she was trying to tell us something," he said.

"What," the vampire replied, "the murderer's name is . . . Sydney Trousers."

Beauregard laughed. What Genevieve had said was not especially funny, but humour from a vampire was unexpected. Not many of the un-dead bothered with jokes.

"Unlikely," he replied. "Mr Boot, perhaps."

"Or a boot-maker. Like Leather Apron."

"Pizer had an alibi for Polly Nicholls. And he left Whitechapel a week ago."

Lestrade was carting Liz Stride off to the mortuary. Beauregard was walking the distance between Berner Street and Mitre Square, and the vampire from Toynbee Hall was tagging along.

Genevieve Dieudonné dressed like a New Woman, tight jacket and simple dress, sensible flat-heeled boots, beret-like cap and waist-length cape. If Great Britain still had an elected parliament, she would have wanted the vote. And, he suspected, she would not have voted for Ruthven.

They arrived at the site of Catherine Eddowes' murder. The bloody patch was guarded by a warm policeman, and the crowds were staying away.

"The Ripper must be a sprinter," she said.

Beauregard checked his watch.

"We beat his time by five minutes, but we knew where we were going. He was presumably just looking for a girl."

"And a private place."

"It's not very private here."

There were faces behind the windows in the court, looking down.

"In Whitechapel, people are practiced at not seeing things."

Genevieve was prowling the tiny walled-in court, as if trying to get the feel of the place.

"You're not like other vampires," he observed.

"No," she agreed.

"How . . ."

"Four hundred and fifty six."

Beauregard was puzzled.

"That's right," she said. "I am not of the Prince Consort's bloodline. My father-in-darkness was Chandagnac, and his mother-in-darkness was Lady Melissa d'Acques, and . . ."

"So all this— " he waved his hand "—is nothing to do with you?"

"Everything is to do with everyone, Mr Beauregard. Vlad Tepes is a sick monster, and his get spread their sickness. That woman this morning is what you can expect of his bloodline . . ."

"You work as a physician?"

She shrugged. "I've picked up a lot of skills over the years. I've been a whore, a soldier, a singer, a geographer, a criminal. Whatever has seemed right. Now, being a doctor is the best I can see."

Beauregard found himself liking this ancient girl. She wasn't like any of the women—warm or un-dead—he knew. Women, whether by choice or from necessity, seemed to stand to one side, watching, passing comments, never acting. Genevieve Dieudonné was not a spectator.

"Is this political?"

Beauregard thought carefully.

"I've asked about the Diogenes Club," she explained. "You're some sort of government office, aren't you?"

"I serve the Crown, yes."

"Well, why your interest in this matter?"

Genevieve stood over the bloody splash that was left of Catherine Eddowes.

"The Queen herself has expressed her concern. If she decrees we try to catch a murderer, then . . ."

"The Ripper might be an anarchist of some stripe," she mused. "Or a die-hard vampire hater."

A little way away from the square, a group of policemen were clustered, Lestrade and Abberline among them, a thin man with a sad moustache and a silk hat at their head. It was Sir Charles Warren, dragged down to a despised quarter of his parish by the killings.

Beauregard sauntered over, the vampire girl with him.

A new-born constable was shifting a square of packing-case away from the wall against which it had been resting. A fat rat, body as big and bloated as a rugby ball, shot out, and darted between the Commissioner's polished shoes, squeaking like rusty nails on a slate.

Lestrade moved aside to let them into the group.

The constable had disclosed a scrawl.

THE VAMPYRES
ARE NOT THE MEN THAT WILL BE
BLAMED FOR NOTHING

"So, obviously the vampires are to be blamed for something," deduced the Commissioner, astutely.

"Could the Ripper be one of us?" asked a distinguished-looking new-born civilian who had come with Sir Charles.

"One of you," Beauregard muttered.

"The man's obviously trying to throw us off," put in Abberline, who was still warm. "That's an educated man trying to make us think he's an illiterate. Only one misspelling, and a double negative not even the thickest coster-monger would actually use."

"Like the letters?" asked Genevieve.

Abberline thought. "Personally, I think the letters were some smart circulation drummer at the *Whitechapel Star* playing silly buggers to drive up sales. This is a different hand, and this was the Ripper. It's too close to be a coincidence."

"The graffito was not here yesterday?" Beauregard asked.

"The beat man swears not."

The constable agreed with the inspector.

"Wipe it off," Sir Charles said.

Nobody did anything.

"There'll be mob rule. We're still few, and the warm are many."

The Commissioner took his own handkerchief to the chalk, and rubbed it away. Nobody protested at the destruction of the evidence.

"There," Sir Charles said, job done. "Sometimes I think I have to do everything myself."

Beauregard saw a narrow-minded impulsiveness that might have passed for stouthearted valour at Rorke's Drift or Lucknow, and understood just how Sir Charles could make a decision that ended in a massacre.

The dignitaries drifted away, back to their cabs and clubs and comfort. And the East End coppers stayed behind to clean up.

"Right," said Lestrade. "I want the cells full by sundown. Haul in every tart, every pimp, every bruiser, every pickpocket. Threaten 'em with whatever you want. Someone knows something, and sooner or later, someone'll talk."

That would please the circle in Limehouse not a bit, Beauregard reflected. Furthermore, Lestrade was wrong. Beauregard had a high enough estimation of the Professor and his colleagues to believe that if any criminal in London knew so much as a hint as to the identity of the Ripper, it would have been passed directly to him. In the week and a half since he had been taken to meet with them, he had heard nothing.

He found himself alone with Genevieve as sun set. She took off her cap.

"There," she said, shaking her hair out, "that's better."

XI

October 22, 1888. *I am keeping Mary Kelly. She is so like Lucy, so like what Lucy became. I have paid her rent up to the end of the month. I visit her when I can, when my work at the Hall permits, and we indulge in our peculiar exchange of fluids.*

The "double event"—hideous expression—has unnerved me, and I think I shall halt my nightwork. It is still necessary, but it is becoming too dangerous. The police are against me, and there are vampires everywhere. Besides, I am learning from Kelly, learning about myself.

She tells me, as we lie on the bed in her lodgings in Miller's Court, that she has gone off the game, that she is not seeing other men. I know she is lying, but do not make an issue of it. I open her pink flesh up and vent myself inside her, and she gently taps my blood, her teeth sliding into me. I have scars on my body, scars that itch like the wound Renfield gave me in Purfleet. I am determined not to turn, not to grow weak.

Money is not important. Kelly can have whatever I have left from my income. Since I came to Toynbee Hall, I've been drawing no salary and heavily subsidising the purchase of medical supplies and other necessaries. There has always been money in my family. No title, but always money.

Stride knew me when the police brought her to the Hall, and she would have identified me if Beauregard had not finished her. Others must have seen me about my nightwork—between Stride and Eddowes, I ran through the streets in a panic, bloodied and with a scalpel in my fist—and there is a not-bad description in the Police Gazette. There are so many fabulations about the Ripper—fuelled by still more silly notes to the press and police—that I can hide unnoticed among them, even if the occasional rumour strikes uncomfortably close.

A patient of mine, an uneducated immigrant named Kosminsky, confessed to me that he was Jack the Ripper, and I duly turned him over to Lestrade for examination. He showed me the file of similar confessions. And somewhere out there is the letter-writer, chortling over his silly red ink and arch jokes. George Lusk, chairman of the Vigilance Committee, was sent half a calf's kidney with a note headed "From Hell", claiming that the enclosure was from one of the dead women. "Tother piece I fried and ate, it was very nise."

I worry about Genevieve. Other vampires have a kind of red fog in their brains, but she is different. I read a piece by Henry Jekyll in The Lancet, speculating on the business of the vampire bloodline, as delicately as possible suggesting that there might be something impure about the royal strain the Prince Consort has imported. So many of Dracula's get are twisted, self-destructing creatures, torn apart by their changing bodies and uncontrollable desires. Royal blood, of course, is notoriously thin. And Jekyll has "disappeared". Lestrade denies that he has been carted off to Devil's Dyke, but many who dare venture an opinion against the Prince Consort seem to get lost in the fog.

I know what I do is right. I was right to save Lucy by cutting off her head, and I have been right to save the others. Nicholls, Schön, Stride, Eddowes. I am right.

But I shall stop.

I am an alienist, and Kelly has made me turn my look back upon myself.

Is my behaviour so different from poor Renfield's, amassing his tiny deaths like a miser hoards pennies? Dracula made a freak of him, as he has made a monster of me.

And I am a monster. Jack the Ripper. I shall be classed with Sweeney Todd, Sawney Beane, Jonathan Wild, Billy Bonney and endlessly served up in the Police Gazette *and* Famous Crimes: Past and Present. *Already, there are penny dreadfuls about Saucy Jack, Red Jack, Spring-Heel'd Jack, Bloody Jack. Soon, there will be music hall turns, sensational melodramas, a wax figure in Madame Tussaud's Chamber of Horrors.*

I meant to destroy a monster, not to become one.

I have made Kelly tell me about Lucy. The story, I am no longer ashamed to realise, excites me. I cannot care for Kelly as herself, so I must care for her for Lucy's sake.

The Lucy I remember is smug and prim and properly flirtatious, delicately encouraging my attentions but then clumsily turning me away when Arthur dangled his title under her nose. Somewhere between that befuddling but enchanting girl and the screaming leech whose head I sawed free of its shoulders was the new-born who turned Kelly. Dracula's get. With each retelling of the nocturnal encounter on the Heath, Kelly adds new details. She either remembers more, or invents them for my sake.

I am not sure I care which.

Sometimes, Lucy's advances to Kelly are tender, seductive, mysterious, with heated caresses before the Dark Kiss. At other times, they are a brutal rape, with needle-teeth shredding flesh and muscle, pain mixed in with the pleasure.

We illustrate with our bodies Kelly's stories.

I can no longer remember the faces of the dead women. There is only Kelly's face. And that becomes more like Lucy with each passing night.

I have bought Kelly clothes similar to those Lucy wore. The nightgown she wears before we couple is very like the shroud in which Lucy was buried. Kelly styles her hair like Lucy's now. Her speech is improving, the Irish accent fading.

Soon, I hesitate to hope, Kelly will be Lucy.

XII

"It's been nearly a month, Charles," the vampire girl ventured, "perhaps it's over?"

Beauregard shook his head.

"No, Genevieve," he said. "Good things come to an end, bad things have to be stopped."

"You're right, of course."

It was well after dark, and they were in the Ten Bells. Beauregard was becoming as familiar with Whitechapel as he had with the other strange territories to which the Diogenes Club had despatched him. He spent his days asleep in Chelsea, and his nights in the East End, with Genevieve, hunting the Ripper. And not catching him.

Everyone was starting to relax. The vigilante groups who had roamed the streets two weeks ago, making mischief and abusing innocents, were still wearing their sashes and carrying coshes, but they spent more time in pubs than the fog. After a month of double- and triple-shifts, policemen were gradually being redistributed back to their regular duties. It was not as if the Ripper did anything to reduce crime elsewhere in the city.

A conspiracy against the Prince Consort had been exposed last week, and, outside Buckingham Palace, Van Helsing's head had company. Shaw, the socialist, was there, and an adventurous young man named Rassendyll. Among the conspirators had been a new-born or two, which added a new colour to the political spectrum. The police were required to exact reprisals upon the conspirators and their families. Devil's Dyke was overcrowded with agitators and insurrectionists. W.T. Stead, an editor who had spoken against the Prince Consort, had been dragged out of his offices by wolfish Carpathians, and torn apart for amusement.

Now, neither Genevieve nor Beauregard drank. They just watched the others. Beside the drunken vigilantes, the pub was full of women, either genuine prostitutes or police agents in disguise. That was one of the several daft schemes that had gone from being laughed at in Scotland Yard to being implemented.

In the Diogenes Club, there was talk of outright rebellion in India and the Far East. A reporter for the *Civil and Military Gazette* had tried to assassinate Varney during an official visit to Lahore, and he—at least—was still at liberty and plotting. Many in her dominions were ceasing to recognise the Queen as their rightful ruler, if only because they sensed that since her resurrection she had not truly worn the crown. Each week, more ambassadors were withdrawn from the Court of St James. The Turks, whose memories were longer than Beauregard had expected, were clamouring for reparations from the Prince Consort, with regard to crimes of war committed against them in the fifteenth century.

Beauregard tried to look at Genevieve without her noticing, without her penetrating his thoughts. In the light, she looked absurdly young. He had to be guarded with her. It was hard to keep his thoughts in rein, and impossible fully to trust any vampire.

"You're right," she said. "He's still out there. He hasn't given up."

"Perhaps the Ripper's taken a holiday?"

"Or been distracted."

"Some say he's a sea captain. He could be on a voyage."

Genevieve thought hard, then shook her head. "No. He's still here. I can sense it."

"You sound like Lees, the psychical fellow."

"It's part of what I am," she explained. "The Prince Consort shapeshifts, but I can sense things. It's to do with our bloodlines. There's a fog around everything, but I can feel the Ripper out there somewhere. He's not finished yet."

"This place is annoying me," he said. "Let's get out, and see if we can do some good."

They had been patrolling like policemen. When not following one of the innumerable false leads that cropped up daily in this case, they just wandered, hoping to come up against a man with a big bag of knives and darkness in his heart. It was absurd, when you thought about it.

"I'd like to call in on the Hall. Jack Seward has a new ladylove, and has been neglecting his duties."

They stood up, and he helped her arrange her cloak on her shoulders.

"Careless fellow," he observed.

"Not at all. He's just driven, obsessive. I'm glad he's found a distraction. He's been heading for a nervous collapse for years. He had a bad time of it when Vlad Tepes first came, I believe, although it's not something be cares to talk about much."

They pushed through the ornately-glassed doors and into the streets. Beauregard shivered in the cold, but Genevieve just breezed through the icy fog as if it were light spring sunshine. He had constantly to remind himself this sharp girl was not human.

Down the street stood a cab, the horse funnelling steam from its nostrils. Beauregard recognised the cabbie.

"What is it?" Genevieve asked, noticing his sudden tension.

"Recent aquaintances," he said.

The door drifted open, creating a swirl in the fog. Beauregard knew they were surrounded. The tramp huddled in the alleyway across the road, the idler hugging himself against the cold, the one he couldn't see in the shadows under the tobacconist's shop. He thumbed the catch of his cane, but did not think he could take them all and look after Genevieve.

Someone leaned out of the cab, and beckoned them. Beauregard, with casual care, walked over.

XIII

"Genevieve Dieudonné," Beauregard introduced her, "Colonel Sebastian Moran, formerly of the First Bangalore Pioneers, author of *Heavy Game of the Western Himalayas*, and one of the greatest scoundrels unhanged . . ."

The new-born in the coach was an angry-looking brute, uncomfortable in evening dress, moustache bristling fiercely. When alive, he must have had the ruddy tan of an "Injah hand", but now he looked like a viper, poison sacs bulging under his chin.

Moran grunted something that might count as an acknowledgement, and ordered them to get into the coach.

Beauregard hesistated, then stepped back to allow her to go first. He was being clever, she realised. If the Colonel meant harm, he would keep an eye on the man he considered a threat. The new-born would not believe her four and a half centuries stronger than he. If it came to it, she could take him apart.

Genevieve sat opposite Moran, and Beauregard took the seat next to her. Moran tapped the roof, and the cab trundled off.

With the motion, the black-hooded bundle next to the Colonel nodded forwards, and had to be straightened up and leaned back.

"A friend?" Beauregard asked.

Moran snorted. Inside the bundle was a man, either dead or insensible.

"What would you say if I told you this was Jack the Ripper?"

"I suppose I'd have to take you seriously. I understand you only hunt the most dangerous game."

Moran grinned like a devil, tiger-fangs under his whiskers.

"Huntin' hunters," he said. "It's the only sport worth talkin' about."

"They say Quatermain and Roxton are better than you with a rifle, and that Russian general who uses the Tartar warbow is the best of all."

The Colonel brushed away the comparisons.

"They're all still warm."

Moran had a stiff arm out, holding back the clumsy bundle.

"We're on our own in this huntin' trip," he said. "The rest of them aren't in it."

Beauregard considered.

"It's been nearly a month since the last matter," the Colonel said. "Jack's finished. But that's not enough for us, is it? If business is to get back to the usual, Jack has to be seen to be finished."

They were near the river. The Thames was a sharp, foul undertaste in the air. All the filth of the city wound up in the river, and was disseminated into the seven seas. Garbage from Rotherhithe and Stepney drifted to Shanghai and Madagascar.

Moran got a grip on the black winding sheet, and wrenched it away from a pale, bloodied face. Genevieve recognised the man.

"Druitt," she said.

"Montague John Druitt, I believe," the Colonel said. "A colleague of yours, with very peculiar nocturnal habits."

This was not right.

Druitt's left eye opened in a rind of blood. He had been badly beaten, but was still alive.

"The police considered him early in the investigation," Beauregard said—a surprise to Genevieve—"but he was ruled out."

"He had easy access," Moran said. "Toynbee Hall is almost dead centre of the pattern made by the murder sites. He fits the popular picture, a crackpot toff with bizarre delusions. Nobody—begging your pardon, ma'am—really believes an educated man works among tarts and beggars out of Christian kindness. And nobody is goin' to object to Druitt hangin' for the slaughter of a handful of whores. He's not exactly royalty, is he? He don't even have an alibi for any of the killings."

"You evidently have close friends at the Yard?"

Moran flashed his feral grin again.

"So, do I extend my congratulations to you and your ladyfriend," the Colonel asked, "have you caught Jack the Ripper?"

Beauregard took a long pause and thought. Genevieve was confused, realising how much had been kept from her. Druitt was trying to say something, but his broken mouth couldn't frame words. The coach was thick with the smell of slick blood, and her own mouth was dry. She had not fed in too long.

"No," Beauregard said. "Druitt will not fit. He plays cricket."

"So does another blackguard I could name. That don't prevent him from bein' a filthy murderer."

"In this case, it does. On the mornings after the second and third and fourth murders, Druitt was on the field. After the double event, he made a half-century and took two wickets. I hardly think he could have managed that if he'd been up all night chasing and killing women."

Moran was not impressed.

"You're beginnin' to sound like that rotten detective. All clues and evidence and deductions. Druitt here is committin' suicide tonight, fillin' his pockets with stones and takin' a swim in the Thames. I dare say the body'll have been bashed about a bit before he's found. But before he does the deed, he'll leave behind a confession. And his handwritin' is goin' to look deuced like that on those bloody crank letters."

Moran made Druitt's head nod.

"It won't wash, Colonel. What if the real Ripper starts killing again?"

"Whores die, Beauregard. It happens often. We found one Ripper, we can always find another."

"Let me guess. Pedachenko, the Russian agent? The police considered him for a moment or two. Sir William Gull, the Queen's physician? The theosophist, Dr Donstan? The solicitor, Soames Forsyte? The cretin, Aron Kosminsky? Poor old Leather Apron Pizer? Dr Jekyll? Prince Eddy? Walter Sickert? Dr Cream? It's a simple matter to put a scalpel into someone's hand and make him up for the part. But that won't stop the killing . . ."

"I didn't take you for such a fastidious sort, Beauregard. You don't mind servin' vampires, or— " a sharp nod at Genevieve "—consortin' with them. You may be warm, but you're chillin' by the hour. Your conscience lets you serve the Prince Consort . . ."

"I serve the Queen, Moran."

The Colonel started to laugh, but—after a flash of razor lightning in the dark of the cab—found Beauregard's sword-cane at his throat.

"I know a silversmith, too," Beauregard said. "Just like Jack."

Druitt tumbled off his seat, and Genevieve caught him. He was broken inside.

Moran's eyes glowed red in the gloom. The silvered length of steel held fast, its point dimpling the Colonel's adam's apple.

"I'm going to turn him," Genevieve said. "He's too badly hurt to be saved any other way."

Beauregard nodded to her, his hand steady.

With a nip, she bit into her wrist, and waited for the blood to well up. If Druitt could drink enough of her blood as she drained him, the transformation would begin.

It was a long time—centuries—since she had had any get. The years had made her cautious, or responsible.

"Another new-born," Moran snorted. "We should've been more selective when it all started."

"Drink," she cooed.

What did she really know about Montague John Druitt? Like her, he was a lay practitioner, not a doctor but with some medical knowledge. She did not even know why a man with some small income and position should want to work in Toynbee Hall. He was not an obsessive philanthropist, like Seward. He was not a religious man, like Booth. Genevieve had taken him for granted as a useful pair of hands. Now, she was going to have to take responsibility for him, possibly for ever.

If he became a monster, like Vlad Tepes or even like Colonel Sebastian Moran, then it would be her fault. She would be killing all the people Druitt killed.

And he had been a suspect. Even if innocent, there was something about Druitt that had made him seem a likely Ripper.

"Drink," she said, forcing the word from her mouth. Her wrist was dripping red.

She held her hand to Druitt's mouth. Her incisors slid from their gumsheaths, and she dipped her head. The scent of Druitt's blood was stinging in her nostrils.

Druitt had a convulsion, and she realised his need was urgent. If he did not drink her blood now, he would die.

She touched her wrist to his mashed lips. He flinched away, trembling.

"No," he gargled, refusing her gift, "no . . ."

A shudder of disgust ran through him, and he died.

"Not everybody wants to live forever at any price," Moran observed. "What a waste."

Genevieve reached across the space between them, and back-handed the Colonel across the face, knocking away Beauregard's cane.

Moran's red eyes shrank, and she could tell he was afraid of her. She was still hungry, having allowed the red thirst to rise in her. She could not drink Druitt's spoiled dead blood. She could not even drink Moran's second- or third-hand blood. But she could relieve her frustration by ripping meat off his face.

"Call her off," Moran spluttered.

One of her hands was at his throat, the other was drawn back, the fingers gathered into a point, sharp talons bunched like an arrowhead. It would be so easy to put a hole in Moran's face.

"It's not worth it," Beauregard said. Somehow, his words cut through her crimson rage, and she held back. "He may be a worm, but he has friends, Genevieve. Friends you wouldn't want to make enemies of."

Her teeth slipped back into her gums, and her sharpened finger-nails settled. She was still itchy for blood, but she was in control again.

Beauregard nodded, and Moran had the coach stop.

The Colonel, his new-born's confidence in shreds, was shaking as they stepped down. A trickle of blood leaked from one eye. Beauregard sheathed his cane, and Moran wrapped a scarf around his pricked neck.

"Quatermain wouldn't have flinched, Colonel," Beauregard said. "Good night, and give my regards to the Professor."

Moran turned his face away into the darkness, and the cab wheeled away from the pavement, rushing into the fog.

Genevieve's head was spinning.

They were back where they had started. Near the Ten Bells. The pub was no quieter now than when they left. Women loitered by the doors, strutting for passersby.

Her mouth hurt, and her heart was hammering. She made fists, and tried to shut her eyes.

Beauregard held his wrist to her mouth.

"Here," he said, "take what you need."

A rush of gratitude made her ankles weak. She almost swooned, but at once dispelled the fog in her mind, concentrating on her need.

She bit him gently, and took as little as possible to slake the red thirst. His blood trickled down her throat, calming her, giving her strength. When it was over, she asked him if it were his first time, and he nodded.

"It's not unpleasant," he commented, neutrally.

"It can be less formal," she said. "Eventually."

"Good night, Genevieve," he said, turning away. He walked into the fog, and left her, his blood still on her lips.

She realised she knew as little about Charles Beauregard as she had about Druitt. He had never really told her why he was interested in the Ripper. Or why he continued to serve his vampire queen.

For a moment, she was frightened. Everyone around her wore a mask, and behind that mask might be . . .

Anything.

XIV

She was who-the-bloody-ever she wanted to be, whoever men wanted her to be. Mary Jane. Marie Jeanette. Or Lucy. She would be Ellen Terry if she had to. Or Queen Victoria.

He sat by her bedside now.

She was telling him again how she had been turned. How his Lucy had come out of the night for her on the Heath, and given her the Dark Kiss. Only now, she was telling him as if she were Lucy, and Mary Jane some other person, some worthless whore . . .

"I was so cold, John, so hungry, so *new* . . ."

It was easy to know Lucy had felt. She had felt the same when she woke from her deep sleep. Only Lucy had woke in a crypt, respectfully laid out. Mary Jane had been on a cart, minutes away from a lime pit. One of the unclaimed dead.

"She was warm, plump, alive, blood pounding in her sweet neck."

He was listening now, nodding his head. She supposed he was mad. But he was a gentleman. And she was good to her, good for her.

"The children hadn't been enough."

Mary Jane had been confused by the new desires. It had taken her weeks to adjust. She had ripped open dogs for their juice. She had not known enough to stay out of the sun, and her skin had turned to painful crackling.

But that was like a dream now. She was beginning to lose Mary Jane's memories. She was Lucy.

"I needed her, John. I needed her blood."

He sat by her bed, reserved and doctorly. Later, she would pleasure him. And she would drink from him.

Each time she drank, she became less Mary Jane and more Lucy. It must be something in his blood.

Since her rebirth, the mirror in her room was useless to her. No one had ever bothered to sketch her picture, so she could easily forget her own face. He had pictures of Lucy, looking like a little girl dressed up in her mother's clothes, and it was Lucy's face she imagined her eyes looked out of.

"I beckoned her from the path," she said, leaning over from the pile of pillows on the bed, her face close to his. "I sang under my breath, and I waved to her. I *wished* her to me, and she came . . ."

She stroked his cheek, and laid her head against his chest.

He was holding his breath, sweating a little, his posture awkward. She could soon make him unbend.

"There were red eyes in front of me, and a voice calling me. I left the path, and she was waiting. It was a cold night, but she wore only a white shift. Her skin was white in the moonlight. Her . . ."

She caught herself.

Mary Jane, she said inside, be careful . . .

He stood up, gently pushing her away, and walked across the room.

Taking a grip of her washstand, he looked at himself in the mirror, trying to find something in his reflection.

She was confused. All her life, she had been giving men what they wanted. Now she was dead, and things were the same.

She went to him, and hugged him from behind. He jumped at her touch, surprised.

Of course, he had not seen her coming.

"John," she cooed at him, "come to bed, John. Make me warm."

He pushed her away again, roughly this time. She was not used to her vampire's strength. Imagining herself still a feeble girl, she was one, a reed easy to break.

"Lucy," he said, emptily, not to her . . .

Anger sparked in her mind.

"I'm not your bloody Lucy Westenra," she shouted. "I'm Mary Jane Kelly, and I don't care who knows it."

"No," he said, reaching into his jacket for something, gripping it hard, "you're not Lucy . . ."

XV

Her touch had changed him. Beauregard had been troubled by dreams since that night. Dreams in which Genevieve Dieudonné, sometimes herself and sometimes a needle-fanged cat, lapped at his blood.

He supposed it had always been in the cards. With the way things were, he would have been tapped by a vampire sooner or later. He was luckier than most, to have given his blood freely rather than have it taken by force.

The fog was thick tonight. And the November cold was like the caress of a razor. Or a scalpel.

Genevieve had taken from him, but given something in return. Something of herself.

He stood outside Toynbee Hall, on the point of entering. He had been here for half an hour. Nothing was that urgent.

She was inside. He *knew*.

He was afraid he wanted her to drink from him again. Not the simple thirst-slaking of an opened wrist, but the full embrace of the Dark Kiss. Genevieve Dieudonné was an extraordinary woman by the standards of any age. Together, they could live through the centuries.

It was a temptation.

A gaudily-painted child, unable to close her mouth over her new teeth, sauntered up to him, and lifted her skirts. He brushed her aside and, sulking, she retreated.

He remembered his duty.

For nearly a fortnight, duty had made him stay away from Toynbee Hall. Now, duty brought him back here.

At the Diogenes Club, he had received a brief note of apology from the Professor, informing him that Colonel Moran had been rebuked for his ill-advised actions. That could hardly be a comfort to Montague Druitt, who had washed ashore at Deptford days ago, face eaten away by fish.

Yet Moran had said something which still ticked away in the back of Beauregard's mind.

Genevieve's lips had been cool, her touch gentle, her tongue roughly pleasant as a cat's. The draining of his blood, so slow and so tender, had been an exquisite sensation, instantly addictive . . .

Toynbee Hall was named for its philanthropic founder. It was a mission to Whitechapel. Arnold Toynbee had said the Britishers of the East End were far more in need of Christian attention than the heathen Africans with whom Dr Livingstone had been so concerned.

The Hall was in the centre of the pattern of the Ripper murders.

Finally, Beauregard overcame his languid confusion, and spurred himself to action. He walked across the narrow street, and slipped into the Hall.

A warm matron sat at a reception desk, devouring the latest Marie Corelli, *Thelma*. Beauregard understood that since she became a new-born, the celebarted authoress's prose style had deteriorated still further. Genevieve had remarked once that vampires were never very creative, all their energies being diverted into the simple prolonging of life.

"Where is Mademoiselle Dieundonné?"

"She is filling in for the director, sir. She should be in Dr Seward's office."

"Thank you."

"Shall you be wanting to be announced?"

"No need to bother, thank you."

The matron frowned, and mentally added another complaint to a list she was keeping of Things Wrong With That Vampire Girl. Beauregard was briefly surprised to be party to her clear and vinegary thoughts, but swept that distraction aside as he made his way to the director's first floor office.

Genevieve was surprised to see him.

"Charles," she said.

She sat at Seward's desk, papers strewn about her. He fancied she was startled, as if found prying where she was not wanted.

"Where have you been?"

He had no answer.

Looking around the room, his eyes were drawn to a device in a glass dust-case. It was an affair of brass boxes, with a large trumpet-like attachment.

"This is an Edison-Bell phonograph, is it not?"

"Jack uses it for medical notes. He has a passion for tricks and toys."

He turned.

"Genevieve . . ."

She was near, now. He had not heard her come out from behind the desk.

"It's all right, Charles. I didn't mean to bewitch you. The symptoms will recede in a week or two. Believe me, I have experience with your condition."

"It's not that . . ."

He could not think along a straight line of reasoning. Butterfly insights fluttered in the back of him mind, never quite caught.

By an effort of will, he concentrated on the pressing matter of the Ripper.

"Why Whitechapel?" he asked. "Why not Soho, or Hyde Park, or anywhere. Vampirism is not limited to this district, nor prostitution. The Ripper hunts here because it is most convenient, because he *is* here. Somewhere, near . . ."

"I've been looking over our records," she said, tapping the pile on the desk. "The victims were all brought in at one time or another."

"It all comes back to Toynbec Hall by so many routes. Druitt and you work here, Stride was brought here, the killings are in a ring about the address, all the dead women were here . . ."

"Could Moran have been right? Could it have been Druitt? There have been no more murders."

Beauregard shook his head. "It's not over yet."

"If only Jack were here."

He made a fist. "We'd have the murderer then."

"No, I mean Jack Seward. He treated all the women. He might know if they had something in common."

Genevieve's words sank into his brain, and lightning swarmed behind his eyes. Suddenly, he *knew* . . .

"They had Dr Seward in common."

"But . . ."

"Dr *Jack* Seward."

She shook her head, but he could tell she was seeing what he saw, coming quickly to a realisation.

They both remembered Elizabeth Stride grasping Dr Seward's ankle. She had been trying to tell them something.

"Are there diaries around here?" Beauregard asked. "Private records, notes, anything? These maniacs are often compelled to keep souvenirs, keepsakes, memorabilia . . ."

"I've been through all his files tonight. They contain only the usual material."

"Locked drawers?"

"No. Only the phonograph cabinet. The wax cylinders are delicate and have to be protected from dust."

Beauregard wrenched the cover off the contraption, and pulled open the drawer of the stand. Its fragile lock splintered.

The cylinders were ranked in tubes, with neatly-inked labels.

"*Nicholls,*" he read aloud, "*Schön, Stride/Eddowes, Kelly, Kelly, Kelly, Lucy . . .*"

Genevieve was by him, delving deeper into the drawer.

"And these . . . *Lucy, Van Helsing, Renfield, Lucy's Tomb.*"

Everyone remembered Van Helsing, and Beauregard even knew Renfield was the Prince Consort's martyred disciple in London. But . . .

"Kelly and Lucy. Who are they? Unknown victims?"

Genevieve was going again through the papers on the desk. She talked as she sorted.

"Lucy, at a guess, was Lucy Westenra, Vlad Tepes' first English conquest, the first of his bloodline here. Dr Van Helsing destroyed her, and Jack Seward, I'll wager, was in with Van Helsing's crowd. As for Kelly . . . well, we have lots of Kellys on our books. But only one who fits our Jack's requirements. Here."

She handed him a sheet of paper, with the details of a patient's treatment.

Kelly, Mary Jane. 13, Miller's Court.

XVI

"Fucking Hell," said Beauregard.

Genevieve had to agree with him.

The stench of dead blood hit her in the stomach like a fist, and she had to hold the doorframe to keep from fainting. She had seen the leavings of murderers before, and blood-muddied battlefields, and plague holes, and torture chambers, and execution sites.

But 13, Miller's Court, was the worst of all.

Dr Seward knelt in the middle of the red ruin barely recognisable as a human being. He was still working, his apron and shirtsleeves dyed red, his silver scalpel flickering in the firelight as he made further pointless incisions.

Mary Kelly's room was a typical cramped lodging. A bed, a chair and a fireplace, with barely enough floor to walk around the bed. Seward's operations had spread the girl across the bed and the floor, and around the walls up to the height of three feet. The cheap muslin curtains were speckled with halfpenny-size dots.

In the grate, a bundle still burned, casting a red light that seared into Genevieve's night-sensitive eyes.

Seward did not seem overly concerned with their intrusion.

"Nearly done," he said, lifting out an eyeball from a pie-shaped expanse that had once been a face, and snipping deftly through the optic nerves. "I have to be sure Lucy is dead. Van Helsing says her soul will not rest until she is truly dead."

He was calm, not ranting.

Beauregard had his pistol out and aimed.

"Put down the knife, and step away from her," he said.

Seward placed the knife on the bedspread, and stood up, wiping his hands on an already-bloody patch of apron.

Mary Kelly was truly dead. Genevieve had no doubt about that.

"It's over," Seward said. "We've beaten him. We've beaten Dracula. The foul contagion cannot spread further."

Genevieve had nothing to say. Her stomach was still a tight fist.

Seward seemed to see Genevieve for the first time.

"Lucy," he said, seeing someone else, somewhere else. "Lucy, it was all for you . . ."

He bent to pick up his scalpel, and Beauregard shot him. In the shoulder.

Seward spun around, his fingers grasping air, and slammed against the wall. He pressed his gloved hand to the wall, and sank downwards, his knees protruding as he tried to make his body shrink. In the wall, a scrap of silver shone where Beauregard's bullet had lodged.

Genevieve had snatched the weapon away from the bed. Its silver blade itched, but she held it by the enamelled grip. It was such a small thing to have done so much damage.

"The shot will have alerted people," Beauregard said. "We have to get him out of here. A mob would tear him apart."

Genevieve hauled Seward upright, and between them they got him into the street. His clothes were sticky and tacky from the drying, foul-smelling gore.

It was nearing morning, and Genevieve was suddenly tired. The cold air did not dispel the throbbing in her head. The image of 13, Miller's Court was imprinted in her mind like a photograph upon paper. She would never, she thought, lose it.

Seward was easy to manipulate. He would walk with them to a police station, or to Hell.

From Hell, that's where the letters had come.

XVII

As soon as they were out of the charnel house, Beauregard made his decision. The women were dead, and Seward was mad. No justice could be served by turning him over to Lestrade.

"Hold him up, Genevieve," he said. "Against the wall."

She knew what he was about, and gave her consent. Seward was propped against the wall of the alley. His face was wearily free of expression. Blood dribbled from his wound.

Beauregard drew his swordcane. The rasp cut through the tiny nightsounds.

"He bit me," the Ripper said, remembering some trivial incident, "the madman bit me."

Seward held out his gloved, swollen hand.

Genevieve nodded, and Beauregard slipped his blade through Seward's heart. The point scraped brickwork. Beauregard withdrew the sword, and sheathed it.

Seward, cleanly dead, crumpled.

"The Prince Consort would have made him immortal, just so he could torture him forever," he said.

Genevieve agreed with him.

"He was mad and not responsible."

"Then who," he asked, "was responsible?"

"The thing who drove him mad."

Beauregard looked up. A cloud had passed from the face of moon, and it shone down through the thinning fog.

He fancied he had seen a bat, large and black, flitting up in the stratosphere.

His duty was not yet discharged.

XVIII

The Queen's carriage had called for her at Toynbee Hall, and a fidgety coachman named Netley was delicately negotiating the way through the cramped streets of Whitechapel. Netley had already picked up Beauregard, from the Diogenes Club. The huge black horse and its discreetly imposing burden would feel less confined once they were on the wider thoroughfares of the city. Now, the carriage was like a panther in Hampton Court Maze, prowling rather than moving as elegantly and speedily as it was meant to. In the night, hostile eyes were aimed at the black coach, and at the coat of arms it bore.

Genevieve noticed Beauregard was somewhat subdued. She had seen him several times since the night of November 9th. Since 13, Miller's Court. She had even been admitted into the hallowed chambers of the Diogenes Club, to give evidence to a private hearing at which Beauregard was called upon to give an account of the death of Dr Seward. She understood the secret ways of government, and realised this tribunal had as much to do with deciding which truths should be concealed as which should be presented to the public at large. The chairman, a venerable and warm diplomat who had weathered many changes of government, took everything in, but gave out no verdict, simply absorbing the information, as each grain of truth shaped the policies of a club that was often more than a club. There were few vampires in the Diogenes Club, and Genevieve wondered whether it might not be a hiding place for the pillars of the *ancien régime*, or a nest of insurrectionists.

An engraved invitation to the Palace had been delivered personally into her hand. As acting director of the Hall, she was busier than ever. A new strain of plague was running through the new-borns of Whitechapel, triggering off their undisciplined shapeshifting powers, creating a horde of short-lived, agonised freaks. But a summons from the Queen and the Prince Consort was not to be ignored.

Presumably, they were to be honoured for their part in ending the career of Jack the Ripper. A private honour, perhaps, but an honour nevertheless.

Genevieve wondered if Beauregard would be proud to meet his sovereign, or if her current state would sadden him. She had heard stories of the situation inside the Palace. And she knew more of Vlad Tepes than most. Among vampires, he had always been the Man Who Would Be King.

The carriage passed through Fleet Street—past the boarded-up and burned-out offices of the nation's great newspapers—and the Strand. There was no fog tonight, just an icy wind.

It had been generally decided, in the ruling cabal of the Diogenes Club, that the identity of the murderer should be witheld, although it was common knowledge that his crimes had come to an end. Arrangements had been made at Scotland Yard, the Commissioner's resignation exchanged for an overseas posting, and Lestrade and Abberline were on fresh cases. Nothing much had changed. Whitechapel was hunting a new madman now, a murderer of brutish disposition and appearance named Edward Hyde who had trampled a small child and then raised his ambitions by shoving a broken walking-stick through the heart of a new-born Member of Parliament. Once he was stopped, another murderer would come along, and another, and another . . .

In Trafalgar Square, there were bonfires. The red light filled the carriage as they passed Nelson's Column. The police kept dousing the fires, but insurrectionists started them up again. Scraps of wood were smuggled in. Items of clothing even were used to fuel the fires. Newborns were superstitiously afraid of fire, and did not like to get too close.

Beauregard looked out with interest at the blazes, heaped around the stone lions. Originally a memorial to the victims of Bloody Sunday, they had a new meaning now. News had come through from India, where there had been another mutiny, with many warm British troops and officials throwing in their lot with the natives. Sir Francis Varney, the unpopular vampire Viceroy, had been dragged from his hiding place at the Red Fort in Delhi by a mob and cast into just such a fire, burned down to ash and bones. The colony was in open revolt. And there were stirrings in Africa and Points East.

Crowds were scuffling by the fires, one of the Prince Consort's Carpathian Guard tossing warm young men about while the Fire Brigade perhaps half-heartedly, tried to train their hoses. Placards were waved and slogans shouted.

JACK STILL RIPS, a graffito read.

The letters were still coming, the red-inked scrawls signed "Jack the Ripper." Now, they called for the warm to rally against their vampire masters. Whenever a new-born was killed, "Jack the Ripper" took the credit. Beauregard had said nothing, but Genevieve suspected that the letters were issued from the Diogenes Club. She saw that a dangerous game was being played in the halls of secret government, factions conspiring against each other, with the ruination of the Prince Consort as an end. Dr Seward might have been mad, but his work had not been entirely wasteful. Even if a monster became a hero, a new Guy Fawkes, a purpose was being served.

She was a vampire, but she was not of the bloodline of Vlad Tepes. That left her, as ever, on the sidelines of history. She had no real

interest either way. It had been refreshing for a while not to have
to pretend to be warm, but the Prince Consort's regime made things
uncomfortable for most of the un-dead. For every noble vampire in his
town house, with a harem of willing blood-slaves, there were twenty
of Mary Kelly, Lilly, or Cathy Eddowes, as miserable as they had
ever been, their vampire attributes addictions and handicaps rather
than powers and potentials.

The carriage, able to breathe at last, rolled down the Mall towards
Buckingham Palace. Insurrectionist leaders hung in chains from
cruciform cages lining the road, some still barely alive. Within
the last three nights, an open battle had raged in St James's Park,
between the warm and the dead.

"Look," Beauregard said, sadly, "there's Van Helsing's head."

Genevieve craned her neck and saw the pathetic lump on the end
of its raised pike. The story was that Abraham Van Helsing was still
alive, in the Prince Consort's thrall, raised high so that his eyes might
see the reign of Dracula over London. The story was a lie. What was
left was a fly-blown skull, hung with ragged strips.

They were at the Palace. Two Carpathians, in midnight black
uniforms slashed with crimson, hauled the huge ironwork frames
aside as if they were silk curtains.

The exterior of the Palace was illuminated. The Union Jack flew,
and the Crest of Dracula.

Beauregard's face was a blank.

The carriage pulled up at the entrance, and a footman opened the
door. Genevieve stepped down first, and Beauregard followed.

She had selected a simple dress, having nothing better and knowing
finery had never suited her. He wore his usual evening dress, and
handed his cape and cane to the servant who took her cloak. A
Carpathian, his face a mask of stiff hair, stood by to watch him
hand over his cane. He turned over his revolver too. Silver bullets
were frowned on at the Court. Smithing with silver was punishable
by death.

The Palace's doors were hauled open in lurches, and a strange
creature—a tailored parti-coloured suit emphasising the extensive
and grotesque malformations of his body, growths the size of loaves
sprouting from his torso, his huge head a knotted turnip in which
human features were barely discernible—admitted them. Genevieve
was overwhelmed with pity for the man, perceiving at once that this
was a warm human being not the fruit of some catastrophically failed
attempt at shapeshifting.

Beauregard nodded to the servant, and said "good evening.
Merrick, is it not?"

A smile formed somewhere in the doughy expanses of Merrick's face, and he returned the greeting, his words slurred by excess slews of flesh around his mouth.

"And how is the Queen this evening?"

Merrick did not reply, but Genevieve imagined she saw an expression in the unreadable map of his features. There was a sadness in his single exposed eye, and a grim set to his lips.

Beauregard gave Merrick a card, and said "compliments of the Diogenes Club." Something conspiratorial passed between the perfectly-groomed gentleman-adventurer and the hideously deformed servant.

Merrick led them down the hallway, hunched over like a gorilla, using one long arm to propel his body. He had one normal arm, which stuck uselessly from his body, penned in by lumpy swellings.

Obviously, it amused Vlad Tepes to keep this poor creature as a pet. He had always had a fondness for freaks and sports.

Merrick knocked on a door.

"Genevieve," Beauregard said, voice just above a whisper, "if what I do brings harm to you, I am sincerely sorry."

She did not understand him. As her mind raced to catch up with him, he leaned over and kissed her, on the mouth, the warm way. She tasted him, and was reminded. The sharing of blood had established a link between them.

The kiss broke, and he stood back, leaving her baffled. Then a door was opened, and they were admitted into the Royal Presences.

Nothing had prepared her for the sty the throne-room had become. Dilapidated beyond belief, its once-fine walls and paintings torn and stained, with the stench of dried blood and human ordure thick in the air, the room was ill-lit by battered chandeliers, and full of people and animals. Laughter and whimpering competed, and the marble floors were thick with filthy discharges. An armadillo rolled by, its rear-parts clogged with its own dirt.

Merrick announced them, his palate suffering as he got their names out. Someone made a crude remark, and gales of laughter cut through the din, then were cut off at a wave of the Prince Consort's ham-sized hand.

Vlad Tepes sat upon the throne, massive as a commemorative statue, his face enormously bloated, rich red under withered gray. Stinking moustaches hung to his chest, stiff with recent blood, and his black-stubbled chin was dotted with the gravy-stains of his last feeding. An ermine-collared cloak clung to his shoulders like the wings of a giant bat; otherwise, he was naked, his body thickly-coated with matted hair, blood and filth clotting on his chest and limbs. His white manhood, tipped scarlet as an adder's tongue, lay coiled like a snake in his lap. His body was swollen like a leech's, his rope-thick veins visibly pulsing.

Beauregard shook in the presence, the smell smiting him like blows. Genevieve held him up, and looked around the room.

"I never dreamed . . ." he muttered, "never . . ."

A warm girl ran across the room, pursued by one of the Carpathians, his uniform in tatters. He brought her down with a swipe of a bear-paw, and began to tear at her back and sides with triple-jointed jaws, taking meat as well as drink.

The Prince Consort smiled.

The Queen was kneeling by the throne, a silver spiked collar around her neck, a massive chain leading from it to a loose bracelet upon Dracula's wrist. She was in her shift and stockings, brown hair loose, blood on her face. It was impossible to see the round old woman she had been in this abused girl. Genevieve hoped she was mad, but feared she was only too well aware of what was going on about her. She turned away, not looking at the Carpathian's meal.

"Majesties," Beauregard said, bowing his head.

Vlad Tepes laughed, an enormous farting sound exploding from his jaggedly-fanged maw. The stench of his breath filled the room. It was everything dead and rotten.

A fastidiously-dressed vampire youth, an explosion of lace escaping at his collar from the tight black shine of his velvet suit, explained to the Prince Consort who these guests were. Genevieve recognised the Prime Minister, Lord Ruthven.

"These are the heroes of Whitechapel," the English vampire said, a fluttering handkerchief before his mouth and nose.

The Prince Consort grinned ferociously, eyes burning like crimson furnaces, moustaches creaking like leather straps.

"The lady and I are acquainted," he said, in surprisingly perfect and courteous English. "We met at the home of the Countess Dolingen of Graz, some hundred years ago."

Genevieve remembered well. The Countess, a snob beyond the grave, had summoned what she referred to as the un-dead aristocracy. The Karnsteins of Styria had been there, pale and uninteresting, and several of Vlad Tepes's Transylvanian associates, Princess Vajda, Countess Bathory, Count Iorga, Count Von Krolock. Also Saint-Germain from France, Villanueva from Spain, Duval from Mexico. At that gathering, Vlad Tepes had seemed an ill-mannered upstart, and his proposition of a vampire crusade, to subjugate petty humanity under his standard, had been ignored. Since then, Genevieve had done her best to avoid other vampires.

"You have served us well, Englishman," the Prince Consort said, praise sounding like a threat.

Beauregard stepped forward.

"I have a gift, majesties," he said, "a souvenir of our exploit in the East End."

Vlad Tepes's eyes gleamed with lust. At heart, he had the philistine avarice of a true barbarian. Despite his lofty titles, he was barely a generation away from the mountain bully-boys his ancestors had been. He liked nothing more than pretty things. Bright, shining toys.

Beauregard took something from his inside pocket, and unwrapped a cloth from it.

Silver shone.

Everyone in the throne room was quieted. Vampires had been feeding in the shadows, noisily suckling the flesh of youths and girls. Carpathians had been grunting their simple language at each other. All went silent.

Fury twisted the Prince Consort's brow, but then contempt and mirth turned his face into a wide-mouthed mask of obscene enjoyment.

Beauregard held Dr Seward's silver scalpel. He had taken it from Genevieve that night. As evidence, she thought.

"You think you can defy me with that tiny needle, Englishman?"

"It is a gift," Beauregard replied. "But not for you."

Genevieve was edging away, uncertain. The Carpathians had detached themselves from their amusements, and were forming a half circle around Beauregard. There was no one between Beauregard and the throne, but, if he made a move towards the Prince Consort, a wall of solid vampireflesh and bone would form.

"For my Queen," Beauregard said, tossing the knife.

Genevieve saw the silver reflect in Vlad Tepes's eyes, as anger exploded dark in the pupils. Then Victoria snatched the tumbling scalpel from the air . . .

It had all been for this moment, all to get Beauregard into the Royal Presence, all to serve this one duty. Genevieve, the taste of him in her mouth, understood.

Victoria slipped the blade under her breast, stapling her shift to her ribs, puncturing her heart. For her, it was over quickly.

With a look of triumph and joy, she fell from her dais, blood gouting from her fatal wound, and rolled down the steps, chain clanking with her.

Vlad Tepes—Prince Consort no more—was on his feet, cloak rippling around him like a thundercloud. Tusklike teeth exploded from his face, and his hands became spear-tipped clusters. Beauregard, Genevieve realised, was dead. But the monster's power was dealt a blow from which it could never recover. The Empire Vlad Tepes had usurped would rise against him. He had grown too arrogant.

The Carpathians were on Beauregard already, talons and mouths red and digging. Genevieve thought she was to die too. Beauregard had tried to keep her from harm by not involving her in his designs. But she had been too stubborn, had insisted on being here, on seeing Vlad Tepes in the lair he had made for himself.

He came down from his throne for her, foul steam pouring from his mouth and nostrils.

But she was older than him. Less blinded by the ignorance of his selfish fantasies. For centuries, he had thought himself special, as a higher being apart from humanity, while she knew she was just a tick in the hide of the warm.

She ducked under his hands, and was not there when he overbalanced, falling to the floor like a felled tree, marble cracking under his face. He was slow in his age, in his bloated state. Too much indulgence. Too much isolation. Veins in his neck burst, spurting blood, and knitted together again.

While Vlad Tepes was scrambling to right himself, the rest of his court were in confusion. Some returned to their bloody pleasure, some fell insensate.

She could do nothing for Beauregard.

Ruthven was uncertain. With the Queen truly dead, things were going to change. He could have barred her way from the palace, but he hesitated—ever the politician—then stood aside.

Merrick had the doors open for her, and she escaped from the infernal heat and stench of the throne-room. He then slammed the doors shut, and put his back to them. He had been part of Beauregard's conspiracy, also willing to give his life for his sovereign. He nodded to the main doors, and made a long howl that might have meant "go."

She saluted the man, and ran from the Palace. Outside, in the night, fires were burning high. The news would soon be spreading.

A spark had touched the gunpowder keg.

Neil Gaiman

Vampire Sestina

Neil Gaiman is the multiple award-winning author of DC Comics' The Sandman *(including the 1991 World Fantasy Award for Best Short Story) and* Black Orchid, *as well as* Violent Cases, Signal to Noise *and numerous other graphic scripts.*

He co-wrote the bestselling humorous novel Good Omens *(with Terry Pratchett), is the author of* The Official Hitch-Hiker's Guide to the Galaxy Companion, *co-devised the* Temps *shared world series, and co-edited* Ghastly Beyond Belief *with Kim Newman and* Now We Are Sick *with Stephen Jones.*

The poem that follows seemed like an atmospheric way to round out this collection.

I wait here at the boundaries of dream,
all shadow-wrapped. The dark air tastes of night,
so cold and crisp, and I wait for my love.
The moon has bleached the colour from her stone.
She'll come, and then we'll stalk this petty world
alive to darkness and the tang of blood.

It is a lonely game, the quest for blood,
but still, a body's got the right to dream

and I'd not give it up for all the world.
The moon has leeched the darkness from the night.
I stand in shadows, staring at her stone:
Undead, my lover . . . O, undead my love?

I dreamt you while I slept today and love
meant more to me than life—meant more than blood!
The sunlight sought me, deep beneath my stone,
more dead than any corpse but still a-dream
until I woke as vapour into night
and sunset forced me out into the world.

For many centuries I've walked the world
dispensing something that resembled love—
a stolen kiss, then back into the night
contented by the life and by the blood.
And come the morning I was just a dream,
cold body chilling underneath a stone.

I said I would not hurt you. Am I stone
to leave you prey to time and to the world?
I offered you a truth beyond your dreams
while all *you* had to offer was your love.
I told you not to worry, and that blood
tastes sweeter on the wing and late at night.

Sometimes my lovers rise to walk the night . . .
Sometimes they lie, a corpse beneath a stone,
and never know the joys of bed and blood
of walking through the shadows of the world;
instead they rot to maggots. O my love
they whispered you had risen, in my dream.

I've waited by your stone for half the night
but you won't leave your dream to hunt for blood.
Goodnight, my love. I offered you the world.

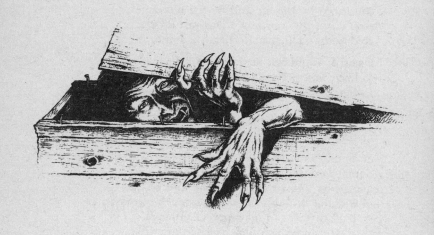